ABOUT THE AUTHOR

Author of over fifty books, Georgette Heyer is one of the best-known and best-loved of all historical novelists, making the Regency period her own. Her first novel, *The Black Moth*, published in 1921, was written at the age of fifteen to amuse her convalescent brother; her last was *My Lord John*. Although most famous for her historical novels, she also wrote eleven detective stories. Georgette Heyer died in 1974 at the age of seventy-one.

Also by Georgette Heyer

Arabella

The Corinthian

Georgette Heyer

arrow books

This edition published by Arrow in 2005

Copyright © Georgette Heyer, 2005

Georgette Heyer has asserted her right under the Copyright, Designs
and Patents Act, 1988 to be identified as the author of this work

Arabella copyright © Georgette Heyer, 1949
The Corinthian copyright © Georgette Heyer, 1940

Arrow
The Random House Group Limited
20 Vauxhall Bridge Road, London SW1V 2SA

Random House Australia (Pty) Limited
20 Alfred Street, Milsons Point, Sydney,
New South Wales 2061, Australia

Random House New Zealand Limited
18 Poland Road, Glenfield,
Auckland 10, New Zealand

Random House (Pty) Limited
Endulini, 5a Jubilee Road, Parktown 2193, South Africa

The Random House Group Limited Reg. No. 954009

www.randomhouse.co.uk

A CIP catalogue record for this book is available from the British Library

Papers used by Random House are natural, recyclable products made from wood
grown in sustainable forests. The manufacturing processes conform to the
environmental regulations of the country of origin

ISBN 0 09 190734 9

Typeset by SX Composing DTP, Rayleigh, Essex
Printed and bound in Great Britain by
Cox & Wyman Ltd, Reading, Berkshire

Arabella

Georgette Heyer

arrow books

One

The schoolroom in the Parsonage at Heythram was not a large apartment, but on a bleak January day, in a household where the consumption of coals was a consideration, this was not felt by its occupants to be a disadvantage. Quite a modest fire in the high, barred grate made it unnecessary for all but one of the four young ladies present to huddle shawls round their shoulders. But Elizabeth, the youngest of the Reverend Henry Tallant's handsome daughters, was suffering from the ear-ache, and, besides stuffing a roasted onion into the afflicted orifice, had swathed her head and neck in an old Cashmere shawl. She lay curled up on an aged sofa, with her head on a worn red cushion, and from time to time uttered a long-suffering sigh, to which none of her sisters paid any heed. Betsy was known to be sickly. It was thought that the climate of Yorkshire did not agree with her constitution, and since she spent the greater part of the winter suffering from a variety of minor ills her delicacy was regarded by all but her Mama as a commonplace.

There were abundant signs, littered over the table in the centre of the room, that the young ladies had retired to this cosy, shabby apartment to hem shirts, but only one of them, the eldest, was thus engaged. In a chair on one side of the fireplace, Miss Margaret Tallant, a buxom fifteen-year-old, was devouring the serial story in a bound volume of *The Ladies' Monthly Museum*, with her fingers stuffed in her ears; and seated opposite to Miss Arabella, her stitchery lying neglected on the table before her, sat

Miss Sophia, reading aloud from another volume of this instructive periodical.

'I must say, Bella,' she remarked, momentarily lowering the book, 'I find this most perplexing! Only listen to what it says here! *We have presented our subscribers with fashions of the newest pattern, not such as shall violate the laws of propriety and decorum, but such as shall assist the smile of good humour, and give an additional charm to the carriage of benevolence. Economy ought to be the order of the day* – And then, if you please, there is a picture of the most ravishing evening-gown – Do but look at it, Bella! – and it says that the Russian bodice is of blue satin, fastened in front with diamonds! *Well!*'

Her sister obediently raised her eyes from the wristband she was hemming, and critically scanned the willowy giantess depicted amongst the Fashion Notes. Then she sighed, and once more bent her dark head over her work. 'Well, if that is their notion of economy, I am sure I couldn't go to London, even if my godmother invited me. And I know she won't,' she said fatalistically.

'You must and you shall go!' declared Sophy, in accents of strong resolution. 'Only think what it may mean to all of us if you do!'

'Yes, but I won't go looking like a dowd,' objected Arabella, 'and if I am obliged to have diamond fastenings to my bodices, you know very well –'

'Oh, stuff! I daresay that is the extreme of fashion, or perhaps they are made of paste! And in any event this is one of the older numbers. I know I saw in one of them that jewelry is no longer worn in the mornings, so very likely – Where is that volume? Margaret, you have it! Do, pray, give it to me! You are by far too young to be interested in such things!'

Margaret uncorked her ears to snatch the book out of her sister's reach. 'No! I'm reading the serial story!'

'Well, you should not. You know Papa does not like us to read romances.'

'If it comes to that,' retorted Margaret, 'he would be excessively grieved to find you reading nothing better than the latest modes!'

They looked at one another; Sophy's lip quivered. 'Dear Meg, do pray give it to me, only for a *moment*!'

'Well, I will when I have finished the *Narrative of Augustus Waldstein*,' said Margaret. 'But *only* for a moment, mind!'

'Wait, I know there is something here to the purpose!' said Arabella, dropping her work to flick over the pages of the volume abandoned by Sophia. '*Method of Preserving Milk by Horse-Radish . . . White Wax for the Nails . . . Human Teeth placed to Stumps . . .* Yes, here it is! Now, listen, Meg! *Where a Female has in early life dedicated her attention to novel-reading she is unfit to become the companion of a man of sense, or to conduct a family with propriety and decorum.* There!' She looked up, the prim pursing of her lips enchantingly belied by her dancing eyes.

'I am sure Mama is not unfit to be the companion of a man of sense!' cried Margaret indignantly. 'And *she* reads novels! And even Papa does not find *The Wanderer* objectionable, or Mrs Edgeworth's *Tales*!'

'No, but he did not like it when he found Bella reading *The Hungarian Brothers*, or *The Children of the Abbey*,' said Sophia, seizing the opportunity to twitch *The Ladies' Monthly Museum* out of her sister's slackened grasp. 'He said there was a great deal of nonsense in such books, and that the moral tone was sadly lacking.'

'Moral tone is not lacking in the serial I am reading!' declared Margaret, quite ruffled. 'Look what it says there, near the bottom of the page! "*Albert! be purity of character your duty!*" I am sure he could not dislike that!'

Arabella rubbed the tip of her nose. 'Well, I think he would say it was fustian,' she remarked candidly. 'But do give the book back to her, Sophy!'

'I will, when I have found what I'm looking for. Besides, it was I who had the happy notion to borrow the volumes from Mrs Caterham, so – Yes, here it is! It says that only jewelry of very plain workmanship is worn in the mornings nowadays.' She added, on a note of doubt: 'I daresay the fashions don't change so very fast, even in London. This number is only three years old.'

3

The sufferer on the sofa sat up cautiously. 'But Bella hasn't got any jewelry, has she?'

This observation, delivered with all the bluntness natural in a damsel of only nine summers, threw a blight over the company.

'I have the gold locket and chain with the locks of Papa's and Mama's hair in it,' said Arabella defensively.

'If you had a tiara, and a – a cestus, and an armlet to match it, it might answer,' said Sophy. 'There is a toilet described here with just those ornaments.'

Her three sisters gazed at her in astonishment. 'What is a cestus?' they demanded.

Sophy shook her head. 'I don't know,' she confessed.

'Well, Bella hasn't got one at all events,' said the Job's comforter on the sofa.

'If she were so poor-spirited as to refuse to go to London for such a trifling reason as that, I would never forgive her!' declared Sophy.

'Of course I would not!' exclaimed Arabella scornfully. 'But I have not the least expectation that Lady Bridlington will invite me, for why should she, only because I am her goddaughter? I never saw her in my life!'

'She sent a very handsome shawl for your christening gift,' said Margaret hopefully.

'Besides being Mama's dearest friend,' added Sophy.

'But Mama has not seen her either – at least, not for years and years!'

'And she never sent Bella anything else, not even when she was confirmed,' pointed out Betsy, gingerly removing the onion from her ear, and throwing it into the fire.

'If your ear-ache is better,' said Sophia, eyeing her with disfavour, 'you may hem this seam for me! I want to draw a pattern for a new flounce.'

'Mama said I was to sit quietly by the fire,' replied the invalid, disposing herself more comfortably. 'Are there any acrostics in those fusty old books?'

4

'No, and if there were I would not give them to anyone so disobliging as you, Betsy!' said Sophy roundly.

Betsy began to cry, in an unconvincing way, but as Margaret was once more absorbed in her serial, and Arabella had drawn Sophia's attention to the picture of a velvet pelisse trimmed lavishly with ermine, no one paid any heed to her, and she presently relapsed into silence, merely sniffing from time to time, and staring resentfully at her two eldest sisters.

They presented a charming picture, as they sat poring over their book, their dark ringlets intermingled, and their arms round each other's waists. They were very plainly dressed, in gowns of blue kerseymere, made high to the throat, and with long tight sleeves; and they wore no other ornaments than a knot or two of ribbons; but the Vicar's numerous offspring were all remarkable for their good looks and had very little need of embellishment. Although Arabella was unquestionably the Beauty of the family, it was pretty generally agreed in the neighbourhood that once Sophia had outgrown the over-plumpness of her sixteen years she might reasonably hope to rival her senior. Each had large, dark, and expressive eyes, little straight noses, and delicately moulded lips; each had complexions which were the envy of less fortunate young ladies, and which owed nothing to Denmark Lotion, Olympian Dew, Bloom of Ninon, or any other aid to beauty advertised in the society journals. Sophia was the taller of the two; Arabella had by far the better figure, and the neater ankle. Sophia looked to be the more robust; Arabella enchanted her admirers by a deceptive air of fragility, which inspired one romantically-minded young gentleman to liken her to a leaf blown by the wind; and another to address a very bad set of verses to her, apostrophising her as the New Titania. Unfortunately, Harry had found this effusion, and had shown it to Bertram, and until Papa had said, with his gentle austerity, that he considered the jest to be outworn, they had insisted on hailing their sister by this exquisitely humorous appellation.

Betsy, brooding over her wrongs, found nothing to admire in

either sister, and was weighing the advantage of cosseting from old Nurse against the possibility of being called upon to amuse Baby Jack, were she to remove herself to the nursery, when the door burst open, and a stout boy of eleven years, in nankeens and a frilled shirt, and with a mop of curly hair, precipitated himself into the room, exclaiming loudly: 'Hallo! Such a kick-up! Mama is with Papa in the study, but *I* know what it's all about!'

'Why, what has happened?' exclaimed Sophia.

'Don't you wish you knew!' said Harry, drawing a piece of twine from his pocket, and beginning to tie it into a complicated knot. 'Watch me tie this one, Meg! I know six of the chief knots now, and if Uncle James does not get Captain Bolton to take me on his next commission it will be the most infamous, swindling thing I ever heard of!'

'But you didn't come to tell us that!' said Arabella. 'What is it?'

'Nothing but one of Harry's hums!' said Margaret.

'No such thing!' retorted her brother. 'Joseph Eccles has been down to the White Hart, and brought back the post with him.' He perceived that he had succeeded in riveting his sisters' attention on himself, and grinned at them. 'Ay, you may stare! There's a letter from London, for Mama. Franked by some lord, too: I saw it.'

Margaret's book slipped from her fingers to the floor; Sophia gave a gasp; and Arabella flew up out of her chair. 'Harry! Not – oh, not from my godmother?'

'Oh, ain't it?' said Harry.

'If it comes from London, it must be from Lady Bridlington!' declared Sophia. 'Arabella, I do believe our fortunes are in a way to being made!'

'I *dare* not suppose it to be possible!' said Arabella, quite faintly. 'Depend upon it, she has written to say she cannot invite me!'

'Nonsense!' replied her practical sister. 'If that were all, pray why should Mama take the letter to my father? I regard the matter as settled already. You are going to London for the Season.'

'Oh, if it could be so indeed!' said Arabella, trembling.

Harry, who had abandoned knot-making in favour of trying to stand on his head, overbalanced at this moment, and fell in a heap on the floor, together with a chair, Sophia's work-box, and a hand-screen, which Margaret had been painting before succumbing to the superior attraction of *The Ladies' Monthly Museum*. Beyond begging him not to be such an ape, none of his sisters censured his clumsiness. He picked himself up, remarking scornfully that only a girl would make such a fuss about a mere visit to London. 'The slowest thing!' he said. 'I should like to know what you think you would do there!'

'Oh, Harry, how can you be so stupid? The balls! The theatres! Assemblies!' uttered Arabella, in choked accents.

'*I* thought you were going there to form an eligible connection,' said Betsy. 'That is what Mama said, for I heard her.'

'Then you had no business to be listening!' said Sophia tartly.

'What's an eligible connection?' demanded Harry, beginning to juggle with several reels of sewing-silk, which had spilled out of the work-box on to the floor.

'I'm sure I don't know!'

'I do,' offered the invalid. 'It's a splendid marriage, of course. And *then* Bella will invite Sophy and Meg and me to stay with her in London, and we shall *all* find rich husbands!'

'That I shall certainly not do, miss!' declared Arabella. 'Let me tell you that no one will invite you anywhere until you have a little more conduct!'

'Well, Mama *did* say it,' argued Betsy, in a whining voice. 'And you need not think I do not know about such things, because –'

Sophia interrupted her ruthlessly. 'If, Betsy, you do not desire me to tell Papa of your shocking lack of delicacy, I advise you to take yourself off to the nursery – where you belong!'

This terrible threat did not fail of its object. Complaining that her sisters were disagreeable cats, Betsy went as slowly from the room as she dared, trailing her shawl behind her.

'She is very sickly,' said Arabella, in an excusing tone.

'She is a precocious brat!' retorted Sophia. 'One would have thought that she would have had more elegance of mind than to be thinking of such things! Oh, Bella, if only you were to be so fortunate as to make a Splendid Marriage! And if Lady Bridlington is to bring you out I am sure I do not see how you can fail to! For,' she added nobly, 'you are by far the prettiest girl *I* have ever seen!'

'Hoo!' interpolated Harry, adding his mite to the conversation.

'Yes,' agreed Margaret, 'but if she must have diamond buttons, and tiaras, and – and those things you spoke of, I don't see how it can be done!'

A damped silence greeted her words. Sophia was the first to recover herself. 'Something,' she announced resolutely, 'will be contrived!'

No one answered her. Arabella and Margaret appeared to be dubiously weighing her pronouncement; and Harry, having discovered a pair of scissors, was pleasurably engaged in snipping short lengths off a skein of darning-wool. Into this pensive silence walked a young gentleman just emerging from adolescence into manhood. He was a handsome youth, fairer than his elder sister, but with something of her cast of countenance; and it was manifest, from the alarming height of his shirt collar, and the disorder of his chestnut locks, that he affected a certain modishness that bordered on dandyism. The Knaresborough tailor who enjoyed his patronage could not aspire to the height of art achieved by Weston or Stultz, but he had done his best, and had indeed been greatly assisted by the admirable proportions of his client. Mr Bertram Tallant set off a coat to advantage, and was blessed with a most elegant pair of legs. These were at the moment encased in a pair of buckskin breeches, but their owner cherished in one of his chests of drawers a pair of yellow pantaloons which he had not yet dared to display to his Papa, but which, he rather fancied, turned him into a veritable Tulip of Fashion. His top-boots, on which he expended much thought and labour, were as refulgent as could be expected of boots belonging to a gentleman whose parents were unhappily unable to supply their second son with the champagne indispensable for a really good blacking; and the points of his shirt-collars, thanks to the loving hands of his sisters, were so stiffly starched that it was only with great difficulty that he could turn his head. Like his elder brother James, at present up at Oxford, prior to taking Orders, he had been educated at Harrow, but he was at present domiciled at home, working under his father's guidance with a view to passing Smalls during the Easter Vacation. This task he had embarked on without enthusiasm, his whole ambition being to obtain a cornetcy in a Hussar regiment. But as this would cost not a penny less than eight hundred pounds, and the termination of the long war with Bonaparte had made promotion unlikely, unless by expensive purchase, Mr Tallant had decided, not unreasonably, that a civil occupation would prove less ruinous than a military career. He intended that Bertram, once provided with a respectable degree, should adorn the Home Office; and any doubts which the volatile disposition of his offspring might have engendered in his mind of his eligibility for that service, he was nearly able to allay by the reflection that Bertram was, after all, not yet eighteen, and that Oxford University, where he himself had passed three scholarly years, would exert a stabilising influence on his character.

The future candidate for Parliament heralded his entrance into the schoolroom with a muted hunting-cry, followed immediately by the announcement that some people were unfairly favoured by fortune.

Arabella clasped both her hands at her breast, and raised a pair of speaking eyes to his face. 'Bertram, is it *indeed* true? Now, don't try to roast me – pray don't!'

'Lord, yes! But who told you?'

'Harry, of course,' replied Sophia. 'The children know everything in this house!'

Mr Bertram Tallant nodded gloomily, and pulled up his sleeves a trifle. 'You don't want him in here: shall I turn him out?' he enquired.

'Ho!' cried Harry, leaping to his feet, and squaring up to his senior in great good-humour. 'A mill!'

'Not in here!' shrieked his sisters, with one accustomed voice.

But as they had no expectation of being attended to, each damsel made a dive to snatch her own particular property out of harm's way. This was just as well, since the room, besides being small, was crowded with knick-knacks. The brothers struggled and swayed together for a brief minute or two, but since Harry, though a lusty lad, was no match for Bertram, he was very soon thrust outside the room, and the door slammed against him. After dealing the scarred panels a few kicks, and threatening his senior with gruesome reprisals, he took himself off, whistling loudly through the convenient gap occasioned by the loss of one of his front teeth; and Bertram was able to remove his shoulders from the door, and to straighten his cravat.

'Well, you are to go,' he informed Arabella. 'I wish I had a rich godmother, that's all! Much old Mrs Calne ever did for me, except to give me a devilish book called the *Christian Comforter*, or some such thing, which was enough to send a fellow to the dogs directly!'

'I must say, I think it was excessively shabby of her,' agreed Margaret. 'Even Papa said that if she had thought you had a taste for such literature, she might have supposed that you would find it upon his shelves.'

'Well, my father knows I have no turn in that direction, and this I will say for him, he don't expect it of me,' said Bertram handsomely. 'He may be devilish straitlaced, and full of old-fashioned notions, but he's a right one at heart, and don't plague one with a pack of humbug.'

'Yes, yes!' said Arabella impatiently, 'but does he know of this letter? Will he let me go?'

'I fancy he don't like it above half, but he said he could not stand in your way, and must trust to your conducting yourself in Society with propriety, and not allowing your head to be turned by frivolity and admiration. And as to that,' Bertram added, with brotherly candour, 'I don't suppose they will think you anything out of the way amongst all the nobs, so there's precious little chance of its happening.'

'No, I am sure they will not,' said Arabella. 'But tell me the whole! What did Lady Bridlington say in her letter?'

'Lord, I don't know! I was trying to make sense of a whole rigmarole of Greek when Mama came in, and I wasn't listening with more than half an ear. I daresay she'll tell it all to you. She sent me to say she wants you in her dressing-room.'

'Good gracious, why could you not have told me that before?' cried Arabella, stuffing the half-finished shirt into a work-bag and flitting out of the room.

The Parsonage, although built on two storeys only, was a large, old-fashioned house, and to reach Mrs Tallant's dressing-room Arabella was obliged to traverse several corridors, all carpeted with a worn drugget, and all equally draughty.

The living of Heythram was respectable, being worth some three hundred pounds a year, in addition to which the present incumbent was possessed of a small independence; but the claims of a numerous family made the recarpeting of passages more a thing to be dreamed of than an allowable expense. The Vicar, himself the son of a landed gentleman, had married the beautiful Miss Theale, who might have been expected to have done better for herself than to have thrown her cap over the windmill for a mere younger son, however handsome he might be. Indeed, it had been commonly said at the time that she had married to disoblige her family, and might, if she had chosen, have caught a baronet on her hook. Instead she had fallen in love with Henry Tallant at first sight. Since his birth was genteel, and her parents had other daughters to dispose of, she had been permitted to have her way; and apart from wishing sometimes that the living were worth more, or that Henry would not put his hand in his pocket for every beggar who crossed his path, she had never given anyone reason to suppose that she regretted her choice. To be sure, she would have liked to have installed into the Parsonage one of the new water-closets, and a Patent Kitchen Range; or, like her brother-in-law up at the Hall, have been able, without feeling the pinch, to have burnt wax candles in all the rooms; but she was a sensible woman, and even when the open fire in the kitchen smoked, and the weather made a visit to the existing water-closet particularly disagreeable, she realised that she was a great deal happier with her Henry than ever she could have been with that almost forgotten baronet. She naturally concurred in his decision that whatever became of their daughters their sons at least must receive every advantage of education; but even while employing every shift of economy to ensure the respectable maintenance of James and Bertram at Harrow she was gradually building her ambitions more and more on the future of her eldest and most beautiful daughter. Without precisely regretting the circumstances which had made it impossible for herself to shine farther afield than York and Scarborough, she was determined that Arabella should not be similarly circumscribed. Perhaps it had been with this hope already at the back of her mind that she had invited her school-friend, Arabella Haverhill, who had contracted such a brilliant match, to stand as godmother to her infant daughter. Certainly her resolve to send the younger Arabella to make her début into society under the aegis of Lady Bridlington was of no very recent date. She had maintained throughout the years an infrequent but regular correspondence with her old friend, and was tolerably certain that fashionable life had in no way impaired the easy good-nature which had characterised the plump and cheerful Miss Haverhill. Lady Bridlington was not herself blessed with daughters – she was, in fact, the mother of only one child, a son, some seven or eight years older than Mrs Tallant's daughter – but from her friend's point of view this was a decided advantage. The mother of a family of hopeful girls, however good-natured, would not be in the least likely to take under her wing yet another young female in search of an eligible husband. But a widow in comfortable circumstances, with a strong inclination for all the amusements of fashion, and no daughters to launch upon the world, might reasonably be supposed to welcome the opportunity of chaperoning a young protégée to the balls, routs, and Assemblies she herself delighted in. Mrs Tallant could not conceive it to be otherwise. Nor was she disappointed. Lady Bridlington, crossing several sheets of gilt-edged notepaper with her sprawling pen, could not imagine why she should not have hit upon the notion herself. She was excessively dull, and liked nothing in the world so much as having young persons about her. It had long been a grief to her, she wrote, that she had no daughter of her own; and as she had no doubt that she would love her dearest Sophia's girl on sight she should await her arrival in the greatest impatience. Mrs Tallant had had no need to mention her object in sending Arabella to town: Henry Tallant might consider that Lady Bridlington's letters betrayed little but folly and frivolity, but her ladyship, however lacking in mental profundity, had plenty of worldly sense. Sophia might rest assured, she wrote, that she would leave no stone unturned to provide Arabella with a suitable husband. Already, she hinted, she had several eligible bachelors in her eye.

It was small wonder, then, that Arabella, peeping into her mother's dressing-room, should have found that admirable lady lost in a pleasant daydream.

'Mama?'

'Arabella! Come in, my love, and close the door! Your godmother has written, and in the kindest way! Dear, dear creature, I knew I might depend upon her!'

'It's true then? I am to go?' Arabella breathed.

'Yes, and she begs I will send you to her as soon as may be contrived, for it seems that Bridlington is travelling on the Continent, and she is quite moped to death, living in that great house all alone. I knew how it must be! She will treat you as her own daughter. And, oh, my dearest child, I never asked it of her, but she has offered to present you at one of the Drawing-rooms!'

This dizzy prospect took from Arabella all power of speech. She could only gaze at her mother, while that lady poured out a list of the delights in store for her.

'Everything I could wish for you! Almack's – I am sure she will be able to procure you a voucher, for she knows all the patronesses! Concerts! The theatre! All the *ton* parties – breakfasts, Assemblies, balls – my love, you will have such opportunities! You can have no notion! Why, she writes that – but never mind that!'

Arabella found her voice. 'But Mama, how shall we contrive? The expense! I cannot – I *cannot* go to London without any clothes to wear!'

'No, indeed!' said Mrs Tallant, laughing. 'That would present a very odd appearance, my love!'

'Yes, Mama, but you know what I mean! I have only two ball dresses, and though they do very well for the Assemblies in Harrowgate, and country parties, I *know* they are not modish enough for Almack's! And Sophy has borrowed all Mrs Caterham's *Monthly Museums*, and I have been looking at the fashions in them, and it is too lowering, ma'am! Everything must be trimmed with diamonds, or ermine, or point-lace!'

'My dear Arabella, don't put yourself in a taking! *That* has all been thought of, I assure you. You must know that I have had this scheme in my mind for many a long day.' She saw her daughter's face of mystification, and laughed again. 'Why, did you think I would send you into society looking like a rustic? I am not quite such a zany, I hope! I have been putting by for this very occasion since I don't know when.'

'Mama!'

'I have a little money of my own, you know,' explained Mrs Tallant. 'Your dear Papa would never use it, but desired me to spend it only as I liked, because I used to be very fond of pretty things, and he never could bear to think I might not have them when I married him. That was all nonsense, of course, and I'm sure I very soon gave up thinking of such fripperies. But I was very glad to have it to spend on my children. And in spite of Margaret's drawing-lessons, and Sophy's music-master, and dearest Bertram's new coat, and those yellow pantaloons which he dare not let Papa see – my love, was there ever such a foolish boy? As though Papa did not know all along! – and having to

14

take poor Betsy to the doctor three times this year, I have quite a little nest-egg saved for you!'

'Oh, Mama, no, no!' cried Arabella, distressed. 'I would rather not go to London at all than that you should be put to such dreadful expense!'

'That is because you are sadly shatterbrained, my dear,' replied her mother calmly. 'I regard it as an investment, and I shall own myself extremely astonished if a great deal of good does not come of it.' She hesitated, looked a little conscious, and said, picking her words: 'I am sure I do not have to tell you that Papa is a Saint. Indeed, I don't suppose there is a better husband or father alive! But he is not at all practical, and when one has eight children to provide for, one must have a little worldly sense, or I don't know how one is to go on. One need have no anxiety about dear James, to be sure; and since Harry is set on going to sea, and his uncle is so obliging as to use his influence in his behalf, *his* future is settled. But I own I cannot be happy about poor Bertram; and where I am to find suitable husbands for all you girls in this restricted neighbourhood, I have not the least notion! Now, that is speaking more plainly than perhaps Papa would like, but you are a sensible puss, Arabella, and I have no scruple in being open with you. If I can but contrive to establish you respectably, you may bring out your sisters, and perhaps, even, if you should be so fortunate as to marry a gentleman of position, you might be able to help Bertram to buy his commission. I do not mean, of course, that your husband should purchase it precisely, but he might very likely have an interest at the Horse Guards, or – or something of the sort!'

Arabella nodded, for it was no news to her that she, as the eldest of four sisters, was expected to marry advantageously. She knew it to be her duty to do so. 'Mama, I will *try* not to disappoint you!' she said earnestly.

Two

*I*t was the candidly expressed opinion of the Vicar's children that Mama must have had a great work to prevail upon Papa to consent to Arabella's going to London. Few things were more reprehensible in his eyes than vanity and pleasure-seeking; and although he never raised any objection to Mama's chaperoning Arabella and Sophia to the Assemblies at Harrowgate, and had even been known to comment favourably upon their gowns, he always impressed upon them that such diversions, innocent in themselves, would, if indulged in to excess, inevitably ruin the character of the most virtuous female. He had himself no taste for society, and had frequently been heard to animadvert severely on the useless and frivolous lives led by ladies of fashion. Moreover, although he was not in the least above enjoying a good joke, he had the greatest dislike of levity, could never be brought to tolerate idle chatter, and if the conversation turned upon worldly trifles would never fail to give it a more proper direction.

But Lady Bridlington's invitation to Arabella did not take the Vicar by surprise. He knew that Mrs Tallant had written to her old friend, and however little he approved of the chief motive behind her resolve to launch her daughter into society, certain of the arguments she employed to persuade him could not but carry weight.

'My dear Mr Tallant,' said his lady, 'do not let us dispute about the merits of an advantageous match! But even you will allow that Arabella is an uncommonly handsome girl!'

Mr Tallant allowed it, adding reflectively that Arabella put him forcibly in mind of what her Mama was at the same age. Mrs Tallant was not impervious to this flattery: she blushed, and looked a little roguishly, but said that he need not try to bamboozle her (an expression she had picked up from her sons).

'All I wish to point out to you, Mr Tallant, is that Arabella is fit to move in the first circles!' she announced.

'My love,' responded the Vicar, with one of his humorous looks, 'if I believed you, I should perhaps consider it my duty to show you that an ambition to move in the first circles, as you call them, could never be an ideal I could wish any of my daughters to aspire to. But as I am persuaded that you have a great many other arguments to advance, I will hold my peace, and merely beg you to continue!'

'Well,' said Mrs Tallant seriously, 'I fancy – but you must tell me if I am mistaken – that you would not regard with any degree of complaisance an alliance with the Draytons of Knaresborough!'

The Vicar was plainly startled, and directed an enquiring look at his spouse.

'Young Joseph Drayton is growing extremely particular in his attentions,' pronounced Mrs Tallant, in a voice of doom. She observed the effect of this, and continued in the blandest way: 'Of course, I am aware that he is considered to be a great catch, for he will inherit all his father's wealth.'

The Vicar was betrayed into an unchristian utterance. 'I could not consent to it! He smells of the shop!'

'Exactly so!' agreed Mrs Tallant, well-satisfied. 'But he has been dangling after Arabella these past six months.'

'Do you tell me,' demanded the Vicar, 'that a daughter of mine encourages his attentions?'

'By no means!' promptly responded the lady. 'Any more than she encourages the attentions of the curate, young Dewsbury, Alfred Hitchen, Humphrey Finchley, or a dozen others! Arabella, my dear sir, is by far the most sought-after belle of these parts!'

'Dear me!' said the Vicar, shaking his head in wonderment. 'I must confess, my love, that none of these young gentlemen would be welcome to me as a son-in-law.'

'Then, perhaps, Mr Tallant, you cherish hopes of seeing Arabella married to her cousin Tom?'

'Nothing,' said the Vicar forcibly, 'could be farther from my wishes!' He recollected himself, and added in a more moderate tone: 'My brother is a very worthy man, according to his lights, and I wish his children nothing but good; but on several counts, which I need not enumerate, I should not desire to see any of my daughters marry their cousins. And, what is more, I am very sure that he has quite other designs for Tom and Algernon!'

'Indeed he has!' corroborated Mrs Tallant cordially. 'He means them to marry heiresses.'

The Vicar bent an incredulous gaze upon her. 'Does my daughter affect any of these young men?' he demanded.

'I fancy not,' replied Mrs Tallant. 'That is to say, she does not show any marked preference for any one of them. But when a girl sees no other gentlemen than those who have been dangling after her ever since she left the schoolroom, what, my dear Mr Tallant, must be the end of it? And young Drayton,' she added musingly, 'is possessed of a considerable fortune. I do not mean that Arabella would consider *that*, but there is no denying that the man who drives a smart curricle, and can afford to be begging a female's acceptance of all the most elegant trifles imaginable, has a decided advantage over his rivals.'

There was a pregnant silence, while all the implications of this speech sank into the Vicar's brain. He said at length, rather wistfully: 'I had hoped that one day a suitable *parti* would present himself, to whom I might have given Arabella with a thankful heart.'

Mrs Tallant threw him an indulgent glance. 'Very likely, my dear, but it would be a great piece of nonsense to pretend that such things happen when one has made not the least push to bring them about! Eligible *partis* do not commonly appear as by magic in country villages: one must go out into the world to find them!' She saw that the Vicar was looking a little pained, and laughed. 'Now, do not tell me that it was otherwise with us, Mr Tallant, for you know very well I met you first at a party in York! I own it was not in the expectation of my falling in love with *you* that my Mama took me there, but in your turn *you* will own that we should never have met if I had sat at home waiting for you!'

He smiled. 'Your arguments are always unanswerable, my love. Yet I cannot entirely like it. I believe Arabella to be a well-behaved girl enough, but she is very young, after all, and I have thought sometimes that her spirits might, lacking wiser guidance, betray her into unbecoming conduct. Under Lady Bridlington's roof, she would, I fear, lead a life gay to dissipation, such as must make her unfit afterwards for rational society.'

'Depend upon it,' said Mrs Tallant soothingly, 'she is by far too well-behaved a girl to occasion us a moment's anxiety. I am sure, too, that her principles are too sound to allow her to lose her head. To be sure, she can be a sad romp, and *that*, my dear sir, is because she has not yet enjoyed the advantages of town polish. I am hopeful of seeing her much improved by a season spent with Bella Bridlington. And if – mind, I only say if! – she were to contract a suitable alliance I am sure you would be as thankful as anyone could be!'

'Yes,' agreed the Vicar, sighing. 'I should certainly be glad to see her comfortably established, the wife of a respectable man.'

'And *not* the wife of young Dewsbury!' interpolated Mrs Tallant.

'Indeed, no! I cannot suppose that any child of mine could attain happiness with a man whom I must – with reluctance – think a very vulgar fellow!'

'In that case, my dear,' said Mrs Tallant, rising briskly to her feet, 'I will write to accept Lady Bridlington's most obliging invitation.'

'You must do as you think right,' he said. 'I have never interfered with what you considered proper for your daughters.'

Thus it was that, at four o'clock on this momentous day, when the Vicar joined his family at the dinner-table, he surprised them by making a humorous reference to Arabella's projected trip. Not even Betsy would have ventured to have mentioned the scheme, for it was generally supposed that he must disapprove of it. But after grace had been said, and the family had disposed themselves about the long table, Arabella began, not very expeditiously, to carve one of the side-dishes, and the Vicar, looking up from his own labours in time to see her place a slightly mangled wing of chicken on a plate, remarked, with a twinkle: 'I think Arabella must take lessons in carving before she goes into society, or she will disgrace us all by her unhandiness. It will not do, you know, my dear, to precipitate a dish into your neighbour's lap, as you seem to be in danger of doing at this moment!'

Arabella blushed, and protested. Sophia, the first to recover from the shock of hearing Papa speak with such good-humour of the London scheme, said: 'Oh, but, Papa, I am sure it will not signify, for ten to one all the dishes are served by the footmen in grand houses!'

'I stand corrected, Sophia,' said the Vicar, with dry meekness.

'Will Lady Bridlington have many footmen?' asked Betsy, dazzled by this vision of opulence.

'One to stand behind every chair,' promptly replied Bertram. 'And one to walk behind Arabella every time she desires to take the air; and two to stand up behind my lady's carriage; and a round dozen, I daresay, to form an avenue in the front hall anytime her ladyship increases her covers for guests. When Arabella returns to us she will have forgotten how to pick up her own handkerchief, mark my words!'

'Well, I don't know how she will go on in such a house!' said Betsy, half-believing him.

'Nor I, indeed!' murmured Arabella.

'I trust she will go on, as you not very elegantly phrase it, my child, exactly as she would in her own home,' said the Vicar.

Silence followed this rebuke. Bertram made a grimace at Arabella across the table, and Harry dug her surreptitiously in the ribs with his elbow. Margaret, who had been wrinkling her brow over her father's words, ventured at last to say: 'Yes, Papa, but I do not precisely see how she can do so! It must be so very different to what we are accustomed to! I should not be surprised, for instance, if she found herself obliged to wear her party-gowns every evening, and I am sure she will not help with the baking, or starch shirts, or feed the chickens, or – or anything of that nature!'

'That was not quite what I meant, my dear,' responded the Vicar repressively.

'Will she not be made to do any work at all?' exclaimed Betsy. 'Oh, how much I wish *I* had a rich godmother!'

This ill-timed remark brought an expression of grave displeasure to the Vicar's face. It was evident to his family that the picture thus conjured up, of a daughter given over wholly to pleasure, was not one he could contemplate with anything but misgiving. Several darkling looks were cast at Betsy, which boded ill for one tactless enough to call down upon her sisters a lecture on the evils of idleness; but before the Vicar could speak, Mrs Tallant had intervened, calling Betsy to order for chattering, and saying cheerfully: 'Well, and I think Papa will agree that Arabella is a good girl, and deserves this indulgence more than any of you. I am sure I do not know how I shall manage without her, for whenever I want a task performed I know I may rely upon her to do it. And, what is a great deal to the point, let me tell you all! – she never shows me a pouting face, or complains that she is bored, or falls into a fit of the sullens because she is obliged to mend her old gown instead of purchasing a new one.'

It could scarcely be expected that this masterly speech would please the three damsels to whom it was pointedly addressed, but it had the happy effect of softening the Vicar's countenance. He glanced at Arabella, who was furiously blushing and holding her head bent over her plate, and said gently: 'Indeed, I am disposed to think that her character is well-established amongst us as one who wants neither sense nor feeling.' Arabella looked up quickly, her eyes brightened by tears. He smiled at her, and said in a teasing voice: 'If she will not let her tongue run like a fiddle-stick, nor express herself in terms which I might almost suppose she learns from her brothers, nor play pranks like a hoyden, I really believe I may indulge the hope that we shall not hear from Lady Bridlington that she is sunk quite beyond reproach in London!'

Such was the relief of his children at escaping one of Papa's homilies that this mild jest was received with a flattering degree of appreciation. Bertram seized the opportunity afforded by the general outcry of laughing protests to inform Betsy in a savage under-voice that if she opened her lips again he would most faithfully drop her in the middle of the duck-pond on the morrow, which promise so terrified her that she sat mumchance throughout the rest of the meal. Sophia, with real nobility of character, then asked Papa to explain something she had read in Sir John Malcolm's *History of Persia*, which the Vicar, whose only personal extravagance was his purchase of books, had lately added to his library. This was a happy inspiration: while her contemporaries gazed at Sophia in stupefaction, the Vicar, becoming quite animated, expounded at length on the subject, quite forgetting the immediate problems of the hour, and reducing his other offspring to a state of speechless indignation by saying, as he rose from the table, that he was glad to find that he had one daughter at least of a scholarly turn of mind.

'And Sophy never read a word of the book!' Bertram said bitterly, when, after enduring an evening in the parlour under the scourge of having passages from Sir John Malcolm's memorable work read aloud to them, he and his two elder sisters had escaped to the sanctuary of the girls' bedchamber.

'Oh, yes, I had!' retorted Sophia, sitting down on the end of her bed, and curling her legs under her in a way that, could her Mama but have seen it, would certainly have called down reproof upon her head.

Margaret, who was always sent up to bed before the appearance of the tea-tray, and thus had been spared the greater part of the evening's infliction, sat up, hugging her knees, and asked simply: 'Why?'

'Well, it was that day that Mama was obliged to go out, and

desired me to remain in the parlour in case old Mrs Farnham should call,' explained Sophia. 'I had nothing else to do.'

After regarding her fixedly for several moments, her brother and sisters apparently decided that the excuse was reasonable, for they abandoned the subject.

'I declare I was ready to sink when Papa said *that* about me!' remarked Arabella.

'Yes, but you know, Bella, he is very absent-minded,' said Sophia, 'and I fancy he had forgotten what you and Bertram did on Boxing Day, and what he said about your inclination for finery, when you pulled the feathers out of Uncle's peacocks to furbish up your old bonnet.'

'Yes, perhaps he had,' agreed Arabella, in a dampened tone. 'But all the same,' she added, her spirits reviving, 'he never said I had no delicacy of principle, which he said to you when he discovered it was you, Sophy, who put one of Harry's trousers-buttons into the bag in Church that Sunday!'

This was so unanswerable that Sophia could think of no retort to make. Bertram said suddenly: 'Well, since it is decided that you are to go to London, Bella, I'll tell you something!'

Seventeen years' intimate knowledge of her younger brother was not enough to restrain Arabella from demanding eagerly: 'Oh, what, pray?'

'You may get a surprise when you are there!' said Bertram, in a voice of mystery. 'Mind, I don't say you will, but you *may*!'

'What can you possibly mean? Tell me, Bertram! – *dearest* Bertram!'

'I'm not such a saphead! Girls always blab everything!'

'I would not! You know I would not! Oh, Bertram!'

'Don't heed him!' recommended Margaret, sinking back on to her pillow. 'It's all humbug!'

'Well, it's not, miss!' said her brother, nettled. 'But you needn't think I mean to tell you, for I don't! But don't be surprised, Bella, if you get a surprise before you have been in London very long!'

This ineptitude naturally threw his sisters into whoops.

23

Unfortunately their mirth reached the ears of old Nurse, who promptly sailed into the room, and delivered herself of a shrill homily on the general impropriety of young gentlemen who sat on the ends of their sisters' beds. Since she was quite capable of reporting this shocking conduct to Mama, Bertram thought it prudent to remove himself, and the symposium came to an abrupt end. Nurse, blowing out the candles, said that if this came to Mama's ears there would be no London for Miss Arabella; but apparently it did not come to Mama's ears, for on the morrow, and indeed on all the succeeding days, nothing was talked of in the Parsonage (except in Papa's presence) but Arabella's entrance into the Polite World.

The first and most pressing consideration was the getting together of a wardrobe suitable for a young lady hopeful of making a successful début. Earnest perusal of the fashion journals had cast Arabella into a mood of despair, but Mama took a more cheerful view of the matter. She commanded the houseboy to summon the ubiquitous Joseph Eccles up to the Parsonage, and desired the pair of them to fetch down from one of the attics two formidable trunks. Joseph, who had been employed by the Vicar since the first year of his marriage as the farm-hand, considered himself the mainstay of the establishment, and was only too ready to oblige the ladies; and he lingered in the dressing-room, proffering counsel and encouragement in the broadest of Yorkshire dialects until kindly but firmly dismissed.

A pleasing aroma of camphor pervaded the air as soon as the lids were raised from the trunks, and the removal of a covering of silver paper disclosed treasures innumerable. The trunks contained the finery which Mama had worn (she said) when she was just such a giddy puss as Arabella. When she had married Papa she had had no occasion for such fripperies, but she had not been able to bring herself to give them away, and had packed them up and well-nigh forgotten all about them.

Three ecstatic gasps shuddered on the air as three rapt young ladies dropped down on their knees beside the trunks, and prepared to rummage to their hearts' content.

There were unimagined delights in the trunks: curled ostrich plumes of various colours; branches of artificial flowers; an ermine tippet (alas, turned sadly yellow with age, but it would serve to trim Sophy's old pelisse!); a loo-mask; a whole package of finest thread-lace; a tiffany cloak, which set Margaret peacocking round the room; several ells of ribbon of a shade which Mama said was called in her young days *opéra brulé*, and quite the rage; scarves of gauze, lace, and blonde, spangled and plain; a box containing intriguing knots of ribbon, whose names Mama could not quite remember, though she rather thought that that pale blue bunch was A Sign of Hope, and the pink bow A Sigh of Venus; point-lace tuckers, and lappet-heads; a feather muff; innumerable fans; sashes; a scarlet-flowered damask mantua petticoat – what a figure Mama must have looked in it! – and a velvet cloak, miraculously lined with sable, which had been a wedding-gift to Mama, but which she had scarcely worn, 'because, my loves, it was finer than anything your aunt possessed, and, after all, she was the Squire's wife, and dreadfully inclined to take a pet, so that I always took care never to give her the least cause to be offended. But it is a beautiful fur, and will make a muff for Arabella, besides trimming a pelisse!'

It was fortunate that Mama was an indulgent parent, and so very fond of a joke, for the trunks contained, besides these treasures, such old-fashioned garments that the three Misses Tallant were obliged to laugh. Fashions had changed a great deal since Mama was a girl, and to a generation accustomed to high-waisted gowns of muslin and crape, with little puff-sleeves, and demure flounces round the hems, the stiff, voluminous silks and brocades Mama had worn, with their elaborate undergowns, and their pads, and their wired bodices, seemed not only archaic, but very ugly too. What was this funny jacket, with all the whalebone? A Caraco? Gracious! And this striped thing, for all the world like a dressing-gown? A lustring sack – well, it was certainly very like a sack, to be sure! Did Mama wear it in *company*? What was in this elegant box? Poudre à la Maréchale! But did Mama then powder her hair, like the picture of

Grandmama Tallant, up at the Hall? Oh, *not* quite like that! A *gray* powder? Oh, Mama, no! And you without a gray hair to your head! How did you dress it? Not cut *at all*? Curls to the waist at the back? And all those rolls and puffs over the ears! How could Mama have had the patience to do it? So odd as it must have looked, too!

But Mama, turning over half-forgotten dresses, grew quite sentimental, remembering that she had been wearing this very gown of green Italian taffeta, over a petticoat of satin, *soupir d'étouffe* (unaccountably missing), when she had first met Papa; remembering the pretty compliment paid to her by that rejected baronet when he had seen her in the white silk waist Sophia was holding up (it had had a book-muslin train, and there should be somewhere a pink silk coat, very smart, which she had worn with it); remembering how shocked her Mama had been when she had seen that rose-coloured Indian muslin underwear which Eliza – your Aunt Eliza, my loves – had brought her from London.

The girls did not know where to look when Mama sighed over a cherry-striped gown, and said how pretty it had been, for really it was quite hideous, and it made them feel almost uncomfortable to think of Mama's being seen abroad in such a garment. It was beyond laughter, so they sat respectfully silent, and were profoundly relieved when suddenly she shook off this unaccustomed mood, and smiled, and said in her own brisk way: 'Well, I daresay you think I must have looked like a dowd, but I assure you I did not! However, none of these brocades is of any use to Arabella, so we will put them up again. But the straw-coloured satin will do famously for a ball-dress, and we may trim it with some of the point-lace.'

There was a dressmaker in High Harrowgate, an elderly Frenchwoman, who had originally come to England as an émigrée from the Revolution. She had very often made dresses for Mrs Tallant and her daughters, and since she had excellent taste, and did not charge extortionate prices, except during the short season, it was decided that she should be entrusted with the task of making all Arabella's gowns. On the first day that the horses could be spared from the farm, Mrs Tallant and her two elder daughters drove to High Harrowgate, taking with them three bandboxes full of the silks, velvets, and laces which had finally been selected from Mrs Tallant's hoard.

Harrowgate, which was situated between Heythram and the large town of Knaresborough, was a watering-place renowned more for the excellent properties of its medicinal springs than for the modishness of its visitors. It consisted of two straggling villages, more than a mile apart, and enjoyed a summer season only. Since upwards of a thousand persons, mostly of valetudinarian habits, visited it then to drink the waters, both villages and their environs boasted more hotels and boarding-houses than private residences. From May till Michaelmas, public balls were held twice a week at the New Assembly Rooms; there was a Promenade, standing in the middle of an agreeable garden; a theatre; and a lending library, much patronised by Mrs Tallant and her daughters.

Mme Dupont was delighted to receive a client in the middle of January, and no sooner learned the reason for the bespeaking of such an extensive wardrobe than she entered into the spirit of the adventure with Gallic enthusiasm, fell into raptures over the silks and satins in the three bandboxes, and spread fashion-plates, and rolls of cambric and muslin and crape before the ladies' eyes. It would be a pleasure, she said, to make for a *demoiselle* with such a *taille* as Mademoiselle Tallant's; already she perceived how Madame's satin polonaise could be transformed into a ball-dress of the most ravishing, while as for the taffeta over-dress – alas, that the elegant toilettes of the last century were no longer in vogue! – she could assure Madame that nothing could be more *comme il faut* than an opera cloak fashioned out of its ample widths, and trimmed with ruched velvet ribbon. As for the cost, that would be a matter for arrangement of the most amicable.

Arabella, who in general had a decided will of her own, as well as very definite ideas on the colour and style of her dresses, was so

27

much shocked by the number of gowns Mama and Mme Dupont seemed to think indispensable for a sojourn in London that she scarcely opened her lips, except to agree in a faint voice with whatever was suggested to her. Even Sophia, who so often earned reproofs from Papa for chattering like a magpie, was awed into comparative silence. Not all her study of the fashion-plates in *The Ladies' Monthly Museum* had prepared her for the dazzling creations sketched in *La Belle Assemblée*. But Mama and Mme Dupont were agreed that only the simplest of these would be *convenable* for such a young lady. One or two ball-dresses of satin, or orange-blossom sarsnet, would be needed for grand occasions, but nothing could be prettier, said Madame, than crape or fine jaconet muslin for the Assemblies at Almack's. Some silver net drapery, perhaps – she had the very thing laid by – or a Norwich shawl, carried negligently across the elbows, would lend a *cachet* to the plainest gown. Then, for a morning half-dress, might she suggest a figured French muslin, with a demi-train? Or perhaps Mademoiselle would prefer a Berlin silk, trimmed with silk floss? For carriage dresses, she would recommend fine cambric, worn with a velvet mantle, and a Waterloo hat, or even a fur bonnet, ornamented – Mademoiselle's colouring made it permissible, even imperative! – with a bunch of cherries.

Morning dresses, afternoon dresses, carriage dresses, walking dresses, ball dresses – it seemed to Arabella and Sophia that the list would never come to an end. 'I cannot imagine how you will find time to wear the half of them!' whispered Sophia.

'Shoes, half-boots, reticules, gloves, stockings,' murmured Mrs Tallant, conning her list. 'Those will do for another day. You must take the greatest care of your silk stockings, my love, for I cannot afford to buy you many pairs! Hats – h'm, yes! What a fortunate thing it was that I kept all my old ostrich feathers! We shall see what we can contrive. I think that will do for today.'

'Mama, what will Bella wear when she goes to the Drawing-room?' asked Sophia.

'*Ah, pour ça, alors, la grande parure!*' cried Madame, her eye brightening.

Mrs Tallant crushed these budding hopes. 'Full dress, to be sure, my dear: satin, I daresay. Feathers, of course. I do not know if hoops are still worn at Court. Lady Bridlington is to make your sister a present of the dress, and I know I may depend upon her to choose just what is right. Come, my dears! If we are to call upon your uncle on our way home it is high time we were off!'

'Call upon my uncle?' repeated Sophia, surprised.

Mrs Tallant coloured slightly, but replied in an airy way: 'Certainly, my love: why should we not? Besides, one should never neglect the observances of civility, and I am sure he would think it very odd in me not to apprise him of Arabella's going to London.'

Sophia knitted her brows a little over this, for although there had always been a good deal of coming and going between the two boys at the Hall, and their young cousins at the Vicarage, visits between their respective parents were rare. The Squire and his brother, while remaining on perfectly amicable terms, scarcely possessed a thought in common, each regarding the other with affectionate contempt; while the late Lady Tallant, besides labouring under all the disadvantages of a jealous temper, had been, even in her charitable brother-in-law's estimation, a very under-bred woman. There were two children of the marriage: Thomas, a bucolic young man of twenty-seven; and Algernon, who held a commission in the –th Regiment, stationed at present in Belgium.

The Hall, which was situated in a pretty little park, about a mile from the village of Heythram, was a commodious, unpretentious house built of the prevailing gray stone of the district. Comfort rather than elegance was the predominant note struck by its furniture and decorations, and it bore, in despite of the ministrations of an excellent housekeeper, the indefinable air of a residence that lacked a mistress. The Squire was more interested in his stables than in his house. He was generally thought to be a warm man, but careful; and although he was fond of his nephews and nieces, and always good-naturedly mounted Bertram during the hunting-season, it was rarely that his affection led him to do more for them than to give them a guinea apiece every Christmas. But he was a hospitable man, and always seemed pleased to welcome his brother's family to his board.

He came bustling out of the house as soon as the Parsonage carriage drew up at his door, and exclaimed in a loud voice: 'Well, well, if it's not Sophia, and the girls! Well, this is a pleasant circumstance! What, only the two of you? Never mind! Come in, and take a glass of wine! Bitter cold, ain't it? Ground's like iron: don't know when we shall get out again, damme if I do!'

Talking all the time, he led the ladies into a square parlour in the front of the house, breaking off his conversation only to shout to someone to bring refreshments into the parlour, and to be quick about it. He then ran his eye over his nieces, and said that they were prettier than ever, and demanded to be told how many beaux they could boast between them. They were spared the necessity of answering this jocular question by his instantly turning to Mrs Tallant, and saying: 'Can't hold a candle to their Mama, though, I swear! I declare, it's an age since I've clapped eyes on you, Sophia! Can't think why you and poor Henry don't come up more often to eat your mutton with me! And how is Henry? Still poring over his books, I dare swear! I never knew such a fellow! But you shouldn't let him keep young Bertram's nose glued to 'em, my dear: that's a good lad – regular devil to go, nothing bookish about him!'

'Bertram is reading for Oxford, Sir John. You know he must do so!'

'Mark my words, he'll do no good there!' said the Squire. 'Better make a soldier of him, as I did with my young rascal. But tell him to come up to the stables here, if he wants to see a rare piece of horseflesh: great rumps and hocks, grand shoulders! Don't mind the boy's trying him, if he likes to, but he's young yet: needs schooling. Does Bertram mean to come out when this frost breaks? Tell him the bay has a splint forming, or you may call me a Dutchman, but he may ride Thunderer, if he chooses.'

'I think,' said Mrs Tallant, with a faint sigh, 'that his Papa does not wish him to hunt any more this season. It quite takes his mind off his book, poor boy!'

'Henry's an old woman,' replied the Squire. 'Ain't it enough for him to have James as bookish as he is himself? Where is that lad? Up at Oxford, eh? Ah well, each man to his taste! Now, that other young rascal of yours – what's his name? Harry! I like the cut of his jib, as he'd say himself. Going to sea, he tells me. How shall you manage it?'

Mrs Tallant explained that one of her brothers was to use his interest in Harry's favour. The Squire seemed satisfied with this, asked jovially after the health of his godson and namesake, and set about pressing cold meat and wine upon his guests. It was some time before any opportunity offered of breaking to him of the visit, but when the spate of his conversation abated a little, Sophia, who could scarcely contain herself for impatience, said abruptly: 'Sir, do you know that Arabella is going to London?'

He stared, first at her, and then at Arabella. 'Eh? What's that you say? How comes this about?'

Mrs Tallant, frowning reprovingly at Sophia, explained the matter. He listened very intently, nodding, and pursing up his lips, as his habit was when he was interested; and after turning it over in his mind for several moments, began to perceive what an excellent thing it was, and to congratulate Arabella upon her good fortune. After he had wished her a great many town-beaux, envied the lucky one who should win her, and prophesied that she would shine down all the London beauties, Mrs Tallant brought his gallantry to an end by suggesting that her daughters would like to go to the housekeeper's room to visit good Mrs Paignton, who was always so kind to them. The style of the Squire's pleasantries was not just to her taste; moreover, she wished to have some private talk with him.

He had a great many questions to ask her, and comments to make. The more he thought about the scheme the better he liked it, for although he was fond of his niece, and considered her a remarkably handsome girl, he did not wish her to become his daughter-in-law. His understanding was not quick, nor had he much power of perception, but it had lately been borne in upon him that his heir had begun to dangle after his cousin in a marked manner: He did not suppose that Tom's affections were deeply engaged, and he was hopeful that if Arabella were removed from the neighbourhood he would soon recover from his mild infatuation, and make some more eligible lady the object of his gallantry. He had a suitable girl in his eye for Tom, but being a fairminded man he was obliged to own that Miss Maria was cast very much in the shade by Arabella. Nothing, therefore, that Mrs Tallant could have told him would have met with more approval from him. He gave the scheme his warmest approbation, and told her that she was a sensible woman.

'Ay, you need not tell me! This is your doing, Sophia! Poor Henry never had a particle of sense! A dear, good fellow, of course, but when a man has a quiverful of children he needs to be a little sharper than Henry. But you have all your wits about you, my dear sister! You are doing just as you should: the girl's uncommon handsome, and should do well for herself. Ay, ay, you will be setting about the wedding preparations before the cat has time to lick her ear! Lady Bridlington, eh? One of the London nobs, I daresay: couldn't be better! But it will cost a great deal!'

'Indeed, you are right, Sir John,' said Mrs Tallant. 'It will cost a very great deal, but when such an opportunity is offered every effort should be made to take advantage of it, I believe.'

'Ay, ay, you will be laying your money out to good purpose!' he nodded. 'But can you trust this fine lady of yours to keep half-pay officers, and such-like, out of the girl's way? It won't do to have her running off with some penniless fellow, you know, and all your trouble wasted!'

The fact that the same thought had more than once crossed her mind did not make this piece of plain-speaking any more agreeable to Mrs Tallant. She considered it extremely vulgar, and replied in a repressive tone that she believed she might depend on Arabella's good sense.

'You had better drop a word of warning in your friend's ear,' said Sir John bluntly. 'You know, Sophia, if that girl of yours were to catch a man of property, and, damme, I don't see why she shouldn't! – it would be a great thing for her sisters! Ay, the more I think on it the better I like it! It is worth all the expense. When does she go? How do you mean to send her?'

'As to that, it is not yet decided, Sir John, but if Mrs Caterham holds by her original scheme, and lets Miss Blackburn go next month – you must know that she is the governess, I daresay – she could travel with Arabella. I believe her home is in Surrey, so she must go to London.'

'But you won't send little Bella on the stage-coach!'

Mrs Tallant sighed. 'My dear sir, the cost of posting is too great to be even thought of! I own, I do not like it, but beggars, you know, cannot be choosers!'

The Squire began to look very thoughtful. 'Well, that won't do,' he said presently. 'No, no, we can't have that! Driving up to your grand friend's house in a hackney! We shall have to contrive a little, Sophia. Now, let me see!'

He sat staring into the fire for some minutes, while his sister-in-law pensively gazed out of the window, and tried not to let her mind dwell on what her sensitive husband's feelings must be, could he but have had the least idea of what she was doing.

'I'll tell you what, sister!' said the Squire suddenly. 'I'll send Bella to London in my travelling carriage, that's what I'll do! No sense in wasting money on posting: it don't matter to the girl if she spends some time on the road. What's more, those post-chaises can't take up all the baggage I'll be bound Bella will have with her. Ay, and this governess of yours will have a box as well, I daresay.'

'Your travelling carriage!' exclaimed Mrs Tallant, rather startled.

'That's it. Never use it myself: it hasn't been out of the coach-house since my poor Eliza died. I'll set the men on to furbish it up: it ain't one of these smart, newfangled barouches, but it's a handsome carriage – I bought it for Eliza, when we were first married, and it has my crest on the panel. You would not be comfortable, sending the girl off with strange post-boys, you know: much better to let my old coachman drive her, and I'll send one of the grooms along to sit up beside him, with a pistol in his pocket in case of highwaymen.' He rubbed his hands together, well-pleased with the scheme, and began to estimate how many days it would take a strong pair of horses – or, at a pinch, even four – to reach London without getting knocked-up. He was inclined to think the plan would answer very well, and that Arabella would not at all object to resting the nags a day here or there upon the road. 'Or she might travel by easy stages, you know!' he said.

Upon reflection, Mrs Tallant perceived that this plan had much to recommend it. Against the evils of lingering in the various posting-houses along the route, must be set the advantages of being driven by a steady, trustworthy coachman, and of being able, as the Squire had pointed out, to carry all the trunks and bandboxes in the carriage, instead of having to send them to town by carrier. She thanked him, therefore, and was still expressing the sense of her obligation to him when the young ladies came back into the room.

The Squire greeted Arabella with great joviality, pinching her cheek, and saying: 'Well, puss, this is a new come-out for you, eh? I'll swear you're in high gig! Now, here's your mother and I have been putting our heads together, and the long and the short of it is you are to go to London in prime style, in your poor aunt's carriage, and Timothy-coachman to drive you. How will that be, my lass?'

Arabella, who had very pretty manners, thanked him, and said everything that was proper. He appeared pleased, told her she might give him a kiss, and he would be satisfied, and suddenly walked out of the room, adjuring her to wait, for he had a little something for her. When he came back, he found his visitors ready to take their leave of him. He shook hands warmly with them all, and pressed into Arabella's a folded banknote, saying: 'There! That is to buy yourself some fripperies with, puss!'

She was quite overcome, for she had not expected anything of the sort; coloured, and stammered that he was by far too kind.

He liked to be thanked, and beamed at her, and pinched her cheek again, very well satisfied with himself and her.

'But, Mama,' said Sophia, when they were driving away from the Hall, 'you will never let poor Arabella go to town in that antiquated carriage of my uncle's!'

'Nonsense!' replied her mother. 'It is a very respectable carriage, and if it is old-fashioned I daresay it is none the worse for that. No doubt you would rather see her dash off in a chaise-and-four, but it would cost as much as fifty or sixty pounds, besides what one must give the postilions, and is not to be thought of. Why, even a pair of horses, so far as we are from London, would mean thirty pounds, and all for what? To be sure, it will be a little slow, but Miss Blackburn will be with your sister, and if they are obliged to stay a day in an inn – to rest the horses, you know – she will be able to look after her, and I may be comfortable in my mind.'

'Mama!' said Arabella faintly. '*Mama!*'

'Good gracious, my love, what is it?'

Arabella dumbly proffered the Squire's banknote. Mrs Tallant took it from her, saying: 'You would like me to take care of it for you, would you? Very well, I will do so, my dear, or you would be squandering it on presents for your brothers and sisters, perhaps!'

'Mama, it is a bill for *fifty pounds!*'

'No!' gasped Sophia.

'Well, that is certainly very generous of your uncle,' said Mrs Tallant. 'If I were you, Arabella, I would embroider a pair of slippers for him before you go away, for you will not like to be backward in any little attention.'

'Oh, no! But I never dreamed – I am sure I did not thank him half enough! Mama, will you take it for my dresses, please?'

'Certainly not. *That* is all provided for. You will find it very much more comfortable in London to have this money by you – indeed, I had hoped your uncle might give you something to spend! There will be little things you may want to purchase, and vails to the servants, you know, and so on. And although your

Papa would not like you to *gamble* precisely, there may be loo-parties, and naturally you would wish to play. In fact, it would be awkward if you did not.'

Sophia opened her eyes at this. 'Papa does not like any of us to play gambling games, ma'am, does he? He says that cards are to blame for many of the evils –'

'Yes, my dear, very likely! But a loo-party is quite a different thing!' said Mrs Tallant, somewhat obscurely. She fidgeted with her reticule for a moment, and then added, a little consciously: 'I should not tease Papa with telling him the whole history of our doings today, girls. Gentlemen do not take the same interest in such things as we do, and I am sure he has very much more important things to think of.'

Her daughters did not pretend to misunderstand her. 'Oh, I would not breathe a word to him!' said Sophia.

'No,' agreed Arabella. 'And *particularly* not about the fifty pounds, for I am sure he would say it was too much, and I must give it back to my uncle! And I don't think I *could*!'

Three

*I*n the end, it was not until after the middle of February that Arabella set out to accomplish the long journey to London. Not only had Mme Dupont taken more time to make the necessary gowns than had been anticipated, but there had been many details to arrange besides; and Betsy had not failed to delay preparations by contracting a putrid sore throat, and low fever. It was felt to be typical of her. While Mrs Tallant still had her hands full, nursing her, Bertram, succumbing to temptation, took French leave of his books and his Papa, and enjoyed a splendid day with the hounds, which culminated in his return to the Parsonage on a farm wagon, with a broken collar-bone. A gloom was thrown over the house for quite a week by this mishap, because the Vicar was not only vexed, but deeply grieved as well. It was not the accident which upset him, for although he did not hunt himself now he had done so regularly in his youth, but (he said) the want of openness in Bertram which had led him to go off without asking permission, or, indeed, even telling his father what he meant to do. The Vicar could not understand such conduct at all, for surely he was not a harsh parent, and surely his sons must know that he did not wish to deprive them of rational enjoyment? He was bewildered, and disturbed, and begged Bertram to explain why he had behaved in such a manner. But it was quite impossible to explain to Papa why one chose rather to play truant, and afterwards take the consequences, than to ask his leave to do something of which one knew well he would not approve.

'How *can* you explain anything to my father?' Bertram demanded of his sisters, in a despairing tone. 'He would only be more hurt than ever, and give one a thundering jaw, and make one feel like the greatest beast in nature!'

'I know,' said Arabella feelingly. 'I think what makes him look so displeased and sad is that he believes you must be afraid of him, and so dared not ask his leave to go. And, of course, one *can't* explain that it isn't *that*!'

'He wouldn't understand if you did,' remarked Sophia.

'Well, exactly so!' said Bertram. 'Besides, you couldn't do it! A pretty botch I should make of telling him that I didn't ask leave because I knew he would look grave, and say I must decide for myself, but did I feel it to be right to go pleasuring when I have examinations to pass – oh, you know the way he talks! The end of it would be that I shouldn't have gone at all! I hate moralising!'

'Yes,' agreed Sophia, 'but the worst of it is that whenever one of us vexes him he very likely falls into the most dreadful dejection, and worries himself with thinking that we are all of us heedless and spoilt, and himself much to blame. I wish he may not forbid you to go to London because of Bertram's wretched folly, Bella!'

'What a bag of moonshine!' exclaimed Bertram scornfully. 'Why the deuce should he, pray?'

It certainly seemed a trifle unreasonable, but when his children next encountered the Vicar, which was at the dinner-table, his countenance wore an expression of settled melancholy, and it was plain that he derived no comfort from the young people's cheerful conversation. A somewhat thoughtless enquiry from Margaret about the exact colour of the ribbons chosen for Arabella's second-best ball-dress provoked him to say that it seemed to him that amongst all his children only James was not wholly given over to levity and frivolity. Unsteadiness of character was what he perceived about him; when he considered that the mere prospect of a visit to London sent all his daughters fashion-mad he must ask himself whether he was not doing very wrong to permit Arabella to go.

A moment's reflection would have convinced Arabella that this was the merest irritation of nerves, but her besetting sin, as her Mama had frequently told her, was the impetuosity which led her into so many scrapes. Alarm at the Vicar's words for an instant suspended every faculty; then she exclaimed hotly: 'Papa! You are unjust! It is too bad!'

The Vicar had never been a severe parent; indeed, he was thought by some to allow his children a shocking degree of licence: but such a speech as this went beyond the bounds of what he would tolerate. His face stiffened to an expression of quelling austerity; he replied in a voice of ice: 'The unwarrantable language you have used, Arabella; the uncontrolled violence of your manner; the want of respect you have shown me – all these betray clearly how unfit you are to be sent into the world!'

Under the table, Sophia's foot kicked Arabella's ankle; across it, Mama's eyes met hers in a warning, reproving look. The colour surged up into her cheeks; her eyes filled; and she stammered: 'I beg your p-pardon, P-papa!'

He returned no answer. Mama broke the uneasy silence by calmly desiring Harry not to eat so fast; and then, just as though nothing untoward had occurred, began to talk to the Vicar about some parish business.

'What a dust you made!' Harry said presently, when the young people had fled to Mama's dressing-room, and poured out the whole story to Bertram, who had had his dinner brought to him there, on the sofa.

'I am *sick* with apprehension!' Arabella said tragically. 'He means to forbid me!'

'Fudge! It was only one of his scolds! Girls are such fools!'

'Ought I to go down and beg his pardon? Oh, no, I dare not! He has shut himself up in the study! What shall I do?'

'Leave it to Mama!' said Bertram, yawning. 'She's as shrewd as she can hold together, and if she means you to go to London, go you will!'

'I would not go to him now, if I were you,' said Sophia. 'You are in such an agitation of spirits that you would be bound to say something unbecoming, or start to cry. And you know how much he dislikes an excess of sensibility! Speak to him in the morning, after prayers!'

This course was decided on. And then, as Arabella afterwards confided to Bertram, it was more dreadful than all the rest! Mama had done her work too well: before the Vicar's erring daughter could utter a word of her carefully rehearsed apology, he had taken her hand, and said with his sweet, wistful smile: 'My child, you must forgive your father. Indeed, I spoke to you with grave injustice yesterday! Alas, that I, who preach moderation to my children, should have so little control over my own temper!'

'Bertram, I had rather by far he had *beaten* me!' said Arabella earnestly.

'Lord, yes!' agreed Bertram, shuddering. 'What a shocking thing! I'm glad I wasn't downstairs! It makes me feel like the devil when he gets to blaming himself. What did you say?'

'I could not utter a word! My voice was *wholly* suspended by tears, as you may imagine, and I was so afraid that he would be vexed with me for not being able to contain my feelings better! But he was not. Only fancy! He took me in his arms, and kissed me, and said I was his dear, good daughter, and oh, Bertram, I'm *not*!'

'Well, you need not put yourself in a pucker for that,' recommended her matter-of-fact brother. 'He won't think it above a day or two. The thing is that his dejected fit is at an end.'

'Oh, yes! But it was much, much worse at breakfast! He would keep on talking to me about the London scheme – teasing me, you know, about the giddy life I should lead there, and saying that I must be sure to write very long letters home, even if I cannot get a frank for them, for he would be so much interested to hear of all my doings!'

Bertram stared at her in undisguised horror. 'He did not!'

'But he did! And in the kindest way, only with that sad look in his eyes – *you* know! until I was ready to give up the whole scheme!'

'My God, I don't wonder at it!'

'No, and to crown all – as though I had not borne enough!' disclosed Arabella, hunting wildly for her handkerchief, 'he said I would want something pretty to wear in London, and he would have a pearl pin he wore when he was a young man made into a ring for me!'

This staggering intelligence made Bertram's jaw drop. After a moment's stupefaction he said resolutely: 'That settles it! I shan't come downstairs today after all. Ten to one, if he saw me he would start to blame himself for my frisk, and I should be driven into running away to enlist, or something, because, you know, a fellow can't stand that kind of thing!'

'No, indeed! I am sure all *my* pleasure has been quite cut-up!'

Since Papa's tender mood of forbearance showed every sign of continuance, Arabella fell into such an abyss of despondency that she was only saved from renouncing the London scheme by the timely intervention of Mama, who gave her thoughts a more cheerful direction by calling her into her bedroom one morning, and saying with a smile: 'I have something to show you, my love, which I think you will like.'

There was a box lying open upon Mama's dressing-table. Arabella blinked at the flash of diamonds, and uttered a long-drawn: 'Oh-h!'

'My father gave them to me,' said Mrs Tallant, sighing faintly. 'Of course I have never worn them of late years, for I have no occasion to. Besides, they are scarcely suitable for a clergyman's wife. But I have had them cleaned, and I mean to lend them to you to take with you to London. And I have asked Papa if he thinks I might give you Grandmama Tallant's pearl necklet, and he sees no objection to it. Your Papa has never cared for sparkling stones, you know, but he thinks pearls both modest and becoming to a female. However, if Lady Bridlington takes you to any dress-parties, which I am sure she will, the diamond set would be just the thing. You see, there is the crescent to set in your hair, and a brooch, and the bracelet as well. Nothing pretentious or vulgar, such as Papa would dislike, but I know the stones are of the finest water.'

41

It was impossible to be dejected after this, or even to contemplate abandoning the London scheme. What with the trimming of hats, hemming of handkerchiefs, embroidering of slippers for the Squire, the arrival of her gowns from Harrowgate, and the knitting of a new purse for Papa, together with all the ordinary duties which fell to her lot, Arabella had no time to indulge in morbid reflections. Everything went on prosperously: the Caterhams' retiring governess expressed herself all willingness to chaperon Arabella on the journey; the Squire discovered that by driving only a few miles out of the way she could spend a day or two with her Aunt Emma, at Arksey, and so rest the horses; Bertram's collar-bone knit itself again; and even Betsy recovered from her sore throat. Not until the Squire's carriage actually stood at the Parsonage gate, waiting to take up the travellers, with all the trunks strapped securely behind it, and Mama's dressing-case (also lent for the occasion) placed tenderly within the vehicle, did the mood of depression again descend upon Arabella. Whether it was Mama's embrace, or Papa's blessing, or Baby Jack's fat little hand waving farewell which overcame her, it would have been hard to say, but her feelings were quite overset, and it was a lady dissolved in tears whom Bertram thrust forcibly into the carriage. It was long before she could be composed again, nor was her companion of much support to her, since an excessive sympathy, coupled, perhaps, with the natural melancholy of a female obliged by circumstances to seek a new post, caused her to weep quite as bitterly in her corner of the capacious carriage.

While familiar landmarks were still to be observed out of the windows, Arabella's tears continued to flow, but by the time the carriage had reached an unknown countryside they had ceased, and after sniffing cautiously at the vinaigrette, proffered in a trembling hand by Miss Blackburn, she was able to dry her wet cheeks, and even to derive a sensible degree of comfort from the opulence of the huge sealskin pillow-muff lying on her lap. This, with the tippet round her throat, had been sent to her with her Aunt Eliza's love – the same who had once given Mama a set of

42

pink Indian muslin underwear. Even though one had never left one's home before, one could not be wholly given over to wretchedness when one's hands were tucked into a muff as large as any depicted in *La Belle Assemblée*. So large, indeed, was it, that Papa – But it would be wiser not to think of Papa, or any of the dear ones at home, perhaps. Better to fix one's attention on the countryside, and one's thoughts on the delights ahead.

To a young lady who had never been farther afield than to York – and that only when Papa had taken her and Sophia to be confirmed in the Minster – every new thing seen on the road was a matter for eager interest and exclamation. To those accustomed to the rapid mode of travel achieved by post-chaises, a journey in a somewhat ponderous carriage drawn by two horses, chosen more for their stamina than their speed, would have seemed slow beyond all bearing. To Arabella it was adventure, while to Miss Blackburn, inured by long custom to the horrors of the stage, it was unlooked-for comfort. Both ladies, therefore, soon settled down to enjoy themselves, thought the refreshments they were offered at the various halts excellent, found nothing to complain of in the beds at the posting-houses, and could not conceive of a more delightful way of undertaking a long journey. They were made very welcome at Arksey, where Aunt Emma received them with the greatest kindness, and the exclamation that Arabella was so like her dear Mama that she had nearly fainted away at the sight of her.

They spent two days at Arksey before taking the road again, and Arabella was quite sorry to leave the large, untidy house, so kind had Aunt Emma been, and so jolly all her cheerful cousins. But Timothy-coachman reported the horses to be quite fresh and ready for the road again, so there could be no lingering. They set forth once more, followed by the shouted good wishes and many hand-wavings of Aunt Emma's family.

After all the fun and the hospitality at Arksey, it did seem to be a little tedious to be sitting all day in a carriage, and once or twice, when a post-chaise-and-four dashed by, or some sporting curricle, with a pair of quick-goers harnessed to it, was encountered, Arabella found herself wishing that the Squire's carriage were not quite so large and unwieldy, and his horses less strengthy and rather more speedy beasts. It would have been pleasant, too, to have been able to have had a fresh pair poled-up when one of Uncle John's cast a shoe, instead of having to wait in a stuffy inn parlour while it was reshod; and Arabella, eating her dinner in the coffee-room of some posting-house, could not quite forbear a look of envy when some smart chaise drove into the courtyard, with horses sweating, and ostlers running out with a fresh team for the impatient traveller. Nor could she help wishing, once she had watched the mail-coach sweep through a turnpike, that Uncle John had provided the groom not with a horse-pistol, for which there did not seem to be the slightest occasion, but with a yard of tin, that he might have blown up for the pike in that same lordly style.

The weather, which had been cold but bright in Yorkshire, worsened as they drove farther south. It was raining in Lincolnshire, and the landscape looked sodden. Not many people were to be seen on the road, and the prospect was so uninviting that Miss Blackburn said that it was a pity they had not had the forethought to provide themselves with a travelling chessboard, with which, in default of looking out of the windows, they might have whiled away the time. At Tuxford they were unlucky enough to find the New Castle Arms without a bed to spare, and were obliged to put up at a smaller and by far less genteel inn, where the sheets had been so ill-aired that Miss Blackburn not only lay and shivered in her bed all night, but arose in the morning with a sore throat, and a tickling at the back of her nose which presaged a cold in the head. Arabella, who, for all her air of fragility, rarely succumbed to minor ailments, was not a penny the worse for the experience, but her north-country soul had been offended by the dust she had seen under her bed, and she was beginning to think that it would be a relief to reach her journey's end. It was vexing to discover, just as she had packed Mama's dressing-case, and was ready to leave the inn, that one of the traces needed repair, for it had been arranged that they should spend the following night at

Grantham, which, the guide-book informed her, lay some twenty-nine or thirty miles on from Tuxford. She hoped very much that the coachman would not decide that his horses could go no farther than to Newark, but since he was something of a despot, and had no opinion of fast travelling, it seemed more than likely that he would. However, the trace was mended in fairly good time, and they reached Newark in time to eat a late luncheon. Here, while he baited his horses, the coachman fell out with one of the ostlers, who asked him whether it was the King's state coach he had there; and this so much affronted him that he was quite as anxious as Arabella to reach Grantham that evening.

It was raining again when they left Newark, and the atmosphere was dank and chilly. Miss Blackburn wrapped herself up in a large shawl, and sniffed unhappily, as her cold gained on her. Even Arabella, who was largely impervious to climatic conditions, suffered a little from the many draughts that crept into the carriage, and wriggled numbed toes inside her half-boots of crimson jean.

The carriage bowled along at a sedate pace for several miles, the tedium being enlivened only at the Balderton turnpike, where, recognising a Johnny Raw in the coachman, the pike-keeper made a spirited attempt to extort a fee from him. But although Timothy-coachman might never have set foot beyond the boundaries of Yorkshire before, he was harder-headed than any of these soft southern folk whom he despised so profoundly, and he knew very well that the ticket bought at the last toll-gate opened all the pikes to him until the next, south of Grantham, was reached. After an exchange of personalities which made Miss Blackburn utter little moans of dismay, and Arabella – regrettably – giggle, he won a signal victory over the pike-keeper, and drove through with a triumphant flourish of his whip.

'Oh, dear, I am becoming so tired of this journey!' confided Arabella. 'I could almost wish to be held up by a highwayman!'

'My dear Miss Tallant, pray do not *think* of such a thing!' shuddered her companion. 'I only hope we may be spared any sort of accident!'

Neither lady's wish was destined to be granted her. No such excitement as a hold-up awaited them, but a little way short of the Marston turnpike the perch of the carriage broke, and the body fell forward upon the box. The Squire's travelling carriage had stood too long in his coach-house.

After the coachman had delivered himself of a long, self-exculpatory monologue, the groom was sent off to take counsel of the pike-keeper, half a mile down the road. When he returned, it was with the pleasing intelligence that no adequate assistance was to be hoped for in the next village: it must be sought in Grantham, five or six miles farther on, where a conveyance could no doubt be hired to fetch the ladies in while the perch was mended, or replaced. The coachman then suggested that his passengers, both of whom were standing by the roadside, should climb up into the carriage again to await deliverance, while the groom took one of the horses and rode on to Grantham. Miss Blackburn was meekly ready to follow this advice, but her charge thought poorly of it.

'What! Sit in that horrid, draughty carriage all that time? I won't do it!' she declared.

'But we cannot continue to stand in the rain, dear Miss Tallant!' said Miss Blackburn.

'Of course we cannot! Either way I am persuaded you would catch your death! There must be a house hereabouts which would lend us shelter! What are those lights over there?'

They plainly shone from the windows of a residence set a little back from the road. The groom volunteered the information that he had noticed some lodge gates a few steps back.

'Good!' said Arabella briskly. 'We will walk up to it, ma'am, and beg them to give us shelter for a little while.'

Miss Blackburn, a timorous soul, protested feebly. 'They would think it so strange of us!'

'No, why should they?' returned Arabella. 'Why, when a carriage had an accident outside *our* gates last year, Papa sent Harry out at once to offer shelter to the travellers! We cannot shiver for an hour or more in that horrid carriage, ma'am, with nothing to do! Besides, I am shockingly hungry, and I should think they would be bound to offer us refreshment, would not you? I am sure it is dinner-time, and past!'

'Oh, I do not think we should!' was all Miss Blackburn had to say, and it seemed so stupid to Arabella that she paid no heed to it, but desired the groom to escort them to the lodge gates before riding off to Grantham. This he did, and the ladies, dismissing him there, trod up the short drive to the house, one of them murmuring disjointed protests, the other perceiving no reason in the world why she should not claim a hospitality anyone in Yorkshire would have been eager to offer.

Four

*I*t was at about this moment that that erratic young sprig of fashion, Lord Fleetwood, fixed his friend, and host, Mr Beaumaris, with a laughing eye, and demanded in a rallying tone: 'Well! You promise me a rare day with the hounds tomorrow – by the by, where do we meet? – but what – *what*, Robert, do you offer me for my entertainment this evening?'

'My cook,' said Mr Beaumaris, 'is generally thought to be an artist in his own line. A Frenchman: I think you will like his way of dressing a Davenport chicken, while some trick he has of flavouring a Benton sauce –'

'What, did you send Alphonse down, then, from London?' interrupted Lord Fleetwood, momentarily diverted.

'Alphonse?' repeated Mr Beaumaris, his finely chiselled brows lifting a little. 'Oh, no! this is another. I don't think I know his name. But I like his way with fish.'

Lord Fleetwood burst out laughing. 'I expect if you discovered a cook with a way of serving game which you liked, you would send him off to that shooting-box of yours, and pay him a king's ransom, only to kick his heels for three parts of the year!'

'I expect I should,' agreed Mr Beaumaris imperturbably.

'*But*,' said his lordship severely, 'I am not to be put off with a cook! I came here in the expectation of finding fair Paphians, let me tell you, and all manner of shocking orgies – wine out of skulls, y'know, and –'

'The lamentable influence of Lord Byron upon society!' interpolated Mr Beaumaris, with a faint, contemptuous smile.

'What? Oh, that poet-fellow that set up such a dust! Myself, I thought him devilish underbred, but of course it don't do to say so. But that's it! Where, Robert, are the fair Paphians?'

'If I had any Paphians in keeping here, you don't imagine, do you, Charles, that I would run the risk of being cut-out by a man of *your* address?' retorted Mr Beaumaris.

Lord Fleetwood grinned at him, but replied: 'None of your gammon to me! It would take ten times my address to cut-out a – a – dash it, a Midas like you!'

'If my memory does not err, all that Midas touched turned to gold,' said Mr Beaumaris. 'I think you mean Croesus.'

'No, I don't! Never heard of the fellow!'

'Well, most of the things I touch have a disheartening way of turning to dross,' said Mr Beaumaris, lightly, but with a note of bitter self-mockery in his languid voice.

This was going a little too deep for his friend. 'Humdudgeon, Robert! You can't bamboozle me! If there are to be no Paphians –'

'I can't conceive why you should have supposed there would be,' interrupted his host.

'Well, I didn't, but I can tell you this, my boy! – that's the latest *on-dit!*'

'Good God! Why?'

'Lord, how should I know? Daresay it's because you won't throw your glove at any of the beauties who have been setting their caps at you any time these five years. What's more, your *chères-amies* are always such devilish high-flyers, dear boy, it puts notions into the heads of all the old tabbies! Think of the Faraglini!'

'I had rather not. The most rapacious female of my acquaintance.'

'But what a face! What a figure!'

'And what a temper!'

'What became of her?' asked his lordship. 'I haven't laid eyes on her since she left your protection.'

'I think she went to Paris. Why? Had you a fancy to succeed me?'

'No, by Jove, I couldn't have stood the nonsense!' said his lordship frankly. 'She'd have had me rolled-up within a month! What did you have to give for those match-grays she used to drive all over town?'

'I can't remember.'

'To tell you the truth,' confided Lord Fleetwood, 'I shouldn't have thought it worth it myself – though I'm not denying she was a curst fine woman!'

'It wasn't.'

Lord Fleetwood regarded him, half-curious, half-amused. 'Is anything worth while to you, Robert?' he asked quizzically.

'Yes, my horses!' retorted Mr Beaumaris. 'And, talking of horses, Charles, what the devil possessed you to buy one of Lichfield's breakdowns?'

'That bay? Now, there's a horse that fairly took my fancy!' said his lordship, his simple countenance lighting up with enthusiasm. 'What a piece of blood and bone! No, really, Robert – !'

'If ever I find myself with a thoroughly unsound animal in my stables,' said Mr Beaumaris ruthlessly, 'I shall offer him to you in the happy certainty that he will take your fancy!'

Lord Fleetwood was still protesting with indignation and vehemence when the butler entered the room to inform his master, rather apologetically, that a carriage had broken down outside his gates, and the two ladies it bore were desirous of sheltering for a short time under his roof.

Mr Beaumaris's cool gray eyes betrayed no emotion, but his mouth seemed for an instant to harden. He said calmly: 'Certainly. There should be a fire in the saloon. Tell Mrs Mersey to wait upon the ladies there.' The butler bowed, and would have withdrawn, but Lord Fleetwood checked him, exclaiming: 'No, no, too shabby by half, Robert! I won't be fobbed off so! What do they look like, Brough? Old? Young? Pretty?'

The butler, inured to his lordship's free and easy ways, replied with unimpaired solemnity that one of the ladies was both young, and – he ventured to think – very pretty.

'I insist on your receiving these females with a proper degree of civility, Robert!' said his lordship firmly. 'Saloon, indeed! Show 'em in, Brough!'

The butler glanced for guidance towards his master, as though he doubted whether the command would be endorsed, but Mr Beaumaris merely said with his usual indifference: 'As you please, Charles.'

'What an ungrateful dog you are!' said Lord Fleetwood, when Brough had left the room. 'You don't deserve your fortune! This is the hand of Providence!'

'I should doubt of their being Paphians,' was all Mr Beaumaris found to say. 'I thought that was what you wanted?'

'Any diversion is better than none!' replied Lord Fleetwood.

'What a singularly infelicitous remark! I wonder why I invited you.'

Lord Fleetwood grinned at him. 'Now, Robert, did you think – *did* you think – to come Tip Street over me? There may be plenty of toadies ready to jump out of their skins at the very thought of being invited to the Nonpareil's house – and no better entertainment offered than a rubber of piquet, I dare swear –'

'You are forgetting the cook.'

'*But*,' continued his lordship inexorably, 'I ain't amongst 'em!'

Mr Beaumaris's habitual aspect was one of coldness, and reserve, but sometimes he could smile in a way that not only softened the austerity of his countenance but lit his eyes with a gleam of the purest amusement. It was not the smile he kept for social occasions – a faintly sardonic curl of the lips, that one – but those who were honoured by a glimpse of it generally revised their first impressions of him. Those who had never seen it were inclined to think him a proud, disagreeable sort of a man, though only the most daring would ever have uttered aloud such a criticism of one who, besides possessing all the advantages of birth and fortune, was an acknowledged leader of society. Lord Fleetwood, no stranger to that smile, saw it dawn now, and grinned more broadly than ever.

'How can you, Charles? When you must know that almost your only claim to fashion is being noticed by me!'

Arabella entered the room to find both its occupants laughing, and thus had the felicity of seeing Mr Beaumaris at his best. That she herself was looking remarkably pretty, with her dusky curls and charming complexion admirably set off by a high-crowned bonnet, with curled ostrich-feather tips, and crimson ribbons tied into a bow under one ear, never entered her head, since Mr Tallant's daughters had always been discouraged from thinking much about their appearance. She paused on the threshold, while the butler murmured her name and Miss Blackburn's, quite unselfconscious, but looking about her with a kind of wide-eyed, innocent interest. She was very much impressed by what she saw. The house was not a large one, but she perceived that it was furnished with a good taste which was as quiet as it was expensive. Her quick scrutiny took in Lord Fleetwood, who had put up an instinctive hand to straighten the Belcher necktie he affected, and passed on to Mr Beaumaris.

Arabella had one brother who aspired to dandyism, and she had thought that she had seen in Harrowgate gentlemen of decided fashion. She now perceived that she had much mistaken the matter. No one she had ever seen approached the elegance of Mr Beaumaris.

Lord Fleetwood, or any of his cronies, could have recognised the tailoring of that coat of olive-green superfine at a glance; Arabella, to whom the magic name of Weston was unknown, was merely aware of a garment so exquisitely cut that it presented all the appearance of having been moulded to its wearer's form. A very good form, too, she noted, with approval. No need of buckram wadding, such as that Knaresborough tailor had inserted into Bertram's new coat, to fill out those shoulders! And how envious Bertram would have been of Mr Beaumaris's fine legs, sheathed in tight pantaloons, with gleaming Hessian boots pulled over them! Mr Beaumaris's shirt-points were not as high as Bertram's, but his necktie commanded the respect of one who had more than once watched her brother's struggles with a far less complicated arrangement. Arabella was not perfectly sure that she admired his style of hairdressing – he affected a Stanhope crop – but she did think him a remarkably handsome man, as he stood there, laughter dying on his lips, and out of his gray eyes.

It was only a moment that he stood thus. She had the impression that he was scanning her critically; then he moved forward, and bowed slightly, and begged, in a rather colourless tone, to know in what way he could be of service to her.

'How do you do?' said Arabella politely. 'I beg your pardon, but the thing is that there has been an accident to my carriage, and – and it is raining, and horridly cold! The groom has rid in to Grantham, and I daresay will bring another carriage out directly, but – but Miss Blackburn has taken a chill, and we should be very much obliged if we might wait here in the warm!'

She was stammering and blushing by the time she came to the end of this speech. Outside, it had seemed the simplest thing in the world to solicit shelter; under Mr Beaumaris's eye, it all at once seemed as though the request were outrageous. To be sure, he was smiling, but it was a very different smile from the one his face had worn when she had entered the room. It was such a very slight curl of the lips, yet there was some quality in it which made her feel ruffled and uncomfortable.

But he said with perfect civility: 'An unfortunate mishap. You must permit me to send you to Grantham in one of my carriages, ma'am.'

Lord Fleetwood, who had been standing staring in the frankest admiration at Arabella, was jerked into action by this speech. Pulling a chair invitingly close to the fire, he exclaimed: 'No, no, come and sit down, ma'am! I can see you are chilled to the bone! Shocking weather for travelling! You will have got your feet wet, I daresay, and *that* will never do, you know! Robert, where have your wits gone a-begging? Why don't you desire Brough to fetch some refreshment for Miss – er – Miss – for the ladies?'

With a look which Arabella was strongly inclined to construe as one of resignation, Mr Beaumaris replied: 'I trust he may be doing so. I beg you will be seated, ma'am!'

But it was Lord Fleetwood who handed Arabella to the chair he had placed, saying solicitously: 'I am sure you are hungry, and will be glad of something to eat!'

'Well, yes, sir,' confessed Arabella, who was very hungry indeed. 'I own, I have been thinking of my dinner for several miles! And no wonder, for I see it is already past five o'clock!'

This naïve speech made his lordship, who never sat down to his dinner before half-past seven at the very earliest, swallow convulsively, but he recovered himself in an instant, and replied without a blink: 'So it is, by Jupiter! You are famished, then! But never mind! Mr Beaumaris here was just saying that dinner would be served in a trice. Weren't you, Robert?'

'Was I?' said Mr Beaumaris. 'I have the wretchedest of memories, but I am sure you are right. I beg you will do me the honour of dining with me, ma'am.'

Arabella hesitated. She could see from her anguished expression that Miss Blackburn thought she should rather accept Mr Beaumaris's first offer; and not the most inveterate of optimists could have read into that languid gentleman's voice anything more than a reluctant civility. But this warm, comfortably furnished room was a most welcome change from the travelling carriage, and the aromas of cooking which had assailed her nostrils as she had crossed the hall had considerably whetted her appetite. She looked a little doubtfully at her host. Again it was Lord Fleetwood who, with his friendly smile and easy manners, clinched the matter. 'Of course they will dine with us! Now, won't you, ma'am?'

'It would be giving too much trouble, sir!' said Miss Blackburn, in a sort of gasp.

'No trouble in the world, ma'am, I assure you! In fact, we are very much obliged to you, for we had been wishing that we were to have company, eh, Robert?'

'Certainly,' agreed Mr Beaumaris. 'Was I not just saying so?'

Miss Blackburn, having undergone a lifetime of slights and snubs, was quick to catch the satirical inflection. She cast him a scared, deprecating look, and coloured. His eyes met hers; he stood looking down at her for a moment, and then said in a much kinder tone: 'I am afraid you are not quite comfortable there, ma'am. Will you not draw nearer to the fire?'

She was thrown into a flutter, and assured him rather disjointedly that she was perfectly comfortable, and himself too good, too obliging! Brough had come into the room with a tray of glasses and decanters, which he set down on a table, and Mr Beaumaris moved towards it, saying: 'You will like to go upstairs with my housekeeper, I daresay, to take off your wet coat, but first you must let me give you a glass of wine.' He began to pour out some Madeira. 'Two extra covers for dinner, Brough – which you will serve immediately.'

Brough thought of the Davenport fowls roasting on the spits in the kitchen, and of the artist in charge of them, and was visibly shaken. 'Immediately, sir?' he said, in a failing voice.

'Let us say, within half-an-hour,' amended Mr Beaumaris, carrying a glass of wine over to Miss Blackburn.

'Yes, sir,' said Brough, and tottered from the room, a broken man.

Miss Blackburn accepted the wine gratefully, but when it was offered to Arabella she declined it. Papa did not like his daughters to taste anything stronger than porter, or the very mild claret-cup served at the Harrowgate Assembly Rooms, and she was a little doubtful of its possible effect on her. Mr Beaumaris did not press her in any way, but set the glass down again, poured out some sherry for himself and his friend, and returned to sit beside Miss Blackburn on the sofa.

Lord Fleetwood, meanwhile, had ensconced himself beside Arabella, and was chatting to her in his inconsequent, cheerful way, which set her quite at her ease. He was delighted to hear that she was on her way to London, hoped to have the pleasure of meeting her there – in the Park, possibly, or at Almack's. He had plenty of anecdotes of *ton* with which to entertain her, and rattled on in an agreeable fashion until the housekeeper came to escort the ladies upstairs.

They were taken to a guest-chamber on the first floor, and handed over there to a housemaid, who brought up hot water for them, and bore their damp coats away to be dried in the kitchen.

'Everything in the first style of elegance!' breathed Miss Blackburn. 'But we should not be dining here! I feel sure we ought not, my dear Miss Tallant!'

Arabella was a little doubtful on this score herself, but as it was now too late to draw back she stifled her misgivings, and said stoutly that she was persuaded there could be no objection. Finding a brush and comb laid out on the dressing-table, she began to tidy her rather tumbled locks.

'They are *most* gentlemanlike,' said Miss Blackburn, deriving comfort from this circumstance. 'Of the first rank of fashion, I daresay. They will be here for the hunting, depend upon it: I collect this is a hunting-box.'

'A hunting-box!' exclaimed Arabella, awed. 'Is it not very large and grand, ma'am, to be that?'

'Oh, no, my dear! Quite a small house! The Tewkesburys, whose sweet children I was engaged to instruct before I removed to Mrs Caterham's establishment, had one much larger, I assure you. This is the Melton country, you must know.'

'Good heavens, are they Melton men, then? Oh, how much I wish Bertram could be here! What I shall have to tell him! I think it is Mr Beaumaris who owns the house: I wonder who the other is? I thought when I first saw him he could not be quite the thing, for that striped waistcoat, you know, and that spotted handkerchief he wears instead of a cravat makes him look like a groom, or some such thing. But when he spoke, of course I knew he was not a vulgar person at all.'

Miss Blackburn, feeling for once in her life pleasantly superior, gave a titter of laughter, and said pityingly: 'Oh, dear me no, Miss Tallant! You will find a great many young gentlemen of fashion wearing much odder clothes than *that*! It is what Mr Geoffrey Tewkesbury – a very modish young man! – used to call *all the crack*!' She added pensively: 'But I must confess that I do not care for it myself, and nor did dear Mrs

Tewkesbury. My notion of a true gentleman is someone like Mr Beaumaris!'

Arabella dragged the comb ruthlessly through a tangle. '*I* thought him a very proud, reserved man!' she declared. 'And not at all hospitable!' she added.

'Oh, no, how can you say so? How very kind and obliging it was of him to place me in the best place, so near the fire! Delightful manners! Nothing high in them at all! I was quite overcome by his condescension!'

It was evident to Arabella that she and Miss Blackburn regarded their host through two very different pairs of spectacles. She preserved an unconvinced silence, and as soon as Miss Blackburn had finished prinking her crimped gray locks at the mirror, suggested that they should go downstairs again. Accordingly they left the room, and crossed the upper hall to the head of the stairway. Mr Beaumaris's fancy had led him to carpet his stairs, a luxury which Miss Blackburn indicated to her charge with one pointing finger and a most expressive glance.

Across the lower hall, the door into the library stood ajar. Lord Fleetwood's voice, speaking in rallying tones, assailed the ladies' ears. 'I swear you are incorrigible!' said his lordship. 'The loveliest of creatures drops into your lap, like a veritable honey-fall, and you behave as though a gull-groper had forced his way into your house!'

Mr Beaumaris replied with disastrous clarity: 'My dear Charles, when you have been hunted by every trick known to the ingenuity of the female mind, you may more readily partake of my sentiments upon this occasion! I have had beauties hopeful of wedding my fortune swoon in my arms, break their bootlaces outside my London house, sprain their ankles when my arm is there to support them, and now it appears that I am to be pursued even into Leicestershire! An accident to her coach! Famous! What a greenhorn she must believe me to be!'

A small hand closed like a vice about Miss Blackburn's wrist. Herself bridling indignantly, she saw Arabella's eyes sparkling, and her cheeks most becomingly flushed. Had she been better acquainted with Miss Tallant she might have taken fright at these signs. Arabella breathed into her ear: 'Miss Blackburn, can I *trust* you?'

Miss Blackburn would have vigorously assured her that she could, but the hand released her wrist, and flew up to cover her mouth. Slightly startled, she nodded. To her amazement, Arabella then picked up her skirts, and fled lightly back to the top of the stairs. Turning there, she began to come slowly down again, saying in a clear, carrying voice: 'Yes, indeed! I am sure I have said the same, dear ma'am, times out of mind! But do, pray, go before me!'

Miss Blackburn, turning to stare at her, with her mouth at half-cock, found a firm young hand in the small of her back, and was thrust irresistibly onward.

'But in spite of all,' said Arabella, 'I prefer to travel with my own horses!'

The awful scowl that accompanied these light words quite bewildered the poor little governess, but she understood that she was expected to reply in kind, and said in a quavering voice: 'Very true, my dear!'

The scowl gave place to an encouraging smile. Any one of Arabella's brothers or sisters would have begged her at this point to consider all the consequences of impetuosity; Miss Blackburn, unaware of the eldest Miss Tallant's besetting fault, was merely glad that she had not disappointed her. Arabella tripped across the hall to that half-open door, and entered the library again.

It was Lord Fleetwood who came forward to receive her. He eyed her with undisguised appreciation, and said: 'Now you will be more comfortable! Devilish dangerous to sit about in a wet coat, y'know! But we are yet unacquainted, ma'am! The stupidest thing! – never can catch a name when it is spoken! That man of Beaumaris's mumbles so that no one can hear him! You must let me make myself known to you, too – Lord Fleetwood, very much at your service!'

'I,' said Arabella, a most dangerous glitter in her eye, 'am Miss Tallant!'

58

His lordship, murmuring polite gratification at being made the recipient of this information, was surprised to find his inanities quite misunderstood. Arabella fetched a world-weary sigh, and enunciated with a scornful curl of her lip: 'Oh yes! *The* Miss Tallant!'

'Th – *the* Miss Tallant?' stammered his lordship, all at sea.

'The rich Miss Tallant!' said Arabella.

His lordship rolled an anguished and an enquiring eye at his host, but Mr Beaumaris was not looking at him. Mr Beaumaris, his attention arrested, was regarding the rich Miss Tallant with a distinct gleam of curiosity, not unmixed with amusement, in his face.

'I had hoped that here at least I might be unknown!' said Arabella, seating herself in a chair a little withdrawn from the fire. 'Ah, you must let me make you known to Miss Blackburn, my – my *dame de compagnie!*'

Lord Fleetwood sketched a bow; Miss Blackburn, her countenance wooden, dropped him a slight curtsy, and sat down on the nearest chair.

'Miss Tallant!' repeated Lord Fleetwood, searching his memory in vain for enlightenment. 'Ah, yes! Of course! Er – I don't think I have ever had the honour of meeting you in town, have I, ma'am?'

Arabella directed an innocent look from him to Mr Beaumaris, and back again, and clapped her hands together with an assumption of mingled delight and dismay. 'Oh, you *did* not know!' she exclaimed. 'I need never have told you! But when you looked *so*, I made sure you were as bad as all the rest! Was anything ever so vexatious? I most particularly desire to be quite unknown in London!'

'My dear ma'am, you may rely on me!' promptly replied his lordship, who, like most rattles, thought himself the model of discretion. 'And Mr Beaumaris, you know, is in the same case as yourself, and able to sympathise with you!'

Arabella glanced at her host, and found that he had raised his quizzing-glass, which hung round his neck on a long black riband, and was surveying her through it. She put up her chin a little, for she was by no means sure that she cared for this scrutiny. 'Indeed?' she said.

It was not the practice of young ladies to put up their chins in just that style if Mr Beaumaris levelled his glass at them: they were more in the habit of simpering, or of trying to appear unconscious of his regard. But Mr Beaumaris saw that there was a decidedly militant sparkle in this lady's eye, and his interest, at first tickled, was now fairly caught. He let his glass fall, and said gravely: 'Indeed! And you?'

'Alas!' said Arabella, 'I am fabulously wealthy! It is the greatest mortification to me! You can have no notion!'

His lips twitched. 'I have always found, however, that a large fortune carries with it certain advantages.'

'Oh, you are a man! I shall not allow you to know anything of the matter!' she cried. 'You cannot know what it means to be the object of every fortune-hunter, courted and odiously flattered only for your wealth, until you are ready to wish that you had not a penny in the world!'

Miss Blackburn, who had hitherto supposed her charge to be a modest, well-behaved girl, barely repressed a shudder. Mr Beaumaris, however, said: 'I feel sure that you underrate yourself, ma'am.'

'Oh, dear me, no!' said Arabella. 'I have too often heard myself pointed out as the rich Miss Tallant to be under any illusion, sir! And it is for this reason that I wish to be quite unknown in London.'

Mr Beaumaris smiled, but as the butler came in just then to announce dinner, he said nothing, but merely offered his arm to Arabella.

The dinner, which consisted of two courses, seemed to Arabella sumptuous beyond her wildest imaginings. No suspicion crossed her mind that her host, after one swift glance at his board, had resigned himself to the knowledge that the reputations of himself and his cook had been placed in jeopardy; or that that artist in the kitchen, having, with strange Gallic imprecations which made his various assistants quake, rent limb from limb two half-roasted Davenport fowls, and flung them into a pan with a béchamel sauce and some tarragons, was even now, as he arranged a basket of pastry on a dish, undecided whether to leave this dishonoured house on the instant, or to cut his throat with the larger carving-knife. Soup à la Reine was removed with fillets of turbot with an Italian sauce; and the chickens à la Tarragon were flanked by a dish of spinach and croûtons, a glazed ham, two cold partridges, some broiled mushrooms, and a raised mutton pie. The second course presented Arabella with an even more bewildering choice, for there was, besides the baskets of pastry, a Rhenish cream, a jelly, a Savoy cake, a dish of salsify fried in butter, an omelette, and some anchovy toast. Mrs Tallant had always prided herself on her housekeeping, but such a repast as this, embellished as it was by elegant garnitures, and subtle sauces, was quite beyond the range of the Vicarage cook. Arabella could not help opening her eyes a little at the array of viands spread before her, but she managed to conceal her awe, and to partake of what was offered to her with a very creditable assumption of unconsciousness. Mr Beaumaris, perhaps loth to degrade his burgundy, or perhaps with a faint, despairing hope of adding piquancy to this commonplace meal, had instructed Brough to serve champagne. Arabella, having already cast discretion to the winds, allowed her glass to be filled, and sipped her way distastefully through it. It had a pleasantly exhilarating effect upon her. She informed Mr Beaumaris that she was bound for the town residence of Lady Bridlington; created several uncles for the simple purpose of endowing herself with their fortunes; and at one blow disposed of four brothers and three sisters who might have been supposed to have laid a claim to a share of all this wealth. She contrived, without precisely making so vulgar a boast, to convey the impression that she was escaping from courtships so persistent as to amount to persecution; and Mr Beaumaris, listening with intense pleasure, said that London was the very place for anyone desirous of escaping attention.

Arabella, embarking recklessly on her second glass of champagne, said that in a crowd one could more easily pass unnoticed than in the restricted society of the country.

'Very true,' agreed Mr Beaumaris.

'*You* never did so!' remarked Lord Fleetwood, helping himself from the dish of mushrooms which Brough presented at his elbow. 'You must know, ma'am, that you are in the presence of the Nonpareil – none other! Quite the most noted figure in society since poor Brummell was done-up!'

'Indeed!' Arabella looked from him to Mr Beaumaris with a pretty air of innocent enquiry. 'I did not know – I might not have heard the name quite correctly, perhaps?'

'My dear Miss Tallant!' exclaimed his lordship, in mock horror. 'Not know the great Beaumaris! The Arbiter of Fashion! Robert, you are quite set down!'

Mr Beaumaris, whose almost imperceptibly lifted finger had brought the watchful Brough to his side, was murmuring some command into that attentive but astonished ear, and paid no heed. His command was passed on to the footman hovering by the side-table, who, being quite a young man, and as yet imperfectly in control of his emotions, betrayed in his startled look some measure of the incredulity which shook his trained soul. The coldly quelling eye of his superior recalled him speedily to a sense of his position, however, and he left the room to carry the stupefying command still farther.

Miss Tallant, meanwhile, had perceived an opportunity to gratify her most pressing desire, which was to snub her host beyond possibility of his recovery. 'Arbiter of Fashion?' she said, in a blank voice. 'You cannot, surely, mean one of the *dandy-set*? I had thought – Oh, I beg your pardon! I expect that in London that is quite as important as being a great soldier, or a statesman, or – or some such thing!'

Even Lord Fleetwood could scarcely mistake the tenor of this artless speech. He gave an audible gasp. Miss Blackburn, whose enjoyment of dinner had already been seriously impaired, refused the partridge, and tried unavailingly to catch her charge's eye. Only Mr Beaumaris, hugely enjoying himself, appeared unmoved. He replied coolly: 'Oh, decidedly! One's influence is so far-reaching!'

'Oh?' said Arabella politely.

'Why, certainly, ma'am! One may blight a whole career by the mere raising of an eyebrow, or elevate a social aspirant to the ranks of the highest *ton* only by leaning on his arm for the length of a street.'

Miss Tallant suspected that she was being quizzed, but the strange exhilaration had her in its grip, and she did not hesitate to cross swords with this expert fencer. 'No doubt, sir, if *I* had ambitions to cut a figure in society *your* approval would be a necessity?'

Mr Beaumaris, famed for his sword-play, slipped under her guard with an unexpected thrust. 'My dear Miss Tallant, *you* need no passport to admit you to the ranks of the most sought-after! Even I could not depress the claims of one endowed with – may I say it? – your face, your figure, and your fortune!'

The colour flamed up into Arabella's cheeks; she choked over the last of her wine, tried to look arch, and only succeeded in looking adorably confused. Lord Fleetwood, realising that his friend had embarked on yet another of his practised flirtations, directed an indignant glance at him, and did his best to engage the heiress's attention himself. He was succeeding quite well when he was thrown off his balance by the unprecedented behaviour of Brough, who, as the second course made its appearance, removed his champagne-glass, replacing it with a goblet, which he proceeded to fill with something out of a tall flagon which his lordship strongly suspected was iced lemonade. One sip was enough alike to confirm this hideous fear and to deprive his lordship momentarily of the power of speech. Mr Beaumaris, blandly swallowing some of the innocuous mixture, seized the opportunity to re-engage Miss Tallant in conversation.

Arabella had been rather relieved to see her wine-glass removed, for although she would have died rather than have owned to it she thought the champagne decidedly nasty, besides making her want to sneeze. She took a revivifying draught of lemonade, glad to discover that in really fashionable circles this mild beverage was apparently served with the second course. Miss Blackburn, better versed in the ways of the *haut ton*, now found herself unable to form a correct judgement of her host. To be plunged from a conviction that he was truly gentlemanlike to a shocked realisation that he was nothing but a coxcomb, and then back again, quite overset the poor little lady. She knew not what to think, but could not forbear casting him a glance eloquent of the warmest gratitude. His eyes encountered hers, but for such a fleeting instant that she could never afterwards be sure whether she had caught the glimmer of an amused smile in them, or whether she had imagined it.

Brough, receiving a message at the door, announced that Madam's groom had brought a hired coach to the house, and desired to know when she would wish to resume her journey to Grantham.

'It can wait,' said Mr Beaumaris, replenishing Arabella's glass. 'A little of the Rhenish cream, Miss Tallant?'

'How long,' demanded Arabella, recalling Mr Beaumaris's odious words to his friend, 'will it take them to mend my own carriage?'

'I understand, miss, that a new pole will be needed. I could not say how long it will be.'

A faint clucking from Miss Blackburn indicated dismay at this intelligence. Mr Beaumaris said: 'A tiresome accident, but I beg you will not distress yourselves! I will send my chaise to pick you up in Grantham at whatever hour tomorrow should be agreeable to you.'

Arabella thanked him, but was resolute in refusing his offer, for which, she assured him, there was not the slightest occasion. If the wheelwright proved too dilatory for her patience she would finish her journey post. 'It will be quite an experience!' she declared truthfully. 'My friends assure me that I am a great deal too old-fashioned in my notions – that quite a respectable degree of comfort is to be found in hired chaises!'

'I perceive,' said Mr Beaumaris, 'that we have much in common, ma'am. But I shall not allow a distaste for hired vehicles to be old-fashioned. Let us rather say that we have a little more nicety than the general run of our fellow-creatures!' He turned his head towards the butler. 'Let a message be conveyed to the wheelwright, Brough, that he will oblige me by repairing Miss Tallant's carriage with all possible expedition.'

Miss Tallant had nothing to do but thank him for his kind offices, and finish her Rhenish cream. That done, she rose from the table, saying that she had trespassed too long on her host's hospitality, and must now take her leave of him, with renewed thanks for his kindness.

'The obligation, Miss Tallant, is all on my side,' he replied. 'I am grateful for the chance which has made us acquainted, and shall hope to have the pleasure of calling upon you in town before many days.'

This promise threw Miss Blackburn into agitation. As she accompanied Arabella upstairs, she whispered: 'My dear Miss Tallant, how *could* you? And now he means to call on you, and you have told him – oh dear, oh dear, what would your Mama say?'

'Pooh!' returned Arabella, brazening it out. 'If he is indeed a rich man, he will not care a fig, or think of it again!'

'*If* he is – Good gracious, Miss Tallant, he must be one of the wealthiest men in the country! When I collected that he was in very truth Mr Beaumaris I nearly swooned where I stood!'

'Well,' said the pot-valiant Arabella, 'if he is so very grand and important you may depend upon it he has not the least intention of calling on me in town. And I am sure I hope he will not, for he is an odious person!'

She refused to be moved from this standpoint, or even to acknowledge that in Mr Beaumaris's person at least no fault could be found. She said that she did not think him handsome, and that she held dandies in abhorrence. Miss Blackburn, terrified that she might, in this alarming mood, betray her dislike of Mr Beaumaris at parting, begged her not to forget what the barest civility rendered obligatory. She added that one slighting word uttered by him would be sufficient to wither any young lady's career at the outset, and then wished that she had held her tongue, since this warning had the effect of bringing the militant sparkle back into Arabella's eyes. But when Mr Beaumaris handed her into the coach, and, with quite his most attractive smile, lightly kissed the tips of her fingers before letting her hand go, she bade him farewell in a shy little voice that gave no hint of her loathing of him.

The coach set off down the drive; Mr Beaumaris turned, and in a leisurely way walked back into his house. He was pounced on in the hall by his injured friend, who demanded to know what the devil he meant by inflicting lemonade upon his guests.

'I don't think Miss Tallant cared for my champagne,' he replied imperturbably.

'Well, if she didn't, she could have refused it, couldn't she?' protested Lord Fleetwood. 'Besides, it was no such thing! She drank two glasses of it!'

'Never mind, Charles, there is still the port,' said Mr Beaumaris.

'Yes, by God!' said his lordship, brightening. 'And, mind, now! I expect the very best in your cellar! A couple of bottles of that '75 of yours, or –'

'Bring it to the library, Brough – something off the wood!' said Mr Beaumaris.

Lord Fleetwood, always the easiest of preys, rose to the bait without a moment's hesitation. 'Here, no, I say!' he cried, turning quite pale with horror. 'Robert! No, really, Robert!'

Mr Beaumaris lifted his bows in the blandest astonishment, but Brough, taking pity on his lordship, said in a soothing tone: 'We have nothing like that in our cellars, I assure your lordship!'

Lord Fleetwood, perceiving that he had once more been gulled, said with strong feeling: 'You deserve I should plant you a facer for that, Robert!'

'Well, if you think you can – !' said Mr Beaumaris.

'I don't,' replied his lordship frankly, accompanying him into

66

the library. 'But that lemonade was a dog's trick to serve me, you know!' His brow puckered in an effort of thought. 'Tallant! . . . Did you ever hear the name before, for I'll swear I never did?'

Mr Beaumaris looked at him for a moment. Then his eyes fell to the snuff-box he had drawn from his pocket. He flicked open the box, and took a delicate pinch between finger and thumb. 'You have never heard of the Tallant fortune?' he said. 'My *dear* Charles — !'

Five

$\mathcal{T}$hanks to Mr Beaumaris's message, which worked so powerfully on the wheelwright as to cause him to ignore the prior claims of three other owners of damaged vehicles, Arabella was only kept waiting for one day in Grantham. Since the Quorn met there on the morning following her encounter with Mr Beaumaris, she was able, from the window of a private parlour at the Angel and Royal Inn, to see just how he looked on horseback. She could have seen how Lord Fleetwood looked too, had she cared, but curiously enough she never even thought of his lordship. Mr Beaumaris looked remarkably well, astride a beautiful thoroughbred, with long, sloping pasterns, and shoulders well laid back. She decided that Mr Beaumaris's seat was as good as any she had ever seen. The tops to his hunting-boots were certainly whiter than a mere provincial would have deemed possible.

The Hunt having moved off, there was nothing for two delayed travellers to do for the rest of the day but stroll about the town, eat their meals, and yawn over the only books to be found in the inn. But by the following morning the Squire's carriage was brought round to the Angel, with a new pole affixed, and the horses well-rested, and the ladies were able to set forward betimes on the last half of their long journey.

Even Miss Blackburn was heartily sick of the road by the time the muddied carriage at last drew up outside Lady Bridlington's house in Park Street. She was sufficiently well acquainted with the metropolis to feel no interest in the various sounds and sights which had made Arabella forget her boredom and her fidgets from the moment that the carriage reached Islington. These, to a young lady who had never seen a larger town than York in her life, were at once enthralling and bewildering. The traffic made her feel giddy, and the noise of post-bells, of wheels on the cobbled streets, and the shrill cries of itinerant vendors of coals, brick-dust, door-mats, and rat-traps quite deafened her. All passed before her wide gaze in a whirl; she wondered how anyone could live in such a place and still retain her sanity. But as the carriage, stopping once or twice for the coachman to enquire the way of nasal and not always polite Cockneys, wound its ponderous way into the more modish part of the town, the din abated till Arabella began even to entertain hopes of being able to sleep in London.

The house in Park Street seemed overpoweringly tall to one accustomed to a rambling two-storeyed country-house; and the butler who admitted the ladies into a lofty hall, whence rose an imposing flight of stairs, was so majestic that Arabella felt almost inclined to apologise for putting him to the trouble of announcing her to her godmother. But she was relieved to find that he was supported by only one footman, and so was able to follow him up with tolerable composure to the drawing-room on the first floor.

Here her qualms were put to flight by the welcome she received. Lady Bridlington, whose plump, pink cheeks were wreathed in smiles, clasped her to an ample bosom, kissed her repeatedly, exclaimed, just as Aunt Emma had, on her likeness to her Mama, and seemed so unaffectedly glad to see her that all constraint was at an end. Lady Bridlington's good-nature extended even to the governess, to whom she spoke with kindness, and perfect civility.

When Mama had known Lady Bridlington, she had been a pretty girl, without more than commonsense, but with such a respectable portion, and with so much vivacity and good-humour, that it was no surprise to her friends when she contracted a very eligible match. Time had done more to enlarge her figure than her mind, and it was not many days before her young charge had discovered that under a superficial worldly wisdom there was little but a vast amount of silliness. Her ladyship read whatever new work of prose or verse was in fashion, understood one word in ten of it, and prattled of the whole; doted on the most admired singers at the Opera, but secretly preferred the ballet; vowed there had never been anything to equal Kean's *Hamlet* on the English stage, but derived considerably more enjoyment from the farce which followed this soul-stirring performance. She was incapable of humming a tune correctly, but never failed to patronise the Concerts of Ancient Music during the season, just as she never failed to visit the Royal Academy every year, at Somerset House, where, although her notion of a good picture was a painting that reminded her forcibly of some person or place with which she was familiar, she unerringly detected the hand of a master in all the most distinguished artists' canvases. Her life seemed to a slightly shocked Arabella to consist wholly of pleasure; and the greatest exertion she ever put her mind to was the securing of her own comfort. But it would have been unjust to have called her a selfish woman. Her disposition was kindly; she liked the people round her to be as happy as she was herself, for that made them cheerful, and she disliked long faces; she paid her servants well, and always remembered to thank them for any extraordinary service they performed for her, such as walking her horses up and down Bond Street in the rain for an hour while she shopped, or sitting up till four or five in the morning to put her to bed after an evening-party; and, provided she was not expected to put herself out for them, or to do anything disagreeable, she was both kind and generous to her friends.

She expected nothing but pleasure from Arabella's visit, and although she knew that in launching the girl into society she was behaving in a very handsome way, she never dwelled on the reflection, except once or twice a day in the privacy of her dressing-room, and then not in any grudging spirit, but merely for the gratifying sensation it gave her of being a benevolent person. She was very fond of visiting, shopping, and spectacles; liked entertaining large gatherings in her own house; and was seldom bored by even the dullest Assembly. Naturally, since every woman of fashion did so, she complained of dreadful squeezes or sadly insipid evenings, but no one who had seen her at these functions, greeting a multitude of acquaintances, exchanging the latest *on-dits*, closely scanning the newest fashions, or taking eager part in a rubber of whist, could have doubted her real and simple enjoyment of them.

To be obliged, then, to chaperon a young lady making her début to a succession of balls, routs, Assemblies, Military Reviews, balloon ascensions, and every other diversion likely to be offered to society during the season, exactly suited her disposition. She spent the better part of Arabella's first evening in Park Street in describing to her all the delightful plans she had been making for her amusement, and could scarcely wait for Miss Blackburn's departure next day before ordering her carriage to be sent round, and taking Arabella on a tour of all the smartest shops in London.

These cast the shops of High Harrowgate into the shade. Arabella was obliged to exercise great self-restraint when she saw the alluring wares displayed in the windows. She was helped a little by her north-country shrewdness, which recoiled from trifles priced at five times their worth, and not at all by her cicerone who, having been blessed all her life with sufficient means to enable her to purchase whatever took her fancy, could not understand why Arabella would not buy a bronze-green velvet hat, trimmed with feathers and a broad fall of lace, and priced at a figure which would have covered the cost of all the hats so cleverly contrived by Mama's and Sophia's neat fingers. Lady Bridlington owned that it was an expensive hat, but she held that to buy what became one so admirably could not be termed an extravagance. But Arabella put it resolutely aside, saying that she had as many hats as she required, and explaining frankly that she must not spend her money too freely, since Papa and Mama could not afford to send her any more. Lady

Bridlington was quite distressed to think that such a pretty girl should not be able to set her beauty off to the best advantage. It seemed so sad that she was moved to purchase a net stocking-purse, and a branch of artificial flowers, and to bestow them on Arabella. She hesitated for a few minutes over a handsome shawl of Norwich silk, but it was priced at twenty guineas, and although this could not be said to be a high price, she remembered that she had one herself, a much better one, for which she had paid fifty guineas, which she could very well lend to Arabella whenever she did not wish to wear it herself. Besides, there would be all the expense of Arabella's Court dress to be borne later in the season, and even though a great deal might be found in her own wardrobe which could be converted to Arabella's needs, the cost was still certain to be heavy. A further inspection of the shawl convinced her that it was of poor quality, not at all the sort of thing she would like to give her young charge, so they left the shop without buying it. Arabella was profoundly relieved, for although she would naturally have liked to have possessed the shawl, it made her very uncomfortable to be in danger of costing her hostess so much money.

Her frankness in speaking of her circumstances made Lady Bridlington a little thoughtful. She did not immediately mention the matter, but when the two ladies sat before the fire in the small saloon that evening, drinking tea, she ventured to put into words some at least of the thoughts which were revolving in her head.

'You know, my dear,' she said, 'I have been considering the best way to set to work, and I have made up my mind to it that as soon as you have grown more used to London – and I am sure it will not be long, for you are such a bright, clever little puss! – I should introduce you, quietly, you know! The season has not yet begun, and London is still very thin of company. And I think that will suit us very well, for you are not used to the way we go on here, and a small Assembly – no dancing, just an evening-party, with music, perhaps, and cards – is the very thing for your first appearance! I mean to invite only a few of my friends, the very people who may be useful to you. You will become acquainted with some other young ladies, and of course with some gentlemen, and that will make it more comfortable, I assure you, when I take you to Almack's, or to some large ball. Nothing can be more disagreeable than to find oneself in a gathering where one does not recognise a single face!'

Arabella could readily believe it, and had nothing but approbation for this excellent scheme. 'Oh, yes, if you please, ma'am! It is of all things what I should like, for I know I shall not know how to go on at first, though I mean to learn as fast as I can!'

'Exactly so!' beamed her ladyship. 'You are a sensible girl, Arabella, and I am very hopeful of settling you respectably, just as I promised your Mama I would!' She saw that Arabella was blushing, and added: 'You won't object to my speaking plain, my love, for I daresay you know how important it is that you should be creditably established. Eight children! I do not know how your poor Mama will ever contrive to get good husbands for your sisters! And boys are such a charge on one's purse! I am sure I do not care to think of what my dear Frederick cost his father and me from first to last! First it was one thing, and then another!'

A serious look came into Arabella's face, as she thought of the many and varied needs of her brothers and sisters. She said earnestly: 'Indeed, ma'am, what you say is very just, and I mean to do my best not to disappoint Mama!'

Lady Bridlington leaned forward to lay her pudgy little hand over Arabella's, and to squeeze it fondly. 'I knew you would feel just as you ought!' she said. 'Which brings me to what I had in mind to say to you!' She sat back again in her chair, fidgeted for a moment with the fringe of her shawl, and then said without looking at Arabella: 'You know, my love, everything depends on first impressions – at least, a great deal does! In society, with everyone trying to find eligible husbands for their daughters, and so many beautiful girls for the gentlemen to choose from, it is in the highest degree important that you should do and say exactly what is right. That is why I mean to bring you out quietly, and not at all until you feel yourself at home in London. For you must know, my dear, that only rustics appear amazed. I am sure I do not know why it should be so, but you may believe that innocent girls from the country are not at all what the gentlemen like!'

Arabella was surprised, for her reading had taught her otherwise. She ventured to say as much, but Lady Bridlington shook her head. 'No, my love, it is not so at all! That sort of thing may do very well in a novel, and I am very fond of novels myself, but they have nothing to do with life, depend upon it! But that was not what I wished to say!' Again she played with the shawl-fringe, saying in a little burst of eloquence: 'I would not, if I were you, my dear, be for ever talking about Heythram, and the Vicarage! You must remember that nothing is more wearisome than to be obliged to listen to stories about a set of persons one has never seen. And though of course you would not prevaricate in any way, it is quite unnecessary to tell everyone – or, indeed, anyone! – of your dear Papa's situation! *I* have said nothing to lead anyone to suppose that he is not in affluent circumstances, for nothing, I do assure you, Arabella, could be more fatal to your chances than to have it known that your expectations are very small!'

Arabella was about to reply rather more hotly than was civil when the recollection of her own conduct in Mr Beaumaris's house came into her mind with stunning effect. She hung her head, and sat silent, wondering whether she ought to make a clean breast of the regrettable affair to Lady Bridlington, and deciding that it was too bad to be spoken of.

Lady Bridlington, misunderstanding the reason for her evident confusion, said hastily: 'If you should be fortunate enough to engage some gentleman's affection, dear Arabella, of course you will tell him just how you are placed, or I shall, and – and, depend upon it, he will not care a button! You must not be thinking that I wish to practise the least deception, for it is no such thing! Merely, it would be foolish, and quite unnecessary, for you to be talking of your circumstances to every chance-met acquaintance!'

'Very well, ma'am,' said Arabella, in a subdued tone.

'I knew you would be sensible! Well, now, I am sure there is no need for me to say anything more to you on this head, and we must decide whom I shall invite to my evening-party. I wonder, my love, if you would see if my tablets are on that little table. And a pencil, if you will be so good!'

These commodities having been found, the good lady settled down happily to plan her forthcoming party. Since the names she recited were all of them unknown to Arabella, the discussion resolved itself into a gentle monologue. Lady Bridlington ran through the greater part of her acquaintance, murmuring that it would be useless to invite the Farnworths, since they had no children; that Lady Kirkmichael gave the shabbiest entertainments, and could not be depended on to invite Arabella, even if she did decide to give a ball for that lanky daughter of hers; that the Accringtons must of course be sent a card, and also the Buxtons – delightful families, both, and bound to entertain largely this season! 'And I mean to invite Lord Dewsbury, and Sir Geoffrey Morecambe, my dear, for there is no saying but what one of them might – And I am sure Mr Pocklington has been hanging out for a wife these two years, not but what he is perhaps a little old – However, we will ask him to come, for there can be no harm in that! Then I must certainly prevail upon dear Lady Sefton to come, for she is one of the patronesses of Almack's, you know; and perhaps Emily Cowper might – And the Charnwoods, and Mr Catwick; and, if they are in town, the Garthorpes . . .'

She rambled on in this style, while Arabella tried to appear interested. But as she could do no more than agree with her hostess when she was appealed to, her attention soon wandered, to be recalled with a jerk when Lady Bridlington mentioned a name she did know.

'And I shall send Mr Beaumaris a card, because it would be such a splendid thing for you, my love, if it were known that he came to your début – for such we may call it! Why, if he were to come, and perhaps talk to you for a few minutes, and seem pleased with you, you would be *made*, my dear! Everyone follows his lead! And perhaps, as there are so few parties yet, he *might* come! I am sure I have been acquainted with him for years, and I knew his mother quite well! She was Lady Mary Caldicot, you know: a daughter of the late Duke of Wigan, and such a beautiful creature! And it is not as though Mr Beaumaris has never been to my house, for he once came to an Assembly here, and stayed for quite half-an-hour! Mind, we must not build upon his accepting, but we need not despair!'

She paused for breath, and Arabella, colouring in spite of herself, was able at last to say: 'I – I am myself a little acquainted with Mr Beaumaris, ma'am.'

Lady Bridlington was so much astonished that she dropped her pencil. 'Acquainted with Mr Beaumaris?' she repeated. 'My love, what *can* you be thinking about? When can you possibly have met him?'

'I – I quite forgot to tell you, ma'am,' faltered Arabella unhappily, 'that when the pole broke – I told you *that*! – Miss Blackburn and I sought shelter in his hunting-box, and – and he had Lord Fleetwood with him, and we stayed to dine!'

Lady Bridlington gasped. 'Good God, Arabella, and you never told me! Mr Beaumaris's house! He actually asked you to dine, and you never breathed a word of it to me!'

Arabella found herself quite incapable of explaining why she had been shy of mentioning this episode. She stammered that it had slipped out of her mind in all the excitement of coming to London.

'Slipped out of your mind?' exclaimed Lady Bridlington. 'You dine with Mr Beaumaris, and at his hunting-box, too, and then talk to me about the excitement of coming to London? Good gracious, child – But, there, you are such a country-mouse, my love, I daresay you did not know all it might mean to you! Did he seem pleased? Did he like you?'

This was a little too much, even for a young lady determined to be on her best behaviour. 'I daresay he disliked me excessively, ma'am, for *I* thought *him* very proud and disagreeable, and I hope you won't ask him to your party on *my* account.'

'Not ask him to my party, when, if he came to it, everyone

would say it was a success! You must be mad, Arabella, to talk so! And do let me beg of you, my dear, never to say such a thing of Mr Beaumaris in public! I daresay he may be a little stiff, but what is that to the purpose, pray? There is no one who counts for more in society, for setting aside his fortune, which is immense, my love, he is related to half the houses in England! The Beaumarises are one of the oldest of our families, while on his mother's side he is a grandson of the Duchess of Wigan – the Dowager Duchess, I mean, which of course makes him cousin to the present Duke, besides the Wainfleets, and – But you would not know!' she ended despairingly.

'I thought Lord Fleetwood most amiable, and gentlemanlike,' offered Arabella, by way of palliative.

'Fleetwood! I can tell you this, Arabella: there is no use in your setting your cap at *him*, for all the world knows that he *must* marry money!'

'I hope, ma'am,' cried Arabella, flaring up, 'that you do not mean to suggest that I should *set my cap* at Mr Beaumaris, for nothing would prevail upon me to do so!'

'My love,' responded Lady Bridlington frankly, 'it would be quite useless for you to do so! Robert Beaumaris may have his pick of all the beauties in England, I daresay! And, what is more, he is the most accomplished flirt in London! But I do most earnestly implore you not to set him against you by treating him with the least incivility! You may think him what you please, but, believe me, Arabella, he could ruin your whole career – and mine, too, if it came to that!' she added feelingly.

Arabella propped her chin in her hand, pondering an agreeable thought. 'Or he could make everything easy for me, ma'am?' she enquired.

'Of course he could – if he chose to do it! He is the most unpredictable creature! It might amuse him to make you the rage of town – or he might take it into his head to say you were not quite in his style – and if once he says *that*, my dear, what man will look twice at you, unless he has already fallen in love with you, which, after all, we *cannot* expect?'

'My dear ma'am,' said Arabella, in dulcet accents, 'I hope I should not be so ill-bred as to be uncivil to *anyone* – even Mr Beaumaris!'

'Well, my dear, I hope not, indeed!' said her ladyship doubtfully.

'I promise I will not be in the least degree uncivil to Mr Beaumaris, if he should come to your party,' said Arabella.

'I am happy to hear you say so, my love, but ten to one he won't come,' responded her ladyship pessimistically.

'He said to me at parting that he hoped to have the pleasure of calling on me in town before many days,' said Arabella disinterestedly.

Lady Bridlington considered this, but in the end shook her head. 'I do not think we should set any store by that,' she said. 'Very likely he said it for politeness' sake.'

'Very likely,' agreed Arabella. 'But if you are acquainted with him, I wish you will send Lord Fleetwood a card for your party, ma'am, for he was excessively kind, and I liked him!'

'Of course I am acquainted with him!' declared Lady Bridlington, quite affronted. 'But do not be setting your heart on him, Arabella, I beg of you! A delightful rattle, but the Fleetwoods are all to pieces, by what I hear, and however much he may flirt with you, I am persuaded he will never make you an offer!'

'Must every man I meet make me an offer?' asked Arabella, controlling her voice with an effort.

'No, my love, and you may depend upon it that they won't!' replied her ladyship candidly. 'In fact, I have had it in mind to warn you against setting your ambitions *too* high! I mean to do all I can for you, but there is no denying that suitable husbands do not grow upon every bush! Particularly, my dear – and I know you will not fly into a miff with me for saying it! – when you have no portion to recommend you!'

In face of her ladyship's conviction, Arabella hardly liked to betray her feelings, so she bit her lip, and was silent. Fortunately, Lady Bridlington's mind was not of a tenacious nature, and as she just then recollected a very important lady whose name must be included amongst the list of invited persons, she forgot about Arabella's matrimonial chances in explaining why it would be folly to omit Lady Terrington from that list. Nothing more was said about Mr Beaumaris, her ladyship having been diverted, by some chance reference of her own, into describing to Arabella the various social treats she had in store for her. In spite of the fact that the season had not yet begun, these were so numerous that Arabella felt almost giddy, and wondered whether, in this round of gaiety, her hostess would find the time to accompany her to Church on Sunday. But in doubting whether Lady Bridlington would go to Church she wronged her: Lady Bridlington would have thought it a very odd thing not to be seen in her pew every Sunday morning, unless, as was very often the case, she chose to attend the service at the Chapel Royal, where, in addition to listening to an excellent sermon, she could be sure of seeing all her more distinguished friends, and even, very often, some member of the Royal Family. This good fortune was hers on Arabella's first Sunday in London, and the circumstance made fine reading for the interested brothers and sisters in Yorkshire, following, as it did (most artistically), descriptions of Hyde Park, and St Paul's Cathedral, and a lively account of the racket and bustle of the London streets.

'*We attended Morning Service at the Chapel Royal, St James's on Sunday,*' wrote Arabella, in a fine, small hand, and on very thin paper, crossing her lines. '*We heard a very good sermon on a text from the Second Epistle to the Corinthians, pray tell dear Papa: He that had gathered much had nothing over; and he that had gathered little had no lack. London is still very thin of company*' – not for nothing had Arabella dutifully attended to her godmother's conversation! – '*but there were a great many fashionables present, and also the Duke of Clarence, who came up to us afterwards, and was very affable, with nothing high in his manner at all.*' Arabella paused, nibbling the end of her pen, and considering the Duke of Clarence. Papa might not care to have his Royal Highness described, but Mama, and Sophy, and Margaret would most certainly wish to know just what he was like, and what he had said. She bent again over her page. '*I do not think one would say that he is precisely handsome,*' she wrote temperately, '*but his countenance is benevolent. His head is a queer shape, and he is inclined to corpulence. He made me think of my uncle, for he talks in just that way, and very loud, and he laughs a great deal. He did me the honour to say that I wore a vastly* fetching *hat: I hope Mama will be pleased, for it was the one with her pink feathers, which she made for me.*' There did not seem to be anything more to be said about the Duke of Clarence, except that he talked quite audibly in Church, and that was information scarcely likely to please the inhabitants of the Vicarage. She read over what she had written, and felt that it might disappoint Mama and the girls. She added a line. '*Lady Bridlington says that he is not near as fat as the Prince Regent, or the Duke of York.*' On this heartening note she ended her paragraph, and embarked on a fresh one.

'*I am growing quite accustomed to London, and begin to know my way about the streets, though of course I do not walk out by myself yet. Lady Bridlington sends a footman with me, just as Bertram said she would, but I see that young females do go alone nowadays, only perhaps they are not of the* haut ton. *This is* very important, *and I am in constant dread that I shall do something improper, such as walking down St James's Street, where all the gentlemen's clubs are, and very* fast, *which of course I do not wish to be thought. Lady Bridlington gives an evening-party, to introduce me to her friends. I shall be all of a quake, for everyone is so grand and fashionable, though perfectly civil, and much kinder than I had looked for. Sophy will like to know that Lord Fleetwood, whom I met on the road, as I wrote to you from Grantham, paid us a morning-visit, to see how I did, which was very amiable and obliging of him. Also Mr Beaumaris, but we were out driving in the Park. He left his card. Lady Bridlington was in transports, and has placed it above all the rest, which I think nonsensical, but I find that that is the way of the World, and makes me reflect on all Papa has said on the subject of Folly, and the Hollowness of Fashionable Life.*' That seemed to dispose satisfactorily of Mr Beaumaris. Arabella dipped her pen in the standish again. '*Lady Bridlington is everything that is kind, and I am persuaded that Lord Bridlington is a very respectable young man, and not at all abandoned to the Pursuit of Pleasure, as Papa feared. His name is*

Frederick. He is travelling in Germany, and has visited a great many of the battlefields. He writes very interesting letters to his Mama, with which I am sure Papa would be pleased, for he seems to feel just as he ought, and moralises on all he sees in a truly elevating way, though rather long.' Arabella perceived that there was little room left on her sheet, and added in a cramped fist: *'I would write more only that I cannot get a frank for this, and do not wish to put Papa to the expense of paying some sixpences for the second sheet. With my love to my brothers and sisters, and my affectionate duty to dear Papa, I remain your loving daughter Arabella.'*

Plenty of promising matter there for Mama and the girls to pore over, and to discuss, even though so much remained unwritten! One could not resist boasting a very little about the compliments paid to one by a Royal Duke, or just mentioning that a fashionable peer of the realm had called to see how one did – not to mention the great Mr Beaumaris, if one had happened to care a fig for that – but one felt quite shy of disclosing even to Mama how very gracious – how amazingly kind – everyone was being to an insignificant girl from Yorkshire.

For so it was. Shopping in Bond Street, driving on clement afternoons in Hyde Park, attending the service at the Chapel Royal, Lady Bridlington naturally encountered friends, and never failed to present Arabella to their notice. Some really forbidding dowagers who might have been expected to have paid scant heed to Arabella unbent in the most gratifying way, quite overpowering her by the kindness of their enquiries, and their insistence that Lady Bridlington should bring her to see them one day. Several introduced their daughters to Arabella, suggesting that she and they might walk in the Green Park some fine morning, so that in less than no time it seemed as though she had a host of acquaintances in London. The gentlemen were not more backward: it was quite a commonplace thing for some stroller in the Park to come up to Lady Bridlington's barouche, and stand chatting to her, and to her pretty protégée; while more than one sprig of fashion, with whom her ladyship was barely acquainted, paid her a morning-visit on what seemed even to one so little given to speculation as Lady Bridlington the slenderest of excuses.

She was a little surprised, but after thinking about it for a few minutes she was as easily able to account for the ladies' civility as the gentlemen's. They were anxious to oblige her. This led her by natural stages to the reflection that she deserved a great deal of credit for having so well advertised Arabella's visit to town. As for the gentlemen, she had never doubted, from the moment of setting eyes on her goddaughter, that that fairy figure and charming countenance could fail to attract instant admiration. Arabella had, moreover, the most enchanting smile, which brought dimples leaping to her cheeks, and was at once mischievous and appealing. Any but the most case-hardened of men, thought Lady Bridlington enviously, would be more than likely, under its intoxicating influence, to behave in a rash manner, however much he might afterwards regret it.

But none of these conclusions quite explained the morning-visits of several high-nosed ladies of fashion, whose civilities towards Lady Bridlington had hitherto consisted of invitations to their larger Assemblies, and bows exchanged from their respective carriages. Lady Somercote was particularly puzzling. She called in Park Street when Arabella was out walking with the three charming daughters of Sir James and Lady Hornsea, and she sat for over an hour with her gratified hostess. She expressed the greatest admiration of Arabella, whom she had met at the theatre with her godmother. 'A delightful girl!' she said graciously. 'Very pretty-behaved, and without the least hint of pretension in her dress or bearing!'

Lady Bridlington agreed to it, and since her mind did not move rapidly it was not until her guest was well into her next observation that she wondered why Arabella should be supposed to show pretension.

'Of good family, I apprehend?' said Lady Somercote, carelessly, but looking rather searchingly at her hostess.

'Of course!' replied Lady Bridlington, with dignity. 'A most respected Yorkshire family!'

Lady Somercote nodded. 'I thought as much. Excellent manners, and conducts herself with perfect propriety! I was particularly pleased with the modesty of her bearing: not the least sign of wishing to put herself forward! And her dress too! Just what I like to see in a young female! Nothing vulgar, such as one too often sees nowadays! When every miss out of the schoolroom is decked out with jewelry, it is refreshing to see one with a simple wreath of flowers in her hair. Somercote was much struck. Indeed, he quite took one of his fancies to her! You must bring her to Grosvenor Square next week, dear Lady Bridlington! Nothing formal, you know: a few friends only, and perhaps the young people may find themselves with enough couples to get up a little dance.'

She waited only for Lady Bridlington's acceptance of this flattering invitation before taking her leave. Lady Bridlington was left with her mind in a whirl. She was shrewd enough to know that more than a compliment to herself must lie behind this unexpected honour, and was at a loss to discover the lady's motive. She was the mother of five hopeful and expensive sons, and it was well known that the Somercote estates were heavily mortgaged. Advantageous marriages were a necessity to the Somercotes' progeny, and no one was more purposeful in her pursuit of a likely heiress than their Mama. For a dismayed instant Lady Bridlington wondered whether, in her anxiety to assist Arabella, she had concealed her circumstances too well. But she could not recall that she had ever so much as mentioned them: indeed, her recollection was that she had taken care never to do so.

The Honourable Mrs Penkridge, calling on her dear friend for the express purpose of bidding her and her protégée to a select Musical Soirée, and explaining, with apologies, how it was due to the stupidity of a secretary that her card of invitation had not reached her long since, spoke in even warmer terms of Arabella. 'Charming! quite charming!' she declared, bestowing her frosted smile upon Lady Bridlington. 'She will throw all our beauties into the shade! That simplicity is so particularly pleasing! You are to be congratulated!'

However perplexed Lady Bridlington might be by this speech,

issuing, as it did, from the lips of one famed as much for her haughtiness as for her acid tongue, it seemed at least to dispose of the suspicion roused in her mind by Lady Somercote's visit. The Penkridges were a childless couple. Lady Bridlington, on whom Mrs Penkridge had more than once passed some contemptuous criticism, was not well-enough acquainted with her to know that almost the only sign of human emotion she had ever been seen to betray was her doting fondness for her nephew, Mr Horace Epworth.

This elegant gentleman, complete to a point as regards side-whiskers, fobs, seals, quizzing-glass, and scented handkerchief, had lately honoured his aunt with one of his infrequent visits. Surprised and delighted, she had begged to know in what way she could be of service to him. Mr Epworth had no hesitation in telling her. 'You might put me in the way of meeting the new heiress, ma'am,' he said frankly. 'Dev'lish fine gal – regular Croesus, too!'

She had pricked up her ears at that, and exclaimed: 'Whom can you be thinking of, my dear Horace? If you mean the Flint chit, I have it for a fact that –'

'Pooh! nothing of the sort!' interrupted Mr Epworth, waving the Flint chit away with one white and languid hand. 'I daresay *she* has no more than thirty thousand pounds! This gal is so rich she puts 'em all in the shade. They call her the Lady Dives.'

'Who calls her so?' demanded his incredulous relative.

Mr Epworth again waved his hand, this time in the direction which he vaguely judged to be northward. 'Oh, up there somewhere, ma'am! Yorkshire, or some other of those dev'lish remote counties! Daresay she's a merchant's daughter: wool, or cotton, or some such thing. Pity, but I shan't regard it: they tell me she's charming!'

'I have heard nothing of this! Who is she? Who told you she was charming?'

'Had it from Fleetwood last night, at the Great-Go,' explained Mr Epworth negligently.

'That rattle! I wish you will not go so often to Watier's,

Horace! I warn you, it is useless to apply to me! I have not a guinea left in the world, and I dare not ask Mr Penkridge to assist you again, until he has forgotten the last time!'

'Put me in the way of meeting this gal, and I'll kiss my fingers to Penkridge, ma'am,' responded Mr Epworth, gracefully suiting the action to the word. 'Acquainted with Lady Bridlington, ain't you? The gal's staying with her.'

She stared at him. 'If Arabella Bridlington had an heiress staying with her she would have boasted of it all over town!'

'No, she wouldn't. Fleetwood particularly told me the gal don't want it known. Don't like being courted for her fortune. Pretty gal, too, by what Fleetwood says. Name of Tallant.'

'I never heard of a Tallant in my life!'

'Lord, ma'am, why should you? Keep telling you she comes from some dev'lish outlandish place in the north!'

'I would not set the least store by anything Fleetwood told me!'

'Oh, it ain't him!' said Mr Epworth cheerfully. 'He don't know the gal's name either. It's the Nonpareil. Knows all about the family. Vouches for the gal.'

Her expression changed; a still sharper look entered her eyes. She said quickly: 'Beaumaris?' He nodded. 'If *he* vouches for her – Is she presentable?'

He looked shocked, and answered in protesting accents: ''Pon my soul, ma'am, you can't be in your senses to ask me such a demned silly question! Now, I put it to you, *would* Beaumaris vouch for a gal that wasn't slap up to the echo?'

'No. No, he would not,' she said decidedly. 'If it's true, and she has no vulgar connections, it would be the very thing for you, my dear Horace!'

'Just what I was thinking myself, ma'am,' said her nephew.

'I will pay Lady Bridlington a morning-visit,' said Mrs Penkridge.

'That's it: do the pretty!' Mr Epworth encouraged her.

'It is tiresome, for I have never been upon intimate terms with her! However, this alters the circumstances! Leave it to me!'

Thus it was that Lady Bridlington found herself the object of Mrs Penkridge's attentions. Since she had never before been honoured with an invitation to one of that lady's more exclusive parties, she was considerably elated, and at once seized the opportunity to invite Mrs Penkridge to her own evening-party. Mrs Penkridge accepted with another of her thin smiles, saying that she knew she could answer for her husband's pleasure in attending the party, and departed, thinking out rapidly some form of engagement for him which would at once spare him an insipid evening, and render it necessary for her to claim her nephew's escort.

Six

*L*ady Bridlington did not expect Arabella's first party to be a failure, since she was a good hostess, and never offered her guests any but the best wines and refreshments, but that it should prove to be a wild success had not even entered her head. She had planned it more with the idea of bringing Arabella to the notice of other hostesses than as a brilliant social event; and although she had certainly invited a good many unattached gentlemen she had not held out the lure of dancing, or of cards, and so had little hope of seeing more than half of them in her spacious rooms. Her main preoccupation was lest Arabella should not be looking her best, or should jeopardise her future by some unconventional action, or some unlucky reference to that regrettable Yorkshire Vicarage. In general, the child behaved very prettily, but once or twice she had seriously alarmed her patroness, either by a remark which betrayed all too clearly the modesty of her circumstances – as when she had asked, in front of the butler, whether she should help to prepare the rooms for the party, for all the world as though she expected to be given an apron and a duster! – or by some impulsive action so odd as to be positively outrageous. Not readily would Lady Bridlington forget the scene outside the Soho Bazaar, when she and Arabella, emerging from this mart, found a heavy wagon stationary in the road, with the one scraggy horse between its shafts straining under an unsparing lash to set it in motion. At one instant a demure young lady had been at Lady Bridlington's side; at the next a flaming fury was confronting the astonished wagoner, commanding him, with a stamp of one little foot, to get down from the wagon at once – *at once!* – and not to *dare* to raise his whip again! He got down, quite bemused, and stood in front of the small fury, an ox of a man, towering above her while she berated him. When he had recovered his wits he attempted to justify himself, but failed signally to pacify the lady. He was a cruel wretch, unfit to be in charge of a horse, and a dolt, besides, not to perceive that one of the wheels was jammed, and through his own bad driving, no doubt! He began to be angry, and to shout Arabella down, but by this time a couple of chairmen, abandoning their empty vehicle, came across the square, expressing, in strong Hibernian accents, their willingness to champion the lady, and their desire to know whether the wagoner wanted to have his cork drawn. Lady Bridlington, all this time, had stood frozen with horror in the doorway of the Bazaar, unable to think of anything else to do than to be thankful that none of her acquaintances was present to witness this shocking affair. Arabella told the chairmen briskly that she would have no fighting, bade the wagoner observe the obstruction against which one of his rear wheels was jammed, herself went to the horse's head, and began to back him. The chairmen promptly lent their aid; Arabella addressed a short, pithy lecture to the wagoner on the folly and injustice of losing one's temper with animals, and rejoined her godmother, saying calmly: 'It is mostly ignorance, you know!'

And although she did, when shown the impropriety of her behaviour, say she was sorry to have made a scene in public, it was evident that she was not in the least penitent. She said that Papa would have told her it was her duty to interfere in such a cause.

But no representations could induce her to say she was sorry for her quite unbecoming conduct two days later, when she entered her bedchamber to find a very junior housemaid, with a swollen face, lighting the fire. It appeared that the girl had the toothache. Now, Lady Bridlington had no desire that any of her servants should suffer the agonies of toothache, and had she been asked she would unquestionably have said that at the first convenient moment the girl should be sent off to have the tooth drawn. The mistress of a large household naturally had a duty to oversee the general well-being of her staff. Indeed, some years previously, when inoculation against cow-pox had been all the rage, she had with her own hands inoculated all the servants at Bridlington, and most of the tenants on the estate. Nearly every great lady had done so: it had been the accepted order of the day. But to bid the sufferer seat herself in the armchair in the best guest-chamber, to give her an Indian silk shawl to wrap round her head; and to disturb one's hostess during the sacred hour of her afternoon-nap by bursting in upon her with a demand for laudanum, was carrying benevolence to quite undesirable lengths. Lady Bridlington did her best to convey the sense of this to Arabella, but she spoke to deaf ears. 'The poor girl is in the most dreadful pain, ma'am!'

'Nonsense, my love! You must not let yourself be imposed upon. Persons of her class always make a to-do about nothing. She had better have the tooth drawn tomorrow, if she can be spared from her work, and –'

'Dear madam, I assure you she is in no case to be toiling up and down all these stairs with coal-scuttles!' said Arabella earnestly. 'She should take some drops of laudanum, and lie down on her bed.'

'Oh, very well!' said her ladyship, yielding to the stronger will. 'But there is no occasion for you to be putting yourself into this state, my dear! And to be asking one of the under-housemaids to sit down in your bedroom, and giving her one of your best shawls –'

'No, no, I have only lent it to her!' Arabella said. 'She is from the country, you know, ma'am, and I think the other servants have not used her as they ought. She was homesick, and so unhappy! And the toothache made it worse, of course. I do believe she wanted someone to be kind to her more than anything else! She has been telling me about her home, and her little sisters and brothers, and –'

'Arabella!' uttered Lady Bridlington. 'Surely you have not been *gossiping with the servants*?' She saw her young guest stiffen, and added hastily: 'You should never encourage persons of her sort to pour out the history of their lives into your ears. I expect you meant it for the best, my dear, but you have no notion how encroaching –'

'I hope, ma'am – indeed, I *know*!' said Arabella, her eyes very bright, and her small figure alarmingly rigid, 'that not one of Papa's children would pass by a fellow-creature in distress!'

It was fast being borne in upon Lady Bridlington that the Reverend Henry Tallant was not only a grave handicap to his daughter's social advancement, but a growing menace to her own comfort. She was naturally unable to express this conviction to Arabella, so she sank back on her pillows, saying feebly: 'Oh, very well, but if people were to hear of it they would think it excessively odd in you, my dear!'

Whatever anyone else might think, it soon became plain that the episode had given her ladyship's upper servants the poorest idea of Arabella's social standing. Her ladyship's personal maid, a sharp-faced spinster who had grown to middle-age in her service, and bullied her without compunction, ventured to hint, while she was dressing her mistress's hair that evening, that it was easy to see Miss was not accustomed to living in large and genteel households.

Lady Bridlington allowed Miss Clara Crowle a good deal of licence, but this was going too far. A pretty thing it would be if the servants, in that odious way they all had of talking about their betters, were to spread such a thing abroad! It would reach the ears of their employers in less than no time, and then the fat would indeed be in the fire! In a few dignified, well-chosen words Lady Bridlington gave her henchwoman to understand that Miss Tallant came from a mansion of awe-inspiring gentility, and was quite above considering appearances. She added, to clinch the matter, that very different customs obtained in the north from those common in London. Miss Crowle, a little cowed, but with a sting yet left in her tongue, sniffed, and said: 'So I have always understood, my lady!' She then encountered her mistress's eyes in the mirror, and added obsequiously: 'Not but what I am sure no one would ever suspicion Miss came from the north, my lady, so prettily as she speaks!'

'Certainly not,' said Lady Bridlington coldly, and quite forgetful of the fact that she had experienced considerable relief, when Arabella had greeted her on her arrival, at finding that no ugly accent marred her soft voice. The dreadful possibility that she might speak with a Yorkshire burr had more than once occurred to her. Had she but known it, she had the Reverend Henry Tallant to thank for his daughter's pure accent. Papa was far too fastidious and cultured a man to permit his children to be slipshod in their speech, even frowning upon the excellent imitations of the farm-hand's conversation, achieved by Bertram and Harry in funning humour.

Miss Clara Crowle might be silenced, but Arabella's reprehensible conduct gave her hostess some serious qualms, and caused her to anticipate her evening-party with less than her usual placidity.

But nothing could have gone off better. To ensure that in appearance at least Arabella should do her credit, Lady Bridlington sent no less a personage than Miss Crowle herself to put the finishing touches to her toilet, rounding off the efforts of the housemaid detailed to wait on her. Miss Crowle was not best pleased when sent off to offer her services to Arabella, but it was many years since she had dressed a young and beautiful lady, and in spite of herself her enthusiasm awoke when she saw how delightfully Arabella's gown of jonquil crape became her, and how tasteful was the spangled scarf hanging over her arms. She saw at a glance that she could scarcely better the simple arrangement of those dark curls, twisted into a high knot on the top of her head, and with the short ringlets allowed to fall over her ears, but she begged Miss to permit her to place her flowers more becomingly. Her cunning hands deftly placed the faggot of artificial roses at just the right angle, and she was so well-satisfied with the result that she said Miss would be quite the belle of the evening, being as she was dark, and the fashion for fair beauties quite outdated.

Arabella, unaware of how greatly Miss Crowle was condescending to her, only laughed, a piece of unconcern that did her no harm in that critical maiden's eyes. Arabella was embarking on her first London party enormously heartened by the arrival, not an hour earlier, of her first London posy of flowers. The exciting box had been carried up to her room immediately, and, when opened, had been found to contain a charming bouquet, tied up – so fortunately! – with long yellow ribbons. Lord Fleetwood's card accompanied the tribute, and was even now propped up against the mirror. Miss Crowle saw it, and was impressed.

Lady Bridlington, presently setting eyes on Arabella just before dinner was announced, was delighted, and reflected that Sophia Theale had always had exquisite taste. Nothing could have set Arabella off to greater advantage than that delicate yellow robe, open down the front over a slip of white satin, and ornamented with clasps of tiny roses to match those in her hair. The only jewelry she wore was the ring Papa had had made for her, and Grandmama's necklet of pearls. Lady Bridlington was half inclined to ring for Clara to fetch down from her own jewel-case two bracelets of gold and pearls, and then decided that Arabella's pretty arms needed no embellishment. Besides, she would be wearing long gloves, so that the bracelets would be wasted.

'Very nice, my love!' she said approvingly. 'I am glad I sent Clara to you. Dear me, where had you those flowers?'

'Lord Fleetwood sent them, ma'am,' replied Arabella proudly.

Lady Bridlington received this information with disappointing composure. 'Did he so? Then at all events we may be sure of seeing *him* here tonight. You know, my love, you must not be expecting a squeeze! I am sure I hope to see my drawing-rooms respectably filled, but it is early in the year still, so you must not be cast-down if you do not see as many people as you might have supposed you would.'

She might have spared her breath. By half-past ten her drawing-rooms were crowded to overflowing, and she was still standing at the head of the stairs receiving late-comers. Nothing, she thought dizzily, had ever been like it! Even the Wainfleets, whom really she had not expected to see, were there; while the haughty Mrs Penkridge, escorted by her dandified nephew, had been amongst the earliest arrivals, unbending amazingly to Arabella, and begging leave to introduce Mr Epworth. Lord Fleetwood, and his crony, Mr Oswald Warkworth, were there, both hovering assiduously near Arabella, very full of gallantry and good spirits; Lady Somercote had brought two of her sons, and the Kirkmichaels their lanky daughter; Lord Dewsbury had failed, but Sir Geoffrey Morecambe was much in evidence, as were also the Accringtons, the Charnwoods, and the Seftons. Lady Sefton, dear creature that she was! had spoken with the greatest kindness to Arabella, and had promised later on to send her a voucher admitting her to Almack's Assembly Rooms. Lady Bridlington felt that her cup was full. It was to overflow. Last of all the guests, arriving after eleven o'clock, when her ladyship, having long since released Arabella from her place at her side, was on the point of abandoning her post and joining her guests in the drawing-rooms, Mr Beaumaris arrived, and came unhurriedly up the stairs. Her ladyship awaited him with a bosom swelling beneath its rich covering of purple satin, and her hand, clasping her fan, trembling slightly under the influence of the accumulated triumphs of this night. He greeted her with his cool civility, and she replied with tolerable composure, thanking him for his kind offices, in Leicestershire, towards her goddaughter.

'A pleasure, ma'am,' said Mr Beaumaris. 'I trust Miss Tallant reached town without further mishaps?'

'Oh, yes, indeed! So obliging of you to have called to enquire after her! We were sorry to have been out. You will find Miss Tallant in one of the rooms. Your cousin, Lady Wainfleet, too, is here.'

He bowed, and followed her into the front drawing-room. A minute later, Arabella, enjoying the attentions of Lord Fleetwood, Mr Warkworth, and Mr Epworth, saw him coming towards her across the room, pausing once or twice on his way to exchange salutations with his friends. Until that moment she had thought Mr Epworth quite the best-dressed man present: indeed, she had been quite dazzled by the exquisite nature of his raiment, and the profusion of rings, pins, fobs, chains, and seals which he wore; but no sooner had she clapped eyes on Mr Beaumaris's tall, manly figure than she realised that Mr Epworth's wadded shoulders, wasp-waist, and startling waistcoat were perfectly ridiculous. Nothing could have been in greater contrast to the extravagance of his attire than Mr Beaumaris's black coat and pantaloons, his plain white waistcoat, the single fob that hung to one side of it, the single pearl set chastely in the intricate folds of his necktie. Nothing he wore was designed to attract attention, but he made every other man in the room look either a trifle overdressed or a trifle shabby.

He reached her side, and smiled, and when she put out her hand raised it fleetingly to his lips. 'How do you do, Miss Tallant?' he said. 'I am happy indeed to have been granted this opportunity of renewing my acquaintance with you.'

'Oh, it is too bad – a great deal too bad!' fluted Mr Epworth, rolling an arch eye at Arabella. 'You and Fleetwood have stolen a march on the rest of us, you know – a shameful thing, 'pon my soul!'

Mr Beaumaris glanced down at him from his superior height, seemed to debate within himself whether this sally was worth the trouble of a reply, to decide that it was not, and turned back to Arabella. 'You must tell me how you like London,' he said. 'It is abundantly plain that London likes you! May I procure you a glass of lemonade?'

94

This offer brought Arabella's chin up, and made her look at him with a distinct challenge in her eyes. She had had plenty of time to discover that it was not the common practice of hosts to sweep the wine from their tables at the end of the first course, and she strongly suspected Mr Beaumaris of quizzing her. He was looking perfectly grave, however, and met her eyes without a shadow of mockery in his own. Before she could answer him, Lord Fleetwood committed a strategical error, and exclaimed: 'Of course! I'll swear you are parched with thirst, ma'am! I will get you a glass immediately!'

'Splendid, Charles!' said Mr Beaumaris cordially. 'Do let me take you a little out of this crush, Miss Tallant!'

He seemed to take her acquiescence for granted, for he did not await a reply, but led her to where a sofa standing against one wall was momentarily unoccupied. How he contrived to find a way through the crowd of chattering guests was a mystery to Arabella, for he certainly did not force a passage. A touch on a man's shoulder, a bow and a smile to a lady, and the thing was done. He sat down beside her on the sofa, seated a little sideways, so that he could watch her face, one hand on the back of the sofa, the other playing idly with his quizzing-glass. 'Does it come up to your expectations, ma'am?' he asked smilingly.

'London? Yes, indeed!' she responded. 'I am sure I was never so happy in my life!'

'I am glad,' he said.

Arabella remembered that Lady Bridlington had warned her against betraying too much enthusiasm: it was unfashionable to appear pleased. She remembered also that she had promised not to make a bad impression on Mr Beaumaris, so she added in a languid tone: 'It is a shocking squeeze, of course, but it is always diverting to meet new people.'

He looked amused, and said with a laugh in his voice: 'No, don't spoil it! Your first answer was charming.'

She eyed him doubtfully for a moment; then her irrepressible dimples peeped out. 'But it is only rustics who own to enjoyment, sir!'

'Is it?' he returned.

'*You*, I am persuaded, do not enjoy such an Assembly as this!'

'You are mistaken: my enjoyment depends on the company in which I find myself.'

'That,' said Arabella naïvely, having thought it over, 'is quite the prettiest thing that has been said to me tonight!'

'Then I can only suppose, Miss Tallant, that Fleetwood and Warkworth were unable to find words to express their appreciation of the exquisite picture you present. Strange! I formed the opinion that they were paying you all manner of compliments.'

She laughed out at that. 'Yes, but it was nonsense! I did not believe a word they said!'

'I hope you believe what *I* say, however, for I am very much in earnest.'

The light tone he used seemed to belie his words. Arabella found him baffling, and directed another of her speculative glances at him. She decided that he must be answered in kind, and said daringly: 'Are you being so obliging as to bring me into fashion, Mr Beaumaris?'

He let his eyes travel round the crowded room, his brows a little raised. 'You do not appear to me to stand in any need of my assistance, ma'am.' He perceived that Lord Fleetwood was edging his way past a knot of people, a glass in his hand, and waited for him to reach the sofa. 'Thank you, Charles,' he said coolly, taking the glass from his lordship, and presenting it to Arabella.

'You,' said Lord Fleetwood, with deep feeling, 'will receive a message from me in the morning, Robert! This is the most barefaced piracy I ever beheld in my life! Miss Tallant, I wish you will send this fellow about his business: his effrontery goes beyond what is allowable!'

'You must learn not to act on impulse,' said Mr Beaumaris kindly. 'A moment's reflection, the least touch of adroitness, and it would have been I who fetched the lemonade and you who had the privilege of sitting beside Miss Tallant on this sofa!'

'But it is Lord Fleetwood who earns my gratitude, for he was the more chivalrous!' said Arabella.

'Miss Tallant, I thank you!'

'You have certainly been amply rewarded, and have now nothing to do but to take yourself off,' said Mr Beaumaris.

'Not for the world!' declared his lordship.

Mr Beaumaris sighed. 'How often I have had to deplore your lack of tact!' he said.

Arabella, sparkling under the influence of all this exciting banter, raised her posy to her nose, and said, with a grateful look cast up at Fleetwood: 'I stand *doubly* in Lord Fleetwood's debt!'

'No, no, it is I who stand in yours, ma'am, since you deigned to accept my poor tribute!'

Mr Beaumaris glanced at the posy, and smiled slightly, but said nothing. Arabella, catching sight of Mr Epworth, who was hovering hopefully in the vicinity, suddenly said: 'Mr Beaumaris, who *is* that oddly dressed man?'

He looked round, but said: 'There are so many oddly dressed men present, Miss Tallant, that I fear I am at a loss. You do not mean poor Fleetwood here?'

'Of course I do not!' exclaimed Arabella indignantly.

'Well, I am sure it would be difficult to find anything odder than that waistcoat he wears. It is very disheartening, for I have really expended a great deal of time in trying to reform his taste. Ah, I think I see whom you must mean! That, Miss Tallant, is Horace Epworth. In his own estimation, he undoubtedly personifies a set of creatures whom I have reason to believe you despise.'

Blushing hotly, Arabella asked: 'Is he a – a dandy?'

'He would certainly like you to think so.'

'Well, if he is,' said Arabella frankly, 'I am sure you are no such thing, and I beg your pardon for saying it that evening!'

'Don't apologise to him, ma'am!' said Lord Fleetwood gaily. 'It is time someone gave him a set-down, and *that*, I assure you, smote him with stunning effect! You must know that he thinks himself a notable Corinthian!'

'What is that, pray?' enquired Arabella.

'A Corinthian, ma'am, besides being a very Tulip of Fashion, is an amateur of sport, a master of sword-play, a deadly fellow with a pistol, a Nonpareil amongst whips, a –'

Mr Beaumaris interrupted this mock-solemn catalogue. 'If you will be such a dead bore, Charles, you will provoke me to explain to Miss Tallant what the world means when it calls you a sad rattle.'

'Well?' demanded Arabella mischievously.

'A fribble, ma'am, not worth your attention!' he replied, rising to his feet. 'I see my cousin over there, and must pay my respects to her.' He smiled, bowed, and moved away; stayed for a minute or two, talking to Lady Wainfleet; drank a glass of wine with Mr Warkworth; complimented his hostess on the success of her party; and departed, having done precisely what he had set out to do, which was to place Miss Tallant's feet securely on the ladder of fashion. The news would be all over town within twenty-four hours that the rich Miss Tallant was the Nonpareil's latest flirt.

'Did you see Beaumaris paying court to that dashed pretty girl?' asked Lord Wainfleet of his wife, as they drove away from Lady Bridlington's house.

'Of course I did!' replied his wife.

'Seemed very taken with her, didn't he? Not in his usual style, was she? I wonder if he means anything?'

'Robert?' said his wife, with something very like a snort. 'If you knew him as well as I do, Wainfleet, you would have seen at one glance that he was amusing himself! *I* know how he looks in just that humour! Someone ought to warn the child to have nothing to do with him! It is too bad for him, for she is nothing but a baby, I'll swear!'

'They're saying in the clubs that she's as rich as a Nabob.'

'So I have heard, but what that has to say to anything I don't know! Robert is quite odiously wealthy, and if ever he marries, which I begin to doubt, it will not be for a fortune, I can assure you!'

'No, I don't suppose it will,' agreed his lordship. 'Why did we go there tonight, Louisa? Devilish flat, that kind of an affair.'

'Oh, shocking! Robert asked me to go. I own I was curious to see his heiress. He said he was going to make her the most sought-after female in London.'

'Sounds like a hum to me,' said his lordship. 'Why should he do so?'

'Exactly what I asked him! He said it might be amusing. There are times, Wainfleet, when I would like to box Robert's ears!'

Seven

Not only in his cousin's bosom were vengeful thoughts nourished against Mr Beaumaris. Lady Somercote, not so doting a mother that she supposed any of her sons would be likely to prove more attractive to the heiress than the Nonpareil, could with pleasure have driven the long diamond pin she wore in her hair between his ribs; Mrs Kirkmichael thought bitterly that he might, considering the number of times she had gone out of her way to be agreeable to him, have bestowed a little of his attention upon her lanky daughter, a gesture which would have cost him nothing, and might have given poor Maria a start in the world; Mr Epworth, uneasily aware that for some inscrutable reason he was consistently cast in the shade by the Nonpareil, went the round of the clubs, saying that he had a very good mind to give Beaumaris a set-down at no very distant date; his aunt recalled that she had once quarrelled violently with Lady Mary Beaumaris, and said that it was from his mother Beaumaris had inherited his flirtatious disposition, adding that she was sorry for the woman he eventually married. Even Mr Warkworth and Lord Fleetwood said that it was rather too bad of the Nonpareil to trifle with the season's biggest catch; while several gentlemen who slavishly copied every detail of Mr Beaumaris's attire wished him safely underground.

There was one voice which was not raised to swell this chorus of disapprobation: Lady Bridlington was in raptures over Mr Beaumaris. She could talk of nothing else throughout the following day. While he sat beside Arabella, not a smile, not a gesture had escaped the good lady's anxious eye. He had paid no heed to any other girl in the room; he had plainly advertised to his world that he found Miss Tallant charming: there was no one in London more amiable, more truly polite, more condescending, or more in her ladyship's good graces! Over and over again she told Arabella that her success was now assured; it was not until her first transports had somewhat abated that she could be rational enough to drop a word of warning in Arabella's ear. But the more she thought of Mr Beaumaris's pronounced attentions to the girl, the more she remembered how many innocent maidens had fallen victims to his spear, the more she became convinced that it was necessary to put Arabella on her guard. So she said in an earnest voice, and with a slightly anxious look in her eye: 'I am persuaded, my love, that you are too sensible a girl to be taken-in! But, you know, I stand to you in place of your Mama, and I think I should tell you that Mr Beaumaris is a most accomplished flirt! No one could be more delighted than I am that he should have singled you out, but it will never do, my dear, if you were to develop a *tendre* in *that* direction! I know I have only to drop a word in your ear, and you will not be offended by it! He is a confirmed bachelor. I could not tell you the number of hearts he has broken! Poor Theresa Howden – she married Lord Congleton some years later – went into a decline, and was the despair of her afflicted parents! They *did* think – and I am sure that nothing could have been more pronounced for all one season than – But no! Nothing came of it!'

Arabella had not been the reigning belle for twenty miles round Heythram without learning to distinguish between the flirt and the man who was in earnest, and she replied instantly: 'I know very well that Mr Beaumaris means nothing by his compliments. Indeed, I am in no danger of being taken-in like a goose!'

'Well, my love, I *hope* you are not!'

'You may be sure I am not. If you do not see any objection,

ma'am, I mean to encourage Mr Beaumaris's attentions, and make the best use I may of them! He believes himself to be amusing himself at my expense; *I* mean to turn him to very good account! But as for losing my heart – No, indeed!'

'Mind, we cannot depend upon his continuing to single you out!' said Lady Bridlington, with unwonted caution. 'If he did, it would be beyond anything great, but there is no saying, after all! However, last night's work was enough to launch you, my dear, and I am *deeply* thankful!' She heaved an ecstatic sigh. 'You will be invited everywhere, I daresay!'

She was quite right. Within one fortnight, she was in the happy position of finding herself with five engagements for the same evening, and Arabella had had to break into Sir John's fifty-pound bill to replenish her wardrobe. She had been seen at the fashionable hour of the Promenade in the Park, sitting beside the Nonpareil, in his high-perch phaeton; she had been almost mobbed at the theatre; she was on nodding terms with all manner of exalted persons; she had received two proposals of marriage; Lord Fleetwood, Mr Warkworth, Mr Epworth, Sir Geoffrey Morecambe, and Mr Alfred Somercote (to mention only the most notable of her suitors) had all entered the lists against Mr Beaumaris; and Lord Bridlington, travelling by fast post all the way, had returned from the Continent to discover what his mother meant by filling his house with unknown females in his absence.

He expressed himself, in measured terms, as being most dissatisfied with Lady Bridlington's explanation. He was a stocky, somewhat ponderous young man, with more sobriety than properly belonged to his twenty-six years. His understanding was not powerful, but he was bookish, and had early formed the habit of acquiring information by the perusal of authoritative tomes, so that by the time he had attained his present age his retentive memory was stocked with a quantity of facts which he was perhaps a little too ready to impart to his less well-read contemporaries. His father's death, while he was still at Eton, coupled with a conviction that his mother stood in constant need of superior male guidance, had added disastrously to his self-consequence. He prided himself on his judgement; was a careful steward of his fortune; had the greatest dislike of anything bordering on the unusual; and deplored the frivolity of those who might have been expected to have been his cronies. His mother's elation at not having spent one evening at home in ten days found no echo in his heart. He could neither understand why she should want to waste her time at social functions, nor why she should have been foolish enough to have invited a giddy girl to stay with her. He was afraid that the cost of all this mummery would be shocking; had Lady Bridlington asked for his counsel, which she might easily have done, he would have advised most strongly against Arabella's visit.

Lady Bridlington was a trifle cast-down by this severity, but since her late husband had left her to the enjoyment of a handsome jointure, out of which she always shared the expenses of the house in Park Street with Frederick, she was able to point out to him that the charge of entertaining Arabella fell upon her, and not upon him. He said that the wish to dictate to his Mama was far from him, but that he must persist in thinking the affair most ill-advised. Lady Bridlington was fond of her only son, but Arabella's success had quite gone to her head, and she was in no mood to listen to sober counsels. She retorted that he was talking a great deal of nonsense; upon which he bowed, compressed his lips, and bade her afterwards remember his words. He added that he washed his hands of the whole business. Lady Bridlington, who had no desire to see him fall a victim to Arabella's charms, was torn between exasperation, and relief that he showed no sign of succumbing to them.

'I will allow her to be a pretty-enough young female,' said Frederick fairmindedly, 'but there is a levity in her bearing which I cannot like, and all this gadding-about which she has led you into is not at all to my taste.'

'Well, I can't conceive why you should have come running home in this foolish way!' retorted his mother.

'I thought it my duty, ma'am,' said Frederick.

'It is a great piece of folly, and people will think it excessively odd in you! No one looked to see you in England again until July at the earliest!'

She was mistaken. No one thought it in the least odd of Lord Bridlington to have curtailed his tour. The opinion of society was pithily summed up by Mrs Penkridge, who said that she had guessed all along that that scheming Bridlington woman meant to marry the heiress to her own son. 'Anyone could have seen how it would be!' she declared, with her mirthless jangle of laughter. 'Such odious hypocrisy, too, to hold to it that she did not expect to see Bridlington in England until the summer! Mark my words, Horace, they will be married before the season is over!'

'Good gad, ma'am, I don't fear Bridlington's rivalry!' said her nephew, affronted.

'Then you are a goose!' said Mrs Penkridge. 'Everything is in his favour! He is the possessor of an honoured name, and a title, which you may depend upon it the girl wants, and – what is a great deal to the point, let me tell you! – he has all the advantage of living in the same house, of being always at hand to minister to her wishes, squire her to parties, and – Oh, it puts me out of all patience!'

But Miss Tallant and Lord Bridlington, from the very moment of exchanging their first polite greetings, had conceived a mutual antipathy which was in no way mitigated by the necessity each was under to behave towards the other with complaisance and civility. Arabella would not for the fortune she was believed to possess have grieved her kind hostess by betraying dislike of her son; Frederick's sense of propriety, which was extremely nice, forbade him to neglect the performance of any attention due to his mother's guest. He could appreciate, and, indeed, since he had a provident mind, applaud Mrs Tallant's ambition to dispose of her daughters creditably; and since his own mother had undertaken the task of finding a husband for Arabella, he was prepared to lend his countenance to her schemes. What shocked and disturbed him profoundly was the discovery, within a week of his home-coming, that every gazetted fortune-hunter in London was dangling after Arabella.

'I am at a loss, ma'am, to guess what you can possibly have said to lead anyone to suppose that Miss Tallant is an heiress!' he announced.

Lady Bridlington, who had several times wondered much the same thing, replied uneasily: 'I never said a word, Frederick! There is not the least reason why anyone should suppose such an absurdity! I own, I was a trifle surprised when – But she is a very pretty girl, you know, and Mr Beaumaris took one of his fancies to her!'

'I have never been intimate with Beaumaris,' said Frederick. 'I do not care for the set he leads, and must deplore his making any modest female the object of his gallantry. The influence he exerts, moreover, over persons whom I should have supposed to have had more –'

'Never mind that!' begged his mother hastily. 'You told me yesterday, Frederick! You may think Beaumaris what you please, but even you will not deny that it lies in his power to bring whom he will into fashion!'

'Very likely, ma'am, but I have yet to learn that it lies in his power to prevail upon such men as Epworth, Morecambe, Carnaby, and – I must add! – Fleetwood, to offer marriage to a female with nothing but her face to recommend her!'

'Not Fleetwood!' protested Lady Bridlington feebly.

'Fleetwood!' repeated Frederick in an inexorable tone. 'I do not mean to say that he is precisely hanging out for a rich wife, but that he cannot afford to marry a penniless girl is common knowledge. Yet his attentions towards Miss Tallant are more marked even than those of Horace Epworth. And this is not all! From hints dropped in my presence, from remarks actually made to me, I am persuaded that the greater part of our acquaintance believes her to be in the possession of a handsome fortune! I repeat, ma'am: what can you have said to have given rise to this folly?'

'But I didn't!' cried poor Lady Bridlington almost tearfully. 'Indeed, I took the greatest pains not to touch on the question of her expectations! It is false to call her penniless, because she is no such thing! With all those children of course the Tallants can do very little for her upon her marriage, but when her father dies – and Sophia, too, for she has some money as well –'

'A thousand or so!' interrupted Frederick contemptuously. 'I beg your pardon, ma'am, but nothing could be more plain to me than that something you have said – inadvertently, I daresay! – has done all this mischief. For mischief I must deem it! A pretty state of affairs it will be if we are to have the world saying – as it will say, once the truth is known! – that you have foisted an impostress upon society!'

This terrible forecast temporarily outweighed in Lady Bridlington's mind the sense of strong injustice the rest of her son's remarks had aroused. She turned quite pale, and exclaimed: 'What is to be done?'

'You may rely upon me, ma'am, to do what is necessary,' replied Frederick. 'Whenever the opportunity offers, I shall say that I have no notion how such a rumour came to be spread about.'

'I suppose you must do so,' agreed his mother dubiously. 'But I do beg of you, Frederick, not to take the whole world into your confidence on the subject! There is not the least need for you to enter into all the details of the poor child's circumstances!'

'It would be quite improper for me to do so, ma'am,' replied Frederick crushingly. '*I* am not responsible for her visit to London! I must point out to you, Mama, that it is *you* who have engaged yourself – unwisely, I consider – to establish her suitably. I am sure I have no desire to prejudice her chances of matrimony. Indeed, since I understand that you mean to keep her with you until some man offers for her, I shall be happy to see her married as soon as possible!'

'I think you are very disagreeable!' said Lady Bridlington, dissolving into tears.

Her peace of mind was quite cut-up. When Arabella came

into the room presently, she found her still dabbing at her eyes, and giving little sniffs. Quite dismayed, Arabella begged to be told the cause of this unhappiness. Lady Bridlington, glad of a sympathetic audience, squeezed her hand gratefully, and without reflection poured forth the sum of her grievances.

Kneeling beside her chair, Arabella listened in stricken silence, her hand lying slackly within Lady Bridlington's. 'It is so unkind of Frederick!' Lady Bridlington complained. 'And so unjust, for I assure you, my dear, I never said such a thing to a soul! How could he think I would do so? It would have been quite wicked to have told such lies, besides being so foolish, and vulgar, and everything that is dreadful! And why Frederick should think I could be so lost to all sense of propriety I am sure I don't know!'

Arabella's head sank; guilt and shame almost overpowered her; she could not speak. Lady Bridlington, misreading her confusion, felt a qualm of conscience at having so unguardedly taken her into her confidence, and said: 'I should not have told you! It is all Frederick's fault, and I daresay he has exaggerated everything, just as he so often does! You must not let it distress you, my love, for even if it were true it would be absurd to suppose such a man as Mr Beaumaris, or young Charnwood, or a great many others I could name, care a button whether you are a rich woman or a pauper! And Frederick will make everything right!'

'How can he do so, ma'am?' Arabella managed to ask.

'Oh, when he sees the opportunity, he will say something to damp such ridiculous notions! Nothing very much, you know, but making light of the story! We need not concern ourselves, and I am sorry I spoke of it to you.'

With all her heart Arabella longed for the courage to confess the whole. She could not. Already Lady Bridlington was rambling on, complaining fretfully of Frederick's unkindness, wondering what cause he had to suppose his mother ill-bred enough to have spread a false tale abroad, and wishing that his father were alive to give him one of his famous scolds. She said instead, in a subdued tone: 'Is that why – why everyone has been so very polite to me, ma'am?'

'Certainly not!' said Lady Bridlington emphatically. 'You must have perceived, my love, how many, many friends I have in London, and you may believe they accepted you out of compliment to me! Not that I mean to say – But before you were at all known, naturally it was my sponsorship that started you in the right way.' She patted Arabella's hand consolingly. 'Then, you know, you are so bright, and pretty, that I am sure it is no wonder that you are so much sought-after. And above all, Arabella, we must remember that the world always follows what is seen to be the mode, and Mr Beaumaris has made you the fashion by singling you out, even driving you in his phaeton, which is an honour indeed, I can tell you!'

Arabella's head was still bowed. 'Does – does Lord Bridlington mean to tell everyone that I – that I have no fortune at all, ma'am?'

'Good gracious, no, child! That would be a fatal thing to do, and I hope he would have more sense! He will merely say it has been greatly exaggerated – enough to frighten away the fortune-hunters, but what will not weigh with an honest man! Do not give it another thought!'

Arabella was unable to obey this injunction. It was long before she could think of anything else. Her impulse was to fly from London, back to Heythram, but hardly had she reached the stage of calculating whether she still possessed enough money to pay her fare on the first coach than all the difficulties attached to such a precipitate retreat presented themselves to her. They were insuperable. She could not bring herself to confess to Lady Bridlington that her own was the wicked, ill-bred tongue accountable for the rumour, nor could she think of any excuse for returning to Yorkshire. Still less could she face the necessity of telling Papa and Mama of her shocking behaviour. She must remain in Park Street until the season came to an end, and if Mama was sadly disappointed at the failure of her schemes, at least Papa would never blame his daughter for returning to her home unbetrothed. She perceived clearly that unless something very wonderful were to happen this must be so, and felt herself guilty indeed.

Not for several hours did her mind recover its tone, but she was both young and optimistic, and after a hearty burst of tears, followed by a period of quiet reflection, she began insensibly to be more hopeful. Something would happen to unravel her difficulties; the odious Frederick would scotch the rumour; people would gradually grow to realise that they had been mistaken. Mr Beaumaris and Lord Fleetwood would no doubt write her down as a vulgar, boasting miss, but she must hope that they had not actually told everyone that it was she who had been responsible for the rumour. Meanwhile there was nothing to be done but to behave as though nothing were the matter. This, to a naturally buoyant spirit, was not so hard a task as might have been supposed: London was offering too much to Arabella for her to be long cast-down. She might fancy all her pleasure destroyed, but she would have been a very extraordinary young woman who could have remembered her difficulties while cards and floral offerings were left every day at the house; while invitations poured in to every form of entertainment known to ingenious hostesses; while every gentleman was eager to claim her hand for the dance; while Mr Beaumaris took her driving in the Park behind his match-grays, and every other young lady gazed enviously after her. Whatever the cause, social success was sweet; and since Arabella was a very human girl she could not help enjoying every moment of it.

She expected to see some considerable diminution in her court once Lord Bridlington had let it be known that her fortune had been grossly exaggerated, and braced herself to bear this humiliation. But although she knew from Lady Bridlington that Frederick had faithfully performed his part, still the invitations came in, and still the unattached gentlemen clustered round her. She took fresh heart, glad to find that fashionable people were not, after all, so mercenary as she had been led to think. Neither she nor Frederick had the smallest inking of the true state of affairs: she because she was too unsophisticated; Frederick because it had never yet occurred to him that anyone could doubt what he said. But he might as well have spared his breath on this occasion. Even Mr Warkworth, a charitably-minded gentleman, shook his head over it, and remarked to Sir Geoffrey Morecambe that Bridlington was doing it rather too brown.

'Just what I was thinking myself,' agreed Sir Geoffrey, scrutinising his necktie in the mirror with a dissatisfied eye. 'Shabby, I call it. Do you think this way I have tied my cravat has something of the look of the Nonpareil's new style?'

Mr Warkworth directed a long, dispassionate stare at it. 'No,' he said simply.

'No, no more do I,' said Sir Geoffrey, sad but unsurprised. 'I wonder what he calls it? It ain't precisely a Mail-coach, and it certainly ain't an Osbaldeston, and though I did think it had something of the look of a *Trône d'amour*, it ain't that either. I can tie every one of *them*.'

Mr Warkworth, whose mind had wandered from this vital subject, said, with a frown: 'Damn it, it *is* shabby! You're right!'

Sir Geoffrey was a little hurt. 'Would you say it was as bad as that, Oswald?'

'I would,' stated Mr Warkworth. 'In fact, the more I think of it the worse it appears to me!'

Sir Geoffrey looked intently at his own image, and sighed. 'Yes, it does. I shall have to go home and change it.'

'Eh?' said Mr Warkworth, puzzled. 'Change what? Good God, dear boy, I wasn't talking about your necktie! Wouldn't dream of saying such a thing to my worst enemy! Bridlington!'

'Oh, him!' said Sir Geoffrey, relieved. 'He's a gudgeon!'

'Oughtn't to be gudgeon enough to think everyone else is one. Tell you what: wouldn't do him any good if he did hoax everybody with that bag of moonshine! She's a devilish fine girl, the little Tallant, and if you ask me she wouldn't have him if he were the only man to offer for her.'

'You can't expect him to know that,' said Sir Geoffrey. 'I shouldn't wonder if he hasn't a suspicion he's a dead bore: in fact, he can't have! Stands to reason: wouldn't prose on as he does, if he knew it!'

Mr Warkworth thought this over. 'No,' he pronounced at last. 'You're wrong. If he don't know he's a dead bore, why does he want to frighten off everyone else? Havey-cavey sort of a business: don't like it! a man ought to fight fair.'

'It ain't that,' replied Sir Geoffrey. 'Just remembered something: the little Tallant don't want it to be known she's as rich as a Nabob. Fleetwood told me: tired of being courted for her money. They were all after her in the north.'

'Oh!' said Mr Warkworth. He asked with vague interest: 'Where does she come from?'

'Somewhere up north: Yorkshire, I believe,' said Sir Geoffrey, inserting a cautious finger into one of the folds of his necktie, and easing it a trifle. 'I wonder if that's better?'

'Well, that's a queer thing. Saw Clayton the other day. *He* comes from Yorkshire, and he don't know the Tallant.'

'No, and Withernsea don't either. Mind you, I won't swear it was Yorkshire! Might have been one of those other devilish rural places – Northumberland, or something. Know what I think?'

'No,' said Mr Warkworth.

'Shouldn't be surprised if she's the daughter of some merchant or other, which would account for it.'

Mr Warkworth looked shocked. 'No, really, dear old boy! Nothing of that sort about the girl! Never heard her utter a word that smelled of the shop!'

'Granddaughter, then,' said Sir Geoffrey, stretching a point. 'Pity, if I'm right, but I'll tell you one thing, Oswald! I wouldn't let it weigh with me.'

Upon consideration, Mr Warkworth decided that he would not either.

Since these views were fairly representative, Arabella was not destined to suffer the mortification of seeing her usual gallants hang back when next she attended the Assembly at Almack's. Lord Bridlington was escorting his mother and her guest, for besides being very correct in such matters, he liked Almack's, and approved of the severity of the rules imposed on the club by its imperious hostesses. A number of his contemporaries said openly that an evening spent at Almack's was the flattest thing in town, but these were frippery fellows with whom Lord Bridlington had little to do.

His politeness led him to engage Miss Tallant for the first country-dance, a circumstance which made the unsuccessful applicants for her hand exchange significant glances. They saw to it that he should have no further opportunity of standing up with her. Not one of them would have believed that he had no desire to do so, much preferring to stroll about the rooms, telling as many people as could be got to listen to him all about his travels abroad.

The waltz, which was still looked at askance by old-fashioned persons, had long since forced its way into Almack's, but it was still the unwritten law that no lady might venture to take part in it unless one of the patronesses had clearly indicated her approval. Lady Bridlington had taken care to impress this important convention upon Arabella's mind, so she refused all solicitations to take the floor when the fiddles struck up for the waltz. Papa would certainly not approve of the dance, she knew: she had never dared to tell him that she and Sophia had learnt the steps from their friends the Misses Caterham, a very dashing pair. So she retired to a chair against the wall, beside Lady Bridlington's, and sat fanning herself, and trying not to look as though she longed to be whirling round the floor. One or two more fortunate damsels, who had watched with disfavour her swift rise to popularity, cast her glances of such pitying superiority that she had to recollect a great many of Papa's maxims before she could subdue the very improper sentiments which entered her breast.

Mr Beaumaris, who had looked in midway through the evening – in fact, a bare ten minutes before the doors were relentlessly shut against late-comers – apparently for no other purpose than to entertain the wife of the Austrian Ambassador, saw Arabella, and was amused, guessing her emotions correctly.

Suddenly he cast one of his quizzical looks at Princess Esterhazy, and said: 'Shall I ask that chit to dance?'

She raised her delicate black brows, a faint smile flickering on her lips. '*Here*, my friend, you are not supreme! I think you dare not.'

'I know I dare not,' said Mr Beaumaris, disarming her promptly. 'That is why I ask you, Princess, to present me to the lady as a desirable partner.'

She hesitated, glancing from him to Arabella, and then laughed, and shrugged. 'Well! She does not put herself forward, after all, and I find her style excellent. Come, then!'

Arabella, startled to find herself suddenly confronted by one of the most formidable patronesses, rose quickly.

'You do not dance, Miss Tallant. May I present Mr Beaumaris to you as a very desirable partner?' said the Princess, with a slightly malicious smile cast at Mr Beaumaris.

Arabella could only curtsy, and blush, and be sorry to find that she was so ill-natured as to be conscious of feelings of ignoble triumph over the ladies who had been kind enough to look pityingly at her.

Mr Beaumaris led her on to the floor, and encircled her waist with one arm, taking her right hand in a light clasp. Arabella was naturally a good dancer, but she felt extremely nervous, partly because she had never attempted the waltz, except in the Misses Caterham's old schoolroom, and partly because it was so strange to be held in such close proximity to a man. For several turns she answered Mr Beaumaris very much at random, being preoccupied with her feet. She was so much shorter than he that her head only just reached his shoulder, and since she felt shy she did not look up, but steadfastly regarded the top of his waistcoat. Mr Beaumaris, who was not in the habit of devoting himself to such very young ladies, found this bashfulness amusing, and not unattractive. After he thought she had had time to recover from it a little, he said: 'It *is* a nice waistcoat, isn't it, Miss Tallant?'

That did make her look up, and quickly too, her face breaking into laughter. She looked so lovely, and her big eyes met his with such a frank, ingenuous expression in them, that he was aware of a stir of something in his heart that was not mere amusement. But he had no intention of going to dangerous lengths with this or any other pretty chit, and he said, in a bantering tone: 'It is customary, you know, to exchange polite conversation during the dance. I have now addressed no fewer than three unexceptionable remarks to you without winning one answer!'

'You see, I am minding my steps,' she confided seriously.

Decidedly this absurd child was a refreshing change from the generality of damsels! Had he been a younger man, he reflected, he might easily have succumbed to her charm. It was fortunate that he was thirty, and no longer to be caught by a pretty face and naïve ways, for he knew well that these would pall on him, and that he wanted something more in the lady whom he would one day marry. He had never yet found just what he was looking for, did not even know what it might prove to be, and was perfectly resigned to his bachelordom.

'It is not at all necessary,' he said. 'You dance delightfully. You do not mean to tell me that this is the first time you have waltzed?'

Miss Tallant certainly did not mean to tell him anything of the sort, and was already regretting her impulsive confidence. 'Good gracious, no!' she said. 'The first time at Almack's, however.'

'I am happy to think, then, that mine was the honour of first leading you on to the floor. You will certainly be besieged by every man present now it is seen that you have no objection to the waltz.'

She said nothing, but fell to studying his waistcoat again. He glanced down at her, a hint of mockery in the smile that hovered about his mouth. 'How does it feel, Miss Tallant, to be the rage of town? Do you enjoy it, or have your northern triumphs given you a distaste for this sort of thing?'

She raised her eyes, and her chin too. 'I am afraid, Mr Beaumaris, that you betrayed what I – what I begged you not to speak of!'

There was a distinctly sardonic look in his eye, but he replied coolly: 'I assure you, ma'am, I have mentioned your circumstances to one person only: Lord Fleetwood.'

'Then it is he who –' She broke off, flushing.

'Very probably,' he agreed. 'You must not blame him, however. Such things are bound to leak out.'

Her lips parted, and then closed again. He wondered what she had so nearly said: whether he was to have been treated to her society manners, or whether she had been about to tell him the truth. On the whole, he was glad that she had thought better of it. If she took him into her confidence, he supposed he would be obliged, in mercy, to bring this game to a close, which would be a pity, since it was providing him with a great deal of entertainment. To have elevated an unknown provincial to the heights of society was an achievement which only one who had no illusions about the world he led could properly appreciate. He was deriving much enjoyment too from observing the efforts of his devoted copyists to win the provincial's hand. As for Arabella herself, Mr Beaumaris shrugged off a momentary compunction. She would no doubt retire in due course to her northern wilds, marry some red-faced squire, and talk for the rest of her life of her brilliant London season. He glanced down at her again, and thought that it would be a pity if she were to retire too soon. Probably, by the end of the London season he would be only too thankful to see her go, but for the present he was very well satisfied to gratify her by a little flirtation.

The music ceased, and he led her off to the floor, to one of the adjoining rooms, where refreshments were served. These were of a very simple nature, the strongest drink offered being a mild claret-cup. Mr Beaumaris procured a glass of lemonade for Arabella, and said: 'You must let me thank you for a delightful few minutes, Miss Tallant: I have seldom enjoyed a dance more.' He received only a slight smile and an inclination of the head in answer to this which were both so eloquent of incredulity that he was delighted. No fool, then, the little Tallant! He would have pursued this new form of sport, in the hope of teasing her into retort, but at that moment two purposeful gentlemen bore down upon them. Arabella yielded to the solicitations of Mr Warkworth, and went off on his arm. Sir Geoffrey Morecambe sighed in a languishing way, but turned his rebuff to good account by seizing the opportunity to ask Mr Beaumaris what he called the arrangement of his neckcloth. He had to repeat the question, for Mr Beaumaris, watching Arabella walk away with Mr Warkworth, was not attending. He brought his gaze to bear on Sir Geoffrey's face, however, at the second time of asking, and raised his brows enquiringly.

'That style you have of tying your cravat!' said Sir Geoffrey. 'I don't perfectly recognise it. Is it something new? Should you object to telling me what you call it?'

'Not in the least,' replied Mr Beaumaris blandly. 'I call it Variation on an Original Theme.'

Eight

Mr Beaumaris's sudden realisation that the little Tallant was no fool underwent no modification during the following days. It began to be borne in upon him that charm he never so wisely she was never within danger of losing her head over him. She treated him in the friendliest fashion, accepted his homage, and – he suspected – was bent upon making the fullest use of him. If he paid her compliments, she listened to them with the most innocent air in the world, but with a look in her candid gaze which gave him pause. The little Tallant valued his compliments not at all. Instead of being thrown into a flutter by the attentions of the biggest matrimonial prize in London, she plainly considered herself to be taking part in an agreeable game. If he flirted with her, she would generally respond in kind, but with so much the manner of one willing to indulge him that the hunter woke in him, and he was quite as much piqued as amused. He began to toy with the notion of making her fall in love with him in good earnest, just to teach her that the Nonpareil was not to be so treated with impunity. Once, when she was apparently not in the humour for gallantry, she actually had the effrontery to cut him short, saying: 'Oh, never mind that! Who was that odd-looking man who waved to you just now? Why does he walk in that ridiculous way, and screw up his mouth so? Is he in pain?'

He was taken aback, for really he had paid her a compliment calculated to cast her into exquisite confusion. His lips twitched, for he had as few illusions about himself as had, to all appearances the lady beside him. 'That,' he replied, 'is Golden Ball, Miss Tallant, one of our dandies, as no doubt you have been told. He is not in pain. That walk denotes his consequence.'

'Good gracious! He looks as though he went upon stilts! Why does he think himself of such consequence?'

'He has never accustomed himself to the thought that he is worth not a penny less than forty thousand pounds a year,' replied Mr Beaumaris gravely.

'What an odious person he must be!' she said scornfully. 'To be consequential for such a reason as that is what I have no patience with!'

'Naturally you have not,' he agreed smoothly.

Her colour rushed up. She said quickly: 'Fortune cannot make the man: I am persuaded you agree with me, for they tell me you are even more wealthy, Mr Beaumaris, and I *will* say this! – you do not give yourself such airs as that!'

'Thank you,' said Mr Beaumaris meekly. 'I scarcely dared to hope to earn so great an encomium from you, ma'am.'

'Was it rude of me to say it? I beg your pardon!'

'Not at all.' He glanced down at her. 'Tell me, Miss Tallant! – Just why do you grant me the pleasure of driving you out in my curricle?'

She responded with perfect composure, but with that sparkle in her eye which he had encountered several times before: 'You must know that it does me a great deal of good socially to be seen in your company, sir!'

He was so much surprised that momentarily he let his hands drop. The grays broke into a canter, and Miss Tallant kindly advised him to mind his horses. The most notable whip in the country thanked her for her reminder, and steadied his pair. Miss Tallant consoled him for the chagrin he might have been supposed to feel by saying that she thought he drove very well. After a stunned moment, laughter welled up within him. His voice shook perceptibly as he answered: 'You are too good, Miss Tallant!'

'Oh, no!' she said politely. 'Shall you be at the masquerade at the Argyll Rooms tonight?'

'I never attend such affairs, ma'am!' he retorted, putting her in her place.

'Oh, then I shall not see you there!' remarked Miss Tallant, with unimpaired cheerfulness.

She did not see him there, but, little though she might have known it, he was obliged to exercise considerable restraint not to cast to the four winds his famed fastidiousness, and to minister to her vanity by appearing at the ball. He did not do it, and hoped that she had missed him. She had, but this was something she would not acknowledge even to herself. Arabella, who had liked the Nonpareil on sight, was setting a strong guard over her sensibilities. He had seemed to her, when first her eyes had alighted on his handsome person, to be almost the embodiment of a dream. Then he had uttered such words to his friend as must shatter for ever her esteem, and had wickedly led her into vulgar prevarication. Now it pleased his fancy to single her out from all the beauties in town, for reasons better known to himself than to her, but which she darkly suspected to be mischievous. No fool, the little Tallant! Not for one moment would she permit herself to indulge the absurd fancy that his court was serious. He might intrude into her meditations, but whenever she was aware of his having done so she was resolute in banishing his image. Sometimes she was strongly of the opinion that he had not believed a word of her boasts on that never to be sufficiently regretted evening in Leicestershire; at others, it seemed as though she had deceived him as completely as she had deceived Lord Fleetwood. It was impossible to fathom the intricacies of his mind, but one thing was certain: the great Mr Beaumaris and the Vicar of Heythram's daughter could have nothing to do with one another, so that the less the Vicar's daughter thought about him the better it would be for her. One could not deny his address, or his handsome face, but one could – and one did – dwell on the many imperfections of his character. He was demonstrably indolent, a spoilt darling of society, with no thought for anything but his fleeting pleasure: a heartless, heedless leader of fashion, given over to selfishness, and every other vice which Papa's daughter had been taught to think reprehensible.

If she missed him at the masquerade, no one would have guessed it. She danced indefatigably the whole night through, refused an offer of marriage from a slightly intoxicated Mr Epworth, tumbled into bed at an advanced hour in the morning, and dropped instantly into untroubled sleep.

She was awakened at a most unseasonable hour by the sudden clatter of fire-irons in the cold hearth. Since the menial who crept into her chamber each morning to sweep the grate, and kindle a new fire there, performed her task with trained stealth, this noise was unusual enough to rouse Arabella with a start. A gasp and a whimper, proceeding from the direction of the fireplace, made her sit up with a jerk, blinking at the unexpected vision of a small, dirty, and tearstained little boy, almost cowering on the hearth-rug, and regarding her out of scared, dilating eyes.

'Good gracious!' gasped Arabella, staring at him. 'Who are you?'

The child cringed at the sound of her voice, and returned no answer. The mists of sleep curled away from Arabella's brain; her eyes took in the soot lying on the floor, the grimed appearance of her strange visitant, and enlightenment dawned on her. 'You must be a climbing-boy!' she exclaimed. 'But what are you doing in my room?' Then she perceived the terror in the pinched and grimed small face, and she said quickly: 'Don't be afraid! Did you lose your way in those horrid chimneys?'

The urchin nodded, knuckling his eyes. He further volunteered the information that ole Grimsby would bash him for it. Arabella, who had had leisure to observe that one side of his face was swollen and discoloured, demanded: 'Is that your master? Does he beat you?'

The urchin nodded again, and shivered.

'Well, he shan't beat you for this!' said Arabella, stretching out her hand for the dressing-gown that was chastely disposed across the chair beside her bed. 'Wait! I am going to get up!'

The urchin looked very much alarmed by this intelligence, and shrank back against the wall, watching her defensively. She slid out of bed, thrust her feet into her slippers, fastened her dressing-gown and advanced kindly upon her visitor. He flung up an instinctive arm, cringing before her. He was clad in disgraceful rags, and Arabella now saw that the ends of his frieze nether-garments were much charred, and that his skinny legs and his bare feet were badly burnt. She dropped to her knees, crying out pitifully: 'Oh, poor little fellow! You have burnt yourself so dreadfully!'

He slightly lowered his protective arm, looking suspiciously at her over it. 'Ole Grimsby done it,' he said.

She caught her breath. 'What!'

'I'm afeard of going up the chimbley,' explained the urchin. 'Sometimes there's rats – big, fierce 'uns!'

She shuddered. 'And he forces you to do so – like that?'

'They most of 'em does,' said the urchin, accepting life as he found it.

She held out her hand. 'Let me see! I will not hurt you.'

He looked wary, but after a moment appeared to consider that she might be speaking the truth, for he allowed her to take one of his feet in her hand. He was surprised when he saw that tears stood in her eyes, for in his experience the gentler sex was more apt to beat one with a broom-handle than to weep over one.

'Poor child, poor child!' Arabella said, a break in her voice. 'You are so thin, too! I am sure you are half-starved! Are you hungry?'

'I'm allus hungry,' he replied simply.

'And cold too!' she said. 'No wonder, in those rags! It is wicked, *wicked*!' She jumped up, and, grasping the bell pull that hung beside the fireplace, tugged it violently.

The urchin uttered another of his frightened whimpers, and said: 'Ole Grimsby 'll beat the daylights out of me! Lemme go!'

'He shan't lay a finger on you!' promised Arabella, her cheeks flushed, and her eyes sparkling through the tears they held.

The urchin came to the conclusion that she was soft in her head. 'Ho!' he remarked bitterly, '*you* don' know old Grimsby! Nor you don' know his ole woman! Broke one of me ribs he did, onct!'

'He shall never do so again, my dear,' Arabella said, turning aside to pull open a drawer in one of the chests. She dragged out the soft shawl which had not so long since been swathed round the head of the sufferer from toothache, and put it round the boy, saying coaxingly: 'There, let me wrap you up till we have had a fire lit! Is that more comfortable, my little man? Now sit down in this chair, and you shall have something to eat directly!'

He allowed himself to be lifted into the armchair, but his expression was so eloquent of suspicion and terror that it wrung Arabella's tender heart. She smoothed his cropped, sandy hair with one gentle hand, and said soothingly: 'You must not be afraid of me: I promise you I will not hurt you, nor let your master either. What is your name, my dear?'

'Jemmy,' he replied, clutching the shawl about him, and fixing her with a frightened stare.

'And how old are you?'

This he was unable to answer, being uninstructed in the matter. She judged him to be perhaps seven or eight years old, but he was so undernourished that he might have been older. While she waited for the summons of the bell to bring her maid to the room, she put more questions to the child. He seemed to have no knowledge of the existence of any parents, volunteering that he was an orphing, on the Parish. When he saw that this seemed to distress her, he tried to comfort her by stating that one Mrs Balham said he was love-begotten. It appeared that this lady had brought him up until the moment when he had passed into the hands of his present owner. An enquiry into Mrs Balham's disposition elicited the information that she was a rare one for jackey, and could half-murder anyone when under the influence of this stimulant. Arabella had no idea what jackey might be, but she gathered that Jemmy's foster-mother was much addicted to strong drink. She questioned Jemmy more closely, and he, gaining confidence, imparted to her, in the most matter-of-fact way, some details of a climbing-boy's life which drove the blood from her cheeks. He told her, with a certain distorted pride, of the violence of one of ole Grimsby's associates, Mr Molys, a master-sweep, who, only a year before, had been sentenced to two years' imprisonment for causing the death of his six-year-old slave.

'Two years!' cried Arabella, sickened by the tale of cruelty so casually unfolded. 'If he had stolen a yard of silk from a mercer's factory they would have deported him!'

Jemmy was not in a position to deny or to corroborate this statement, and preserved a wary silence. He saw that the young lady was very angry, and although her wrath did not seem to be directed against himself his experience had taught him to run no unnecessary risks of being suddenly knocked flying against the wall. He shrank into the corner of the chair therefore, and clutched the shawl more tightly round his person.

A discreet knock fell on the door, and a slightly flustered and considerably startled housemaid entered the room. 'Was it you rang, miss?' she asked, in astonished accents. Then her eye alighted on Arabella's visitor, and she uttered a genteel shriek. 'Oh, miss! What a turn it gave me! The young varmint to give you such a fright! It's the chimney-sweep's boy, miss, and him looking for him all over! You come with me this instant, you wicked boy, you!'

Jemmy, recognising a language he understood, whined that he had not meant to do it.

'Hush!' Arabella said, dropping her hand on one bony little shoulder. 'I know very well it is the sweep's boy, Maria, and if you look at him you will see how he has been used! Go downstairs, if you please, and fetch me some food for him directly – and send someone up to kindle the fire here!'

Maria stared at her as though she thought she had taken leave of her senses. 'Miss!' she managed to ejaculate. 'A dirty little *climbing-boy*?'

'When he has been bathed,' said Arabella quietly, 'he will not be dirty. I shall need plenty of warm water, and the bath, if you please. But first a fire, and some milk and food for the poor child!'

The affronted handmaid bridled. 'I hope, miss, you do not expect *me* to wash that nasty little creature! I'm sure I don't know what her ladyship would say to such goings-on!'

'No,' said Arabella, 'I expect nothing from you that I might expect from a girl with a more feeling heart than yours! Go and do what I have asked you to do, and desire Becky to come upstairs to me!'

'Becky?' gasped Maria.

'Yes, the girl who had the toothache. And when you have brought up food – some bread-and-butter, and some meat will do very well, but do not forget the milk! – you may send someone to tell Lord Bridlington that I wish to see him at once.'

Maria gulped, and stammered: 'But, miss, his lordship is abed and asleep!'

'Well, let him be wakened!' said Arabella impatiently.

'Miss, I dare not for my life! His orders were no one wasn't to disturb him till nine o'clock, and he won't come, not till he has shaved himself, and dressed, not his lordship!'

Arabella considered the question, and finally came to the conclusion that it might be wiser to dispense with his lordship's assistance for the time being. 'Very well,' she said. 'I will dress immediately, then, and see the sweep myself. Tell him to wait!'

'See the sweep – dress – Miss, you won't never! With that boy watching you!' exclaimed the scandalised Maria.

'Don't be such a fool, girl!' snapped Arabella, stamping her foot. 'He's scarcely older than my little brother at home! Go away before you put me out of all patience with you!'

This, however, Maria could not be persuaded to do until she had arranged a prim screen between the wondering Jemmy and his hostess. She then tottered away to spread the news through the house that Miss was raving mad, and likely to be taken off to Bedlam that very day. But since she did not dare to thwart a guest so much petted by her mistress, she delivered Arabella's message to Becky, and condescended to carry up a tray of food to her room.

Jemmy, still huddled in the big chair, was bewildered by the unprecedented turn of events, and understood nothing of what was intended towards him. But he perfectly understood the significance of a plate of cold beef, and half a loaf of bread, and his sharp eyes glistened. Arabella, who had flung on her clothes at random, and done up her hair in a careless knot, settled him down to the enjoyment of his meal, and sallied forth to do battle with the redoubtable Mr Grimsby, uneasily awaiting her in the front hall.

The scene, conducted under the open-mouthed stare of a footman in his shirt-sleeves, two astonished and giggling maids, and the kitchen-boy, was worthy of a better audience. Mr Beaumaris, for instance, would have enjoyed it immensely. Mr Grimsby, knowing that the sympathies of those members of the household he had so far encountered were with him, and seeing that his assailant was only a chit of a girl, tried at the outset to take a high line, rapidly cataloguing Jemmy's many vices, and adjuring Arabella not to believe a word the varmint uttered. He soon discovered that what Arabella lacked in inches she more than made up for in spirit. She tore his character to shreds and warned him of his ultimate fate; she flung Jemmy's burns and bruises in his face, and bade him answer her if he dared. He did not dare. She assured him that never would she permit Jemmy to go back to him, and when he tried to point out his undoubted rights over the boy she looked so fierce that he backed before her. She said that if he wished to talk of his rights he might do so before a magistrate, and at these ominous words all vestige of fight went out of him. The misfortune which had overtaken his friend, Mr Molys, was still fresh in his mind, and he desired to have no dealings with an unjust Law. There was no doubt that a young lady living in a house of this style would have those at her back who could, if she urged them to it, make things very unpleasant for a poor chimney-sweep. The course for a prudent man to follow was retreat: climbing-boys were easily come by, and Jemmy had never been a success. Mr Grimsby, his back bent nearly double, edged himself out of the house, trying to assure Arabella in one breath that she might keep Jemmy and welcome, and that, whatever the ungrateful brat might say, he had been like a father to him.

Flushed with her triumph, Arabella returned to her room, where she found Jemmy, the plate of meat long since disposed of, eyeing with a good deal of apprehension the preparations for his ablutions. A capacious hip-bath stood before the fire, into which Becky was emptying the last of three large brass cans of hot water. Whatever Becky might think of climbing-boys, she had conceived a slavish adoration of Arabella, and she declared her willingness to do anything Miss might require of her.

'First,' said Arabella briskly, 'I must wash him, and put basilicum ointment on his poor little feet and legs. Then I must get him some clothes to wear. Becky, do you know where to procure suitable clothes for a child in London?'

Becky nodded vigorously, twisting her apron between her fingers. She ventured to say that she had sent home a suit for her brother Ben which Mother had been ever so pleased with.

'Have you little brothers? Then you will know just what to buy for this child!' Arabella said. 'A warm jacket, and some smalls, and a shirt – oh, and some shoes and stockings! Wait! I will give you the money, and you shall go and procure the things immediately!'

'If you please, miss,' said Becky firmly, 'I think I ought to help you wash him first.' She added sapiently: 'Likely he'll struggle, miss – not being used to it.'

She was quite right. Jemmy fought like a tiger to defend his person from the intended rape, and was deaf alike to coaxings and to reassurances. But the two damsels before him had not helped to bring up their respective young brothers for nothing. They stripped Jemmy of his rags, heedless of his sobs and his protests, and they dumped him, wildly kicking, in the bath, and ruthlessly washed every inch of his emaciated small person.

It was not to be expected that Jemmy's howls would not be heard beyond the confines of the room. They were lusty, and they penetrated to Lady Bridlington's ears. It was inconceivable to the good lady that they could really be emanating from within her house, as they seemed to be, and she was just about to ring her bell, and desire Clara Crowle to send away whatever child it was who was screaming in the street, when the howls ceased (Jemmy had been lifted out of the bath, and wrapped in a warm towel), and she sank back again in her bed. Not long after this, Miss Crowle came softly in with her breakfast-tray, and the pleasing intelligence that Miss Arabella was out of her mind, and had got a dirty little boy in her room, and wouldn't let him go, not whatever anyone said. Hardly had her ladyship grasped the essential points of the story poured into her bemused ears than Arabella herself came in. Her visit made it necessary for Miss Crowle to revive her mistress with hartshorn-and-water, and to burn pastilles, for it brought on a nervous spasm of alarming intensity. Lady Bridlington now understood that she was expected not only to house a boy picked out of the gutter, but to pursue his late master by every means in her power. Arabella talked of the Law, and of magistrates; of cruelties which made it almost impossible for Lady Bridlington even to swallow her coffee; and of what Papa would say must be done in so shocking a case. Lady Bridlington moaned, and said faintly: 'But you cannot! The boy must be given back to his master! You don't understand these things!'

'Cannot?' cried Arabella, her eyes flashing. '*Cannot*, ma'am? I beg your pardon, but it is you who have not understood! When you have seen the dreadful marks on the poor little soul's back – and his ribs almost breaking through his skin! – you will not talk so!'

'No, no, Arabella, for heaven's sake – !' begged her godmother. 'I won't have you bring him in here! Where is Frederick? My dear, of course it is all very dreadful, and we will see what can be done, but do, pray, wait until I am dressed! Clara, where is his lordship?'

'His lordship, my lady,' responded Clara with relish, 'having partaken of his breakfast, has gone riding in the Park, as is his custom. His lordship's gentleman happening to mention that Miss had a climbing-boy in her room, his lordship said as how he must be sent off at once.'

'Well, he will not be!' said Arabella, not mincing matters.

Lady Bridlington, reflecting that it was just like Frederick to issue orders in this foolish style, and leave others to see them carried out, decided to postpone any further discussion until he should be present to lend her his support. She persuaded Arabella to go away, looked with distaste at her breakfast-tray, and begged Clara, in a failing voice, to give her her smelling-salts.

When Lord Bridlington returned from his morning exercise, he was displeased to learn that nothing had so far been done about the climbing-boy, except that Miss had sent one of the under-servants out to buy him a suit of clothes. He was still frowning over this when his Mama came downstairs, and almost fell upon his neck. 'Thank heaven you are come at last!' she uttered. 'What can have induced you to go out with the house in this uproar? I am driven nearly distracted! She wants me to employ the boy as a page!'

Frederick led her firmly into the saloon on the ground-floor, and shut the door upon the interested butler. He then demanded an explanation of an affair which he said he was at a loss to understand. His mother was in the middle of giving him one when Arabella came into the room, leading the washed and clothed Jemmy by the hand.

'Good-morning, Lord Bridlington!' she said calmly. 'I am glad you are come home, for you will best be able to help me to decide what I ought to do with Jemmy here.'

'I can certainly do so, Miss Tallant,' he answered. 'The boy must of course go back where he belongs. It was most improper of you, if you will permit me to say so, to interfere between him and his master.'

He encountered a look which surprised him. 'I do not permit

anyone, Lord Bridlington, to tell me that in rescuing a helpless child from the brutality of a monster I am doing what is improper!' said Arabella.

'No, no, my dear, of course not!' hastily interposed Lady Bridlington. 'Frederick did not mean – But, you see, there is nothing one can do in these sad cases! That is – I am sure Frederick will speak to the man – give him a good fright, you know!'

'Really, Mama –'

'And Jemmy?' demanded Arabella. 'What will you do with him?'

His lordship looked distastefully at the candidate for his protection. Jemmy had been well scrubbed, but not the most thorough application of soap and water could turn him into a well-favoured child. He had a sharp little face, a wide mouth, from which a front tooth was missing, and a very snub nose. His short, ragged hair was perfectly straight, and his ears showed a tendency to stick out from his head.

'I do not know what you expect me to do!' said his lordship fretfully. 'If you had any knowledge of the laws governing apprentices, my dear Miss Tallant, you would know that it is quite impossible to steal this boy away from his master!'

'When the master of an apprentice misuses a boy as this child has been misused,' retorted Papa's daughter, 'he renders himself liable to prosecution! What is more, this man knows it, and I assure you he does not expect to have Jemmy returned to him!'

'I suppose you think I should adopt the boy!' said Frederick, goaded.

'No, I do not think that,' replied Arabella, her voice a little unsteady. 'I only think that you might – show some compassion for one so wretchedly circumstanced!'

Frederick coloured hotly. 'Well, of course I am excessively sorry, but –'

'Do you know that his master lights a fire in the grate beneath him, to force him up the chimney?' interrupted Arabella.

'Well, I don't suppose he would go up if – Yes, yes, shocking, I know, but chimneys must be swept, after all, or what would become of us all?'

'Oh, that Papa were here!' Arabella cried. 'I see that it is useless to talk to you, for you are selfish and heartless, and you care for nothing but your own comfort!'

It was at this inopportune moment that the door was opened, and the butler announced two morning-callers. He afterwards explained this lapse, which he felt quite as acutely as his mistress, by saying that he had supposed Miss to be still upstairs with That Boy. Frederick made a hasty gesture indicative of his desire that the visitors should be excluded, but it was too late. Lord Fleetwood and Mr Beaumaris walked into the room.

Their reception was unusual. Lady Bridlington gave vent to an audible moan; her son stood rooted to the floor in the middle of the room, his face flushed, and his whole appearance that of a man who had been stuffed; and Miss Tallant, also very much flushed, bit her lip, and turned on her heel, leading a small urchin over to a chair by the wall, and bidding him gently to sit down on it, and to be a good boy.

Lord Fleetwood blinked upon this scene; Mr Beaumaris's brows went up, but he gave no other sign of surprise, merely bowing over Lady Bridlington's nerveless hand, and saying: 'How do you do? I trust we don't intrude? I called in the hope of persuading Miss Tallant to drive to the Botanical Gardens with me. They tell me the spring flowers are quite a sight there.'

'You are very obliging, sir,' said Arabella curtly, 'but I have more important affairs to attend to this morning.'

Lady Bridlington pulled herself together. 'My love, we can discuss all that later! I am sure it would do you good to take the air! Do but send that – that child down to the kitchen, and –'

'Thank you, ma'am, but I do not stir from the house until I have settled what is to be done with Jemmy.'

Lord Fleetwood, who had been regarding Jemmy with frank curiosity, said: 'Jemmy, eh? Er – friend of yours, Miss Tallant?'

'No. He is a climbing-boy who came by mistake down the

chimney of my bedchamber,' Arabella replied. 'He has been most shamefully used, and he is only a child, as you may see – I daresay not more than seven or eight years old!'

The warmth of her feelings brought a distinct tremor into her voice. Mr Beaumaris looked curiously at her.

'No, really?' said Lord Fleetwood, with easy sympathy. 'Well, that's a great deal too bad! Shocking brutes, some of these chimney-sweeps! Ought to be sent to gaol!'

She said impulsively: 'Yes, that is what I have been telling Lord Bridlington, only he seems not to have the least understanding!'

'Arabella!' implored Lady Bridlington. 'Lord Fleetwood can have no interest in such matters!'

'Oh, I assure you, ma'am!' said his lordship. 'I am interested in anything that interests Miss Tallant! Rescued the child, did you? Well, upon my soul, I call it a devilish fine thing to do! Not as though he was a taking brat, either!'

'What does that signify?' said Arabella contemptuously. 'I wonder how taking, my lord, you or I should be had we been brought up from infancy by a drunken foster-mother, sold while still only babies to a brutal master, and forced into a hateful trade!'

Mr Beaumaris moved quietly to a chair a little removed from the group in the centre of the room, and stood leaning his hands on the back of it, his eyes still fixed on Arabella's face.

'No, no! Exactly so!' hastily said Lord Fleetwood.

Lord Bridlington chose, unwisely, to intervene at this point. 'No doubt it is just as you say, ma'am, but this is hardly a topic for my mother's sitting-room! Let me beg of you –'

Arabella turned on him like a flash, her eyes bright with tears, her voice unsteady with indignation. 'I will not be silenced! It is a topic that should be discussed in every Christian lady's sitting-room! Oh, I mean no disrespect, ma'am! You have not thought – you cannot have thought! Had you seen the wounds on this child's body you could not refuse to help him! I wish I had made you come into my room when I had him naked in the bath! Your heart must have been touched!'

'Yes, but, Arabella, my heart *is* touched!' protested her afflicted godmother. 'Only I don't want a page, and he is much too young, and such an ugly little thing! Besides, the sweep will very likely claim him, because, whatever you may think, if the boy is apprenticed to him, which he must be –'

'You may make your mind easy on that score, ma'am! His master will never dare to lay claim to him. He knows very well that he is in danger of being taken before a magistrate, for I told him so, and he did not doubt me! Why, he cringed at the very word, and backed himself out of the house as fast as he could!'

Mr Beaumaris spoke at last. 'Did you confront the sweep, Miss Tallant?' he asked, an odd little smile flickering on his lips.

'Certainly I did!' she replied, her glance resting on him for an indifferent moment.

Lady Bridlington was suddenly inspired. 'He must go to the Parish, of course! Frederick, *you* will know how to set about it!'

'No, no, he must not!' Arabella declared. 'That would be worse than anything, for what will they do with him, do you suppose, but set him to the only trade he knows? And he is afraid of those dreadful chimneys! If it were not so far away, I would send him to Papa, but how could such a little boy go all that way alone?'

'No, certainly not!' said Lord Fleetwood. 'Not to be thought of!'

'Lord Bridlington, surely, surely you would not condemn a child to such a life as he has endured?' Arabella begged, her hands going out in a pleading gesture. 'You have so *much*!'

'Of course he wouldn't!' declared Fleetwood rashly. 'Now, come, Bridlington!'

'But why should I?' demanded Frederick. 'Besides, what could I do with the brat? It is the greatest piece of nonsense I ever had to listen to!'

'Lord Fleetwood, will *you* take Jemmy?' asked Arabella,

turning to him beseechingly.

His lordship was thrown into disorder. 'Well, I don't think –
You see, ma'am – Fact of the matter is – Dash it, Lady
Bridlington's right! The Parish! That's the thing!'

'Unworthy, Charles!' said Mr Beaumaris.

The much goaded Lord Bridlington rounded on him. 'Then,
if that is what you think, Beaumaris, perhaps *you* will take the
wretched brat!'

Then it was that Mr Beaumaris, looking across the room at
Arabella, all flushed cheeks and heaving bosom, astonished the
company, and himself as well. 'Yes,' he said. 'I will.'

Nine

These simple words struck the ears of his audience with stunning effect. Lord Fleetwood's jaw dropped; Lady Bridlington's and her son's rather protuberant eyes started at Mr Beaumaris; and Arabella stared at him in amazement. It was she who broke the silence. '*You?*' she said, the incredulity in her tone leaving him in no doubt of her opinion of his character.

A rather rueful smiled twisted his lips. 'Why not?' he said.

Her eyes searched his face. 'What would you do with him?' she demanded.

'I haven't the smallest notion,' he confessed. 'I hope you may be going to tell me what I am to do with him, Miss Tallant.'

'If I let you take him, you would throw him on the Parish, like Lord Fleetwood!' she said bitterly.

His lordship uttered an inarticulate protest.

'I have a great many faults,' replied Mr Beaumaris, 'but, believe me, you may trust my pledged word! I will neither throw him on the parish, nor restore him to his master.'

'You must be mad!' exclaimed Frederick.

'You would naturally think so,' said Mr Beaumaris, flicking him with one of his disdainful glances.

'Have you considered what people would be bound to say?' Frederick said.

'No, nor do I propose to burden my head with anything that interests me so little!' retorted Mr Beaumaris.

Arabella said in a softened voice: 'If you mean it indeed, sir, you will be doing the very kindest thing – perhaps the best thing you have ever done, and, oh, I *thank* you!'

'Certainly the best thing I have ever done, Miss Tallant,' he said, with that wry smile.

'What will you do with him?' she asked again. 'You must not be thinking that I mean you to adopt him as your own, or anything of that nature! He must be brought up to a respectable trade, only I do not know what would be the best for him!'

'Perhaps,' suggested Mr Beaumaris, 'he has views of his own on the subject. What, Jemmy, would you choose to do?'

'Yes, what would you like to do when you are a man?' said Arabella, turning to kneel beside Jemmy's chair, and speaking in a coaxing tone. 'Tell me!'

Jemmy, who had been following all this with an intent look in his face, had no very clear idea of what it was about, but his quick, cockney mind had grasped that none of these swells, not even the stout, cross one, intended any harm to him. The scared expression in his eyes had given place to one of considerable acuteness. He answered his protectress without hesitation. 'Give ole Grimsby a leveller!' he said.

'Yes, my dear, and so you shall, and I hope you will do the same by everyone like him!' said Arabella warmly. 'But how would you choose to earn your living?'

Mr Beaumaris's lips twitched appreciatively. So the little Tallant had brothers, had she?

Lady Bridlington was looking bewildered, and her son disgusted. Lord Fleetwood, accepting Arabella's unconsciously betrayed knowledge of boxing-cant without question, looked Jemmy over critically, and gave it as his opinion that the boy was not the right build for a bruiser.

'Of course not!' said Arabella. 'Think, Jemmy! What could you do, do you suppose?'

The urchin reflected, while the company awaited his pleasure. 'Sweep a crossing,' he pronounced at last. 'I could 'old the gen'lemen's 'orses, then.'

'Hold the gentlemen's horses?' repeated Arabella. Her eye brightened. 'Are you fond of horses, Jemmy?'

Jemmy nodded vigorously. Arabella looked round in triumph. 'Then I know the very thing!' she said. 'Particularly since it is you who are to take charge of him, Mr Beaumaris!'

Mr Beaumaris waited in deep foreboding for the blow to fall.

'He must learn to look after horses, and then, as soon as he is a little older, you may employ him as your Tiger!' said Arabella radiantly.

Mr Beaumaris, whose views on the folly of entrusting blood-cattle to the guardianship of small boys were as unequivocal as they were well-known, replied without a tremor: 'To be sure I may. The future now being provided for –'

'But you never drive with a Tiger up behind you!' exclaimed Lord Bridlington. 'You have said I know not how many times –'

'I do wish, Bridlington, that you would refrain from interrupting with these senseless comments,' said Mr Beaumaris.

'But that child is far too young to be a Tiger!' pointed out Lady Bridlington.

Arabella's face fell. 'Yes, he is,' she said regretfully. 'Yet it would be the very thing for him, if only we knew what to do with him in the meantime!'

'I think,' said Mr Beaumaris, 'that in the meantime I had better convey him to my own house, and place him in the charge of my housekeeper, pending further discussion between us, Miss Tallant.'

He was rewarded with a glowing look. 'I did not know you would be so kind!' said Arabella. 'It is a splendid notion, for the poor little fellow needs plenty of good food, and I am sure he must get it in your house! Listen, Jemmy, you are to go with this gentleman, who is to be your new master, and be a good boy, and do as he bids you!'

Jemmy, clutching a fold of her dress, was understood to say that he preferred to remain with her. She bent over him, patting his shoulder. 'No, you cannot stay with me, my dear, and I am sure you would not like it half so well if you could, for you must know that he has a great many horses, and will very likely let you see them. Did you come here in your curricle, sir?' Mr

Beaumaris bowed. 'Well, there, do you hear that, Jemmy?' said Arabella, in a heartening tone. 'You are to drive away in a carriage, behind a pair of beautiful gray horses!'

'I am driving my chestnuts today,' said Mr Beaumaris apologetically. 'I am so sorry, but I feel I should perhaps mention it!'

'You did very right,' said Arabella approvingly. 'One should never tell untruths to children! Chestnuts, Jemmy, glossy brown horses! How grand you will feel sitting up behind them!'

Apparently the urchin felt that there was much in what she said. He released her gown, and directed his sharp gaze upon his new owner. 'Proper good 'uns?' he asked suspiciously.

'Proper good 'uns,' corroborated Mr Beaumaris gravely.

Jemmy slid from the chair. 'You ain't slumming me? You won't go a-givin' of me back to ole Grimsby?'

'No, I won't do that. Come and take a look at my horses!'

Jemmy hesitated, glancing up at Arabella, who at once took his hand, and said: 'Yes, let us go and see them!'

When Jemmy beheld the equipage being led up and down the street, his eyes widened, and he drew a shuddering breath of ecstasy. 'That's a bang-up set-out, that is!' he said. 'Will I drive them 'orses, guv'nor?'

'You will not,' said Mr Beaumaris. 'You may sit up beside me, however.'

'Yessir!' said Jemmy, recognising the voice of authority.

'Up with you, then!' Mr Beaumaris said, lifting him into the curricle. He turned, and found that Arabella was holding her hand out to him. He took it in his, and held it for a moment.

'I wish I might find the words to thank you!' she said. 'You will let me know how he goes on.'

'You may rest easy on that head, Miss Tallant,' he said, bowing. He took the reins in his hand, and mounted into the carriage, and looked down maliciously at Lord Fleetwood, who had accompanied them out of the house, and was just taking his leave of Arabella. 'Come, Charles!'

Lord Fleetwood started, and said hurriedly: 'No, no, I'll walk! No need to worry about me, my dear fellow!'

'Come, Charles!' repeated Mr Beaumaris gently.

Lord Fleetwood, aware of Arabella's eyes upon him, sighed, and said: 'Oh, very well!' and climbed into the curricle, wedging Jemmy between himself and Mr Beaumaris.

Mr Beaumaris nodded to his gaping groom, and steadied the chestnuts as they sprang forward. 'Coward,' he remarked.

'It ain't that I'm a coward!' protested his lordship. 'But we shall have all the fools in London staring after us! I can't think what's come over you, Robert! You're never going to keep this brat in Mount Street! If it leaks out, and it's bound to, I suppose you know everyone will think it's a by-blow of yours?'

'The possibility had crossed my mind,' agreed Mr Beaumaris. 'I am sure I ought not to let it weigh with me: Miss Tallant certainly would not.'

'Well, damn it, I think that prosy fool, Bridlington, was right for once in his life! You've gone stark, staring mad!'

'Very true: I have known it this half-hour and more.'

Lord Fleetwood looked at him in some concern. 'You know, Robert, if you're not careful you'll find yourself walking to the altar before you're much older!' he said.

'No, she has the poorest opinion of me,' replied Mr Beaumaris. 'I perceive that my next step must be to pursue the individual known to us as "ole Grimsby".'

'What?' gasped Fleetwood. 'She never asked that of you!'

'No, but I feel she expects it of me.' He saw that the mention of the sweep's name had made Jemmy look up at him in quick alarm, and said reassuringly: 'No, I am not going to give you to him.'

'Robert, never in all the years I've known you have I seen you make such a cake of yourself!' said his friend, with brutal frankness. 'First you let the little Tallant bamboozle you into saddling yourself with this horrid brat, and now you talk of meddling with a chimney-sweep! *You!* Why, it's unheard of!'

'Yes, and, what is more, I have a shrewd suspicion that a benevolent career is going to prove extremely wearing,' said Mr Beaumaris thoughtfully.

'I see what it is,' said Fleetwood, after regarding his profile for a few moments. 'You're so piqued she don't favour you you'll go to any lengths to fix your interest with the girl!'

'I will,' said Mr Beaumaris cordially.

'Well, you'd better take care what you are about!' said his worldly-wise friend.

'I will,' said Mr Beaumaris again.

Lord Fleetwood occupied himself during the rest of the short drive in delivering a severe lecture on the perfidy of those who, without having any serious intentions, attempted to cut out their friends with the season's most notable catch, adding, for good measure, a lofty condemnation of hardened rakes who tried to deceive innocent country maidens.

Mr Beaumaris listened to him with the utmost amiability, only interrupting to applaud this last flight of eloquence. 'That's very good, Charles,' he said approvingly. 'Where did you pick it up?'

'Devil!' said his lordship, with feeling. 'Well, I wash my hands of you – and I hope she will lead you a pretty dance!'

'I have a strong premonition,' replied Mr Beaumaris, 'that your hope is likely to be realised.'

Lord Fleetwood gave it up, and as Mr Beaumaris saw no reason to take him into his confidence, what little time was left before Mount Street was reached was occupied in discussing the chances of the newest bruiser in his forthcoming fight with an acknowledged champion.

Mr Beaumaris, at this stage, would have been chary of confiding in anyone the precise nature of his intentions. He was by no means sure that he knew what they were himself, but that he had called in Park Street for precisely the reasons described by his friend, and, when confronted by the vision of Arabella fighting for the future of her unattractive protégé, had undergone an enlightenment so blinding as almost to deprive him of his senses, was certain. No consideration of the conduct to be expected of a delicately nurtured female had stopped her. She knew no discomfiture when two gentlemen of fashion had arrived to find her embroiled in the concerns of an urchin far beneath the notice of any aspirant to social heights. No, by God! thought Mr Beaumaris exultantly, she showed us what she thought of such frippery fellows as we are! We might have gone to the devil for all she cared. *I* might have made her a laughing-stock only by recounting the story – as I could! Lord, yes, as I *could*! Did she know it? Would she have cared? Not a farthing, the little Tallant! But I must stop Charles spreading this all over town.

Mr Beaumaris, hunting now in earnest, was by far too experienced a sportsman to pursue his quarry too closely. He let several days pass before making any attempt to approach Arabella. When next he encountered her it was at a ball given by the Charnwoods. He asked her to stand up with him for one of the country-dances, but when the moment for taking their places in the set came, led her to a sofa, saying: 'Shall you object to sitting down with me instead? One can never converse in comfort while dancing, and I must consult you about our urchin.'

'No, indeed!' she said warmly. 'I have been so anxious to know how he goes on!' She seated herself, holding her fan in her clasped hands, and raised her eyes to his face in an enquiring look. 'Is he well? Is he happy?'

'As far as I have been able to ascertain,' replied Mr Beaumaris carefully, 'he is not only fast recovering the enjoyment of excellent health, but is achieving no common degree of felicity by conduct likely to deprive me of the services of most of my existent staff.'

Arabella considered this. Mr Beaumaris watched appreciatively the wrinkling of her thoughtful brow. 'Is he very naughty?' she asked presently.

'According to the report of my housekeeper, Miss Tallant – but I daresay she is not to be at all believed! – he is the embodiment of too many vices for me to enumerate.'

She seemed to accept this with unimpaired calm, for she nodded understandingly.

'Pray do not think that I should dream of burdening you with anything so unimportant as the complaints of a mere housekeeper!' begged Mr Beaumaris. 'Nothing but the most urgent of exigencies could have prevailed upon me to open my lips to you upon this subject!' She looked startled, and enquiring: 'You see,' he said apologetically, 'it is Alphonse!'

'Alphonse?'

'My chef,' explained Mr Beaumaris. 'Of course, if you say so, ma'am, he shall go! But I must own that his departure would cause me grave concern. I do not mean to say that my life would be shattered, precisely, for no doubt there *are* other chefs who have his way with a soufflé, and who do not take such violent exception to the raids of small boys upon the larder!'

'But this is quite absurd, Mr Beaumaris!' said Arabella severely. 'You must have been indulging Jemmy beyond what is right! I daresay he is excessively ill-behaved: it is always so, unless their spirits are utterly broken, and we must be thankful that his are not!'

'Very true!' agreed Mr Beaumaris, entranced by this wisdom. 'I will at once present this view of the matter to Alphonse.'

Arabella shook her head. 'Oh, no! it would not be of the least avail, I daresay! Foreigners,' she said largely, 'have no notion how to manage children! What is to be done?'

'I cannot help feeling,' said Mr Beaumaris, 'that Jemmy would benefit by country air.'

This suggestion found favour. 'Nothing could be better for him!' agreed Arabella. 'Besides, there is no reason why he should tease you, I am sure! Only how may it be contrived?'

Much relieved at having so easily cleared this fence, Mr Beaumaris said: 'The notion did just cross my mind, ma'am, that if I were to take him into Hampshire, where I have estates, no doubt some respectable household might be found for him.'

'One of your tenants! The very thing!' exclaimed Arabella. 'Quite a simple cottage, mind, and a sensible woman to take care of him! Only I am afraid she would have to be paid a small sum to do it.'

Mr Beaumaris, who felt that no sum could be too large for the ridding of his house of one small imp who threatened to disrupt it, bore up nobly under the warning, and said that he had envisaged this possibility, and was prepared to meet it. It then occurred to Arabella that he might reasonably expect so great an heiress as herself to bear the charge of her protégé; and she embarked on a tangled explanation of why she could not at present do so. Mr Beaumaris interrupted her speech when it showed signs of becoming ravelled beyond hope. 'No, no, Miss Tallant!' he said. 'Do not deny me this opportunity to perform a charitable action, I beg of you!'

So Arabella very kindly refrained from doing so, and bestowed so grateful a smile upon him that he felt himself to have been amply rewarded.

'Are you quite in disgrace with Lady Bridlington?' he asked quizzically.

She laughed, but looked a little guilty. 'I *was*,' she owned. 'But since she has seen that the story has not got about, she has forgiven me. She was persuaded that everyone would be laughing at me. As though I would care for such a thing as that, when I had but done my duty!'

'Certainly not!'

'Do you know, I had begun to believe that everyone in town – all the grand people, I mean – were quite heartless, and selfish?' she confided. 'I am afraid I was not quite civil to you – indeed, Lady Bridlington assures me that I was shockingly rude! – but then, you see, I had no notion that you were not like all the rest. I beg your pardon!'

Mr Beaumaris had the grace to acknowledge a twinge of conscience. It led him to say: 'Miss Tallant, I did it in the hope of pleasing you.'

Then he wished that he had curbed his tongue, for her confiding air left her, and although she talked easily for a few more minutes he was fully aware that she had withdrawn from him again.

He was able to retrieve his position a few days later, and took care not to jeopardise it again. When he returned from a visit to his estates he called in Park Street to give Arabella comfortable tidings of Jemmy, whom he had foisted on to a retired servant of his own. She was a little concerned lest the town-bred waif should feel lost and unhappy in the country, but when he informed her that the last news he had of Jemmy, before leaving Hampshire, was that he had let a herd of bullocks out of the field where they were confined, pulled the feathers from the cock's tail, tried to ride an indignant pig round the yard, and eaten a whole batch of cakes newly baked by his kind hostess, she perceived that Jemmy was made of resilient stuff, and laughed, and said that he would soon settle down, and learn to be a good boy.

Mr Beaumaris agreed to it, and then played his trump card. He thought Miss Tallant would like to know that he had taken steps to ensure the well-being of Mr Grimsby's future apprentices.

Arabella was delighted. 'You have brought him to justice!'

'Well, not quite that,' confessed Mr Beaumaris. He saw the disappointed look in her eye, and added hastily: 'You know, I could not feel that to be appearing in a court of law was just what you would like. Then, too, when it is a question of apprentices one is apt to find oneself confronted with all manner of difficulties in the way of removing boys from their masters. It seemed best, therefore, to drop a word in Sir Nathaniel Conant's ear. He is the Chief Magistrate, and as I have some acquaintance with him the thing was easy. Mr Grimsby will take care how he disregards a warning from Bow Street, I assure you.'

Arabella was a little sorry to think that Mr Grimsby was not to be cast into gaol, but being a sensible girl she readily appreciated the force of Mr Beaumaris's arguments, and told him that she was very much obliged to him. She sat pondering deeply for some moments, while he watched her, wondering what now was in her head. 'It should be the business of people with interest and fortune to enquire into such things!' she said suddenly. 'No one seems to care a button in a great city like this! I have seen such dreadful sights since I came to London – such beggary, and misery, and such countless ragged children who seem to have no parents and no homes! Lady Bridlington does not care to have anything of that nature spoken about, but, oh, I would like so much to be able to help such children as poor Jemmy!'

'Why don't you?' he asked coolly.

Her eyes flew to his; he knew that he had been too blunt: she would not tell him the truth about herself. Nor did she. After a tiny pause, she said: 'Perhaps, one day, I shall.'

He wondered whether her godmother had warned her against him, and when she excused herself from dancing with him at the next Assembly was sure of it.

But the warning came from Lord Bridlington. Mr Beaumaris's marked attentions to Arabella, including, as they had, so extraordinary a gesture as the adoption of Jemmy, had aroused the wildest hopes in Lady Bridlington's shallow brain. If any of his previous amatory adventures had led him to perform a comparable deed, she at least had never heard of it. She began to indulge the fancy that his intentions were serious, and had almost written to give Mrs Tallant a hint of it when Lord Bridlington dashed her hopes.

'You would do well, ma'am, to put your young friend a little on her guard with Beaumaris,' he said weightily.

'My dear Frederick, and so I did, at the outset! But he has become so particular in his attentions, showing such a decided preference for her, and trying to fix his interest with her by every means in his power, that I really begin to think he has formed a lasting attachment! Only fancy if she were to form such a connection, Frederick! I declare, I should feel it as much as if she were my own child! For it will be all due to me, you know!'

'You would be very unwise to put such a notion into the girl's head, Mama,' he said, cutting short these rhapsodies. 'I can tell you this: Beaumaris's intimates don't by any means regard his pursuit of Miss Tallant in that light!'

'No?' she said, in a faltering tone.

'Far otherwise, ma'am! They are saying that it is all pique, because she does not appear to favour him above any other. I must say, I should not have expected her to have shown such good sense! You must know that men of his type, accustomed as he is to being courted and flattered, are put very much on their mettle by a rebuff from any female who has not been so foolish as to pick up the handkerchief they have carelessly tossed towards her. It puts me out of all patience to see anyone so spoiled and caressed! But be that as it may, you should know, Mama, that bets are being laid and taken at White's against Miss Tallant's holding out against this siege!'

'How odious men are!' exclaimed Lady Bridlington indignantly.

Odious they might be, but if they were laying bets of that nature at the clubs there was nothing for a conscientious chaperon to do but warn her charge once more against lending too credulous an ear to an accomplished flirt. Arabella assured her that she had no intention of doing so.

'No, my dear, very likely not,' replied her ladyship. 'But there is no denying that he is a very attractive man: I am conscious of it myself! Such an air! such easy address! But it is of no use to think of that! I am sadly afraid that it is a kind of sport with him to make females fall in love with him.'

'*I* shall not do so!' declared Arabella. 'I like him very well, but, as I told you before, I am not such a goose as to be taken-in by him!'

Lady Bridlington looked at her rather doubtfully. 'No, my love, I hope not indeed. To be sure, you have so many admirers that we need not consider Mr Beaumaris. I suppose – you will not be offended at my asking, I know! – I suppose no eligible gentleman has proposed to you?'

Quite a number of gentlemen, eligible and ineligible, had proposed to Arabella, but she shook her head. She might acquit some of her suitors of having designs on her supposed wealth, but two among them at least would never have offered for her hand, she was very sure, had they known her to be penniless; and the courtships of several notorious fortune-hunters made it impossible for her to believe that Lord Bridlington's well-meaning efforts had in any way scotched that dreadful rumour.

She felt her situation to be unhappy indeed. Easter was almost upon them, and there had been plenty of time for her, with the opportunities which had been granted to her, to have fulfilled her Mama's ambitions. She felt guilty, for it had cost Mama so much money, which she could ill-afford, to send her to London, so that the least a grateful daughter could have done would have been to have repaid her by accepting some respectable offer of marriage. She could not do it. She cared for none of those who had proposed to her, and although that, she supposed, ought not to weigh too heavily in the scales when balanced against the benefits that would accrue to the dear brothers and sisters, she was resolved to accept no offer from anyone ignorant of her true circumstances. Perhaps there was still to come into her life some suitor to whom it would be possible to confess the whole, but he had not yet appeared, and, pending his arrival, it was with relief that Arabella turned to Mr Beaumaris, who, whatever his intentions might be, certainly coveted no fortune.

Mr Beaumaris offered her every facility to turn to him, but he could scarcely congratulate himself on the outcome. The smallest attempt at gallantry had the effect of transforming her from the confiding child he found so engaging into the society damsel who was ready enough to fence lightly with him, but who showed him quite clearly that she wanted none of his practised love-making. And when Lady Bridlington had repeated much of her son's warning, not omitting to mention the fact that Mr Beaumaris's friends knew him to be merely trifling, Mr Beaumaris found Miss Tallant even more elusive. He was reduced to employing an ignoble stratagem, and, having been obliged to visit his estates on a matter of business, sought Arabella out upon his return, and told her that he wished to consult her again about Jemmy's future. In this manner, he lured her to drive out with him in his curricle. He drove her to Richmond Park, and she raised no objection to this, though he had not previously taken her farther afield than Chelsea. It was a fine, warm afternoon, with the sun so brightly shining that Arabella ventured to wear a very becoming straw hat, and to carry a small sunshade with a very long handle, which she had seen in the Pantheon Bazaar, and had not been able to resist purchasing. She said, as Mr Beaumaris handed her up into the curricle, that it was very kind of him to drive her into the country, since she liked it of all things, and was able to think herself, while in that great park, many miles from town.

'Do you know Richmond Park, then?' he asked.

'Oh, yes!' replied Arabella cheerfully. 'Lord Fleetwood drove me there last week; and then, you know, the Charnwoods got up a party, and we all went in three barouches. And tomorrow, if it is fine, Sir Geoffrey Morecambe is to take me to see the Florida Gardens.'

'I must count myself fortunate, then, to have found you on a day when you had no other engagement,' remarked Mr Beaumaris.

'Yes, I am out a great deal,' agreed Arabella. She unfurled the sunshade, and said: 'What was it that you wished to tell me about Jemmy, sir?'

'Ah, yes, Jemmy!' he said. 'Subject to your consent, Miss Tallant, I am making – in fact, I have made – a trifling change in his upbringing. I fear he will never come to any good under Mrs Buxton's roof, and still more do I fear that if he remained there he would shortly be the death of her. At least, so she informed me when I went down to Hampshire the day before yesterday.'

She gave him one of her warm looks. 'How very kind that was of you! Did you go all that way on that naughty boy's account?'

Mr Beaumaris was sorely tempted. He glanced down at his companion, met her innocently enquiring gaze, hesitated, and then said: 'Well, no, Miss Tallant! I had business there.'

She laughed. 'I thought it had been that.'

'In that case,' said Mr Beaumaris, 'I am glad I did not lie to you.'

'How can you be so absurd? As though I should wish you to put yourself to so much trouble! What has Jemmy been doing?'

'It would sadden you to know: Mrs Buxton is persuaded that he is possessed of a fiend. The language he employs, too, is not such as she is accustomed to. I regret to say that he has also alienated my keepers, who have quite failed to impress upon him the impropriety of disturbing my birds, or, I may add, of stealing pheasants' eggs. I cannot imagine what he can want with them.'

'Of course he should be punished for doing so! I daresay he has not enough employment. One must remember that he has been used to work and should be made to do so now. It is not at all good for anyone to be perfectly idle.'

'Very true, ma'am,' agreed Mr Beaumaris meekly.

Miss Tallant was not deceived. She looked sharply up at him, and bit her lip, saying after a moment: 'We are speaking of *Jemmy*!'

'I hoped we were,' confessed Mr Beaumaris.

'You are being nonsensical,' said Arabella, with some severity. 'What is to be done with him?'

'I found, upon enquiry, that the only person who is inclined to regard him favourably is my head groom, who says that his way with the horses is quite remarkable. It appears that he has been for ever slipping off to the stables, where, for a wonder, he comports himself unexceptionably. Wrexham was so much impressed by finding him – er – hobnobbing with a bay stallion generally thought to be extremely dangerous, that he came up to represent to me the propriety of handing the boy over to him to train. He is a childless man, and since he expressed his willingness to house Jemmy, I thought it better to fall in with his schemes. I hardly think Jemmy's language will shock him, and I am encouraged to hope, from what I know of Wrexham, that he will know how to keep the boy in order.'

Arabella approved so heartily of this arrangement, that he took the risk of saying in a melancholy tone: 'Yes, but if it succeeds, I shall be at a loss to think of a pretext for getting you to drive out with me.'

'Dear me, have I shown myself so reluctant?' said Arabella, raising her eyebrows. 'I wonder why you will talk so absurdly, Mr Beaumaris? You may depend upon it that I shall take care to be seen every now and then in your company, for I cannot be so sure of my credit as to run the risk of having it said that the Nonpareil has begun to find me a dead bore!'

'You stand in no such danger, Miss Tallant, believe me.' He drew in his horses for a sharp bend in the road, and did not speak again until the corner was negotiated. Then he said: 'I am afraid that you deem me a very worthless creature, ma'am. What am I to do to convince you that I can be perfectly sensible?'

'There is not the least need: I am sure that you can,' she replied amicably.

After that she became interested in the countryside, and from that passed to her forthcoming presentation. This event was to take place in the following week, and already her dress had been sent home from the skilful costumier who had altered an old gown of Lady Bridlington's to the present mode. Miss Tallant did not tell Mr Beaumaris that, naturally, but she did describe its magnificence to him, and found him both sympathetic and knowledgeable. He asked her what jewels she would wear with it, and she replied, in a very grand way: 'Oh, nothing but diamonds!' and was promptly ashamed of herself for having said it, although it was perfectly true.

'Your taste is always excellent, Miss Tallant. Nothing could be more displeasing to a fastidious eye than a profusion of jewelry. I must congratulate you on having exerted so beneficial an influence over your contemporaries.'

'I?' she gasped, quite startled, and half-suspecting him of quizzing her.

'Certainly. The total lack of ostentation which characterises your appearance is much admired, I assure you, and is beginning to be copied.'

'You cannot be serious!'

'But of course I am serious! Had you not noticed that Miss Accrington has left off that shocking collar of sapphires, and that Miss Kirkmichael no longer draws attention to the limitations of her figure by a profusion of chains, brooches, and necklaces which I should have supposed her to have chosen at random from an over-stocked jewel-box?'

There was something so irresistibly humorous to Arabella in the thought that her straitened circumstances had been at the root of a new mode that she began to giggle. But she would not tell Mr Beaumaris why she sat chuckling beside him. He did not press her for an explanation, but as they had by this time reached the Park, suggested that she might like to walk on the grass for a little way, while the groom took charge of the curricle. She assented readily, and while they strolled about, Mr Beaumaris told her something of that home of his in Hampshire. The bait failed. Miss Tallant confined her remarks on her own home to descriptions of the Yorkshire scene, and would not be lured into exchanging family reminiscences.

'I collect that your father is still alive, ma'am? You mentioned him, as I remember, on the day that you adopted Jemmy.'

'Did I? Yes, indeed he is alive and I wished for him very much that day, for he is the best man in the world, and he would have known just what was right to be done!'

'I shall hope to have the pleasure of making his acquaintance one day. Does he come to London at all?'

'No, never,' replied Arabella firmly. She could not imagine that Mr Beaumaris and Papa would have the least pleasure in one another's acquaintance, thought that the conversation was getting on to dangerous ground, and reverted to her society manner.

This was maintained during most of the drive back to London, but when the open country was left behind, and the curricle was passing once more between rows of houses, it deserted her abruptly. In the middle of a narrow street, the grays took high-bred exception to a wagon with a tattered and flapping canvas roof, which was drawn up to one side of the road. There was barely room for the curricle to slip past this obstruction, and Mr Beaumaris, his attention all on his horses, failed to take notice of a group of youths bending over some object on the flag-way, or to heed the anguished yelp which made Arabella, casting aside the light rug which covered her legs, cry out: 'Oh, stop!' and shut her sunshade with a snap.

The grays were mincing past the wagon; Mr Beaumaris did indeed pull them up, but Arabella did not wait for the curricle to come to a standstill, but sprang hazardously down from it. Mr Beaumaris, holding his sidling, snorting pair in an iron hand, took one quick glance over his shoulder, saw that Arabella was dispersing the group on the flag-way by the vigorous use of her sunshade, and snapped: 'Go to their heads, fool!'

His groom, still perched up behind, and apparently dumb-founded by Miss Tallant's strange conduct, came to himself with a start, jumped down, and ran round to hold the grays. Mr Beaumaris sprang down, and descended swiftly upon the battleground. Having scientifically knocked two louts' heads together, picked up the third lout by his collar and the seat of his frieze breeches, and thrown him into the road, he was able to see what had aroused Miss Tallant's wrath. Crouched, shivering and whimpering, on the flag-way, was a small, sandy-coated mongrel, with a curly tail, and one ear disreputably flying.

'Those wicked, brutal, *fiends*!' panted Miss Tallant, cheeks and eyes in a glow. 'They were *torturing* the poor little thing!'

'Take care! He may snap at you!' Mr Beaumaris said quickly, seeing her about to kneel down beside the dog. 'Shall I thrash them all soundly?'

At these words, the two smaller boys departed precipitately, the two whose heads were still ringing drew circumspectly out of range of Mr Beaumaris's long-lashed whip, and the bruised youth in the road whined that they weren't doing any harm, and that all his ribs were busted.

'How badly have they hurt him?' Miss Tallant asked anxiously. 'He cries when I touch him!'

Mr Beaumaris pulled off his gloves, and handed them to her, together with his whip, saying: 'Hold those for me, and I'll see.'

She obediently took them, and watched anxiously while he went over the mongrel. She saw with approval that he handled the little creature firmly and gently, in a way that showed he knew what he was about. The dog whined, and uttered little cries, and cowered, but he did not offer to snap. Indeed, he feebly wagged his disgraceful tail, and once licked Mr Beaumaris's hand.

'He is badly bruised, and has one or two nasty sores, but there are no bones broken,' Mr Beaumaris said, straightening himself. He turned to where the two remaining youths were standing, poised on the edge of flight, and said sternly: 'Whose dog is this?'

'It don't belong to no one,' he was sullenly informed. 'It goes all over, stealing things off of the rubbish-heaps: yes, *and* out of the butcher's shop!'

'I seen 'im in Chelsea onct with 'alf a loaf of bread,' corroborated the other youth.

The accused crawled to Mr Beaumaris's elegantly shod feet, and pawed one gleaming hessian appealingly.

'Oh, see how intelligent he is!' cried Arabella, stooping to fondle the animal. 'He knows he has you to thank for his rescue!'

'If he knows that, I think little of his intelligence, Miss Tallant,' said Mr Beaumaris, glancing down at the dog. 'He certainly owes his life to you!'

'Oh, no! I could never have managed without your help! Will you be so obliging as to hand him up to me, if you please?' said Arabella, prepared to climb into the curricle again.

Mr Beaumaris looked from her to the unkempt and filthy mongrel at his feet, and said: 'Are you quite sure that you want to take him with you, ma'am?'

'Why, of course! You do not suppose that I would leave him here, for those wretches to torment as soon as we were out of sight! Besides, you heard what they said! He has no master – no one to feed him, or to take care of him! Please give him to me!'

Mr Beaumaris's lips twitched, but he said with perfect gravity: 'Just as you wish, Miss Tallant!' and picked up the dog by the scruff of its neck. He saw Miss Tallant's arms held out to receive her new protégé, and hesitated. 'He is very dirty, you know!'

'Oh, what does that signify? I have soiled my dress already, with kneeling on the flag-way!' said Arabella impatiently.

So Mr Beaumaris deposited the dog on her lap, received his whip and gloves from her again, and stood watching with a faint smile while she made the dog comfortable, and stroked its ears, and murmured soothingly to it. She looked up. 'What do we wait for, sir?' she asked, surprised.

'Nothing at all, Miss Tallant!' he said, and got into the curricle.

Miss Tallant, continuing to fondle the dog, spoke her mind with some force on the subject of persons who were cruel to animals, and thanked Mr Beaumaris earnestly for his kindness in knocking the horrid boys' heads together, a violent proceeding which seemed to have met with her unqualified approval. She then occupied herself with talking to the dog, and informing him of the splendid dinner he should presently be given, and the warm bath which he would (she said) so much enjoy. But after a time she became a little pensive, and relapsed into meditative silence.

'What is it, Miss Tallant?' asked Mr Beaumaris, when she showed no sign of breaking the silence.

'Do you know,' she said slowly, 'I have just thought – Mr Beaumaris, something tells me that Lady Bridlington may not like this dear little dog!'

Mr Beaumaris waited in patient resignation for his certain fate to descend upon him.

Arabella turned impulsively towards him. 'Mr Beaumaris, do you think – *would* you – ?'

He looked down into her anxious, pleading eyes, a most rueful twinkle in his own. 'Yes, Miss Tallant,' he said. 'I would.'

Her face broke into smiles. '*Thank* you!' she said. 'I knew I might depend upon you!' She turned the mongrel's head gently towards Mr Beaumaris. 'There, sir! That is your new master, who will be very kind to you! Only see how intelligently he looks, Mr Beaumaris! I am sure he understands. I daresay he will grow to be quite devoted to you!'

Mr Beaumaris looked at the animal, and repressed a shudder. 'Do you think so indeed?' he said.

'Oh, yes! He is not, perhaps, a very *beautiful* little dog, but mongrels are often the cleverest of all dogs.' She smoothed the creature's rough head, and added innocently: 'He will be company for you, you know. I wonder you do not have a dog already.'

'I do – in the country,' he replied.

'Oh, sporting dogs! They are not at all the same.'

Mr Beaumaris, after another look at his prospective companion, found himself able to agree with this remark with heartfelt sincerity.

'When he has been groomed, and has put some flesh on his bones,' pursued Arabella, serene in the conviction that her sentiments were being shared, 'he will look very different. I am quite anxious to see him in a week or two!'

Mr Beaumaris drew up his horses outside Lady Bridlington's house. Arabella gave the dog a last pat, and set him on the seat beside his new owner, bidding him stay there. He seemed a little undecided at first, but being too bruised and battered to leap down into the road, he did stay, whining loudly. However, when Mr Beaumaris, having handed Arabella up to the door, and seen her admitted into the house, returned to his curricle, the dog stopped whining, and welcomed him with every sign of relief and affection.

'Your instinct is at fault,' said Mr Beaumaris. 'Left to myself, I should abandon you to your fate. That, or tie a brick round your neck, and drown you.'

His canine admirer wagged a doubtful tail, and cocked an ear. 'You are a disgraceful object!' Mr Beaumaris told him. 'And what does she expect me to do with you?' A tentative paw was laid on his knee. 'Possibly, but let me tell you that I know your sort! You are a toadeater, and I abominate toadeaters. I suppose, if I sent you into the country, my own dogs would kill you on sight.'

The severity in his tone made the dog cower a little, still looking up at him with the expression of a dog anxious to understand.

'Have no fear!' Mr Beaumaris assured him, laying a fleeting hand on his head. 'She clearly wishes me to keep you in town.

Did it occur to her, I wonder, that your manners, I have no doubt at all, leave much to be desired? Do your wanderings include the slightest experience of the conduct expected of those admitted into a gentleman's house? Of course they do not!' A choking sound from his groom made him say over his shoulder: 'I hope you like dogs, Clayton, for you are going to wash this specimen.'

'Yes, sir,' said his grinning attendant.

'Be very kind to him!' commanded Mr Beaumaris. 'Who knows? He may take a liking to you.'

But at ten o'clock that evening, Mr Beaumaris's butler, bearing a tray of suitable refreshments to the library, admitted into the room a washed, brushed, and fed mongrel, who came in with something as near a prance as could be expected of one in his emaciated condition. At sight of Mr Beaumaris, seeking solace from his favourite poet in a deep winged chair by the fire, he uttered a shrill bark of delight, and reared himself up on his hind legs, his paws on Mr Beaumaris's knees, his tail furiously wagging, and a look of beaming adoration in his eyes.

Mr Beaumaris lowered his Horace. 'Now, what the devil – ?' he demanded.

'Clayton brought the little dog up, sir,' said Brough. 'He said as you would wish to see how he looked. It seems, sir, that the dog didn't take to Clayton, as you might say. Very restless, Clayton informs me, and whining all the evening.' He watched the dog thrust his muzzle under Mr Beaumaris's hand, and said: 'It's strange the way animals always go to you, sir. Quite happy now, isn't he?'

'Deplorable,' said Mr Beaumaris. 'Down, Ulysses! Learn that my pantaloons were not made to be pawed by such as you!'

'He'll learn quick enough, sir,' remarked Brough, setting a glass and a decanter down on the table at his master's elbow. 'You can see he's as sharp as he can stare. Would there be anything more, sir?'

'No, only give this animal back to Clayton, and tell him I am perfectly satisfied with his appearance.'

'Clayton's gone off, sir. I don't think he can have understood that you wished him to take charge of the little dog,' said Brough.

'I don't think he can have wanted to understand it,' said Mr Beaumaris grimly.

'As to that, sir, I'm sure I couldn't say. I doubt whether the dog will settle down with Clayton, him not having a way with dogs like he has with horses. I'm afraid he'll fret, sir.'

'Oh, my God!' groaned Mr Beaumaris. 'Then take him down to the kitchen!'

'Well, sir, of course – if you say so!' replied Brough doubtfully. 'Only there's Alphonse.' He met his master's eye, apparently had no difficulty in reading the question in it, and said: 'Yes, sir. Very French he has been on the subject. Quite shocking, I'm sure, but one has to remember that foreigners are queer, and don't like animals.'

'Very well,' said Mr Beaumaris, with a resigned sigh. 'Leave him, then!'

'Yes, sir,' said Brough, and departed.

Ulysses, who had been thoroughly, if a little timidly, inspecting the room during this exchange, now advanced to the hearth-rug again, and paused there, suspiciously regarding the fire. He seemed to come to the conclusion that it was not actively hostile, for after a moment he curled himself up before it, heaved a sigh, laid his chin on Mr Beaumaris's crossed ankles, and disposed himself for sleep.

'I suppose you imagine you are being a companion to me,' said Mr Beaumaris.

Ulysses flattened his ears, and gently stirred his tail.

'You know,' said Mr Beaumaris, 'a prudent man would draw back at this stage.'

Ulysses raised his head to yawn, and then snuggled it back on Mr Beaumaris's ankles, and closed his eyes.

'You may be right,' admitted Mr Beaumaris. 'But I wonder what next she will saddle me with?'

Ten

When Arabella had parted from Mr Beaumaris at the door of Lady Bridlington's house, the butler who had admitted her informed her that two gentlemen had called to see her, and were even now awaiting her in the smaller saloon. This seemed to her a trifle unusual, and she looked surprised. The butler explained the matter by saying that one of the young gentlemen was particularly anxious to see her, since he came from Yorkshire, and would not be unknown to her. A horrid fear gripped Arabella that she was now to be exposed to the whole of London, and it was with an almost shaking hand that she picked up the visiting-card from the salver the butler was holding out to her. But the name elegantly inscribed upon it was unknown to her: she could not recall ever having heard of, much less met, a Mr Felix Scunthorpe.

'*Two* gentlemen?' she said.

'The other young gentleman, miss, did not disclose his name,' replied the butler.

'Well, I suppose I must see them,' Arabella decided. 'Pray tell them that I shall be downstairs directly! Or is her ladyship in?'

'Her ladyship has not yet returned, miss.'

Arabella hardly knew whether to be glad or sorry. She went up to her room to change her soiled gown, and came down again some few minutes later hoping that she had schooled her face not to betray her inward trepidation. She entered the saloon in a very stately way, and looked rather challengingly across it. There were, as the butler had warned her, two young gentlemen standing by the window. One was a slightly vacuous looking youth, dressed with extreme nicety, and holding, besides his tall hat, an ebony cane, and an elegant pair of gloves; the other was a tall, loose-limbed boy, with curly dark hair, and an aquiline cast of countenance. At sight of him, Arabella uttered a shriek, and ran across the room to cast herself upon his chest. '*Bertram!*'

'Here, I say, Bella!' expostulated Bertram, recoiling. 'Mind what you are about, for the lord's sake! My neckcloth!'

'Oh, I beg your pardon, but I am so *glad* to see you! But how is this? Bertram, Papa is not in town?'

'Good God, no!'

'Thank heaven!' Arabella breathed, pressing her hands to her cheeks.

Her brother found nothing to wonder at in this exclamation. He looked her over critically, and said: 'Just as well he ain't, for he'd be bound to give you one of his scolds for dressing-up as fine as fivepence! I must say, Bella, you're turned out in prime style! Slap up to the mark, ain't she, Felix?'

Mr Scunthorpe, much discomposed at being called upon to give an opinion, opened and shut his mouth once or twice, bowed, and looked despairing.

'He thinks you're complete to a shade,' explained Bertram, interpreting these signs. 'He ain't much of a dab with the petticoats, but he's a great gun, I can tell you! Up to every rig and row in town!'

Arabella looked at Mr Scunthorpe with interest. He presented the appearance of a very mild young man; and although his fancy waistcoat bespoke the man of fashion, he seemed to her to lack address. She bowed politely, which made him blush very much, and fall into a fit of stuttering. Bertram, feeling that some further introduction might be considered desirable by his sister, said: 'You don't know him: he was at Harrow with me. He's older than I am, but he's got no brains, y'know: never could learn anything! I ran into him in the High.'

'The High?' repeated Arabella.

'Oxford, you know!' said Bertram loftily. 'Dash it, Bella, you can't have forgot I've been up to take my Smalls!'

'No, indeed!' she said. 'Sophy wrote that you were gone there, and that poor James was unable to accompany you, because of the jaundice. I was so sorry! But how did you go on, Bertram? Do you think you have passed?'

'Lord, I don't know! There was one devilish paper – but never mind that now! The thing is that I met old Felix here, the very man I wanted!'

'Oh, yes?' Arabella said, adding with a civil smile: 'Were you up for Smalls too, sir?'

Mr Scunthorpe appeared to shrink from such a suggestion, shaking his head, and making a sound in his throat which Arabella took to be a negative.

'Of course he wasn't!' said Bertram. 'Don't I keep telling you he can't learn anything? He was visiting some friends in Oxford! He found it pretty dull work, too, didn't you, Felix? They would take him to blue-parties, all professors, and Bagwigs, and the poor fellow couldn't follow the stuff they talked. Shabby thing to do to him, for he was bound to make a cake of himself in that sort of company! However, that's not what I want to talk about. The thing is, Bella, that Felix is going to show me all the sights, because he's at home to a peg in London – been on the town ever since they threw him out of Harrow.'

'And Papa gave his consent?' exclaimed Arabella.

'As a matter of fact,' said Bertram airily, 'he don't know I'm here.'

'Doesn't know you're here?' cried Arabella.

Mr Scunthorpe cleared his throat. 'Given him the bag,' he explained. He added: 'Only thing to do.'

Arabella turned his eyes wonderingly towards her brother. He looked a little guilty, but said: 'No, you can't say I've given him the bag!'

Mr Scunthorpe corrected himself. 'Hoaxed him.'

Bertram seemed to be about to take exception to this too, but after beginning to refute it he broke off, and said: 'Well, in a way I suppose I did.'

'Bertram, you must be mad!' cried Arabella, pale with dismay. 'When Papa knows you are in town, and without leave –'

'The thing is he won't know it,' interrupted Bertram. 'I wrote a letter to Mama, telling her I had met my friend Felix, and he had invited me to stay with him. So they won't be in a fret when I don't go back immediately, and they won't know where I am, because I didn't give my direction. And that brings me to what I particularly want to warn you about, Bella! I'm going by the name of Anstey while I'm in town, and while I don't mind if you tell this godmother of yours that I'm a friend of yours, you are not to say I'm your brother! She'd be bound to write and tell my mother, and then the fat would be in the fire!'

'But, Bertram, how can you *dare*?' asked Arabella, in an awed voice. 'Papa will be so angry!'

'Yes, I know. I shall get a rare trimming, but I shall have had a bang-up time first, and I can stand a lick or two after,' said Bertram cheerfully. 'I made up my mind I'd do it, before you came to town. Do you remember my telling you that you might get a surprise? I'll swear you never thought *this* would be it!'

'No, indeed I did not!' Arabella said, sinking into a chair. 'Oh, Bertram, I am quite in a quake! I cannot understand any of it! How can you afford to be staying in London? Are you Mr Scunthorpe's guest?'

'No, no, poor old Felix ain't standing the huff! I won a ticket in a lottery! Only think of it, Bella! A hundred pounds!'

'A lottery! Good God, what would Papa say if he knew *that*?'

'Oh, he would kick up no end of a bobbery, of course, but I shan't tell him. And, you know, once I had won it the only thing to be done was to spend it, because you must see I had to get rid of it before Papa found I had it!' He saw that his sister was looking horrified, and said indignantly: 'I must say, I don't see why you would grudge it to me! I daresay you are having a capital time yourself!'

'No, no, how could you think I would grudge you *anything*,

160

Bertram? But to have you in town, and to be obliged to pretend I am not your sister, and to deceive Papa and Mama –' She stopped, remembering her own situation. 'Oh, Bertram, how *wicked* we are!'

Mr Scunthorpe looked very much alarmed at this, but Bertram said: 'Fudge! It's not telling lies precisely just not to mention that you have seen me when you write to Mama!'

'You do not know! It is worse than that!' whispered Arabella. 'Bertram, I am in such a scrape!'

He stared at her. 'You are? How is this?' He saw her glance towards his friend, and said: 'You needn't mind Felix: he's no gabster!'

Arabella was easily able to believe this, but she not unnaturally felt reluctant to disclose her story to one who was a stranger to her, even though she had already realised that if he was not to betray her unwittingly he must be taken some way at least into her confidence. Mr Scunthorpe tweaked his friend's sleeve. 'Must help your sister out of the scrape, dear boy. Happy to be of service!'

'I am very much obliged to you, sir, but no one can help me out of it!' said Arabella tragically. 'If only you will be so kind as not to betray me!'

'Of course he won't betray you!' declared Bertram. 'What in thunder have you been about, Bella?'

'Bertram, everyone believes me to be a great heiress!' disclosed Arabella, in a stricken tone.

He stared at her for a moment, and then burst out laughing. 'You goosecap! I'll wager they don't! Why, Lady Bridlington knows you are not! You don't mean that she put such a tale about?'

She shook her head. '*I* said it!' she confessed.

'*You* said it? What the devil made you do such a thing? However, I don't suppose anyone believed you!'

'They do believe it. Lord Bridlington says that every gazetted fortune-hunter in town is dangling after me – and, oh, Bertram, it is true! I have refused *five* offers already!'

The idea that there could be found five gentlemen ready to marry his sister struck Bertram as being exquisitely humorous, and he went off into another burst of laughter. Arabella was obliged to confess the whole, since he seemed so incredulous. Her narrative was rather disjointed, since he interpolated so many questions; and at one point a considerable digression was caused by Mr Scunthorpe, who, having regarded her fixedly for some moments, suddenly became loquacious, and said: 'Beg pardon, ma'am, but did you say Mr Beaumaris?'

'Yes. He and Lord Fleetwood.'

'The Nonpareil?'

'Yes.'

Mr Scunthorpe drew a breath, and turned to address his friend. 'You hear that, Bertram?'

'Well, of course I heard it!'

'Didn't think you could have. You see this coat of mine?'

Both Tallants stared at his coat in some bewilderment.

'Got my man to copy the lapels of one Weston made for the Nonpareil,' said Mr Scunthorpe, with simple pride.

'Good God, what has that to say to anything?' demanded Bertram.

'Thought you might be interested,' explained Mr Scunthorpe apologetically.

'Never mind him!' Bertram told his sister. 'If it wasn't just like you, Bella, to fly into a miff, and go off into one of your crazy starts! Mind, I don't say I blame you! Did he spread the story over London?'

'I think it was Lord Fleetwood who did that. Mr Beaumaris told me once that he had not discussed the matter with anyone but Lord Fleetwood. Sometimes I have wondered whether – whether he had guessed the truth, but I cannot believe that he has, for he would despise me dreadfully, I am sure, if he knew how odiously I behaved, and certainly not stand up with me at all the balls – for he very seldom dances! – or take me out driving in his curricle.'

Mr Scunthorpe looked very much impressed. 'He does that?'

'Oh, yes!'

Mr Scunthorpe nodded portentously at Bertram. 'You know what, dear boy? All the crack, your sister! Not a doubt of it. Knows all the best people. Drives out with the Nonpareil. Good thing she said she was an heiress.'

'Oh, no, no, I wish I had never done so, for it has made everything so uncomfortable!'

'Now, Bella, that's gammon! I know you! Don't you try to tell me you don't like being all the go, because I wouldn't believe you if you did!' said Bertram, with brotherly candour.

Arabella thought it over. Then she gave a reluctant smile. 'Well, yes, perhaps I do like it, but when I remember the cause of it I do indeed wish I had never said such a thing! Only consider what a fix I am in! If the truth were known now I should be utterly discredited! No one would even *bow* to me, I daresay, and I have the greatest dread that Lady Bridlington would send me home in disgrace! And then Papa would know, and – Bertram, I had almost rather throw myself into the river than have him know such a thing of me!'

'Lord, yes!' he agreed, with a shudder. 'But it won't come to that! If anyone asks *me* any prying questions, I shall say you are well known to me, and so will Felix!'

'Yes, but that is not all!' Arabella pointed out. 'I can never, never accept any offer made to me, and what Mama will think of such selfishness I dare not consider! For she so much hoped that I should form an eligible connection, and Lady Bridlington is bound to tell her that – that quite a number of *very* eligible gentlemen have paid me the most marked attentions!'

Bertram knit his brows over this. 'Unless – No, you're right, Bella; devilish awkward fix! You would have to tell the truth, if you accepted an offer, and ten to one he'd cry off. What a tiresome girl you are, to be sure! Dashed if I see what's to be done! Do you, Felix?'

'Very difficult situation,' responded Mr Scunthorpe, shaking his head. 'Only one thing to be done.'

'What's that?'

Mr Scunthorpe gave a diffident cough. 'Just a little thing that occurred to me. Daresay you won't care about it: can't say I care about it myself, but can't hang back when a lady's in a fix.'

'But what *is* it?'

'Mind, only a notion I had!' Mr Scunthorpe warned him. 'You don't like it: you say so! *I* don't like it, but ought to offer.' He perceived that the Tallants were quite mystified, blushed darkly, and uttered in a strangled voice: 'Marriage!'

Arabella stared at him for a moment, and then went into a peal of mirth. Bertram said scornfully: 'Of all the cork-brained notions – ! *You* don't want to marry Bella!'

'No,' conceded Mr Scunthorpe. 'Promised I would help her out of the scrape, though!'

'What's more,' Bertram said severely, 'those trustees of yours would never let you! You're not of age.'

'Talk them over,' said Mr Scunthorpe hopefully.

However, Arabella, thanking him for his kind offer, said that she did not think they would suit. He seemed grateful, and relapsed into the silence which appeared to be natural to him.

'I daresay I shall hit upon something,' said Bertram. 'I'll think about it, at all events. Should I stay to do the pretty to this godmother of yours, do you think?'

Arabella urged him strongly to do so. She was inclined to grieve over his necessary incognito, but he told her frankly that it would not at all suit him to be for ever gallanting her to the *ton* parties. 'Very dull work!' he said. 'I know you are gone civility-mad since you came to town, but it's not in my line.' He then enumerated the sights he meant to see in London, and since these seemed to consist mostly of such innocuous entertainments as Astley's Amphitheatre, the Royal Menagerie at the Tower, Madame Tussaud's Waxworks, Napoleon's carriage, on view at Bullock's Museum, a look-in at Tattersall's, the departure of the Brighton coaches from the White Horse Cellar, and the forthcoming Military Review in Hyde Park, his anxious sister's worst qualms were allayed. At first sight he had seemed to her to have grown a great deal older, for he was wearing a sophisticated waistcoat, and had brushed his hair in a new style; but when he told her about the peep-show which had diverted him so much in Coventry Street, and expressed a purely youthful desire to witness that grand spectacle, *The Burning Of Moscow* (supported by Tight-rope Walking, and an Equestrian Display), she could feel that he was still boy enough not to hanker after the more sophisticated and by far more dangerous amusements to be found in London. But, then, as he confidentially informed Mr Scunthorpe, when they presently left Park Street together, females took such foolish notions into their heads that it would have been ridiculous to have disclosed to her that he had an equally ardent desire to see a bout of fisticuffs at the Fives-court, to blow a cloud with all the Corinthians at the Daffy Club, to penetrate the mysteries of the Royal Saloon, and the Peerless Pool, and certainly to put in an appearance at the Opera – not, he hastened to assure his friend, because he wanted to listen to music, but because he was credibly informed that to stroll in the Fops' Alley was famous sport, and all the go. Since he had decided, very prudently, to put up at one of the City inns, where, if he chose, he could be sure of a tolerable dinner at the Ordinary, which was very moderately priced, he entertained reasonable hopes of being able to afford all these diversions. But first, he perceived, it was necessary to buy a much higher-crowned and more curly-brimmed beaver to set on his head; a pair of Hessians with tassels; a fob, and perhaps a seal; and certainly a pair of natty yellow gloves. Without these adjuncts to a gentleman's costume he would look like a Johnny Raw. Mr Scunthorpe agreed, and ventured to point out that a driving-coat with only two shoulder-capes was thought, in well-dressed circles, to be a paltry affair. He said he would take Bertram along to his own man, a devilish clever tailor, even though he had not acquired the fame of a Weston or a Stultz. However, as the great advantage of patronising this rising man lay in the assurance that he would be willing to rig out any friend of Mr Scunthorpe's on tick, Bertram raised no objection to jumping into a hackney at once, and telling the jarvey to drive with all speed to Clifford

Street. Mr Scunthorpe vouched for it that Swindon's art would give his friend quite a new touch, and as this seemed extremely desirable to Bertram, he thought he could hardly lay out a substantial sum of money to better advantage. Mr Scunthorpe then imparted to him a few useful hints, particularly warning him against such extravagances of style as must give rise to the suspicion that he belonged to the extreme dandy-set frowned upon by the real Pinks of the *Ton*. Beyond question, the finest model for any aspiring gentleman to copy was the Nonpareil, that Go amongst the Goers. This put Bertram in mind of something which had been slightly troubling his mind, and he said: 'I say, Felix, do you think my sister should be driving about the town with him? I don't mind telling you I don't like it above half!'

Here Mr Scunthorpe was able at once to allay his qualms: for a lady to drive in a curricle or a phaeton, with a groom riding behind, was unexceptionable. 'Mind, it would not do for a female to go in a tilbury!' he said.

His brotherly concern relieved, Bertram abandoned the question, merely remarking that he would give a monkey to see his father's face if he knew how rackety Bella had become.

Arrived in Clifford Street, they obtained instant audience of Mr Swindon, who was so obliging as to bring out his pattern-card immediately, and to advise his new client on the respective merits of Superfine and Bath Suiting. He thought six capes would be sufficient for a light drab driving-coat, an opinion in which Mr Scunthorpe gravely concurred, explaining to Bertram that it would never do for him to ape the Goldfinches, with their row upon row of capes. Unless one was an acknowledged Nonesuch, capable of driving to an inch, or one of the Melton men, it was wiser, he said, to aim at neatness and propriety rather than the very height of fashion. He then bent his mind to the selection of a cloth for a coat, and although Bertram had not intended to order a new coat, he was persuaded to do so, as much by the assertion of Mr Swindon that a single-breasted garment of corbeau-coloured cloth, with wide lapels, and silver buttons, would set his person off to advantage, as by the whispered assurance of his friend that the snyder always gave his clients long credit. Indeed, Mr Scunthorpe was rarely troubled with his tailor's account, since that astute man of business was well aware that being a fatherless minor Mr Scunthorpe's considerable fortune was held in trust by tight-fisted guardians, who doled him out a beggarly allowance. Nothing so ungenteel as cost or payment was mentioned during the session in Clifford Street, so that Bertram left the premises torn between relief and a fear that he might have pledged his credit for a larger sum than he could afford to pay. But the novelty and excitement of a first visit to the Metropolis soon put such untimely thoughts to rout, while a lucky bet at the Fives-court clearly showed the novice the easiest way of raising the wind.

A close inspection of such sprigs of fashion as were to be seen at the Fives-court made Bertram very glad to think he had bespoken a new coat, and he confided to Mr Scunthorpe that he would not visit the haunts of fashion until his clothes had been sent home. Mr Scunthorpe thought this a wise decision, and, as it was of course absurd to suppose that Bertram should kick his heels at the City inn which enjoyed his patronage, he volunteered to show him how an evening full of fun and gig could be spent in less exalted circles. This entertainment, beginning as it did in the Westminster Pit, where it seemed to the staring Bertram that representatives of every class of society, from the Corinthian to the dustman, had assembled to watch a contest between two dogs; and proceeding by way of the shops of Tothill Fields, where adventurous bucks tossed off noggins of Blue Ruin, or bumpers of heavy wet, in company with bruisers, prigs, coal-heavers, Nuns, Abbesses, and apple-women, to a coffee-shop, ended in the watch-house, Mr Scunthorpe having become bellicose under the influence of his potations. Bertram, quite unused to such quantities of liquor as he had imbibed, was too much fuddled to have any very clear notion of what circumstance it was that had excited his friend's wrath, though he had a vague idea that it was in some way connected with the advances being made by a gentleman in Petersham trousers towards a lady who had terrified him earlier in the proceedings by laying a palpable lure for him. But when a mill was in progress it was not his part to enquire into the cause of it, but to enter into the fray in support of his cicerone. Since he was by no means unlearned in the noble art of self-defence, he was able to render yeoman service to Mr Scunthorpe, no proficient, and was in a fair way to milling his way out of the shop when the watch, in the shape of several Charleys, all springing their rattles, burst in upon them and, after a spirited set-to, overpowered the two peacebreakers, and hailed them off to the watch-house. Here, after considerable parley, conducted for the defence by the experienced Mr Scunthorpe, they were admitted to bail, and warned to present themselves next day in Bow Street, not a moment later than twelve o'clock. The night-constable then packed them both into a hackney, and they drove to Mr Scunthorpe's lodging in Clarges Street, where Bertram passed what little was left of the night on the sofa in his friend's sitting-room. He awoke later with a splitting headache, no very clear recollection of the late happenings, but a lively dread of the possible consequences of what he feared had been a very bosky evening. However, when Mr Scunthorpe's man had revived his master, and he emerged from his bedchamber, he was soon able to allay any such misgivings. 'Nothing to be in a fret for, dear boy!' he said. 'Been piloted to the lighthouse scores of times! Watchman will produce broken lantern in evidence – they always do it! – you give false name, pay fine, and all's right!'

So, indeed, it proved, but the experience a little shocked the Vicar's son. This, coupled with the extremely unpleasant after-effects of drinking innumerable flashes of lightning, made him determine to be more circumspect in future. He spent several days in pursuing such harmless amusements as witnessing a badger drawn in a menagerie in Holborn, losing his heart to Miss O'Neill from a safe position in the pit, and being introduced by Mr Scunthorpe into Gentleman Jackson's exclusive Boxing School in Bond Street. Here he was much impressed by the manners and dignity of the proprietor (whose decision in all matters of sport, Mr Scunthorpe informed him, was accepted as final by patrician and plebeian alike), and was gratified by a glimpse of such notable amateurs as Mr Beaumaris, Lord Fleetwood, young Mr Terrington, and Lord Withernsea. He had a little practise with the single-stick with one of Jackson's assistants, felt himself honoured by receiving a smiling word of encouragement from the great Jackson himself, and envied the assurance of the Goes who strolled in, exchanged jests with Jackson, who treated them with the same degree of civility as he showed to his less exalted pupils, and actually enjoyed bouts with the ex-champion himself. He was quick to see that no consideration of rank or consequence was enough to induce Jackson to allow a client to plant a hit upon his person, unless his prowess deserved such a reward; and from having entered the saloon with a feeling of superiority he swiftly reached the realisation that in the Corinthian world excellence counted for more than lineage. He heard Jackson say chidingly to the great Nonpareil himself (who stripped to remarkable advantage, he noticed) that he was out of training; and from that moment his highest ambition was to put on the gloves with this peerless master of the art.

At the end of a week, Mr Swindon, urged thereto by Mr Scunthorpe, delivered the new clothes, and, after purchasing such embellishments to his costume as a tall cane, a fob, and a Marseilles waistcoat, Bertram ventured to show himself in the Park, at the fashionable hour of five o'clock. Here he had the felicity of seeing Lord Coleraine, Georgy à Cockhorse, prancing down Rotten Row on his mettlesome steed; Lord Morton, on his long-tailed gray; and, amongst the carriages, Tommy Onslow's curricle; a number of dashing gigs and tilburies; the elegant barouches of the ladies; and Mr Beaumaris's yellow-winged phaeton-and-four, which he appeared to be able to turn within a space so small as to seem impossible to any mere whipster. Nothing would do for Bertram after that but to repair to the nearest jobmaster's stables, and to arrange for the hire of a showy chestnut hack. Whatever imperfections might attach to the bearing and style of a young gentleman from the country, Bertram knew himself to be a bruising rider, and in this guise determined to show himself to the society which his sister already adorned.

As luck would have it, he encountered her on the day when he first sallied forth, mounted upon his hired hack. She was sitting up beside Mr Beaumaris in his famous phaeton, animatedly describing to him the scene of the Drawing-room in which she had taken so humble a part. This event had necessarily occupied her thoughts so much during the past week that she had been able to spare very few for the activities of her adventurous brother. But when she caught sight of him, trotting along on his chestnut hack, she exclaimed, and said impulsively: 'Oh, it is – Mr Anstey! Do pray stop, Mr Beaumaris!'

He drew up his team obediently, while she waved to Bertram. He brought his hack up to the phaeton, and bowed politely, only slightly quizzing her with his eyes. Mr Beaumaris, glancing indifferently at him, caught this arch look, became aware of a slight tension in the trim figure beside him, and looked under his lazy eyelids from one to the other.

'How do you do? How do you go on?' said Arabella, stretching out her hand in its glove of white kid.

Bertram bowed over it very creditably, and replied: 'Famously! I mean to come – I mean to visit you some morning, Miss Tallant!'

'Oh, yes, please do!' Arabella looked up at her escort, blushed, and stammered: 'May I p-present Mr Anstey to you, Mr Beaumaris? He – he is a friend of mine!'

'How do you do?' responded Mr Beaumaris politely. 'From Yorkshire, Mr Anstey?'

'Oh, yes! I have known Miss Tallant since I was in short coats!' grinned Bertram.

'You will certainly be much envied by Miss Tallant's numerous admirers,' responded Mr Beaumaris. 'Are you staying in town?'

'Just a short visit, you know!' Bertram's gaze reverted to the team harnessed to the phaeton, all four of them on the fret. 'I say, sir, that's a bang-up team you have in hand!' he said, with all his sister's impulsiveness. 'Oh, don't look at this hack of mine – showy, but I never crossed a greater slug in my life!'

'You hunt, Mr Anstey?'

'Yes, with my uncle's pack, in Yorkshire. Of course, it is not like the Quorn country, or the Pytchley, but we get some pretty good runs, I can tell you!' Bertram confided.

'Mr Anstey,' interrupted Arabella, fixing him with a very compelling look, 'I think Lady Bridlington has sent you a card for her ball: I hope you mean to come!'

'Well, you know, Bel – Miss Tallant!' said Bertram, with disastrous lack of gallantry, 'that sort of mummery is not much in my line!' He perceived an anguished expression in her eyes, and added hastily: 'That is, delighted, I am sure! Yes, yes, I shall be there! And I shall hope to have the honour of standing up with you!' he ended punctiliously.

Mr Beaumaris was obliged to pay attention to his team, but he did not miss the minatory note in Arabella's voice as she said: 'I collect we are to have the pleasure of receiving a visit from you *tomorrow*, sir!'

'Oh!' said Bertram. 'Yes, of course! As a matter of fact, I shall be taking a look-in at Tattersall's, but – Yes, to be sure! I'll come to visit you all right and tight!'

He then doffed his new hat, and bowed, and rode off at an easy canter. Arabella appeared to be conscious that some explanation was called for. She said airily: 'You must know, sir, that we have been brought up almost as – as brother and sister!'

'I thought perhaps you had,' responded Mr Beaumaris gravely.

She glanced sharply up at his profile. He seemed to be wholly absorbed in the task of manoeuvring the phaeton through a gap between a dowager's landaulet and a smart barouche with a crest on the panel. She reassured herself with the reflection that whereas she favoured her Mama, Bertram was said to be the image of what the Vicar had been at the same age, and said: 'But I was telling you about the Drawing-room, and how graciously the Princess Mary smiled at me! She was wearing the most magnificent toilet I ever saw in my life! Lady Bridlington tells me that when she was young she was thought to be the most handsome of all the princesses. I thought she looked to be very good-natured.'

Mr Beaumaris agreed to it, reserving to himself his enjoyment in hearing this innocent description of the Regent's most admired sister. Miss Tallant, entrancing him with one of her unguarded moments of naïvety, then told him of the elegant, gilt-edged card of invitation which had arrived that very day in Park Street from no less a personage than the Lord Chamberlain, who informed Lady Bridlington that he was commanded by his Royal Highness the Prince Regent to invite her, and Miss Tallant, to a Dress-party at Carlton House on Thursday next, to have the honour of meeting (in large capitals) Her Majesty The Queen. He said that he should be on the look-out for her at Carlton House, and refrained from observing that the Regent's parties, planned as they were on a magnificent scale which offended the taste of such arbiters of true elegance as himself, were amongst the worst squeezes in town, and had even been known to include such vulgarities as a fountain playing in the middle of the dinner-table to which he had himself been bidden.

He entered into her feelings upon this event with far more sympathy than did Bertram, when he presented himself in Park Street on the following afternoon. Lady Bridlington having retired, as she always did, to her couch, to recruit her energies for an evening to be spent at no fewer than four different parties, Arabella was able to enjoy the luxury of a tête-à-tête with her favourite brother. While acknowledging handsomely that he was glad to think of her being invited to Carlton House, he said that he supposed there would be a vast rout of fashionables present, and that for himself he preferred to spend his evenings in a simpler style. He further begged her not to favour him with a description of the gown she meant to wear. She perceived that he was not much interested in her social triumphs, and turned willingly enough to his own chosen amusements. He was slightly evasive on this subject, replying to her questions in general terms. His experience of the female sex had not led him to indulge his imagination with the belief that even an adoring sister would regard with favour such delights as a visit to Cribb's Parlour, where he had actually handled the Champion's famous silver cup, presented to him after his last fight, some years previously, against Molyneux, the Black; the blowing of a cloud at the Daffy Club, surrounded by young Bloods of the Fancy, veterans of the Ring, promising novices, and an array of portraits hanging round the walls of past champions whose very names filled him with awe; or a lounge through the famous Saloon at Covent Garden, where the bold, ogling glances of the Cyprians who made this haunt their hunting-ground both shocked and terrified him. Nor did he tell her of an assignation he had made with a new acquaintance, encountered at Tattersall's that very morning. He had seen at a glance that Mr Jack Carnaby was quite the thing – almost a Tulip of Fashion, in fact, if dress and air were anything to judge by – but something warned him that Arabella would regard with horror his approaching introduction into a snug little gaming-house under the auspices of this gentleman. It would be of very little use to assure her that he was going merely for the experience, and had not the least intention of gaming away his precious blunt; even his knowledgeable cicerone had shaken his head over this new scheme, and had uttered cryptic warnings against ivory-turners and Greek banditti, adding that his uncle and principal trustee held that it was a good flat that was never down. He said that he had himself proved the truth of this excellent maxim, but since he owned, upon enquiry, that nothing was known to Mr Carnaby's discredit, Bertram paid scant heed to his advice. Mr Carnaby led him to a discreet house in Pall Mall, where, upon knocking in a certain fashion on the door, they were inspected through a grille, and finally admitted. Nothing could have been further removed from Bertram's expectations of what a gaming-hell would be like than the decorous house in which he found himself. The various servants were all very respectable men, with quiet manners, and it would have been hard to have found a more civil or obliging host than the proprietor. Never having indulged in any game more dashing than whist, Bertram spent some time in looking-on, but when he thought he had mastered the rules governing hazard, he ventured to join that table, armed with a modest rouleau. He soon perceived that Mr Scunthorpe had been quite at fault in his talk of Fulhams, and up-hills, for he enjoyed a run of astonishing luck, and came away at last with his pocket so full of guineas that he had no longer any need to worry over his growing expenses. A lucky bet at Tattersall's on the following day put him in a fair way to thinking himself at home on the Turf and at the Table, and it was not to be expected that he would lend any but an impatient ear to Mr Scunthorpe's dark prophecy that having got into Tow Street he would end up in the clutch of a Bum-trap.

'Know what my uncle says?' Mr Scunthorpe demanded. 'They always let a flat win the first time he goes to a hell. Hedge off, dear boy! they'll queer you on that suit!'

'Oh, fudge!' retorted Bertram. 'I hope I'm not such a gudgeon as to dip too deeply! I'll tell you what, Felix, I *would* like to play just once at Watier's, if you could contrive it for me!'

'What?' gasped Mr Scunthorpe. 'Dear old boy, they would never let you set foot inside the Great-Go, upon my honour they would not! Why, I've never played there myself! Much better go to Vauxhall! Might meet your sister there! See the Grand Cascade! Listen to the Pandean band! All the crack, you know!'

'Oh, dull work, when I might be trying my luck at faro!' said Bertram.

Eleven

From the Daffy Club to Limmer's Hotel in Conduit Street was an inevitable step for any young gentleman interested in the Fancy to take. Here were to be found all the Pets of the Ring, and the Corinthians who patronised them. Bertram went there under the auspices of Mr Scunthorpe, who was anxious to turn his friend's thoughts away from more dangerous haunts. He had begun to acquire acquaintances in London, and was thus in the proud position of exchanging greetings with several of the men present. He and Mr Scunthorpe sat down in one of the boxes, and Mr Scunthorpe painstakingly pointed out to him all the notabilities he could see, including a very down-the-road looking man who, he whispered, could be trusted to tip a man the office what to back in any race. He then excused himself, and bore down upon this knowledgeable person, and became absorbed in conversation with him. While he was thus engaged, Bertram saw Mr Beaumaris stroll in with a party of friends, but as he had by this time fully grasped the exalted position occupied by the Nonpareil he was flattered beyond measure when, after raising his glass and regarding him through it for a moment, Mr Beaumaris walked across the sanded floor, and sat down at his table, saying with a slight smile: 'Did I not meet you in the Park the other day? Mr – er – Anstey, I believe?'

Bertram acknowledged it, flushing shyly; but when Mr Beaumaris added casually: 'You are related to Miss Tallant, I collect?' he made haste to deny any relationship, adding that

Miss Tallant was quite above his touch. Mr Beaumaris accepted this without comment, and asked him where he was putting up in town. Bertram saw no harm in disclosing his direction, or even in telling Mr Beaumaris that this was his first visit to the Metropolis.

It was the expressed opinion of Mr Jack Carnaby that the Nonpareil was a haughty, disagreeable kind of man, but Bertram was unable to trace the least sign of haughtiness, or of reserve, in his manners. Mr Beaumaris's intimates could have informed Mr Tallant that while no one could be more snubbing, no one, on the other hand, could be – when he chose – more sympathetic. In less than no time, Bertram, forgetting his bashfulness, was confiding far more to his grand new acquaintance than he had the least idea of. Mr Beaumaris, himself a Melton man, complimented him on his seat on a horse, and any barrier Bertram might have raised between himself and the author of his sister's predicament crumbled at this touch. He was led on to describe the country over which he hunted, the exact locality of Heythram, and his own impossible ambitions, without having the smallest suspicion that all this information was being skilfully extracted from him. He told Mr Beaumaris about Smalls, and his hopes of adorning the Home Office, and when Mr Beaumaris said, with a humorous lift to one eyebrow, that he should not have supposed him to have had parliamentary ambitions, he blurted out his real ambition, ending by saying wistfully: 'But it can't be, of course. Only I would have liked of all things to have been able to have joined a cavalry regiment!'

'I think you would do very well in a cavalry regiment,' agreed Mr Beaumaris, rising, as Mr Scunthorpe came back to the table. 'Meanwhile, do not draw the bustle with too much of a vengeance during this visit of yours to London!' He nodded to Mr Scunthorpe, and walked away, leaving that gentleman to explain to Bertram with the utmost earnestness just how greatly he had been honoured.

But Mr Beaumaris, quelling the ecstatic advances of his canine admirer, an hour or two later, said: 'If you had any real regard for me, Ulysses, you would be greeting me with condolences rather than with these uncalled-for raptures.'

Ulysses, considerably plumper, and with his flying ear more rebellious than ever, and his tail even more tightly curled over his back, stretched worshipfully before the god of his idolatry, and uttered an encouraging bark. After that he bustled to the door of the library, and plainly invited Mr Beaumaris to enter, and partake of refreshment there. Brough, tenderly relieving his master of his long cloak, and his hat and gloves, remarked that it was wonderful how knowing the little dog was.

'It is wonderful what encouragement he has received from my staff to continue to burden me with his unwanted presence in my house!' retorted Mr Beaumaris acidly.

Brough, who had dealt with Mr Beaumaris for many years, permitted himself to give what in a lesser personage would have been a grin, and to say; 'Well, sir, if I had *known* you wanted him chased off, I'm sure I'd have done my best! Not but what he's so devoted to you that I doubt if he'd have gone, setting aside that it would go to my heart to chase off a dog that handles Alphonse like this one does.'

'If that misbegotten animal has been upsetting Alphonse, I'll wring his neck!' promised Mr Beaumaris.

'Oh, no, sir, nothing of that sort! When you're out, and Ulysses comes downstairs (as come he does), he behaves to Alphonse as though he hadn't had a bite to eat in a month, nor wouldn't think of touching so much as a scrap of meat he found on the kitchen floor. Well, as I said to Mrs Preston, if ever a dog could speak, that one does, telling Alphonse as plain as a Christian that he's the only friend he's got in the world. Quite won Alphonse over, he has. In fact, when two nice loin chops was found to be missing, Alphonse would have it the undercook was accusing the dog of having stolen them only to cover up his own carelessness, and Ulysses sitting there looking as if he didn't know what a chop tasted like. He buried the bones under the rug in your study, sir, but I have removed them.'

'You are not only an ill-favoured specimen,' Mr Beaumaris

informed Ulysses severely, 'but you have all the faults of the under-bred: toadeating, duplicity, and impudence!'

Ulysses sat down to relieve the irritation of a healing wound by a hearty scratch. He was rebuked, and since he had heard that note in Mr Beaumaris's voice before – as when he had expressed a vociferous desire to share his bedchamber with him – he stopped scratching, and flattened his ears placatingly.

Mr Beaumaris poured himself out a glass of wine, and sat down with it in his favourite chair. Ulysses sat before him, and sighed deeply. 'Yes, I daresay,' said Mr Beaumaris, 'but I have something better to do than to spend my time spreading ointment on your sores. You should remember, moreover, that you cannot be permitted to meet your benefactress again until you are entirely healed.' Ulysses yawned at him, and lay down with his head on his paws, as one who found the conversation tedious. Mr Beaumaris stirred him with one foot. 'I wonder if you are right?' he mused. 'A month ago I should have been sure of it. Yet I let her saddle me with a foundling-brat, and a mongrel-cur – you will forgive my plain speaking, Ulysses! – and I am now reasonably certain that neither of you is destined to be the most tiresome of my responsibilities. Do you suppose that that wretched youth is masquerading under a false name for reasons of his own, or in support of her pretensions? Do not look at me like that! You may consider that experience should have taught me wisdom, but I do not believe that it was all a clever plot to inveigle me into declaring myself. I am not even sure that she regards me with more than tolerance. In fact, Ulysses, I am not very sure of anything – and I think I will pay my grandmother a long overdue visit.'

In pursuance of this resolve, Mr Beaumaris sent for his curricle next morning. Ulysses, who had shared his breakfast, bundled ahead of him down the steps of his house, leaped into the curricle, and disposed himself on the passenger's seat with all the air of a dog born into the purple.

'*No!*' said Mr Beaumaris forcibly. Ulysses descended miserably from the curricle, and prostrated himself on the flag-way. 'Let me tell you, my friend,' said Mr Beaumaris, 'that I have a certain reputation to maintain, which your disreputable appearance would seriously jeopardise! Do not be alarmed! – I am not, alas, going out of your life for ever!' He climbed into the curricle, and said: 'You may stop grinning, Clayton, and let 'em go!'

'Yes, sir!' said his groom, obeying both these behests, and swinging himself expertly up on to the curricle as it passed him. After a minute to two, having twice glanced over his shoulder, he ventured to inform Mr Beaumaris that the little dog was following him.

Mr Beaumaris uttered an oath, and reined in his reluctant pair. The faithful hound, plodding valiantly along, with heaving ribs, and several inches of tongue hanging from his parted jaws, came up with the curricle, and once more abased himself in the road. 'Damn you!' said Mr Beaumaris. 'I suppose you are capable of following me all the way to Wimbledon! It now remains to be seen whether my credit is good enough to enable me to carry you off. Get up!'

Ulysses was very much out of breath, but at these words he mustered up enough strength to scramble into the curricle once more. He wagged a grateful tail, climbed on to the seat beside Mr Beaumaris, and sat there panting blissfully. Mr Beaumaris read him a short lecture on the evils of blackmail, which sorely tried the self-control of his groom, discouraged him peremptorily from hurling a challenge at a mere pedestrian dog in the gutter, and proceeded on his way to Wimbledon.

The Dowager Duchess of Wigan, who was the terror of four sons, three surviving daughters, numerous grandchildren, her man of business, her lawyer, her physician, and a host of dependants, greeted her favourite grandson characteristically. He found her imbibing nourishment in the form of slices of toast dipped in tea, and bullying the unmarried daughter who lived with her. She had been a great belle in her day, and the ravages of her former beauty were still discernible in the delicate bones of her face. She had a way of looking at her visitors with an eagle-like stare, had never been known to waste politeness on anyone, and was scathingly contemptuous of everything modern. Her children were inordinately proud of her, and lived in dread of her periodical commands to them to present themselves at her house. Upon her butler's ushering Mr Beaumaris into her morning-room, she directed one of her piercing looks at him, and said: 'Oh! So it's you, is it? Why haven't you been to see me since I don't know when?'

Mr Beaumaris, bowing deeply over her hand, replied imperturbably: 'On the occasion of my last visit, ma'am, you told me you did not wish to see me again until I had mended my ways.'

'Well, have you?' said the Duchess, conveying another slip of soaked toast to her mouth.

'Certainly, ma'am: I am in a fair way to becoming a philanthropist,' he replied, turning to greet his aunt.

'I don't want any more of *them* about me,' said her grace. 'It turns my stomach enough already to have to sit here watching Caroline at her everlasting knitting for the poor. In *my* day, we gave 'em vails, and there was an end to it. Not that I believe you. Here, take this pap away, Caroline, and ring the bell! Maudling one's inside with tea never did any good to anyone yet, and never will. I'll tell Hadleigh to fetch up a bottle of Madeira – the lot your grandfather laid down, not that rubbish Wigan sent me t'other day!'

Lady Caroline removed the tray, but asked her parent in a shrinking tone if she thought that Dr Sudbury would approve.

'Sudbury's an old woman, and you're a fool, Caroline!' replied the Duchess. 'You go away, and leave me to talk to Robert! I never could abide a pack of females hangin' round me!' she added, as Lady Caroline gathered up her knitting: 'Tell Hadleigh the *good* Madeira! He knows. Well, sir, what have you to say for yourself now you *have* had the impudence to show your face here again?'

Mr Beaumaris, closing the door behind his aunt, came back into the room, and said with deceptive meekness that he was happy to find his grandmother in such excellent health and spirits.

'Graceless jackanapes!' retorted the Duchess with relish. She ran her eye over his handsome person. 'You look very well – at least, you would if you didn't make such a figure of yourself in that rig! When I was a girl, no gentleman would have dreamed of paying a social call without powder, let me tell you! Enough to make your grandfather turn in his grave to see what you've all come to, with your skimpy coats, and your starched collars, and not a bit of lace to your neckcloth, or your wristbands! If you can sit down in those skin-tight breeches, or pantaloons, or whatever you call 'em, do so!'

'Oh, yes, I can sit down!' said Mr Beaumaris, disposing himself in a chair opposite to hers. 'My pantaloons, like Aunt Caroline's gifts to the poor, are knitted, and so adapt themselves reasonably well to my wishes.'

'Ha! Then I'll tell Caroline to knit you a pair for Christmas. That'll send her into hysterics, for a bigger prude I never met!'

'Very likely, ma'am, but as I am sure that my aunt would obey you, however much her modesty was offended, I must ask you to refrain. The embroidered slippers which reached me last Christmas tried me high enough. I wonder what she thought I should do with them?'

The Duchess gave a cackle of laughter. 'Lord bless you, she don't *think*! You shouldn't send her handsome gifts.'

'I send you very handsome gifts,' murmured Mr Beaumaris, 'but you never reciprocate!'

'No, and I never shall. You've got more than's good for you already. What have you brought me this time?'

'Nothing at all – unless you have a fancy for a mongrel-dog?'

'I can't abide dogs, or cats either. Fifty thousand a year if you've a penny, and you don't bring me as much as a posy! Out with it, Robert! What did you come for?'

'To ask you whether you think I should make a tolerable husband, ma'am.'

'What?' exclaimed her grace, sitting bolt upright in her chair, and grasping the arms with her frail, jewelled hands. 'You're never going to offer for the Dewsbury girl?'

'Good God, no!'

'Oh, so that's yet another idiot who's wearing the willow for you, is it?' said her grace, who had her own ways of discovering what was going on in the world from which she had retired. 'Who is it now? One of these days you'll go a step too far, mark my words!'

'I think I have,' said Mr Beaumaris.

She stared at him, but before she could speak her butler had entered the room, staggering under a specimen of the ducal plate which her grace had categorically refused to relinquish to the present Duke, on the twofold score that it was her personal property, and that he shouldn't have married anyone who gave his mother such a belly-ache as that die-away ninny he had set in her place. This impressive tray Hadleigh set down on the table, casting, as he did so, a very expressive look at Mr Beaumaris. Mr Beaumaris nodded his understanding, and rose, and went to pour out the wine. He handed his grandmother a modest half-glass, to which she instantly took exception, demanding to know whether he had the impertinence to suppose that she could not carry her wine.

'I daresay you can drink me under the table,' replied Mr Beaumaris, 'but you know very well it's extremely bad for your health, and also that you cannot bully me into pandering to your outrageous commands.' He then lifted her disengaged hand to his lips, and said gently: 'You are a rude and an overbearing old woman, ma'am, but I hope you may live to be a hundred, for I like you so much better than any other of my relatives!'

'I daresay that's not saying much,' she remarked, rather pleased by this audacious speech. 'Sit down again, and don't try to hoax me with any of your faradiddles! I can see you're going to make a fool of yourself, so you needn't wrap it up in clean linen! You haven't come here to tell me you're going to marry that brass-faced lightskirt you had in keeping when I last saw you?'

'I have not!' said Mr Beaumaris.

'Just as well, for laced mutton being brought into the family is what I won't put up with! Not that I think you're fool enough for that.'

'Where *do* you learn your abominable expressions, ma'am?' demanded Mr Beaumaris.

'*I* don't belong to your mealy-mouthed generation, thank God! Who is she?'

'If I did not know from bitter experience, ma'am, that nothing occurs in London but what you are instantly aware of it, I should say that you had never heard of her. She is – or at any rate, she says she is – the latest heiress.'

'Oh! Do you mean the chit that that silly Bridlington woman has staying with her? I'm told she's a beauty.'

'She *is* beautiful,' acknowledged Mr Beaumaris. 'But that's not it.'

'Well, what is it?'

He reflected. 'She is the most enchanting little wretch I ever encountered,' he said. 'When she is trying to convince me that she is up to every move in the social game, she contrives to appear much like any other female, but when, as happens all too often for my comfort, her compassion is stirred, she is ready to go to any lengths to succour the object of her pity. If I marry her, she will undoubtedly expect me to launch a campaign for the alleviation of the lot of climbing-boys, and will very likely turn my house into an asylum for stray curs.'

'Oh, she will, will she?' said her grace, staring at him with knit brows. 'Why?'

'Well, she has already foisted a specimen of each on to me,' he explained. 'No, perhaps I wrong her. Ulysses she certainly foisted on to me, but the unspeakable Jemmy I actually offered to take under my protection.'

The Duchess brought her hand down on the arm of her chair. 'Stop trying to gammon me!' she commanded. 'Who is Ulysses, and who is Jemmy?'

'I have already offered to make you a present of Ulysses,' Mr Beaumaris reminded her. 'Jemmy is a small climbing-boy whose manifest wrongs Miss Tallant is determined to set right. I wish you might have heard her telling Bridlington that he cared for nothing but his own comfort, like all the rest of us; and asking poor Charles Fleetwood to imagine what his state might now be had he been reared by a drunken foster-mother, and sold into slavery to a sweep. Alas that I was not privileged to witness her encounter with the sweep! I understand that she drove him from the house with threats of prosecution. I am not at all surprised that he cowered before her: I have seen her disperse a group of louts.'

'She sounds to me an odd sort of a gal,' remarked her grace. 'Is she a lady?'

'Unquestionably.'

'Who's her father?'

'That, ma'am, is a mystery I have hopes that you may be able to unravel.'

'I?' she exclaimed. 'I don't know what you think I can tell you!'

'I have reason to believe that her home is within easy reach of Harrowgate, ma'am, and I recall that you visited that watering-place not so very long ago. You may have seen her at an Assembly – I suppose they do have Assemblies at Harrowgate? – or have heard her family spoken of.'

'Well, I didn't!' replied her grace bitterly. 'What's more I don't want to hear anything more about Harrowgate! A nasty, cold, shabby-genteel place, with the filthiest waters I ever tasted in my life! They did me no good at all, as anyone but a fool like that snivelling leech of mine would have known from the outset! Assemblies, indeed! It's no pleasure to me to watch a parcel of country-dowds dancing this shameless waltz of yours! Dancing! *I* could give you another name for it!'

'I have no doubt that you could, ma'am, but I must beg you to spare my blushes! Moreover, for one who is for ever railing against the squeamishness of the modern miss, your attitude towards the waltz seems a trifle inconsistent.'

'I don't know anything about consistency,' retorted her grace, with perfect truth, 'but I do know indecency when I see it!'

'We are wandering from the point,' said Mr Beaumaris firmly.

'Well, I never met any Tallants in Harrowgate, or anywhere else. When I wasn't trying to swallow something that no one is ever going to make me believe wasn't drained off from the kennels, I was sitting watching your aunt knot a fringe in the most uncomfortable hole of a lodging I've been in yet! Why, I had to take all my own bed-linen with me!'

'You always do, ma'am,' said Mr Beaumaris, who had several times been privileged to see the start of one of the Duchess's impressive journeys. 'Also your own plate, your favourite chair, your steward, your –'

'I don't want any of your impudence, Robert!' interrupted her grace. 'I don't always *have* to take 'em!' She gave her shawl a twitch. 'It's nothing to me whom you marry,' she said. 'But why you must needs dangle after a wealthy woman beats me!'

'Oh, I don't think she has any fortune at all!' replied Mr Beaumaris coolly. 'She only said she had to put me in my place.'

He came under her eagle-stare again. 'Put you in your place? Are you going to tell me, sir, that she ain't tumbling over herself to catch you?'

'Far from it. She holds me at arm's length. I cannot even be sure that she has even the smallest *tendre* for me.'

'Been seen in your company often enough, hasn't she?' said her grace sharply.

'Yes, she says it does her a great deal of good socially to be seen with me,' said Mr Beaumaris pensively.

'Either she's a devilish deep 'un,' said her grace, a gleam in her eye, 'or she's a good gal! Lord, I didn't think there was one of these niminy-piminy modern gals alive that had enough spirit not to toadeat you! Should I like her?'

'Yes, I think you would, but to tell you the truth, ma'am, I don't care a button whether you like her or not.'

Surprisingly, she took no exception to this, but nodded, and said: 'You'd better marry her. Not if she ain't of gentle blood, though. You ain't a Caldicot of Wigan, but you come of good stock. I wouldn't have let your mother marry into your family if it hadn't been one of the best – not for five times the settlements your father made on her!' She added reminiscently: 'A fine gal, Maria: I liked her better than any other of my brats.'

'So did I,' agreed Mr Beaumaris, rising from his chair. 'Shall I propose to Arabella, risking a rebuff, or shall I address myself to the task of convincing her that I am not the incorrigible flirt she has plainly been taught to think me?'

'It's no use asking me,' said her grace unhelpfully. 'It wouldn't do you any harm to get a good set-down, but I don't mind your bringing the gal to see me one day.' She held out her hand to him, but when he had punctiliously kissed it, and would have released it, her talon-like fingers closed on his, and she said: 'Out with it, sir! What's vexing you, eh?'

He smiled at her. 'Not precisely that, ma'am – but I have the stupidest wish that she would tell me the truth!'

'Pooh, why should she?'

'I can think of only one reason, ma'am. That is what vexes me!' said Mr Beaumaris.

Twelve

On his way home from Wimbledon, Mr Beaumaris drove up Bond Street, and was so fortunate as to see Arabella, accompanied by a prim-looking maidservant, come out of Hookham's Library. He pulled up immediately, and she smiled, and walked up to the curricle, exclaiming: 'Oh, how much better he looks! I told you he would! Well, you dear little dog, do you remember me, I wonder?'

Ulysses wagged his tail in a perfunctory manner, suffered her to stretch up a hand to caress him, but yawned.

'For heaven's sake, Ulysses, try to acquire a little polish!' Mr Beaumaris admonished him.

Arabella laughed. 'Is that what you call him? Why?'

'Well, he seemed, on the evidence, to have led a roving life, and judging by the example we saw it must have been adventurous,' explained Mr Beaumaris.

'Very true!' She watched Ulysses look up adoringly into his face, and said: 'I knew he would grow to be attached to you: only see how he looks at you!'

'His affection, Miss Tallant, threatens to become a serious embarrassment.'

'Nonsense! I am sure you must be fond of him, or you would not take him out with you!'

'If that is what you think, ma'am, you can have no idea of the depths to which he can sink to achieve his own ends. Blackmail is an open book to him. He is well aware that I dare not deny him, lest I should lose what little reputation I may have in your eyes.'

'How absurd you are! I knew, as soon as I saw how well you handled him, that you know just how to use a dog. I am so glad you have kept him with you.'

She gave Ulysses a last pat, and stepped back on to the flag-way. Mr Beaumaris said: 'Will you not give me the pleasure of driving you to your door?'

'No, indeed, it is only a step!'

'No matter: send your maid home! Ulysses adds his entreaties to mine.'

As Ulysses chose this moment to scratch one ear, this made her laugh.

'Mere bashfulness,' explained Mr Beaumaris, stretching down his hand. 'Come!'

'Very well – since Ulysses wishes it so much!' she said, taking his hand, and climbing into the curricle. 'Mr Beaumaris will see me home, Maria.'

He spread a light rug across her knees, and said over his shoulder: 'I have recalled, Clayton, that I need something from the chemist's. Go and buy me a – a gum-plaster! You may walk home.'

'Very good, sir,' said the groom, at his most wooden, and sprang down into the road.

'A *gum-plaster*?' echoed Arabella, turning wide eyes of astonishment upon Mr Beaumaris. 'What in the world can you want with such a thing, sir?'

'Rheumatism,' said Mr Beaumaris defiantly, setting his horses in motion.

'*You*? Oh, no, you must be quizzing me!'

'Not at all. I was merely seeking an excuse to be rid of Clayton. I hope Ulysses will prove himself an adequate chaperon. I have something to say to you, Miss Tallant, for which I do not desire an audience.'

She had been stroking the dog, but her hands were stilled at this, and the colour receded from her cheeks. Rather breathlessly, she asked: 'What is it?'

'Will you do me the honour of becoming my wife?'

She was stunned, and for a moment could not utter a word. When she was able to control her voice a little, she said: 'I think you *must* be quizzing me.'

'You must know that I am not.'

She trembled. 'Yes, yes, let us say that that was all it was, if you please! I am very much obliged to you, but I cannot marry you!'

'May I know why you cannot, Miss Tallant?'

She was afraid that she was about to burst into tears, and answered in a shaken tone: 'There are many reasons. Pray believe it is impossible!'

'Are you quite sure that these reasons are insuperable?' he asked.

'Quite, quite sure! Oh, please do not urge me further! I had never dreamed – it never entered my head – I would not for the world have given you cause to suppose – Oh, *please* say no more, sir!'

He bowed, and was silent. She sat staring down at her clasped hands in great agitation of spirit, her mind in a turmoil, tossed between surprise at such a declaration, coming from one whom she had believed to have been merely amusing himself, and the shock of realising, for the first time, that there was no one she would rather marry than Mr Beaumaris.

After a slight pause, he said in his usual calm way: 'I believe there is always a little awkwardness attached to such situations as this in which we now find ourselves. We must strive not to allow it to overcome us. Is Lady Bridlington's ball to rank amongst the season's greatest squeezes?'

She was grateful to him for easing the tension, and all the discomfort of the moment, and tried to reply naturally. 'Yes, indeed, it is! I am sure quite three hundred cards of invitation have been sent out. Shall – shall you find time to look in, I wonder?'

'Yes, and shall hope that even though you will not *marry* me you may be persuaded to *dance* with me.'

She replied she scarcely knew what: it was largely inaudible. He shot a quick look at her averted profile, hesitated, and then said nothing. They had reached Park Street by this time, and in another moment he had handed her down from the curricle.

'Do not come with me to the door! I know you do not like to leave your horses!' she said, in a hurried tone. 'Good-bye! I shall see you at the ball.'

He waited until he had seen her admitted into the house, and then got into the curricle again, and drove off. Ulysses nudged his nose under his arm. 'Thank you,' he said dryly. 'Do you think I am unreasonable to wish that she would trust me enough to tell me the truth?'

Ulysses sighed heavily; he was rather sleepy after his day in this country.

'I suppose I shall end by telling her that I have known it all along. And yet – Yes, Ulysses, I am quite unreasonable. Did it seem to you that she was not as indifferent to me as she would have had me believe?'

Understanding that something was expected of him, his admirer uttered a sound between a yelp and a bark, and furiously wagged his tail.

'You feel that I should persevere?' said Mr Beaumaris. 'I was, in fact, too precipitate. You may be right. But if she had cared at all, would she not have told me the truth?'

Ulysses sneezed.

'At all events,' remarked Mr Beaumaris, 'she was undoubtedly pleased with me for bringing you out with me.'

Whether it was due to this circumstance, or to Ulysses' unshakeable conviction that he was born to be a carriage-dog, Mr Beaumaris continued to take him about. Those of his intimates who saw Ulysses, once they had recovered from the initial shock, were of the opinion that the Nonpareil was practising some mysterious jest on society, and only one earnest imitator went so far as to adopt an animal of mixed parentage to ride in his own carriage. He thought that if the Nonpareil was setting a new fashion it would become so much the rage that it might be difficult hereafter to acquire a suitable mongrel. But Mr Warkworth, a more profound thinker, censured this act as being rash and unconsidered. 'Remember when the Nonpareil wore a dandelion in his buttonhole three days running?' he said darkly. 'Remember the kick-up there was, with every saphead in town running round to all the flower-women for dandelions, which they hadn't got, of course. Stands to reason you couldn't buy dandelions! Why, poor Geoffrey drove all the way to Esher looking for one, and Altringham went to the trouble of rooting up half-a-dozen out of Richmond Park, and having a set-to with the keeper over it, and then planting 'em in his window-boxes. Good idea, if they *had* become the mode: clever fellow, Altringham! – but of course the Nonpareil was only hoaxing us! Once he had the whole lot of us decked out with them, he never wore one again, and a precious set of gudgeons we looked! Playing the same trick again, if you ask me!'

Only in one quarter did unhappy results arise from the elevation of Ulysses. The Honourable Frederick Byng, who had for years been known by the sobriquet of Poodle Byng from his habit of driving everywhere with a very highly-bred and exquisitely shaved poodle sitting up beside him, encountered Mr Beaumaris in Piccadilly one afternoon, and no sooner clapped eyes on his disreputable companion than he pulled up his horses all standing, and spluttered out: 'What the devil – ?'

Mr Beaumaris reined in his own pair, and looked enquiringly over his shoulder. Mr Byng, his florid countenance suffused by an angry flush, was engaged in backing his curricle, jabbing at his horses' mouths in a way that showed how greatly moved he was. Once alongside the other curricle, he glared at Mr Beaumaris, and demanded an explanation.

'Explanation of what?' said Mr Beaumaris. 'If you don't take care, you'll go off in an apoplexy one of these days, Poodle! What's the matter?'

Mr Byng pointed a trembling finger at Ulysses. 'What's the meaning of *that*?' he asked belligerently. 'If you think I'll swallow any such damned insult – !'

He was interrupted. The two dogs, who had been eyeing one another measuringly from their respective vehicles, suddenly succumbed to a mutual hatred, uttered two simultaneous snarls, and leaped for one another's throats. Since the curricles were too far apart to allow them to come to grips, they were obliged to vent their feelings in a series of hysterical objurgations, threats, and abuse, which drowned the rest of Mr Byng's furious speech.

Mr Beaumaris, holding Ulysses by the scruff of his neck, laughed so much that he could hardly speak: a circumstance which did nothing to mollify the outraged Mr Byng. He began to say that he should know how to answer an attempt to make him ridiculous, but was obliged to break off in order to command his dog to be quiet.

'No, no, Poodle, don't call me out!' said Mr Beaumaris, his shoulders still shaking. 'Really, I had no such intention! Besides, we should only make fools of ourselves, going out to Paddington in the cold dawn to exchange shots over a pair of dogs!'

Mr Byng hesitated. There was much in what Mr Beaumaris said; moreover Mr Beaumaris was acknowledged to be one of the finest shots in England, and to call him out for a mere trifle would be an act of sheer foolhardiness. He said suspiciously: 'If you're not doing it to make a laughing-stock of me, why *are* you doing it?'

'Hush, Poodle, hush! You are treading on delicate ground!' said Mr Beaumaris. 'I cannot bandy a lady's name about in the open street!'

'What lady? I don't believe a word of it! Why can't you make that damned mongrel be quiet?'

In lamentable contrast to his well-trained adversary, who was now seated virtuously beside his master again, and affecting a maddening deafness, Ulysses, convinced that he had cowed the contemptible dandy, was hurling extremely ignoble taunts at him. Mr Beaumaris cuffed him, but although he cowered under the avenging hand he was quite unrepentant, and resumed his threats with unabated fervour.

'It is all jealousy, Poodle!' Mr Beaumaris said soothingly. 'The hatred of the vulgar for the aristocrat! I think we had better part, don't you?'

Mr Byng gave an angry snort, and drove off. Mr Beaumaris released Ulysses, who shook himself, sighed his satisfaction, and looked up for approbation. 'Yes, you will, I perceive, ruin me yet,' said Mr Beaumaris severely. 'If I am any judge of the matter, you picked your language up in the back-slums, and have probably been the associate of dustmen, coal-heavers, bruisers, and other such low persons! You are quite unfit for polite circles.'

Ulysses lolled his tongue out, and grinned cheerfully.

'At the same time,' said Mr Beaumaris, relenting, 'I daresay you would have made mincemeat of the creature, and I must own that I am not entirely out of sympathy with you. But poor Poodle will certainly cut me for a week at least.'

However, at the end of five days Mr Byng unbent, adopting a tolerant attitude towards Ulysses. It had been borne in upon him that to drive past the Nonpareil's curricle, staring rigidly ahead, was provocative of just the amusement amongst his acquaintances which he particularly wished to discourage.

Mr Beaumaris and Miss Tallant met again in the dazzling splendour of the Circular Room at Carlton House, on the night of the Regent's Dress-party. Arabella was so much impressed by the elegance of the sky-blue draperies, and the almost intolerable glare of a huge cut-glass chandelier, reflected, with its myriads of candles, in four large pier-glasses, that she momentarily forgot her last meeting with Mr Beaumaris, and greeted him by saying impulsively: 'How do you do? I have never seen anything like it in my life! Each room is more magnificent than the last!'

He smiled. 'Ah, but have you yet penetrated to the Conservatory, Miss Tallant? Our Royal host's *chef d'oeuvre*, believe me! Let me take you there!'

By this time she had recollected under what circumstances they had parted, so short a time previously, and her colour had risen. Many tears had been shed over the unhappy circumstance which had made it impossible for her to accept Mr Beaumaris's suit, and it had required all the excitement of a party at Carlton House to make her forget for one evening that she was the most miserable girl alive. She hesitated now, but Lady Bridlington was nodding and beaming, so she placed her hand on Mr Beaumaris's arm, and went with him through a bewildering number of apartments, all full of people, up the grand stairway, and through several saloons and antechambers. In the intervals of bowing to acquaintances, and occasionally exchanging a word of greeting, Mr Beaumaris entertained her with an account of Ulysses' quarrel with Mr Byng's poodle, and this made her laugh so much that a good deal of her constraint vanished. The Conservatory made her open her eyes very wide indeed, as well it might. Mr Beaumaris watched her, a look of amusement in his face, while she gazed silently round the extraordinary structure. Finally, she drew a breath, and uttered one of her unexpectedly candid remarks. 'Well, I don't know why he should call it a Conservatory, for it is a great deal more like a cathedral, and a very bad one too!' she said.

He was delighted. 'I thought you would be pleased with it,' he said, with deceptive gravity.

'I am not at all pleased with it,' replied Arabella severely. 'Why is there a veil over that statue?'

Mr Beaumaris levelled his glass at Venus Asleep, under a shroud of light gauze. 'I can't imagine,' he confessed. 'No doubt one of Prinny's flashes of taste. Would you like to ask him? Shall I take you to find him?'

Arabella declined the offer hastily. The Regent, an excellent host, had already managed to spend a minute or two in chat with nearly every one of his guests, and although Arabella was storing up the gracious words he had uttered to her, and meant to send home to the Vicarage an exact account of his amiability, she found conversation with such an exalted personage rather overpowering. So Mr Beaumaris took her back to Lady Bridlington, and after staying beside her for a few minutes was buttonholed by a gentleman in very tight satin knee-breeches, who lisped that the Duchess of Edgeware commanded his instant attendance. He bowed, therefore, to Arabella, and moved away, and although she several times afterwards caught a glimpse of him, he was always engaged with friends, and did not again approach her. The rooms began to seem hot, and overcrowded; the company the most boring set of people imaginable; and the vivacious, restless, and scintillating Lady Jersey, who flirted with Mr Beaumaris for quite twenty minutes, an odious creature.

Lady Bridlington's ball was the next social event of importance. This promised to be an event of more than ordinary brilliance, and although the late Lord Bridlington, to gratify an ambitious bride, had added a ballroom and a conservatory to the back of the house, it seemed unlikely that all the guests who had accepted her ladyship's invitation could be accommodated without a degree of overcrowding so uncomfortable as to mark the evening as an outstanding success. An excellent band had been engaged for the dancing, Pandean pipes were to play during the supper, extra servants were hired, police-officers and link-boys warned to make Park Street their special objective, and refreshments to supplement the efforts of Lady Bridlington's distracted cook ordered from Gunter's. For days before the event, housemaids were busy moving furniture, polishing the crystal chandeliers, washing the hundreds of spare glasses unearthed from a storeroom in the basement, counting and recounting plates and cutlery, and generally creating an atmosphere of bustle and unrest in the house. Lord Bridlington, who combined an inclination for ceremonious hospitality with a naturally frugal mind, was torn between complacency at having drawn to his house all the most fashionable persons who adorned the *ton*, and a growing conviction that the cost of the party would be enormous. The bill for wax candles alone threatened to rise to astronomical heights, and not his most optimistic calculations of the number of glasses of champagne likely to be drunk reduced the magnums that must be ordered to a total he could contemplate with anything but gloom. But his self-esteem was too great to allow of his contemplating for more than a very few minutes the expedient of eking out the precious liquor by making it into an iced cup. Cups there must certainly be, as well as lemonade, orgeat, and such milder beverages as would please the ladies, but unless the party were to fall under the stigma of having been but a shabby affair after all the best champagne must flow throughout the evening in unlimited quantities. His mind not being of an order to question his own consequence, his gratification on the whole outweighed his misgivings, and if a suspicion did enter his head that he had Arabella to thank for the flattering number of acceptances which poured into the house, he was easily able to banish it. His mother, rather shrewder than he, gave honour where it was due, and, in a fit of reckless extravagance, was moved to order a new gown for Arabella from her own expensive dressmaker. But she was not, after all, so sadly out of pocket over the transaction, since a very few words whispered into the ear of Mme Dumaine were enough to convince that astute woman of business that the réclame of designing a toilette for the great Miss Tallant would fully justify her in making a substantial reduction in the price of a gown of figured lace over a white satin robe, with short, full, plaited sleeves, fastened down the front with pearl buttons to match the edging of pearls to the overdress. Arabella, ruefully surveying the depredations caused by a succession of parties to her glove-drawer, was obliged to purchase a new pair of long white gloves, as well as new satin sandals, and a length of silver net to drape round her shoulders in the style known as à l'Ariane. There was not very much left, by this time, of the Squire's handsome present to her; and when she considered how impossible her own folly had made it for her to requite her family's generosity in the only way open to a personable young female, she was overcome by feelings of guilt and remorse, and could not refrain from shedding tears. Nor could she refrain from indulging her fancy with the contemplation of the happiness which might even now have been hers, had she not allowed her temper to lead her so grossly to deceive Mr Beaumaris. This was a thought more bitter than all the rest, and it was only by the resolute exercise of her commonsense that she was able to regain some degree of calm. It was not to be supposed that the haughty Mr Beaumaris, related as he was to so many noble houses, so distinguished in his bearing, so much courted, and so much pursued, would ever have looked twice at a girl from a country Vicarage, with neither fortune nor connection to recommend her to his notice.

It was therefore with mixed feelings that Arabella awaited the arrival of the first guests on the appointed night. Lady Bridlington, thinking that she looked a little hagged (as well she might, after a week of such nerve-racking preparation) had tried to persuade her to allow Miss Crowle to rub a little – a *very* little! – rouge into her cheeks, but after one look at the result of this delicate operation Arabella had washed it away, declaring that never would she employ such aids to beauty as must, could he but see them, destroy for ever Papa's affection for his eldest daughter. Lady Bridlington pointed out, very reasonably, that there could be no fear of Papa's seeing them, but as Arabella remained adamant, and showed alarming signs of being about to burst into tears, she pressed her no more, consoling herself with the reflection that even without her usual blooming colour her goddaughter could not fail to appear lovely in the exquisite gown of Mme Dumaine's making.

One cause at least for satisfaction was granted to Arabella: although some guests might arrive early, and leave betimes to attend another function; others walk in past two o'clock, having relegated Lady Bridlington's ball to the third place on their list of the evening's engagements, so that the ball was rendered chaotic by the constant comings and goings, and Park Street echoed hideously for hours to the shouts of My lord's carriage! or My lady's chair! and heated police-officers quarrelled with vociferous link-boys, and chairmen exchanged insults with coachmen, Bertram arrived punctually at ten o'clock, and nobly remained throughout the proceedings.

He had recklessly ordered an evening dress from the obliging Mr Swindon, rightly deeming the simple garments he had brought with him from Heythram quite inadequate to the occasion. Mr Swindon had done well by him, and when Arabella saw him mount the stairway between the banks of flowers which she had helped all day to revive by frequent sprinklings of water, her heart swelled with pride in his appearance. His dark blue coat set admirably across his shoulders; his satin knee-breeches showed scarcely a crease; and nothing could have been more chaste than his stockings or his waistcoat. With his dark, curly locks rigorously brushed into the fashionable Brutus, his handsome, aquiline countenance interestingly pale from the nervousness natural to a young gentleman attending his first *ton* party, he looked almost as distinguished as the Nonpareil himself. Arabella, fleetingly clasping his hand, bestowed on him so speaking a look of admiration that he was betrayed into a grin so boyish and attractive as to cause another early arrival to demand of her companion, who was that handsome boy?

Emboldened by the intensive coaching of a noted French dancing-master, whom he had found the time to visit, he claimed his sister's hand for the first waltz, and, being a graceful youth, taught by the athletic sports at Harrow to move with precision and a complete control over his limbs, acquitted himself so well that Arabella was moved to exclaim: 'Oh, Bertram, how elegantly you dance! Do, pray, let us make up a set for the quadrille, and dance together in it!'

This, however, he did not feel himself capable of doing. It was true that he had acquired the rudiments of the more simple steps, but he doubted his ability to go through the *grande ronde* or the *pas de zéphyr* without muffing these figures. Gazing up into his face, it occurred to Arabella that he too was looking a trifle hagged. She anxiously asked him if he were quite well, and he assured her that he had never been better in his life, very creditably refraining from confiding to her that his adventurous career had made so deep a hole in his purse that the question of how he was to meet his liabilities had been causing him some sleepless nights. Since she had not seen him since a furtive assignation in the Mall one morning, under the vague chaperonage of the nursemaids who aired their charges there, and bought glasses of milk for them, fresh from the cows that lent so rural an air to the scene, she could not but feel uneasy about him. The faint rakishness that now hung about him did nothing to allay her fears, and she rather unjustly blamed Mr Scunthorpe for setting his feet upon a path Papa would certainly not have wished him to tread. She had formed no very favourable opinion of Mr Scunthorpe, and, with the praiseworthy notion of introducing Bertram into better company, made him known to one of the most disinterested of her admirers, young Lord Wivenhoe, heir to an affluent Earldom, and known to the greater part of London as Chuffy Wivenhoe, an affectionate sobriquet earned for him by his round, good-humoured countenance. This lively young nobleman, although he had not so far offered for her hand, formed one of Arabella's court, and was one of her favourites, being blessed with ingenuous manners and an overflowing friendliness. She introduced Bertram to him with the best of intentions, but had she known that the engaging Chuffy had been reared by a misguided parent according to the principles laid down by the late Mr Fox's father, she might have refrained from so doing. In spite of every evidence to disprove them, the Earl of Chalgrove held Lord Holland's maxims in high esteem, and blandly encouraged his heir to indulge in every extravagance that captured his erratic fancy, discharging his gaming-debts as cheerfully as he discharged the bills that poured in from his tailor, his coachbuilder, his hatter, and a host of other tradesmen who enjoyed his patronage.

The two young gentlemen took an instant liking to one another. Lord Wivenhoe was some years Bertram's senior, but his mind was as youthful as his countenance, whereas Bertram's aquiline features, and superiority of intellectual attainment, added several years to his true age. They found themselves with much in common, and before they had enjoyed one another's society for more than a very few minutes had arranged to go together to a forthcoming race-meeting.

Meanwhile, Miss Tallant's pleasure in dancing with her young friend from Yorkshire had not passed unnoticed. Gloom was struck into several hearts that had cherished hopes of winning the heiress, for not the most sanguine amongst her suitors could persuade himself that she had ever smiled up into his face with such unshadowed affection as she bestowed upon Bertram, or had talked so much or so confidentially to him. It struck that acute observer, Mr Warkworth, that there was an elusive resemblance between the pair. He mentioned the matter to Lord Fleetwood, who had been so fortunate as to secure the promise of Arabella's hand for the quadrille, and was being incorrigibly blind to the claims of the less well-favoured damsels who had not been solicited to waltz, and were consequently chatting animatedly together in gilt chairs placed round the walls of the ballroom.

Lord Fleetwood stared hard at the Tallants for a minute or two, but could perceive no likeness, which, indeed, existed more in an occasional expression than in their lineaments. 'No, dash it!' he said. 'The little Tallant ain't got a beak of a nose!'

Mr Warkworth acknowledged it, and excused his lapse by explaining that it was only a sudden notion he had taken into his head.

Mr Beaumaris did not arrive until after midnight, and consequently failed to secure a waltz with Arabella. He seemed to be in one of his more inaccessible moods, and, having exerted himself to say a few civil things to his hostess, to dance once with a lady to whom she presented him, and once with his cousin, Lady Wainfleet, occupied himself in strolling through the various saloons, talking languidly to acquaintances, and surveying the company through his quizzing-glass with a faintly bored air. After about half-an-hour, when two sets were forming for a country-dance, he went in search of Arabella, who had disappeared from the ballroom in the direction of the conservatory, at the end of the last dance, accompanied by Mr Epworth, who protested that there had never been such a jam in the history of London balls, and offered to procure her a cooling glass of lemonade. Whether he redeemed this promise or not, Mr Beaumaris never knew, but when he walked into the conservatory a few minutes later, it was to find Arabella shrinking back in a chair in a state of the greatest discomfort, and trying to disengage her hands from the fervent clasp of Mr

Epworth, romantically on his knees before her. Everyone else having left the conservatory to take their places in the new sets, the enterprising Mr Epworth, fortified by liberal doses of Lord Bridlington's champagne, had seized the opportunity once more to press his suit upon the heiress. Mr Beaumaris entered in time to hear her utter in a tone of distress: 'Oh, pray do not! Mr Epworth, I implore you, get up! I am very much obliged to you, but I shall never, never change my mind! It is ungentlemanly of you to tease me like this!'

'Do try not to be such a dead bore, Epworth!' said Mr Beaumaris, with his usual sangfroid. 'I came to ask you if you would stand up with me for the next dance, Miss Tallant.'

She was blushing furiously, and returned rather an incoherent answer. Mr Epworth, considerably mortified at having been found in such a posture by one whose contempt he dreaded, got to his feet, muttered something about taking his leave, and left the conservatory. Mr Beaumaris, taking her fan from Arabella's hand, unfurled it, and began gently to wave it beside her heated countenance. 'How many times has he proposed to you?' he enquired conversably. 'How very ridiculous he looked, to be sure!'

She was obliged to laugh, but said warmly: 'He is the most odious little man, and seems to think he has only to persevere to make me receive his advances with complaisance!'

'You must make allowances for him,' said Mr Beaumaris. 'If he did not believe you to be a wealthy woman he would cease to trouble you.'

Her bosom swelled; she said in a low, shaking voice: 'Had it not been for *you*, sir, he would never have known it!'

He was silent, as much from disappointment as from the rueful knowledge that although Fleetwood's had been the tongue which had spread the rumour, it had been his own idly malicious words which had convinced Fleetwood of the truth of Arabella's claim.

After a moment, she said in a subdued tone: 'Shall we take our places in the set?'

'No, the numbers must by now be made up,' he replied, continuing to fan her.

'Oh! Well – well, perhaps we should go back into the ballroom, at all events!'

'Don't be alarmed!' said Mr Beaumaris, with a touch of asperity. 'I have not the smallest intention of embarrassing you by kneeling at your feet!'

Her colour rushed up again; she turned away her head in confusion, her lip slightly trembling. Mr Beaumaris shut the fan, and gave it back to her. He said gently: 'I am not, I hope, such a coxcomb as to distress you by repeated solicitations, Miss Tallant, but you may believe that I am still of the same mind as I was when I made you an offer. If your sentiments should undergo a change, one word – one look! – would be sufficient to apprise me of it.' She lifted her hand in a gesture imploring his silence. 'Very well,' he said. 'I shall say no more on that head. But if you should stand in need of a friend at any time, let me assure you that you may depend upon me.'

These words, delivered, as they were, in a more earnest tone than she had yet heard him use, almost made her heart stand still. She was tempted to take the risk of confessing the truth; hesitated, as the dread of seeing his expression change from admiration to disgust took possession of her; turned her eyes towards him; and then hurriedly rose to her feet, as another couple entered the conservatory. The moment was lost; she had time not only to recollect what might be the consequences if Mr Beaumaris treated her second confidence with no more respect than he had treated her first; but also to recall every warning she had received of the danger of trusting him too far. Her heart told her that she might do so, but her scared brain recoiled from the taking of any step that might lead to exposure, and to disgrace.

She went back into the ballroom with him; he relinquished her to Sir Geoffrey Morecambe, who came up to claim her; and within a very few minutes had taken leave of his hostess, and left the party.

Thirteen

*B*ertram's acquaintance with Lord Wivenhoe prospered rapidly. After a day spent together at the races, each was so well pleased with the other that further assignations were made. Lord Wivenhoe did not trouble to enquire into his new friend's age, and Bertram naturally did not confess that he was only just eighteen years old. Wivenhoe drove him to Epsom in his curricle, with a pair of dashing bays harnessed in the bar, and finding that Bertram was knowledgeable on the subject of horseflesh, good-naturedly offered to hand over the ribbons to him. So well did Bertram handle the pair, and at such a spanking pace did he drive them, showing excellent judgement in the feathering of his corners, and catching the thong of his whip just as the Squire had taught him, that he needed no other passport to Wivenhoe's favour. Any man who could control the kind of prime cattle his lordship liked must be a capital fellow. When he could do so without abating his cheerful conversation he was clearly a right 'un, at home to a peg, and worthy of the highest regard. After some very interesting exchanges of reminiscences about incurable millers, roarers, lungers, half-bred blood-cattle, gingers, and slugs, which led inevitably to still more interesting stories of the chase, during the course of which both gentlemen found themselves perfectly in accord in their contempt of such ignoble persons as roadsters and skirters, and their conviction that the soundest of all maxims was, Get over the ground if it breaks your neck, formality was at an end between them, and his lordship was not only begging Bertram to call him Chuffy, as everyone else did, but promising to show him some of the rarer sights in town.

Bertram's fortunes, ever since he had come to London, had fluctuated in a bewildering manner. His first lucky evening with what he had swiftly learnt to refer to as St Hugh's Bones had started him off on a career that seriously alarmed his staider friend, Mr Scunthorpe. He had been encouraged by his luck to order a great many things from the various shops and warehouses where Mr Scunthorpe was known, and although a hat from Baxter's, a pair of boots from Hoby's, a seal from Rundell and Bridge, and a number of trifling purchases, such as a walking cane, a pair of gloves, some neckcloths, and some pomade for his hair were none of them really expensive, he had discovered, with a slight shock, that when added together they reached rather an alarming total. There was also his bill at the inn to be taken into account, but since this had not so far been presented he was able to relegate it to the very back of his mind.

The success of that first evening's play had not been repeated: in fact, upon the occasion of his second visit to the discreet house in Pall Mall he had been a substantial loser, and had been obliged to acknowledge that there might have been some truth in Mr Scunthorpe's dark warning. He was quite shrewd enough to realise that he had been a pigeon amongst hawks, but he was inclined to think that the experience would prove of immense value to him, since he was not one to be twice caught with the same lure. Playing billiards with Mr Scunthorpe at the Royal Saloon, he was approached by an affable Irishman, who applauded his play, and offered to set him a main or two, or to accompany him to a snug little ken where a penchant for faro, or rouge-et-noir, could be enjoyed. It was quite unnecessary for Mr Scunthorpe to whisper in his ear that this was a nibble from an ivory-turner: Bertram had no intention of going with the plausible Irishman, had scented a decoy the moment he saw him, and was very well-pleased with himself for being no longer a flat, but, on the contrary, a damned knowing one. A pleasantly convivial evening at Mr Scunthorpe's lodging, with several rubbers of whist to follow an excellent dinner, convinced him that he had a natural aptitude for cards, a belief that was by no means shaken by the vicissitudes of fortune which followed this initiation. It would be foolish, of course, to frequent gaming-hells, but once a man had made friends in town there were plenty of unexceptionable places where he could enjoy every form of gaming, from whist to roulette. On the whole, he rather thought he was lucky at the tables. He was quite sure that he was lucky on the Turf, for he had several very good days. It began to be a regular habit with him to look in at Tattersall's, to watch how the sporting men bet their money there, and sometimes to copy them, in his modest way, or at others to back his own choice. When he became intimate with Chuffy Wivenhoe, he accompanied him often, either to advise him on the purchase of a prad, to watch some ruined man's breakdowns being sold, or to lay out his blunt on a forthcoming race. Once he had fallen into the way of going with Wivenhoe it was impossible to resist spending a guinea for the privilege of being made free of the subscription-room; and once the very safe man whom his lordship patronised saw the company he kept it was no longer necessary for him to do more than record his bets, just as the Bloods did, and wait for settling-day either to receive his gains, or to pay his losses. It was all so pleasant, and every day was so full of excitement, that it went to his head, and if he was sometimes seized by panic, and felt himself to be careering along at a pace he could no longer control, such frightening moments could not endure when Chuffy was summoning him to come and try the paces of a capital goer, or Jack Carnaby carrying him off to the theatre, or the Fives-court, or the Daffy Club. None of his new friends seemed to allow pecuniary considerations to trouble them, and since they all appeared to be constantly on the brink of ruin, and yet contrived, by some fortunate bet, or throw of the dice, to come about again, he began to fall insensibly into the same way of life, and to think that it was rustic to treat a temporary insolvency as more than a matter for jest. It did not occur to him that the tradesmen who apparently gave Wivenhoe and Scunthorpe unlimited credit would not extend the same consideration to a young man whose circumstances were unknown to them. The first hint he received of the different light in which he was regarded came in the form of a horrifying bill from Mr Swindon. He could not believe at first that he could possibly have spent so much money on two suits of clothes and an overcoat, but there did not seem to be any disputing Mr Swindon's figures. He asked Mr Scunthorpe, in an airy way, what he did if he could not meet his tailor's account. Mr Scunthorpe replied simply that he instantly ordered a new rig-out, but however much Bertram had been swept off his feet he retained enough native shrewdness to know that this expedient would not answer in his case. He tried to get rid of a very unpleasant feeling at the pit of his stomach by telling himself that no tailor expected to be paid immediately, but Mr Swindon did not seem to be conversant with this rule. After a week he presented his bill a second time, accompanied by a courteous letter indicating that he would be much obliged by an early settlement of his account. And then, as though they had been in collusion with Mr Swindon, other tradesmen began to send in their bills, so that in less than no time one of the drawers in the dressing-table in Bertram's bedroom was stuffed with them. He managed to pay some of them, which made him feel much easier, but just as he was convincing himself that with the aid of a judicious bet, or a short run of luck, he would be able to clear himself from debt altogether, a polite but implacable gentleman called to see him, waited a good hour for him to come in from a ride in the Park, and then presented him with a bill which he said he knew had been overlooked. Bertram managed to get rid of him, but only by giving him some money on account, which he could ill-spare, and after an argument which he suspected was being listened to by the waiter hovering round the coffee-room door. This fear was shortly confirmed by the landlord's sending up his account with the Red Lion next morning. Matters were becoming desperate, and only one way of averting disaster suggested itself to Bertram. It was all very well for Mr Scunthorpe to advise against racing and gaming: what Mr Scunthorpe did not understand was that merely to abstain from these pastimes would in no way solve the difficulty. If Mr Scunthorpe found himself at Point Non Plus he had trustees who, however much they might rate him, would certainly come to his rescue. It was quite unthinkable that Bertram should appeal to his father for assistance: he would rather, he thought, cut his throat, for not only did the very thought of laying such a collection of bills before the Vicar appal him, but he knew very well that the settlement of them must seriously embarrass his father. Nor would it any longer be of any use to sell his watch, or that seal he had bought, or the fob that hung beside it from his waistband: in some inexplicable way his expenses seemed to have been growing ever larger since he had begun to frequent the company of men of fashion. A vague, and rather dubious notion of visiting a moneylender was vetoed by Mr Scunthorpe, who told him that since the penalties attached to the lending of money at interest to minors were severe, not even Jew King could be induced to advance the smallest sum to a distressed client under age. He added that he had once tried that himself, but that the cents-per-cent were all as sharp as needles, and seemed to smell out a fellow's age the moment they clapped eyes on him. He was concerned, though not surprised, to learn of Bertram's having got into Queer Street, and had the quarter not been so far advanced that he himself was at a standstill, he would undoubtedly have offered his friend instant relief, for he was one, his intimates asserted, who dropped his blunt like a generous fellow. Unfortunately he had no blunt to drop, and knew from past experience that an application to his trustees would result in nothing but unfeeling advice to him to rusticate at his house in Berkshire, where his Mama would welcome him with open arms. To do him justice,

Bertram would have been exceedingly reluctant to have accepted pecuniary assistance from any of his friends, since he saw no prospect, once he had returned to Yorkshire, of being able to reimburse them. There was only one way of getting clear, and that was the way of the Turf and the Table. He knew it to be hazardous, but as he could not see that it was possible for him to be in a worse case than he was already, it was worth the risk. Once he had paid his debts he rather thought that he should bring his visit to London to an end, for although he had enjoyed certain aspects of it enormously, he by no means enjoyed insolvency, and was beginning to realise that to stand continually on the edge of a financial precipice would very soon reduce him to a nervous wreck. An interview with a creditor who was not polite at all, but, on the contrary, extremely threatening, had shaken him badly: unless he made a speedy recovery it could only be a matter of days before the tipstaffs would be on his heels, even as Mr Scunthorpe had prophesied.

It was at this stage in his career that two circumstances occurred which seemed to hold out hopes of delivery. A fortunate evening playing faro for modest stakes encouraged him to think that his luck had turned again; and Chuffy Wivenhoe, earwigged by a jockey at Tattersall's, passed on to him the name of the *certain bet* thus disclosed. It really seemed as though Providence was at last aiding Bertram. It would be madness not to bet a substantial amount on the horse, for if it won he would have solved all his difficulties at one blow, and would have enough money left over to pay for his fare back to Yorkshire on the stage-coach. When Wivenhoe laid his own bet, he followed suit, and tried not to think of the predicament he would be in on settling-day if that infallible jockey had for once in his life been mistaken in his judgement.

'I'll tell you what, Bertram,' said Wivenhoe, as they strolled out of the subscription-room together, 'if you should care for it, I'll take you along with me to the Nonesuch Club tonight: all the go, y'know, and devilish exclusive, but they'll let you in if you come with me.'

'What is it?' Bertram asked.

'Oh, faro and hazard, for the most part! It was started by some of the great guns only this year, because Watier's is becoming damned flat: they say it won't last much longer – never been the same since Brummell had to run for it! The Nonesuch is devilish good sport, I can tell you. There ain't many rules, for one thing, and though most of the men bet pretty heavily, the patrons fixed the minimum stake at twenty guineas, and there's only one faro-table. What's more, it ain't a shabby business enterprise, like half the gaming-clubs, and if you want to play hazard you appoint the croupier from amongst your set, and someone will always volunteer to call the odds. None of these paid croupiers and groom-porters, which make the Great-Go more like a hotel than a social club. The whole idea is to make it a friendly affair, keep out the scaff and raff, and do away with all the rules and regulations which get to be such a dead bore! For instance, there's no damned syndicate running the faro-bank: they take it in turns, the well-breeched swells, like Beaumaris, and Long Wellesley Pole, and Golden Ball, and Petersham, and the rest of that set. Oh, it's the Pink of the Mode, I can tell you – top-of-the-trees!'

'I'd like to go with you,' Bertram said, 'only – Well, the fact is I'm none too plump in the pocket just now! Had a shocking run of luck!'

'Oh, no need to fret over that!' said his insouciant friend. 'I keep telling you it ain't like Watier's! No one cares whether you bet twenty guineas or a hundred! You come: a man's luck is bound to change if he sticks to it – one of the things my governor told me, and *he* should know!'

Bertram was undecided, but since he was already engaged to dine at Long's Hotel with Lord Wivenhoe there was no need for him to return a definite answer to the invitation until he had thought it over rather more carefully. His lordship said that he should depend upon him, and there the matter for the moment rested.

It was not to be supposed that Bertram's protracted sojourn in

London was causing his sister no anxiety. Arabella was very anxious indeed, for although she was not taken into his confidence she could not doubt, from his appearance, that he was spending money far more lavishly than the winning of a hundred pounds in a lottery justified him in doing. She seldom set eyes on him, and when they did meet she could not think that he was looking well. Late nights, unaccustomed potations, and worry, were taking their toll. But when she told him that he was looking fagged to death, and implored him to return to Yorkshire, he was able to retort with a good deal of truth that she was not particularly blooming herself. It was true. Her bright colour had faded a little, and her eyes had begun to seem a trifle large for her face, etched in, as they were, with shadows. Lord Bridlington, observing this, ascribed it to the absurd exigencies of a London season, and moralised on the folly of females with social ambitions. His mother, who had not failed to take note of the fact that her charge was no longer driving in the Park so frequently with Mr Beaumaris, and had developed a habit of evading his visits to the house, drew more correct conclusions, but failed signally to induce Arabella to confide in her. Whatever Frederick chose to say, Lady Bridlington was by this time convinced that the Nonpareil was very much in earnest, and she could not imagine what could be holding Arabella back from encouraging his advances. Divining that her reasons would be quite inexplicable to the good lady, Arabella preferred to keep her own counsel.

It had not escaped the notice of the Nonpareil that his tiresome love was not enjoying her customary good-looks and spirits, nor was it unknown to him that she had lately refused three advantageous offers of marriage, since the rejected suitors made no secret of the fact that their hopes were quite cut-up. She had excused herself from dancing with him at Almack's, but three times during the course of the evening he had been aware that her eyes were following him.

Mr Beaumaris, rhythmically drawing Ulysses' flying ear through his hand – a process which reduced Ulysses to a state of blissful idiocy – said meditatively: 'It is a melancholy reflection, is it not, that at my age I can be such a fool?'

Ulysses, his eyes half-closed, his senses swooning in ecstasy, gave a sigh which his god might, if he chose, interpret as one of sympathy.

'What if she proves to be the daughters of a tradesman?' said Mr Beaumaris. 'I do owe something to my name, you know. It might even be worse, and surely I am too old to be losing my head for a pretty face!'

Since his hand was still, Ulysses nudged him. Mr Beaumaris resumed his steady pulling of that shameful ear, but said: 'You are quite right: it is not her pretty face. Do you believe her to be entirely indifferent to me? Is she really afraid to confess the truth to me? She must not be – no, Ulysses, she must not be! Let us look on the darker side! Is she ambitious to acquire a title? If that is so, why, then, has she sent poor Charles to the rightabout? You believe her to be aiming higher? But she cannot suppose that Witney will come up to scratch! Nor do I think that your suspicions are correct, Ulysses.'

Ulysses, catching the note of severity in his voice, cocked an anxious eye at him. Mr Beaumaris took his muzzle in his hand, and gently shook it. 'What do you advise me to do?' he asked. 'It appears to me that I have reached Point Non Plus. Should I –' He broke off, and rose suddenly to his feet, and took a turn about the room. 'What a saphead I am!' he said. 'Of course! Ulysses, your master is a fool!' Ulysses jumped up to place his forepaws against those elegant pantaloons, and uttered a protesting bark. All this walking about the room, when Mr Beaumaris might have been better employed, was not at all to his taste. 'Down!' commanded Mr Beaumaris. 'How many more times am I to request you not to sully the purity of my garments by scrabbling at them with your ignoble, and probably dirty, paws? Ulysses, I shall be leaving you for a space!'

Ulysses might find this a little beyond him, but he fully understood that his hour of bliss was at an end, and so lay down in an attitude of resignation. Mr Beaumaris's subsequent actions filled him with vague disquiet, for although he was unacquainted with the significance of portmateaux, some instinct warned him that they boded no good to little dogs. But these inchoate fears were as nothing when compared to the astonishment, chagrin, and dismay suffered by that peerless gentleman's gentleman, Mr Painswick, when he apprehended that his employer proposed to leave town without the support and expert ministration of a valet whom every Tulip of Fashion has at one time or another attempted to suborn from his service. He had accepted with equanimity the information that his master was going out of town for perhaps as much as a week, and was already laying out, in his mind, the raiment suitable for a sojourn at Wigan Park, or Woburn Abbey, or Belvoir, or perhaps Cheveley, when the full horror of the event burst upon him. 'Put up enough shirts and neckcloths to last me for seven days,' said Mr Beaumaris. 'I'll travel in riding-dress, but you may as well pack the clothes I have on, in case I should need them. I shan't take you with me.'

It took a full minute for the sense of his pronouncement to penetrate to the mind of his valet. He was shocked, and could only gaze at Mr Beaumaris in stupefaction.

'Tell 'em to have my travelling-chaise, and the bays, at the door by six o'clock,' said Mr Beaumaris. 'Clayton can accompany me for the first couple of stages, and bring the horses home.'

Mr Painswick found his voice. 'Did I understand you to say, sir, that you would not be requiring Me?' he asked.

'You did,' responded Mr Beaumaris.

'May I enquire, sir, who then is to wait upon you?' demanded Mr Painswick, in a voice of ominous quiet.

'I am going to wait upon myself,' replied Mr Beaumaris.

Mr Painswick accorded this attempt at humour the perfunctory smile it deserved. 'Indeed, sir? And who, if you please, will press your coat for you?'

'I suppose they are accustomed to pressing coats at the posting-houses,' said Mr Beaumaris indifferently.

'If you can call it pressing,' said Mr Painswick darkly. 'Whether you will be pleased with the result, sir, is, if I may be permitted to say so, Another Matter.'

Mr Beaumaris then said something so shocking that it gave his henchman, as he afterwards reported to Brough, a Very nasty Spasm. 'I daresay I shan't,' he said, 'but it won't signify.'

Mr Painswick looked searchingly at him. He did not bear the appearance of one bordering on delirium, but there could be little doubt that his case was serious. Mr Painswick spoke in the tone of one soothing a refractory patient. 'I think, sir, it will be best for me to accompany you.'

'I have already told you that I don't need you. You may have a holiday.'

'I should not, sir, have the Heart to enjoy it,' returned Mr Painswick, who invariably spent his holidays in indulging nightmarish visions of his understudy's sending Mr Beaumaris forth with his clothes improperly brushed, his boots dulled by neglect, or, worst of all, a speck of mud on the skirts of his driving-coat. 'If I may say so without offence, sir, you cannot Go Alone!'

'And if *I* may say so without offence, Painswick,' retorted Mr Beaumaris, 'you are being foolish beyond permission! I will readily own that you keep my clothes in excellent order – I should not continue to bear with you, if you did not – and that the secret of imparting a gloss to my Hessians, which you so jealously guard, makes you not wholly undeserving of the extortionate wage I pay you; but if you imagine that I am unable to dress myself creditably without your assistance, your powers of self-deception must be greater than even I was aware of! Upon occasion – and merely to reward you! – I have permitted you to shave me: I allow you to help me into my coats, and to hand me my neckcloth. But at no time, Painswick, have I allowed you to dictate to me what I should wear, to brush my hair, or to utter a word – a sound! – while I am engaged in arranging that neckcloth! I shall do very well without you. But you must put up enough neckcloths to allow for some failures.'

Mr Painswick swallowed these insults, but tried one last, desperate throw. 'Your Boots, sir! You will never use a *jack*!'

'Certainly not,' said Mr Beaumaris. 'Some menial shall pull them off for me.'

Mr Painswick gave a groan. 'With greasy hands, sir! And only I know what it means to get a thumb-mark off your Hessians!'

'He shall handle them through gloves,' promised Mr Beaumaris. 'You need not lay out my knee-breeches: I am going to the Nonesuch Club tonight.' He added, possibly to atone for his harshness: 'Don't wait up for me, but call me at five o'clock tomorrow morning!'

Mr Painswick responded in a voice trembling with suppressed passion: 'If, sir, you choose to dispense with my services upon your journey, I am sure it is not for me to utter a word of criticism, nor would I so far demean myself as to remonstrate with you, whatever my feelings may be. But retire from my post before I have put you to bed, sir, and removed your raiment for proper attention, nothing will prevail upon me to do!'

'As you please,' said Mr Beaumaris, unmoved. 'Far be it from me to interfere in your determination to become a martyr in my cause!'

Mr Painswick could only throw him a look of searing reproach, being, as he afterwards confided to Brough, unable to trust himself to say more. It had been Touch and Go with him, he said, whether he remained another day in the service of one so lost to the sense of what was due to himself and his valet. Brough, who was perfectly well-aware that wild horses would not have parted his colleague from Mr Beaumaris, sympathised in suitable terms, and produced a bottle of Mr Beaumaris's second-best port. The healing properties of port, when mixed with a judicious quantity of gin, soon exercised a beneficial effect upon Mr Painswick's wounded feelings, and remarking that there was nothing like a glass of flesh-and-blood for setting a man up, he settled down to discuss with his crony and rival all the possible reasons that might be supposed to underlie Mr Beaumaris's rash and unbecoming conduct.

Mr Beaumaris, meanwhile, after dining at Brooks's, strolled across St James's Street towards Ryder Street, where the Nonesuch Club was established. Thus it was that when, rather later in the evening, Bertram Tallant entered the faro-room under the protective chaperonage of Lord Wivenhoe, Mr Beaumaris was afforded an excellent opportunity of estimating in just what manner Miss Tallant's enterprising young relative had been spending his time in London.

Two circumstances had decided Bertram in favour of visiting the Nonesuch Club. The first was the news that that sure winner, Fear-not-Victorious, had been unplaced in his race; the second the discovery of twenty-pound bill amongst the tangle of accounts in the dressing-table. Bertram had seat staring at it quite numbly for some minutes, not even wondering how he had come to mislay it. He had suffered a terrible shock, for he had argued himself into believing that Fear-not-Victorious was bound to win, and had not seriously considered how he was to meet his creditor at Tattersall's on Monday if the animal were unplaced. The utter impossibility of meeting him at all burst upon him with shattering effect, so that he felt sick with apprehension, and could see nothing but a hideous vision of the Fleet Prison, where he would no doubt languish for the rest of his days, since it did not appear to him that his father could be expected to do more for so depraved a son than to expunge his name from the family tree, and forbid all mention of him at the Vicarage.

Rendered reckless by this last, and most crushing blow, he rang the bell for the waiter, and demanded a bottle of brandy. It was then borne in upon him that orders had been issued in the tap not to supply him with any liquor for which he did not put down his blunt. Flushing darkly, he drove his hand into his breeches' pocket, and dragged out his last remaining handful of coins. Throwing one of these on the table, he said: 'Fetch it, damn you! – and you may keep the change!'

This gesture a little relieved his feelings, and the first glass of brandy, tossed at one gulp down his throat, had a still more heartening effect upon him. He looked again at the twenty-pound bill, still clasped between his fingers. He remembered that Chuffy had named twenty pounds as the minimum stake permitted to punters at the Nonesuch. Such a coincidence was surely too marked to be ignored. The second glass of brandy convinced him that here in his hand lay his last chance of saving himself from irretrievable ruin and disgrace.

Not being accustomed to drinking neat brandy, he was obliged before setting out for Long's Hotel to swallow a damper in the form of a glass of porter. This had a sobering effect and the walk through the streets to Long's put him in tolerable shape to do justice to *maintenon* cutlets, and the hotel's famed Queensbury hock. He had made up his mind to be guided by Fate. He would lay down his twenty guineas upon a card chosen at random from the livret: if it turned up, he would take it for a sign that his luck had changed at last, and play on until he had covered all his debts; if he lost, he would be very little worse off than he was already, and could, at the worst, cut his throat, he supposed.

When he and Lord Wivenhoe entered the faro-room at the Nonesuch, Mr Beaumaris, holding the bank, had just completed a deal, and had tossed the pack on to the floor. He raised his eyes, as a waiter laid a fresh pack before him, and looked straight across to the door. The lure of hazard had drawn all but one other of the club's doyens from the room, and that one, Lord Petersham, was lost in one of his fits of deep abstraction.

Damn Petersham! Thought Mr Beaumaris, on the horns of a dilemma. Why must he choose this of all moments to dream of tea?

That amiable but vague peer, perceiving Lord Wivenhoe, smiled upon him with the doubtful air of one who seemed to recollect seeing his face before. If he took notice of a youthful stranger within the sacred precincts of the club, he gave no sign of it. Mr Warkworth stared very hard at Bertram, and then glanced towards the head of the table. Lord Fleetwood, filling his glass, frowned, and also looked to the Nonpareil.

Mr Beaumaris gave an order to the waiter to bring him another bottle of burgundy. One blighting word from him, and the stranger would have nothing to do but bow himself out with what dignity he could muster. There was the rub: the boy would be unbearably humiliated, and one could not trust that young fool, Wivenhoe, to smooth over the rebuff. He would be far more likely to kick up a dust over the exclusion of one his friends, placing the unhappy Bertram in a small more intolerable position.

Lord Wivenhoe, finding places for himself and Bertram at the table, was casually making Bertram known to his neighbours. One of these was Fleetwood, who favoured Bertram with a curt nod, and again looked under his brows at the Nonpareil; the other, like most of the men in the room, was content to accept any friend of Chuffy's without question. One of the older men said something under his breath about babes and sucklings, but not loudly enough to be overheard.

Mr Beaumaris glanced round the table. 'Stakes, gentlemen,' he said calmly.

Bertram, who had changed his bill for one modest rouleau, thrust it in a quick movement towards the queen in the livrat. Other men were placing their bets; someone said something which made his neighbour laugh; Lord Petersham sighed deeply, and deliberately pushed forward several large rouleaus, and ranged them about his chosen cards; then he drew a delicately enamelled snuff-box from his pocket, and helped himself to a pinch of his latest blend. A pulse was beating so hard in Bertram's throat that it almost hurt him; he swallowed, and fixed his eyes on Mr Beaumaris's hand, poised above the pack before him.

The boy has been having some deep doings, thought Mr Beaumaris. Shouldn't wonder if he's rolled-up! What the devil possessed Chuffy Wivenhoe to being him here?

The bets were al placed; Mr Beaumaris turned up the first card, and placed it to the right of the pack.

'Scorched again!' remarked Fleetwood, one of whose bets stood by the card's counterpart.

Mr Beaumaris turned up the Carte Anglaise, and laid it down to the left of the pack. The Queen of Diamonds danced before Bertram's eyes. For a dizzy moment he could only stare at the card; the he looked up, and met Mr Beaumaris's cool gaze, and smiled waveringly. That smile told Mr Beaumaris quite as much as he had need to know, and did noting to increase his enjoyment of the evening ahead of him. He picked up the rake beside him, and pushed two twenty-guinea rouleaus across the table. Lord Wivenhoe called for wine for himself and his friend, and settled down to plunge with his usual recklessness.

For half-an-hour the luck ran decidedly in Bertram's favour, and Mr Beaumaris was encouraged to hope that he would rise form the table a winner. He was drinking fairly steadily, a flush of excitement in his cheeks, his eyes, glittering a little in the candlelight, fixed on the cards. Lord Wivenhoe sat cheerfully losing beside him. He was soon punting on tick, scrawling his vowels, and tossing them over to the bank. Other men, Bertram noticed, did the same. There was quite a pile of paper before Mr Beaumaris.

The luck veered. Three times did Bertram bet heavily on the bank's card. He was let with only two rouleaus, and staked them both, sure that the bank could not win his money four times in succession. It could. To his own annoyance, Mr Beaumaris turned up the identical card.

From then, on, he accepted with an unmoved countenance, vowel upon vowel from Bertram. It was quite impossible to tell the boy either that he would not take his vouchers, or that he would be well-advised to go home. It was even doubtful whether Bertram would have listened to him. He was in the grip of a gamester's madness, betting recklessly, persuaded by one lucky chance that the luck smiled upon him again, convinced when he lost that ill-fortune could not last. That he had the least idea of the sum he already owed the bank, Mr Beaumaris cynically doubted.

The evening broke up rather earlier than usual, Mr Beaumaris having warned the company that he did not sit after two o'clock, and Lord Petersham sighing that he did not think he should take the bank over tonight. Wivenhoe, undaunted by his losses, said cheerfully: 'In the basket again! What do I owe, Beaumaris?'

Mr Beaumaris silently handed his vowels to him. While his lordship did rapid sums in mental addition, Bertram, the flush dying out of his cheeks, sat staring at the paper still lying in front of Mr Beaumaris. He said jerkily: 'And I?' And stretched out his hand.

'Dipped, badly dipped!' said Wivenhoe, shaking his head. 'I'll send you a draught on my bank, Beaumaris. The devil was in it tonight!'

Other men were totting up their losses; there was a noise of lighthearted conversation dining in Bertram's ears; he found that his vowels totalled six hundred pounds, a sum that seemed vast to him, almost incredible. He pulled himself together, pride coming to his rescue, and rose. He looked very white now, and ridiculously boyish, but he held his head well up, and spoke to Mr Beaumaris perfectly calmly. 'I may have to keep you waiting for a few days, sir,' he said. 'I – I have no banking accommodation in London, and must send to Yorkshire for funds!'

What do I do now? Wondered Mr Beaumaris. Tell the boy the only use I have for his vowels is as shaving-papers? No: he would enact me a Cheltenham tragedy. Besides, the fright may do him a world of good. He said: 'There is no hurry, Mr Anstey. I am going out of town tomorrow for a week, or five days. Come and see me at my house – let us say, next Thursday. Anyone will tell you my direction. Where are you putting up?'

Bertram replied mechanically: 'At the Red Lion, in the City, sir.'

'Robert!' called Fleetwood, from the other side of the room, where he was engaged in a lively argument with Mr Warkworth. 'Robert, come and bear me out! *Robert!*'

'Yes, in a moment!' Mr Beaumaris returned. He detained Bertram a moment longer. 'Don't fail!' he said. 'I shall expect to see you on Thursday.'

He judged it to be impossible to say more, for there were people all round them, and it was plain that the boy's pride would not brook a suggestion that his gaming-debts should be consigned to the flames.

But he was still frowning when he reached his house, some time later. Ulysses, gambolling and squirming before him, found that his welcome was not receiving acknowledgement, and barked at him. Mr Beaumaris bent, and patted him absentmindedly. 'Hush! I am not in the mood for these transports!' he said. 'I was right when I told you that you were not destined to be the worst of my responsibilities, was I not? I think I ought to have set the boy's mind at ease: one never knows, with boys of that age – and I didn't like the look in his face. All to pieces, I have little doubt. At the same time, I'll be damned if I'll go out again at this hour of night. A night's reflection won't hurt him.'

He picked up the branch of candles that stood upon the hall-table, and carried it into his study, and to his desk by the window. Seeing him sit down, and open the ink-standish, Ulysses indicated his sentiments by yawning loudly.' Don't let me keep you up!' said Mr Beaumaris, dipping a pen in the standish, and drawing a sheet of paper towards himself.

Ulysses cast himself on the floor with a flop, gave one or two whines, bethought him of a task left undone, and began zealously to clean his forepaws.

Mr Beaumaris wrote a few rapid lines, dusted his sheet, shook of the sand, and was just about to fold the missive, when he paused. Ulysses looked up hopefully. 'Yes, in a minute,' said Mr Beaumaris. 'If he has quite outrun the constable –' He laid down the paper, drew out a fat pocket-book from his inner pocket, and extracted from it a bill for a hundred pounds. This he folded up in his letter, sealed the whole with a wafer, and directed it. Then he rose, and to Ulysses' relief indicated that he was now ready to go to bed. Ulysses, who slept every night on the mat outside his door, and regularly, as a matter of form, challenged Painswick's right to enter that sacred apartment each morning, scampered ahead of him up the stairs. Mr Beaumaris found his valet awaiting him, his expression a nice mixture of wounded sensibility, devotion to duty, and long-suffering. He gave the sealed letter into his hand. 'See that that is delivered to a Mr Anstey, at the Red Lion, somewhere in the City, tomorrow morning,' he said curtly. 'In person!' he added.

Fourteen

Not for three days did any news of the disasters which had overtaken Bertram reach his sister. She had written to beg him to meet by the Bath Gate in the Green Park, and had sent the letter by the Penny Post. When he neither appeared at the rendezvous, nor replied to her letter, she began to be seriously alarmed, and was trying to think of a way of visiting the Red Lion without her godmother's knowledge when Mr Scunthorpe sent up his card, at three o'clock one afternoon. She desired the butler to show him into the drawing-room, and went down immediately from her bed-chamber to receive him.

It did not at once strike her that he was looking preternaturally solemn; she was too eager to learn tidings of Bertram, and went impetuously towards him wit her hand held out, exclaiming: 'I am so very glad you have called to see me, sir! I have been so much worried about my brother! Have you news of him? Oh, do not tell me he is ill?'

Mr Scunthorpe bowed, cleared his throat, and grasped her hand spasmodically. In a somewhat throaty voice he replied: 'No, ma'am. Oh, no! Not *ill*, precisely!'

Her eyes eagerly scanned his face. She now perceived that his countenance wore an expression of deep melancholy, and felt immediately sick with apprehension. She managed to say: 'Not – not – *dead?*'

'Well, no, he ain't dead,' replied Mr Scunthorpe, but hardly in a reassuring tones. 'I suppose you might say it ain't as bad as that. Though, mind you, I wouldn't say he wont' be dead, if we don't take care, because when a fellow takes to – But never mind that!'

'Never mind it?' cried Arabella, pale with a alarm. 'Oh, what can be the matter? Pray, pray tell me instantly!'

Mr Scunthorpe looked at her uneasily. 'Better have some smelling-salts,' he suggested. 'No wish to upset a lady. Nasty shock. Daresay you'd like a glass of hartshorn and water. Ring for a servant!'

'No, no, I need nothing! Pray do not! Only put me out of this agony of suspense!' Arabella implored him, clinging with both hands to the back of a chair.

Mr Scunthorpe cleared his throat again. 'Thought it best to come to you,' he said. 'Sister. Happy to be of service myself, but at a standstill. Temporary, of course, but there it is. Must tow poor Bertram out of the River Tick!'

'River?' gasped Arabella.

Mr Scunthorpe perceived that he had been misunderstood. He made haste to rectify this. 'No, no, not drowned!' he assured her. 'Swallowed a spider!'

'Bertram has swallowed a spider?' Arabella repeated, in a dazed voice.

Mr Scunthorpe nodded. 'That's it,' he said. 'Blown up at Point Non Plus. Poor fellow knocked into horse-nails!'

Arabella's head was by this time in such a whirl that she was uncertain whether her unfortunate brother had fallen into the river, or had been injured in some explosion, or was more mildly, suffering from an internal disorder. Her pulse was tumultuous; the most agitating reflections made it impossible for her to speak above a whisper. She managed to utter: 'Is he dreadfully hurt? Have they taken him to a hospital?'

'Not a case for a hospital, ma'am,' said Mr Scunthorpe. 'More likely to be screwed up.'

This pronouncement, conjuring up the most horrid vision of a coffin, almost deprived Arabella of her senses. Her eyes started at Mr Scunthorpe in a look of painful enquiry. 'Screwed up?' she repeated faintly.

'The Fleet,' corroborated Mr Scunthorpe, sadly shaking his head. 'Told him how it would be. Wouldn't listen. Mind, if the thing had come off right, he could have paid down his dust, and no harm done. Trouble was, it didn't. Very rarely does, if you ask me.'

The gist of this speech, gradually penetrating to Arabella's understanding, brought some of the colour back to her face. She sank into a chair, her legs trembling violently, and said. 'Do you mean he is in *debt?*'

Mr Scunthorpe looked at her in mild surprise. 'Told you so, ma'am!' he pointed out.

'Good God, how could I possibly guess –? Oh, I have been so afraid that something of the sort must happen! Thank you for coming to me, sir! You did very right!'

Mr Scunthorpe blushed. 'Always happy to be of service!'

'I must go to him!' Arabella said. 'Will you be so kind as to escort me? I do not care to take my maid on such an errand, and I think perhaps I should not go alone.'

'No, wouldn't do at all,' Mr Scunthorpe agreed. But better not go, ma'am! Not the thing for you. Delicate female – shabby neighbourhood! Take a message.'

'Nonsense! Do you think I have never been to the City? Only wait until I have fetched a bonnet, and a shawl! We may tack a hackney, and be there before Lady Bridlington comes downstairs.'

'Yes, but – Fact is, ma'am, he ain't at the Red Lion!' said Mr Scunthorpe, much disturbed.

She had sprung up from her chair, but at this she paused. 'Not? But how is this? Why has he left the inn?'

'Couldn't pay his shot,' explained Mr Scunthorpe apologetically. 'Left his watch. Silly thing to do. Might have come in useful.'

'Oh!' she cried out, horror in her voice. 'Is it as bad as *that?*'

'Worse!' said Mr Scunthorpe gloomily. 'Got queered sporting his blunt on the table. Only hadn't enough blunt. Took to signing vowels, and ran aground.'

'*Gaming!*' Arabella breathed, in a shocked voice.

'Faro,' said Mr Scunthorpe. 'Mind, no question of any Greeking transactions! No fuzzing, or handling the concavesuit! Not but what it makes it worse, because a fellow has to be dashed particular in all matters of play and pay, if he goes to the Nonesuch. All the go, I assure you: Corinthian club – best of good *ton*! They play devilish huge there – above my touch!'

'Then it was not you who took him to such a place!'

'Couldn't have been,' said Mr Scunthorpe simply. 'Not a member. Chuffy Wivenhoe.'

'Lord Wivenhoe! Oh, what a fool I have been!' cried Arabella. 'It was I who made him known to Lord Wivenhoe!'

'Pity,' said Mr Scunthorpe, shaking his head.

'But how wicked of him to have led Bertram to such a place! Oh, how could he have done so? I had no suspicion – I thought him so agreeable, and gentlemanlike –!'

'Polite to a point,' agreed Mr Scunthorpe. 'Very good sort of a man: very well-liked. Daresay he did it for the best.'

'How could he think so?' Arabella said hotly.

'Very exclusive club,' he pointed out.

She said impatiently. 'It is of no use for us to argue on that head. Where is Bertram?'

'Don't think you'd know the place, ma'am. It's – it's near Westminster!'

'Very well, let us go there at once!'

In considerable agitation, Mr Scunthorpe said: 'No, dash it! Can't take a lady to Willow Walk! You don't quite understand, ma'am! Poor Bertram – couldn't pay his shot – not a meg on him – duns in his pocket – tipstaffs after him – had to give 'em all the bag! Can't quite make out exactly how it was, but think he must have gone back to the Red Lion when he left the nonesuch, because he has his portmanteau with him. Seems to have bolted for it to Tothill Fields. Very low back-slum, ma'am. Silly fellow ought to have come and knocked me up – happy to have given him my sofa!'

'Good God, why did he not?'

225

He coughed in an embarrassed way. 'Might have been a little bit on the go,' he said diffidently. 'Scared of being pounded by the tipstaffs, too. Come to think of it, might easily be if he stayed with me. Dashed tradesmen know he's a friend of mine! At all events, ha ain't with me – didn't send me word where he was till this morning – feeling too blue-devilled, I daresay. Don't blame him: would myself!'

'Oh, poor Bertram, poor Bertram!' she cried, wringing her hands. 'I do not care where he is, see him I must, if I have to go to this Willow Walk alone!'

'Good God, ma'am, mustn't do that!' he exclaimed, appalled. 'Very rough set of coves in Willow Walk! Besides –' He paused, looking acutely uncomfortable. 'Not quite himself!'

'Oh, he must be ill with worry, and despair! Nothing would keep me from him at a such a time! I will fetch my bonnet, and we may be off directly!'

'Ma'am, he won't like it!' Mr Scunthorpe said desperately. 'Very likely be ready to murder me only for telling you! You *can't* see him!'

'Why can I not?'

'He's been in the sun a trifle! You see – very understandable thing to do! – shot the cat!'

'*Shot the cat?*'

'Can't blame him!' Mr Scunthorpe pleaded. 'Wouldn't have told you, if you hadn't been so set on seeing him! Felt desperate – shot the cat – felt better – kept on swallowing balls of fire – result, looking as queer as Dick's hatband, when I saw him!'

'Do you mean that he has been drinking?' demanded Arabella. 'What, in heaven's name, is a ball of fire?'

'Brandy,' said Mr Scunthorpe. 'Devilish bad brandy too. Told him to make Blue Ruin the preferred suit. Safer.'

'Every word you say makes me the more determined to go to him!' declared Arabella.

'Assure you much better to send him some blunt, ma'am!'

'I will take him all I have, but oh, it is so little! I cannot think yet what is to be done!'

Mr Scunthorpe pointed significantly to the ceiling. 'You don't think the old lady –?' he suggested delicately.

She shook her head. 'Oh, no, no! Impossible!'

Mr Scunthorpe looked a little thoughtful. 'In that case, ma'am, better take you to him. Talking very wildly this morning. No saying what he might do.'

She almost ran to the door. 'We have not a moment to waste, then!'

'No, no!' he assured her. 'No need to be on the fret! Won't cut his throat today! Told the girl to hide his razor.'

'What girl?'

He became very much confused, blushed, and uttered: 'Girl he sent to my lodging with a message. Been looking after him.'

'Oh, God bless her!' Arabella cried fervently. 'What is her name? How much I must owe her!'

As the lady in question had introduced herself to Mr Scunthorpe as Leaky Peg, he was obliged to take refuge in prevarication, and to hope devoutly that they would not encounter her in Willow Walk. He said that he had not caught her name. Arabella seemed a little disappointed, but since this was no time for wasting over trifles she said no more, but ran out of the room to fetch her bonnet and shawl.

It was impossible for her to leave the house without the butler's being aware of it, but although he looked surprised, he made no comment, and in a few minutes' time she and Mr Scunthorpe were seated in a ramshackle hackney coach, which seemed as though, many years before, it had formed part of a nobleman's equipage, but which had fallen into sad decay. The coverings to the seats and the squabs were tattered and dirty, and the vehicle smelled strongly of beer and old leather. These evils Arabella scarcely noticed, in such a turmoil was her mind. It was a struggle to support her spirits at all; she felt ready to sink; and was unable, while in such a state of agitation, to form any plan for Bertram's relief. The only solution which had so far presented itself to her mind was an instinctive impulse, no sooner thought of than recoiled from, to send off an express to Heythram. Mr

Scunthorpe's suggestion of applying to Lady Bridlington she well knew to be useless, nor would her pride tolerate the putting of herself under such added obligation to her godmother. Wild notions of selling Mama's diamonds, and the pearl necklet that had belong to Grandmama Tallant, could not, she knew, be entertained, for these trinkets were not hers to dispose of at will.

Beside her, Mr Scunthorpe, feeling vaguely that her spirits required support, tried to entertain her by pointing out, conscientiously, the various places of interest the hackney drove past. She scarcely heeded him, but when they reached Westminster, began to look about her a little, insensibly cheered by the respectability of the neighbourhood. But the hackney lumbered on, and in a surprisingly short space of time it was hard to realise that she must be within a stone's throw of the Abbey, so squalid were her surroundings. An unlucky attempt made by Mr Scunthorpe to divert her, by pointing out an ugly brick structure which he said was the Tothill Fields Bridewell, made her shudder so alarmingly that he hastily informed her that it was so crammed to overflowing with felons that there was no room for another soul behind its walls. A row of squat, almshouses was the next object of interest to be seen. This was followed by a charity school, but the district seemed to Arabella to be largely composed of wretched hovels, ancient mansions, fallen into depressing decay, and a superfluity of taverns. Frowsy looking women stood in the doorways of some of the hovels; half-naked urchins turned cartwheels on the dirty cobbles, in the hope of gaining largesse from persons well-breeched enough to travel in hackney coaches; at one corner, a fat woman, seated behind an iron cauldron appeared to be dispensing tea to a curiously ill-assorted crowd of persons, ranging from bricklayers to bedisened young women; various street-cries echoed in the narrow streets, from offers of coal to entreaties for old iron; and the male population seemed to consist entirely of scavengers, sweeps, and unidentifiable persons with blue jowls, and mufflers round their necks in place of collars.

After passing the entrances to several noisome alleys, the

hackney turned into Willow Walk, and proceeded down it for some way before drawing up outside a dingy house, whose windows showed, besides fluttering oddments of washing hung out to dry, several broken panes of glass. In the open doorway, and old woman sat in a rocking-chair, puffing at a clay pipe, and engaged in conversation with a younger female, who held a squalling infant on one arm, which she from time to time shook, or refreshed from a black bottle, from which she herself took frequent pulls. Arabella had no positive knowledge of what was in that black bottle, but that it must contain strong liquor she felt convinced. The thought of Bertram was momentarily banished from her head; as Mr Scunthorpe handed her down from the hackney, and punctiliously brushed off the straws that clung to the flounce of her simple cambric dress, she opened her reticule, hunted in it for a shilling, and astonished the mother of the infant by pressing it into her hand, and saying earnestly: 'Pray buy the baby some milk! Oh, pray do not give it that horrid stuff!'

Both women stared at her with fallen jaws. The old Irishwoman, the first to regain command over her faculties, burst into a cackle of mirth, and informed her that she was talking to no less a personage than Quartern Sue. This conveyed little to Arabella, but while she was still puzzling over the appellation, Quartern Sue, recovering from her stupefaction, had launched forth into a catalogue of her embarrassments, and was holding her hand cupped suggestively. Mr Scunthorpe, beads of sweat standing upon his brow, took it upon himself to hustle his charge into the house, whispering to her that she must not get into talk with such ill-famed women. Quartern Sue, never one to let slip an opportunity, followed them, her beggar's whine rising to a crescendo, but was repulsed at the foot of a rickety, uncarpeted stairway by a strapping young woman, with a tousle of greasy yellow hair, a countenance which not all the ravages of gin had entirely deprived of comeliness, and a tawdry dress, stained in various places, and with the bodice cut so low as to reveal glimpses of dirty shift. This lady, having driven Quartern Sue forth by a series of remarks, not one of which was intelligible to

Arabella, turned and confronted the genteel visitors with a belligerent look on her face, and her arms set widely akimbo. She demanded of Mr Scunthorpe, with whom she appeared to be acquainted, what he meant by brining a flash mort to the ken. Mr Scunthorpe uttered the one word, Sister! in strangled accents, upon which the blonde beauty turned a pair of fierce, bloodshot eyes upon Arabella, and ejaculated: 'Ho! Sister, is it?'

'Girl who brought me the message!' explained Mr Scunthorpe in a blushful aside to Arabella.

The blond beauty needed no other passport to Arabella's favour. If she was conscious – as she could hardly have failed to have been – of the strong aroma of daffy which hung about the person of Leaky Peg, she gave no sign of it, but started forward, with her hands held out, and impulsive words on her lips. 'Oh, are you the girl who has been kind to my brother? You must let me thank you! I can never, never repay you! Mr Scunthorpe here has been telling me that it was you who took care of him when he – when he came to this place!'

Leaky Peg stared very hard at her for a moment, and then pugnaciously: 'I found the covey on the mop, blue as megrim, see? And him no more than a mouth! Half flash and half foolish, that's him. Strike me, I don't know what I see in the hick!'

'Miss Tallant, better come upstairs!' said the anguished Mr Scunthorpe, to whom Leaky Peg's vocabulary was rather more intelligible than to Arabella.

'You dub your mummer, you death's head on a mopstick!' Leaky peg advised him. 'Leave me and the swell mort be!' She turned back to Arabella, and said roughly: 'Lurched, ain't he? He tells me there's a fastener out after him. He hadn't so much as a meg in his truss when I come up with him in the boozing-ken. I took him along with me – strike me if I know why!' She jerked her thumb towards the stairs. 'You want to take him away: this ain't his lay, nor it ain't mine neither! Spouting a kid's mish all to buy him mutton and smash, which he don't eat! Me! You take him off; you're welcome!'

Gathering from these words that Leaky Peg had been keeping

Bertram supplied with food, Arabella, tears standing in her eyes, seized one of her hands, and pressed it fervently between both her own, saying: 'How good you are! Indeed, I thank you! He is only a boy, you know, and what must have become of him without you I dare not think!'

'Well, it's little enough I got from it!' remarked Leaky Peg caustically. 'You and him with your breakteeth words! You get up them dancers, you and that moulder alongside you that looks like a toothdrawer! First door on the right: stale-drunk, he is, but he ain't backt yet!'

With these heartening words she turned on her heel, and strode out of the house, driving before her Quartern Sue, who had had the temerity to venture on to the threshold again. Mr Scunthorpe made haste to usher Arabella up the stairs, saying reproachfully: 'Shouldn't talk to her, ma'am! Not at all the thing! Assure you!'

'The thing!' she exclaimed scornfully. 'She has a kind heart, sir!'

Abashed, Mr Scunthorpe begged pardon, and tapped at a door at the head of the stairs.

Bertram's voice sounded from within the room, and without waiting for her escort to usher her in Arabella lifted the latch and quickly entered.

The apartment, which looked out on to a filthy yard, where lean cats prowled amongst garbage-heaps, was small, rather dark, and furnished with a sagging bed pushed up against one wall, a deal table, two wooden chairs, and a strip of threadbare carpet. The remains of a loaf of bread, a heel of cheese, together with a glass, a jug, and an empty bottle stood on the table; and on the mantelshelf, presumably placed there by Leaky Peg, was a cracked mug containing a wilting bunch of flowers. Bertram, who was stretched on the bed, raised himself on his elbow as the door opened, an apprehensive look in his face. He was fully dressed, but was wearing a handkerchief knotted round his neck, and looked both ill and unkempt. When he saw Arabella, he uttered something like a sob, and struggled up, and to his feet. 'Bella!'

She was in his arms on the word, unable to prevent herself from bursting into tears, but passionately clasping him to her. His breath reeked of spirits, but although this shocked her, she did not recoil from him, but hugged him more tightly still. 'You should not have come!' he said unsteadily. 'Felix, how *could* you have brought her here?'

'Warned her she wouldn't like it,' Mr Scunthorpe excused himself. 'Very set on seeing you!'

Bertram gave a groan. 'I did not mean you to know!'

She disengaged herself, wiped her tears away, and sat down on one of the chairs. 'Bertram, you know that is nonsense!' she said. 'Whom should you turn to if not to me? I am so sorry! What you must have suffered in this dreadful house!'

'Pretty, ain't it?' he said jeeringly. 'I don't know how I came here: Leaky Peg brought me. You may as well know, Bella, I was so foxed I don't remember anything that happened after I bolted from the Red Lion!'

'No, I quite see,' she said. 'But, Bertram, pray do not go on drinking! It is all so bad, and that makes it worse! You look sadly out of sorts, and no wonder! Have you a sore throat, dearest?'

He flushed, his hand going instinctively to the handkerchief round his neck. 'This! Oh, no! Gammoning the draper, my dear!' He saw her look of bewilderment, and added, with a short laugh: 'You would be surprised at the cant I have learnt from my hosts here! I've become a spouter – at least Peg manages the business for me! Pawned, Bella, pawned! Shan't have a rag to my back soon – not that that will signify!'

Mr Scunthorpe, seated on the edge of the bed, exchanged a meaning look with Arabella. She said briskly: 'It would signify very much! We must think what is to be done. Only tell me what you owe!'

He was reluctant to divulge the sum, but she insisted, and after a little while he blurted out: 'It comes to more than seven hundred pounds! There is no possibility of my being able to get clear!'

She was aghast for she had not supposed that he could owe

232

nearly so much. The sum seemed vast beyond belief, so that she could not be surprised when Bertram, casting himself into the other chair, began to talk in a wild way of putting a period to his existence. She let him run on, guessing that his despair needed the relief of just such mad outpourings, and having no very real fear that he would put his violent threats into execution. While he talked she cudgelled her brains for a solution to his difficulties, only lending half an ear to him, but patting his hand soothingly from time to time. Mr Scunthorpe intervened at last, saying with great commonsense: 'Don't think you ought to jump into the river, dear old boy. Sister wouldn't like it. Bound to leak out. Your governor might not like it either: never can tell!'

'No, indeed!' Arabella said. 'You must not talk of it any more, Bertram. You know how wicked it would be!'

'Well, I suppose I shan't kill myself,' Bertram said, a shade sulkily. 'Only, I can tell you this: I'll never face my father with *this*!'

'No, no!' she agreed. 'Seven hundred pounds! Bertram how has it been possible?'

'I lost six hundred at faro,' he said, dropping his head in his hands. 'The rest – Well, there was the tailor, and the horse I hired, and what I owe at Tatt's, and my shot at the inn – oh, a dozen things! Bella, what am I to do?'

He sounded much more like the younger brother she knew when he spoke like that, a scared look in his face, and in his voice an unreasoning dependence on her ability to help him out of a scrape.

'Bills don't signify,' pronounced Mr Scunthorpe. 'Leave town: won't be followed. Not been living under your own name. Gaming debts another matter. Got to raise the wind for that. Debt of honour.'

'I know it, curse you!'

'But all debts are debts of honour!' Arabella said. 'Indeed, you should pay your bills first of all!'

A glance passed between the two gentlemen, indicative of their mutual agreement not to waste breath in arguing with a

233

female on a subject she would clearly never understand. Bertram passed his hand over his brow, heaving a short sigh, and saying: 'There's only one thing to be done. I have thought it all over, Bella, and I mean to enlist, under a false name. If they won't have me as a trooper, I'll join a line regiment. I should have done it yesterday, when I first thought of it, only that there's something I must do first. Affair of honour. I shall write to my father, of course, and I daresay he will utterly cast me off, but that can't be helped!'

'How can you think so?' Arabella cried hotly. 'Grieved he must be – oh, I dare not even think of it! – but you must know that never, never would he do such an unchristian thing as to cast you off! Oh, do not write to him yet! Only give me time to think what I can do! If Papa knew that you owed all that money, I am very sure he would pay ever penny of it, though it ruined him!'

'How can you suppose I would be such a gudgeon as to tell him *that*? No! I shall tell him that my whole mind is set on the army, and I had as lief start in the ranks as not!'

This speech struck far more dismay into Arabella's heart than his previous talk of committing suicide, for to take the King's shilling seemed to her a likely thing for him to do. She uttered, hardly above a whisper: 'No, no!'

'It must be, Bella,' he said. 'I'm sure the army is all I'm fit for, and I cannot show my face again with a load of debt hanging over me. Particularly a debt of honour! O God, I think I must have been mad!' His voice broke, and he could not speak for a moment. In the end he contrived to summon up the travesty of a smile, and to say: 'Pretty pair, aint' we? Not that *you* did anything as wrong as I have.'

'Oh, I have behaved so dreadfully!' she exclaimed. 'It is even my fault that you are reduced to these straits! Had I never presented you to Lord Wivenhoe –'

'That's fudge!' he said quickly. 'I had been to gaming-houses before I met him. He was not to know I wasn't as well-blunted as that set of his! I ought not to have gone with him to the Nonesuch. Only I had lost money on a race, and I thought – I hoped – Oh, talking pays no toll! But to say it was your fault is all gammon!'

'Bertram, who won your money at the Nonesuch?' she asked.

'The bank. It was faro.'

'Yes, but someone holds the bank!'

'The Nonpareil.'

She stared at him. 'Mr Beaumaris?' she gasped. He nodded. 'Oh, no, do not say so! How could he have let you – No, no, Bertram!'

'She sounded so much distressed that he was puzzled. 'Why the devil shouldn't he?'

'You are only a boy! He must have known! And to accept notes of hand from you! Surely he might have refused to do so much at least!'

'You don't understand!' he said impatiently. 'I went there with Chuffy, so why should he refuse to let me play?'

Mr Scunthorpe nodded. 'Very awkward situation, ma'am. Devilish insulting to refuse a man's vowels.'

She could not appreciate the niceties of the code evidently shared by both gentlemen, but she could accept that they must obtain in male circles. 'I must think it wrong of him,' she said. 'But never mind! The thing is that he is – that I am particularly acquainted with him! Don't be in despair, Bertram! I am persuaded that if I were to go to him, explain that you are not of age, and not a rich man's son, he will forgive the debt!'

She broke off, for there was no mistaking the expressions of shocked disapprobation in both Bertram's and Mr Scunthorpe's faces.

'Good God, Bella, what will you say next!'

'But, Bertram, indeed he is not proud and disagreeable, as so many people think him! I – I have found him particularly kind, and obliging!'

'Bella, this is a *debt of honour*! If it takes my life long to do it, I must pay it, and so I shall tell him!'

Mr Scunthorpe nodded judicial approval of this decision.

'Spend your life paying six hundred pounds to a man who is

so wealthy that I daresay he regards it no more than you would a shilling?' cried Arabella. 'Why, it is absurd!'

Bertram looked despairingly at his friend. Mr Scunthorpe said painstakingly: 'Nothing to do with it, ma'am. Debt of honour is a debt of honour. No getting away from that.'

'I cannot agree! I own, I do not like to do it, but I *could* do it, and I know he would never refuse me!'

Bertram grasped her wrist. 'Listen, Bella! I daresay you don't understand – in fact, I can see that you don't! – but if you dared to do such a thing I swear you'd never seem my face again! Besides, even if he did tear up my vowels I should still think myself under an obligation to redeem them! Next you will be suggesting that you should ask him to pay those damned tradesmen's bills for me!'

She coloured guiltily, for some such idea had just crossed her mind. Suddenly, Mr Scunthorpe, whose face a moment before had assumed a cataleptic expression, uttered three pregnant words. 'Got a notion!'

The Tallants looked anxiously at him, Bertram with hope, his sister more than a little doubtfully.

'Know what they say?' Mr Scunthorpe demanded. 'Bank always wins!'

'I know that,' said Bertram bitterly. 'If that's all you have to say –'

'Wait!' said Mr Scunthorpe. 'Start one!' He saw blank bewilderment in the two faces confronting him, and added, with a touch of impatience: 'Faro!'

'Start a faro-bank?' said Bertram incredulously. 'You must be mad! Why, even if it were not the craziest thing I ever heard of, you can't run a faro-bank without capital!'

'Thought of that,' said Mr Scunthorpe, not without pride. 'Go to my trustees. Go at once. Not a moment to be lost.'

'Good God, you don't suppose they would let you touch your capital for such a cause as that?'

'Don't see why not!' argued Mr Scunthorpe. 'Always trying to add to it. Preaching at me for ever about improving the estate!

236

Very good way of doing it: wonder they haven't thought of it for themselves. Better go and see my uncle at once.'

'Felix, you're a gudgeon!' said Bertram irritably. 'No trustee would let you do such a thing! And even if they would, good God, we neither of us want to spend our lives running a faro-bank!'

'Shouldn't have to,' said Mr Scunthorpe, sticking obstinately by his guns. 'Only want to clear you of debt! One good night's run would do it. Close the bank then.'

He was so much enamoured of this scheme that it was some time before he could be dissuaded from trying to promote it. Arabella, paying very little heed to the argument, sat wrapped in her own thoughts. That these were by no means pleasant would have been apparent, even to Mr Scunthorpe, had he been less engrossed in the championing of his own plans, for not only did her hands clench and unclench in her lap, but her face, always very expressive, betrayed her. But by the time Bertram had convinced Mr Scunthorpe that a faro-bank would not answer, she was sufficiently mistress of herself again to excite no suspicion in either gentleman's breast.

She turned her eyes towards Bertram, who had sunk back, after his animated argument, into a state of hopeless gloom. 'I shall think of something,' she said. 'I *know* I shall contrive to help you! Only please, please do not enlist, Bertram! Not yet! Only if I should fail!'

'What do you mean to do?' he demanded. 'I shan't enlist until I have seen Mr Beaumaris, and – and explained to him how it is! That I *must* do. I – I told him I had no funds in London, and should be obliged to send into Yorkshire for them, so he asked me to call at his house on Thursday. It is of no use to look at me like that, Bella! I couldn't tell him I was done-up, and had no means of paying him, with them all there, listening to what we were saying! I would have died rather! Bella, have you any money? Could you spare me enough to get my shirt back? I can't go to see the Nonpareil like this!'

She thrust her purse into his hand. 'Yes, yes of course! If only

237

I had not bought those gloves, and the shoes, and the new scarf! There are only ten guineas left, but it will be enough to make you more comfortable until I have thought how to help you, won't it? Do, do remove from this dreadful house! I saw quite a number of inns on our way, and one or two of them looked to be respectable!'

It was plain that Bertram would be only too ready to change his quarters, and after a brief dispute, in which he was very glad to be worsted, he took the purse, gave her a hug, and said that she was the best sister in the world. He asked wistfully whether she thought Lady Bridlington might be induced to advance him seven hundred pounds, on a promise of repayment over a protracted period, but although she replied cheerfully that she had no doubt that she could arrange something of the sort, he could not deceive himself into thinking it possible, and sighed. Mr Scunthorpe, prefixing his remark with one of his deprecating coughs, suggested that as the hackney had been told to wait for them, he and Miss Tallant ought, perhaps, to be taking their leave. Arabella was much inclined to go at once in search of a suitable hostelry for Bertram, but was earnestly dissuaded, Mr Scunthorpe promising to attend to this matter himself, and also to redeem Bertram's raiment from the pawnbroker's shop. The brother and sister then parted, clinging to one another in such a moving way that Mr Scunthorpe was much affected by the sight, and had to blow his nose with great violence.

Arabella's first action on reaching Park Street again was to run up to her bedchamber, and without pausing to remove her bonnet to sit down at the little table in the window, and prepare to write a letter. But in spite of the evident urgency of the matter she had no sooner written her opening words than all inspiration appeared to desert her, and she sat staring out of the window, while the ink dried on her pen. At last she drew a breath, dipped the pen in the standish again, and resolutely wrote two lines. Then she stopped, read them over, tore up the paper, and drew a fresh sheet towards her.

It was some time before she had achieved a result that satisfied her, but it was done at last, and the letter sealed up with a wafer. She then rang the bell-pull, and upon a housemaid's coming in answer to the summons desired the girl to send Becky to her, if she could be spared from her duties. When Becky presently appeared, shyly smiling and twisting her hands together in her apron, Arabella held out the letter, and said: 'If you please, Becky, do you think you could contrive to slip out, and – and carry that to Mr Beaumaris's house? You might say that I have asked you to go on an errand for me, but – but I shall be very much obliged to you if you will not disclose to anyone what it is!'

'Oh, miss!' breathed the handmaid, scenting a romance. 'As though I would say a word to a living soul!'

'Thank you! If – if Mr Beaumaris should be at home, I should be glad if you would wait for an answer to the letter!'

Becky nodded her profound understanding of this, assured Arabella that she might trust her through fire and water, and departed.

Nothing could have been more conspiratorial than her manner of entering Arabella's room half-an-hour later, but she brought bad news: Mr Beaumaris had gone into the country three days ago, and had said that he might be away from London for a week.

Fifteen

M r BEAUMARIS returned to his London house in time to partake of a late breakfast on Tuesday morning, having been absent for six days. It had been considered probable by his dependants that he would be away for a full week, but as he rarely gave any positive information on his movements, counted no cost, and had accustomed his highly-paid servants to live in a constant state of expectation of being obliged, at a moment's notice, to provide suitable entertainment for himself, or for a score of guests, his premature arrival caused no one any dismay. It caused one member of his household a degree of joy bordering on delirium. A ragged little mongrel, whose jauntily curled tail had been clipped unhappily between his legs for six interminable days, and who had spent the major part of this time curled into a ball on the rug outside his master's door, refusing all sustenance, including plates of choice viands prepared by the hands of the great M. Alphonse himself, came tumbling down the stairs, uttering canine shrieks, and summoned up enough strength to career madly round in circles before collapsing in an exhausted, panting heap at Mr Beaumaris's feet. It spoke volumes for the light in which Mr Beaumaris's whims were regarded by his retainers that the condition to which his disreputable protégé had wilfully reduced himself brought every member of the household who might have been considered in some way responsible into the hall to exonerate himself from all blame. Even M. Alphonse mounted the stairs from his basement kingdom to describe to Mr Beaumaris in detail the chicken-broth, the ragout of rabbit, the shin of beef, and the marrow-bone with which he had tried to tempt Ulysses' vanished appetite. Brough broke in on his Gallic monologue to assure Mr Beaumaris that he for one had left nothing undone to restore Ulysses' interest in life, even going to the lengths of importing a stray cat into the house, in the hope that this outrage would galvanise one notoriously unsympathetic towards all felines to activity. Painswick, with a smug air that rendered him instantly odious to his colleagues, drew attention to the fact that it had been his superior understanding of Ulysses' processes of thought which Mr Beaumaris had to thank for his finding himself still in possession of his low-born companion: he had conceived the happy notion of giving Ulysses one of Mr Beaumaris's gloves to guard.

Mr Beaumaris, who had picked Ulysses up, paid no heed to all these attempts at self-justification, but addressed himself to his adorer. 'What a fool you are!' he observed. 'No, I have the greatest dislike of having my face licked, and must request you to refrain. Quiet, Ulysses! quiet! I am grateful to you for your solicitude, but you must perceive that I am in the enjoyment of my customary good health. I would I could say the same of you. You have once more reduced yourself to skin and bone, my friend, a process which I shall take leave to inform you I consider as unjust as it is ridiculous. Anyone setting eyes on you would suppose that I grudged you even the scraps from my table!' He added, without the slightest change of voice, and without raising his eyes from the creature in his arms: 'You would also appear to have bereft by household of its senses, so that the greater part of it, instead of providing me with the breakfast I stand in need of, is engaged in excusing itself from any suspicion of blame and – I may add – doing itself no good thereby.'

Ulysses, to whom the mere sound of Mr Beaumaris's voice was ecstasy, looked adoringly up into his face, and contrived to lick the hand that was caressing him. On his servants, Mr Beaumaris's voice operated in quite another fashion: they dispersed rapidly, Painswick to lay out a complete change of raiment; Brough to set the table in the breakfast-parlour; Alphonse to carve at lightning speed several slices of a fine York ham, and to cast eggs and herbs into a pan; and various underlings to grind coffee-beans, cut bread, and set kettles on to boil. Mr Beaumaris tucked Ulysses under one arm, picked up the pile of letters from the table in the hall, and strolled with them into his library. To the zealous young footman who hastened to fling open the door for him, he said: 'Food for this abominable animal!' – a command which, relayed swiftly to the kitchen, caused M. Alphonse to command his chief assistant instantly to abandon his allotted task, and to prepare a dish calculated to revive the flagging appetite of a Cambacérès.

Mr Beaumaris, tossing a pile of invitations and bills aside, came upon a billet which had not been delivered through the medium of the Penny Post, and which was superscribed, *urgent.* The writing, certainly feminine, was unknown to him. 'Now, what have we here, Ulysses?' he said, breaking the wafer.

They had not very much. '*Dear Mr Beaumaris,*' ran the missive, *I should be very much obliged to you if you would do me the honour of calling in Park Street as soon as may be convenient to you, and requesting the butler to inform me of the event. I remain, Ever yours most sincerely, Arabella Tallant.*'

This model of the epistolary art, which had caused Miss Tallant so much heart-searching, and so many ruined sheets of hot-pressed notepaper, did not fail of its effect. Mr Beaumaris cast aside the rest of his correspondence, set Ulysses down on the floor, and bent his powerful mind to the correct interpretation of these few, heavily underlined, words. He was still engaged on this task when Brough entered the room to announce that his breakfast awaited him. He carried the letter into the parlour, and propped it against the coffee-pot, feeling that he had not yet got to the bottom of it. At his feet, Ulysses, repairing with enthusiasm the ravages of his protracted fast, was rapidly consuming a meal which might have been judged excessive for the satisfaction of the appetite of a boa-constrictor.

'This,' said Mr Beaumaris, 'was delivered here three days ago, Ulysses!'

Ulysses, whose keen olfactory sense had discovered the chicken giblets cunningly hidden in the middle of his plate, could spare no more than a perfunctory wag of the tail for this speech; and to Mr Beaumaris's subsequent demand to know what could be in the wind he returned no answer at all. Mr Beaumaris pushed away the remains of his breakfast, a gesture which was shortly to operate alarmingly on the sensibilities of the artist below stairs, and waved aside his valet, who had just entered the room. 'My town dress!' he said.

'I have it ready, sir,' responded Painswick, with dignity. 'There was just one matter which I should perhaps mention.'

'Not now,' said Mr Beaumaris, his eyes still bent upon Miss Tallant's tantalising communication.

Painswick bowed, and withdrew. The matter was not, in his fastidious estimation of sufficient importance to justify him in intruding upon his employer's evident preoccupation; nor did he broach it when Mr Beaumaris presently came upstairs to change his riding-dress for the blue coat, yellow pantaloons, chaste waistcoat, and gleaming Hessians with which he was wont to gratify the eyes of beholders in the Metropolis. This further abstention was due, however, more to the sense of irretrievable loss which had invaded his soul on the discovery that a shirt was missing from Mr Beaumaris's execrably packed portmanteau than from a respect for his master's abstraction. He confined his conversation to bitter animadversions on the morals of inn-servants, and the depths of depravity to which some unknown boots had sunk in treating Mr Beaumaris's second-best pair of Hessians with a blacking fit only to be used on the footwear of country squires. He could hardly flatter himself that Mr Beaumaris, swiftly and skilfully arranging the folds of his neckcloth in the mirror, or delicately paring his well-cared-for finger-nails, paid the least heed to his discourse, but it served in some measure to relieve his lacerated feelings.

Leaving his valet to repair the damage to his wardrobe, and his faithful admirer to sleep off the effects of a Gergantuan meal, Mr Beaumaris left the house, and walked to Park Street. Here he was met by the intelligence that my lord, my lady, and Miss Tallant had gone out in the barouche to the British Museum, where Lord Elgin's much disputed marbles were now being exhibited, in a wooden shed built for their accommodation. Mr Beaumaris thanked the butler for this information, called up a passing hackney, and directed the jarvey to drive him to Great Russell Street.

He found Miss Tallant, her disinterested gaze fixed upon a sculptured slab from the Temple of Nike Apteros, enduring a lecture from Lord Bridlington, quite in his element. It was Lady Bridlington who first perceived his tall, graceful figure advancing across the saloon, for since she had naturally seen the collection of antiquities when it was on view at Lord Elgin's residence in Park Lane, and again when it was removed to Burlington House, she felt herself to be under no obligation to look at it a third time, and was more profitably engaged in keeping a weather eye cocked for any of her acquaintances who might have elected to visit the British Museum that morning. Upon perceiving Mr Beaumaris, she exclaimed in accents of delight: 'Mr Beaumaris! What a lucky chance, to be sure! How do you do? How came you not to be at Kirkmichael's Venetian Breakfast yesterday? Such a charming party! I am persuaded you must have enjoyed it! Six hundred guests – only fancy!'

'Amongst so many, ma'am, I am flattered to know that you remarked my absence,' responded Mr Beaumaris, shaking hands. 'I have been out of town for some days, and only returned this morning. Miss Tallant! 'Servant, Bridlington!'

Arabella, who had started violently upon hearing his name uttered, and quickly turned her head, took his hand in a clasp which seemed to him slightly convulsive, and raised a pair of strained, enquiring eyes to his face. He smiled reassuringly down into them, and bent a courteous ear to Lady Bridlington, who was making haste to assure him that she had come to the

Museum merely to show the Grecian treasure to Arabella, who had not been privileged to see them on their *first* showing. Lord Bridlington, not averse from any aggrandisement to his audience, began in his consequential way to expound his views on the probable artistic value of the fragments, a recreation which would no doubt have occupied him for a considerable period of time had Mr Beaumaris not cut him short by saying, in his most languid way; 'The pronouncements of West, and of Sir Thomas Lawrence, must, I imagine, have established the ësthetic worth of these antiquities. As to the *propriety* of their acquisition, we may, each one of us, hold to our own opinion.'

'Mr Beaumaris, do you care to visit Somerset House with us?' interrupted Lady Bridlington. 'I do not know how it comes about that we were not there upon Opening Day, but such a rush of engagements have we been swept up in that I am sure it is a wonder we have time to turn round! Arabella, my love, I daresay you are quite tired of staring at all these sadly damaged bits of frieze, or whatever it may be called – not but what I declare I could feast my eyes on it for ever! – and will be glad to look at pictures for a change!'

Arabella assented to it, throwing so beseeching a look at Mr Beaumaris that he was induced to accept a seat in the barouche.

During the drive to the Strand, Lady Bridlington was too much occupied in catching the eyes of chance acquaintances, and drawing their attention to the distinguished occupant of one of the back seats by bowing and waving to them, to have much time for conversation. Arabella sat with her eye downcast, and her hand fidgeting with the ribands tied round the handle of her sunshade; and Mr Beaumaris was content to watch her, taking due note of her pallor, and the dark shadows beneath her eyes. It was left to Lord Bridlington entertain the company, which he did very willingly, prosing uninterruptedly until the carriage turned into the courtyard of Somerset House.

Once inside the building, Lady Bridlington, whose ambitions had for some time been centred on promoting a match between Arabella and the Nonpareil, seized the first opportunity that offered of drawing Frederick away from the interesting pair. She stated her fervent desire to see the latest example of Sir Thomas Lawrence's art, and dragged him away from a minute inspection of the President's latest enormous canvas to search for this fashionable masterpiece.

'In what way can I serve you, Miss Tallant?' said Mr Beaumaris quietly.

'You – you had my letter?' faltered Arabella, glancing fleetingly up into his face.

'This morning. I went instantly to Park Street, and, apprehending that the matter was of some urgency, followed you to Bloomsbury.'

'How kind – how *very* kind you are!' uttered Arabella, in accents which could scarcely have been more mournful had she discovered him to have been a monster of cruelty.

'What is it, Miss Tallant?'

Bearing all the appearance of one rapt in admiration of the canvas before her, she said: 'I daresay you may have forgot all about it, sir, but – but you told me once – that is, you were so obliging as to say – that if my sentiments underwent a change –'

Mr Beaumaris mercifully intervened to put an end to her embarrassment. 'I have certainly not forgotten it,' he said. 'I perceive Lady Charnwood to be approaching, so let us move on! Am I to understand, ma'am, that your sentiments *have* undergone a change?'

Miss Tallant, obediently walking on to stare at one of the new Associates' *Probationary Pictures* (described in her catalogue as 'An Old Man soliciting a Mother for Her Daughter who was shewn Unwilling to consent to so disproportionate a match') said baldly: 'Yes.'

'My surroundings,' said Mr Beaumaris, 'make it impossible for me to do more than assure you that you have made me the happiest man in England, ma'am;

'Thank you,' said Arabella, in a stifled tone. 'I shall try to be a – to be a comfortable wife, sir!'

Mr Beaumaris's lips twitched, but he replied with perfect

gravity: 'For my part, I shall try to be an unexceptionable husband, ma'am!'

'Oh, yes, I am *sure* you will be!' said Arabella naïvely. 'If only –'

'If only –?' prompted Mr Beaumaris, as she broke off.

'Nothing!' she said hastily. 'Oh, dear, there is Mr Epworth!'

'A common bow in passing will be enough to damp his pretensions,' said Mr Beaumaris. 'If that does not suffice, I will look at him through my glass.'

This made her give an involuntary gurgle of laughter, but an instant later she was serious again, and evidently struggling to find the words with which to express herself.

'What very awkward places we do choose in which to propose to one another!' remarked Mr Beaumaris, guiding her gently towards a red-plush couch. 'Let us hope that if we sit down, and appear to be engrossed in conversation no one will have the bad manners to interrupt us!'

'I do not know what you must think of me!' said Arabella.

'I expect I had better not tell you until we find ourselves in a more retired situation,' he replied. 'You always blush so delightfully when I pay you compliments that it might attract attention to ourselves.'

She hesitated, and then turned resolutely towards him, tightly gripping his sunshade, and saying: 'Mr Beaumaris, you do *indeed* wish to marry me?'

'Miss Tallant, I do *indeed* wish to marry you!' he asserted.

'And – and you are so wealthy that my – my fortune can mean nothing to you?'

'Nothing at all, Miss Tallant.'

She drew an audible breath. 'Then – will you marry me at once?' she asked.

Now, what the devil's the meaning of this? thought Mr Beaumaris, startled. Can that damned young cub have been getting up to more mischief since I left town?

'At once?' he repeated, voice and countenance quite impassive.

'Yes!' said Arabella desperately. 'You must know that I have the greatest dislike of – of all *formality*, and – and the nonsense that always accompanies the announcement of an engagement! I – I should wish to be married very quietly – in fact, in the strictest secrecy – and before anyone has guessed – that I have accepted your very obliging offer!'

The wretched youth must have been deeper under the hatches than I guessed, thought Mr Beaumaris, and still she dare not tell me the truth! Does she really mean to carry out this outrageous suggestion, or does she only think that she means it? A virtuous man would undoubtedly, at this juncture, disclose that there is not the smallest need for these measures. What very unamusing lives virtuous men must lead!

'You may think it off of me, but I have always thought it would be so very romantic to elope!' pronounced Papa's daughter defiantly.

Mr Beaumaris, whose besetting sin was thought by many to be his exquisite enjoyment of the ridiculous, turned a deaf ear to the promptings of his better self, and replied instantly. 'How right you are! I wonder I should not have thought of an elopement myself! The announcement of the engagement of two such notable figures as ourselves must provoke a degree of comment and congratulation which would not be at all to our taste!'

'Exactly so!' nodded Arabella, relieved to find that he saw the matter in so reasonable a light.

'Consider, too, the chagrin of such as Horace Epworth!' said Mr Beaumaris, growing momently more enamoured of the scheme. 'You would be driven to distraction by their ravings!'

'Well, I do think I might be,' said Arabella.

'There is not a doubt of it. Moreover, the formality of making application to your father for permission to address you is quite antiquated, and we shall do well to dispense with it. If some little feeling still exists in the minds of old-fashioned persons against marrying minors out of hand, it need not concern us, after all.'

'N-no,' agreed Arabella, rather doubtfully. 'Do you think people will – will be very much shocked, sir?'

'No,' said Mr Beaumaris, with perfect truth. 'No one will be in the least shocked. When would you like to elope?'

'Would tomorrow be too soon?' asked Arabella anxiously.

Mr Beaumaris might wish that his love would give him her confidence, but it would have been idle to have denied that he was hugely enjoying himself. Life with Arabella would contain few dull moments; and although her estimate of his morals was unflattering enough to have discomposed any man of sensibility it left his withers unwrung, since he was well-aware that her assumption of his readiness to behave in so improper a fashion sprang from an innocence which he found enchanting. He replied with great promptness: 'Not a moment too soon! But for the recollection that there are one or two preparations which perhaps I should make I should have suggested that we should leave this building together at once.'

'No, that would be impossible,' said Arabella seriously. 'In fact – I do not know very much about such things, but I cannot but feel that it will be excessively difficult for me to escape from Park Street without anyone's knowing! For I must carry a valise with me, at least, besides my dressing-case, and how may it be contrived? Unless I crept out at dead of night, of course, but it would have to be very late indeed, for the porter always waits up for Lord Bridlington to come in. And I might fall asleep,' she added candidly.

'I have a constitutional dislike of eloping at dead of night,' said Mr Beaumaris firmly. 'Such exploits entail the use of rope-ladders, I am credibly informed, and the thought of being surprised perhaps by the Watch in the very act of throwing this up to your window I find singularly unnerving.'

'Nothing,' said Arabella, 'would prevail upon me to climb down a rope-ladder! Besides, my bedroom is at the back of the house.'

'Perhaps,' said Mr Beaumaris, 'you had better leave me to make the necessary arrangements.'

'Oh, yes!' responded Arabella gratefully. 'I am sure you will know just how it should be contrived!'

This reflection upon his past career Mr Beaumaris bore with an unmoved countenance. 'Just so, Miss Tallant,' he said gravely. 'Now, it occurs to me that, tomorrow being Wednesday, there will be a gala night at Vauxhall Gardens.'

'Yes, Lady Bridlington thought at one time of taking me to it,' agreed Arabella. 'But then, you know, she recalled that it is the night of the party at Uxbridge House.'

'A very dull affair, I have no doubt. I shall invite Lady Bridlington – and Bridlington, I suppose – to do me the honour of joining *my* party at Vauxhall. You will naturally be included in this invitation, and at a convenient moment during the course of the evening, we shall slip away together to the street entrance, where my chaise will be awaiting us.'

Arabella considered this proposition, and discovered two objections to it. 'Yes, but how very odd it would seem to Lady Bridlington if you were to go away in the middle of your own party!'

The reflection that Lady Bridlington might well deem this eccentricity the least odd feature of the affair Mr Beaumaris kept to himself. He said: 'Very true. A note shall be delivered to her after our departure.'

'Well, I suppose that would be better than nothing,' Arabella conceded. 'Oh, will she ever forgive me for treating her so?' This involuntary exclamation seemed to escape her without her knowledge. She raised the second of her objections. 'And in any event it will not answer, because I cannot take a valise to Vauxhall!'

'That you will also leave to me,' said Mr Beaumaris.

'But you cannot call in Park Street to fetch it!' she pointed out.

'Certainly not.'

'And I will *not* elope without a change of clothes, or my hairbrushes, or my tooth-powder!' declared Arabella.

'Most improper,' agreed Mr Beaumaris. 'All these things shall be forthcoming.'

'You cannot buy such things for me!' gasped Arabella, shocked.

'I assure you I should enjoy doing it.'

She stared at him, and then exclaimed wretchedly: 'How dreadful it all is! I never, never thought I should come to this! I daresay it seems the merest commonplace to you, but to me – But I see that it is of no use to cavil!'

The tell-tale muscle at the corner of Mr Beaumaris's mouth quivered, and was sternly repressed. 'Well, perhaps not precisely commonplace,' he said. 'It so happens that I have not previously eloped with anyone. However, to a man of ordinary ingenuity the affair should not prove impossible to achieve creditably, I trust. I perceive Mrs Penkridge, who is hoping to catch either your eye or mine. We shall permit her to do so, and while she asks you to say if you do not think Nollekens's bust over there most like, I shall go in search of Lady Bridlington, and engage her to bring you to Vauxhall tomorrow evening.'

'Oh, pray do not! I dislike Mrs Penkridge excessively!' she whispered.

'Yes, an odious woman, but impossible to avoid,' he returned.

Seeing him rise to his feet, Mrs Penkridge bore down upon him, her acidulated smile on her lips. Mr Beaumaris greeted her with his smooth civility, stayed for perhaps a minute, and then, to Arabella's indignation, made his bow, and went off in the direction of the next room.

Either Lady Bridlington proved hard to find, or he must have fallen a victim of her garrulity, Arabella thought, for it seemed a very long time before she set eyes on him again. When he did reappear, Lady Bridlington was walking beside him, wreathed in smiles. Arabella made her excuses to Mrs Penkridge, and went across to her godmother, who greeted her with the cheerful intelligence that Mr Beaumaris had formed the most delightful scheme for an evening at Vauxhall. 'I did not scruple to accept, my love, for I knew you would like it of all things!' she said.

'Yes,' said Arabella, feeling that she was now committed to an irrevocable and reprehensible course which she would no doubt regret her life long. 'I mean, oh yes! how very agreeable!'

Sixteen

Upon leaving Somerset House, Mr Beaumaris got into a hackney, and drove to the Red Lion inn. What he learned at that hostelry threw abundant light on to Arabella's conduct. Since he had his own reasons for believing Arabella's heart to have been won long since, he was not in the east wounded by the discovery that she proposed to marry him as means of rescuing her brother from debt, but, on the contrary, considerably amused. Having paid Bertram's bill at the inn, and received his watch back from the landlord, he returned to his own house in yet another hackney.

The same delight in the ridiculous which had made him wear a dandelion in his button-hole for three consecutive days for no better purpose than to enjoy the discomfiture of his misguided friends and copyists made him deeply appreciative of the situation in which he now found himself; and he beguiled the tedium of the drive to Mount Street in wondering when it would cross his absurd love's mind that the disclosure, following hard upon the wedding-ceremony, that she required a large sum of money from him without a moment's loss of time, might be productive of a little awkwardness. He could not resist picturing the scene, and was still laughing softly when he reached his house, a circumstance which considerably surprised his butler.

'Send round to the stables for my Tilbury, will you, Brough?' he said. 'And desire Painswick – oh, you're there, are you?' he added, as his valet descended the stairs. 'I want to hear no more about missing shirts, on which excessively boring subject I can see from your expression you are prepared to discourse at length, but you may tell me this! Where is the letter I gave into your hands to be delivered at the Red Lion, to a Mr Anstey, and why did you not tell me that it had not been so delivered?'

'You may perhaps recall, sir,' said Painswick reproachfully, 'that I mentioned to you while you sat at breakfast that there was a matter which I deemed it my duty to bring to your notice. Upon which, sir, you said, Not now.'

'Did I?' I had no idea you could be so easily silenced. Where is the letter?'

'I placed it, sir, at the bottom of the pile that was awaiting you on the table here,' replied Painswick, tacitly disclaiming further responsibility.

'In that case it is in the library. Thank you: that is all.'

Ulysses, who had been lying stretched out in the library, enjoying the sleep of the replete, awoke at Mr Beaumaris's entrance, yawned, got up, shook himself, sneezed several times, stretched, and indicated by his cocked ears and wagging tail that he was now ready for any adventure.

'I am glad to see you restored to your usual self,' said Mr Beaumaris, running through the mass of his neglected correspondence, and picking up his own letter to Bertram. 'You know, you should not have dissuaded me from going out again that evening! Just look what has come of it! And yet I don't know. I would not have missed this morning's interview for a thousand pounds! I suppose you think that I am behaving very badly? I am, of course, but do me the justice to own that she deserves it for being such an adorable little fool!'

Ulysses wagged his tail. He was not only willing to do Mr Beaumaris justice, but presently indicated his readiness to accompany him on whatever expedition he had in mind.

'It would be useless to suggest, I suppose, that you are occupying Clayton's seat?' said Mr Beaumaris, mounting into his tilbury.

Clayton, grinning, expressed himself as being agreeable to

taking the little dog on his knees, but Mr Beaumaris shook his head.

'No, no, I fear he would not like it. I shan't need you,' he said, and drove off, remarking to his alert companion: 'We are now faced with the wearing task of tracking down that foolish young man's inarticulate friend, Felix Scunthorpe. I wonder whether, in the general medley, there is any bloodhound strain in you?'

He drew blank at Mr Scunthorpe's lodging, but on being informed that Mr Scunthorpe had mentioned that he was going to Boodle's, drove at once to St James's Street, and was so fortunate as to catch sight of his quarry, walking up the flag-way. He reined in, and called imperatively: 'Scunthorpe!'

Mr Scunthorpe had naturally perceived who was driving a spanking chestnut between the shafts of the tilbury, but as he had no expectations of being recognised by the Nonpareil this summons surprised him very much. He was even a little doubtful, and said cautiously: 'Me, sir?'

'Yes, you. Where is young Tallant?' he saw an expression of great wariness descend upon Mr Scunthorpe's face, and added impatiently: 'Come, don't be more of a fool than you can help? You don't suppose I am going to hand him over to the tipstaffs, do you?'

'Well, he's at the Cock,' disclosed Mr Scunthorpe reluctantly. 'That is to say,' he corrected himself, suddenly recalling his friend's incognito, 'he is, if you mean Mr Anstey.'

'Have you any brothers?' demanded Mr Beaumaris.

'No,' said Mr Scunthorpe, blinking at him. 'Only child.'

'You relieve my mind. Offer my congratulations to your parents!'

Mr Scunthorpe thought this over, with knit brow, but could make nothing of it. He put Mr Beaumaris right on one point. 'Only one parent,' he said. 'Father died three months after I was born.'

'Very understandable,' said Mr Beaumaris. 'I am astonished that he lingered on for so long. Where is this Cock you speak of?'

'Thing is – not sure I ought to tell you!' said Mr Scunthorpe.

'Take my word for it, you will be doing your misguided friend an extremely ill-turn if you don't tell me!'

'Well, it's at the corner of Duck Lane, Tothill Fields,' confided Mr Scunthorpe, capitulating.

'Good God!' said Mr Beaumaris, and drove off.

The Cock inn, however, though a small, squat building, proved to be more respectable than its situation had led Mr Beaumaris to suppose. Duck Lane might abound in filth of every description, left to rot in the road, but the Cock seemed to be moderately clean, and well-kept. It even boasted an ostler, who emerged from the stable to gape at the tilbury. When he understood that the swell handling the ribbons had not merely stopped to enquire the way, but really did desire him to take charge of his horse and carriage, a vision of enormous largesse danced before his eyes, and he hastened to assure this noble client that he was ready to bestow his undivided attention on the equipage.

Mr Beaumaris then descended from the tilbury, and walked into the tap of the inn, where his appearance caused a waterman, a jarvey off duty, two bricklayer's labourers, a scavenger, and the landlord to break off their conversation in mid-sentence to stare a him.

'Good-morning!' said Mr Beaumaris. 'You have a Mr Anstey putting up here, I think?'

The landlord, recovering from his surprise, came forward, bowing several times. 'Yes, your honour! Oh, yes, indeed, your honour! – Chase that cur out of here, Joe! – If your honour will –'

'Do nothing of the sort, Joe!' interrupted Mr Beaumaris.

'Is he *yours* sir?' gasped the landlord.

'Certainly he is mine. A rare specimen: his family tree would surprise you! Is Mr Anstey in?'

'He'll be up in his room, sir. Keeps hisself *to* himself, in a manner of speaking. If your honour would care to step into the parlour, I'll run up and fetch him down before the cat can lick her ear.'

255

'No, take me up to him,' said Mr Beaumaris. 'Ulysses, do stop hunting for rats! We have no time to waste on sport this morning! Come to heel!'

Ulysses, who had found a promising hole in one corner of the tap, and was snuffing at it in a manner calculated to keep its occupant cowering inside it for the next twenty-four hours at least, regretfully obeyed this command, and followed Mr Beaumaris up a steep, narrow stairway. The landlord scratched on one of the three doors at the top of this stair, a voice bade him come in, and Mr Beaumaris, nodding dismissal to his guide, walked in, shut the door behind him, and said cheerfully: 'How do you do? I hope you don't object to my dog?'

Bertram, who had been sitting at a small table, trying for the hundredth time to hit upon some method of solving his difficulties, jerked up his head, and sprang to his feet, as white as his shirt. '*Sir*!' he uttered, grasping the back of his chair with one shaking hand.

Ulysses, misliking his tone, growled at him, but was called to order. 'How many more times am I to speak to you about your total lack of polish, Ulysses?' said Mr Beaumaris severely. 'Never try to pick a quarrel with a man under his own roof! Lie down at once!' He drew off his gloves, and tossed them on to the bed. 'What a very tiresome young man you are!' he told Bertram amiably.

Bertram, his face now as red as a beetroot, said in a choked voice: 'I was coming to your house on Thursday, as you bade me!'

'I'm sure you were. But if you hadn't been so foolish as to leave the Red Lion so – er – hurriedly, there would not have been the slightest need for this rustication of yours. *You* would not have worried yourself half-way to Bedlam, and *I* should not have been obliged to bring Ulysses to a locality you can see he does not care for.'

Bertram glanced in a bewildered way towards Ulysses, who was sitting suggestively by the door, and said: 'You don't understand, sir. I – I was rolled up! It was that, or – or prison, I suppose!'

256

'Yes, I rather thought you were,' agreed Mr Beaumaris. 'I sent a hundred pound banknote to you the next morning, together with my assurance that I had no intention of claiming from you the vast sums you lost to me. Of course, I should have done very much better to have told you so at the time – and better still to have ordered you out of the Nonesuch at the outset! But you will agree that the situation was a trifle awkward.'

'Mr Beaumaris,' said Bertram, with considerable difficulty, 'I c-can't redeem my vowels now, but I pledge you my word that I *will* redeem them! I was coming to see you on Thursday, to tell you the whole, and – and to beg your indulgence!'

'Very proper,' approved Mr Beaumaris. 'But it is not my practice to win large sums of money from schoolboys, and you cannot expect me to change my habits only to accommodate your conscience, you know. Shall we sit down, or don't you trust the chairs here?'

'Oh, I beg pardon!' Bertram stammered, flushing vividly. 'Of course! I don't know what I was thinking about! Pray, will you take this chair, sir? But it will not do! I must and I will – Oh, can I offer you any refreshment? They haven't anything much here, except beer and porter, and gin, but if you would care for some gin –'

'Certainly not, and if that is how you have been spending your time since last I saw you I am not surprised that you are looking burned to the socket.'

'I haven't been – at least, I did at first, only it was brandy – but not – not lately,' Bertram muttered, very shamefaced.

'If you drank the brandy sold in this district, you must have a constitution of iron to be still alive,' remarked Mr Beaumaris. 'What's the sum total of your debts? Or don't you know?'

'Yes, but – *You* are not going to pay my debts, sir!' A dreadful thought occurred to him; he stared very hard at his visitor, and demanded: 'Who told you where I was?'

'Your amiable but cork-brained friend, of course.'

'*Scunthorpe?*' Bertram said incredulously. 'It was not – it was not someone else?'

'No, it was not someone else. I have not so far discussed the matter with your sister, if that is what you mean?'

'How do you know she is my sister?' Bertram said, staring at him harder than ever. 'Do you say that Scunthorpe told you that too?'

'No, I guessed it from the start. Have you kept your bills? Let me have them!'

'Nothing would induce me to!' cried Bertram hotly. 'I mean, I am very much obliged to you, sir, and it's curst good of you, but you must *see* that I couldn't accept such generosity! Why, we are almost strangers! I cannot conceive why you should think of doing such a thing for me!'

'Ah, but we are not destined to remain strangers!' explained Mr Beaumaris. 'I am going to marry your sister.'

'Going to marry *Bella*?' Bertram said.

'Certainly. You perceive that that puts the whole matter on quite a different footing. You can hardly expect me either to win money from my wife's brother at faro, or to bear the odium of having a relative in the Fleet. You really must consider *my* position a little, my dear boy.'

Bertram's lip quivered. 'I see what it is! She *did* go to you, and *that* is why – But if you think, sir, that I have sunk so low I would let Bella sacrifice herself only to save me from disgrace –'

Ulysses, taking instant exception to the raised voice, sprang to Mr Beaumaris's side, and barked a challenge at Bertram. Mr Beaumaris dropped a hand on his head. 'Yes, very rude, Ulysses,' he agreed. 'But never mind! Bear in mind that it's not everyone who holds me in such high esteem as you do!'

Much confused, Bertram stammered: 'I didn't mean – I beg your pardon! I only meant – She never said a word of this to me!'

'Didn't she? How secretive females are, to be sure! Perhaps she felt that her parents should be the first persons to learn the news.'

'Well, I suppose she *might*,' Bertram said doubtfully. 'But considering she said she couldn't marry anyone, because she made 'em all think she was an heiress –'

'She didn't make me think anything of the sort,' said Mr Beaumaris.

'Oh, I *see*!' said Bertram, his brow clearing. 'Well, I must say, sir, I'm dashed glad, because I had a notion she liked you more than all the rest! I – I wish you very happy! And, of course, I do see that it makes a difference to my debt to *you*, only I don't think I should let you pay the other debts, because it is not in the least your affair, and –'

'Now, don't let us go into all that again!' begged Mr Beaumaris. 'Just tell me what you propose to do if I don't pay your debts!'

'I thought of enlisting in a cavalry regiment, if they would take me,' confessed Bertram. 'Under an assumed name, of course!'

'I should think that a cavalry regiment would suit you very well,' said Mr Beaumaris. 'But it will be very much more comfortable for you, and for all of us, if you join it under your own name, and as a cornet. What do you want? A Hussar regiment?'

These incredible words made Bertram turn first red, and then white, swallow convulsively, and finally blurt out: 'You *c-couldn't* mean that! After *this* I – Oh, sir, *do* you mean it?'

'Yes, of course, but give me your bills!'

'I don't deserve anyone should do anything for me!' Bertram said, overcome.

'The bills!'

Bertram, already floating in some beatific dream, started, and said: 'The bills! Oh! Oh, yes, I have them all here – only you will be very much shocked to see how much I have spent, and –'

'Nothing ever shocks me,' replied Mr Beaumaris, holding out a hand. He stuffed the sheaf of crumpled papers into the pocket of his driving-coat, and said: 'I will settle all these so that none of your creditors will know that it was not you who paid them. Do you owe anything in this neighbourhood beyond your shot here?'

Bertram shook his head. 'No, for Bella gave me all the money she had, when she came to see me. I am afraid you would not have liked her doing so, sir, and nor did I, but Felix brought her, like the saphead he is! It – It was a horrid place, and I think I ought to tell you that it was all my fault that she ever went to such a back-slum!'

'You fill me with dismay,' said Mr Beaumaris. 'I do trust she did not set eyes on any destitute person whom she may feel it to be her duty to befriend?'

'Well, I don't *think* she did,' Bertram replied. 'Felix did say that she told a woman they all call Quartern Sue not to give her baby gin to drink, and gave her a shilling to buy it some milk. And I am excessively sorry, sir, and I would not have had it happen for the world, but Felix says that they walked smash into Leaky Peg, who – who took me to the place when I was so castaway I didn't know even where I was, or how I came there. She – she *was* very good to me, in her way, you know, and Bella got it into her head she owed her a debt of gratitude for looking after me! But that's all right, because I gave Peg five pounds out of the money Bella left for me!'

'Heaven help me!' said Mr Beaumaris. 'She will undoubtedly expect me to house this doxy! *Leaky Peg*, did you say? Good God!'

'No, no, sir, of course she won't!' exclaimed Bertram. 'Why *should* she?'

'Because that is her invariable practice,' said Mr Beaumaris bitterly. 'You don't suppose, do you, that I voluntarily adopted that animal over there?'

'You don't mean Bella gave him to you? Well, that's a great deal too bad of her! I must say, I thought it was a queer sort of a dog for *you* to have, sir!'

'The whole of London thinks it is a queer sort of a dog for me to have. Even the landlord of this tavern tried to chase him from the taproom!' He drew out his pocketbook, and extracted from it several banknotes, and pushed them across the table. 'There you are: pay your shot here, redeem whatever lies in pawn, and book yourself the boxseat on the first stage to Harrowgate. I believe the northern-bound coaches leave at some godless hour of the morning, so you had better spend tonight at whatever inn they set out from. A few days in the fresh air will, I trust, repair the ravages of all the brandy you imbibed, and make it possible for you to meet your father without arousing suspicion.'

Bertram tried to speak, failed, tried once more, and managed to say in a very gruff voice: 'I c-can't thank you as I should, and of course I know it is for Bella's sake! But I *can* do one thing, and I will! I shall confess the whole to my father, sir, and – and if he says I may not join a Hussar regiment, after behaving so badly, well – well it will serve me right!'

'Yes,' said Mr Beaumaris, 'that is very noble of you, of course, but I have always found it to be an excellent plan, before one indulges in an orgy of expiation, to consider whether the recipient of the sort of confession you have in mind may not be made to suffer a great deal of quite unnecessary pain.'

Bertram was silent for a moment, as this sank into his brain. 'You don't think I should tell my father, sir?'

'I not only don't think you should: I utterly forbid you to mention the matter to him.'

'I don't quite like to deceive him,' Bertram said shyly. 'You see –'

'I am sure you don't, so if your mind is set on doing penance, that will serve your turn excellently. You have been staying in Berkshire with Scunthorpe. Just bear that in mind, and forget that you have ever been within ten miles of London!' He rose, and held out his hand. 'Now I must go. Don't harrow yourself with thinking that you have broken all the ten commandments! You have only done what four out of five young fools do, if set loose upon the town. Incidentally, you have acquired a deal of valuable experience, and when next you come to London you will do much better.'

'I shall never be able to show my face in London again, sir,' said Bertram wistfully. 'But thank you!'

'Nonsense! A few years' service, and you will become a dashing Captain, I daresay, with a fine pair of military whiskers. No one will recognise you. By the way, don't call to take leave of our sister: she is very much occupied today. I will tell her that you are safely despatched to Yorkshire. Ulysses, stop scratching! Do try to be a little more worthy of me! Yes, we are now going, but it is quite unnecessary, and, indeed, extremely uncivil, to caper about in that joyful fashion!' He picked up his gloves, shook hands, and walked to the door, but bethought him of something, and put a hand into his inner pocket. 'Association with that hound – the boon companion of every prig in town, I have not a shadow of doubt – is fast undermining my morals. Your watch, Bertram!'

Seventeen

_M_ r BEAUMARIS'S subsequent proceedings, during the short space of time that elapsed before his elopement, were many and varied, but although they included precise instructions to his coachman and his postilion, and a drive out of London, there was one curious omission: he took no steps to procure a special licence, so that it was to be inferred that he contemplated a flight to the Border, and a ceremony performed across the anvil at Gretna Green: a departure from the canons of good taste which would have staggered any of his associates who had had the least suspicion of his clandestine intentions. But as no one who met him detected anything out of the ordinary in his demeanour no one except his prospective bride speculated at all on the course of action he meant to pursue.

Arabella, naturally enough, employed every moment that was unoccupied by social engagements in a great deal of speculation, but as she was wholly ignorant of the rules governing hasty marriages the need of a special licence did not occur to her. She certainly supposed that she would be driven to Gretna Green, and, having once accepted this hateful necessity, resolutely turned her thoughts away from it. Romantic though such an adventure might be, no young lady, reared, as she had been, in the strictest propriety, could embark on it without feeling herself to have sunk to irreclaimable depths of depravity. How she was ever to explain such conduct to the satisfaction of Papa was an unanswerable question. Only the thought of Bertram's predicament in any way sustained her. She snatched ten minutes between seeing a balloon-ascent and dressing for a more than ordinarily splendid ball, in scribbling a letter to Bertram, assuring him that he need only wait patiently at the Cock for a few more days before he should infallibly be rescued from all his embarrassments.

Of Mr Beaumaris she saw nothing until she met him at Vauxhall Gardens. He was not present at the ball on the night previous to their assignation, a circumstance of which she hardly knew whether to be glad or sorry.

Perhaps it was fortunate that Lady Bridlington's plans for their amusement left her with so little time for reflection. The indulgence of a quiet hour or two in her own bedchamber was not granted her. Try as she would she was unable to stay awake after that splendid ball, and only awoke next morning when Maria drew back her window-blinds. The day was full to overflowing with engagements: she was dressing for Mr Beaumaris's Vauxhall Gardens party, before, as it seemed to her, she well realised what she was about.

It so happened that through the press of invitations which had showered down upon the house in Park Street Arabella had never before visited the famous gardens. They took sculls across the river, to enter by the water-gate, and at any other time she must have been transported by the sight which met her eyes. The gardens, which were laid out in groves and colonnades, were lit (as Lord Bridlington instructively informed her) by no fewer than thirty-seven thousand lamps, some of them suspended in graceful festoons between the pillars of the colonnades. The orchestra, detected across the principal grove, was established in a giant kiosk, glittering all over with coloured lights; there was a spacious pavilion, lined with mirrors, which formed the principal supper-room for those who did not care to go to the expense of hiring one of the boxes which opened on to the various colonnades; a Rotunda, where excellent concerts were held throughout the season; several magnificent fountains; and innumerable walks where lovers could lose themselves at will.

Mr Beaumaris met his guests at the water-entrance, and conducted them to the Rotunda, where, since it was past eight o'clock, the concert was already in progress. Arabella could scarcely meet his eyes, but forced herself to look up once, very fleetingly, into his face. He smiled at her, but no private speech passed between them.

After the first act of the concert, at about ten o'clock, a bell rang, and those who had no ear for music poured into the Rotunda to witness the marvels of the Grand Cascade. Even though feelings of guilt were in danger of overcoming her, Arabella could not help uttering an exclamation of delight when a dark curtain arose to reveal a rural scene, done in miniature, but amazingly life-like, of a cascade, a watermill, a bridge, and a succession of coaches, wagons, and other vehicles passing with every appearance of verisimilitude across the stage. Even the sound of the wheels, and the rush of the waters was ingeniously counterfeited, so that she thought it no matter for wonder that people should visit Vauxhall three and four times only to see this marvel.

When the curtain descended again, Mr Beaumaris suggested that his guests might like to partake of supper instead of waiting to hear the second part of the concert. This being agreed to, they edged their way out of the row where they were sitting and strolled down one of the colonnades to the supper-box which had been hired for their accommodation. This was in an excellent position, not too close to the orchestra in the kiosk to make conversation a labour, and commanding a splendid view of the principal grove. No one, of course, could visit Vauxhall without eating the wafer-thin slices of ham for which the suppers were famous, or tasting the rack-punch; but in addition to these delicacies Mr Beaumaris had ordered a meal so excellently chosen as to tempt the most fugitive appetite. Even Arabella, whose appetite had deserted her several days before, could enjoy the chicken, cooked before her eyes in a chafing-dish; and was persuaded to toy with a trifle. Mr Beaumaris prepared a peach for her with his own hands, and since an imminent elopement was no excuse, she believed, for a present lapse of good manners, she ate this too, smiling shyly and gratefully at him. She found little to say beyond the merest commonplace throughout supper, but this silence passed unnoticed in the spate of Lord Bridlington's discourse. He kindly explained to the ladies the mechanism which produced the wonders of the Grand Cascade; sketched the history of the Gardens; extensively examined their claim to be considered a development of the old Spring Gardens; and disposed of the tradition which linked the district with the name of Guy Fawkes. He was only interrupted when it became necessary to exchange greetings with some acquaintance who happened to walk past the box; and since his mother murmured encouraging remarks every now and then, and Mr Beaumaris, with great self-control, forbore to utter one of his blighting snubs, he enjoyed himself very much, and was sorry when his host suggested that Miss Tallant would like to see the Fireworks.

He was allowed to take Arabella on his arm on their way to the part of the grounds whence these could best be seen, while Mr Beaumaris followed beside Lady Bridlington, but just as he had secured two excellent places he found himself, quite how he did not know, supplanted, and was obliged to attend to his Mama, who did not like her situation, and insisted on his finding her a place where her view of the set-pieces would not be obscured by the head-dress of a lady who favoured immensely tall ostrich plumes.

Arabella momentarily forgot her troubles in enchantment, and clapped her hands when the rockets soared skywards, and burst into stars. Mr Beaumaris, inured to fireworks, derived even more entertainment through watching her round-eyed delight; but after the first of the set-pieces had burnt itself out, he consulted his watch, and said gently: 'Shall we go, Miss Tallant?'

These words brought her to earth with a shock. An impulse to tell him that she had changed her mind had to be sternly repressed, and all the miseries poor Bertram must be enduring recalled. She clutched her taffeta cloak round her, and said nervously: 'Oh, yes! Is it already time? Yes, let us go at once!'

There was not the least difficulty in detaching themselves unnoticed from a crowd of persons all intent upon the evolutions of a giant Catherine-wheel; Arabella laid a cold hand on Mr Beaumaris's arm, and went with him down an alley, past the Fountain of Neptune, most tastefully illuminated, along one of the colonnades, and so to the land-entrance. Several carriages were awaiting their owners here, and amongst them Mr Beaumaris's travelling chaise, with a pair of horses harnessed to it, and his head-coachman, and one postilion in attendance. Neither of these individuals betrayed the smallest surprise at seeing a lady on his master's arm, and although Arabella was too much embarrassed to raise her eyes she was aware that they were conducting themselves as though this elopement were an everyday occurrence in their lives. They sprang to well-trained activity as soon as they saw their master; the cloths were swept from the back of Mr Beaumaris's high-bred horses; the steps of the chaise were let down, the doors opened, and Mr Beaumaris handed his bride tenderly up into the luxurious vehicle. So little time had she been kept waiting in the road that she did not even look to see whether any baggage was strapped to the back of the chaise. Mr Beaumaris paused only to exchange a word with the coachman, and then sprang up, and took his place beside Arabella on the comfortably cushioned seat; the doors were shut on them; the postilion swung himself into the saddle, and the equipage moved forward.

Mr Beaumaris spread a soft rug over Arabella's legs, and said: 'I have a warmer cloak here: may I put it round your shoulders?'

'Oh, no, thank you! I am quite warm!' Arabella said nervously.

He took her hand, and kissed it. After a moment she drew it away, and sought desperately for something to say to relieve the tension of the moment.

'How very well-sprung your chaise is, sir!' she achieved.

'I am glad you are pleased with it,' he responded, in the same polite tone which she had used. 'I remembered, of course, that we are alike in detesting hired vehicles.'

'Are – are we?' she said doubtfully. 'I mean, of course –'

'We exchanged opinions, the first time we met, on the only tolerable way of travel,' Mr Beaumaris reminded her.

This recollection not unnaturally deprived her of speech. Mr Beaumaris, most obligingly, forbore to press her for an answer, but talked agreeably about the concert they had heard that night. Arabella, who had experienced a few moments' panic on finding herself shut up with her bridegroom in a chaise, travelling to an unknown but probably remote, destination, was overwhelmingly grateful to him for behaving precisely as though he were escorting her home from some place of entertainment. She had been much afraid that he would perhaps have tried to make love to her. She had not much experience in such matters, but it had occurred to her that a gentleman starting on an elopement might expect some demonstration of affection from his beloved. A week earlier, safe in the darkness of her bedchamber, her cheek on a damp pillow, Arabella had owned to herself that life could hold no greater happiness for her than for Mr Beaumaris to take her in his arms; now, miserably conscious of her duplicity, she could imagine nothing more unnerving. But Mr Beaumaris, surely the calmest of runaway-bridegrooms, showed no desire to succumb to his ardour. Finding that he was being answered in monosyllables, he presently gave up trying to engage Arabella in genteel conversation, and leaned back in his corner of the chaise, his head a little turned against the squabs behind it towards her, so that he could watch her face in the dim moonlight that penetrated into the vehicle. Arabella was scarcely aware the he had stopped talking to her. She was lost in her own thoughts, seated bolt upright, and clinging with one hand to the strap that hung from the wall of the chaise beside her. She could see the postilion bobbing up and down before her, and, when the cobbles were left behind, was vaguely conscious of having left the streets and to be driving through the countryside. In what direction they were travelling, or where she would find herself at the first halt, she had no idea, nor were these the questions that troubled her mind. The impropriety of her conduct she had from the start known to be unforgivable; what now filled her with repugnance was the sudden realisation that in marrying Mr Beaumaris while he still laboured under a misapprehension she was treating him so shabbily that it was doubtful if he would ever pardon her, much less continue to regard her with even a shred of affection. At this melancholy reflection a small sob escaped her, which had the effect of making Mr Beaumaris say; 'What is it, my love?'

'Nothing! Nothing!' whispered Arabella, much agitated.

To her relief, he appeared to accept this, for he said no more. She decided, in a wave of remorse, that he was the greatest gentleman of her acquaintance, with the best manners, the most delicate forbearance, and quite the kindest disposition. It was at this point that the moment for which Mr Beaumaris had been waiting arrived. All at once Arabella wondered how soon after the wedding-ceremony she could break the news to him that she required him not only to forgive her brother's debt to him, but also to bestow a hundred pounds on him for the settlement of all his other liabilities; and what words she could find with which most unexceptionably to express this urgent necessity. There were no such words, as a very little cudgelling of her brain sufficed to convince her. She could not imagine how she could ever have been foolish enough to have supposed that the thing could be done, or that such a confession could be made without afterwards rendering it impossible for her to convince him that she did indeed love him.

These, and still more disagreeable thoughts, were jostling one another in Arabella's frightened mind when the pace at which they were travelling seemed sensibly to slacken. The chaise swung round at so sharp an angle that only her clutch on the strap saved Arabella from being thrown on to Mr Beaumaris's shoulder. It proceeded for a very little way, and then drew up. Arabella turned towards the dupe beside her, and said breathlessly: 'I cannot! I cannot! Mr Beaumaris, I am *very* sorry, but it was all a mistake! Please take me back to London at once! Oh, please take me back!'

Mr Beaumaris received his daunting request with a remarkable degree of composure, merely replying, as the door of the chaise was opened: 'Shall we discuss this matter in a more private spot? Let me assist you to alight, my love!'

'Please take me back! I – I don't want to elope, after all!' said Arabella, in an urgent whisper.

'Then we won't elope,' returned Mr Beaumaris reassuringly. 'I must own that I think it quite unnecessary for us to do so. Come!'

Arabella hesitated, but since he seemed determined that she should descend for the chaise, and perhaps wanted to rest his horses, she allowed him to hand her down. They seemed to be standing before a large building, but it showed none of the welcoming lights to be expected of a posting-inn, nor had the chaise driven into a courtyard. At the top of a flight of broad, shallow stone steps a large door opened, and a beam of light from the interior of the building showed Arabella neat flower-beds flanking the entrance. Before she had recovered from the surprise of finding herself at what was plainly a private resident, Mr Beaumaris had led her up the steps, and into a lofty hall, furnished in a massive style, and lit by candles in wall-chandeliers. An elderly butler bowed them in, and said: 'Good-evening sir.' One powdered and liveried footman divested Mr Beaumaris of his cloak, another relieved him of his hat and gloves.

Arabella stood turned to stone as all the implications of her surroundings burst upon her. Mr Beaumaris's soothing assurance to her that they would not elope now became invested with the most sinister significance, and it was a pathetically white and frightened face which she turned towards him. He smiled at her, but before either of them had time to speak, the butler had informed Mr Beaumaris that he would find the Yellow Saloon in readiness; and a most respectable-looking housekeeper, with neat white hair under a starched cap, had appeared upon the scene, and was dropping a curtsy to Arabella.

'Good-evening, miss! Good-evening, Mr Robert! Please to

take Miss into the saloon, while I see that the maids unpack her trunk! You will find a nice fire, for I am sure Miss must be chilled after the drive, so late as it is. Let me take your cloak, miss! I shall bring up a glass of hot milk directly: I am sure you will be glad of it.'

The promise of a glass of hot milk, which hardly seemed to be in keeping with the hideous vision of seduction and rape which had leapt to her mind, a little reassured Arabella. One of the footmen had thrown open a door at the back of the hall; Mr Beaumaris possessed himself of a trembling, icy little hand, and said: 'I want to make you known to Mrs Watchet, my love, who is a very old friend of mine. Indeed, one of my earliest allies!'

'Now, Master Robert! I'm sure I am very happy to see you here, miss – and mind, now, don't let Master Robert keep you out of your bed till all hours!'

The fear that Master Robert had quite different intentions receded still farther. Arabella summoned up a smile, said something in a shy little voice, and allowed her self to be led into a saloon, fitted up in the first style of elegance, and offering her all the comfort of a small fire, burning in a brightly polished grate.

The door was softly closed behind them; Mr Beaumaris drew a chair invitingly forward, and said: 'Come and sit down, Miss Tallant! You know, I cannot but be glad that you have decided after all not to elope with me. To tell you the truth, there is one circumstance at least that makes me reluctant to proceed with you to Scotland – a journey that would occupy six or seven days, I daresay, before we found ourselves back in London.'

'Oh!' said Arabella, sitting down primly on the edge of the chair, and regarding him out of scared, doubtful eyes.

'Yes,' said Mr Beaumaris, 'Ulysses!'

Her eyes widened. 'Ulysses?' she repeated blankly.

'The animal you were so obliging as to bestow upon me,' he explained. 'Most unfortunately, he has developed so marked a predilection for my society that he frets himself to skin and bone if I am absent from him for more than a night. I did not quite like to bring him with me upon our elopement, for I can discover no precedent for taking a dog with one upon such an occasion, and one scarcely cares to violate the conventions at such a moment.'

The door opened just then to admit Mrs Watchet, who came in, carrying a glass of steaming milk on a silver tray. This, with a plate of macaroon, she set down on a small table at Arabella's elbow, telling her that when she had drunk it, and said goodnight to Master Robert, she should be escorted upstairs to her bed-chamber. With a slightly severe injunction to Mr Beaumaris not to keep Miss talking to him too long, she then curtsied herself out of the room

'Sir!' said Arabella desperately, as soon as they were alone again: 'What is this house to which you have brought me?'

'I have brought you to my grandmother's house, at Wimbledon,' he replied. 'She is a very old lady, and keeps early hours, so you must forgive her for not being downstairs to receive you. You will meet her tomorrow morning. My aunt, who lives with her, would undoubtedly have sat up to receive you had she not gone a few days ago to stay with one of her sisters for a short time.'

'Your grandmother's house?' exclaimed Arabella, almost starting from her chair. 'Good God, why have you brought me to such a place, Mr Beaumaris?'

'Well, you know,' he explained, 'I could not but feel that it was possible you might think better of that notion of eloping. Of course, if, after a night's repose, you still believe we should go to Gretna Green, I assure you I shall escort you there, whatever Ulysses' claims upon me may be. For myself, the more I consider the matter, the more I am convinced that we should do better to steel ourselves to meet the felicitations of our friends, and announce our betrothal in the columns of the society journals in the accepted manner.'

'Mr Beaumaris,' interrupted Arabella, pale but resolute, 'I cannot marry you!' She added, on another of her small sobs: 'I don't know why you should ever have wanted to marry me, but –'

'I have lost my entire fortune on 'Change, and must instantly repair it,' he interrupted promptly.

Arabella rose jerkily, and confronted him. 'I have not a penny in the world!' she announced.

'In that case,' responded Mr Beaumaris, maintaining his clam, 'you really have no choice in the matter: you must obviously marry me. Since we are being frank with one another, I will confess that my fortune is still intact.'

'I deceived you! I am not an heiress!' Arabella said, feeling that he could not have understood her words.

'You never deceived me for a moment,' said Mr Beaumaris, smiling at her in a way which made her tremble still more violently.

'I *lied* to you!' cried Arabella, determined to bring him to a sense of her iniquities.

'Most understandable,' agreed Mr Beaumaris. 'But I am really quite uninterested in heiresses.'

'Mr Beaumaris,' said Arabella earnestly, 'the whole of London believes me to be a wealthy woman!'

'Yes, and since the whole of London must certainly continue in that belief, you have, as I have already pointed out to you, no choice but to marry me,' he said. '*My* fortune, happily, is so large that *your* lack of fortune need never be suspected.'

'Oh, why didn't you tell me you knew the truth?' she cried, wringing her hands.

He possessed himself of them, and held them lightly. 'My dearest goose, why didn't you trust me, when I assured you that you might?' he countered. 'I have cherished throughout the belief that you would confide in me, and you see I was quite right. So certain was I that you would not, when the time actually came, run off with me in this absurd fashion, that I visited my grandmother yesterday, and told her the whole story. She was very much diverted, and commanded me to bring you to stay for a few days with her. I hope you will not object to this: she frightens half the world, but you will have me to support you through the ordeal.'

Arabella pulled her hands resolutely away, and turned from him to hide her quivering lips, and suffused eyes. 'It is worse than you know!' she said, in a stifled tone. 'When you know all the truth, you will not wish to marry me! I have been worse than untruthful: I have been shameless! I can never marry you, Mr Beaumaris!'

'This is most disturbing,' he said. 'Not only have I sent the notice of our betrothal to the *Gazette*, and the *Morning Post*, but I have obtained your father's consent to our marriage.'

At this, she spun round to face him again, a look of utter astonishment in her face. '*My father's consent?*' she repeated incredulously.

'It is usual, you know,' explained Mr Beaumaris apologetically.

'But you do not know my father!'

'On the contrary. I made his acquaintance last week, and spent two most agreeable nights at Heythram,' he said.

'But – Did Lady Bridlington tell you?'

'No, not Lady Bridlington. Your brother let slip the name of his home once, and I have an excellent memory. I am sorry, by the way, that Bertram should have been having such an uncomfortable time during my absence from town. That was quite my fault: I should have sought him out, and settled his difficulties before I left for Yorkshire. I did write to him, but he had unfortunately departed from the Red Lion before the delivery of my letter. However, you won't find that the experience has harmed him, so I must hope to be forgiven.'

Her cheeks were now very much flushed. 'You know it all then! Oh, what must you think of me? I asked you to marry me because – because I wanted you to give me seven hundred pounds to save poor Bertram from a debtor's prison!'

'I know you did,' said Mr Beaumaris cordially. 'I don't know how I contrived to keep my countenance. When did it occur to you, my ridiculous little love, that to demand a large sum of money from your bridegroom as soon as the ring was on your finger might be a trifle awkward?'

'Just now – in your chaise!' she confessed, covering her face with her hands. 'I couldn't do it! I have behaved very, very badly, but when I realised what I was about – oh, indeed, I knew I could never do it!'

'We have both behaved very badly,' he agreed. 'I encouraged Fleetwood to spread the news that you were a great heiress: I even allowed him to suppose that I knew all about your family. I thought it would be amusing to see whether I could make you the rage of London – and I blush to confess it, my darling: it *was* amusing! Nor do I really regret it in the least, for if I had not set out on this most reprehensible course we might never have come much in one another's way again, after our first meeting, and I might never have discovered that I had found the very girl I had been looking for for so long.'

'No, no, how can you say so?' she exclaimed, large tears standing on the ends of her lashes. 'I came to London in the hope of – of contracting an eligible marriage, and I asked you to marry me because you are so very rich! You *could* not wish to marry such an odious creature!'

'No, perhaps I couldn't,' he replied. 'But although you may have forgotten that when I first addressed myself to you, you declined my offer, I have not. If wealth was all your object, I can't conceive what should have induced you to do so! It seemed to me that you were not entirely indifferent to me. All things considered, I decided that my proper course was to present myself to your parents without further loss of time. And I am very glad I did so, for not only did I spend a very pleasant time at the Vicarage, but I also enjoyed a long talk with your mother – By the way, do you know how much you resemble her? More, I think than any of your brothers and sisters, though they are all remarkably handsome. But, as I say, I enjoyed a long talk with her, and was encouraged to hope, from what she told me, that I had not been mistaken in thinking you were not indifferent to me.'

'I never wrote a word to Mama, or even to Sophy, about – about – not being indifferent to you!' Arabella said involuntarily.

'Well, I do not know how that may be,' said Mr Beaumaris, 'but Mama and Sophy were not at all surprised to receive a visit from me. Perhaps you may have mentioned me rather frequently in your letters, or perhaps Lady Bridlington gave Mama a hint that I was the most determined of your suitors.'

The mention of her godmother made Arabella start, and exclaim: 'Lady Bridlington! Good God, I left a letter for her on the table in the hall, telling her of the dreadful thing I had done, and begging her to forgive me!'

'Don't disturb yourself, my love: Lady Bridlington knows very well where you are. Indeed, I found her most helpful, particularly when it came to packing what you would need for a brief sojourn at my grandmother's house. She promised that her own maid should attend to the matter while we were listening to that tedious concert. I daresay she has long since told that son of hers that he may look for the notice of our engagement in tomorrow's *Gazette*, together with the intelligence that we have both of us gone out of town to stay with the Dowager Duchess of Wigan. By the time we reappear in London, we must hope that our various acquaintances will have grown so accustomed to the news that we shall not be quite overwhelmed by their astonishment, their chagrin, or their felicitations. But I am strongly of the opinion that you should permit me to escort you home to Heythram as soon as possible: *you* will naturally wish your father to marry us, and *I* am extremely impatient to carry off my wife without any loss of time. My darling, what in the world have I said to make you cry?'

'Oh, nothing, nothing!' sobbed Arabella. 'Only that I don't deserve to be so happy, and I n-never was indifferent to you, though I t-tried very hard to be, when I thought you were only trifling with m-me!'

Mr Beaumaris then took her firmly into his arms, and kissed her; after which she derived much comfort from clutching the lapel of his elegant coat, and weeping into his shoulder. None of the very gratifying things which Mr Beaumaris murmured into

276

the curls that were tickling his chin had any other effect on her than to make her sob more bitterly than ever, so he presently told her that even his love for her could not prevail upon him to allow her to ruin his favourite coat. This changed her tears to laughter, and after he had dried her face, and kissed her again, she became tolerably composed, and was able to sit down on the sofa beside him, and to accept from him the glass of tepid milk which he told her she must drink if she did not wish to incur Mrs Watchet's displeasure. She smiled mistily, and sipped the milk, saying after a moment: 'And Papa gave his consent! Oh, what will he say when he knows the whole? What did you tell him?'

'I told him the truth,' replied Mr Beaumaris.

Arabella nearly dropped the glass. 'All the truth?' she faltered, dismay in her face.

'All of it – oh, not the truth about Bertram! His name did not enter into our conversation, and I strictly charged him, when I sent him off to Yorkshire, not to divulge one word of his adventures. Much as I like and esteem your father, I cannot feel that any good purpose would be served by distressing him with *that* story. I told him the truth about you and me.'

'Was he – dreadfully displeased with me?' asked Arabella, in a small, apprehensive voice.

'He was, I fear, a little grieved,' owned Mr Beaumaris. 'But when he understood that you would never have announced yourself to have been an heiress had you not overheard me talking like a coxcomb to Charles Fleetwood, he was soon brought to perceive that I was even more to blame for the deception than you.'

'*Was* he?' said Arabella doubtfully.

'Drink your milk, my love! Certainly he was. Between us, your Mama and I were able to show him that without my prompting Charles would never have spread the rumour abroad, and that once the rumour had been so spread it was impossible for you to deny it, since naturally no one ever asked you if it were true. I daresay he may give you a little scold, but I am quite sure you are already forgiven.'

'Did he forgive you too?' asked Arabella, awed.

'*I* had all the merit of making the confession,' Mr Beaumaris pointed out virtuously. 'He forgave me freely. I cannot imagine why you should look so much surprised: I found him in every way delightful, and have seldom enjoyed an evening more than the one I spent conversing with him in his study, after your Mama and Sophy had gone to bed. Indeed, we sat talking until the candles guttered in their sockets.'

Arabella's awed expression became even more marked. 'Dear sir, what – what did you talk *about?*' she enquired, quite unable to visualise Papa and the Nonpareil hob-nobbing together.

'We discussed certain aspects of Wolf's *Prolegomena ad Homerum*, a copy of which work I changed to see upon his bookshelf,' replied Mr Beaumaris calmly. 'I myself picked up a copy when I was in Vienna last year, and was much interested in Wolf's theory that more than one hand was employed in the writing of the *Iliad* and the *Odyssey.*'

'Is – is *that* what the book is about?' asked Arabella.

He smiled, but replied gravely: 'Yes, that is what it is about – though your father, a far more profound scholar than I am, found the opening chapter, which treats of the proper methods to be used in the recension of ancient manuscripts, of even more interest. He took me a little out of my depth there, but I hope I may have profited by his very just observations.'

'Did you *enjoy* that?' demanded Arabella, much impressed.

'Very much. In spite of my frippery ways, you know, I do occasionally enjoy rational conversation, just as I can spend a very agreeable evening playing at lottery-tickets with Mama, and Sophy, and the children.'

'You did not do *that!*' she cried. 'Oh, you are quizzing me! You must have been shockingly bored!'

'Nothing of the sort! The man who could be bored in the midst of such a lively family as yours must be an insufferable fellow, above being pleased by anything. By the by, if that uncle of yours does not come up to scratch, we must do something towards helping Harry to achieve his burning ambition to become a second Nelson. Not the eccentric uncle who died, and left you his entire fortune, but the one who still lives.'

'Oh, pray don't speak of that dreadful fortune ever again!' begged Arabella, hanging down her head.

'But I must speak of it!' objected Mr Beaumaris. 'Since I presume that we shall frequently be inviting the various members of your family to stay with us, and can hardly pass them all off as heirs and heiress, *some* explanation of your superior circumstances must be forthcoming! Your Mama – an admirable woman! – and I decided that the eccentric uncle would serve our turn very well. We were further agreed, quite tacitly, you know, that it will be unnecessary, and, indeed, quite undesirable, to mention the matter to Papa.'

'Oh, no it would never do to tell him that!' she said quickly. 'He would not like it at all, and when he is grieved with any of us – Oh, if only he does not discover the scrape Bertram fell into, and if only Bertram didn't fail to pass that examination at Oxford, which I am much afraid he may have, because it did not sound to me as though –'

'It is not the slightest consequences,' he interrupted. 'Bertram – though Papa does not yet know it – is not going to Oxford: he is going to join a cavalry regiment, where he will feel very much more at home, and, I daresay, become a great credit to us all.'

At this, Arabella caught his hand in her free one, and kissed it, exclaiming, with a sob in her voice: 'How good you are! How much, much *too* good you are, my *dear* Mr Beaumaris!'

'*Never*,' said Mr Beaumaris, snatching his hand away, and taking Arabella into his arms so urgently that the rest of the milk in the glass was spilt over her gown, *Never*, Arabella, dare to do such a thing again! And don't talk such fustian to me, or persist in calling me Mr Beaumaris!'

'Oh, I must!' protested Arabella, into his shoulder. 'I can't call you – I can't call you – Robert!'

'You have called me Robert very prettily, and you will find, if you persevere, that it will rise quite easily to your lips in a very short space of time.'

'Well, if it will please you, I will *try* to say it,' said Arabella. She sat up suddenly, as a thought occurred to her, and said in her impulsive way: 'Oh, Mr Beaumaris – I mean, dear Robert! – there was an unfortunate female, called Leaky Peg, in that horrid house where I went to see poor Bertram, and she was so very kind to him! Do you think –?'

'No, Arabella,' said Mr Beaumaris firmly. 'I do not!'

She was disappointed, but docile. 'No?' she said.

'No,' said Mr Beaumaris, drawing her back into his arm.

'I thought we might have taken her away from that dreadful place,' suggested Arabella, smoothing his coat-lapel with a coaxing hand.

'I am quite sure you did, my love, but while I am prepared to receive into my household climbing-boys and stray curs, I must draw the line at a lady rejoicing in the name of Leaky Peg.'

'You don't think she might learn to become a housemaid, or something of that sort? You know –'

'I only know two things,' interrupted Mr Beaumaris. 'The first is that she is not going to make the attempt in any house of mine; and the second, and by far the more important, is that I adore you, Arabella!'

Arabella was so much pleased by this disclosure that she lost interesting Leaky Peg, and confined herself to the far more agreeable task of convincing Mr Beaumaris that his very obliging sentiments were entirely reciprocated.

The
Corinthian

Georgette Heyer

arrow books

One

The company, ushered by a disapproving butler into the yellow saloon of Sir Richard Wyndham's house in St James's Square, comprised two ladies and one reluctant gentleman. The gentleman, who was not much above thirty years of age, but sadly inclined to fat, seemed to feel the butler's disapproval, for upon that dignified individual's informing the elder of the two ladies that Sir Richard was not at home, he cast a deprecating glance at him, not in the least the glance of a peer of the realm upon a menial, but an age-old look of one helpless man to another, and said in a pleading tone: 'Well, then, don't you think, Lady Wyndham – ? Louisa, hadn't we better – ? I mean, no use going in, my love, is there?'

Neither his wife nor his mother-in-law paid any attention to this craven speech. 'If my brother is gone out, we will await his return,' said Louisa briskly.

'Your poor Papa was always out when one wanted him,' complained Lady Wyndham. 'It is very affecting to me to see Richard growing every day more like him.'

Her fading accents were so lachrymose that it seemed probable that she would dissolve into tears upon her son's doorstep. George, Lord Trevor, was uneasily aware of a hand-kerchief, clutched in one thin, gloved hand, and put forward no further objection to entering the house in the wake of the two ladies.

Declining all offers of refreshment, Lady Trevor escorted her parent into the Yellow Saloon, settled her comfortably upon a satin sofa, and announced her intention of remaining in St James's Square all day, if need be. George, with a very clear idea, born of sympathy, of what would be his brother-in-law's emotions upon returning to his residence to find a family deputation in possession of it, said unhappily: 'You know, I don't think we should, really I don't! I don't like it above half. I wish you would drop this notion you've taken into your heads'

His wife, who was engaged in stripping off her lavender-kid gloves, threw him a look of indulgent contempt. 'My dear George, if *you* are afraid of Richard, let me assure you that *I* am not.'

'Afraid of him! No, indeed! But I wish you will consider that a man of nine-and-twenty won't relish having his affairs meddled with. Besides, he will very likely wonder what the deuce it has to do with me, and I'm sure I can't tell him! I wish I had not come.

Louisa ignored this remark, considering it unworthy of being replied to, which indeed it was, since she ruled her lord with a rod of iron. She was a handsome woman, with a great deal of decision in her face, and a leavening gleam of humour. She was dressed, not perhaps in the height of fashion, which decreed that summer gauzes must reveal every charm of a lady's body, but with great elegance and propriety. Since she had a very good figure, the prevailing mode for high-waisted dresses, with low-cut bodices, and tiny puff-sleeves, became her very well: much better, in fact, than skin-tight pantaloons, and a long-tailed coat became her husband.

Fashion was not kind to George. He looked his best in buckskin breeches and top-boots, but he was unfortunately addicted to dandyism, and pained his friends and relatives by adopting every extravagance of dress, spending as much time over the arrangement of his cravat as Mr Brummell himself, and squeezing his girth into tight stays which had a way of creaking whenever he moved unwarily.

The third member of the party, reclining limply on the satin sofa, was a lady with quite as much determination as her daughter, and a far more subtle way of getting her wishes attended to. A widow of ten years' standing, Lady Wyndham enjoyed the frailest health. The merest hint of opposition was too much for the delicate state of her nerves; and anyone, observing her handkerchief, her vinaigrette, and the hartshorn which she usually kept by her, would have had to be stupid indeed to have failed to appreciate their sinister message. In youth, she had been a beauty; in middle age, everything about her seemed to have faded: hair, cheeks, eyes, and even her voice, which was plaintive, and so gentle that it was a wonder it ever made itself heard. Like her daughter, Lady Wyndham had excellent taste in dress, and since she was fortunate enough to possess a very ample jointure she was able to indulge her liking for the most expensive fal-lals of fashion without in any way curtailing her other expenses. This did not prevent her from thinking herself very badly off, but she was able to enjoy many laments over her straitened circumstances without feeling the least real pinch of poverty, and to win the sympathy of her acquaintances by dwelling sadly on the injustice of her late husband's will, which had placed his only son in the sole possession of his immense fortune. The jointure, her friends deduced hazily, was the veriest pittance.

Lady Wyndham, who lived in a charming house in Clarges Street, could never enter the mansion in St James's Square without suffering a pang. It was not, as might have been supposed from the look of pain she always cast upon it, a family domicile, but had been acquired by her son only a couple of years before. During Sir Edward's lifetime, the family had lived in a much larger, and most inconvenient house in Grosvenor Square. Upon Sir Richard's announcement that he proposed to set up an establishment of his own, this had been given up, so that Lady Wyndham had been able ever since to mourn its loss without being obliged to suffer any longer its inconveniences. But however much she might like her own house in Clarges Street it was not to be supposed that she could bear with equanimity her son's inhabiting a far larger house in St James's Square; and when every other source of grievance failed her, she

3

always came back to that, and said, as she said now, in an ill-used voice: 'I cannot conceive what he should want with a house like this!'

Louisa, who had a very good house of her own, besides an estate in Berkshire, did not in the least grudge her brother his mansion. She replied: 'It doesn't signify, Mama. Except that he must have been thinking of marriage when he bought it. Would you not say so, George?'

George was flattered at being thus appealed to, but he was an honest, painstaking person, and he could not bring himself to say that he thought Richard had had any thought of marriage in his head, either when he had bought the house, or at any other time.

Louisa was displeased. 'Well!' she said, looking resolute, 'he must be brought to think of marriage!'

Lady Wyndham lowered her smelling-salts to interpolate: 'Heaven knows I would never urge my boy to do anything distasteful, but it has been an understood thing for years that he and Melissa Brandon would seal the long friendship between our families with the Nuptial Tie!'

George goggled at her, and wished himself otherwise.

'If he doesn't wish to marry Melissa, I'm sure I should be the last person to press her claim,' said Louisa. 'But it is high time that he married someone, and if he has no other suitable young female in his eye, Melissa it must be.'

'I do not know how to face Lord Saar,' bemoaned Lady Wyndham, raising the vinaigrette to her nose again. 'Or poor dear Emily, with three girls besides Melissa to dispose of, and none of them more than passable. Sophia has spots, too.'

'I do not consider Augusta hopeless,' said Louisa fairly. 'Amelia, too, may improve.'

'Squints!' said George.

'A slight cast in one eye,' corrected Louisa. 'However, we are not concerned with that. Melissa is an extremely handsome creature. No one can deny *that*!'

'And such a desirable connection!' sighed Lady Wyndham. 'Quite one of the best families!'

4

'They tell me Saar won't last another five years, not at the rate he's going now,' said George. 'Everything mortgaged up to the hilt, and Saar drinking himself into his grave! They say his father did the same.'

Both ladies regarded him with disfavour. 'I hope, George, you do not mean to imply that Melissa is addicted to the bottle?' said his wife.

'Oh no, no! Lord, no, I never thought of such a thing! I'm sure she's an excellent young woman. But this I will say, Louisa: I don't blame Richard if he don't want her!' said George defiantly. 'Myself, I'd as soon marry a statue!'

'I must say,' conceded Louisa, 'she is a trifle cold, perhaps. But it is a very delicate position for her, you'll allow. It has been understood since both were children that she and Richard would make a match of it, and *she* knows that as well as *we* do. And here is Richard, behaving in the most odious way! I am out of all patience with him!'

George rather liked his brother-in-law, but he knew that it would be foolhardy to defend him, so he held his peace. Lady Wyndham took up the tale of woe. 'Heaven forbid that I should force my only son to a disagreeable marriage, but I live in hourly dread of his bringing home some dreadful, low-born creature on his arm, and expecting me to welcome her!'

A vision of his brother-in-law crossed George's mind's eye. He said doubtfully: 'Really, you know, I don't think he'll do that, ma'am.'

'George is quite right,' announced Louisa. 'I should think the better of Richard if he did. It quite shocks me to see him so impervious to every feminine charm! It is a great piece of nonsense for him to dislike the opposite sex, but one thing is certain: dislike females he may, but he owes a duty to the name, and marry he must! I am sure I have been at pains to introduce him to every eligible young woman in town, for I am by no means set on his marrying Melissa Brandon. Well! He would not look twice at any of them, so if that is the mind he is in, Melissa will suit him very well.'

5

'Richard thinks they all want him for his money,' ventured George.

'I dare say they may. What has that to say to anything, pray? I imagine you do not mean to tell me that Richard is romantic!'

No, George was forced to admit that Richard was not romantic.

'If I live to see him suitably married, I can die content!' said Lady Wyndham, who had every expectation of living for another thirty years. 'His present course fills my poor mother's heart with foreboding!'

Loyalty forced George to expostulate. 'No, really, ma'am! Really, I say! There's no harm in Richard, not the least in the world, 'pon my honour!'

'He puts me out of all patience!' said Louisa. 'I love him dearly, but I despise him with all my heart! Yes, I do, and I do not care who hears me say so! He cares for nothing but the set of his cravat, the polish on his boots, and the blending of his snuff!'

'His horses!' begged George unhappily.

'Oh, his horses! Very well! Let us admit him to be a famous whip! He beat Sir John Lade in their race to Brighton! A fine achievement indeed!'

'Very handy with his fives!' gasped George, sinking but game.

'*You* may admire a man for frequenting Jackson's Saloon, and Cribb's Parlour! *I* do not!'

'No, my love,' George said. 'No, indeed, my love!'

'And I make no doubt you see nothing reprehensible in his addiction to the gaming-table! But I had it on the most excellent authority that he dropped three thousand pounds at one sitting at Almack's!'

Lady Wyndham moaned, and dabbed at her eyes. 'Oh, do not say so!'

'Yes, but he's so devilish wealthy it can't signify!' said George.

'Marriage,' said Louisa, 'will put a stop to such fripperies.'

The depressing picture this dictum conjured up reduced George to silence. Lady Wyndham said, in a voice dark with mystery: 'Only a mother could appreciate my anxieties. He is at a dangerous age, and I live from day to day in dread of what he may do!'

George opened his mouth, encountered a look from his wife, shut it again, and tugged unhappily at his cravat.

The door opened; a Corinthian stood upon the threshold, cynically observing his relatives. 'A thousand apologies,' said the Corinthian, bored but polite. 'Your very obedient servant, ma'am. Louisa, yours! My poor George! Ah – was I expecting you?'

'Apparently not!' retorted Louisa, bristling.

'No, you weren't. I mean, they took it into their heads – *I* couldn't stop them!' said George heroically.

'I thought I was not,' said the Corinthian, closing the door, and advancing into the room. 'But my memory, you know, my lamentable memory!'

George, running an experienced eye over his brother-in-law, felt his soul stir. 'B'gad, Richard, I like that! That's a devilish well-cut coat, 'pon my honour, it is! Who made it?'

Sir Richard lifted an arm, and glanced at his cuff. 'Weston, George, only Weston.'

'George!' said Louisa awfully.

Sir Richard smiled faintly, and crossed the room to his mother's side. She held out her hand to him, and he bowed over it with languid grace, just brushing it with his lips. 'A thousand apologies, ma'am!' he repeated. 'I trust my people have looked after you – er – *all* of you?' His lazy glance swept the room. 'Dear me!' he said. 'George, you are near to it: oblige me, my dear fellow, by pulling the bell!'

'We do not need any refreshment, I thank you, Richard,' said Louisa.

The faint, sweet smile silenced her as none of her husband's expostulations had ever done. 'My dear Louisa, you mistake – I assure you, you mistake! George is in the most urgent need of – er – stimulant. Yes, Jeffries, I rang. The Madeira – oh, ah! and some ratafia, Jeffries, if you please!'

'Richard, that's the best Waterfall I've ever seen!' exclaimed

George, his admiring gaze fixed on the intricate arrangement of the Corinthian's cravat.

'You flatter me, George; I fear you flatter me.'

'Pshaw!' snapped Louisa.

'Precisely, my dear Louisa,' agreed Sir Richard amiably.

'Do not try to provoke me, Richard!' said Louisa, on a warning note. 'I will allow your appearance to be everything that it should be – admirable, I am sure!'

'One does one's poor best,' murmured Sir Richard.

Her bosom swelled. 'Richard, I could hit you!' she declared.

The smile grew, allowing her a glimpse of excellent white teeth. 'I don't think you could, my dear.'

George so far forgot himself as to laugh. A quelling glance was directed upon him. 'George, be quiet!' said Louisa.

'I must say,' conceded Lady Wyndham, whose maternal pride could not quite be overborne, 'there is no one, except Mr Brummell, of course, who looks as well as you do, Richard.'

He bowed, but he did not seem to be unduly elated by this encomium. Possibly he took it as his due. He was a very notable Corinthian. From his Wind-swept hair (most difficult of all styles to achieve), to the toes of his gleaming Hessians, he might have posed as an advertisement for the Man of Fashion. His fine shoulders set off a coat of superfine cloth to perfection; his cravat, which had excited George's admiration, had been arranged by the hands of a master; his waistcoat was chosen with a nice eye; his biscuit-coloured pantaloons showed not one crease; and his Hessians with their jaunty gold tassels, had not only been made for him by Hoby, but were polished, George suspected, with a blacking mixed with champagne. A quizzing-glass on a black ribbon hung round his neck; a fob at his waist; and in one hand he carried a Sèvres snuff-box. His air proclaimed his unutterable boredom, but no tailoring, no amount of studied nonchalance, could conceal the muscle in his thighs, or the strength of his shoulders. Above the starched points of his shirt-collar, a weary, handsome face showed its owner's disillusionment. Heavy lids drooped over grey eyes which were intelligent enough, but only to observe the vanities of the world; the smile which just touched that resolute mouth seemed to mock the follies of Sir Richard's fellow men.

Jeffries came back into the room with a tray, and set it upon a table. Louisa waved aside the offer of refreshment, but Lady Wyndham accepted it, and George, emboldened, by his mother-in-law's weakness, took a glass of Madeira.

'I dare say,' said Louisa, 'that you are wondering what we are here for.'

'I never waste my time in idle speculation,' replied Sir Richard gently. 'I feel sure that you are going to tell me what you are here for.'

'Mama and I have come to speak to you about your marriage,' said Louisa, taking the plunge.

'And what,' enquired Sir Richard, 'has George come to speak to me about?'

'That too, of course!'

'No, I haven't!' disclaimed George hurriedly. 'You know I said I'd have nothing to do with it! I never wanted to come at all!'

'Have some more Madeira,' said Sir Richard soothingly.

'Well, thank you, yes, I will. But don't think I'm here to badger you about something which don't concern me, because I'm not!'

'Richard!' said Lady Wyndham deeply, 'I dare no longer meet Saar face to face!'

'As bad as that, is he?' said Sir Richard. 'I haven't seen him myself these past few weeks, but I'm not at all surprised. I fancy I heard something about it, from someone – I forget whom. Taken to brandy, hasn't he?'

'Sometimes,' said Lady Wyndham, 'I think you are utterly devoid of sensibility!'

'He is merely trying to provoke you, Mama. You know perfectly well what Mama means, Richard. When do you mean to offer for Melissa?'

There was a slight pause. Sir Richard set down his empty wine-glass, and flicked with one long finger the petals of a flower in a bowl on the table. 'This year, next year, sometime – or never, my dear Louisa.'

'I am very sure she considers herself as good as plighted to you,' Louisa said.

Sir Richard was looking down at the flower under his hand, but at this he raised his eyes to his sister's face, in an oddly keen, swift look. 'Is that so?'

'How should it be otherwise? You know very well that Papa and Lord Saar designed it so years ago.'

The lids veiled his eyes again. 'How medieval of you!' sighed Sir Richard.

'Now, don't, pray, take me up wrongly, Richard! If you don't like Melissa, there is no more to be said. But you do like her – or if you don't, at least *I* never heard you say so! What Mama and I feel – and George, too – is that it is time and more that you were settled in life.'

A pained glance reproached Lord Trevor. '*Et tu, Brute?*' said Sir Richard.

'I swear I never said so!' declared George, choking over his Madeira. 'It was all Louisa. I dare say I may have agreed with her. *You* know how it is, Richard!'

'I know,' agreed Sir Richard, sighing. 'You too, Mama?'

'Oh Richard, I live only to see you happily married, with your children about you!' said Lady Wyndham, in trembling tones.

A slight, unmistakable shudder ran through the Corinthian. 'My children about me . . . Yes. Precisely, ma'am. Pray continue!'

'You owe it to the name,' pursued his mother. 'You are the last of the Wyndhams, for it's not to be supposed that your Uncle Lucius will marry at this late date. There is Melissa, dear girl, the very wife for you! So handsome, so distinguished – birth, breeding: everything of the most desirable!'

'Ah – your pardon, ma'am, but do you include Saar, and Cedric, not to mention Beverley, under that heading?'

'That's exactly what I say!' broke in George. '"It's all very well," I said, "and if a man likes to marry an iceberg it's all one to me, but you can't call Saar a desirable father-in-law, damme if you can! While as for the girl's precious brothers," I said, "they'll ruin Richard inside a year!"'

'Nonsense!' said Louisa. 'It is understood, of course, that Richard would make handsome settlements. But as for his being responsible for Cedric's and Beverley's debts, I'm sure I know of no reason why he should!'

'You comfort me, Louisa,' said Sir Richard.

She looked up at him not unaffectionately. 'Well, I think it is time to be frank, Richard. People will be saying next that you are playing fast and loose with Melissa, for you must know the understanding between you is an open secret. If you had chosen to marry someone else, five, ten years ago, it would have been a different thing. But so far as I am aware your affections have never even been engaged, and here you are, close on thirty, as good as pledged to Melissa Brandon, and nothing settled!'

Lady Wyndham, though in the fullest agreement with her daughter, was moved at this point to defend her son, which she did by reminding Louisa that Richard was only twenty-nine after all.

'Mama, Richard will be thirty in less than six months. For I,' said Louisa with resolution, 'am turned thirty-one.'

'Louisa, I am touched!' said Sir Richard. 'Only the deepest sisterly devotion, I am persuaded, could have wrung from you such an admission.'

She could not repress a smile, but said with as much severity as she could muster: 'It is no laughing matter. You are no longer in your first youth, and you know as well as I do that it is your duty to think seriously of marriage.'

'Strange,' mused Sir Richard, 'that one's duty should be invariably so disagreeable.'

'I know,' said George, heaving a sigh. 'Very true! very true indeed!'

'Pooh! nonsense! What a coil you make of a simple matter!' Louisa said. 'Now, if I were to press you to marry some romantical miss, always wanting you to make love to her, and

11

crying her eyes out every time you chose to seek your amusements out of her company, you might have reason to complain. But Melissa – yes, an iceberg, George, if you like, and what else, pray, is Richard? – Melissa, I say, will never plague you in *that* way.'

Sir Richard's eyes dwelled inscrutably upon her face for a moment. Then he moved to the table and poured himself out another glass of Madeira.

Louisa said defensively: 'Well, you don't *wish* her to cling about your neck, I suppose?'

'Not at all.'

'And you are not in love with any other woman, are you?'

'I am not.'

'Very well, then! To be sure, if you were in the habit of falling in and out of love, it would be a different matter. But, to be plain with you, you are the coldest, most indifferent, selfish creature alive, Richard, and you will find in Melissa an admirable partner.'

Inarticulate clucking sounds from George, indicative of protest, caused Sir Richard to wave a hand towards the Madeira. 'Help yourself, George, help yourself!'

'I must say, I think it most unkind in you to speak to your brother like that,' said Lady Wyndham. 'Not but what you *are* selfish, dear Richard. I'm sure I have said so over and over again. But so it is with the greater part of the world! Everywhere one turns one meets with nothing but ingratitude!'

'If I have done Richard an injustice, I will willingly ask his pardon,' said Louisa.

'Very handsomely said, my dear sister. You have done me no injustice. I wish you will not look so distressed, George: your pity is quite wasted on me, I assure you. Tell me, Louisa: have you reason to suppose that Melissa expects me to – er – pay my addresses to her?'

'Certainly I have. She has been expecting it any time these five years!'

Sir Richard looked a little startled. 'Poor girl!' he said. 'I must have been remarkably obtuse.'

His mother and sister exchanged glances. 'Does that mean that you will think seriously of marriage?' asked Louisa.

He looked thoughtfully down at her. 'I suppose it must come to that.'

'Well, for my part,' said George, defying his wife, 'I would look around me for some other eligible female! Lord, there are dozens of 'em littering town! Why, I've seen I don't know how many setting their caps at you! Pretty ones, too, but you never notice them, you ungrateful dog!'

'Oh yes, I do,' said Sir Richard, with a curl of the lips.

'*Must* George be vulgar?' asked Lady Wyndham tragically.

'Be quiet, George! And as for you, Richard, I consider it in the highest degree nonsensical for you to take up that attitude. There is no denying that you're the biggest catch on the Marriage Mart – Yes, Mama, that is vulgar too, and I beg your pardon – but you have a lower opinion of yourself than I credit you with if you can suppose that your fortune is the only thing about you which makes you a desirable *parti*. You are generally accounted handsome – indeed, no one, I believe, could deny that your person is such as must please; and when you will take the trouble to be conciliating there is nothing in your manners to disgust the nicest taste.'

'This encomium, Louisa, almost unmans me,' said Sir Richard, much moved.

'I am perfectly serious. I was about to add that you often spoil everything by your odd humours. I do not know how you should expect to engage a female's affection when you never bestow the least distinguishing notice upon any woman! I do not say that you are uncivil, but there is a languor, a reserve in your manner, which must repel a woman of sensibility.'

'I am a hopeless case indeed,' said Sir Richard.

'If you want to know what I think, which I do not suppose you do, so you need not tell me so, it is that you are spoilt, Richard. You have too much money, you have done everything you wished to do before you are out of your twenties; you have been courted by match-making Mamas, fawned on by toadies, and indulged by all the world. The end of it is that you are bored to death. There! I have said it, and though you may not thank me for it, you will admit that I am right.'

'Quite right,' agreed Sir Richard. 'Hideously right, Louisa!'

She got up. 'Well, I advise you to get married and settle down. Come, Mama! We have said all we meant to say, and you know we are to call in Brook Street on our way home. George, do you mean to come with us?'

'No,' said George. 'Not to call in Brook Street. I daresay I shall stroll up to White's presently.'

'Just as you please, my love,' said Louisa, drawing on her gloves again.

When the ladies had been escorted to the waiting barouche, George did not at once set out for his club, but accompanied his brother-in-law back into the house. He preserved a sympathetic silence until they were out of earshot of the servants, but caught Sir Richard's eye then, in a very pregnant look, and uttered the one word: 'Women!'

'Quite so,' said Sir Richard.

'Do you know what I'd do if I were you, my boy?'

'Yes,' said Sir Richard.

George was disconcerted. 'Damn it, you can't know!'

'You would do precisely what I shall do.'

'What's that?'

'Oh – offer for Melissa Brandon, of course,' said Sir Richard.

'Well, I wouldn't,' said George positively. 'I wouldn't marry Melissa Brandon for fifty sisters! I'd find a cosier armful, 'pon my soul I would!'

'The cosiest armful of my acquaintance was never so cosy as when she wanted to see my purse-strings untied,' said Sir Richard cynically.

George shook his head. 'Bad, very bad! I must say, it's enough to sour any man. But Louisa's right, you know: you ought to get married. Won't do to let the name die out.' An idea occurred to him. 'You wouldn't care to put it about that you'd lost all your money, I suppose?'

'No,' said Sir Richard, 'I wouldn't.'

'I read somewhere of a fellow who went off to some place where he wasn't known. Devil of a fellow he was: some kind of a foreign Count, I think. I don't remember precisely, but there was a girl in it, who fell in love with him for his own sake.'

'There would be,' said Sir Richard.

'You don't like it?' George rubbed his nose, a little crestfallen. 'Well, damme if I know what to suggest!'

He was still pondering the matter when the butler announced Mr Wyndham, and a large, portly, and convivial-looking gentleman rolled into the room, ejaculating cheerfully: 'Hallo, George! You here? Ricky, my boy, your mother's been at me again, confound her! Made me promise I'd come round to see you, though what the devil she thinks I can do is beyond me!'

'Spare me!' said Sir Richard wearily. 'I have already sustained a visit from my mother, not to mention Louisa.'

'Well, I'm sorry for you, my boy, and if you take my advice you'll marry that Brandon-wench, and be done with it. What's that you have there? Madeira? I'll take a glass.'

Sir Richard gave him one. He lowered his bulk into a large armchair, stretched his legs out before him, and raised the glass. 'Here's a health to the bridegroom!' he said, with a chuckle. 'Don't look so glum, nevvy! Think of the joy you'll be bringing into Saar's life!'

'Damn you,' said Sir Richard. 'If you had ever had a shred of proper feeling, Lucius, you would have got married fifty years ago, and reared a pack of brats in your image. A horrible thought, I admit, but at least I should not now be cast for the rôle of Family Sacrifice.'

'Fifty years ago,' retorted his uncle, quite unmoved by these insults, 'I was only just breeched. This is a very tolerable wine, Ricky. By the way, they tell me young Beverley Brandon's badly dipped. You'll be a damned public benefactor if you marry that girl. Better let your lawyer attend to the settlements, though. I'd be willing to lay you a monkey Saar tries to bleed you white. What's the matter with you, George? Got the toothache?'

'I don't like it,' said George. 'I told Louisa so at the outset, but you know what women are! Myself, I wouldn't have Melissa Brandon if she were the last woman left single.'

'What, she ain't the spotty one, surely?' demanded Lucius, concerned.

'No, that's Sophia.'

'Oh, well, nothing to worry about then! You marry the girl, Ricky: you'll never have any peace if you don't. Fill up your glass, George, and we'll have another toast!'

'What is it this time?' enquired Sir Richard, replenishing the glasses. 'Don't spare me!'

'To a pack of brats in your image, nevvy: here's to 'em!' grinned his uncle.

Two

Lord Saar lived in Brook Street with his wife, and his family of two sons and four daughters. Sir Richard Wyndham, driving to his prospective father-in-law's house twenty-four hours after his interview with his own parent, was fortunate enough to find Saar away from home, and Lady Saar, the butler informed him, on her way to Bath with the Honourable Sophia. He fell instead into the arms of the Honourable Cedric Brandon, a rakish young gentleman of lamentable habits, and a disastrous charm of manner.

'Ricky, my only friend!' cried the Honourable Cedric, dragging Sir Richard into a small saloon at the back of the house. 'Don't tell me you've come to offer for Melissa! They say good news don't kill a man, but *I* never listen to gossip! M'father says ruin stares us in the face. Lend me the money, dear boy, and I'll buy myself a pair of colours, and be off to the Peninsula, damme if I won't! But listen to me, Ricky! *Are* you listening?' He looked anxiously at Sir Richard, appeared satisfied, and said, wagging a solemn finger: 'Don't do it! There isn't a fortune big enough to settle *our* little affairs: take my word for it! Have nothing to do with Beverley! They say Fox gamed away a fortune before he was twenty-one. Give you my word, he was nothing to Bev, nothing at all. Between ourselves, Ricky, the old man has taken to brandy. H'sh! Not a word! Mustn't tell tales about m'father! But run, Ricky! That's my advice to you: *run*!'

'Would you buy yourself a pair of colours, if I gave you the money?' asked Sir Richard.

'Sober, yes; drunk, no!' replied Cedric, with his wholly disarming smile. 'I'm very sober now, but I shan't be so for long. Don't give me a groat, dear old boy! Don't give Bev a groat! He's a bad man. Now, when I'm sober I'm a good man – but I ain't sober above six hours out of the twenty-four, so you be warned! Now I'm off. I've done my best for you, for I like you, Ricky, but if you go to perdition in spite of me, I'll wash my hands of you. No, damme, I'll sponge on you for the rest of my days! Think, dear boy, think! Bev and your very obedient on your doorstep six days out of seven – duns – threats – wife's brothers done-up – pockets to let – wife in tears – nothing to do but pay! Don't do it! Fact is, we ain't worth it!'

'Wait!' Sir Richard said, barring his passage. 'If I settle your debts, will you go to the Peninsula?'

'Ricky, it's you who aren't sober. Go home!'

'Consider, Cedric, how well you would look in Hussar uniform!'

An impish smile danced in Cedric's eyes. 'Wouldn't I just! But at this present I'd look better in Hyde Park. Out of the way, dear boy! I've a very important engagement. Backed a goose to win a hundred-yard race against a turkey-cock. Can't lose! Greatest sporting event of the season!'

He was gone on the words, leaving Sir Richard, not, indeed, to run, as advised, but to await the pleasure of the Honourable Melissa Brandon.

She did not keep him waiting for long. A servant came to request him to step upstairs, and he followed the man up the wide staircase to the withdrawing-room on the first floor.

Melissa Brandon was a handsome, dark-haired young woman, a little more than twenty-five years old. Her profile was held to be faultless, but in full face her eyes were discovered to be rather too hard for beauty. She had not, in her first seasons, lacked suitors, but none of the gentlemen attracted by her undeniable good looks, had ever, in the cock-fighting phrase of her graceless elder brother, come up to scratch. As he bowed over her hand, Sir Richard remembered George's iceberg simile, and at once banished it from his obedient mind.

'Well, Richard?'

Melissa's voice was cool, rather matter-of-fact, just as her smile seemed more a mechanical civility than a spontaneous expression of pleasure.

'I hope I see you well, Melissa?' Sir Richard said formally.

'Perfectly, I thank you. Pray sit down! I apprehend that you have come to discuss the question of our marriage.'

He regarded her from under slightly raised brows. 'Dear me!' he said mildly. 'Someone would appear to have been busy.'

She was engaged upon some stitchery, and went on plying her needle with unruffled composure. 'Do not let us beat about the bush!' she said. 'I am certainly past the age of being missish, and you, I believe, may rank as a sensible man.'

'Were you ever missish?' enquired Sir Richard.

'I trust not. I have no patience with such folly. Nor am I romantic. In that respect, we must be thought to be well-suited.'

'Must we?' said Sir Richard, gently swinging his gold-handled quizzing-glass to and fro.

She seemed amused. 'Certainly! I trust you have not, at this late date, grown sentimental! It would be quite absurd!'

'Senility,' pensively observed Sir Richard, 'often brings sentiment in its train. Or so I have been informed.'

'We need not concern ourselves with that. I like you very well, Richard, but there is just a little nonsense in your disposition which makes you turn everything to jest. I myself am of a more serious nature.'

'Then in *that* respect, we cannot be thought to be well-suited,' suggested Sir Richard.

'I do not consider the objection insuperable. The life you have chosen to lead up till now has not been such as to encourage serious reflection, after all. I dare say you may grow more dependable, for you do not want for sense. *That*, however, must be left to the future. At all events, I am not so unreasonable as to feel the difference in our natures to be an impassable barrier to marriage.'

'Melissa,' said Sir Richard, 'will you tell me something?'

She looked up. 'Pray, what do you wish me to tell you?'

'Have you ever been in love?' asked Sir Richard.

She coloured slightly. 'No. From my observation, I am thankful that I have not. There is something excessively vulgar about persons under the sway of strong emotions. I do not say it is *wrong*, but I believe I have something more of fastidiousness than most, and I find such subjects extremely distasteful.'

'You do not,' Sir Richard drawled, 'envisage the possibility of – er – falling in love at some future date?'

'My dear Richard! With whom, pray?'

'Shall we say with myself?'

She laughed. 'Now you are being absurd! If you were told that it would be necessary to approach me with some show of love-making, you were badly advised. Ours would be a marriage of convenience. I could contemplate nothing else. I like you very well, but you are not at all the sort of man to arouse those warmer passions in my breast. But I see no reason why *that* should worry either of us. If *you* were romantic, it would be a different matter.'

'I fear,' said Sir Richard, 'that I must be very romantic.'

'I suppose you are jesting again,' she replied, with a faint shrug.

'Not at all. I am so romantic that I indulge my fancy with the thought of some woman – doubtless mythical – who might desire to marry me, not because I am a very rich man, but because – you will have to forgive the vulgarity – because she loved me!'

She looked rather contemptuous. 'I should have supposed you to be past the age of fustian, Richard. I say nothing against love, but, frankly, love-matches seem to me a trifle beneath us. One would say you had been hobnobbing with the bourgeoisie at Islington Spa, or some such low place! I do not forget that I am a Brandon. I dare say we are very proud; indeed, I hope we are!'

'That,' said Sir Richard dryly, 'is an aspect of the situation which, I confess, had not so far occurred to me.'

She was amazed. 'I had not thought it possible! I imagined

everyone knew what we Brandons feel about our name, our birth, our tradition!'

'I hesitate to wound you, Melissa,' said Sir Richard, 'but the spectacle of a woman of your name, birth, and tradition, cold-bloodedly offering herself to the highest bidder is not one calculated to impress the world with a very strong notion of her pride.'

'This is indeed the language of the theatre!' she exclaimed. 'My duty to my family demands that I should marry well, but let me assure you that even *that* could not make me stoop to ally myself with one of inferior breeding.'

'Ah, this is pride indeed!' said Sir Richard, faintly smiling.

'I do not understand you. You must know that my father's affairs are in such case as – in short –'

'I am aware,' Sir Richard said gently. 'I apprehend it is to be my privilege to – er – unravel Lord Saar's affairs.'

'But of course!' she replied, surprised out of her statuesque calm. 'No other consideration could have prevailed upon me to accept your suit!'

'This,' said Sir Richard, pensively regarding the toe of one Hessian boot, 'becomes a trifle delicate. If frankness is to be the order of the day, my dear Melissa, I must point out to you that I have not yet – er – proffered my suit.'

She was quite undisturbed by this snub, but replied coldly: 'I did not suppose that you would so far forget what is due to our positions as to approach *me* with an offer. We do not belong to *that* world. You will no doubt seek an interview with my father.'

'I wonder if I shall?' said Sir Richard.

'I imagine that you most certainly will,' responded the lady, snipping her thread. 'Your circumstances are as well known to me as mine are to you. If I may say so bluntly, you are fortunate to be in a position to offer for a Brandon.'

He looked meditatively at her, but made no remark. After a pause, she continued: 'As for the future, neither of us, I trust, would make great demands upon the other. You have your amusements: they do not concern me, and however much my reason may deprecate your addiction to pugilism, curricle-racing, and deep basset –'

'Pharaoh,' he interpolated.

'Very well, pharaoh: it is all one. However much I may deprecate such follies, I say, I do not desire to interfere with your tastes.'

'You are very obliging,' bowed Sir Richard. 'Bluntly, Melissa, I may do as I please if I will hand you my purse?'

'That is putting it bluntly indeed,' she replied composedly. She folded up her needlework, and laid it aside. 'Papa has been expecting a visit from you. He will be sorry to hear that you called while he was away from home. He will be with us again to-morrow, and you may be sure of finding him, if you care to call at – shall we say eleven o'clock?'

He rose. 'Thank you, Melissa. I feel that my time has not been wasted, even though Lord Saar was not here to receive me.'

'I hope not, indeed,' she said, extending her hand. 'Come! We have had a talk which must, I feel, prove valuable. You think me unfeeling, I dare say, but you will do me the justice to admit that I have not stooped to unworthy pretence. Our situation is peculiar, which is why I overcame my reluctance to discuss the question of our marriage with you. We have been as good as betrothed these five years, and more.'

He took her hand. 'Have you considered yourself betrothed to me these five years?' he enquired.

For the first time in their interview her eyes failed to meet his. 'Certainly,' she replied.

'I see,' said Sir Richard, and took his leave of her.

He put in a belated appearance at Almack's that evening. No one, admiring his *point-de-vice* appearance, or listening to his lazy drawl, could have supposed him to be on the eve of making the most momentous decision of his life. Only his uncle, rolling into the club some time after midnight, and observing the dead men at his elbow, guessed that the die had been cast. He told George Trevor, whom he found just rising from the basset-table, that Ricky was taking it hard, a pronouncement which distressed

22

George, and made him say: 'I have not exchanged two words with him. Do you tell me he has actually offered for Melissa Brandon?'

'I'm not telling you anything,' said Lucius. 'All I say is that he's drinking hard and plunging deep.'

In great concern, George seized the first opportunity that offered of engaging his brother-in-law's attention. This was not until close on three o'clock, when Sir Richard at last rose from the pharaoh-table, and Sir Richard was not, by that time, in the mood for private conversation. He had lost quite a large sum of money, and had drunk quite a large quantity of brandy, but neither of these circumstances was troubling him.

'No luck, Ricky?' his uncle asked him.

A somewhat hazy but still perfectly intelligent glance mocked him. 'Not at cards, Lucius. But think of the adage!'

George knew that Sir Richard could carry his wine as well as any man of his acquaintance, but a certain reckless note in his voice alarmed him. He plucked at his sleeve, and said in a lowered tone: 'I wish you will let me have a word with you!'

'Dear George – my very dear George!' said Sir Richard, amiably smiling. 'You must be aware that I am not – quite – sober. No words to-night.'

'I shall come round to see you in the morning, then,' said George, forgetting that it was already morning.

'I shall have the devil of a head,' said Sir Richard.

He made his way out of the club, his curly-brimmed hat at an angle on his head, his ebony cane tucked under one arm. He declined the porter's offer to call up a chair, remarking sweetly: 'I am devilish drunk, and I shall walk.'

The porter grinned. He had seen many gentlemen in all the various stages of inebriety, and he did not think that Sir Richard, who spoke with only the faintest slurring of his words, and who walked with quite wonderful balance, was in very desperate straits. If he had not known Sir Richard well, he would not, he thought, have seen anything amiss with him, beyond his setting off in quite the wrong direction for St James's Square. He felt constrained to call Sir Richard's attention to this, but begged pardon when Sir Richard said: 'I know. The dawn is calling me, however. I am going for a long, long walk.'

'Quite so, sir,' said the porter, and stepped back.

Sir Richard, his head swimming a little from sudden contact with the cool air, strolled aimlessly away in a northerly direction.

His head cleared after a while. In a detached manner, he reflected that it would probably begin to ache in a short time, and he would feel extremely unwell, and not a little sorry for himself. At the moment, however, while the fumes of brandy still wreathed about his brain, a curious irresponsibility possessed him. He felt reckless, remote, divorced from his past and his future. The dawn was spreading a grey light over the quiet streets, and the breeze fanning his cheeks was cool, and fresh enough to make him glad of his light evening cloak. He wandered into Brook Street, and laughed up at the shuttered windows of Saar's house. 'My gentle bride!' he said, and kissed his fingers in the direction of the house. 'God, what a damned fool I am!'

He repeated this, vaguely pleased with the remark, and walked down the long street. It occurred to him that his gentle bride would scarcely be flattered, if she could see him now, and this thought made him laugh again. The Watch, encountered at the north end of Grosvenor Square, eyed him dubiously, and gave him a wide berth. Gentlemen in Sir Richard's condition not infrequently amused themselves with a light-hearted pastime known as Boxing the Watch, and this member of that praiseworthy force was not anxious to court trouble.

Sir Richard did not notice the Watch, nor, to do him justice, would he have felt in the least tempted to molest him if he had noticed him. Somewhere, in the recesses of his brain, Sir Richard was aware that he was the unluckiest dog alive. He felt very bitter about this, as though all the world were in league against him; and, as he branched off erratically down a quiet side street, he was cynically sorry for himself, that in ten years spent in the best circles he had not had the common good fortune to meet one female whose charms had cost him a single hour's sleep. It did not seem probable that he would be more fortunate in the future. 'Which, I suppose,' remarked Sir Richard to one of the new gas-lamps, 'is a – is a consummation devoutly to be wished, since I am about to offer for Melissa Brandon.'

It was at this moment that he became aware of a peculiar circumstance. Someone was climbing out of a second-storey window of one of the prim houses on the opposite side of the street.

Sir Richard stood still, and blinked at this unexpected sight. His divine detachment still clung to him; he was interested in what he saw, but by no means concerned with it. 'Undoubtedly a burglar,' he said, and leaned nonchalantly on his cane to watch the end of the adventure. His somewhat sleepy gaze discovered that whoever was escaping from the prim house was proposing to do so by means of knotted sheets, which fell disastrously short of the ground. '*Not* a burglar,' decided Sir Richard, and crossed the road.

By the time he had reached the opposite kerbstone, the mysterious fugitive had arrived, somewhat fortuitously, at the end of his improvised rope, and was dangling precariously above the shallow area, trying with one desperate foot to find some kind of a resting-place on the wall of the house. Sir Richard saw that he was a very slight youth, only a boy, in fact, and went in a leisurely fashion to the rescue.

The fugitive caught sight of him as he descended the area-steps, and gasped with a mixture of fright and thankfulness: 'Oh! Could you help me, please? I didn't know it was so far. I thought I should be able to jump, only I don't think I can.'

'My engaging youth,' said Sir Richard, looking up at the flushed face peering down at him. 'What, may I ask, are you doing on the end of that rope?'

'*Hush!*' begged the fugitive. 'Do you think you could catch me, if I let go?'

'I will do my poor best,' promised Sir Richard.

The fugitive's feet were only just above his reach, and in

another five seconds the fugitive descended into his arms with a rush that made him stagger, and almost lose his balance. He retained it by a miracle, clasping strongly to his chest an unexpectedly light body.

Sir Richard was not precisely sober, but although the brandy fumes had produced in his brain a not unpleasant sense of irresponsibility, they had by no means fuddled his intellect. Sir Richard, his chin tickled by curls, and his arms full of fugitive, made a surprising discovery. He set the fugitive down, saying in a matter-of-fact voice: 'Yes, but I don't think you are a youth, after all.'

'No, I'm a girl,' replied the fugitive, apparently undismayed by his discovery. 'But, please, will you come away before they wake up?'

'Who?' asked Sir Richard.

'My aunt – all of them!' whispered the fugitive. 'I am very much obliged to you for helping me – and do you think you could untie this knot, if you please? You see, I had to tie my bundle on my back, and now I can't undo it. And where is my hat?'

'It fell off,' said Sir Richard, picking it up, and dusting it on his sleeve. 'I am not quite sober, you know – in fact, I am drunk – but I cannot help feeling that this is all a trifle – shall we say – irregular?'

'Yes, but there was nothing else to be done,' explained the fugitive, trying to look over her own shoulder at what Sir Richard was doing with the recalcitrant knot.

'Oblige me by standing still!' requested Sir Richard.

'Oh, I am sorry! I can't think how it worked right round me like that. Thank you! I am truly grateful to you!'

Sir Richard was eyeing the bundle through his quizzing-glass. '*Are* you a burglar?' he enquired.

A chuckle, hastily choked, greeted this. 'No, of course I'm not. I couldn't manage a bandbox, so I had to tie all my things up in a shawl. And now I think I must be going, if you please.'

'Drunk I undoubtedly am,' said Sir Richard, 'but some

remnants of sanity still remain with me. You cannot, my good child, wander about the streets of London at this hour of night, and dressed in those clothes. I believe I ought to ring that bell, and hand you over to your – aunt, did you say?'

Two agitated hands clasped his arm. 'Oh, *don't*!' begged the fugitive. '*Please* don't!'

'Well, what am I to do with you?' asked Sir Richard.

'Nothing. Only tell me the way to Holborn!'

'Why Holborn?'

'I have to go to the White Horse Inn, to catch the stagecoach for Bristol.'

'That settles it,' said Sir Richard. 'I will not set you a foot on your way until I have the whole story from you. It's my belief you are a dangerous criminal.'

'I am not!' said the fugitive indignantly. 'Anyone with the veriest speck of sensibility would feel for my plight! I am escaping from the most odious persecution.'

'Fortunate child!' said Sir Richard, taking her bundle from her. 'I wish I might do the same. Let us remove from this neighbourhood. I have seldom seen a street that depressed me more. I can't think how I came here. Do you feel that our agreeable encounter would be improved by an exchange of names, or are you travelling incognita?'

'Yes, I shall have to make up a name for myself. I hadn't thought of that. My real name is Penelope Creed. Who are you?'

'I,' said Sir Richard, 'am Richard Wyndham, wholly at your service.'

'Beau Wyndham?' asked Miss Creed knowledgeably.

'Beau Wyndham,' bowed Sir Richard. 'Is it possible that we can have met before?'

'Oh no, but of course I have heard of you. My cousin tries to tie his cravat in a Wyndham Fall. At least, that is what he says it is, but it looks like a muddle to me.'

'Then it is *not* a Wyndham Fall,' said Sir Richard firmly.

'No, that's what I thought. My cousin tries to be a dandy, but he has a face like a fish. They want me to marry him.'

'What a horrible thought!' said Sir Richard, shuddering.

'I told you you would feel for my plight!' said Miss Creed. 'So would you now set me on my way to Holborn?'

'No,' replied Sir Richard.

'But you must!' declared Miss Creed, on a note of panic. 'Where are we going?'

'I cannot walk about the streets all night. We had better repair to my house to discuss this matter.'

'No!' said Miss Creed, standing stock-still in the middle of the pavement.

Sir Richard sighed. 'Rid yourself of the notion that I cherish any villainous designs upon your person,' he said. 'I imagine I might well be your father. How old are you?'

'I am turned seventeen.'

'Well, I am nearly thirty,' said Sir Richard.

Miss Creed worked this out. 'You couldn't possibly be my father!'

'I am far too drunk to solve arithmetical problems. Let it suffice that I have not the slightest intention of making love to you.'

'Well, then, I don't mind accompanying you,' said Miss Creed handsomely. 'Are you really drunk?'

'Vilely,' said Sir Richard.

'No one would credit it, I assure you. You carry your wine very well.'

'You speak as one with experience in these matters,' said Sir Richard.

'My father was used to say that it was most important to see how a man behaved when in his cups. My cousin becomes excessively silly.'

'You know,' said Sir Richard, knitting his brows, 'the more I hear of this cousin of yours the more I feel you should not be allowed to marry him. Where are we now?'

'Piccadilly, I think,' replied Miss Creed.

'Good! I live in St James's Square. Why do they want you to marry your cousin?'

'Because,' said Miss Creed mournfully, 'I am cursed with a large fortune!'

Sir Richard halted in the middle of the road. 'Cursed with a large fortune?' he repeated.

'Yes, indeed. You see, my father had no other children, and I believe I am most fabulously wealthy, besides having a house in Somerset, which they won't let me live in. When he died I had to live with Aunt Almeria. I was only twelve years old, you see. And now she is persecuting me to marry my cousin Frederick. So I ran away.'

'The man with a face like a fish?'

'Yes.'

'You did quite right,' said Sir Richard.

'Well, I think I did.'

'Not a doubt of it. Why Holborn?'

'I told you,' replied Miss Creed patiently. 'I am going to get on the Bristol coach.'

'Oh! Why Bristol?'

'Well, I'm not going to Bristol precisely, but my house is in Somerset, and I have a very great friend there. I haven't seen him for nearly five years, but we used to play together, and we pricked our fingers – mixing the blood, you know – and we made a vow to marry one another when we were grown-up.'

'This is all very romantic,' commented Sir Richard.

'Yes, isn't it?' said Miss Creed enthusiastically. 'You are not married, are you?'

'No. Oh, my God!'

'Why, what is the matter?'

'I've just remembered that I am going to be.'

'Don't you want to be?'

'No.'

'But no one could force *you* to be married!'

'My good girl, you do not know my relatives,' said Sir Richard bitterly.

'Did they talk to you, and talk to you, and *talk* to you? And say

29

it was your duty? And plague your life out? And cry at you?' asked Miss Creed.

'Something of the sort,' admitted Sir Richard. 'Is that what your relatives did to you?'

'Yes. So I stole Geoffrey's second-best suit, and climbed out of the window.'

'Who is Geoffrey?'

'Oh, he is my other cousin! He is at Harrow, and his clothes fit me perfectly. Is this your house?'

'This is my house.'

'But wait!' said Miss Creed. 'Will not the porter be sitting up to open the door to you?'

'I don't encourage people to sit up for me,' said Sir Richard, producing from his pocket a key, and fitting it into the lock.

'But I expect you have a valet,' suggested Miss Creed, hanging back. 'He will be waiting to help you to bed.'

'True,' said Sir Richard. 'But he will not come to my room until I ring the bell. You need have no fear.'

'Oh, in that case – !' said Miss Creed, relieved, and followed him blithely into the house.

A lamp was burning in the hall, and a candle was placed on a marble-topped table, in readiness for Sir Richard. He kindled it by thrusting it into the lamp, and led his guest into the library. Here there were more candles, in chandeliers fixed to the wall. Sir Richard lit as many of these as seemed good to him, and turned to inspect Miss Creed.

She had taken off her hat, and was standing in the middle of the room, looking interestedly about her. Her hair, which clustered in feathery curls on the top of her head, and was somewhat raggedly cut at the back, was guinea-gold; her eyes were a deep blue, very large and trustful, and apt at any moment to twinkle with merriment. She had a short little nose, slightly freckled, a most decided chin, and a pair of dimples.

Sir Richard, critically observing her, was unimpressed by these charms. He said: 'You look the most complete urchin indeed!'

She seemed to take this as a tribute. She raised her candid eyes to his face, and said: 'Do I? Truly?'

His gaze travelled slowly over her borrowed raiment. 'Horrible!' he said. 'Are you under the impression that you have tied that – that travesty of a cravat in a Wyndham Fall?'

'No, but the thing is I have never tied a cravat before,' she explained.

'That,' said Sir Richard, 'is obvious. Come here!'

She approached obediently, and stood still while his expert fingers wrought with the crumpled folds round her neck.

'No, it is beyond even my skill,' he said at last. 'I shall have to lend you one of mine. Never mind; sit down, and let us talk this matter over. My recollection is none of the clearest, but I fancy you said you were going into Somerset to marry a friend of your childhood.'

'Yes, Piers Luttrell,' nodded Miss Creed, seating herself in a large arm-chair.

'Furthermore, you are just seventeen.'

'Turned seventeen,' she corrected.

'Don't quibble! And you propose to undertake this journey as a passenger on an Accommodation coach?'

'Yes,' agreed Miss Creed.

'And, as though this were not enough, you are going alone?'

'Of course I am.'

'My dear child,' said Sir Richard, 'drunk I may be, but not so drunk as to acquiesce in this fantastic scheme, believe me.'

'I don't think you are drunk,' said Miss Creed. 'Besides, it has nothing to do with you! You cannot interfere in my affairs merely because you helped me out of the window.'

'I didn't help you out of the window. Something tells me I ought to restore you to the bosom of your family.'

Miss Creed turned rather white, and said in a small, but very clear voice: 'If you did that it would be the most cruel – the most treacherous thing in the world!'

'I suppose it would,' he admitted.

There was a pause. Sir Richard unfobbed his snuff-box with a flick of one practised finger, and took a pinch. Miss Creed swallowed, and said: 'If you had ever *seen* my cousin, you would understand.'

He glanced down at her, but said nothing.

'He has a wet mouth,' said Miss Creed despairingly.

'That settles it,' said Sir Richard, shutting his snuff-box. 'I will escort you to your childhood's friend.'

Miss Creed blushed. 'You? But you can't!'

'Why can't I?'

'Because – because I don't know you, and I can very well go by myself, and – well, it's quite absurd! I see now that you *are* drunk.'

'Let me inform you,' said Sir Richard, 'that missish airs don't suit those clothes. Moreover, I don't like them. Either you will travel to Somerset in my company, or you will go back to your aunt. Take your choice!'

'Do please consider!' begged Miss Creed. 'You know I am obliged to travel in the greatest secrecy. If you went with me, no one would know what had become of you.'

'No one would know what had become of me,' repeated Sir Richard slowly. 'No one – my girl, you have no longer any choice: I am going with you to Somerset!'

Three

As no argument produced the least effect on Sir Richard's suddenly reckless mood, Miss Creed abandoned her conscientious attempt to dissuade him from accompanying her on her journey, and owned that his protection would be welcome. 'It is not that I am afraid to go by myself,' she explained, 'but, to tell you the truth, I am not quite used to do things all alone.'

'I should hope,' said Sir Richard, 'that you are not quite used to travelling in the common stage either.'

'No, of course I am not. It will be quite an adventure! Have you ever travelled by stagecoach?'

'Never. We shall travel post.'

'Travel post? You must be mad!' exclaimed Miss Creed 'I dare say you are known at every posting-inn on the Bath road. We should be discovered in a trice. Why, I had thought of all that even before you made up your mind to join me! My cousin Frederick is too stupid to think of anything, but my Aunt Almeria is not, and I make no doubt she will guess that I have run away to my own home, and follow me. That is one of the reasons why I made up my mind to journey in the stage. She will enquire for me at the posting-houses, and no one will be able to give her the least news of me. And just think what a bustle there would be if it were discovered that we had been travelling about the country together in a post-chaise!'

'Does it seem to you that there would be less impropriety in our travelling in the stage?' enquired Sir Richard.

33

'Yes, much less. In fact, I do not see that it is improper at all, for how can I prevent your booking a seat in a public vehicle, if you wish to do so? Besides, I have not enough money to hire a post-chaise.'

'I thought you said you were cursed with a large fortune?'

'Yes, but they won't let me have anything but the most paltry allowance until I come of age, and I've spent most of this month's pin-money.'

'I will be your banker,' said Sir Richard.

Miss Creed shook her head vigorously. 'No, indeed you will not! One should never be beholden to strangers. I shall pay everything for myself. Of course, if you are set against travelling by the stage, I do not see what is to be done. Unless –' she broke off as an idea occurred to her, and said, with sparkling eyes: 'I have a famous notion! You are a notable whip, are you not?'

'I believe I am accounted so,' replied Sir Richard.

'Well, supposing you were to drive in your own curricle? Then I could get up behind, and pretend to be your Tiger, and hold the yard of tin, and blow up for the change and –'

'No!' said Sir Richard.

She looked disappointed. 'I thought it would be exciting. However, I dare say you are right.'

'I am right,' said Sir Richard. 'The more I think of it, the more I see that there is much to be said for the stagecoach. At what hour did you say that it leaves town?'

'At nine o'clock, from the White Horse Inn, in Fetter Lane. Only we must go there long before that, on account of your servants. What is the time now?'

Sir Richard consulted his watch. 'Close on five,' he replied.

'Then we have not a moment to lose,' said Miss Creed. 'Your servants will be stirring in another hour. But you can't travel in those clothes, can you?'

'No,' he said, 'and I can't travel with that cravat of yours either, or that abominable bundle. And, now I come to look at you more particularly, I never saw hair worse cut.'

'You mean the back, I expect,' said Miss Creed, unresentful of

34

these strictures. 'Luckily, it has always been short in front. I had to chop the back bits off myself, and I could not well see what I was about.'

'Wait here!' commanded Sir Richard, and left the room.

When he returned it was more than half an hour later, and he had shed his evening-dress for buckskin breeches, and top-boots, and a coat of blue superfine cloth. Miss Creed greeted him with considerable relief. 'I began to fear you had forgotten me, or fallen asleep!' she told him.

'Nothing of the sort!' said Sir Richard, setting a small cloak-bag and a large portmanteau down on the floor. 'Drunk or sober, I never forget my obligations. Stand up, and I will see what I can do towards making you look more presentable.'

He had a snowy white cravat over one arm, and a pair of scissors in his hand. A few judicious snips greatly improved the appearance of Miss Creed's head, and by the time a comb had been ruthlessly dragged through her curls, forcing rather than coaxing them into a more manly style, she began to look quite neat, though rather watery-eyed. Her crumpled cravat was next cast aside, and one of Sir Richard's own put round her neck. She was so anxious to see how he was arranging it that she stood on tiptoe to catch a glimpse of herself in the mirror hanging above the mantelpiece, and got her ears boxed.

'*Will* you stand still?' said Sir Richard.

Miss Creed sniffed, and subsided into dark mutterings. However, when he released her, and she was able to see the result of his handiwork, she was so pleased that she forgot her injuries, and exclaimed: 'Oh, how nice I look! Is it a Wyndham Fall?'

'Certainly not!' Sir Richard replied. 'The Wyndham Fall is not for scrubby schoolboys, let me tell you.'

'I am not a scrubby schoolboy!'

'You look like one. Now put what you have in that bundle into the cloak-bag, and we'll be off.'

'I have a very good mind not to go with you,' said Miss Creed, glowering.

'No, you haven't. You are now my young cousin, and we are wholly committed to a life of adventure. What did you say your name was?'

'Penelope Creed. Most people call me Pen, but I ought to have a man's name now.'

'Pen will do very well. If it occasions the least comment, you will say that it is spelt with two N's. You were named after that Quaker fellow.'

'Oh, that is a very good idea! What shall I call you?'

'Richard.'

'Richard who?'

'Smith – Jones – Brown.'

She was engaged in transferring her belongings from the Paisley shawl to the cloak-bag. 'You don't look like any of those. What shall I do with this shawl?'

'Leave it,' replied Sir Richard, gathering up some gleaming scraps of guinea-gold hair from the carpet, and casting them to the back of the fireplace. 'Do you know, Pen Creed, I fancy you have come into my life in the guise of Providence?'

She looked up enquiringly. 'Have I?' she said doubtfully.

'That, or Disaster,' said Sir Richard. 'I shall know which when I am sober. But, to tell you the truth, I don't care a jot! *En avant, mon cousin!*'

It was past midday when Lady Trevor, accompanied by her reluctant husband, called at her brother's house in St James's Square. She was admitted by the porter, obviously big with news, and handed on by him to the butler. 'Tell Sir Richard that I am here,' she commanded, stepping into the Yellow Saloon.

'Sir Richard, my lady, is not at home,' said the butler, in a voice pregnant with mystery.

Louisa, who had extracted from her lord a description of Sir Richard's proceedings at Almack's on the preceding night, snorted. 'You will tell him that his sister desires to see him,' she said.

'Sir Richard, my lady, is not upon the premises,' said the butler, working up to his climax.

'Sir Richard has trained you well,' said Louisa dryly. 'But I am not to be put off so! Go and tell him that I wish to see him!'

'Sir Richard, my lady, did not sleep in his bed last night!' announced the butler.

George was surprised into indiscreet comment. 'What's that? Nonsense! He wasn't as foxed as that when *I* saw him!'

'As to that, my lord,' said the butler, with dignity, 'I have no information. In a word, my lord, Sir Richard has vanished.'

'Good Gad!' ejaculated George.

'Fiddle-de-dee!' said Louisa tartly. 'Sir Richard, as I suppose, is in his bed!'

'No, my lady. As I informed your ladyship, Sir Richard's bed has not been slept in.' He paused, but Louisa only stared at him. Satisfied with the impression he had made, he continued: 'The evening attire which Sir Richard was wearing yesterday was found by his man, Biddle, upon the floor of his bedroom. Sir Richard's second-best top-boots, a pair of buckskins, a blue riding-coat, his drab overcoat, and a fawn coloured beaver, have all disappeared. One is forced to the conclusion, my lady, that Sir Richard was called away unexpectedly.'

'Gone off without his valet?' George demanded in a stupefied tone.

The butler bowed. 'Precisely so, my lord.'

'Impossible!' George said, from the heart.

Louisa, who had been frowning over these tidings, said in a brisk voice: 'It is certainly very odd, but there is no doubt some perfectly reasonable explanation. Pray, are you certain that my brother left no word with *any* member of his household?'

'None whatsoever, my lady.'

George heaved a deep sigh, and shook his head. 'I warned you, Louisa! I *said* you were driving him too hard!'

'You said nothing of the sort!' snapped Louisa, annoyed with him for talking so indiscreetly before a palpably interested servant. 'To be sure, he may well have mentioned to us that he

37

was going out of town, and we have forgotten the circumstance.'

'How can you say so?' asked George, honestly puzzled. 'Why, didn't you have it from Melissa Brandon herself that he was to call –'

'That will do, George!' said Louisa, quelling him with a look so terrible that he quailed under it. 'Tell me, Porson,' she resumed, turning again to the butler, 'has my brother gone in his post-chaise, or is he driving himself?'

'None of Sir Richard's vehicles, my lady, sporting or otherwise, is missing from the stables,' said Porson, relishing the cumulative effect of his disclosures.

'He is riding, then!'

'I have ascertained from the head groom, my lady, that none of Sir Richard's horses has been abstracted. The head groom has not seen Sir Richard since yesterday morning.'

'Good Gad!' muttered George, his eyes starting with dismay at the hideous thought which presented itself to him. 'No, no, he would not do that!'

'Be quiet, George! For heaven's sake, be quiet!' Louisa cried sharply. 'Why, what nonsensical notion have you taken into your head? I am sure it is most provoking of Richard to slip off like this, but as for – I won't have you say such things! Ten to one, he has gone off to watch some odious sporting event: prize-fighting, I dare say! He will be home presently.'

'But he didn't sleep at home!' George reminded her. 'And I'm bound to say he wasn't cold stone sober when he left Almack's last night. I don't mean he was badly foxed, but you know what he's like when he's –'

'I am thankful to say that I know nothing of the kind!' retorted Louisa. 'If he was not sober, it would account for his erratic behaviour.'

'Erratic behaviour! I must say, Louisa, that is a fine way to talk when poor Ricky may be at the bottom of the river,' exclaimed George, roused to noble courage.

She changed colour, but said faintly: 'How can you be so absurd? Don't say such things, I beg of you!'

The butler coughed. 'I beg your lordship's pardon, but if I might say so, Sir Richard would hardly change his raiment for the execution of – of what I apprehend your lordship means.'

'No. No, very true! He would not, of course!' agreed George, relieved.

'Moreover, my lord, Biddle reports that Sir Richard's drawers and wardrobe have been ransacked, and various articles of clothing abstracted. Upon going to rouse Sir Richard this morning, Biddle found his room in the greatest disorder, as though Sir Richard had made his preparations for a journey in haste. Furthermore, my lord, Biddle informed me that a port-manteau and a small cloak-bag are missing from the cupboard in which they are customarily kept.'

George gave a sudden croak of laughter. 'Bolted, by Gad! Yoicks! gone awa-ay!'

'*George!*'

'I don't care!' said George defiantly. 'I'm devilish glad he has bolted!'

'But there was no need!' Louisa said, forgetting that Porson was in the room. 'No one was constraining him to marry –' she caught Porson's eye, and stopped short.

'I should inform your ladyship,' said Porson, apparently deaf to her indiscreet utterance, 'that there were several other Peculiar Circumstances attached to Sir Richard's disappearance.'

'Good heavens, you talk as though he has been spirited away by magic!' said Louisa impatiently. 'What circumstances, my good man?'

'If your ladyship will excuse me, I will fetch them for your inspection,' said Porson, and bowed himself out.

Husband and wife were left to stare at one another in perplexity.

'Well!' said George, not without satisfaction, 'you see now what comes of plaguing a man out of his mind!'

'I didn't! George, it is unjust of you to say so! Pray, how could *I* force him to offer for Melissa if he did not wish to? I am persuaded his flight has nothing whatever to do with that affair.'

'No man will bear being teased to do something he don't want to do,' said George.

'Then all I have to say is that Richard is a bigger coward than I would have believed possible! I am sure, if only he had told me frankly that he did not wish to marry Melissa I should not have said another word about it.'

'Ha!' ejaculated George, achieving a sardonic laugh.

He escaped reproof by Porson's coming back into the room, bearing certain articles which he laid carefully upon the table. In great astonishment, Lord and Lady Trevor gazed at a Paisley shawl, a crumpled cravat, and some short strands of guinea-gold hair, curling appropriately enough into a shape resembling a question-mark.

'What in the world – ?' exclaimed Louisa.

'These articles, my lady, were discovered by the under-footman upon his entering the library this morning,' said Porson. 'The shawl, which neither Biddle nor myself can remember to have seen before, was lying on the floor; the cravat had been thrown into the grate; and the – er – lock of hair – was found under the shawl.'

'Well, upon my word!' said George, putting up his glass the better to inspect the articles. He pointed his glass at the cravat. 'That tells its own tale! Poor Ricky must have come in last night in a bad state. I dare say his head was aching: mine would have been, if I had drunk half the brandy he tossed off yesterday. I see it all. There he was, pledged to call on Saar this morning – no way out of it – head on fire! He tugged at his cravat, felt as though he must choke, and ruined the thing – and no matter how far gone he was, Ricky would never wear a crumpled necktie! There he was, sitting in a chair, very likely, and running his hands through his hair, in the way a man does –'

'Richard never yet disarranged his hair, and no matter how drunk he may have been, he did not pull a curl of *that* colour out of his own head!' interrupted Louisa. 'Moreover, it has been cut off. Anyone can see that!'

George levelled his glass at the gleaming curl. A number of

emotions flitted across his rather stolid countenance. He drew a breath. 'You're quite right, Louisa,' he said. 'Well, I never would have believed it! The sly dog!'

'You need not wait, Porson!' Louisa said sharply.

'Very good, my lady. But I should perhaps inform your ladyship that the under-footman found the candles burning in the library when he entered it this morning.'

'I cannot see that it signifies in the least,' replied Louisa, waving him aside.

He withdrew. George, who was holding the curl in the palm of his hand, said: 'Well, *I* can't call anyone to mind with hair of this colour. To be sure, there were one or two opera-dancers, but Ricky's not at all the sort of man to want 'em to cut off their hair for him. But there's no doubt about one thing, Louisa: this curl was a keepsake.'

'Thank you, George, I had already realized that. Yet I thought I knew all the respectable women of Richard's acquaintance! One would say that kind of keepsake must have belonged to his salad days. I am sure he is much too unromantic now to cherish a lock of hair!'

'And he threw it away,' George said, shaking his head. 'You know, it's devilish sad, Louisa, upon my word it is! Threw it away, because he was on the eve of offering for that Brandon-iceberg!'

'Very affecting! And having thrown it away, he then ran away himself – not, you will admit, making any offer at all! And where did the shawl come from?' She picked it up as she spoke, and shook it out. 'Extremely creased! Now why?'

'Another keepsake,' George said. 'Crushed it in his hands, poor old Ricky – couldn't bear the recollections it conjured up – flung it away!'

'Oh, fiddle!' said Louisa, exasperated. 'Well, Porson, what is it now?'

The butler, who had come back into the room, said primly: 'The Honourable Cedric Brandon, my lady, to see Sir Richard. I thought perhaps your ladyship would wish to receive him.'

'I don't suppose he can throw the least light on this mystery, but you may as well show him in,' said Louisa. 'Depend upon it,' she added to her husband, when Porson had withdrawn himself again, 'he will have come to learn why Richard did not keep his engagement with Saar this morning. I am sure I do not know what I am to say to him!'

'If you ask me, Cedric won't blame Richard,' said George. 'They tell me he was talking pretty freely at White's yesterday. Foxed, of course. How you and your mother can want Ricky to marry into that family is what beats me!'

'We have known the Brandons all our lives,' Louisa said defensively. 'I don't pretend that –' She broke off, as the Honourable Cedric walked into the room, and stepped forward, with her hand held out. 'How do you do, Cedric? I am afraid Richard is not at home. We – think he must have been called away suddenly on urgent affairs.'

'Taken my advice, has he?' said Cedric, saluting her hand with careless grace. ' "You run, Ricky! Don't do it!" that's what I told him. Told him I'd sponge on him for the rest of his days, if he was fool enough to let himself be caught.'

'I wonder that you should talk in that vulgar way!' said Louisa. 'Of course he has not *run*! I dare say he will be back any moment now. It was excessively remiss of him not to have sent a note round to inform Lord Saar that he could not wait on him this morning, as he had engaged himself to do, but –'

'You've got that wrong,' interrupted Cedric. 'No engagement at all. Melissa told him to call on m'father; he didn't say he would. Wormed it out of Melissa myself an hour ago. Lord, you never saw anyone in such a rage! What's all this?' His roving eye had alighted on the relics laid out upon the table. 'A lock of hair, by Jove! Devilish pretty hair too!'

'Found in the library this morning,' said George portentously, ignoring his wife's warning frown.

'Here? Ricky?' demanded Cedric. 'You're bamming me!'

'No, it is perfectly true. We cannot understand it.'

Cedric's eyes danced. 'By all that's famous! Who'd have

thought it, though? Well, that settles our affairs! Devilish inconvenient, but damme, I'm glad he's bolted! Always liked Ricky – never wanted to see him bound for perdition with the rest of us! But we're done-up now, and no mistake! The diamonds have gone.'

'What?' Louisa cried. 'Cedric, not the Brandon necklace?'

'That's it. Last sheet-anchor thrown out to the windward – gone like that!' He snapped his fingers in the air, and laughed. 'I came to tell Ricky I'd accept his offer to buy me a pair of colours, and be off to the Wars.'

'But how? Where?' gasped Louisa.

'Stolen. My mother took it to Bath with her. Never would stir without the thing, more's the pity! *I* wonder m'father didn't sell it years ago. Only thing he didn't sell, except Saar Court, and that'll have to go next. My mother wouldn't hear of parting with the diamonds.'

'But Cedric, how stolen? Who took it?'

'Highwaymen. My mother sent off a courier post-haste to m'father. Chaise stopped somewhere near Bath – two fellows with masks and horse-pistols – Sophia screeching like a hen – my mother swooning – outriders taken by surprise – one of 'em winged. And off went the necklace. Which is what I can't for the life of me understand.'

'How terrible! Your poor Mama! I am so sorry! It is an appalling loss!'

'Yes, but how the devil did they find the thing?' said Cedric. 'That's what I want to know.'

'But surely if they took Lady Saar's jewel-case –'

'The necklace wasn't in it. I'll lay my last shilling on that. My mother had a hiding-place for it – devilish cunning notion – always put it there when she travelled. Secret pocket behind one of the squabs.'

'Good Gad, do you mean to say someone divulged the hiding-place to the rascals?' said George.

'Looks mighty like it, don't it?'

'Who knew of it? If you can discover the traitor, you may yet get the necklace back. Are you sure of all your servants?'

'I'm sure none of them – Lord, I don't know!' Cedric said, rather hastily. 'My mother wants the Bow Street Runners set on to it, but m'father don't think it's the least use. And now here's Ricky bolted, on top of everything! The old man will go off in an apoplexy!'

'Really, Cedric, you must not talk so of your Papa!' Louisa expostulated. 'And we don't know that Richard has – has *bolted*! Indeed, I am sure it's no such thing!'

'He'll be a fool if he hasn't,' said Cedric. 'What do you think, George?'

'I don't know,' George answered. 'It is very perplexing. I own, when I first heard of his disappearance – for you must know that he did not sleep in his bed last night, and when *I* saw him he was foxed – I felt the gravest alarm. But –'

'Suicide, by God!' Cedric gave a shout of laughter. 'I must tell Melissa that! Driven to death! Ricky! Oh, by all that's famous!'

'Cedric, you are quite abominable!' said Louisa roundly. 'Of course Richard has not committed suicide! He has merely gone away. I'm sure I don't know where, and if you say anything of the sort to Melissa I shall never forgive you! In fact, I beg you will tell Melissa nothing more than that Richard has been called away on an urgent matter of business.'

'What, can't I tell her about the lock of yaller hair? Now, don't be a spoil-sport, Louisa!'

'Odious creature!'

'We believe the lock of hair to be a relic of some long-forgotten affair,' said George. 'Possibly a boy-and-girl attachment. It would be gross impropriety to mention it beyond these walls.'

'If it comes to that, old fellow, what about the gross impropriety of poking and prying into Ricky's drawers?' asked Cedric cheerfully.

'We did no such thing!' Louisa cried. 'It was found upon the floor in the library!'

'Dropped? Discarded? Seems to me Ricky's been leading a double life. I'd have said myself he never troubled much about females. Won't I roast him when I see him!'

'You will do nothing of the sort. Oh dear, I wish to heaven I knew where he has gone, and what it all means!'

'I'll tell you where he's gone!' offered Cedric. 'He's gone to find the yaller-haired charmer of his youth. Not a doubt of it! Lord, I'd give a monkey to see him, though. Ricky on a romantic adventure!'

'Now you are being absurd!' said Louisa. 'If one thing is certain, it is that Richard has not one grain of romance in his disposition, while as for adventure –! I dare say he would shudder at the mere thought of it. Richard, my dear Cedric, is first, last, and always a man of fashion, and he will never do anything unbefitting a Corinthian. You may take my word for *that*!'

Four

The man of fashion, at that precise moment, was sleeping heavily in one corner of a huge green-and-gold Accommodation coach, swaying and rocking on its ponderous way to Bristol. The hour was two in the afternoon, the locality Calcot Green, west of Reading and the dreams troubling the repose of the man of fashion were extremely uneasy. He had endured some waking moments, when the coach had stopped with a lurch and a heave to take up or to set down passengers, to change horses, or to wait while a laggardly pike-keeper opened a gate upon the road. These moments had seemed to him more fraught with nightmare even than his dreams. His head was aching, his eyeballs seemed to be on fire, and a phantasmagoria of strange, unwelcome faces swam before his outraged vision. He had shut his eyes again with a groan, preferring his dreams to reality, but when the coach stopped at Calcot Green to put down a stout woman with a tendency to asthma, sleep finally deserted him, and he opened his eyes, blinked at the face of a precise-looking man in a suit of neat black, seated opposite him, ejaculated: 'Oh, my God!' and sat up.

'Is your head *very* bad?' asked a solicitous and vaguely familiar voice in his ear.

He turned his head, and encountered the enquiring gaze of Miss Penelope Creed. He looked at her in silence for a few moments; then he said: 'I remember. Stagecoach – Bristol. Why, oh why, did I touch the brandy?'

46

An admonitory pinch made him recollect his surroundings. He found that there were three other persons in the coach, seated opposite to him, and that all were regarding him with interest. The precise-looking man, whom he judged to be an attorney's clerk, was frankly disapproving; a woman in a poke-bonnet and a paduasoy shawl nodded to him in a motherly style, and said that he was like her second boy, who could not abide the rocking of the coach either; and a large man beside her, whom he took to be her husband, corroborated this statement by enunciating in a deep voice: 'That's right!'

Instinct took Sir Richard's hand to his cravat; his fingers told him that it was considerably crumpled, like the tails of his blue coat. His curly-brimmed beaver seemed to add to the discomfort of his aching head; he took it off, and clasped his head in his hands, trying to throw off the lingering wisps of sleep. 'Good God!' he said thickly. 'Where are we?'

'Well, I am not quite sure, but we have passed Reading,' replied Pen, rather anxiously surveying him.

'Calcot Green, that's where we are,' volunteered the large man. 'Stopped to set down someone. They ain't a-worriting theirselves over the time-bill, that's plain. I dare say the coachman's stepped down for a drink.'

'Ah, well!' said his wife tolerantly. 'It'll be thirsty work, setting up on the box in the sun like he has to.'

'That's right,' agreed the large man.

'If the Company was to hear of it he would be turned off, and very rightly!' said the clerk, sniffing. 'The behaviour of these stagecoach-men is becoming a scandal.'

'I'm sure there's no call for people to get nasty if a man falls behind his time-bill a little,' said the woman. 'Live and let live, that's what I say.'

Her husband assented to this in his usual fashion. The coach lurched forward again, and Pen said, under cover of the noise of the wheels and the horses' hooves: 'You kept on telling me that you were drunk, and now I see that you were. I was afraid you would regret coming with me.'

47

Sir Richard raised his head from his hands. 'Drunk I most undoubtedly must have been, but I regret nothing except the brandy. When does this appalling vehicle reach Bristol?'

'It isn't one of the fast coaches, you know. They don't engage to cover much above eight miles an hour. I think we ought to be in Bristol by eleven o'clock. We seem to stop such a number of times, though. Do you mind very much?'

He looked down at her. 'Do you?'

'To tell you the truth,' she confided, 'not a bit! I am enjoying myself hugely. Only I don't want you to be made uncomfortable all for my sake. I quite see that you are sadly out-of-place in a stagecoach.'

'My dear child, you had nothing whatever to do with my present discomfort, believe me. As for *my* being out-of-place, what, pray, are you?'

The dimples peeped. 'Oh, *I* am only a scrubby schoolboy, after all!'

'Did I say that?' She nodded. 'Well, so you are,' said Sir Richard, looking her over critically. 'Except for – Did I tie that cravat? Yes, I thought I must have. What in the world have you got there?'

'An apple,' replied Pen, showing it to him. 'The fat woman who got out just now gave it to me.'

'You are not going to sit there munching it, are you?' demanded Sir Richard.

'Yes, I am. Why shouldn't I? Would you like a bit of it?'

'I should not!' said Sir Richard.

'Well, I am excessively hungry. That was the one thing we forgot.'

'What was?'

'Food,' said Pen, digging her teeth into the apple. 'We ought to have provided ourselves with a basket of things to eat on the journey. I forgot that the stage doesn't stop at posting-houses, like the mail-coaches. At least, I didn't forget exactly, because I never knew it.'

'This must be looked to,' said Sir Richard. 'If you are hungry, you must undoubtedly be fed. What are you proposing to do with the core of that apple?'

'Eat it,' said Pen.

'Repellent brat!' said Sir Richard, with a strong shudder.

He leaned back in his corner, but a tug at his sleeve made him incline his head towards his companion.

'I told these people that you were my tutor,' whispered Pen.

'Of course, a young gentleman in his tutor's charge *would* be travelling in the common stage,' said Sir Richard, resigning himself to the rôle of usher.

At the next stage, which was Woolhampton, he roused himself from the languor which threatened to possess him, alighted from the coach, and showed unexpected competence in procuring from the modest inn a very tolerable cold meal for his charge. The coach awaited his pleasure, and the attorney's clerk, whose sharp eyes had seen Sir Richard's hand go from his pocket to the coachman's ready palm, muttered darkly of bribery and corruption on the King's Highway.

'Have some chicken,' said Sir Richard amiably.

The clerk refused this invitation with every evidence of contempt, but there were several other passengers, notably a small boy with adenoids, who were perfectly ready to share the contents of the basket on Pen's knees.

Sir Richard had good reason to know that Miss Creed's disposition was extremely confiding; during the long day's journey he discovered that she was friendly to a fault. She observed all the passengers with a bright and wholly unself-conscious gaze; conversed even with the clerk; and showed an alarming tendency to become the life and soul of the party. Questioned about herself, and her destination, she wove, zest-fully, an entirely mendacious story, which she embroidered from time to time with outrageous details. Sir Richard was ruthlessly applied to for corroboration, and, entering into the spirit of the adventure, added a few extempore details himself. Pen seemed pleased with these, but was plainly disappointed at his refusal to join her in keeping the small boy with adenoids amused.

He leaned back in his corner, lazily enjoying Miss Creed's flights into the realms of fancy, and wondering what his mother and sister would think if they knew that he was travelling to an unknown destination, by stagecoach, accompanied by a young lady as unembarrassed by this circumstance as by her male attire. A laugh shook him, as he pictured Louisa's face. His head had ceased aching, but although the detachment fostered by brandy had left him, he still retained a feeling of delightful irresponsibility. Sober, he would certainly not have set forth on this absurd journey, but having done so, drunk, he was perfectly willing to continue it. He was, moreover, curious to learn more of Pen's history. Some farrago she had told him last night: his recollection of it was a trifle hazy, but there had surely been something about an aunt, and a cousin with a face like a fish.

He turned his head slightly on the dingy squabs of the coach, and watched, from under drooping eyelids, the animated little face beside him. Miss Creed was listening, apparently keenly interested, to a long and involved recital of the illness which had lately prostrated the motherly woman's youngest-born. She shook her head over the folly of the apothecary, nodded wisely at the efficiency of an age-old nostrum compounded of strange herbs, and was on the point of capping this recipe with one in use in her own family when Sir Richard's foot found hers, and trod on it.

It was certainly time to check Miss Creed. The motherly woman stared at her, and said that it was queer-and-all to meet a young gentleman so knowledgeable.

'My mother,' said Pen, blushing, 'has been an invalid for many years.'

Everyone looked solicitous, and a desiccated female in the far corner of the coach said that no one could tell *her* anything about illness.

This remark had the effect of diverting attention from Pen, and as the triumphant lady plunged into the history of her sufferings, she sat back beside Sir Richard, directing up at him a look quite as mischievous as it was apologetic.

The lawyer's clerk, who had not yet forgiven Sir Richard for bribing the coachman, said something about the license allowed to young persons in these days. He contrasted it unfavourably with his own upbringing, and said that if he had a son he would not pamper him by giving him a tutor, but would send him to school. Pen said meekly that Mr Brown was very strict, and Sir Richard, correctly identifying Mr Brown with himself, lent colour to her assertion by telling her sternly not to chatter.

The motherly woman said that she was sure the young gentleman brightened them all up, and for her part she did not hold with people being harsh with children.

'That's right,' agreed her spouse. 'I never wanted to break any of *my* young 'uns' spirits: I like to see 'em up-and-coming.'

Several of the passengers looked reproachfully at Sir Richard, and, that no doubt of his severity might linger in their minds, Pen subsided into crushed silence, folding her hands on her knees, and casting down her eyes.

Sir Richard saw that he would figure for the rest of the journey as an oppressor, and mentally rehearsed a speech which was destined for Miss Creed's sole edification.

She disarmed him by falling asleep with her cheek against his shoulder. She slept between one stage and the next, and when roused by the coach's halting with its usual lurch, opened her eyes, smiled drowsily up at Sir Richard and murmured: 'I'm glad you came. Are you glad you came?'

'Very. Wake up!' said Sir Richard, wondering what more imprudent remarks might be hovering on her tongue.

She yawned, and straightened herself. An altercation seemed to be in progress between the guard and someone standing in the inn-yard. A farmer, who had boarded the coach at Calne, and was seated beside Pen, said that he thought the trouble was that the would-be passenger was not upon the way-bill.

'Well, he cannot come inside, that is certain!' said the thin woman. 'It is shocking, the way one is crowded already!'

'Where are we?' enquired Pen.

'Chippenham,' responded the farmer. 'That's where the Bath road goes off, see?'

She sat forward to look out of the window. 'Chippenham already? Oh yes, so it is! I know it well.'

Sir Richard cocked an amused eye at her. '*Already?*' he murmured.

'Well, I have been asleep, so it seems soon to me. Are you very weary, sir?'

'By no means. I am becoming entirely resigned.'

The new passenger, having apparently settled matters with the guard, at this moment pulled open the door, and tried to climb up into the coach. He was a small, spare man, in a catskin waistcoat, and jean-pantaloons. He had a sharp face, with a pair of twinkling, lashless eyes set deep under sandy brows. His proposed entrance into the coach was resolutely opposed. The thin woman cried out that there was no room; the lawyer's clerk said that the way the Company over-loaded its vehicles was a scandal; and the farmer recommended the newcomer to climb on to the roof.

'There ain't an inch of room up there,' protested the stranger. 'Lord, I don't take up much space! Squeeze up, coves!'

'Full-up! Try the boot!' said the farmer.

'Cast your winkers over me, cull: I don't take up no more room than what a bodkin would!' pleaded the stranger. 'Besides, there's a set of flash young coves on the roof. I'd be mortal afraid to sit with 'em, so I would!'

Sir Richard, casting an experienced eye over the man, mentally wrote him down as one probably better known to the Bow Street Runners than to himself. He was not surprised, however, to hear Miss Creed offering to squeeze up to make room, for he had, by this time, formed a very fair estimate of his charge's warmheartedness.

Pen, edging close to Sir Richard, coaxed the farmer to see for himself that there was room enough for one more passenger. The man in the catskin waistcoat grinned at her, and hopped into the coach. 'Dang me if I didn't think you was a flash cull too!' he said, squeezing himself into the vacant place. 'I'm obliged to ye, young shaver. When coves do Jimmy Yarde a service he don't forget it neither.'

The lawyer, who seemed to have much the same opinion of Mr Yarde as that held by Sir Richard, sniffed, and folded his hands tightly on the box which he held on his knees.

'Lord bless you!' said Mr Yarde, observing this gesture with a tolerant smile, '*I* ain't no boman prig!'

'What's a boman prig?' asked Pen innocently.

'There, now! If you ain't a werry suckling!' said Mr Yarde, almost disconcerted. 'A boman prig, young gentleman, is what I trust you'll never be. It's a cove as ends up in Rumbo – ah, and likely on the Nubbing Cheat afore he's much older!'

Much intrigued, Pen demanded a translation of these strange terms. Sir Richard, having pondered and discarded the notion of commanding her to exchange places with him, lay back and listened with lazy enjoyment to her initiation into the mysteries of thieves' cant.

A party of young gentlemen, who had been spectators of a cock-fight held in the district, had been taken up at Chippenham, and had crowded on to the roof. From the sounds preceding thence, it seemed certain that they had been refreshing themselves liberally. There was a good deal of shouting, some singing, and much drumming with heels upon the roof. The motherly woman and the thin spinster began to look alarmed, and the lawyer's clerk said that the behaviour of modern young men was disgraceful. Pen was too deeply engaged in conversation with Jimmy Yarde to pay much heed to the commotion, but when, after the coach had rumbled on for another five miles, the pace was suddenly accelerated, and the top-heavy vehicle bounced over ruts and pot-holes, and swung perilously first to one side and then to the other, she broke off her enthralling discourse, and looked enquiringly at Sir Richard.

A violent lurch flung her into his arms He restored her to her own seat, saying dryly: 'More adventure for you. I hope you are enjoying it?'

'But what is happening?'

'I apprehend that one of the would-be sprigs of fashion above has taken it into his head to tool the coach,' he replied.

'Lord ha' mercy!' exclaimed the motherly woman. 'Do you mean that one of they pesky, drunken lads is a-driving of us, sir?'

'So I should suppose, ma'am.'

The spinster uttered a faint shriek. 'Good God, what will become of us?'

'We shall end, I imagine, in the ditch,' said Sir Richard, with unruffled calm.

Babel at once broke forth, the spinster demanding to be let out at once, the motherly woman trying to attract the coachman's notice by hammering against the roof with her sunshade, the farmer sticking his head out of the window to shout threats and abuse, Jimmy Yarde laughing, and the lawyer's clerk angrily demanding of Sir Richard why he did not *do* something?

'What would you wish me to do?' asked Sir Richard, steadying Pen with a comfortingly strong arm.

'Stop the coach! Oh, sir, pray stop it!' begged the motherly woman.

'Bless your heart, ma'am, it'll stop of its own this gait!' grinned Jimmy Yarde.

Hardly had he spoken than a particularly sharp bend in the road proved to be too much for the amateur coachman's skill. He took the corner too wide, the near-hind wheels mounted a slight bank, and skidded down the farther side into a deep ditch, and everyone inside the vehicle was flung rudely over. There were screams from the women, oaths from the farmer, the cracking noise of split wood, and the shatter of broken glass. The coach lay at a crazy angle with sprigs of thorn-hedge thrusting in through the broken windows.

Pen, whose face was smothered in the many capes of Sir Richard's drab driving-coat, gasped, and struggled to free herself from a hold which had suddenly clamped her to Sir Richard's side. He relaxed it, saying: 'Hurt, Pen?'

'No, not in the least! Thank you so very much for holding me! Are you hurt?'

A splinter of glass had cut his cheek slightly, but since he had been holding on to the leather arm-rest hanging in the corner of the coach, he had not been thrown, like everyone else, off his seat. 'No, only annoyed,' he replied. 'My good woman, this is neither the time nor the place for indulging in a fit of the vapours!'

This acid rider was addressed to the spinster, who, finding herself pitch-forked on top of the lawyer's clerk, had gone off into strong hysterics.

'Here, let me get my dabblers on to that there door!' said Jimmy Yarde, hoisting himself up by seizing the opposite arm-rest. 'Dang me if next time I travel in a rattler I don't ride on the roof, flash-culls or no!'

The coach not having collapsed quite on to its side, but being supported by the bank and the hedge bordering the ditch, it was not difficult to force open the door, or to climb out through it. The spinster had indeed to be lifted out, since she had stiffened all over, and would do nothing but scream and drum her heels, but Pen scrambled out with an agility which scorned helping hands, and the motherly woman said that provided every gentleman would turn his back upon her she would engage to get out by herself too.

It was now considerably after nine o'clock, but although the sun had gone, the summer sky was still light, and the air warm. The travellers found themselves on a deserted stretch of road, a couple of miles short of the little town of Wroxhall, and rather more than thirty miles from Bristol. The most cursory inspection of the coach was enough to convince them that it would need extensive repairs before being able to take the road again; and Sir Richard, who had gone immediately to the horses, returned to Pen's side in a few moments with the news that one of the wheelers had badly strained a tendon. He had been right in thinking that the reins had been handed over to one of the outside passengers. To tool the coach was a common enough pastime amongst young men who aspired to be whips, but that any paid coachman could have been foolish enough to relinquish his seat to an amateur far gone in drink was incomprehensible, until the coachman's own condition had been realized.

Pen, who was sitting on Sir Richard's portmanteau, received the news of complete breakdown with perfect equanimity, but all the other inside passengers burst into vociferous complaint, and besieged the guard with demands to be instantly conveyed to Bristol, by means unspecified. Between his indignation at his colleague's gross misconduct, and his exasperation at being shouted at by six or seven persons at once, the unfortunate man was for some time incapable of collecting his wits, but presently it was suggested that if the travellers would only be patient, he would ride back on one of the leaders to Chippenham, and there try to procure some sort of a vehicle to convey them to Wroxhall, where they would be obliged to remain until the next Accommodation coach to Bristol picked them up there early on the following morning.

Several persons decided to set forward on foot for Wroxhall at once, but the spinster was still having hysterics, the motherly woman said that her corns would not permit of her tramping two miles, and the lawyer's clerk held to it that he had a right to be conveyed to Bristol that night. There was a marked tendency in one or two persons to turn to Sir Richard, as being plainly a man accustomed to command. This tendency had the effect of making Sir Richard, not in the least gratified, walk over to Pen's side, and say languidly, but with decision: 'This, I fancy, is where we part company with our fellow-travellers.'

'Yes, do let us!' assented Pen blithely. 'You know, I have been thinking, and I have a much better scheme now. We won't go to Bristol at all!'

'This is very sudden,' said Sir Richard. 'Do I understand you to mean that you have made up your mind to return to London?'

'No, no, of course not! Only now that we have broken down I think it would be silly to wait for another coach, because very

56

likely we should be overtaken by my aunt. And I never really wanted to go to Bristol, after all.'

'In that case, it seems perhaps a pity that we came so far upon the road to it,' said Sir Richard.

Her eyes twinkled. 'Stupid! I mean, my home is not in Bristol, but near to it, and I think it would be much better, besides being like a real adventure, to walk the rest of the way.'

'Where is your home?' demanded Sir Richard.

'Well, it is near Queen Charlton, not far from Keynsham, you know.'

'I don't,' said Sir Richard. 'This is your country, not mine. How far, in your judgment, is Queen Charlton from where we now are?'

'I'm not *entirely* sure,' replied Pen cautiously. 'But I shouldn't think it could be above fifteen, or, at the most twenty miles, going 'cross country.'

'Are you proposing to walk twenty miles?' said Sir Richard.

'Well, I dare say it is not as much. As the crow flies, I expect it is only about ten miles off.'

'You are not a crow,' said Sir Richard damningly. 'Nor, I may add, am I. Get up from that portmanteau!'

She rose obediently. 'I think I could quite well walk twenty miles. Not all at once, of course. What *are* we going to do?'

'We are going to retrace our steps along the road until we come to an inn,' replied Sir Richard. 'As I remember, there was one, about a couple of miles back. Nothing would induce me to make one of this afflictive coach-party!'

'I must own, I am a little tired of them myself,' admitted Pen. 'Only I won't go to a posting-house!'

'Make yourself easy on that score!' said Sir Richard grimly. 'No respectable posting-house would open its doors to us in this guise.'

This made Pen giggle. She put forward no further opposition, but picked up the cloak-bag, and set out beside Sir Richard in the direction of Chippenham.

None of the coach-passengers noticed their departure, since

all were fully occupied, either in reviling the coachman, or in planning their immediate movements. The bend in the road soon shut them off from sight of the coach, and Sir Richard then said: 'And now you may give me that cloak-bag.'

'Well, I won't,' said Pen, holding on to it firmly. 'It is not at all heavy, and you have your portmanteau to carry already. Besides, I feel more like a man every moment. What shall we do when we reach the inn?'

'Order supper.'

'Yes, and after that?'

'Go to bed.'

Pen considered this. 'You don't think we should set forward on our journey at once?'

'Certainly not. We shall go to bed like Christians, and in the morning we shall hire a conveyance to carry us to Queen Charlton. A private conveyance,' he added.

'But –'

'Pen Creed,' said Sir Richard calmly, 'you cast me for the rôle of bear-leader, and I accepted it. You drew a revolting picture of me which led everyone in that coach to regard me in the light of a persecutor of youth. Now you are reaping the harvest of your own sowing.'

She laughed. 'Are you going to persecute me?'

'Horribly!' said Sir Richard.

She tucked a confiding hand in his arm, and gave a little skip. 'Very well, I will do as you tell me. I'm very glad I met you: we are having a splendid adventure, are we not?'

Sir Richard's lips twitched. Suddenly he burst out laughing, standing still in the middle of the road, while Pen doubtfully surveyed him.

'But what is the matter with you?' she asked.

'Never mind!' he said, his voice still unsteady with mirth. 'Of course we are having a splendid adventure!'

'Well, I think we are,' she said, stepping out beside him again. 'Piers will be so surprised when he sees me!'

'I should think he would be,' agreed Sir Richard. 'You are

quite sure that you don't regret coming in search of him, I suppose?'

'Oh yes, quite! Why, Piers is my oldest friend! Didn't I tell you that we made a vow to be married?'

'I have some recollection of your doing so,' he admitted. 'But I also recollect that you said you hadn't seen him for five years.'

'No, that is true, but it doesn't signify in the least, I assure you.'

'I see,' said Sir Richard, keeping his inevitable reflections to himself.

They had not more than two miles to go before they reached the inn Sir Richard had seen from the window of the coach. It was a very small hostelry, with a weather-beaten sign creaking on its chains, a thatched roof, and only one parlour, besides the common tap-room.

The landlord, upon hearing of the breakdown of the stage-coach, accepted the travellers' unconventional arrival without surprise. It was growing dark by this time, and it was not until Sir Richard had stepped into the inn, and stood in the light of a hanging lamp, that the landlord was able to obtain a clear view of him. Sir Richard had chosen for the journey a plain coat and serviceable breeches, but the cut of the blue cloth, the high polish on his top-boots, the very style of his cravat, and the superfluity of capes on his drab over-coat all proclaimed so unmistakably the gentleman of fashion that the landlord was obviously taken aback, and looked from him to Pen with considerable suspicion.

'I shall require a bedroom for myself, and another for my nephew,' said Sir Richard. 'Also some supper.'

'Yes, sir. Did your honour say you was travelling on the Bristol-stage?' asked the landlord incredulously.

'Yes,' said Sir Richard raising his brows. 'I did say so. Have you any objection?'

'Oh no, sir! no, I'm sure!' replied the landlord hastily. 'Your honour said supper! I'm afraid we – we aren't in the habit of entertaining the Quality, but if your honour would condescend to a dish of ham and eggs, or maybe a slice of cold pork, I'll see to it on the instant!'

Sir Richard having graciously approved the ham and eggs, the landlord bowed him into the stuffy little parlour, and promised to have the only two guest-chambers the inn possessed immediately prepared. Pen, directing a conspiratorial look at Sir Richard, elected to follow the portmanteau and the cloak-bag upstairs. When she reappeared a slatternly maid-servant had spread supper on the table in the parlour, and Sir Richard had succeeded in forcing open two of its tiny windows. He turned, as Pen came in, and asked: 'What in heaven's name have you been doing all this time? I began to think you had deserted me.'

'Desert you! Of course I wouldn't do anything so silly! The thing was, I could see the landlord had noticed your clothes, so I thought of a famous tale to tell him. That's why I went off with him. I knew he would try to discover from me why you were travelling on the stagecoach.'

'And did he?'

'Yes, and I told him that you had had reverses on 'Change and had fallen on evil times,' said Pen, drawing up her chair to the table.

'Oh!' said Sir Richard. 'Was he satisfied with that?'

'Perfectly. He said he was very sorry. And then he asked where we were bound for. I said, for Bristol, because *all* the family had lost its money, and so I had had to be taken away from school.'

'You have the most fertile imagination of anyone of my acquaintance,' said Sir Richard. 'May I ask what school you have been gracing?'

'Harrow. Afterwards I wished I had said Eton, because my cousin Geoffrey is at Harrow, and I don't like him. I wouldn't go to his school.'

'I suppose it is too late to change the school now,' Sir Richard said, in a regretful tone.

She looked up quickly, her fascinating smile crinkling the corners of her eyes. 'You are laughing at me.'

'Yes,' admitted Sir Richard. 'Do you mind?'

'Oh no, not a bit! No one laughs in my aunt's house. I like it.'

'I wish,' said Sir Richard, 'you would tell me more about this aunt of yours. Is she your guardian?'

'No, but I have had to live with her ever since my father died. I have no real guardian, but I have two trustees. On account of my fortune, you understand.'

'Of course, yes: I was forgetting your fortune. Who are your trustees?'

'Well, one is my uncle Griffin – Aunt Almeria's husband, you know – but he doesn't signify, because he does just what Aunt tells him. The other is my father's lawyer, and he doesn't signify either.'

'For the same reason?'

'I don't know, but I shouldn't wonder at it in the least. Everyone is afraid of Aunt Almeria. Even I am, a little. That's why I ran away.'

'Is she unkind to you?'

'N-no. At least, she doesn't ill-treat me, but she is the kind of woman who always gets her own way. Do you know?'

'I know,' Sir Richard said.

'She talks,' explained Pen. 'And when she is displeased with one, I must say that it is very uncomfortable. But one should always be just, and I do not blame her for being so set on my marrying Fred. They are not very rich, you see, and of course Aunt would like Fred to have all my fortune. In fact, I am very sorry to be so disobliging, particularly as I have lived with the Griffins for nearly five years. But, to tell you the truth, I didn't in the least want to, and as for marrying Fred, I could *not*! Only when I suggested to Aunt Almeria that I would much prefer to give my fortune to Fred, and *not* marry him, she flew into a passion, and said I was heartless and shameless, and cried, and talked about nourishing vipers in her bosom. I thought that was unjust of her, because it was a very handsome offer, don't you agree?'

'Very,' said Sir Richard. 'But perhaps a trifle – shall we say, crude?'

'Oh!' Pen digested this. 'You mean that she did not like my *not* pretending that Fred was in love with me?'

61

'I think it just possible,' said Sir Richard gravely.

'Well, I am sorry if I wounded her feelings, but truly I don't think she has the least sensibility. I only said what I thought. But it put her in such a rage that there was nothing for it but to escape. So I did.'

'Were you locked in your room?' enquired Sir Richard.

'Oh no! I daresay I should have been if Aunt had guessed what I meant to do, but she would never think of such a thing.'

'Then – forgive my curiosity! – why did you climb out of the window?' asked Sir Richard.

'Oh, that was on account of Pug!' replied Pen sunnily.

'Pug?'

'Yes, a horrid little creature! He sleeps in a basket in the hall, and he *always* yaps if he thinks one is going out. That would have awakened Aunt Almeria. There was nothing else I could do.'

Sir Richard regarded her with a lurking smile. 'Naturally not. Do you know, Pen, I owe you a debt of gratitude?'

'Oh?' she said, pleased, but doubtful. 'Why?'

'I thought I knew your sex. I was wrong.'

'Oh!' she said again. 'Do you mean that I don't behave as a delicately bred female should?'

'That is one way of putting it, certainly.'

'It is the way Aunt Almeria puts it.'

'She would, of course.'

'I am afraid,' confessed Pen, 'that I am not very well-behaved. Aunt says that I had a lamentable upbringing, because my father treated me as though I had been a boy. I ought to have been, you understand.'

'I cannot agree with you,' said Sir Richard. 'As a boy you would have been in no way remarkable; as a female, believe me, you are unique.'

She flushed to the roots of her hair. 'I *think* that is a compliment.'

'It is,' Sir Richard said, amused.

'Well, I wasn't sure, because I am not out yet, and I do not know any men except my uncle and Fred, and they don't pay compliments. That is to say, not like that.' She looked up rather shyly, but chancing to catch sight of someone through the window, suddenly exclaimed: 'Why, there's Mr Yarde!'

'Mr who?' asked Sir Richard, turning his head.

'You can't see him now: he has gone past the window. You *must* remember Mr Yarde, sir! He was the odd little man who got into the coach at Chippenham, and used such queer words that I could not perfectly understand him. Do you suppose he can be coming to this inn?'

'I sincerely trust not!' said Sir Richard.

Five

*H*is trust was soon seen to have been misplaced, for after a few minutes the landlord came into the room, to ask apologetically whether the noble gentleman would object to giving up one of his rooms to another traveller. 'I told him as how your honour had bespoke both bedchambers, but he is very wishful to get a lodging, sir, so I told him as how I would ask your honour if, maybe, the young gentleman could share your honour's chamber – there being two beds, sir.

Sir Richard, meeting Miss Creed's eye for one pregnant moment, saw that she was struggling with a strong desire to burst out laughing. His own lips quivered, but before he could answer the landlord, the sharp face of Mr Jimmy Yarde peered over that worthy's shoulder.

Upon recognizing the occupants of the parlour, Mr Yarde seemed to be momentarily taken aback. He recovered himself quickly, however, to thrust his way into the parlour with a very fair assumption of delight at encountering two persons already known to him. 'Well, if it ain't my young chub!' he exclaimed. 'Dang me if I didn't think the pair of you had loped off to Wroxhall!'

'No,' said Sir Richard. 'It appeared to me that Wroxhall would be over-full of travellers to-night.'

'Ay, you're a damned knowing one, ain't you? Knowed it the instant I clapped my glaziers on you. And right you are! Says I to myself, "Wroxhall's no place for you, Jimmy, my boy!"'

'Was the thin woman still having the vapours?' asked Pen.

'Lordy, young chub, she were stretched out as stiff as a corpse when I loped off, and no one knowing what to do to bring her to her senses. Ah, and mighty peevy I thought myself, to hit on the notion of coming to this ken – not knowing as you had bespoke all the rooms afore me.'

His bright face shifted to Sir Richard's unpromising countenance. 'Unfortunate!' said Sir Richard politely.

'Ah, now!' wheedled Mr Yarde, 'you wouldn't go for to out-jockey Jimmy Yarde! Lordy, it's all of eleven o'clock, and the light gone. What's to stop your doubling up with the young shaver?'

'If your honour would condescend to allow the young gentleman to sleep in the spare bed in your honour's chamber?' interpolated the landlord in an ingratiating tone.

'No,' said Sir Richard. 'I am an extremely light sleeper, and my nephew snores.' Ignoring an indignant gasp from Pen, he turned to Mr Yarde. 'Do you snore?' he asked.

Jimmy grinned. 'Not me! I sleep like a babby, so help me!'

'Then you,' said Sir Richard, 'may share my room.'

'Done!' said Jimmy promptly. 'Spoke like a rare gager, guv'nor, which I knew you was. Damme, if I don't drain a clank to your very good health!'

Resigning himself to the inevitable, Sir Richard nodded to the landlord, and bade Jimmy draw up a chair.

Not having boarded the stagecoach when Pen had announced Sir Richard to be her tutor, Jimmy apparently accepted her new relationship without question. He spoke of her to Sir Richard as 'your nevvy,' drank both their healths in gin-and-water bespoken by Sir Richard, and seemed to be inclined to make a night of it. He became rather loquacious over his second glass of daffy, and made several mysterious references to Files, and those engaged on the Dub-lay, and the Kidd. Various embittered strictures on Flash Culls led Sir Richard to infer that he had lately been working in partnership with persons above his own social standing, and did not mean to repeat the experience.

Pen sat drinking it all in, with her eyes growing rounder and rounder, until Sir Richard said that it was time she was in bed. He escorted her out of the parlour to the foot of the stairs, where she whispered to him in the tone of one who has made a great discovery: 'Dear sir, I don't believe he is a respectable person!'

'No,' said Sir Richard. 'I don't believe it either.'

'But is he a *thief*?' asked Pen, shocked.

'I should think undoubtedly. Which is why you will lock your door, my child. Is it understood?'

'Yes, but are you sure you will be safe? It would be dreadful if he were to cut your throat in the night!'

'It would indeed,' Sir Richard agreed. 'But I can assure you he won't. You may take this for me, if you will, and keep it till the morning.'

He put his heavy purse into her hand. She nodded. 'Yes, I will. You will take great care, will you not?'

'I promise,' he said, smiling. 'Be off now, and don't tease yourself over my safety!'

He went back to the parlour, where Jimmy Yarde awaited him. Being called upon to join Mr Yarde in a glass of daffy, he raised not the slightest objection, although he very soon suspected Jimmy of trying to drink him under the table. As he refilled the glasses for the third time, he said apologetically: 'Perhaps I ought to warn you that I am accounted to have a reasonably strong head. I should not like you to waste your time, Mr Yarde.'

Jimmy was not at all abashed. He grinned, and said: 'Ah, I said you was a peevy cull! Knowed it as soon as I clapped my daylights on to you. You learned to drink Blue Ruin in Cribb's parlour!'

'Quite right,' said Sir Richard.

'Oh, I knowed it, bless your heart! "That there gentry-cove would peel remarkably well," I says to myself. "And a handy bunch of fives he's got." Never you fret, guv'nor: Jimmy Yarde's no green 'un. What snabbles me, though, is how you come to be travelling in the common rumble.'

Sir Richard gave a soft laugh suddenly. 'You see, I have lost all my money,' he said.

'Lost all your money?' repeated Jimmy, astonished.

'On 'Change,' added Sir Richard.

The light, sharp eyes flickered over his elegant person. 'Ah, you're trying to gammon me! What's the lay?'

'None at all.'

'Dang me if I ever met such a cursed rum touch!' A suspicion crossed his mind. 'You ain't killed your man, guv'nor?'

'No. Have you?'

Jimmy looked quite alarmed. 'Not me, guv'nor, not me! I don't hold with violence, any gait.'

Sir Richard helped himself to a leisurely pinch of snuff. 'Just the Knuckle, eh?'

Jimmy gave a start, and looked at him with uneasy respect. 'What would the likes of you know about the Knuckle?'

'Not very much, admittedly. I believe it means the filching of watches, snuff-boxes, and such-like from the pockets of the unsuspecting.'

'Here!' said Jimmy, looking very hard at him across the table, 'you don't work the Drop, do you?'

Sir Richard shook his head.

'You ain't a Picker-up, or p'raps a Kidd?'

'No,' said Sir Richard. 'I am quite honest – what you, I fancy, call a Flat.'

'I don't!' Jimmy said emphatically. 'I never met a flat what was so unaccountable knowing as what you are, guv'nor; and what's more I hope I don't meet one again!'

He watched Sir Richard rise to his feet, and kindle his bed-room candle at the guttering one on the table. He was frowning in a puzzled way, clearly uncertain in his mind. 'Going to bed, guv'nor?'

Sir Richard glanced down at him. 'Yes. I did warn you that I am a shockingly light sleeper, did I not?'

'Lord, you ain't got no need to fear *me*!'

'I am quite sure I have not,' smiled Sir Richard.

When Jimmy Yarde, an hour later, softly tiptoed into the low-pitched bed-chamber above the parlour, Sir Richard lay to all appearances peacefully asleep. Jimmy edged close to the bed, and stood watching him, and listening to his even breathing.

'Don't drop hot tallow on me, I beg!' said Sir Richard, not opening his eyes.

Jimmy Yarde jumped, and swore.

'Quite so,' said Sir Richard.

Jimmy Yarde cast him a look of venomous dislike, and in silence undressed, and got into the neighbouring bed.

He awoke at an early hour, to hear roosters crowing from farm to farm in the distance. The sun was up, but the day was still misty, and the air very fresh. The bed creaked under him as he sat up, but it did not rouse Sir Richard. Jimmy Yarde slid out of it cautiously, and dressed himself. On the dimity-covered table by the window, Sir Richard's gold quizzing-glass and snuff-box lay, carelessly discarded. Jimmy looked wistfully at him. He was something of a connoisseur in snuff-boxes, and his fingers itched to slip this one into his pocket. He glanced uncertainly towards the bed. Sir Richard sighed in his sleep. His coat hung over a chair within Jimmy's reach. Keeping his eyes on Sir Richard, Jimmy felt in its pockets. Nothing but a handkerchief rewarded his search. But Sir Richard had given no sign of returning consciousness. Jimmy picked up the snuff-box, and inspected it. Still no movement from the bed. Emboldened, Jimmy dropped it into his capacious pocket. The quizzing-glass swiftly followed it. Jimmy went stealthily towards the door. As he reached it, a yawn made him halt in his tracks, and spin round.

Sir Richard stretched, and yawned again. 'You're up early, my friend,' he remarked.

'That's right,' said Jimmy, anxious to be gone before his theft could be discovered. 'I'm not one for lying abed on a fine summer's morning. I'll get a breath of air before I have my breakfast. Daresay we'll meet downstairs, eh, guv'nor?'

'I daresay we shall,' agreed Sir Richard. 'But in case we don't, I'll relieve you of my snuff-box and my eyeglass now.'

Exasperated, Jimmy let fall the modest bundle which contained his nightgear. 'Dang me, if I ever met such a leery cove in all my puff!' he said. 'You never saw me lift that lobb!'

'I warned you that I was a shockingly light sleeper,' said Sir Richard.

'Bubbled by a gudgeon!' said Jimmy disgustedly, handing over the booty. 'Here you are: there's no need for you to go calling in any harman, eh?'

'None at all,' replied Sir Richard.

'Damme, you're a blood after my own fancy, guv'nor! No hard feeling?'

'Not the least in the world.'

'I wish I knew what your lay might be,' Jimmy said wistfully, and departed, shaking his head over the problem.

Downstairs he found Pen Creed, who had also awakened early. She bade him a cheerful good-morning, and said that she had been out, and was of the opinion that it was going to be a hot day. When he asked her if she and her uncle meant to board the next stagecoach to Bristol, she replied prudently that her uncle had not yet told her what they were going to do.

'You are bound for Bristol, ain't you?' enquired Jimmy.

'Oh yes!' said Pen, with a beautiful disregard for the truth.

They were standing in the taproom, which, at that hour of the morning, was empty, and just as Pen was beginning to say that she wanted her breakfast, the landlady came through the door leading from the kitchen, and asked them if they had heard the news.

'What news?' Pen asked uneasily.

'Why, everyone's in quite a pucker up at Wroxhall, us being quiet folk, and not used to town-ways. But there's my boy Jim come in saying there's one of they Bow Street Runners come down by the Mail. What he may want, surely to goodness there's none of us knows! They do say as how he stopped off at Calne, and come on easy-like to Wroxhall. And there he be, poking his nose into respectable houses, and asking all manner of questions! Well, what I say is, *we've* nothing to hide, and he may come here if he pleases, but he will learn nothing.'

'Is he coming here?' asked Pen, in a faint voice.

'Going to all the inns hereabout, by what they tell me,' responded the landlady. 'Jem took the notion into his head it's all along of the stagecoach which you and your good uncle was on, sir, for seemingly he's been asking a mort of questions about the passengers. Our Sam looks to see him here inside of half an hour. "Well," I says, "let him come, for I'm an honest woman, and there's never been a word said against the house, not to my knowledge!" Your breakfast will be on the table in ten minutes, sir.'

She bustled into the parlour, leaving Pen rather pale, and Jimmy Yarde suddenly thoughtful. 'Runners, eh?' said that worthy, stroking his chin. 'There now!'

'I have never seen one,' said Pen, with a creditable show of nonchalance. 'It will be most interesting. I wonder what he can want?'

'There's no telling,' replied Jimmy, his lashless eyes dwelling upon her in a considering stare. 'No telling at all. Seems to me, though, he won't be wanting a flash young chub like you.'

'Why, of course not!' replied Pen, forcing a laugh.

'That's what I thought,' said Jimmy, transferring his gaze to the long coat which had been flung across one of the tables. 'Might that be your toge, young shaver?'

'Yes, but I didn't need it after all. It is much warmer outside than I thought it would be.'

He picked it up, shook out its folds, and gave it to her. 'Don't you go leaving things about in common taprooms!' he said austerely. 'There's plenty of files – ah, even in these quiet parts! – would be glad to get their dabblers on to a good toge like that.'

'Oh yes! Thank you! I'll take it upstairs!' said Pen, glad of an opportunity to escape.

'You couldn't do better,' approved Jimmy. 'Then we'll have a bit of food, and though I don't hold with harmen in general – which is to say, with Law-officers, young shaver – why, I'm a peacable man, and if any such be wishful to search me, they're welcome.'

He strolled into the parlour, with the air of one whose

conscience is clean, and Pen hurried off upstairs, to tap urgently on Sir Richard's door.

His voice called to her to come in, and she entered to find him putting the finishing touches to his cravat. He met her eyes in the mirror, and said: 'Well, brat?'

'Sir, we must leave this place instantly!' said Pen impetuously. 'We are in the greatest danger!'

'Why? Has your aunt arrived?' asked Sir Richard, preserving his calm.

'Worse!' Pen declared. 'A Bow Street Runner!'

'Ah, I thought you were a house-breaker in the first place!' said Sir Richard, shaking his head..

'I am not a house-breaker! You know I am not!'

'If the Runners are after you, it is obvious to me that you are a desperate character,' he replied, slipping his snuff-box into his pocket. 'Let us go downstairs, and have some breakfast.'

'Please, dear sir, be serious! I am sure that my Aunt must have set the Runner on to me!'

'My dear child, if there is any one thing more certain than another it is that Bow Street has never heard of your existence. Don't be silly!'

'Oh!' She heaved a sigh of relief. 'I do trust you are right, but it is just the sort of thing Aunt Almeria would do!'

'You are the best judge of that, no doubt, but you may take it from me that it is not in the least the sort of thing a Bow Street Runner would do. You will probably find that the man he wants is our friend Mr Yarde.'

'Yes, at first I thought that too, but he says the Runner is welcome to search him if he wants to.'

'Then it is safe to assume that Mr Yarde has disposed of whatever booty it was he ran off with. Breakfast!'

In considerable trepidation, Pen followed him down to the parlour. They found Jimmy Yarde discussing a plate of cold beef. He greeted Sir Richard with a grin and a wink, obviously quite unabashed by his previous encounter with him that morning, to which he referred in the frankest terms. 'When I meet up with a leery cove, I don't bear malice,' he announced, raising a tankard of ale. 'So here's your wery good health, guv'nor, and no hard feelings!'

Sir Richard seemed to be rather bored, and merely nodded. Jimmy Yarde fixed him with a twinkling eye, and said: 'And no splitting to any harman about poor old Jimmy boning your lobb, because he never did, and you know well it's in your pocket at this wery moment. What's more,' he added handsomely, 'I wouldn't fork you now I has your measure, guv'nor, not for fifty Yellow Boys!'

'I'm glad of that,' said Sir Richard.

'No splitting?' Jimmy said, his head on one side.

'Not if I am allowed to eat my breakfast in peace,' replied Sir Richard wearily.

'All's bowman then!' said Jimmy, 'and not another word will you hear from me, guv'nor, till we gets to Bristol. Damme if I don't ride outside the rattler, just to oblige you!'

Sir Richard looked meditatively at him, but said nothing. Pen sat down facing the window, and watched the road for signs of a Bow Street Runner.

Contrary to the landlady's expectations, the Runner did not reach the inn until some little time after the breakfast covers had been removed, and Jimmy Yarde had strolled out to lounge at his ease on a bench set against the wall of the hostelry.

The Runner entered the inn by way of the yard at the back of it, and the first person he encountered was Sir Richard, who was engaged in settling his account with the landlord. Miss Creed, at his elbow, drew his attention to the Runner's arrival by urgently twitching his coat sleeve. He looked up, with raised brows, saw the newcomer, and lifted his quizzing-glass.

'Beg your pardon, sir,' said the Runner, touching his hat. 'Me not meaning to intrude, but being wishful to speak with the landlord.'

'Certainly,' said Sir Richard, his brows still expressive of languid surprise.

'At your convenience, sir: no hurry, sir!' said the Runner, retreating to a discreet distance.

The sigh which escaped Miss Creed was one of such profound relief that it was plain her alarms had not until that moment been allayed. Sir Richard finished paying his shot, and with a brief: 'Come, Pen!' tossed over his shoulder, left the taproom.

'He didn't come to find me!' breathed Pen.

'Of course he didn't.'

'I couldn't help being a little alarmed. What shall we do now, sir?'

'Shake off your very undesirable travelling-acquaintance,' he replied briefly.

She gave a gurgle. 'Yes, but how? I have *such* a fear that he means to go with us to Bristol.'

'But we are not going to Bristol. While he is being interrogated by that Runner, we, my child, are going to walk quietly out by the back door, and proceed by ways, which I trust will not prove as devious as the tapster's description of them, to Colerne. There we shall endeavour to hire a vehicle to carry us to Queen Charlton.'

'Oh, famous!' cried Pen. 'Let us go at once!'

Five minutes later they left the inn unobtrusively, by way of the yard, found themselves in a hayfield, and skirted it to a gate leading into a ragged spinney.

The village of Colerne was rather less than three miles distant, but long before they had reached it Sir Richard was tired of his portmanteau. 'Pen Creed, you are a pestilent child!' he told her.

'Why, what have I done?' she asked, with one of her wide, enquiring looks.

'You have hailed me from my comfortable house –'

'I didn't! It was you who *would* come!'

'I was drunk.'

'Well, that was not my fault,' she pointed out.

'Don't interrupt me! You have made me travel for miles in a conveyance smelling strongly of dirt and onions –'

'That was the fat woman's husband,' interpolated Pen. 'I noticed it myself.'

'No one could have failed to notice it. And I am not partial to onions. You drew a portrait of me which led everyone in the coach to regard me in the light of an oppressor of innocent youth –'

'Not the thin, disagreeable man. *He* wanted me to be oppressed.'

'He was a person of great discrimination. Not content with that, you pitchforked me into what threatens to be a life-friendship with a pickpocket, to escape from whose advances I am obliged to tramp five miles, carrying a portmanteau which is much heavier than I had supposed possible. It only remains for me to become embroiled in an action for kidnapping, which I feel reasonably assured your aunt will bring against me.'

'Yes, and now I come to think of it, I remember that you said you were going to be married,' said Pen, quite unimpressed by these strictures. 'Will she be very angry with you?'

'I hope she will be so very angry that she will wish never to see my face again,' said Sir Richard calmly. 'In fact, brat, that reflection so far outweighs all other considerations that I forgive you the rest.'

'I think you are a very odd sort of person,' said Pen. 'Why did you ask her to marry you, if you did not wish to?'

'I didn't. During the past two days that is the only folly I have not committed.'

'Well, why did you mean to ask her, then?'

'*You* should know.'

'But you are a man! No one could make you do anything you did not choose to do!'

'They came mighty near it. If you had not dropped out of the window into my arms, I have little doubt that I should at this moment be receiving the congratulations of my acquaintance.'

'Well, I must say I do not think you are at all just to me, then, to call me a pestilent child! I saved you – though, indeed, I didn't know it – from a horrid fate.'

74

'True. But need I have been saved in a noisome stagecoach?'

'That was part of the adventure. Besides, I explained to you at the outset why I was travelling on the stage. You must own that we are having a very exciting time! And, what is more, you have had more adventure than I, for you actually shared a room with a real thief!'

'So I did,' said Sir Richard, apparently much struck by this circumstance.

'And I can plainly see a cottage ahead of us, so I expect we have reached Colerne,' she said triumphantly.

In a few moments, she was found to have been right. They walked into the village, and fetched up at the best-looking inn.

'Now, what particular lie shall we tell here?' asked Sir Richard.

'A wheel came off our post-chaise,' replied Pen promptly.

'Are you never at a loss?' he enquired, regarding her in some amusement.

'Well, to tell you the truth I haven't had very much experience,' she confided.

'Believe me, no one would suspect that.'

'No, I must say I think I was quite born to be a vagabond,' she said seriously.

The story of the faulty wheel was accepted by the landlord of the Green Man without question. If he thought it strange that the travellers should have left the main highway to brave the perils of rough country lanes, his mild surprise was soon dissipated by the announcement that they were on their way to Queen Charlton, and had attempted to find a shorter road. He said that they would have done better to have followed the Bristol road to Cold Ashton, but that perhaps they were strangers in these parts?

'Precisely,' said Sir Richard. 'But we are going to visit friends at Queen Charlton, and we wish to hire some sort of a vehicle to carry us there.'

The smile faded from the landlord's face when he heard this, and he shook his head. There were no vehicles for hire at Colerne. There was, in fact, only one suitable carriage, and that his own gig. 'Which I'd be pleased to let out to your honour if I had but a man to send with it. But the lads is all out haymaking, and I can't go myself. Maybe the blacksmith could see what's to be done to patch up your chaise, sir?'

'Quite useless!' said Sir Richard truthfully. 'The wheel is past repairing. Moreover, I instructed my postilion to ride back to Wroxhall. What will you take for lending your gig to me without a man to go with it?'

'Well, sir, it ain't that so much, but how will I get it back?'

'Oh, one of Sir Jasper's grooms will drive it back!' said Pen. 'You need have no fear on that score!'

'Would that be Sir Jasper Luttrell, sir?'

'Yes, indeed, we are going on a visit to him.'

The landlord was plainly shaken. Sir Jasper was apparently well-known to him; on the other hand Sir Richard was not. He cast him a doubtful, sidelong look, and slowly shook his head.

'Well, if you won't let out your gig on hire, I suppose I shall have to buy it,' said Sir Richard.

'Buy my gig, sir?' gasped the landlord, staggered.

'And the horse too, of course,' added Sir Richard, pulling out his purse.

The landlord blinked at him. 'Well, I'm sure, sir! If that's the way it is, I don't know but what I could let you drive the gig over yourself – seeing as how you're a friend of Sir Jasper. Come to think of it, I won't be needing it for a couple of days. Only you'll have to rest the old horse afore you send him back, mind!'

Sir Richard raised no objection to this, and after coming to terms with an ease which led to the landlord's expressing the wish that there were more gentlemen like Sir Richard to be met with, the travellers had only to wait until the cob had been harnessed to the gig, and led round to the front of the inn.

The gig was neither smart nor well-sprung, and the cob's gait was more sure than swift, but Pen was delighted with the whole equipage. She sat perched up beside Sir Richard, enjoying the hot sunshine, and pointing out to him the manifold superiorities of the Somerset countryside over any other county.

They did not reach Queen Charlton until dusk, since the way to it was circuitous, and often very rough. When they came within sight of the village, Sir Richard said: 'Well, brat, what now? Am I to drive you to Sir Jasper Luttrell's house?'

Pen, who had become rather silent during the last five miles of their drive, said with a little gasp: 'I have been thinking that perhaps it would be better if I sent a message in the morning! It is not Piers, you know, but, though I did not think of her at the time, it – it has occurred to me that perhaps Lady Luttrell may not perfectly understand . . .'

Her voice died away unhappily. She was revived by Sir Richard's saying in matter-of-fact tones: 'A very good notion. We will drive to an inn.'

'The George was always accounted the best,' offered Pen. 'I have never actually been inside it, but my father was used to say its cellars were excellent.'

The George was discovered to be an ancient half-timbered hostelry with beamed ceilings, and wainscoted parlours. It was a rambling house, with a large yard, and many chintz-hung bed-rooms. There was no difficulty in procuring a private parlour, and by the time Pen had washed the dust of the roads from her face, and unpacked the cloak-bag, her spirits, which had sunk unaccountably, had begun to lift again. Dinner was served in the parlour, and neither the landlord nor his wife seemed to recognize in the golden-haired stripling the late Mr Creed's tomboyish little girl.

'If only my aunt does not discover me before I have found Piers!' Pen said, helping herself to some more raspberries.

'We will circumvent her. But touching this question of Piers, do you – er – suppose that he will be able to extricate you from your present difficulties?'

'Well, he will have to, if I marry him, won't he?'

'Undoubtedly. But – you must not think me an incorrigible wet blanket – it is not precisely easy to be married at a moment's notice.

'Isn't it? I didn't know,' said Pen innocently. 'Oh well, I dare say we shall fly to Gretna Green then! We used to think that would be a splendid adventure.'

'Gretna Green in those clothes?' enquired Sir Richard, levelling his quizzing-glass at her.

'Well, no, I suppose not. But when Piers has explained it all to Lady Luttrell, I expect she will be able to get some proper clothes for me.'

'You do not entertain any doubts of Lady Luttrell's – er – receiving you as her prospective daughter-in-law?'

'Oh no! She was always most kind to me! Only I did think that perhaps it would be better if I saw Piers first.'

Sir Richard, who had so far allowed himself to be borne along resistless on the tide of this adventure, began to perceive that it would shortly be his duty to wait upon Lady Luttrell, and to give her an account of his dealings with Miss Creed. He glanced at that young lady, serenely finishing the last of the raspberries, and reflected, with a wry smile, that the task was not going to be an easy one.

A servant came in to clear away the dishes presently. Pen at once engaged him in conversation and elicited the news that Sir Jasper Luttrell was away from home.

'Oh! But not Mr Piers Luttrell?'

'No, sir, I saw Mr Piers yesterday. Going to Keynsham, he was. I do hear as he has a young gentleman staying with him – a Lunnon gentleman, by all accounts.'

'Oh!' Pen's voice sounded rather blank. As soon as the man had gone away, she said: 'Did you hear that, sir? It makes it just a little awkward, doesn't it?'

'Very awkward,' agreed Sir Richard. 'It seems as though we have now to eliminate the gentleman from London.'

'I wish we could. For I am sure my aunt will guess that I have come home, and if she finds me before I have found Piers, I am utterly undone.'

'But she will not find you. She will only find me.'

'Do you think you will be able to fob her off?'

'Oh, I think so!' Sir Richard said negligently. 'After all,

she would scarcely expect you to be travelling in my company, would she? I hardly think she will demand to see my nephew.'

'No, but what if she does?' asked Pen, having no such dependence on her aunt's forbearing.

Sir Richard smiled rather sardonically. 'I am not, perhaps, the best person in the world of whom to make – ah – impertinent demands.'

Pen's eyes lit with sudden laughter. 'Oh, I do hope you will talk to her like that, and look at her just *so*! And if she brings Fred with her, he will be quite overcome, I dare say, to meet you face to face. For you must know that he admires you excessively. He tries to tie his cravat in a Wyndham Fall, even!'

'That, in itself, I find an impertinence,' said Sir Richard.

She nodded, and lifted a hand to her own cravat. 'What do you think of mine, sir?'

'I have carefully refrained from thinking about it at all. Do you really wish to know?'

'But I have arranged it just as you did!'

'Good God!' said Sir Richard faintly. 'My poor deluded child!'

'You are teasing me! At least it was not ill enough tied to make you rip it off my neck as you did when you first met me!'

'You will recall that we left the inn in haste this morning,' he explained.

'I am persuaded *that* would not have weighed with you. But you put me in mind of a very important matter. You paid my reckoning there.'

'Don't let that worry you, I beg.'

'I am determined to pay everything for myself,' Pen said firmly. 'It would be a shocking piece of impropriety if I were to be beholden for money to a stranger.'

'True. I had not thought of that.'

She looked up with her sudden bright look of enquiry. 'You are laughing at me again!'

He showed her a perfectly grave countenance. 'Laughing? I?'

'I know very well you are. You may make your mouth prim, but I have noticed several times that you laugh with your eyes.'

'Do I? I beg your pardon!'

'Well, you need not, for I like it. I would not have come all this way with you if you had not had such smiling eyes. Isn't it odd how one knows if one can trust a person, even if he is drunk?'

'Very odd,' he said.

She was hunting fruitlessly through her pockets. 'Where can I have put my purse? Oh, I think I must have put it in my overcoat!'

She had flung this garment down on a chair, upon first entering the parlour, and stepped across the room to feel in the capacious pockets.

'Are you seriously proposing to count a few miserable shillings into my hand?'

'Yes, indeed I am. Oh, here it is!' She pulled out a leather purse with a ring round its neck, from one pocket, stared at it, and exclaimed: 'This is not my purse!'

Sir Richard looked at it through his glass. 'Isn't it? It is certainly not mine, I assure you.'

'It is very heavy. I wonder how it can have come into my pocket? Shall I open it?'

'By all means. Are you quite sure it is not your own?'

'Oh yes, quite!' She moved to the table, tugging at the ring. It was a little hard to pull off, but she managed it after one or two tugs, and shook out into the palm of her hand a diamond necklace that winked and glittered in the light of the candles.

'*Richard!*' gasped Miss Creed, startled into forgetting the proprieties again. 'Oh, I beg your pardon! But look!'

'I am looking, and you have no need to beg my pardon. I have been calling you Pen these two days.'

'Oh, that is another matter, because you are so much older!'

He looked at her somewhat enigmatically. 'Am I? Well, never mind. Do I understand that this gaud does not belong to you?'

'Good gracious, no! I never saw it before in my life!'

'Oh!' said Sir Richard. 'Well, it is always agreeable to have problems solved. Now we know why your friend Mr Yarde had no fear of the Bow Street Runner.'

Six

*P*en let the necklace slip through her fingers on to the table. 'You mean that he stole it, and then – and then put it in *my* pocket? But, sir, this is terrible! Why – why, that Runner will next come after us!'

'I think it more likely that Mr Yarde will come after us.'

'Good God!' Pen said, quite pale with dismay. 'What are we to do?'

He smiled rather maliciously. 'Didn't you desire to meet with a real adventure?'

'Yes, but – Oh, do not be absurd and teasing, I beg of you! What shall we do with the necklace? Couldn't we throw it away somewhere, or hide it in a ditch?'

'We could, of course, but it would surely be a trifle unfair to the owner?'

'I don't care about that,' confessed Pen. 'It would be dreadful to be arrested for thieving, and I know we shall be!'

'Oh, I trust not!' Sir Richard said. He straightened the necklace, where it lay on the table, and looked down at it with a slight frown creasing his brow. 'Yes,' he said meditatively. 'I have seen you before. Now, *where* have I seen you before?'

'Do please put it away!' begged Pen. 'Only think if a servant were to come into the room!'

He picked it up. 'My lamentable memory! Alas, my lamentable memory! Where, oh, *where* have I seen you?'

'Dear sir, if Jimmy Yarde finds us, he will very likely cut our throats to get the necklace back!'

'On the contrary, I have his word for it that he is opposed to all forms of violence.'

'But when he does not discover it in my pocket, where he placed it – and now I come to think of it, he actually had my coat in his hands – he must guess that we have discovered it!'

'Very likely he will, but I cannot see what profit there would be in his cutting our throats.' Sir Richard restored the necklace to its leather purse, and dropped it into his pocket. 'We have now nothing to do but to await the arrival of Jimmy Yarde. Perhaps – who knows? – we may induce him to divulge the ownership of the necklace. Meanwhile, this parlour is very stuffy, and the night remarkably fine. Do you care to stroll out with me to admire the stars, brat?'

'I suppose,' said Pen defiantly, 'that you think I am very poor-spirited!'

'Very,' agreed Sir Richard, his eyes glinting under their heavy lids.

'I am not afraid of anything,' Pen announced. 'Merely, I am *shocked*!'

'A waste of time, believe me. Are you coming?'

'Yes, but it seems to me as though you have put a live coal in your pocket! What if some dishonest person were to steal it from you?'

'Then we shall be freed from all responsibility. Come along!'

She followed him out into the warm night. He appeared to have banished all thought of the necklace from his mind. He pointed various constellations out to her, and, drawing her hand through his arm, strolled with her down the street, past the last straggling cottages, into a lane redolent of meadowsweet.

'I suppose I was poor-spirited,' Pen confided presently. 'Shall you feel obliged to denounce poor Jimmy Yarde to the Runner?'

'I hope,' said Sir Richard dryly, 'that Mr Piers Luttrell is a gentleman of resolute character.'

'Why?'

'That he may be able to curb your somewhat reckless friendliness.'

'Well, I haven't seen him for five years, but it was always I who thought of things to do.'

'That is what I feared. Where does he live?'

'Oh, about two miles farther down this road! *My* home is on the other side of the village. Should you like to see it?'

'Immensely, but not at the moment. We will now retrace our steps, for it is time that you were in bed.'

'I shan't sleep a wink.'

'I trust that you are mistaken, my good child – in fact, I am reasonably certain that you are.'

'And to add to everything,' said Pen, unheeding, 'Piers has got a horrid man staying with him! I don't know what is to be done.'

'In the morning,' said Sir Richard soothingly, 'we will attend to all these difficulties.'

'In the morning, very likely, Aunt Almeria will have discovered me.'

On this gloomy reflection, they retraced their steps to the inn. Its shuttered windows cast golden gleams out into the quiet street, several of them standing open to let in the cool night air. Just as they were about to pass one of them on their way to the inn door, a voice spoke inside the room, and to her astonishment, Sir Richard suddenly gripped Pen's arm, and brought her to a dead halt. She started to enquire the reason for this sudden stop, but his hand across her mouth choked back the words.

The voice from within the house said with a slight stammer: 'You c-can't come up to C-Crome Hall, I tell you! It's b-bad enough as it is. G-Good God, man, if anyone were to see me sneaking off to meet you here they'd p-precious soon smell a rat!'

A more robust voice answered: 'Maybe I've been smelling rats myself, my young buck. Who was it foisted a partner on to me, eh? Were the pair of ye meaning to cheat Horace Trimble? Were ye, my bonny boy?'

'You fool, you let yourself be b-bubbled!' The stammerer said furiously. 'Then you c-come here – enough to ruin everything! I tell you I d-daren't say! And don't come up to C-Crome Hall again, damn you! I'll m-meet you tomorrow, in the spinney down the road. 'Sblood, he can't have g-gone far! Why don't you go to B-Bristol if he didn't b-break back to London? Instead of c-coming here to insult me!'

'I insult you! By the powers, that's rich!' A full-throated laugh followed the words, and the sound of a chair being dashed back on a wooden floor.

'Damn your impudence! You've b-bungled everything, and now you c-come blustering to me! *You* were to arrange everything! *I* was to l-leave all to you! Finely you've arranged it! And n-now you expect m-me to set all to rights!'

'Softly, my buck! softly! You're crowing mighty loud, but I did my part of the business all right and tight. It was the man you were so set on that bubbled me, and that makes me think, d'ye hear? It makes me think mighty hard. Maybe you'd better think too – and if you've a notion in your head that Horace Trimble's a green 'un, get rid of it! See?'

'Hush, for G-God's sake! You d-don't know who may be listening! I'll m-meet you to-morrow, at eleven, if I c-can shake off y-young Luttrell. We must think what's to be done!'

A door opened and was hastily shut again. Sir Richard pulled Pen back into the shadows beyond the window, and, a moment later, a slight, cloaked figure came out of the inn, and strode swiftly away into the darkness.

The warning pressure on Pen's arm held her silent, although she was by this time agog with excitement. Sir Richard waited until the dwindling sound of footsteps had died in the distance, and then strolled on with Pen's hand still tucked in his arm, past the open window to the inn-door. Not until they stood in their own parlour again did Pen allow herself to speak, but as soon as the door was shut behind them, she exclaimed: 'What did it mean? He spoke of "Young Luttrell" – did you hear him? It must be the man who is staying with him! But who was the other man, and what were they talking about?'

Sir Richard did not appear to be attending very closely. He was standing by the table, a frown between his eyes, and his mouth rather grim. Suddenly his gaze shifted to Pen's face, but what he said seemed to her incomprehensible. 'Of course!' he muttered softly. 'So *that* was it!'

'Oh, *do* tell me!' begged Pen. '*What* was it, and why did you stop when you heard the stammering-man speak? Do you – is it possible that you know him?'

'Very well indeed,' replied Sir Richard.

'Good heavens! And it is he who is visiting Piers! Dear sir, does it seem to you that everything is becoming a trifle awkward?'

'Extremely so,' said Sir Richard.

'Well, that is what I thought,' said Pen. 'First we are saddled with a stolen necklace, and now we discover that a friend of yours is staying with Piers!'

'Oh no, we do not!' said Sir Richard. 'That young gentleman is no friend of mine! Nor, I fancy, is his presence in this neighbourhood unconnected with that necklace. If I do not mistake, Pen, we have become enmeshed in a plot from which it will take all my ingenuity to extricate us.'

'I have ingenuity too,' said Miss Creed, affronted.

'Not a scrap,' responded Sir Richard calmly.

She swallowed this, saying in a small voice: 'Very well, if I haven't, I haven't, but I wish you will explain.'

'I feel sure you do,' said Sir Richard: 'But the truth is that I cannot. Not only does it appear to me to be a matter of uncommon delicacy, but it is also for the moment – a little obscure.'

She sighed. 'It does not seem fair, because it was I who found the necklace, after all! Who is the stammering-man? You may just as well tell me that, because Piers will, you know.'

'Certainly. The stammering-man is the Honourable Beverley Brandon.'

'Oh! I don't know him,' said Pen, rather disappointed.

'You are to be congratulated.'

'Is he an enemy of yours?'

'An enemy! No!'

'Well, you seem to dislike him very cordially.'

'That does not make him my enemy. To be exact, he is the

younger brother of the lady to whom I was to have been betrothed.'

Pen looked aghast. 'Good God, sir, can he have come in search of you?'

'No, nothing of that kind. Indeed, Pen, I can't tell you more, for the rest is conjecture.' He met her disappointed look, and smiled down at her, gently pinching her chin. 'Poor Pen! Forgive me!'

A little colour stole up to the roots of her hair. 'I do not mean to tease you. I expect you will tell me all about it when – when it isn't conjecture.'

'I expect I shall,' he agreed. 'But that will not be tonight, so be off with you to bed, child!'

She went, but was back again a few minutes later, round-eyed and breathless. 'Richard! He has found us! I have seen him! I am certain it was he!'

'Who?' he asked.

'Jimmy Yarde, of course! It was so hot in my room that I drew back the curtains to open the window, and the moon was so bright that I stood looking out for a minute. And there he was, directly below me! I could not mistake. And the worst is that I fear he saw me, for he drew back at once into the shadow of the house!'

'Did he indeed?' There was a gleam in Sir Richard's eye. 'Well, he is here sooner than I expected. A resourceful gentleman, Mr Jimmy Yarde!'

'But what are we going to do? I am not in the least, afraid, but I should like to be told what you wish me to do!'

'That is very easily done. I wish you to exchange bed-chambers with me. Show yourself again at the window of your own room, if you like, but on no account pull back the blinds in mine. I have a very earnest desire to meet Mr Jimmy Yarde.'

Her dimples peeped. 'I see! like the fairy-story! "Oh, Grandma, what big teeth you have!" *What* an adventure we are having! But you will take care, won't you, sir?'

'I will.'

'And you will tell me all about it afterwards?'

'Perhaps.'

'If you don't,' said Pen, with deep feeling, 'it will be the most unjust thing imaginable!'

He laughed, and, seeing that there was no more to be got out of him, she went away again.

An hour later, the candlelight vanished from the upper room with the open casements and the undrawn blinds, but it was two hours before Mr Yarde's head appeared above the window-sill, and not a light shone in the village.

The moon, sailing across a sky of deepest sapphire, cast a bar of silver across the floor of the chamber, but left the four-poster bed in shadow. The ascent, by way of the porch-roof, a stout drain-pipe, and a gnarled branch of wistaria, had been easy, but Mr Yarde paused before swinging a leg over the sill. His eye, trying to penetrate the darkness, encountered a drab driving-coat, hanging over the back of a chair placed full in the shaft of moonlight. He knew that coat, and a tiny sigh escaped him. He hoisted himself up, and noiselessly slid into the room. He had left his shoes below, and his stockinged-feet made no sound on the floor, as he crept across it.

But there was no heavy leather sack-purse in the pocket of the driving-coat.

He was disappointed, but he had been prepared for disappointment. He stole out of the moonlight to the bedside, listening to the sound of quiet breathing. No tremor disturbed its regularity, and after listening to it for a few minutes, he bent, and began cautiously to slide his hand under the dimly-seen pillow. The other, his right, grasped a muffler, which could be readily clapped over a mouth opened to utter a startled cry.

The cry, hardly more than a croak, strangled at birth, was surprised out of himself, however, for, just as his sensitive fingers felt the object for which they were seeking, two iron hands seized him by the throat, and choked him.

He tore quite unavailingly at the hold, realizing through the drumming in his ears, the bursting of his veins, and the pain in his temples, that he had made a mistake, that the hands crushing the breath out of him certainly did not belong to any stripling.

Just as he seemed to himself to be losing possession of his senses, the grip slackened, and a voice he was learning to hate, said softly: 'Your error, Mr Yarde!'

He felt himself shaken and suddenly released, and, being quite powerless to help himself, fell to the floor and stayed there, making odd crowing noises as he got his wind back. By the time he had recovered sufficiently to struggle on to one elbow, Sir Richard had cast off the coverlet, and sprung out of bed. He was dressed in his shirt and breeches, as Mr Yarde's suffused eyes saw, as soon as Sir Richard had relit the candle by his bed.

Sir Richard laid aside the tinder-box, and glanced down at Mr Yarde. Jimmy's vision was clearing; he was able to see that Sir Richard's lips had curled into a somewhat contemptuous smile. He began gingerly to massage his throat, which felt badly bruised, and waited for Sir Richard to speak.

'I warned you that I was a shockingly light sleeper,' Sir Richard said.

Jimmy cast him a malevolent look, but made no answer.

'Get up!' Sir Richard said. 'You may sit on that chair, Mr Yarde, for we are going to enjoy a heart-to-heart talk.'

Jimmy picked himself up. A glance in the direction of the window was enough to convince him that he would be intercepted before he could reach it. He sat down and drew the back of his hand across his brow.

'Don't let us misunderstand one another!' Sir Richard said. 'You came to find a certain diamond necklace, which you hid in my nephew's coat this morning. There are just three things I can do with you. I can deliver you up to the Law.'

'You can't prove I come to fork the necklace, guv'nor,' Jimmy muttered.

'You think not? We may yet see. Failing the Bow Street Runner – but I feel he would be happy to take you into custody – I fancy a gentleman of the name of Trimble – ah, Horace

Trimble, if my memory serves! – would be even happier to relieve me of you.'

The mention of this name brought an expression of great uneasiness into Jimmy's sharp countenance. 'I don't know him! Never heard of any such cove!'

'Oh yes, I think you have!' said Sir Richard.

'I ain't done you any harm, guv'nor, nor intended any! I'll cap downright –'

'You needn't: I believe you.'

Jimmy's spirits began to lift. 'Dang me if I didn't say you was a leery cove! You wouldn't be hard on a cull!'

'That depends on the – er – cull. Which brings me, Mr Yarde, to the third course I might – I say, might, Mr Yarde – pursue. I can let you go.'

Jimmy gasped, swallowed, and muttered hoarsely: 'Spoke like the gentry-cove you are, guv'nor!'

'Tell me what I want to know, and I will let you go,' said Sir Richard.

A wary look came into Jimmy's eyes. 'Spilt, eh? Lord bless you, there ain't anything to tell you!'

'It will perhaps make it easier for you if I inform you that I am already aware that you have been working in – somewhat uneasy partnership – with Mr Horace Trimble.'

'Cap'n Trimble,' corrected Jimmy.

'I should doubt it. He, I take it, is the – er – flash cull – whom you referred to last night.'

'I don't deny it.'

'Furthermore,' said Sir Richard, 'the pair of you were working for a young gentleman with a pronounced stammer. Ah, for a Mr Brandon, to be precise.'

Jimmy had changed colour. 'Stow your whids and plant 'em!' he growled. 'You're too leery for me, see? Damme if I know what your lay is!'

'That need not concern you. Think it over, Mr Yarde! Will you be handed over to Captain Trimble, or do you choose to go as you came, through that window?'

Jimmy sat for a moment, still gently rubbing his throat, and looking sideways at Sir Richard. 'Damn all flash culls!' he said at last. 'I'll whiddle the whole scrap. I ain't a bridle-cull, see? What *you* calls the High Toby. That ain't my lay: I'm a rum diver. Maybe I've touched the rattler now and then, but I never went on the bridle-lay, not till a certain gentry-cove, which we knows of, tempted me. And I wish I hadn't, see? Five hundred Yellow Boys I was promised, but not a grig will I get! He's a rare gager, that gentry-cove! Dang me if I ever works with such again! He's a bad 'un, guv'nor, you can lay your last megg on that!'

'I am aware. Go on!'

'There's an old gentry-mort going to Bath, see? Lord love you, she was his own mother! Now, that's what I don't hold with, but it ain't none of my business. Me and Cap'n Trimble holds up the chaise by Calne, or thereabouts. The necklace is in a hiding-place behind one of the squabs – ah, and rum squabs they was, all made out of red silk!'

'Mr Brandon knew of this hiding-place, and told you?'

'Lord love you, he made naught of that, guv'nor! We was to snaffle the necklace, and pike on the bean, see?'

'Not entirely.'

'Lope off as fast we could. Now, I don't hold with violence, any gait, nor that stammering young chub neither. But Cap'n Trimble looses off his pops, and one of the outriders gets it in the wing. While the Cap'n's a-covering the coves with his pops, I dubs the jigger – opens the door – and finds a couple of gentry-morts, hollering fit to rouse the countryside. I don't take nothing but the necklace, see? I'm a peevy cove, and this ain't my lay. I don't like it. We pikes, and Cap'n Trimble he pushes his pop into my belly, and says to hand over the necklace. Well, I does so. I'm a peevy cove. I don't hold with violence. Now, the lay is that we take them sparklers to that flash young boman prig, which is taking cover down here, with a regular green 'un, which he gets to know at Oxford. All's Bob, then! But I'm leery, see? Seems to me I'm working with a flash file, and if he makes off with the sparklers, which I suspicion he will, my young chub don't tip me my earnest. I forks the cove. Bristol's the place for me, I thinks, and I gets on to the werry same rattler which you and your nevvy's a-riding in. When that harman from Bow Street comes along, I thinks there's a fastner out for me, and I tips the cole to Adam Tiler, as you might say.'

'You placed the necklace in my nephew's pocket?'

'That's it, guv'nor. No harman won't suspicion a young shaver like him, I thinks. But you and he lopes off unbeknownst, and I comes to this place. Oh, I knew you was a peevy cull! So I touts the case, see?'

'No.'

'Runs my winkers over the house,' said Jimmy impatiently. 'I see your young shaver at this werry window – I should have remembered that you was a peevy cove, guv'nor.'

'You should indeed. However, you have told me what I wish to know, and you are now at liberty to – er – pike on the bean.'

'Spoke like the gentry-cove you are!' said Jimmy hoarsely. 'I'm off! And no hard feelings!'

It did not take him long to climb out of the window. He waved his hand with cheerful impudence, and disappeared from Sir Richard's sight.

Sir Richard undressed, and went to bed.

The boots, who brought up his blue coat in the morning, and his top-boots, was a little surprised to find that he had exchanged bedchambers with his supposed nephew, but accepted his explanation that he disliked his original apartment with only an inward shrug. The Quality, he knew, were full of whims and oddities.

Sir Richard looked through his glass at his coat, which he had sent downstairs to be pressed, and said he felt sure the unknown presser had done his best. He next levelled the eyeglass at his top-boots, and sighed. But when he was asked if there were anything amiss, he said No, nothing: it was good for a man to be removed occasionally from civilization.

The top-boots stood side by side, glossily black and without a speck upon them of dust, or mud. Sir Richard shook his head sadly, and sighed again. He was missing his man, Biddle, in whose ingenious brain lay the secret of polishing boots so that you could see your face reflected in them.

But to anyone unacquainted with the art of Biddle Sir Richard's appearance, when he presently descended the stairs, left little to be desired. There were no creases in the blue coat, his cravat would have drawn approval from Mr Brummell himself, and his hair was brushed into that state of cunning disorder known as the Wind-swept Style.

As he rounded the bend in the stair-case, he heard Miss Creed exchanging friendly salutations with a stranger. The stranger's voice betrayed his identity to Sir Richard, whose eyes managed, for all their sleepiness, to take very good stock of Captain Trimble.

Sir Richard came down the last flight in a leisurely fashion, and interrupted Miss Creed's harmless remarks, by saying in his most languid tone: 'My good boy, I wish you will not converse with strangers. It is a most lamentable habit. Rid yourself of it, I beg!'

Pen looked round in surprise. It occurred to her that she had not known that her protector could sound so haughty, or look so – yes, so insufferably proud!

Captain Trimble turned too. He was a fleshy man, with a coarse, florid sort of good-looks, and a rather loud taste in dress. He said jovially: 'Oh, I don't mind the lad's talking to me!'

Sir Richard's hand sought his quizzing-glass, and raised it. It was said in *haut-ton* circles that the two deadliest weapons against all forms of pretension were Mr Brummell's lifted eyebrow, and Sir Richard Wyndham's quizzing-glass. Captain Trimble, though thick-skinned, was left in no doubt of its blighting message. His cheeks grew dark, and his jaw began to jut belligerently.

'And who might you be, my fine buck?' he demanded.

'I might be a number of different persons,' drawled Sir Richard.

Pen's eyes were getting rounder and rounder, for it appeared to her that this new and haughty Sir Richard was deliberately trying to provoke Captain Trimble into quarrelling with him.

For a moment it seemed as though he would succeed. Captain Trimble started forward, with his fists clenched, and an ugly look on his face. But just as he was about to speak, his expression changed, and he stopped in his tracks, and ejaculated: 'You're Beau Wyndham! Well, I'll be damned!'

'The prospect,' said Sir Richard, bored, 'leaves me unmoved.'

With the discovery of Sir Richard's identity, the desire to come to blows with him seemed to have deserted the Captain. He gave a somewhat unconvincing laugh, and said that there was no offence.

The quizzing-glass focused upon his waistcoat. A shudder visibly shook Sir Richard. 'You mistake – believe me, you mistake, sir. That waistcoat is an offence in itself.'

'Oh, I know you dandies!' said the Captain waggishly. 'You're full of quips. But we shan't quarrel over a little thing like that. Oh, no!'

The quizzing-glass fell. 'I am haunted by waistcoats,' Sir Richard complained. 'There was something with tobine stripes at Reading, horrible to any person of taste. There was a mustard-coloured nightmare at – Wroxham was it? No. I fancy, if memory serves me, Wroxham was rendered hideous by a catskin disaster with pewter buttons. The mustard-coloured nightmare came later. And now, to crown all –'

'Catskin?' interrupted Captain Trimble, his eyes fixed intently upon that disdainful countenance. 'Catskin, did you say?'

'Pray do not keep on repeating it!' said Sir Richard. 'The very thought of it –'

'Look'ee, sir, I'm by way of being interested in a cat-skin waistcoat myself! Are you sure it was at Wroxham you saw it?'

'A catskin waistcoat on its way to Bristol,' said Sir Richard dreamily.

'Bristol! Damme, I never thought – I thank you, Sir Richard! I thank you very much indeed!' said Captain Trimble, and plunged down the passage leading to the stable-yard at the back of the inn.

Sir Richard watched him go, a faint, sweet smile on his lips. 'There, now!' he murmured. 'An impetuous gentleman, I fear. Let it be a lesson to you, brat, not to confide too much in strangers.'

'I didn't!' said Pen. 'I merely –'

'But he did,' Sir Richard said. 'A few chance words let fall from my tongue, and our trusting acquaintance is already calling for his horse. I want my breakfast.'

'But why have you sent him to Bristol?' Pen demanded.

'Well, I wanted to get rid of him,' he replied, strolling into the parlour.

'I thought you were trying to pick a quarrel with him.'

'I was, but he unfortunately recognized me. A pity. It would have given me a good deal of pleasure to have put him to sleep. However, I dare say it has all turned out for the best. I should have been obliged to have tied him up somewhere, which would have been a nuisance, and might have led to future complications. I shall be obliged to leave you for a short space this morning, by the way.'

'Do, please, sir, stop being provoking!' begged Pen. 'Did you see Jimmy Yarde last night, and what happened?'

'Oh yes, I saw him! Really, I don't think anything of particular moment happened.'

'He didn't try to murder you?'

'Nothing so exciting. He tried merely to recover the diamonds. When he – er – failed to do so, we enjoyed a short conversation, after which he left the inn, as unobtrusively as he had entered it.'

'Through the window, you mean. Well, I am glad you let him go, for I could not help liking him. But what are we going to do now, if you please?'

'We are now going to eliminate Beverley,' replied Sir Richard, carving the ham.

'Oh, the stammering-man! How shall we do that? He

sounded very disagreeable, but I don't think we should eliminate him in a rough way, do you?'

'By no means. Leave the matter in my hands, and I will engage for it that he will be eliminated without the least pain or inconvenience to anyone.'

'Yes, but then there is the necklace,' Pen pointed out. 'I feel that before we attend to anything else we ought to get rid of it. Only fancy if you were to be found with it in your pocket!'

'Very true. But I have arranged for that. The necklace belongs to Beverley's mother, and he shall restore it to her.'

Pen laid down her knife and fork. 'Then that explains it all! I thought that stammering-man had more to do with it than you would tell me. I suppose he hired Jimmy Yarde, and that other person, to steal the necklace?' She wrinkled her brow. 'I don't wish to say rude things about your friends, Richard, but it seems to me very wrong of him – most improper!'

'Most,' he agreed.

'Even *dastardly*!'

'I think we might call it dastardly.'

'Well, that is what it seems to me. I see now that there is a great deal in what Aunt Almeria says. She considers that there are terrible pitfalls in Society.'

Sir Richard shook his head sadly. 'Alas, too true!'

'And vice,' said Pen awfully. 'Profligacy, and extravagance, you know.'

'I know.'

She picked up her knife and fork again. 'It must be very exciting,' she said enviously.

'Far be it from me to destroy your illusions, but I feel I should inform you that stealing one's mother's diamonds is not the invariable practice of members of the *haut ton*.'

'Of course not. I know *that*!' said Pen with dignity. She added in persuasive tones: 'Shall I come with you when you go to meet the stammering-man?'

'No,' answered Sir Richard, not mincing matters.

'I thought you would say that. I wish I were really a man.'

'I still should not take you with me.'

'Then you would be very selfish, and disagreeable, and altogether abominable!' declared Pen roundly.

'I think I am,' reflected Sir Richard, recalling his sister's homily.

The large eyes softened instantly, and as they scanned Sir Richard's face a slight flush mounted to Pen's cheeks. She bent over her plate again, saying in a gruff little voice: 'No, you are not. You are very kind, and obliging, and I am sorry I teased you.'

Sir Richard looked at her. He seemed to be about to speak, but she forestalled him, adding buoyantly: 'And when I tell Piers how well you have looked after me, he will be most grateful to you, I assure you.'

'Will he?' said Sir Richard, at his dryest. 'I am afraid I was forgetting Piers.'

Seven

*T*he spinney down the road, referred to by Beverley in his assignation with Captain Trimble, was not hard to locate. A careless question put to one of the ostlers elicited the information that it formed part of the grounds of Crome Hall. Leaving Pen to keep a sharp look-out for signs of an invasion by her relatives, Sir Richard set out shortly before eleven o'clock, to keep Captain Trimble's appointment. The impetuous Captain had indeed called for his horse, and had set off in the direction of Bristol, with his cloak-bag strapped on to the saddle. He had paid his shot, so it did not seem as though he contemplated returning to Queen Charlton.

At the end of a ten-minute walk, Sir Richard reached the outskirts of the spinney. A gap in the hedge showed him a trodden path through the wood, and he followed this, glad to be out of the strong sunlight. The path led to a small clearing, where a tiny stream ran between clumps of rose-bay willow herb in full flower. Here a slightly built young gentleman, dressed in the extreme of fashion, was switching pettishly with his cane at the purple heads of the willow-herb. The points of his collar were so monstrous as to make it almost impossible for him to turn his head, and his coat fitted him so tightly that it seemed probable that it must have needed the combined efforts of three strong men to force him into it. Very tight pantaloons of a delicate biscuit-hue encased his rather spindly legs, and a pair of tasselled Hessians sneered at their sylvan surroundings.

The Honourable Beverley Brandon was not unlike his sister

Melissa, but the classic cast of his features was spoiled by a pasty complexion, and a weakness about mouth and chin not shared by Melissa. He turned, as he heard the sound of approaching footsteps, and started forward, only to be fetched up short by the sight, not of Captain Trimble's burly figure, but of a tall, well-built gentleman in whom he had not the slightest difficulty in recognizing his prospective brother-in-law.

He let his malacca cane drop from suddenly nerveless fingers. His pale eyes started at Sir Richard. 'W-w-what the d-devil?' he stammered.

Sir Richard advanced unhurriedly across the clearing. 'Good-morning, Beverley,' he said, in his pleasant, drawling voice.

'W-what are *you* d-doing here?' Beverley demanded, the wildest surmises chasing one another through his brain.

'Oh, enjoying the weather, Beverley, enjoying the weather! And you?'

'I'm staying with a friend. F-fellow I knew up at Oxford!'

'Indeed?' Sir Richard's quizzing-glass swept the glade, as though in search of Mr Brandon's host. 'A delightful rendezvous! One would almost suspect you of having an assignation with someone!'

'N-no such thing! I was j-just taking the air!'

The quizzing-glass was levelled at him. Sir Richard's pained eye ran over his person. 'Putting the countryside to scorn, Beverley? Strange that you who care so much about your appearance should achieve such lamentable results! Now, Cedric cares nothing for his, but – er – always looks the gentleman.'

'You have a d-damned unpleasant tongue, Richard, b-but you needn't think I'll put up with it j-just because you've known me for y-years!'

'And how,' enquired Sir Richard, faintly interested, 'do you propose to put a curb on my tongue?'

Beverley glared at him. He knew quite as well as Captain Trimble that Sir Richard's exquisite tailoring and languid bearing were deceptive; that he sparred regularly with

Gentleman Jackson, and was accounted one of the best amateur heavyweights in England. 'W-what are you d-doing here?' he reiterated weakly.

'I came to keep your friend Trimble's appointment with you,' said Sir Richard, removing a caterpillar from his sleeve. Ignoring a startled oath from Mr Brandon, he added: 'Captain Trimble – by the way, you must tell me sometime where he acquired that unlikely title – found himself obliged to depart for Bristol this morning. Rather a hasty person, one is led to infer.'

'D-damn you, Richard, you mean you sent him off! W-what do you know about Trimble, and why did –'

'Yes, I fear that some chance words of mine may perhaps have influenced him. There was a man in a catskin waistcoat – dear me, there seems to be a fatal spell attached to that waistcoat! You look quite pale, Beverley.'

Mr Brandon had indeed changed colour. He shouted: 'S-stop it! So Yarde split, d-did he? Well, w-what the d-devil has it to do with you, hey?'

'Altruism, Beverley, sheer altruism. You see, your friend Yarde – you know, I cannot congratulate you on your choice of tools – saw fit to hand the Brandon diamonds into my keeping.'

Mr Brandon looked quite stupefied. 'Handed them to *you*? Yarde d-did that? B-but how d-did you know he had them? How *c-could* you have known?'

'Oh, I didn't!' said Sir Richard, taking snuff.

'B-but if you didn't know, why d-did you constrain him – oh, what the d-devil does all this m-mean?'

'You have it wrong, my dear Beverley. I didn't constrain him. I was, in fact, an unwitting partner in the crime. I should perhaps explain that Mr Yarde was being pursued by a Runner from Bow Street.'

'A Runner!' Mr Brandon began to look ashen. 'Who set them on? G-god damn it, I –'

'I have no idea. Presumably your respected father, possibly Cedric. In Mr Yarde's picturesque but somewhat obscure language, he – er – tipped the cole to Adam Tiler. Have I that right?'

'How the d-devil should I know?' snapped Brandon.

'You must forgive me. You seem to me to be so familiar with – er – thieves and – er – swashbucklers, that I assumed that you were conversant also with thieving cant.'

'D-don't keep on talking about thieves!' Beverley said, stamping his foot.

'It is an ugly word, isn't it?' agreed Sir Richard.

Beverley ground his teeth, but said in a blustering voice: 'Very well! I *did* t-take the damned necklace! If you m-must know, I'm d-done up, ruined! But you n-needn't take that psalm-singing t-tone with me! If I d-don't sell it, my father will soon enough!'

'I don't doubt you, Beverley, but I must point out to you that you have forgotten one trifling circumstance in your very engaging explanation. The necklace belongs to your father.'

'I c-consider it's family property. It's folly to keep it w-when we're all of us aground! D-damn it, I was forced to take the thing! *You* don't know w-what it is to be in the p-power of a d-damned cent-per-cent! If the old m-man would have p-parted, this wouldn't have happened! I told him a m-month ago I hadn't a feather to fly with, but the old fox wouldn't c-come up to scratch. I tell you, I've no c-compunction! He lectured me as though he himself w-weren't under hatches, which, by God, he is! Deep b-basset's been *his* ruin; m-myself, I prefer to g-go to perdition with a d-dice-box.' He gave a reckless laugh, and suddenly sat down on the moss-covered stump of a felled tree, and buried his face in his hands.

'You are forgetting women, wine, and horses,' said Sir Richard unemotionally. 'They also have played not inconsiderable rôles in this dramatic progress of yours. Three years ago you were once again under the hatches. I forget what it cost to extricate you from your embarrassments, but I do seem to recall that you gave your word you would not again indulge in – er – quite so many excesses.'

'Well, I'm n-not expecting *you* to raise the w-wind for me this time,' said Beverley sulkily.

'What's the figure?' Sir Richard asked.

'How should I know? I'm n-not a damned b-banking clerk! T-twelve thousand or so, I dare say. If you hadn't spoiled my g-game, I c-could have settled the whole thing.'

'You delude yourself. When I encountered your friend Yarde he was making for the coast with the diamonds in his pocket.'

'Where are they now?'

'In my pocket,' Sir Richard said coolly.

Beverley lifted his head. 'L-listen, Richard, you're not a b-bad fellow! Who's to know you ever had the d-diamonds in your hands? It ain't your affair: give them to m-me, and forget all about the rest! I swear I'll n-never breathe a w-word to a soul!'

'Do you know, Beverley, you nauseate me? As for giving you the diamonds, I have come here with exactly that purpose.'

Beverley's hand shot out. 'I d-don't care what you think of m-me! Only hand the n-necklace over!'

'Certainly,' Sir Richard said, taking the leather purse out of his pocket. 'But you, Beverley, will give them back to your mother.'

Beverley stared at him. 'I'll be d-damned if I will! You fool, how could I?'

'You may concoct what plausible tale you please: I will even engage myself to lend it my support. But you will give back the necklace.'

A slight sneer disfigured Beverley's face. 'Oh, j-just as you l-like! Hand it over!'

Sir Richard tossed the purse over to him. 'Ah, Beverley! Perhaps I should make it clear to you that if, when I return to town, it has not been restored to Lady Saar I shall be compelled to – er – split on you.'

'You won't!' Beverley said, stowing the purse away in an inner pocket. 'M-mighty pretty behaviour for a b-brother-in-law!'

'But I am not your brother-in-law,' said Sir Richard gently.

'Oh, you n-needn't think I don't know you're g-going to m-marry Melissa! Our scandals will become yours too. I think you'll keep your m-mouth shut.'

'I am always sorry to disappoint expectations, but I have not the smallest intention of marrying your sister,' said Sir Richard, taking another pinch of snuff.

Beverley's jaw dropped. 'You d-don't mean she w-wouldn't have you?'

'No, I don't mean that.'

'B-but it's as g-good as settled!'

'Not, believe me, by me.'

'The d-devil!' Beverley said blankly.

'So you see,' pursued Sir Richard, 'I should have no compunction whatsoever in informing Saar of this episode.'

'You w-wouldn't split on me to my f-father!' Beverley cried, jumping up from the tree-stump.

'That, my dear Beverley, rests entirely with you.'

'But, d-damn it, m-man, I *can't* give the d-diamonds back! I tell you I'm d-done – up, fast aground!'

'I fancy that to have married into your family would have cost me considerably more than twelve thousand pounds. I am prepared to settle your debts – ah, for the last time, Beverley!'

'D-devilish good of you,' muttered Beverley. 'G-give me the money, and I'll settle 'em myself.'

'I fear that your intercourse with Captain Trimble has led you to credit others with his trusting disposition. I, alas, repose not the slightest reliance on your word. You may send a statement of your debts to my town house. I think that is all – except that you will be recalled to London suddenly, and you will leave Crome Hall, if you are wise, not later than to-morrow morning.'

'Blister it, I w-won't be ordered about by y-you! I'll leave w-when I choose!'

'If you don't choose to do so in the morning, you will leave in the custody of a Bow Street Runner.'

Beverley coloured hotly. 'By G-God, I'll p-pay you for this, Richard!'

'But not, if I know you, until I have settled your debts,' said Sir Richard, turning on his heel.

Beverley stood still, watching him walk away down the path, until the undergrowth hid him from sight. It was several minutes before it occurred to him that although Sir Richard had been unpleasantly frank on some subjects, he had not divulged how or why he came to be in Queen Charlton.

Beverley frowned over this. Sir Richard might, of course, be visiting friends in the neighbourhood, but apart from a house belonging to some heiress or other, Crome Hall was the only country seat of any size for several miles. The more Beverley considered the matter, the more inexplicable became Sir Richard's presence. From a sort of sullen curiosity, he passed easily to a mood of suspicion, and began to think that there was something very odd about the whole affair, and to wonder whether any profit could be made out of it.

He was not in the least grateful to Sir Richard for promising to pay his debts. He certainly wished to silence his more rapacious creditors, but he would have considered it a stupid waste of money to settle any bill which could possibly be held over to some later date. Moreover, the mere payment of his debts would not line his pockets, and it was hard to see how he was to continue to support life in the manner to which he was accustomed.

He took the necklace out, and looked at it. It was a singularly fine specimen of the jeweller's art, and several of the stones in it were of a truly formidable size. It was worth perhaps twice twelve thousand pounds. One did not, of course, find it easy to obtain the real value of stolen goods, but even if he had been forced to sell it for as little as twenty thousand pounds he would still have been eight thousand pounds in pocket, since there was no longer the least necessity to share the proceeds with Horace Trimble. Trimble, Beverley thought, has bungled the affair, and deserved nothing. If only Richard could be silenced, Trimble need never know that the necklace had been recovered from Jimmy Yarde, and it could be sold to the sole advantage of the only one of the three persons implicated in its theft who had a real right to it.

The more he reflected on these lines, and the longer he gazed at the diamonds, the more fixed became Beverley's conviction that Sir Richard, instead of assisting him in his financial difficulties, had actually robbed him of eight thousand pounds, if not more. A burning sense of injury possessed him, and if he could at that moment have done Sir Richard an injury, without incurring any himself, he would certainly have jumped at the chance.

But short of lying in wait for him, and shooting him, there did not seem to be anything he could do to Richard, with advantage; and although he would have been very glad to have heard of Richard's sudden death, and would have thought it, quite sincerely, a judgment on him, his murderous inclination was limited, to do him justice, to a strong wish that Richard would fall out of a window, and break his neck, or be set upon by armed highwaymen, and summarily slain. At the same time, there was undoubtedly something queer about Richard's being in this remote village, and it might be worth while to discover what had brought him to Queen Charlton.

Sir Richard, meanwhile, walked back to the village, arriving at the George in time to see a couple of sweating horses being led into the stable, and a postchaise being pushed into one corner of the roomy yard. He was therefore fully prepared to encounter strangers in the inn, and any doubts of their identity were set at rest upon his stepping into the entrance-parlour, and perceiving a matron with an imposing front seated upon one of the oaken settles, and vigorously fanning her heated countenance. At her elbow stood a stockily built young gentleman with his hair brushed into a Brutus, mopping his brow. He had somewhat globular eyes of no particular colour, and when seen in profile bore a distinct likeness to a hake.

The same unfortunate resemblance was to be observed, though in a less pronounced degree, in Mrs Griffin. The lady was built on massive lines, and appeared to be feeling the heat. Possibly a travelling costume of purple satin trimmed with a quantity of sarsenet, and worn under a spencer, and a voluminous cloak of drab merino cloth, might have contributed to her discomfort. Her locks were confined in a round cap, and over this she wore a beehive bonnet of moss-straw, trimmed with enough plumes to remind Sir Richard forcibly of a hearse. The landlord was standing in front of her in an attitude of concern, and as Sir Richard stepped into the entrance-parlour, she said in tones of strong resolution: 'You are deceiving me! I demand to have this – this youth brought before me!'

'But, Mama!' said the stocky young man unhappily.

'Silence, Frederick!' pronounced the matron.

'But consider, Mama! If the – the young man the landlord speaks of is travelling with his uncle, he could not possibly be – be my cousin, could he?'

'I do not believe a word of what this man says!' declared Mrs Griffin. 'I should not wonder if he had been bribed.'

The landlord regretfully said that no one had tried to bribe him.

'Pshaw!' said Mrs Griffin.

Sir Richard judged it to be time to call attention to his own presence. He walked forward in the direction of the staircase.

'Here is the gentleman!' said the landlord, with a good deal of relief. 'He will tell for himself that what I've said is the truth, ma'am.'

Sir Richard paused, and glanced with raised eyebrows from Mrs Griffin to her son, and from Mr Frederick Griffin to the landlord. 'I beg your pardon?' he drawled.

The attention of the Griffins instantly became focused upon him. The gentleman's eyes were riveted to his cravat; the lady, taking in his air of elegance, was plainly shaken.

'If your honour pleases!' said the landlord. 'The lady, sir, is come in search of a young gentleman, which has run away from school, the same being her ward. I've told her that I have but one young gentleman staying in the house, and him your honour's nephew, and I'd be glad if you'd bear me out, sir.'

'Really,' said Sir Richard, bored, 'I don't know whom you have staying in the house besides myself and my nephew.'

'The question is, *have* you a nephew?' demanded Mrs Griffin.

Sir Richard raised his quizzing-glass, surveyed her through it, and bowed slightly. 'I was certainly under the impression that I had a nephew, ma'am. May I ask in what way he interests you?'

'If he *is* your nephew, I have no interest in him whatsoever,' declared the matron handsomely.

'Mama!' whispered her son, anguished. 'Recollect, I beg of you! A stranger! No proof! The greatest discretion!'

'I am quite distracted!' said Mrs Griffin, shedding tears.

This had the effect of driving the landlord from the room, and of flustering Mr Griffin. Between trying to pacify his parent, and excusing such odd behaviour to the elegant stranger, he became hotter than ever, and floundered in a morass of broken phrases. The look of astonishment on Sir Richard's face, the pained lift of his brows, quite discomposed him, and he ended by saying: 'The truth is my mother is sadly overwrought!'

'My confidence has been betrayed!' interpolated Mrs Griffin, raising her face from her damp handkerchief.

'Yes, Mama: precisely so! Her confidence has been betrayed, sir, by – by the shocking conduct of my cousin, who has –'

'I have nourished a viper in my bosom!' said Mrs Griffin.

'Just so, Mama. She has nourished – at least, not quite that, perhaps, but it is very bad, very upsetting to a lady of delicate sensibility!'

'All my life,' declaimed Mrs Griffin, 'I have been surrounded by ingratitude!'

'Mama, you cannot be surrounded by – and in any case, you know it is not so! Do, pray, calm yourself! I shall claim your indulgence, sir. The circumstances are so peculiar, and my cousin's behaviour has exerted so strong an effect upon my poor mother that – in short –'

'It is the impropriety of it which is worse than anything!' said Mrs Griffin.

'Exactly so, Mama. You see, it is the impropriety, sir – I mean, my mother is not quite herself.'

'I shall never,' announced the matron, 'hold up my head again! It is my belief that this person is in league with her!'

'Mama, most earnestly I implore you –!'

'Her?' repeated Sir Richard, apparently bewildered.

'Him!' corrected Mr Griffin.

'You must forgive me if I do not perfectly understand you,' said Sir Richard. 'I apprehend that you have – er – mislaid a youth, and have come –'

'Precisely so, sir! We mis – at least, no, no, we did not mislay him, of course!'

'Ran away!' uttered Mrs Griffin, emerging from the handkerchief for a brief instant.

'Ran away,' corroborated her son.

'But in what way,' enquired Sir Richard, 'does this concern me, sir?'

'Not at all, sir, I assure you! No such suspicion is cherished by me, upon my word!'

'What suspicion?' asked Sir Richard, still more bewildered.

'None sir, none in the world! That is just what I was saying. I have no suspicion –'

'But I have!' said Mrs Griffin, in much more robust tones. 'I accuse you of concealing the truth from me!'

'Mama, do but consider! You cannot – you know you cannot insult this gentleman by insinuating –'

'In the execution of my duty there is nothing I cannot do!' responded his mother nobly. 'Besides, I do not know him. I mistrust him.'

Mr Griffin turned wretchedly to Sir Richard: 'You see, sir, my mother –'

'Mistrusts me,' supplied Sir Richard.

'No, no, I assure you! My mother is sadly put out, and scarcely knows what she is saying.'

'I am in the fullest possession of my faculties, I thank you, Frederick!' said Mrs Griffin, gathering strength.

'Of course, of course, Mama! But the agitation – the natural agitation –'

'If he is speaking the truth,' interrupted Mrs Griffin, 'let him summon his nephew to stand before me!'

'Ah, I begin to understand you!' said Sir Richard. 'Is it

possible, ma'am, that you suspect my nephew of being your errant ward?'

'No, no!' said Griffin feebly.

'Yes!' declared his mother.

'But Mama, only consider what such a thought must imply!' said Mr Griffin in a frenzied aside.

'I can believe anything of that unnatural creature!'

'I should doubt very much whether my nephew is upon the premises,' said Sir Richard coldly. 'He was engaged to spend the day with friends, upon an expedition of pleasure. However, if he should not yet have left the house, I will engage to – er – allay all these heart burnings.'

'If he has run out to escape us, I shall await his return!' said Mrs Griffin. 'And so I warn you!'

'I admire your resolution, ma'am, but I must point out to you that your movements are of no possible interest to me,' said Sir Richard, stepping over to the bell, and jerking it.

'Frederick!' said Mrs Griffin. 'Will you stand by and hear your mother being insulted by one whom I strongly suspect of being a dandy?'

'But Mama, indeed, it is no concern of ours if he is!'

'Perhaps,' said Sir Richard, in arctic tones, 'it may be of service if I make myself known to you, ma'am. My name is Wyndham.'

Mrs Griffin received this information with every appearance of disdain, but its effect upon her son was staggering. His eyes seemed to be in danger of bursting out of their sockets; he started forward, and ejaculated in tones of deepest reverence: 'Sir! is this possible? Have I the honour of addressing Sir Richard Wyndham?'

Sir Richard bowed slightly.

'The celebrated whip?' asked Mr Griffin.

Sir Richard bowed again.

'The creator of the Wyndham Fall?' pursued Mr Griffin, almost overcome.

Tired of bowing, Sir Richard said: 'Yes.'

'Sir,' said Mr Griffin, 'I am happy to make your acquaintance! My name is Griffin!'

'How do you do?' murmured Sir Richard, holding out his hand.

Mr Griffin clasped it. 'I wonder I should not have recognized you. Mama, we have been quite mistaken. This is none other than the famous Sir Richard Wyndham – the friend of Brummell, you know! You must have heard me – you must have heard him spoken of. It is quite impossible that he can know anything of my cousin's whereabouts.'

She seemed to accept this, though with obvious reluctance. She looked Sir Richard over with disfavour, and said paralysingly: 'I have the greatest dislike of all forms of dandyism, and I have ever deplored the influence exerted by the Bow-Window set upon young men of respectable upbringing. However, if you are indeed Sir Richard Wyndham, I dare say you would not object to showing my son how to arrange his cravat in what he calls the Wyndham Fall, so that he need no longer spoil every neckcloth in his drawer before achieving a result which I consider lamentable.'

'Mama!' whispered the unhappy Mr Griffin. 'I beg of you!'

The entrance of a servant, in answer to the bell's summons came as a timely interruption. Upon being asked to discover whether Sir Richard's nephew were in the house, he was able to reply that the young gentleman had left the inn some time previously.

'Then I fear there is nothing for you to do but to await his return,' said Sir Richard, addressing himself to Mrs Griffin.

'We should not dream of – Mama, there can be no doubt that she – he – did not come here after all. Lady Luttrell disclaims all knowledge, remember, and *she* must certainly have known if my cousin had come into this neighbourhood.'

'If I could think that she had gone to cousin Jane, all would not yet be lost!' said Mrs Griffin. 'Yet it is possible? I fear the worst!'

'This is all very perplexing,' complained Sir Richard. 'I was under the impression that this mysterious truant was of the male sex.'

'Frederick, my nerves can stand no more!' said Mrs Griffin, surging to her feet. 'If you mean to drag me the length of England again, I must insist upon being permitted the indulgence of half an hour's solitude first!'

'But Mama, it was not I who would come here!' expostulated Mr Griffin.

Sir Richard again rang the bell, and this time desired that a chambermaid should be sent to him. Mrs Griffin was presently consigned to the care of an abigail, and left the room majestically, commanding hot water to wash with, tea, and a decent bedchamber.

Her son heaved a sigh of relief. 'I must beg pardon, Sir Richard! You must allow me to beg your pardon!'

'Not at all,' said Sir Richard.

'Yes, yes, I insist! Such an unfortunate misunderstanding! An explanation is due to you! A slip of the tongue, you know, but my mother is labouring under strong emotion, and does not quite heed what she says. You noticed it: indeed, no one could wonder at your surprise! The unhappy truth, sir is that my cousin is not a boy, but – in a word, sir – a female!'

'This explanation, Mr Griffin, is quite unnecessary, believe me.'

'Sir,' said Mr Griffin earnestly, 'as a Man of the World, I should value your opinion! Concealment is useless: the truth must be discovered in the end. What, sir, would you think of a member of the Weaker Sex who assumed the disguise of a man, and left the home of her natural protector by way of the window?'

'I should assume,' replied Sir Richard, 'that she had strong reasons for acting with such resolution.'

'She did not wish to marry me,' said Mr Griffin gloomily.

'Oh!' said Sir Richard. 'Well, I'm sure I can't see why she should be so set against me, but that's not it, sir. The thing is that here's my mother determined to find her, and to make her marry me, and so hush up the scandal. But I don't like it above half. If she dislikes the notion so much, I don't think I ought to marry her, do you?'

'Emphatically not!'

'I must say I am very glad to hear you say that, Sir Richard!' said Mr Griffin, much cheered. 'For you must know that my mother has been telling me ever since yesterday that I must marry her now, to save her name. But I think she would very likely make me uncomfortable, and nothing could make up for that, in my opinion.'

'A lady capable of escaping out of a window in the guise of a man would quite certainly make you more than uncomfortable,' said Sir Richard.

'Yes, though she's only a chit of a girl, you know. In fact, she is not yet out. I am very happy to have had the benefit of the opinion of a Man of the World. I feel that I can rely on your judgment.

'On my judgment you might, but in nothing else, I assure you,' said Sir Richard. 'You know nothing of me, after all. How do you know that I am not now concealing your cousin from you?'

'Ha-ha! Very good, upon my word! Very good, indeed!' said Mr Griffin, saluting a jest of the first water.

Eight

The Griffins did not leave Queen Charlton until the cool of the afternoon, and by the time he saw their chaise off the premises of the George, Sir Richard was heartily sick of the company of surely one of his most devout worshippers. No sign was seen of Pen, who had no doubt fled the house upon the Griffins' arrival. What sustenance she had snatched up to bear her strength up through a long day Sir Richard had no means of knowing.

Mrs Griffin, tottering downstairs to partake of light refreshment, found her son hanging upon Sir Richard's bored lips. Upon hearing that he had divulged the secret of Pen's identity, she first showed a dangerous tendency to swoon, but upon being supplied with a glass of ratafia by Sir Richard, revived sufficiently to pour out her wrongs into his ear.

'What I ask myself,' she said dramatically, 'has become of that tiresome girl? Into what company may she have fallen? I see that you, Sir Richard, are a person of sensibility. Conceive of my feelings! What – I say, *what* if my unfortunate niece should have fallen into the hands of some *Man*?'

'What indeed!' said Sir Richard.

'She must marry him. When I think of the care, the hopes, the maternal fondness I have lavished – but it is ever so! There is no gratitude in the world to-day.'

Upon this gloomy reflection, she ordered her chaise to be got ready to bear her instantly to Chippenham. She would have remained at Queen Charlton for the night, she explained, only that she suspected the sheets.

Sir Richard, having seen her off, walked down the street, to cool his heated brow, and to consider the intricacies of his position.

It was while he was absent that Miss Creed and the Honourable Beverley Brandon, approaching the George from widely divergent angles, but with identical circumspection, came face to face in the entrance-parlour.

They eyed one another. A few moments' conversation with the tapster had put Beverley in possession of information which he found sufficiently intriguing to make him run the risk of perhaps encountering Captain Trimble in entering the inn, and prosecuting further enquiries about Sir Richard Wyndham. Sir Richard, the tapster had told him, was putting up at the George with his nephew.

Now, Sir Richard's nephew, as Beverley knew well, was a lusty young gentleman not yet breeched. He did not mention this circumstance to the tapster, but on hearing that the mysterious nephew in question was a youth in his teens, he pricked up his ears, and penetrated from the tap-room into the main parlour of the inn.

Here Pen, entering the George cautiously from the stable-yard, came plump upon him. Never having seen his face, she did not at once recognize him, but when, after an intent stare, he moved towards her, saying with a slight stammer: 'How d-do you do? I think you m-must be Wyndham's n-nephew?' she had no doubt of his identity.

She was no fool, and she realized at once that anyone well-acquainted with Sir Richard must be aware that she was not his nephew. She replied guardedly: 'Well, I call him my uncle, because he is so much older than I am, but in point of fact we are cousins only. Third cousins,' she added, making the relationship as remote as she could.

A smile which she did not quite like lingered on Beverley's rather slack mouth. Mentally, he was reviewing Sir Richard's family, but he said with great affability: 'Oh, indeed? Ch-charmed to make your acquaintance, Mr-er-er?'

'Brown,' supplied Pen, regretting that she had not thought to provide herself with a more unusual surname.

'Brown,' bowed Beverley, his smile widening. 'It is a great p-pleasure to me to m-meet any connection of W-Wyndham's. In such a remote spot, too! Now d-do tell me! What b-brings you here?'

'Family affairs,' answered Pen promptly. 'Uncle Richard – Cousin Richard, I mean, only I have always been in the way of calling him uncle, you understand – very kindly undertook to come with me.'

'So it was on y-your account that he came to Queen Ch-Charlton!' said Beverley. 'That is most interesting!' His eyes ran over her in a way that made her feel profoundly ill-at-ease. 'M-*most* interesting!' he repeated. 'P-pray present my c-compliments to Wyndham, and tell him that I perfectly understand his reasons for choosing such a secluded locality!'

He bowed himself out with a flourish, leaving Pen in a state of considerable trepidation. In the tap-room, he called for paper, ink, a pen, and some brandy, and sat down at a table in one corner to write a careful letter to Sir Richard. It took time, for he was not apt with a pen, and much brandy, but it was finished at last to his satisfaction. He looked round rather owlishly for wafers, but the tapster had brought him none, so he folded the note into a screw, wrote Sir Richard's name on it in a flourishing scrawl, and told the tapster to give it to Sir Richard upon his return to the inn. After that he went away, not quite steadily, but full of chuckling glee at his own ingenuity.

The tapster, who was busy serving drinks, left the twisted note on the bar while he hurried to the other end of the room with beer for a clamorous party of country-men. It was here that Captain Trimble, coming into the tap-room from the stableyard, found it.

Captain Trimble, who had spent a fruitless day in attempting to discover some trace of Jimmy Yarde in Bristol, was hot, and tired, and in no very good temper. He sat down on a high stool at the bar, and began to wipe his face with a large handkerchief.

It was as he was restoring the handkerchief to his pocket that the note, and its superscription, caught his eye. He was well-acquainted with Mr Brandon's handwriting, and he recognized it at once. It did not at first surprise him that Mr Brandon should have written to Sir Richard Wyndham; he supposed them to be of the same fashionable set. But as he looked idly down at the screw of paper thoughts of the wild-goose chase upon which Sir Richard had sent him took strong possession of his mind, and he wondered, not for the first time during that exasperating day, whether Sir Richard could have had a motive in dispatching him to Bristol. The note began to assume a sinister aspect; suspicion darkened the already warm colour in the Captain's cheeks; and after staring at the note for a minute, he cast a quick look round, saw that no one was watching him, and deftly palmed it.

The tapster came back to the bar, but by the time he had recollected the note, Captain Trimble had retired to a high-backed settle by the empty fireplace, and was calling for a can of ale. At a convenient moment, he unscrewed the twist of paper, and read its contents.

'My very dear Richard,' had written Mr Brandon, *'I am desolated to find that you have gone out. I should like to continue our conversation. When I tell you that I have been privileged to meet your nephew, my dear Richard, I feel that you will appreciate the wisdom of meeting me again. You would not wish me to talk, but a paltry twelve thousand is not enough to close my mouth, which, however, I am willing to do, tho' not for a less sum than I have it in my power to obtain by Other Means. Should you wish to discuss this delicate matter, I shall be in the spinney at ten o'clock this evening. If you do not come there, I shall understand that you have Withdrawn your Objection to my disposing of Certain Property as I choose, and I fancy that it would be Unwise of you to mention our dealings in this matter to anyone, either now or later.'*

Captain Trimble read this missive twice before folding it again into its original twist. The mention of Pen he found obscure, and of no particular interest. There was apparently a disreputable secret in some way connected with Sir Richard's young nephew, but the Captain did not immediately perceive what profit was to be made out of it. Far more arresting was the thinly veiled reference to the Brandon necklace. The Captain's eyes smouldered as he thought this over, and his massive jaw worked a little. He had suspected Beverley's good faith from the moment that Jimmy Yarde had been thrust on him as an accomplice. The matter seemed as clear as crystal now. Beverley and Yarde had hatched a plot to cheat him of his share in the fortune, and when Beverley had been raving against him for blundering – very convincingly he had raved too – he had actually had the necklace in his pocket. Well, Mr Brandon would have to learn that it was not wise to try to bubble Horace Trimble, and still less wise to leave unsealed notes lying about in a common tap-room. As for Sir Richard, the Captain found his part in these tortuous proceedings very difficult to fathom. He seemed to know something about the diamonds, but he was far too wealthy a man, the Captain considered, to have the least interest in their worth in terms of guineas. But Sir Richard had undoubtedly meddled in the affair, and the Captain wished with all his heart that he could discover a way to pay him in full for his interference.

Captain Trimble was naturally a man of violence, but although he would have liked very much to spoil Sir Richard's handsome face, he wasted no more than a couple of minutes over this pleasing dream. Sir Richard, if it came to fisticuffs, would enjoy the encounter far more than would his assailant. A more determined assault, on a dark night, by a couple of stout men armed with clubs, might have a better chance of success, but even this scheme had a drawback. Sir Richard had been set upon twice before, by hardy rogues who planned to rob him. He had not been robbed, and he had not been attacked again. He was marked down by every cut-throat and robber in the Rogues' Calendar as dangerous, one who carried pistols, and could draw and fire with a speed and a deadly accuracy which made him a most undesirable man to molest.

Regretfully, the Captain decided that Sir Richard must be left alone, for the present, at all events.

By this time the tapster had discovered the loss of Mr Brandon's note. Everyone in the room disclaimed all knowledge of its whereabouts. Captain Trimble drained his can, and carried it over to the bar. As he set it down, he said: 'Isn't that a bit of paper I see?'

No one could see anything, but that might have been because the Captain bent so quickly to pick it up. When he straightened himself, the screw of paper was between his fingers. The tapster took it with a word of thanks, and gave it to one of the waiters, who had come into the tap-room for a pint of burgundy, and told him to deliver it to Sir Richard. Captain Trimble, quite as well-pleased as Beverley had been, betook himself to the coffee-room, and ordered a sustaining meal.

Sir Richard, meanwhile, had returned to the inn. He found Pen awaiting him in the parlour, curled up in a big chair and eating an apple. 'This passion for munching raw fruit!' he remarked. 'You look a very urchin.'

She twinkled at him. 'Well, I am hungry. Did you – did you have a pleasant day with my Aunt Almeria, sir?'

'I hope with all my heart,' said Sir Richard, eyeing her with some severity, 'that *you* spent the day in the greatest possible discomfort. I wish it had rained.'

'I didn't. I visited my home, and I went to all the *particular* places Piers and I used to hide in, when people wanted us to do our lessons. Only I hadn't anything to eat.'

'I am glad,' said Sir Richard. 'Do you know that I have not only found myself in a position where I was forced to lie, and dissemble, and practise the most shocking deceit, but I have also been obliged to consort for five hours with one of the most commonplace young cubs it has ever been my ill-fortune to meet?'

'I knew Fred would come with my aunt! Doesn't he look just like a fish, sir?'

'Yes, a hake. But you cannot divert me from what I wish to say. Half an hour's conversation with your aunt has convinced me that you are an unprincipled brat.'

'Did she say unkind things of me?' Miss Creed wrinkled her

brow. 'I don't think I am *unprincipled*, precisely.'

'You are a menace to all law-abiding and respectable citizens,' said Sir Richard.

She seemed gratified. 'I didn't think I was as important as that.'

'Look what you have done to me!' said Sir Richard.

'Yes, but I don't think you are very law-abiding or respectable,' objected Pen.

'I was once, but it seems a long time ago.'

She finished her apple. 'Well, I am sorry you are feeling cross, for I think I should tell you something which you may not be pleased about.'

He looked at her with misgiving. 'Let me know the worst!'

'It was the stammering-man,' said Pen, not very lucidly. 'Of course, I quite see that I should have been more careful.'

'You mean Beverley Brandon. What has he been doing?'

'Well, you see, he came here. And just at that very same moment, I chanced to walk into the inn, and – and we met.'

'When was this?'

'Oh, not long ago! You were gone out. Only he seemed to know me.'

'Seemed to know you?'

'Well, he said surely I must be your nephew,' Pen explained.

Sir Richard had been listening to her with a gathering frown. He said now, with a grim note which she had not before heard in his voice: 'Beverley knows very well that the only nephew I have is a child in short petticoats.'

'Oh, have you got a nephew?' enquired Pen, diverted.

'Yes. Never mind that. What did you reply?'

'Well, I think I was quite clever,' said Pen hopefully. 'Naturally, I knew who he must be, as soon as he spoke; and I guessed, of course, that he must know I am not your nephew. Because even if some people think I have no ingenuity, I am not at all stupid,' she added, with a darkling look.

'Does that rankle?' His countenance had relaxed a little. 'Never mind! go on!'

'I said that in point of fact you were not my uncle, but I called you so because you were a great deal older than I. I said that you were my third cousin. Then he asked me why we had come to Queen Charlton, and I said it was on account of family affairs, though I would rather have pointed out that it was extremely ill-bred and inquisitive of him to ask me such questions. And after that he went away.'

'Did he indeed? Did he say what had brought him here in the first place?'

'No. But he gave me a message for you, which I did not quite like.'

'Well?'

'It sounded sinister to me,' said Pen, preparing him for the worst.

'I can well believe it.'

'And the more I think of it the more sinister it appears to me. He said I must present his compliments to you, and tell you that he perfectly understands your reason for coming to such a secluded spot.'

'The devil!' said Sir Richard.

'I was afraid you would not be excessively pleased,' Pen said anxiously. 'Do you suppose that it means that he knows who I am?'

'Not that, no,' Sir Richard replied.

'Perhaps,' suggested Pen, 'he guessed that I am not a boy?'

'Perhaps.'

She thought the matter over. 'Well, I don't see what else he could possibly have meant. But Jimmy Yarde never suspected me, and I conversed with him far more than I did with this disagreeable stammering-man. How very unfortunate it is that we should have met someone who knows you well!'

'I beg your pardon?' said Sir Richard, putting up his glass.

She looked innocently up at him. 'On account of his being aware that you have no nephew or cousin like me, I mean.'

'Oh!' said Sir Richard, lowering the glass. 'I see. Don't let it worry you!'

'Well, it does worry me, because I see now that I have been imprudent. I should not have let you come with me. It has very likely placed you in an awkward situation.'

'That aspect of it had not occurred to me,' said Sir Richard, faintly smiling. 'The imprudence was mine. I ought to have handed you over to your aunt at our first meeting.'

'Do you wish you had?' asked Pen wistfully.

He looked down at her for an instant. 'No.'

'Well, I'm glad, because if you had tried to, I would have run away from you.' She lifted her chin from her cupped hands. 'If you are not sorry to be here, do not let us give it another thought! It is so very fatiguing to go on being sorry about something which one has done. Did you order any dinner, sir?'

'I did. Duck and peas.'

'Good!' said Pen, with profound satisfaction. 'Where has Aunt Almeria gone, do you suppose?'

'To Chippenham, and then to Cousin Jane.'

'To Cousin Jane? Good gracious, why?'

'To see whether you have taken refuge with her, I imagine.'

'With Cousin Jane!' Pen exclaimed. 'Why, she is the most odious old woman, and takes snuff!'

Sir Richard, who had just opened his own box, paused. 'Er — do you consider that an odious habit?' he asked.

'In a female, I do. Besides, she spills it on her clothes. Ugh! Oh, I did not mean you, sir!' she added, with a ripple of sudden laughter. 'You do it with such an air!'

'Thank you!' he said.

A waiter came in to lay the covers for dinner, and presented a small, twisted note to Sir Richard on a large tray.

He picked it up unhurriedly, and spread it open. Pen, anxiously watching him, could detect nothing in his face but boredom. He read the note through to the end, and consigning it to his pocket, glanced towards Pen. 'Let me see: what were we discussing?'

'Snuff,' replied Pen, in a hollow voice.

'Ah, yes! I myself use King's Martinique, but there are many

121

who consider it a trifle light in character.'

She returned a mechanical answer, and upon the waiter's leaving the room, interrupted Sir Richard's description of the proper way to preserve snuff in good condition, by demanding impetuously: 'Who was it from, sir?'

'Don't be inquisitive!' said Sir Richard calmly.

'You can't deceive me! I feel sure it was from that hateful man.'

'It was, but there is no occasion for you to trouble your head over it, believe me.'

'Only tell me! Does he mean to do you some mischief?'

'Certainly not. It would, in all events, be a task quite beyond his power.'

'I feel very uneasy.'

'So I perceive. You will be the better for your dinner.'

The waiter came in with the duck at that opportune moment, and set it upon the table. Pen was, in fact, so hungry that her thoughts were instantly diverted. She made a very good dinner, and did not again refer to the note.

Sir Richard, maintaining a flow of easy conversation, seemed to be wholly devoid of care, but the note had annoyed him. There was very little fear, he considered, of Beverley's being able to harm Miss Creed, since he could have no knowledge of her identity; and his veiled threat of exposing Sir Richard was a matter of indifference to that gentleman. But he would certainly meet Beverley in the spinney at the proposed hour, for it now became more than ever necessary to despatch him to London immediately. While he remained in the neighbourhood there would be no question of delivering Pen into Lady Luttrell's care, and although Sir Richard had not the least desire to relinquish his self-appointed guardianship of that enterprising damsel, he was perfectly well aware that he must do so, and without any loss of time.

Accordingly, he sent her to bed shortly after half-past-nine, telling her that if she were not tired she deserved to be. She went without demur, so probably her day spent in the open had made her sleepy. He waited until a few minutes before ten o'clock, and then took his hat and walking-cane, and strolled out of the inn.

There was a full moon, and not a cloud to be seen in the sky. Sir Richard had no difficulty in seeing his way, and soon came to the track through the wood. It was darker here, for the trees held out the moonlight. A rabbit scuttled across the path, an owl hooted somewhere at hand, and there were little rustlings in the undergrowth, but Sir Richard was not of a nervous disposition, and did not find these sounds in anyway disturbing.

But he was hardly prepared to come upon a lady lying stretched across the path, immediately round a bend in it. This sight was, indeed, so unexpected that it brought him up short. The lady did not move, but lay in a crumpled heap of pale muslin and darker cloak. Sir Richard, recovering from his momentary surprise, strode forward, and dropped on to his knee beside her. It was too dark under the trees for him to be able to distinguish her features clearly, but he thought she was young. She was not dead, as he had at first feared, but in a deep faint. He began to chafe her hands, and had just bethought him of the tiny stream which he had observed that morning, when she showed signs of returning consciousness. He raised her in his arms, hearing a sigh flutter past her lips. A moan succeeded the sigh; she said something he could not catch, and began weakly to cry.

'Don't cry!' Sir Richard said. 'You are quite safe.'

She caught her breath on a sob, and stiffened in his hold. He felt her little hands close on his arm. Then she began to tremble.

'No, there is nothing to frighten you,' he said in his cool way. 'You will be better directly.'

'Oh!' The exclamation sounded terrified. 'Who are you? Oh, let me go!'

'Certainly I will let you go, but are you able to stand yet? You do not know me, but I am perfectly harmless, I assure you.'

She made a feeble attempt to struggle up, and succeeded only in crouching on the path in a woebegone huddle, saying through her sobs: 'I must go! Oh, I must go! I ought not to have come!'

'That I can well believe,' said Sir Richard, still on his knee beside her. 'Why did you come? Or is that an impertinent question?'

It had the effect of redoubling her sobs. She buried her face in her hands, shuddering, and rocking herself to and fro, and gasping out unintelligible phrases.

'Well!' said a voice behind Sir Richard.

He looked quickly over his shoulder. 'Pen! What are you doing here?'

'I followed you,' replied Pen, looking critically down at the weeping girl. 'I brought a stout stick too, because I thought you were going to meet the odious stammering-man, and I feel sure he means to do you a mischief. Who is this?'

'I haven't the slightest idea,' replied Sir Richard. 'And presently I shall have something to say to you on the subject of this idiotic escapade of yours! My good child, can't you stop crying?'

'What is she doing here?' asked Pen, unmoved by his strictures.

'Heaven knows! I found her lying on the path. How does one make a female stop crying?'

'I shouldn't think you could. She's going to have a fit of the vapours, I expect. And I do *not* see why you should hug people, if you don't know who they are.'

'I was not hugging her.'

'It looked like it to me,' argued Pen.

'I suppose,' said Sir Richard sardonically, 'you would have had me step over her, and walk on?'

'Yes, I would,' replied Pen promptly.

'Don't be a little fool! The girl had fainted.'

'Oh!' Pen moved forward. 'I wonder what made her do that? You know, it all seems extremely odd to me.'

'It seems quite as odd to me, let me tell you.' He laid his hand on the sobbing girl's shoulder. 'Come! You will not help matters by crying. Can't you tell me what has happened to upset you so?'

The girl made a convulsive effort to choke back her hysterical tears, and managed to utter: 'I was so frightened!'

'Yes, that I had realized. What frightened you?'

'There was a man!' gasped the girl. 'And I hid, and then another man came, and they began to quarrel, and I dared not move for fear they should hear me, and the big one hit the other, and he fell down and lay still, and the big one took something out of his pocket, and went away, and oh, oh, he passed so close I c-could have touched him only by stretching out my hand! The other man never moved, and I was so frightened I ran, everything went black, and I think I fainted.'

'Ran away?' repeated Pen in disgusted accents. 'What a poor-spirited thing to do! Didn't you go to help the man who was knocked down?'

'Oh no, no, no!' shuddered the girl.

'I must say, I don't think you deserve to have such an adventure. And if I were you I wouldn't continue sitting in the middle of the path. It isn't at all helpful, and it makes you look very silly.'

This severe speech had the effect of angering the girl. She reared up her head, and exclaimed: 'How dare you? You are the rudest young man I ever met in my life!'

Sir Richard put his hand under her elbow, and assisted her to her feet. 'Ah – accept my apologies on my nephew's behalf, ma'am!' he said, with only the faintest quiver in his voice. 'A sadly ill-conditioned boy! May I suggest to you that you should rest on this bank for a few moments, while I go to investigate the – er – scene of the assault you so graphically described? My nephew – who has, you perceive, provided himself with a stout stick – will charge himself with your safety.'

'I'll come with you,' said Pen mutinously.

'You will – for once in your life – do as you are told,' said Sir Richard, and, lowering the unknown on to the bank, strode on down the track towards the clearing in the wood.

Here the moonlight bathed the ground in its cold silver light. Sir Richard had no doubt that he would find Beverley Brandon, either stunned, or recovering from the effects of the blow which had felled him, but as he stepped into the clearing he saw not only one man lying still on the ground, but a second on his knees beside him.

Sir Richard trod softly, and it was not until he had approached to within a few feet of the little group that the kneeling man heard his footsteps, and looked quickly over his shoulder. The moonlight drained the world of colour, but even allowing for this the face turned towards Sir Richard was unnaturally pallid. It was the face of a very young man, and perfectly strange to Sir Richard.

'Who are you?' The question was shot out in a hushed, rather scared voice. The young man started to his feet, and took up an instinctively defensive pose.

'I doubt whether my name will convey very much to you, but, for what it is worth, it is Wyndham. What has happened here?'

The boy seemed quite distracted, and replied in a shaken tone: 'I don't know. I found him here – like this. I – I think he's dead!'

'Nonsense!' said Sir Richard, putting him out of his way, and in his turn kneeling beside Beverley's inanimate body. There was a bruise on the livid brow, and when Sir Richard raised Beverley his head fell back in a way that told its own tale rather horribly. Sir Richard saw the tree-stump, and realized that Beverley's head must have struck it. He laid his body down again, and said without the least vestige of emotion: 'You are perfectly right. His neck is broken.'

The boy dragged a handkerchief out of his pocket, and wiped his brow with it. 'My God, who did it? – I – I didn't, you know!'

'I don't suppose you did,' Sir Richard replied, rising to his feet, and dusting the knees of his breeches.

'But it's the most shocking thing! He was staying with me, sir!'

'Oh!' said Sir Richard, favouring him with a long, penetrating look.

'He's Beverley Brandon – Lord Saar's younger son!'

'I know very well who he is. You, I apprehend, are Mr Piers Luttrell?'

'Yes. Yes, I am. I knew him up at Oxford. Not very well, because I – well, to tell you the truth, I never liked him much. But a week ago he arrived at my home. He had been visiting friends, I think. I don't know. But of course I – that is, my mother and I – asked him to stay, and he did. He has not been quite well – seemed to be in need of rest, and – and country air. Indeed, I can't conceive how he comes to be here now, for he retired to his room with one of his sick headaches. At least, that was what he told my mother.'

'Then you did not come here in search of him?'

'No, no! I came – The fact is, I just came out to enjoy a stroll in the moonlight,' replied Piers, in a hurry.

'I see.' There was a dry note in Sir Richard's voice.

'Why are *you* here?' demanded Piers.

'For the same reason,' Sir Richard answered.

'But you know Brandon!'

'That circumstance does not, however, make me his murderer.'

'Oh no! I did not mean – but it seems so strange that you should both be in Queen Charlton!'

'I thought it tiresome, myself. My errand to Queen Charlton did not in any way concern Beverley Brandon.'

'Of course not! I didn't suppose – Sir, since you didn't kill him, and I didn't, who – who did, do you suppose? For he did not merely trip and fall, did he? There is that bruise on his forehead, and he was lying face upwards, just as you saw him. Someone struck him down!'

'Yes, I think someone struck him down,' agreed Sir Richard.

'I suppose you do not know who it might have been, sir?'

'I wonder?' Sir Richard said thoughtfully.

Piers waited, but as Sir Richard said no more, but stood looking frowningly down at Beverley's body, he blurted out: 'What ought I to do? Really, I do not know! I have no experience in such matters. Perhaps you could advise me?'

'I do not pretend to any very vast experience myself, but I suggest that you should go home.'

'But we can't leave him here – can we?'

'No, we can't do that. I will inform the magistrate that there is – er – a corpse in the wood. No doubt he will attend to it.'

'Yes, but I don't wish to run away, you know,' Piers objected. 'It is the most devilish, awkward situation, but of course I don't dream of leaving you to – to explain it all to the magistrate. I shall have to say that it was I who found the body.'

Sir Richard, who knew that the affair was one of extreme delicacy, and who had been wondering for several minutes in what way it could be handled so as to spare the Brandons as much humiliation as possible, did not feel that the entry of Piers Luttrell into the proceedings would facilitate his task. He cast another of his searching looks over the young man, and said: 'Your doing so would serve no useful purpose, I believe. You had better leave it to me.'

'You know something about it!'

'Yes, I do. I am on terms of – er – considerable intimacy with the Brandons, and I know a good deal about Beverley's activities. There is likely to be a peculiarly distasteful scandal arising out of this murder.'

Piers nodded. 'I was afraid of that. You know, sir, he was not at all the thing, and he knew some devilish odd people. A man came up to the house, enquiring for him only yesterday – a seedy sort of bully: I dare say you may be familiar with the type. Beverley did not like it above half, I could see.'

'Were you privileged to meet this man?'

'Well, I saw him: I didn't exchange two words with him. The servant came to tell Beverley that a Captain Trimble had called to see him, and Beverley was so much put out that I – well, I fear I did rather wonder what was in the wind.'

'Ah!' said Sir Richard. 'The fact that you have met Trimble may – or may not – prove useful. Yes, I think you had better go home, and say nothing about this. No doubt the news of Beverley's death will be conveyed to you to-morrow morning.'

'But what shall I tell the constable, sir?'

'Whatever he asks you,' replied Sir Richard.

'Shall I say that I found Beverley here, with you?' asked Piers doubtfully.

'I hardly think that he will ask you that question.'

'But will he not wonder how it came about that I did not miss Beverley?'

'Did you not say that Beverley gave it out that he was retiring to bed? Why should you miss him?'

'To-morrow morning?'

'Yes, I think you might miss him at the breakfast-table,' conceded Sir Richard.

'I see. Well, if you feel it to be right, sir, I – I own I would rather not divulge that I was in the wood tonight. But what must I say if I am asked if I know you?'

'You don't know me.'

'N-no. No, I don't, of course,' said Piers, apparently cheered by this reflection.

'That is a pleasure in store for you. I came into this neighbourhood for the purpose of – er – making your acquaintance, but this seems hardly the moment to enter upon a matter which I have reason to suspect may prove extremely complicated.'

'You came to see *me*?' said Piers, astonished. 'How can this be?'

'If,' said Sir Richard, 'you will come to see me at the "George" to-morrow – a very natural action on your part, in view of my discovery of your guest's corpse – I will tell you just why I came to Queen Charlton in search of you.'

'I am sure I am honoured – but I cannot conceive what your business with me may be, sir!'

'That,' said Sir Richard, 'does not surprise me nearly as much as my business is likely to surprise you, Mr Luttrell!'

Nine

*H*aving got rid of Piers Luttrell, who, after peering at his watch surreptitiously, and several times looking about him as though in the expectation of seeing someone hiding amongst the trees, went off, rather relieved but much bewildered, Sir Richard walked away to rejoin Pen and the unknown lady. He found only Pen, seated on the bank with an air of aloof virtue, her hands folded primly on her knees. He paused, looking her over with a comprehending eye. 'And where,' he asked in conversational tones, 'is your companion?'

'She chose to go home,' responded Pen. 'I dare say she grew tired of waiting for you to come back.'

'Ah, no doubt! Did you by any chance, suggest to her that she should do so?'

'No, because it was not at all necessary. She was very anxious to go. She said she wished she had not come.'

'Did she tell you why she had come?'

'No. I asked her, of course, but she is such a silly little missish thing that she would do nothing but cry, and say she was a wicked girl. Do you know what I think, Richard?'

'Probably.'

'Well, it's my belief she came to meet someone. She seems to me exactly the sort of female who would feel romantic just because there is a full moon. Besides, why else should she be here at this hour?'

'Why indeed?' agreed Sir Richard. 'I apprehend that you have little sympathy to spare for such folly?'

'None at all,' said Pen. 'In fact, I think it's silly, besides being improper.'

'You are severe!'

'I can tell by your voice that you are laughing at me. I expect you are thinking of my climbing out of a window. But *I* was not going to meet a lover by moonlight! Such stuff!'

'Fustian,' nodded Sir Richard. 'Did she disclose the identity of her lover?'

'No, but she said her own name was Lydia Daubenay. And no sooner had she told me that than she went off into another taking, and said she was distracted, and wished she had not told me. Really, I was quite glad when she decided to go home without waiting for you.'

'Yes, I had rather gathered the impression that her company was not agreeable to you. I suppose it hardly signifies. She did not appear to me to be the kind of young woman who could be trusted to bear a still tongue in her head.'

'Well, I don't know,' said Pen thoughtfully. 'She was so frightened I quite think she may not say a word about the adventure. I have been considering the matter, and it seems to me that she must be in love with someone whom her parents do not wish her to marry.'

'That,' said Sir Richard, 'seems to be a fair conclusion.'

'So that I shouldn't be at all surprised if she conceals the fact that she was in the wood to-night. By the way, was it the stammering-man?'

'It was, and Miss Daubenay was right in her suspicion: he is dead.'

Miss Creed accepted this with fortitude. 'Well, if he is, I can tell you who killed him. That girl told me all over again how it happened, and there is no doubt that the other man was Captain Trimble. And he did it to get the necklace!'

'Admirable!' said Sir Richard.

'It is as plain as a pikestaff. And now that I come to think of it, it may very likely be all for the best. Of course, I am sorry for the stammering-man, but you can't deny that he was a very disagreeable person. Besides, I know perfectly well that he was threatening you. That is why I followed you. Now we are rid of the whole affair!'

'Not quite, I fear. You must not think that I am unmoved by your heroic behaviour, but I could wish that you had gone to bed, Pen.'

'Yes, but I find that most unreasonable of you,' objected Pen. 'It seems to me that you want to keep all the adventure for yourself!'

'I appreciate your feelings,' said Sir Richard, 'but I would point out to you that your situation is a trifle – shall we say irregular? – and that we have been at considerable pains to excite no undue attention. Hence that abominable stagecoach. The last thing in the world I desire is to see you brought forward as a witness to this affair. If Miss Daubenay does not disclose her share in it, you may yet escape notice, but, to tell you the truth, I place little dependence on Miss Daubenay's discretion.'

'Oh!' said Pen, digesting this. 'You think there may be a little awkwardness if it should be discovered that I am not a boy? Perhaps we had better leave Queen Charlton?'

'No, that would indeed be fatal. We are now committed to this adventure. I am going to inform the local magistrate that I have discovered a corpse in this spinney. As you have encountered Miss Daubenay, upon whose discretion we have decided to place no reliance, I shall mention the fact that you accompanied me upon my evening stroll, and we must trust that no particular notice will be taken of you. By the way, brat, I think you had better become my young cousin – my remote young cousin.'

'Ah!' said Miss Creed, gratified. 'My own story!'

'Your own story.'

'Well, I must say I am glad you don't wish to run away,' she confided. 'You cannot conceive how much I am enjoying myself! I dare say it is otherwise with you, but, you see, I have had such a very dull life up till now! And I'll tell you another thing, Richard: naturally I am very anxious to find Piers, but I think we had better not send any word to him until we have finished this adventure.'

He was silent for a moment. 'Are you very anxious to find Piers?' he asked at last.

'Of course I am! Why, that is why we came!'

'Very true. I was forgetting. You will see Piers tomorrow morning, I fancy.'

She got up from the bank. 'I shall see him to-morrow? But how do you know?'

'I should have mentioned to you that I have just had the felicity of meeting him.'

'Piers?' she exclaimed. 'Here? In the wood?'

'Over Beverley Brandon's body.'

'I thought I heard voices! But how did he come to be here? And why didn't you bring him to me directly?'

Sir Richard took time over his answer. 'You see, I was under the impression that Miss Daubenay was still with you,' he explained.

'Oh, I see!' said Pen innocently. 'Yes, indeed, you did quite right! We don't want her to be included in our adventure. But did you tell Piers about me?'

'The moment did not seem to be propitious,' confessed Sir Richard. 'I told him to come to visit me at the "George" to-morrow morning, and on no account to divulge his presence in the wood to-night.'

'What a surprise it will be to him when he finds me at the George!' said Pen gleefully.

'Yes,' said Sir Richard. 'I think it will be – a surprise to him.'

She fell into step beside him on their way back to the road. 'I am glad you did not tell him! I suppose he had come to look for the stammering-man? I can't conceive how he could have had such a disagreeable person to visit him!'

Sir Richard, who had rarely, during the twenty-nine years of his existence, found himself at a loss, now discovered that he was totally incapable of imparting his own suspicions to his trusting companion. Apparently, it had not occurred to her that the sentiments of her old play-fellow might have undergone a change; and so fixed in her mind was a five-year-old pact of betrothal that it had not entered her head to question either its durable qualities, or its desirability. She evidently considered herself plighted to Piers Luttrell, a circumstance which had no doubt had much to do with her friendly acceptance of Sir Richard's companionship. Phrases of warning half-formed themselves in Sir Richard's brain, and were rejected. Piers would have to do his explaining; Sir Richard could only hope that upon coming face to face with him after a lapse of years, Pen might discover that as he had outgrown a childhood's fancy, so too had she.

They entered the George together. Pen went up to bed at a nod from Sir Richard, but Sir Richard rang the bell for a servant. A sleepy waiter came in answer to the summons, and, upon being asked for the direction of the nearest magistrate, said that Sir Jasper Luttrell was the nearest, but was away from home. He knew of no other, so Sir Richard desired him to fetch the landlord to him, and sat down to write a short note to whom it might concern.

When the landlord came into the parlour, Sir Richard was shaking the sand off the single sheet of paper. He folded it, and sealed it with a wafer, and upon being told that Mr John Philips, of Whitchurch, was the nearest available magistrate, wrote this gentleman's name on the note. As he wrote, he said in his calm way: 'I shall be obliged to you if you will have this letter conveyed directly to Mr Philips.'

'To-night, sir?'

'To-night. Mr Philips will, I imagine, come back with your messenger. If he asks for me, show him into this room. Ah, and landlord!'

'Sir?'

'A bowl of rum punch. I will mix it myself.'

'Yes, sir! Immediately, sir!' said the landlord, relieved to receive such a normal command.

He lingered for a moment, trying to summon up sufficient

resolution to ask the fine London gentleman why he wanted to see a magistrate thus urgently. Sir Richard's quizzing-glass came up, and the landlord withdrew in haste. The waiter would have followed him, but was detained by Sir Richard's uplifted forefinger.

'One moment! Who gave you the note which you delivered to me this evening?'

'It was Jem, sir – the tapster. It was when I went up to the bar for a pint of burgundy for a gentleman dining in the coffee-room that Jem gave it to me. It was Captain Trimble who picked it up off the ground, where it was a-laying. It got swep' off the bar, I dessay, sir, the tap-room being crowded at the time, and Jem with his hands full.'

'Thank you,' said Sir Richard. 'That is all.'

The waiter went away considerably mystified. Sir Richard, on the other hand, felt that the mystery had been satisfactorily explained, and sat down to await the landlord's return with the ingredients for a bowl of punch.

Mr Philips' residence was situated some five miles from Queen Charlton, and it was consequently some time before the clatter of horses' hooves in the street heralded his arrival. Sir Richard was squeezing the lemon into the punch-bowl when he was ushered into the parlour, and looked up fleetingly to say: 'Ah, how do you do? Mr Philips, I apprehend?'

Mr Philips was a grizzled gentleman with a harassed frown, and a slight paunch.

'Your servant, sir! Have I the honour of addressing Sir Richard Wyndham?'

'Mine, sir, is the honour,' said Sir Richard absently, intent upon his punch.

'Sir,' said Mr Philips, 'your very extraordinary communication – I may say, your unprecedented disclosure – has, as you perceive, brought me immediately to enquire into this incredible affair!'

'Very proper,' said Sir Richard. 'You will wish to visit the scene of the crime, I imagine. I can give you the direction, but no doubt the village constable is familiar with the locality. The body, Mr Philips, is – or was – lying in the clearing in the middle of the spinney, a little way down the road.'

'Do you mean to tell me, sir, that this story is true?' demanded the magistrate.

'Certainly it is true. Dear me, did you suppose me to be so heartless as to drag you out at this hour on a fool's errand? Are you in favour of adding the juice of one or of two lemons?'

Mr Philips, whose eyes had been critically observing Sir Richard's proceedings, said, without thinking: 'One! One is enough!'

'I feel sure you are right,' said Sir Richard.

'You know, sir, I must ask you some questions about this extraordinary affair!' said Philips, recollecting his errand.

'So you shall, sir, so you shall. Would you like to ask them now, or after you have disposed of the body?'

'I shall first repair to the scene of the murder,' declared Philips.

'Good!' said Sir Richard. 'I will engage to have the punch ready against your return.'

Mr Philips felt that this casual way of treating the affair was quite out of order, but the prospect of returning to a bowl of hot rum punch was so agreeable that he decided to overlook any trifling irregularity. When he returned to the inn, half an hour later, he was feeling chilled, for it was now past midnight and he had not taken his overcoat with him. Sir Richard had caused a fire to be kindled in the wainscoted parlour, and from the bowl on the table, which he was stirring with a long-handled spoon, there arose a very fragrant and comforting aroma. Mr Philips rubbed his hands together, and could not refrain from ejaculating: 'Ha!'

Sir Richard looked up, and smiled. His smile had won more hearts than Mr Philips', and it had a visible effect on that gentleman.

'Well, well, well! I won't deny that's a very welcome smell, Sir Richard! A fire, too! Upon my word, I'm glad to see it!

Gets chilly at night, very chilly! A bad business, sir! a very bad business!'

Sir Richard ladled the steaming brew into two glasses, and gave one to the magistrate. 'Draw up a chair to the fire, Mr Philips. It is, as you say, a very bad business. I should tell you that I am intimately acquainted with the family of the deceased.'

Mr Philips fished Sir Richard's note out of his pocket. 'Yes, yes, just as I supposed, sir. I do not know how you would otherwise have furnished me with the poor man's name. You know him, in fact. Precisely! He was travelling in your company, perhaps?'

'No,' said Sir Richard, taking a chair on the opposite side of the fireplace. 'He was staying with a friend who lives in the neighbourhood. The name was, I think, Luttrell.'

'Indeed! This becomes more and more – But pray continue, sir! You were not, then, together?'

'No, nothing of the sort. I came into the West Country in family affairs. I need not burden you with them, I think.'

'Quite, quite! Family affairs: yes! Go on, sir! How came you to discover Mr Brandon's body?'

'Oh, by accident! But it will be better, perhaps, if I recount my share in this affair from its start.'

'Certainly! Yes! Pray do so, sir! This is a remarkably good bowl of punch, I may say.'

'I am generally thought to have something of a knack with a punch-bowl,' bowed Sir Richard. 'To go back, then, to the start! You have no doubt heard, Mr Philips, of the Brandon diamonds?'

From the startled expression in the magistrate's eyes, and the slight dropping of his jaw, it was apparent that he had not. He said: 'Diamonds? Really, I fear – No, I must confess that I had not heard of the Brandon diamonds.'

'Then, I should explain that they make up a certain famous necklace, worth, I dare say, anything you like.'

'Upon my word! An heirloom! Yes, yes, but in what way –'

'While on my way to Bristol with a young relative of mine, a slight accident befell our coach, and we were forced to put up for the night at a small inn near Wroxham. There, sir, I encountered an individual who seemed to me – but I am not very well-versed in these matters – a somewhat questionable character. How questionable I did not know until the following morning, when a Bow Street Runner arrived at the inn.

'Good God, sir! This is the most – But I interrupt you!'

'Not at all,' said Sir Richard politely. 'I left the inn while the Runner was interrogating this individual. It was not until my young cousin and I had proceeded some way on our journey that I discovered in my pocket a purse containing the Brandon necklace.'

The magistrate sat bolt upright in his chair. 'You amaze me, sir! You astonish me! The necklace in your pocket? Really, I do not know what to say!'

'No,' agreed Sir Richard, rising and refilling his guest's glass. 'I was rather taken aback myself. In fact, it was some time before I could think how it came to be there.'

'No wonder, no wonder! Most understandable, indeed! You recognized the necklace?'

'Yes,' said Sir Richard, returning to his chair. 'I recognized it, but – really, I am amazed at my own stupidity! – I did not immediately connect it with the individual encountered near Wroxham. The question was then not so much how it came to be in my possession, as how to restore it to Lord Saar with the least possible delay. I could picture Lady Saar's dismay at such an irreparable loss! Ah – a lady of exquisite sensibility, you understand!'

The magistrate nodded his comprehension. The rum punch was warming him quite as much as the fire, and he had a not unpleasant sensation of mixing with exalted persons.

'Happily – or perhaps I should say, in the light of future events, *unhappily*,' continued Sir Richard, 'I recalled that Beverley Brandon – he was Saar's younger son, I should mention – was staying in this neighbourhood. I repaired instantly to this inn, therefore, and, being fortunate enough to meet Brandon just beyond the village, gave the necklace to him without further ado.'

The magistrate set down his glass. 'You gave the necklace to him? Did he know that it had been stolen?'

'By no means. He was as astonished as I was, but engaged himself to restore it immediately to his father. I considered the matter satisfactorily settled – Saar, you know, having the greatest dislike of any kind of notoriety, such as must accrue from the theft, and the subsequent proceedings.'

'Sir!' said Mr Philips, 'do you mean to imply that this unfortunate young man was murdered for the sake of the necklace?'

'That,' said Sir Richard, 'is what I fear may have happened.'

'But this is shocking! Upon my word, sir, I am quite dumbfounded! – what – who can have known that the necklace was in his possession?'

'I should have said that no one could have known it, but, upon consideration, I imagine that the individual who hid it in my pocket may well have followed me to this place, waiting for an opportunity to get it back into his possession.'

'True! very true! You have been spied upon! Yet you have not seen that man in Queen Charlton?'

'Do you think he would – er – let me see him?' enquired Sir Richard, evading this question.

'No. No, indeed! Certainly not! But this must be looked to!'

'Yes,' agreed Sir Richard, pensively swinging his eyeglass on the end of its ribbon. 'And I think you might, with advantage, look to the sudden disappearance from this inn of a flashy person calling himself Captain Trimble, Mr Philips.'

'Really, sir! This becomes more and more – Pray, what reason have you for supposing that this man may be implicated in the murder?'

'Well,' said Sir Richard slowly, 'some chance words which I let fall on the subject of – ah – waistcoats, sent Captain Trimble off hot-foot to Bristol.'

The magistrate blinked, and directed an accusing glance

towards his half-empty glass. A horrid suspicion that the rum punch had affected his understanding was dispelled, however, by Sir Richard's next words.

'My acquaintance at the inn near Wroxham wore a catskin waistcoat. A casual reference to this circumstance had the surprising effect of arousing the Captain's curiosity. He asked me in what direction the man in the catskin waistcoat had been travelling, and upon my saying that I believed him to be bound for Bristol, he left the inn – er – incontinent.'

'I see! yes, yes, I see! An accomplice!'

'My own feeling,' said Sir Richard, 'is that he was an accomplice who had been – er – bubbled.'

The magistrate appeared to be much struck by this. 'Yes! I see it all! Good God, this is a terrible affair! I have never been called upon to – But you say this Captain Trimble went off to Bristol, sir?'

'He did. But I have since learned, Mr Philips, that he was back at this inn at six o'clock this evening. Ah! I should, I see, say *yesterday* evening,' he added with a glance at the clock on the mantelpiece.

Mr Philips drew a long breath. 'Your disclosures, Sir Richard, open up – are in fact, of such a nature as to – Upon my word, I never thought – But the murder! You discovered this, sir?'

'I discovered Brandon's body,' corrected Sir Richard.

'How came you to do this, sir? You had a suspicion? You –'

'None at all. It was a warm evening, and I stepped out to enjoy a stroll in the moonlight. Chance alone led my footsteps to the wood where I found my unfortunate young friend's body. It is only since making that melancholy discovery that I have pieced together the – er – evidence.'

Mr Philips had a hazy idea that chance had played an over-important part in Sir Richard's adventures, but he was aware that the punch he had drunk had slightly clouded his intellect. He said guardedly: 'Sir, the story you have unfolded is of a nature which – in short, it must be carefully sifted. Yes, indeed. Carefully sifted! I must request you not to remove from this neighbourhood until I have had time – pray do not misunderstand me! There is not the least suggestion, I assure you, of –'

'My dear sir, I don't misunderstand you, and I have no intention of removing from this inn,' said Sir Richard soothingly. 'I am aware that you have, so far, only my word for it that I am indeed Richard Wyndham.'

'Oh, as to that, I am sure – no suggestion of disbelieving – But my duty is prescribed! You will appreciate my position, I am persuaded!'

'Perfectly!' said Sir Richard. 'I shall hold myself wholly at your disposal. You, as a man of the world, will, I am assured, appreciate the need of the exercise of – ah – the most delicate discretion in handling this affair.'

Mr Philips, who had once spent three weeks in London, was flattered to think that the imprint of that short sojourn was pronounced enough to be discernible to such a personage as Beau Wyndham, and swelled with pride. Native caution, however, warned him that his investigation had better be postponed to a more sober moment. He rose to his feet with careful dignity, and set his empty glass down on the table. 'I am obliged to you!' he pronounced. 'I shall wait upon you to-morrow – no, to-day! I must consider this affair. A terrible business! I think one may say, a terrible business!'

Sir Richard agreed to this, and after a meticulous exchange of courtesies, Mr Philips took his leave. Sir Richard snuffed the candles, and went up to bed, not dissatisfied with his night's work.

In the morning, Pen was first down. The day was fine, and her cravat, she flattered herself, very well tied. There was a suggestion of a prance about her gait as she sallied forth to inspect the weather. Sir Richard, no believer in early rising, had ordered breakfast for nine o'clock, and it was as yet only eight. A maid-servant was engaged in sweeping the floor of the private parlour, and a bored waiter was spreading clean cloths over the tables in the coffee-room. As Pen passed through the entrance-parlour, the landlord, who was conversing in low tones with a gentleman unknown to her, looked round, and exclaimed: 'Here is the young gentleman himself, sir!'

Mr Philips, confronted with the biggest crime ever committed within the limits of his jurisdiction, had perhaps imbibed too strong a brew of rum punch on the previous evening, but he was a zealous person, and, in spite of awaking with a very bad head, he had lost no time in getting out of his comfortable bed, and riding back to Queen Charlton to continue his investigations. As Pen paused, he stepped forward, and bade her a civil good-morning. She responded, wishing that Sir Richard would come downstairs; and upon Mr Philips' asking her, in a tone of kindly patronage, whether she was Sir Richard's young cousin, assented, and hoped that the magistrate would not ask for her name.

He did not. He said: 'Now, you were with Sir Richard when he discovered this very shocking crime, were you not, young man?'

'Well, not precisely,' said Pen.

'Oh? How is that?'

'I was, and I wasn't,' Pen explained, with an earnestness which robbed the words of flippancy. 'I didn't see the body.'

'No? Just tell me exactly what happened. No need to feel any alarm, you know! If you walked out with your cousin, how came you to have separated?'

'Well, sir, there was an owl,' confided Pen unblushingly.

'Come, come! An *owl*?'

'Yes: my cousin said that too.'

'Said what?'

'Come, come! He is not interested in bird-life.'

'Ah, I see! You collect eggs, eh? That's it, is it?'

'Yes, and also I like to watch birds.'

Mr Philips smiled tolerantly. He wondered how old this slim boy was, and thought it a pity the young fellow should be so effeminate; but he was a country man himself, and dimly he could recall the bird-watching days of his youth. 'Yes, yes, I understand! You went off on your own to try to catch a glimpse of this owl: well, I have done the same in my time! And so you were not with your good cousin when he reached the clearing in the wood?'

'No, but I met him on his return, and of course he told me what he had found.'

'I dare say, but hearsay, my boy, is not evidence,' said Mr Philips, nodding dismissal.

Pen made for the door, feeling that she had extricated herself from a difficult situation with aplomb. The landlord ran after her with a sealed letter. 'If I was not forgetting! I beg pardon, sir, but a young person brought this for you not an hour ago. Leastways, it was for a young gentleman of the name of Wyndham. Would that be in mistake for yourself, sir?'

Pen took the letter, and looked at it with misgiving. 'A young person?' she repeated.

'Well, sir, it was one of the servant-girls from Major Daubenay's.'

'Oh!' said Pen. 'Oh, very well! Thank you!'

She passed out into the village street, and after dubiously regarding the direction on the note, which was to – 'Wyndham Esq.,' and written in a round schoolgirl's hand, she broke the seal, and spread open the single sheet.

'*Dear Sir,*' the letter began, primly enough, '*The Unfortunate Being whom you befriended last night, is in Desperate Case, and begs that you will come to the little orchard next to the road at eight o'clock punctually, because it is vital that I should have Private Speech with you. Do not fail. Your obliged servant,*

Lydia Daubenay.'

It was plain that Miss Daubenay had written this missive in considerable agitation. Greatly intrigued, Pen enquired the way to Major Daubenay's house of a baker's boy, and set off down the dusty road.

By the time she had reached the appointed rendezvous it was half-past eight, and Miss Daubenay was pacing up and down impatiently. A thick, high hedge shut the orchard off from sight of the house, and a low wall enclosed it from the road. Pen climbed on to this without much difficulty, and was greeted by an instant accusation: 'Oh, you are so late! I have been waiting ages!'

'Well, I am sorry, but I came as soon as I had read your letter,' said Pen, jumping down into the orchard. 'Why do you wish to see me?'

Miss Daubenay wrung her hands, and uttered in tense accents: 'Everything has gone awry. I am quite distracted! I don't know what to do!'

Pen betrayed no particular solicitude at this moving speech, but critically looked Miss Daubenay over.

She was a pretty child, about the same age as Pen herself, but shorter, and much plumper. She had a profusion of nut-brown ringlets, a pair of fawn-like brown eyes, and a soft rosebud of a mouth. She was dressed in a white muslin dress, high-waisted, and frilled about the ankles, and with a great many pale-blue bows of ribbon with long fluttering ends. She raised her melting eyes to Pen's face, and breathed: 'Can I trust you?'

Miss Creed was a literal-minded female, and instead of responding with promptness and true chivalry, she replied cautiously: 'Well, probably you can, but I am not sure till I know what it is that you want.'

Miss Daubenay seemed a little daunted for a moment, and said in a soft moan: 'I am in such a taking! I have been very, very silly!'

Pen found no difficulty in believing this. She said: 'Well, don't stand there wringing your hands! Let us sit down under that tree.'

Lydia looked doubtful. 'Will it not be damp?'

'No, of course not! Besides, what if it were?'

'Oh, the grass might stain my dress!'

'It seems to me,' said Pen severely, 'that if you are bothering about your dress you cannot be in such great trouble.'

'Oh, but I am!' said Lydia, sinking down on to the turf, and clasping her hands at her bosom. 'I do not know what you will say, or what you will think of me! I must have been mad!

Only, you were kind to me last night, and I thought I could trust you!'

'I dare say you can,' said Pen. 'But I wish you will tell me what is the matter, because I have not yet had any breakfast, and –'

'If I had thought that you would be so unsympathetic I would never, never have sent for you!' declared Lydia in tremulous accents.

'Well, it is very difficult to be sympathetic when a person will do nothing but wring her hands, and say the sort of things there really is no answer to,' said Pen reasonably. 'Do start at the beginning!'

Miss Daubenay bowed her head. 'I am the most unhappy creature alive!' she announced. 'I have the misfortune to be secretly betrothed to one whom my father will not tolerate.'

'Yes, I thought you were. I suppose you went to meet him in the wood last night?'

'Alas, it is true! But do not judge me hastily! He is the most unexceptionable – the most –'

'If he is unexceptionable,' interrupted Pen, 'why won't your father tolerate him?'

'It is all wicked prejudice!' sighed Lydia. 'My father quarrelled with his father, and they don't speak.'

'Oh! What did they quarrel about?'

'About a piece of land,' said Lydia mournfully.

'It sounds very silly.'

'It is silly. Only *they* are perfectly serious about it, and they do not care a fig for *our* sufferings! We have been forced to this hateful expedient of meeting in secret. I should tell you that my betrothed is the *soul* of honour! Subterfuge is repugnant to him, but what can we do? We love each other!'

'Why don't you run away?' suggested Pen practically.

Startled eyes leapt to hers. 'Run where?'

'To Gretna Green, of course.'

'Oh, I could not! Only think of the scandal!'

'I do think you should try not to be so poor-spirited. However, I dare say you can't help it.'

'You are the rudest boy I ever met!' exclaimed Lydia, 'I declare I wish I had not sent for you!'

'So do I, because this seems to me a silly story, and not in the least my concern,' said Pen frankly. 'Oh, pray don't start to cry! There, I am sorry! I didn't mean to be unkind! But why *did* you send for me?'

'Because, though you are rude and horrid, you did not seem to me like other young men, and I thought you would understand, and not take advantage of me.'

Pen gave a sudden mischievous chuckle. 'I shan't do *that*, at all events! Oh dear, I am getting so hungry! Do tell me why you sent for me!'

Miss Daubenay dabbed her eyes with a wisp of a handkerchief. 'I was so distracted last night I scarce knew what I was doing! And when I reached home, the most dreadful thing happened! Papa saw me! Oh, sir, he accused me of having gone out to meet P – to meet my betrothed, and said I should be packed off again to Bath this very day, to stay with my Great-Aunt Augusta. The horridest, most disagreeable old woman! Nothing but backgammon, and spying, and everything of the most hateful! Sir, I felt myself to be in desperate case! Indeed, I said it before I had time to recollect the consequences!'

'Said what?' asked Pen, patient but bored.

Miss Daubenay bowed her head again. 'That it was not – not *that* man I had gone to meet, but another, whom I had met in Bath, when I was sent to Great-Aunt Augusta to – to cure me of what Papa called my *infatuation*! I said I had been in the habit of meeting this other man c-clandestinely, because I thought that would make Papa afraid to send me back to Bath, and might perhaps even reconcile him to the Real Man.'

'Oh!' said Pen doubtfully. 'And did it?'

'No! He said he did not believe me.'

'Well, I must say I'm not surprised at that.'

'Yes, but in the end he did, and now I wish I had never said it. He said if there was Another Man, who was it?'

'You ought to have thought of that. He was bound to ask that question, and you must have looked very silly when you could not answer.'

'But I did answer!' whispered Miss Daubenay, apparently overcome.

'But how could you, if there wasn't another man?'

'I said it was you!' said Miss Daubenay despairingly.

Ten

The effect of this confession upon Pen was not quite what Miss Daubenay had expected. She gasped, choked, and went off into a peal of laughter. Affronted, Miss Daubenay said: 'I don't see what there is to laugh at!'

'No, I dare say you don't,' said Pen, mopping her eyes. 'But it is excessively amusing for all that. What made you say anything so silly?'

'I couldn't think of anything else to say. And as for its being *silly*, you may think me very ill-favoured, but I have already had *several* suitors!'

'I think you are very pretty, but I am not going to be a suitor,' said Pen firmly.

'I don't want you to be! For one thing, I find you quite odiously rude, and for another you are much too young, which is why I chose you, because I thought I should be quite safe in so doing.'

'Well you are, but I never heard of anything so foolish in my life! Pray, what was the use of telling your father such fibs?'

'I told you,' said Lydia crossly. 'I scarcely knew what I was saying, and I thought – But everything has gone awry!'

Pen looked at her with misgiving. 'What do you mean?'

'Papa is going to wait on your cousin this morning.'

'What!' exclaimed Pen.

Lydia nodded. 'Yes, and he is not angry at all. He is pleased!'

'Pleased? How can he be pleased at your holding clandestine meetings with a strange man?'

'To be sure, he did say that that was very wrong of me. But he asked me your name. Of course I don't know it, but your cousin told me his name was Wyndham, so I said yours was too.'

'But it isn't!'

'Well, how was I to know that?' demanded Lydia, aggrieved. 'I had to say something!'

'You are the most unprincipled girl in the world! Besides, why should he be pleased just because you said my name was Wyndham?'

'Apparently,' said Lydia gloomily, 'the Wyndhams are all fabulously wealthy.'

'You must tell him without any loss of time I am *not* a Wyndham, and that I haven't any money at all!'

'How can I tell him anything of the kind? I think you are being most unreasonable! Do but consider! If I said now that I had been mistaken in your name he would suppose you to have been trifling with me!'

'But you cannot expect me to pretend to be in love with you!' Pen said, aghast.

Lydia sniffed. 'Nothing could be more repulsive to me than such a notion. I am already sorry that I mentioned you to Papa. Only I *did*, and now I don't know what to do. He would be so angry if he knew that I had made it all up!'

'Well, I am very sorry, but it seems to me quite your own fault, and I wash my hands of it,' said Pen.

She glanced at Miss Daubenay's flower-like countenance, and made a discovery. Miss Daubenay's soft chin had acquired a look of obstinacy; the fawn-like eyes stared back at her with a mixture of appeal and determination. 'You can't wash your hands of it. I told you that Papa was going to seek an interview with your cousin to-day.'

'You must stop him.'

'I can't. You don't know Papa!'

'No, and I don't want to know him,' Pen pointed out.

'If I told him it had all been lies, I do not know what he might not do. I won't do it! I don't care what you may say: I *won't*!'

149

'Well, I shall deny every word of your story.'

'Then,' said Lydia, not without triumph, 'Papa will do something dreadful to you, because he will think it is you who are telling lies!'

'It seems to me that unless he is a great fool he must know you well enough by now to guess that it is *you* who have told lies!' said Pen, with asperity.

'It's no use being disagreeable and rude,' said Lydia. 'Papa thinks you followed me to Queen Charlton.'

'You mean you told him so,' said Pen bitterly.

'Yes, I did. At least, he asked me, and I said yes before I had had time to think.'

'Really, you are the most brainless creature! Do you *never* think?' said Pen, quite exasperated. 'Just look what a coil you've created! Either your Papa is coming to ask me what my intentions are, or – which I think a great deal more likely – to complain to Richard about my conduct! Oh dear, whatever will Richard say to this fresh disturbance?'

It was plain that all this meant nothing to Miss Daubenay. For form's sake, she repeated that she was very sorry, but added: 'I hoped you would be able to help me. But you are a boy! You don't understand what it means to be persecuted as I am!'

This remark could not but strike a chord of sympathy. 'As a matter of fact, I do know,' said Pen. 'Only, if helping you means offering for your hand, I won't do it. The more I think of it, the more ridiculous it seems to me that you should have dragged me into it. How could such an absurd tale possibly be of use?'

Lydia sighed. 'One does not think of those things in the heat of the moment. Besides, I didn't really mean to drag you in. It – it just happened.'

'I don't see how it could have happened if you didn't mean it.'

'One thing led to another,' Lydia explained vaguely. 'Almost before I knew it, the whole story had – had grown up. Of course I don't wish you to offer for my hand, but I do think you might pretend you want to, so that Papa shan't suspect me of telling lies.'

'No!' said Pen.

'I think you are very unkind,' whimpered Lydia. 'I shall be sent back to Bath, and Great-Aunt Augusta will spy on me, and I shall never see Piers again!'

'Who?' Pen's head was jerked round. '*Who* will you never see again?'

'Oh, please do not ask me! I did not mean to mention his name!'

'Are you –' Pen stopped, rather white of face, and started again: 'Are you betrothed to Piers Luttrell?'

'You know him!' Miss Daubenay clasped ecstatic hands.

'Yes,' said Pen, feeling as though the pit of her stomach had suddenly vanished. 'Yes, I know him.'

'Then you will help me!'

Miss Creed's clear blue eyes met Miss Daubenay's swimming brown ones. Miss Creed drew a long breath. 'Is – is Piers indeed in love with you?' she asked incredulously.

Miss Daubenay bridled. 'You need not sound so surprised! We have been plighted for a whole year! Why do you look so oddly?'

'I beg your pardon,' apologized Pen. 'But how he must have changed! It is very awkward!'

'Why?' asked Lydia, staring.

'Well, it – it – you wouldn't understand. Has he been meeting you in woods for a whole year?'

'No, because Papa sent me to Bath, and Sir Jasper forbade him to see me any more, and even Lady Luttrell said we were too young. But we love each other!'

'It seems extraordinary,' said Pen, shaking her head. 'You know, I find it very hard to believe!'

'You are the horridest boy! It is perfectly true, and if you know Piers you may ask him for yourself! I wish I had never clapped eyes on you!'

'So do I,' replied Pen frankly.

Miss Daubenay burst into tears. Pen surveyed her with interest, and asked presently in the voice of one probing mysteries: 'Do you always cry as much as this? Do you – do you cry at Piers?'

'I don't cry *at* people!' sobbed Miss Daubenay. 'And if Piers knew how horrid you have been to me he would very likely knock you down!'

Pen gave a hiccup of laughter. This incensed Lydia so much that she stopped crying, and dramatically commanded Pen to leave the orchard immediately. However, when she discovered that Pen was only too ready to take her at her word, she ran after her, and clasped her by the arm. 'No, no, you cannot go until we have decided what is to be done. You won't – oh, you *can't* be cruel enough to deny my story to Papa!'

Pen considered this. 'Well, provided you won't expect me to offer for you –'

'No, no, I promise I won't!'

Pen frowned. 'Yes, but it's of no use. There is only one thing for it: you will have to run away.'

'But –'

'Now, don't begin to talk about the scandal, and spoiling your dress!' begged Pen. 'For one thing, it is odiously missish, and for another Piers will never be able to bear it.'

'Piers,' said Miss Daubenay, with swelling bosom, 'thinks me Perfect!'

'I haven't seen Piers for a long time, but he *can't* have grown up as stupid as that!' Pen pointed out.

'Yes, he – oh, I hate you, I hate you!' cried Lydia, stamping her foot. 'Besides, how can I run away?'

'Oh, Piers will have to arrange it! If Richard doesn't object, I daresay I may help him,' Pen assured her. 'You will have to escape at dead of night, of course, which puts me in mind of a very important thing: you will need a rope-ladder.'

'I haven't a rope-ladder,' objected Lydia.

'Well, Piers must make one for you. If he throws it up to your window, you could attach it securely, could you not, and climb down it?'

'I would rather escape by the door,' said Lydia, gazing helplessly up at her.

'Oh, very well, but it seems rather tame! However, it is quite your own affair. Piers will be waiting for you with a post-chaise-and-four. You will leap up into it, and the horses will spring forward, and you will fly for the Border! I can see it all!' declared Pen, her eyes sparkling.

Lydia seemed to catch a little of her enthusiasm. 'To be sure, it does sound romantic,' she admitted. 'Only it is a great way to the Border, and everyone would be so cross with us!'

'Once you were married that wouldn't signify.'

'No. No, it wouldn't, would it? But I don't think Piers has any money.'

'Oh!' Pen's face fell. 'That certainly makes it rather awkward. But I daresay we shall contrive something.'

Lydia said: 'Well, if you don't mind, I would prefer *not* to go to Gretna, because although it would be romantic I can't help thinking it would be very uncomfortable. Besides, I couldn't have any attendants, or a wedding-dress, or a lace veil, or any-thing.'

'Don't chatter!' said Pen. 'I am thinking.'

Lydia was obediently silent.

'We must soften your father's heart!' declared Pen at length.

Lydia looked doubtful. 'Yes, I should like that of all things, but how?'

'Why, by making him grateful to Piers, of course!'

'But why should he be grateful to Piers? He says Piers is a young cub.'

'Piers,' said Pen, 'must rescue you from deadly peril.'

'Oh no, please!' faltered Lydia, shrinking. 'I should be frightened! And just think how dreadful it would be if he didn't rescue me!'

'What a little goose you are!' said Pen scornfully. 'There won't be any real danger!'

'But if there is no danger, how can Piers –'

'Piers shall rescue you from me!' said Pen.

Lydia blinked at her. 'I don't understand. How can Piers –'

'Do stop saying "How can Piers"!' Pen begged. 'We must make your father believe that I am a penniless young man without any prospects at all, and then we will run away together!'

'But I don't want to run away with you!'

'No, stupid, and I don't want to run away with you! It will just be a Plot. Piers must ride after us, and catch us, and restore you to your Papa. And he will be so pleased that he will let you marry Piers after all! Because Piers has very good prospects, you know.'

'Yes, but you are forgetting Sir Jasper,' argued Lydia.

'We can't possibly be plagued by Sir Jasper,' said Pen impatiently. 'Besides, he is away. Now, don't make any more objections! I must go back to the George, and warn Richard. And I will consult with Piers as well, and I daresay we shall have it all arranged in a trice. I will meet you in the spinney this evening, to tell you what you must do.'

'Oh no, no, no!' shuddered Lydia. 'Not the spinney! I shall never set foot there again!'

'Well, here, then, since you are so squeamish. By the way, did you tell your Papa the whole? I mean, how you saw Captain Trimble kill the stammering-man?'

'Yes, of course I did, and he says I must tell it to Mr Philips! It is so dreadful for me! To think that my troubles had put it out of my head!'

'What a tiresome girl you are!' exclaimed Pen. 'You should not have said a word about it! Ten to one, we shall get into a tangle now, because Richard has already told Mr Philips *his* story, and I have told him mine, and now you are bound to say something quite different. Did you mention Richard to your Papa?'

'No,' confessed Lydia, hanging her head. 'I just said that I ran away.'

'Oh well, in that case perhaps there will be no harm done!' said Pen optimistically. 'I am going now. I will meet you here again after dinner.'

'But what if they watch me, and I cannot slip away?' cried Lydia, trying to detain her.

Pen had climbed on to the wall, and now prepared to jump down into the road. 'You must think of something,' she said sternly, and vanished from Miss Daubenay's sight.

When Pen reached the George Sir Richard had not only finished his breakfast, but was on the point of sallying forth in search of his errant charge. She came into the parlour, flushed and rather breathless, and said impetuously: 'Oh, Richard, such an adventure! I have such a deal to tell you! All our plans must be changed!'

'This is very sudden!' said Sir Richard. 'May I ask where you have been?'

'Yes, of course,' said Pen, seating herself at the table, and spreading butter lavishly on a slice of bread. 'I have been with that stupid girl. You would not believe that anyone could be so silly, sir!'

'I expect I should. What has she been doing, and why did you go to see her?'

'Well, it's a long story, and *most* confused!'

'In that case,' said Sir Richard, 'perhaps I shall unravel it more easily if you do not tell it to me with your mouth full.'

Her eyes lit with laughter. She swallowed the bread-and-butter, and said: 'Oh, I'm sorry! I am so hungry, you see.'

'Have an apple,' he suggested.

She twinkled responsively. 'No, thank you, I will have some of that ham. Dear sir, what in the world do you suppose that wretched girl did?'

'I have no idea,' said Sir Richard, carving several slices of the ham.

'Why, she told her Papa that she had gone into the spinney last night to meet *me*!'

Sir Richard laid down the knife and fork. 'Good God, why?'

'Oh, for such an idiotic reason that it is not worth recounting! But the thing is, sir, that her Papa is coming to see you about it this morning. She hoped, you see, that if she said she had been in the habit of meeting me clandestinely in Bath –'

'In Bath?' interrupted Sir Richard in a faint voice.

'Yes, she said we had been meeting for ever in Bath, on account of her Great-Aunt Augusta, and not wishing to be sent there again. I quite understand *that*, but –'

'Then your understanding is very much better than mine,' said Sir Richard. 'So far I have not been privileged to understand one word of this story. What has her Great-Aunt Augusta to do with it?'

'Oh, they sent Lydia to stay with her, you see, and she did not like it! She said it was all backgammon and spying. I could not but feel for her over that, for I know exactly what she means.'

'I am glad,' said Sir Richard, with emphasis.

'The thing is, that she thought if she told her Papa that she had met me clandestinely in Bath, he would not send her there again.'

'This sounds to me remarkably like mania in an acute form.'

'Yes, so it did to me. But there is worse to come.' She says that instead of being angry, her Papa is inclined to be pleased!'

'The madness seems to be inherited.'

'That is what I thought, but it appears that Lydia told her Papa that my name was Wyndham, and now he thinks that perhaps she is on the brink of making a Good Match!'

'Good God!'

'I knew you would be surprised. And there is another circumstance too, which turns everything topsy-turvy.' She glanced up fleetingly from her plate, and said with a little difficulty: 'I discovered something which – which quite took me aback. She told me whom she went to meet in the wood last night.'

'I see,' said Sir Richard.

She flushed. 'Did you – did you know, sir?'

'I guessed, Pen.'

She nodded. 'It was stupid of me not to suspect. To tell you the truth, I thought – However, it doesn't signify. I expect you did not like to tell me.'

'Do you mind very much?' he asked abruptly.

'Well, I – it – You see, I had it fixed in my mind that Piers – and I – So I daresay it will take me just a little while to grow accustomed to it, besides having all my plans overset. But never mind that! We have now to consider what is to be done to help Piers and Lydia.'

'We?' interpolated Sir Richard.

'Yes, because I quite depend on you to persuade Lydia's Papa that I am not an eligible suitor. That is most important!'

'Do you mean to tell me that this insane person is coming here to obtain my consent to your marriage with his daughter?'

'I think he is coming to discover how much money I have, and whether my intentions are honourable,' said Pen, pouring herself out a cup of coffee. 'But I daresay Lydia mistook the whole matter, for she is amazingly stupid, you know, and perhaps he is coming to complain to you about my shocking conduct in meeting Lydia in secret.'

'I foresee a pleasing morning,' said Sir Richard dryly.

'Well, I must say I think it will be very amusing,' Pen admitted. 'Because – why, what is the matter, sir?'

Sir Richard had covered his eyes with one hand. 'You think it will be very amusing! Good God!'

'Oh, now you are laughing at me again!'

'Laughing! I am recalling my comfortable home, my ordered life, my hitherto stainless reputation, and wondering what I can ever have done to deserve being pitchforked into this shameless imbroglio! Apparently, I am to go down to history as one who not only possessed a cousin who was a monster of precocious depravity, but who actually aided and abetted him in attempting to seduce a respectable young female.'

'No, no!' said Pen earnestly. 'Nothing of the kind, I assure you! I have it all arranged in the best possible way, and *your* part will be everything of the most proper!'

'Oh, well, in *that* case – !' said Sir Richard, lowering his hand.

'Now I know you are laughing at me! I am going to be the only son of a widow.'

'The unfortunate woman has all my sympathy.'

'Yes, because I am very wild, and she can do nothing with me. That is why you are here, of course. I cannot but see that I don't look quite old enough to be an eligible suitor. Do you think I do, sir?'

'No, I don't. In fact, I should not be surprised if Lydia's parent were to arrive with a birch-rod.'

'Good gracious, how dreadful! I never thought of that! Well, I shall depend upon you.'

'You may confidently depend upon me to tell Major Daubenay that his daughter's story is a farrago of lies.'

Pen shook her head. 'No, we can't do that. I said just the same myself, but you must see how difficult it would be to persuade Major Daubenay that we are speaking the truth. Consider, sir! She told him that I had followed her here, and I must admit it looks very black, because I *was* in the spinney last night, and you know we cannot possibly explain the real story. No, we must make the best of it. Besides, I quite feel that we ought to help Piers, if he does indeed wish to marry such a foolish creature.'

'I have not the slightest desire to help Piers, who seems to me to be behaving in a most reprehensible fashion.'

'Oh no, indeed he cannot help it! I see that I had better tell you their whole story.'

Without giving Sir Richard time to protest, she launched into a rapid and colourful account of the young lovers' tribulations. The account, being freely embellished with her own comments, was considerably involved, and Sir Richard several times interrupted it to crave enlightenment on some obscure point. At the end of it, he remarked without any noticeable display of enthusiasm: 'A most affecting history. For myself, I find the theme of Montague and Capulet hopelessly outmoded, however.'

'Well, I have made up my mind to it that there is only one thing for them to do. They must elope.'

Sir Richard, who had been playing with his quizzing-glass, let it fall, and spoke with startling severity. 'Enough of this! Now, understand me, brat, I will engage to fob off the irate father, but there it must end! This extremely tedious pair of lovers may elope to-morrow for anything I care, but I will have no hand in it, and I will not permit you to have a hand in it either. Do you see?'

Pen looked speculatively at him. There was no smile visible in his eyes, which indeed looked much sterner than she had ever believed they could. Plainly, he would not lend any support to her scheme of eloping with Miss Daubenay herself. It would be better, decided Pen, to tell him nothing about this. But she was not one to let a challenge rest unanswered, and she replied with spirit: 'You may do as you choose, but you have *no* right to tell me what I must or must not do! It is not in the least your affair.'

'It is going to be very much my affair,' replied Sir Richard.

'I don't understand what you can possibly mean by saying anything so silly!'

'I daresay you don't, but you will.'

'Well, we won't dispute about that,' said Pen pacifically.

He laughed suddenly. 'Indeed, I hope we shan't!'

'And you won't tell Major Daubenay that Lydia's story was false?'

'What do you want me to tell him?' he asked, succumbing to the coaxing note in her voice, and the pleading look in her candid eyes.

'Why, that I have been with my tutor in Bath, but that I was so troublesome that my Mama –'

'The widow?'

'Yes, and *now* you will understand why she is a widow!'

'If you are supposed to favour your mythical father, I do understand. He perished on the gallows.'

'That is what Jimmy Yarde calls the Nubbing Cheat.'

'I daresay it is, but I beg you won't.'

'Oh, very well! Where was I?'

'With your tutor.'

'To be sure. Well, I was so troublesome that my Mama sent you to bring me home. I expect you are a trustee, or something of that nature. And you may say all the horridest things about me to Major Daubenay that you like. In fact, you had better tell him that I am *very* bad, besides being quite a pauper.'

'Have no fear! I will draw such a picture of you as must make him thankful that his daughter has escaped becoming betrothed to such a monster.'

'Yes, do!' said Pen cordially. 'And then I must see Piers.'

'And then?' asked Sir Richard.

She sighed. 'I haven't thought of that yet. Really, we have so much on our hands that I cannot be teased with thinking of any more plans just now!'

'Will you let me suggest a plan to you, Pen?'

'Yes, certainly, if you can think of one. But first I should like to see Piers, because I still cannot quite believe that he truly wishes to marry Lydia. Why, she does nothing but cry, Richard!'

Sir Richard looked down at her enigmatically. 'Yes,' he said. 'Perhaps it would be better if you saw Piers first. People – especially young men – change a great deal in five years, brat.'

'True,' she said, in a melancholy tone. 'But *I* didn't change!'

'I think perhaps you did,' he said gently.

She seemed unconvinced, and he did not press the point. The waiter came in to clear away the covers, and hardly had he left the parlour than Major Daubenay's card was brought to Sir Richard.

Pen, changing colour, exclaimed: 'Oh dear, now I wish I weren't here! I suppose I can't escape now, can I?'

'Hardly. You would undoubtedly walk straight into the Major's arms. But I won't let him beat you.'

'Well, I hope you won't!' said Pen fervently. 'Tell me quickly, how does a person look depraved? *Do* I look depraved?'

'Not in the least. The best you can hope for is to look sulky.'

She retired to a chair in the corner, and sprawled in it, trying to scowl. 'Like this?'

'Excellent!' approved Sir Richard.

A minute later, Major Daubenay was ushered into the parlour. He was a harassed-looking man, with a high colour, and upon finding himself confronted by the tall, immaculate figure of a Corinthian, he exclaimed: 'Good Gad! You *are* Sir Richard Wyndham!'

Pen, glowering in the corner, could only admire the perfection of Sir Richard's bow. The Major's slightly protuberant eyes discovered her. 'And *this* is the young dog who has been trifling with my daughter!'

'*Again?*' said Sir Richard wearily.

The Major's eyes started at him. 'Upon my soul, sir! Do you tell me that this – this young scoundrel is in the habit of seducing innocent females?'

'Dear me, is it as bad as that?' asked Sir Richard.

'No, sir, it is not!' fumed the Major. 'But when I tell you that my daughter has confessed that she went out last night to meet him clandestinely in a wood, and has met him many times before in Bath –'

Up came Sir Richard's quizzing-glass. 'I condole with you,' he said. 'Your daughter would appear to be a young lady of enterprise.'

'My daughter,' declared the Major, 'is a silly little miss! I do not know what young people are coming to! This young man – dear me, he looks no more than a lad! – is, I understand, a relative of yours?'

'My cousin,' said Sir Richard. 'I am – er – his mother's trustee. She is a widow.'

'I see that I have come to the proper person!' said the Major.

Sir Richard raised one languid hand. 'I beg you will acquit me of all responsibility, sir. My part is merely to remove my cousin from the care of a tutor who has proved himself wholly incapable of controlling his – er – activities, and to convey him to his mother's home.'

'But what are you doing in Queen Charlton, then?' demanded the Major.

It was plain that Sir Richard considered the question an impertinence. 'I have acquaintances in the neighbourhood, sir. I scarcely think I need trouble you with the reasons which led me to break a journey which cannot be other than – er – excessively distasteful to me. Pen, make your bow!'

'Pen?' repeated the Major, glaring at her.

'He was named after the great Quaker,' explained Sir Richard.

'Indeed! Then I would have you know, sir, that his behaviour scarcely befits his name!'

'You are perfectly right,' agreed Sir Richard. 'I regret to say that he has been a constant source of anxiety to his widowed parent.'

'He seems very young,' said the Major, scanning Pen critically.

'But, alas, old in sin!'

The Major was slightly taken aback. 'Oh, come, come, sir! I daresay it is not as bad as that! One must make allowances for young people. To be sure, it is very reprehensible, and I do not by any means exonerate my daughter from blame, but the springtime of life, you know, sir! Young people take such romantic notions into their heads – not but what I am excessively shocked to learn of clandestine meetings! But when two young persons fall in love, I believe –'

'In love!' interpolated Sir Richard, apparently thunderstruck.

'Well, well, I daresay you are surprised! One is apt to fancy the birds always too young to leave the nest, eh? But –'

'Pen!' said Sir Richard, turning awfully upon his supposed cousin. 'Is it possible that you can have made serious advances towards Miss Daubenay?'

'I never offered *marriage*,' said Pen, hanging her head.

The Major seemed to be in danger of suffering an apoplexy. Before he could recover the power of speech, Sir Richard had intervened. Upon the Major's bemused ears fell a description of Pen's shameless precocity that caused the object of it to turn away hastily to hide her laughter. According to Sir Richard's malicious tongue, Bath was strewn with her innocent victims. When Sir Richard let fall the information that this youthful moral leper was without means or expectations, the Major found enough breath to declare that the whelp ought to be horsewhipped.

'Precisely my own view,' bowed Sir Richard.

'Upon my word, I had not dreamed of such a thing! Penniless, you say?'

'Little better than a pauper,' said Sir Richard.

'Good Gad, what an escape!' gasped the Major. 'I do not know what to say! I am aghast!'

'Alas!' said Sir Richard, 'his father was just such another! The same disarming air of innocence hid a wolfish heart.'

'You appal me!' declared the Major. 'Yet he looks a mere boy!'

Pen, feeling that it was time she bore a part in the scene, said with an air of innocence which horrified the Major: 'But if Lydia says I offered marriage, it is not true. It was all mere trifling. I do not wish to be married.'

This pronouncement once more bereft the Major of speech. Sir Richard's forefinger banished Pen to her corner, and by the time the outraged parent ceased gobbling, he had once more taken charge of the situation. He agreed that the whole affair must at all costs be hushed up, promised to deal faithfully with Pen, and finally escorted the Major out of the parlour, with assurances that such depravity should not go unpunished.

Pen, who had been struggling with an overwhelming desire to laugh, went off into a peal of mirth as soon as the Major was out of earshot, and had, in fact, to grasp a chair-back to support herself. In this posture she was discovered by Mr Luttrell, who, as soon as Sir Richard and the Major had passed through the entrance-parlour, oblivious of his presence there, bounced in upon Pen, and said through shut teeth: 'So! You think it damned amusing, do you, you little cur? Well, I do *not*!'

Pen raised her head, and through brimming eyes saw the face of her old playmate swim before her.

Mr Luttrell, stuttering with rage, said menacingly: 'I heard you! I could not help but hear you! So you didn't intend marriage, eh? You – you *boast* of having t-trifled with an innocent female! And you think you c-can get off scot-free, do you? *I'll* teach you a lesson!'

Pen discovered to her horror that Mr Luttrell was advancing

upon her with his fists clenched. She dodged behind the table, and shrieked: 'Piers! Don't you *know* me? Piers, look at me! I'm *Pen*!'

Mr Luttrell dropped his fists, and stood gaping. 'Pen?' he managed to utter. '*Pen?*'

Eleven

They stood staring at one another. The gentleman found his voice first, but only to repeat in accents of still deeper amazement: '*Pen?* Pen Creed?'

'Yes, indeed I am!' Pen assured him, keeping the table between them.

His fists unclenched. 'But – but what are you doing here? And in those clothes? I don't understand!'

'Well, it's rather a long story,' Pen said.

He seemed slightly dazed. He ran his hand through his hair, in a gesture she knew well, and said: 'But Major Daubenay – Sir Richard Wyndham –'

'They are both part of the story,' replied Pen. She had been looking keenly at him, and thinking that he had not greatly changed, and she added: 'I should have known you anywhere! Have I altered so much?'

'Yes. At least, I don't know. It's your hair, I suppose, cut short like that, and – and those clothes!'

He sounded shocked, which made her think that perhaps he had changed a little. 'Well, I truly am Pen Creed,' she said.

'Yes, I see that you are, now that I have had time to look at you. But I cannot understand it! I could not help hearing some of what was said, though I tried not to – until I heard Miss Daubenay's name!'

'Please, Piers, don't fly into a rage again!' Pen said rather nervously, for she distinctly heard his teeth grind together. 'I can explain everything!'

'I do not know whether I am on my head or my heels!' he complained. 'You have been imposing on her! How could you do such a thing? *Why* did you?'

'I haven't!' said Pen. 'And I must say, I do think you might be a little more glad to see me!'

'Of course I am glad! But to come here masquerading as a boy, and playing pranks on a defenceless – *That* was why she failed last night!'

'No, it wasn't! She saw the stammering-man killed, and ran away, you stupid creature!'

'How do you know?' he asked suspiciously.

'I was there, of course.'

'With her?'

'Yes, but –'

'You *have* been imposing on her!'

'I tell you it's no such thing! I met her by the merest chance.'

'Tell me this!' commanded Piers. 'Does she know that you are a girl?'

'No, but –'

'I knew it!' he declared. 'And I distinctly heard the Major say that she had met you in Bath! I don't know why you did it, but it is the most damnable trick in the world! And Lydia – deceiving me – encouraging your advances – oh, my eyes are open now!'

'If you say another word, I shall box your ears!' said Pen indignantly. 'I would not have believed you could have grown into such a stupid, tiresome creature! I never met Lydia Daubenay in my life until last night, and if you don't believe me you may go and ask her!'

He looked rather taken aback, and said in an uncertain tone: 'But if you did not know her, how came you to be with her in the wood last night?'

'That was chance. The silly little thing swooned, and I –'

'She is not a silly little thing!' interrupted Piers, firing up.

'Yes, she is, very silly. For what must she do, upon reaching home, but tell her Papa that it was not you she had gone to meet, but me!'

This announcement surprised him. His bewildered grey eyes sought enlightenment in Pen's face; he said with a rueful grin: 'Oh Pen, do sit down and explain! You never could tell a story so that one could make head or tail of it!'

She came away from the table, and sat down on the window-seat. After a pained glance at her attire, Piers seated himself beside her. Each took critical stock of the other, but whereas Pen looked Piers frankly over, he surveyed her rather shyly, and showed a tendency to avert his gaze when it encountered hers.

He was a well-favoured young man, not precisely handsome, but with a pleasant face, a good pair of shoulders, and easy, open manners. Since he was four years her senior, he had always seemed to her, in the old days, very large, far more experienced than herself, and quite worthy of being looked up to. She was conscious, as she sat beside him on the window-seat of a faint feeling of disappointment. He seemed to her little more than a boy, and instead of assuming his old mastery in his dealings with her, he was obviously shy, and unable to think of anything to say. Their initial encounter had of course been unfortunate, but Pen thought that he might, upon discovering her identity, have exhibited more pleasure at meeting her again. She felt forlorn all at once, as though a door had been shut in her face. A vague suspicion that what was behind the shut door was not what she had imagined only made her the more melancholy. To hide it, she said brightly: 'It is such an age since I saw you, and there is so much to say! I don't know where to begin!'

He smiled, but there was a pucker between his brows. 'Yes, indeed, but it seems so strange! Why did she say she had gone out to meet you, I wonder?'

It was apparent to Pen that Miss Daubenay possessed his thoughts to the exclusion of everyone else. Repressing a strong desire to favour him with her opinion of that young lady, she recounted as briefly as she could what had passed between her and Lydia in the orchard. Any expectation she might have had of his viewing his betrothed's conduct in the same light as she did was banished by his exclaiming rapturously: 'She is such an innocent little thing! It is just like her to have said that! I see it all now!'

This was too much for Pen. 'Well, I think it was a ridiculous thing to have said.'

'You see, she knows nothing of the world, Pen,' he said earnestly. 'Then, too, she is impulsive! Do you know, she always makes me think of a bird?'

'A goose, I suppose,' said Pen somewhat tartly.

'I meant a wild bird,' he replied, with dignity. 'A fluttering, timid, little –'

'She didn't seem to me very timid,' Pen interrupted. 'In fact, I thought she was extremely bold to ask a perfectly strange young man to pretend to be in love with her.'

'You don't understand her. She is so trusting! She needs someone to take care of her. We have loved one another ever since our first meeting. We should have been married by now if my father had not picked a foolish quarrel with the Major. Pen, you cannot think what our sufferings have been! There seems to be no end to them! We shall never induce our fathers to consent to our marriage, never!'

He sank his head in his hands with a groan, but Pen said briskly: 'Well, you will have to marry without their consent. Only you both of you seem to be so poor-spirited that you will do nothing but moan, and meet in woods! Why don't you elope?'

'Elope! You don't know what you are saying, Pen! How could I ask that fragile little thing to do anything of the sort? The impropriety, too! I am persuaded she would shrink from the very thought of it!'

'Yes, she did,' agreed Pen. 'She said she would not be able to have attendants, or a lace veil.'

'You see, she has been very strictly reared – has led the most sheltered life! Besides, why should she not have a lace veil, and – and those things which females set store by?'

'For my part,' Pen said, 'I would not care a fig for such fripperies if I loved a man!'

'Oh, you are different!' said Piers. 'You were always more like a boy than a girl. Just look at you now! *Why* are you masquerading as a boy? It seems to me most peculiar, and not quite the thing, you know.'

'There were circumstances which – which made it necessary,' said Pen rather stiffly. 'I had to escape from my aunt's house.'

'Well, I still don't see why –'

'Because I was forced to climb out of a window!' snapped Pen. 'Moreover, I could not travel all by myself as a female, could I?'

'No, I suppose you could not. Only you should not be travelling by yourself at all. What a madcap you are!' A thought occurred to him; he glanced down at Pen with a sudden frown. 'But you were with Sir Richard Wyndham when I came in, and you seemed to be on mighty close terms with him, too! For heaven's sake, Pen, what are you about? How do you come to be in his company?'

The interview with her old playmate seemed to be fraught not only with disappointment, but with unforeseen difficulties as well. Pen could not but realize that Mr Luttrell was not in sympathy with her. 'Oh, that – that is too long a story to tell!' she replied evasively. 'There were reasons why I wished to come home again, and – and Sir Richard would not permit me to go alone.'

'But, Pen!' He sounded horrified. 'You are surely not travelling with him?'

His tone swept away adventure, and invested her exploit instead with the stigma of impropriety. She coloured hotly, and was searching her mind for an explanation that would satisfy Piers when the door opened, and Sir Richard came into the room.

One glance at Mr Luttrell's rigidly disapproving countenance; one glimpse of Pen's scarlet cheeks and over-bright eyes, were enough to give Sir Richard a very fair notion of what had been taking place in the parlour. He closed the door, saying in his pleasant drawl: 'Ah, good-morning, Mr Luttrell! I trust the – er – surprising events of last night did not rob you of sleep?'

A sigh of relief escaped Pen. With Sir Richard's entrance the reeling world seemed, miraculously, to have righted itself. She left the window-seat, and went instinctively towards him. 'Sir, Piers says – Piers thinks –' She stopped, and raised a hand to her burning cheek.

Sir Richard looked at Piers with slightly raised brows. 'Well?' he said gently. 'What does Piers say and think?'

Mr Luttrell got up. Under that ironical, tolerant gaze, he too began to blush. 'I only said – I only wondered how Pen comes to be travelling in your company!'

Sir Richard unfobbed his snuff-box, and took a pinch. 'And does no explanation offer itself to you?' he enquired.

'Well, sir, I must say it seems to me – I mean –'

'Perhaps I should have told you,' said Sir Richard drawing Pen's hand through his arm, and holding it rather firmly, 'that you are addressing the future Lady Wyndham.'

The hand twitched in Sir Richard's, but in obedience to the warning pressure of his fingers Miss Creed remained silent.

'Oh, I see!' said Piers, his brow clearing. 'I beg pardon! It is famous news indeed! I wish you very happy! But – but why must she wear those clothes, and what are you doing here? It still seems very odd to me! I suppose since you are betrothed it may be argued that – But it is most eccentric, sir, and I do not know what people may say!'

'As we have been at considerable pains to admit no one but yourself into the secret of Pen's identity, I hardly think that people will say anything at all,' replied Sir Richard calmly. 'If the secret were to leak out – why, the answer is that we are a very eccentric couple!'

'It will never leak out through me!' Piers assured him. 'It is no concern of mine, naturally, but I can't help wondering what should have brought you here, and why Pen had to get out of a window. However, I don't mean to be inquisitive, sir. It was only that – having known Pen all my life, you see!'

It was Miss Creed's turn now to give Sir Richard's hand a warning pinch. In fact, so convulsive was her grip that he glanced down at her with a reassuring little smile.

'I am afraid I cannot tell you our reasons for coming here,' he said. 'Certain circumstances arose which made the journey necessary. Pen's attire, however, is easily explained. Neither of us wished to burden ourselves with a duenna upon a mission of – er – extreme delicacy; and the world, my dear Luttrell, being a censorious place, it was judged expedient for Pen to pretend to be, instead of my affianced wife, my young cousin.'

'To be sure, yes! of course!' said Piers, mystified, but overborne by the Corinthian's air of assurance.

'By now,' said Sir Richard, 'we should be on our way back to London, had it not been for two unfortunate circumstances. For one of these, you, I must regretfully point out to you, are responsible.'

'I?' gasped Piers.

'You,' said Sir Richard, releasing Pen's hand. 'The lady to whom you, I apprehend, are secretly betrothed, has, in a somewhat misguided attempt to avert suspicion from the truth informed her parent that Pen is the man with whom she had an assignation in the spinney last night.'

'Yes, Pen told me that. Indeed, I wish she had not done it, sir, but she is so impulsive, you know!'

'So I have been led to infer,' said Sir Richard. 'Unhappily, since I am for the present compelled to remain in Queen Charlton, her impulsiveness has rendered our situation a trifle awkward.'

'Yes, I see that,' owned Piers. 'I am very sorry for it, sir. But must you remain here?'

'Yes,' replied Sir Richard. 'No doubt it has escaped your memory, but a murder was committed in the spinney last night. It was I who discovered Brandon's body, and conveyed the news to the proper quarter.'

Piers looked troubled at this, and said: 'I know, sir, and I do not like it above half! For, in point of fact, *I* first found Beverley, only you told me not to say so!'

'I hope you did not?'

'No, because it is so excessively awkward, on account of Miss

Daubenay's presence in the spinney! But if she has said that she went there to meet Pen –'

'You had better continue to preserve a discreet silence, my dear boy. The knowledge that you also were in the spinney would merely confuse poor Mr Philips. You see, I have the advantage of knowing who killed Brandon.'

'I think,' said Pen judicially, 'we ought to tell Piers about the diamond necklace, sir.'

'By all means,' agreed Sir Richard.

The history of the diamond necklace, as recounted by Miss Creed, made Mr Luttrell forget for a few moments his graver preoccupations. He seemed very much more the Piers of her childhood when he exclaimed: 'What an adventure!' and by the time he had described to her his surprise at receiving a visit from Beverley, whom he had known but slightly up at Oxford; and had exchanged impressions of Captain Horace Trimble, they were once more upon very good terms. Sir Richard, who thought that his own interests would best be served by allowing Pen uninterrupted intercourse with Mr Luttrell, soon left them to themselves; and after Piers had once more felicitated Pen on her choice of a husband – felicitations which she received in embarrassed silence – the talk soon returned to his own difficulties.

She listened to his enraptured description of Miss Daubenay with as much patience as she could muster, but when he begged her not to divulge her sex to the lady for fear lest her nice sense of propriety might suffer too great a shock, she was so much incensed that she was betrayed into giving him her opinion of Miss Daubenay's morals and manners. A pretty squabble at once flared up, and might have ended in Piers' stalking out of Pen's life for ever had she not remembered, just as he reached the door, that she had engaged herself to further his pretensions to Lydia's hand.

It took a few moments' coaxing to persuade him to relax his air of outraged dignity, but when it was borne in upon him that Lydia had summoned Pen to her side that morning, he did seem to feel that such forward conduct called for an explanation. Pen waved his excuses aside, however. 'I don't mind that, if only she would not cry so much!' she said.

Mr Luttrell said that his Lydia was all sensibility, and deprecated, with obvious sincerity, a suggestion that a wife suffering from an excess of sensibility might prove to be a tiresome acquisition. As he seemed to feel that the support of Lydia was his life's work, Pen abandoned all thought of trying to wean him from his attachment to the lady, and announced her plans for his speedy marriage.

These palpably took Mr Luttrell aback. Lydia's refusal to elope with him he regarded as natural rather than craven, and when Pen's false-abduction scheme was enthusiastically described to him he said that she must be mad to think of such a thing.

'I declare I have a good mind to wash my hands of the whole affair!' said Pen. 'Neither of you has the courage to make the least push in the matter! The end of it will be that your precious Lydia will be married to someone else, and then you will be sorry!'

'Oh, don't suggest such a thing!' he begged. 'If only my father would be a little conciliating! He used to like the Major well enough before they quarrelled.'

'You must soften the Major's heart.'

'Yes, but how?' he asked. 'Now, don't, pray, suggest any more foolish abduction schemes, Pen! I daresay you think them very fine, but if you would but consider the difficulties! No one would ever believe we had not planned it all, because if she eloped with you she would not then wish to marry me, now, would she?'

'No, but we could say that I had forcibly abducted her. Then you could rescue her from me.'

'How should I know that you had abducted her?' objected Piers. 'And just think what a pucker everyone would be in! No, really, Pen, it won't answer! Good God, I should have to fight a duel with you, or something of that nature! I mean, how odd it would look if all I did was to take Lydia home!'

'Well, so we could!' said Pen, her eyes brightening, as new horizons swam into her ken. 'I could have my arm in a sling, and say that you had wounded me! Oh, do let us, Piers! It would be such a famous adventure!'

'You don't seem to me to have changed in the least!' said Piers, in anything but a complimentary tone. 'You are the most complete hand indeed! I cannot conceive how you came to be betrothed to a man of fashion like Wyndham! You know, you will have to mend your ways! In fact, I cannot conceive of your being married at all! You are a mere child.'

Another quarrel might at this point have sprung up between them, had not Sir Richard come back into the room just then, with Mr Philips in his wake. He was looking faintly amused, and the instant expression of extreme trepidation which transformed the countenances of the youthful couple by the window made his lips twitch involuntarily. However, he spoke without a tremor in his voice. 'Ah, Pen! Would you explain, if you please, your – er – owl story, to Mr Philips?'

'Oh!' said Pen, blushing furiously.

The magistrate looked severely across at her. 'From the information I have since received, young man, I am forced to the conclusion that your story was false.'

Pen glanced towards Sir Richard. Instead of coming to her rescue, he smiled maliciously, and said: 'Stand up, my boy, stand up, when Mr Philips addresses you!'

'Oh yes, of course!' said Pen, rising in a hurry. 'I beg pardon! My owl-story! Well, you see, I did not know what to say when you asked why I had not been with my cousin last night.'

'Did not know what to say! You had only one thing to say, and that was the truth!' said Mr Philips austerely.

'I could not,' replied Pen. 'A lady's reputation was at stake!'

'So I am informed. Well, I do not say that I do not sympathize with your motive, but I must warn you, sir, that any further prevarication on your part may lead to serious trouble. Serious trouble! I say nothing of your conduct in meeting Miss Daubenay in a manner I can only describe as clandestine. It is no

174

concern of mine, no concern at all, but if you were a son of mine – However, that is neither here nor there! Fortunately –' He cast a reproachful glance at Sir Richard – 'fortunately, I repeat, Miss Daubenay's evidence corroborates the information that this shocking crime was perpetrated by a person corresponding with the description furnished me of the man Trimble. Were it not for this circumstance – for I will not conceal from you that I am far from being satisfied! Very far indeed! You must permit me to say, Sir Richard, that your presence in the spinney last night points to your having positively aided and abetted your cousin in his reprehensible – But I am aware that *that* is Major Daubenay's concern!'

'No, no, you have it wrong!' Pen assured him. 'My cousin was searching for me! In fact, he was very angry with me for going to the spinney, were you not, Richard?'

'I was,' admitted Sir Richard. 'Very.'

'Well, the whole affair seems to me very strange!' said Philips. 'I will say no more than that *yet*!'

'You behold me – er – stricken with remorse,' said Sir Richard.

The magistrate snorted, jerked a bow, and took himself off.

'My reputation! oh, my reputation!' mourned Sir Richard. 'Horrible and unprincipled brat, *why* the owl?'

'Well, I had to say something!' Pen pointed out.

'I am afraid,' said Piers, conscience-stricken, 'that it is a *little* Lydia's fault. But indeed, sir, she meant no harm!'

'I know,' said Sir Richard. 'She is so impulsive! I feel a hundred years old.'

He went out on the words, and Pen at once rounded on Mr Luttrell, saying in accusing accents: 'There! You see now what your precious Lydia has done!'

'She is no worse than you are! In fact, not as bad!' retorted Piers. '*She* would not masquerade about the country as a boy! I do not wonder at Sir Richard's feeling a hundred years old. If I were betrothed to you, I should feel the same!'

Miss Creed's eyes flashed. 'Well, I will tell you something,

Piers Luttrell! I have got a cousin with a face like a fish, and *he* wants to marry me, which is why I escaped out a window. *But* – do you hear me? – I would a great deal rather marry him than you. If I had to marry you, I would drown myself! You are stupid, and rude, and spiritless!'

'Merely because I have a little common sense,' began Piers, very stiff, and rather flushed.

He was interrupted. A waiter came in with the news that a Young Person desired instant speech with Mr Wyndham.

Correctly divining this mythical being to be herself, Pen said: 'What can that nonsensical girl want now? I wish I had never come to Queen Charlton! Oh, very well! Show the young person in!'

'Good God, can it be Lydia?' exclaimed Piers, when the waiter had withdrawn.

The young person was not Miss Daubenay, but her personal maid, a rosy damsel, who appeared to be strongly imbued with her mistress's romantic ideals. She came in heavily veiled, and presented Pen with a sealed letter. While Pen tore it open, and read its agitated message, Piers besieged the girl with urgent questions, to which, however, she only replied with evasive answers, punctuated by giggles.

'Good gracious!' exclaimed Pen, deciphering Miss Daubenay's scrawl. 'Matters are now desperate! She says she will elope with you.'

'What?' Piers abandoned the servant, and strode to Pen's side. 'Here, give it to me!'

Pen warded him off. 'She says they are going to send her to the Wilds of Lincolnshire.'

'Yes, yes, that is where her grandmother lives! When does she go?'

'I can't read it – oh yes, I see! To-morrow morning, with her Papa. She says I am to tell you to arrange for the elopement this evening, without fail.'

'Good God!' Piers snatched the letter from her, and read it for himself. 'Yes, you are right: she does say tomorrow morning!

Pen, if she goes, it will be the end of everything! I never meant to do anything so improper as to elope with her, but I have now no choice! It is not as though her parents disapprove of me, or – or that I am not eligible. If *that* were so, it would be different. But until they quarrelled – however, talking is to no purpose!' He turned to the maidservant, who had by this time put back her veil, and was listening to him with her mouth open. 'Are you in your mistress's confidence?' he demanded.

'Oh yes, sir!' she assured him, adding with another giggle: 'Though the master would tear me limb from limb if he knew I was taking letters to you, sir.'

Piers ignored this somewhat exaggerated statement. 'Tell me, is your mistress indeed resolved upon this course?'

'Oh!' said the damsel, clasping her plump hands together, 'she was never more resolved in her life, sir! "I must Fly!" she says to me, clean distracted. "Lucy," she says, "I am Utterly Undone, for All is Discovered!" So I popped on my bonnet, sir, and slipped out when Cook's back was turned, "for," says my poor young mistress, with tears standing in her eyes fit to break anyone's heart, "if I am whisked off to Lincolnshire, I shall die!" And so she will sir, no question!'

Pen sat down again, hugging her knees. 'Nothing could be better!' she declared. 'I always liked the notion of your eloping to Gretna Green. In fact, it was my suggestion. Only, Lydia told me that you have no money, Piers. Shall we make Richard pay for the post-chaise?'

'Certainly not!' he replied. 'Of course I have enough money for *that*!'

'I think you ought to have four horses,' she warned him. 'Posting charges are very high, you know.'

'Good God, Pen, I'm not penniless! Lydia meant only that I am dependent upon my father. If he refuses to forgive us, I shall be obliged to find some genteel occupation, but I am persuaded that once the deed is done he will very soon come round. Oh, Pen! is she not an angel? I am quite overcome! Is it not affecting that she should trust me so implicitly?'

177

Pen opened her eyes at this. 'Why shouldn't she?' she asked, surprised.

'Why shouldn't she? Really, Pen, you don't understand in the least! Think of her placing her life, honour, all, in my care!'

'I don't see anything wonderful in that,' replied Pen contemptuously. 'I think it would be a great deal more extraordinary if she didn't trust you.'

'I remember now that you never had much sensibility,' said Piers. 'You are such a child!' He turned again to the interested abigail. 'Now, Lucy, attend to me! You must take a letter back to your mistress, and assure her besides that I shall not fail. Are you prepared to accompany us to Scotland?'

She gaped at him for a moment, but however strange the idea might have been to her it apparently pleased her, for she nodded vehemently, and said: 'Oh yes, sir, thank you, sir!'

'Who ever heard of taking a maid on an elopement?' demanded Pen.

'I will not ask Lydia to fly with me without some female to go with her!' declared Piers nobly.

'Dear me, I should think she would wish the girl at Jericho!'

'Lydia is quite unused to waiting upon herself,' said Piers. 'Moreover, the presence of her maid must lend respectability to our flight.'

'Has she a little lap-dog she would like to take with her too?' asked Pen innocently.

Piers cast her a quelling look, and stalked across the room to a small writing-table near the window. After testing the pen that lay on it, mending it, and dipping it in the standish, he then sat while the ink dried on it, frowning over what he should write to his betrothed. Finally, he dipped the pen in the standish once more, and began to write, punctuating his labour with reminders to Lucy to see that her mistress had a warm cloak, and did not bring too many bandboxes with her.

'Or the parrot,' interpolated Pen.

'Lor', sir, Miss Lydia hasn't got any parrot!'

'If you don't hold your tongue, Pen –'

'No little lap-dog either?' Pen asked incredulously.

'No, sir, 'deed, no! There's only her love-birds, the pretty things, and her doves!'

'Well, you will not have room in the chaise for a dove-cot, but you should certainly bring the love-birds,' said Pen, with an irrepressible chuckle.

Piers flung down his pen. 'Another word from you, and I'll put you out of the room!'

'No, you won't, because this is a private parlour, and you are nothing but a guest in it.'

'But will I tell Miss to bring the love-birds?' asked Lucy, puzzled.

'No!' said Piers. 'Oh, do stop, Pen! You are driving me distracted! Listen, I have told Lydia that I will have a chaise waiting in the lane behind the house at midnight. Do you think that is too early? Will her parents go to her room as late as that?'

'No, sir, that they won't!' said Lucy. 'The Major does be such a one for retiring early! He'll be in bed and asleep by eleven, take my word for it, sir!'

'Fortunately, it is moonlight,' Piers said, shaking sand over his letter. 'Listen, Lucy! I depend upon you to see that your mistress goes early to bed; she must get what sleep she can! And you must wake her at the proper time, do you understand? Can I trust you to pack for her, and to bring her safely to me?'

'Oh, yes, sir!' replied Lucy, bobbing a curtsey. 'For I wouldn't be left to face the Major, not for ever so!'

'You had best go back to the house with all possible speed,' Piers said, applying a wafer to the folded letter, and handing it to her. 'Mind, now! that letter must not fall into the wrong hands!'

'If anyone tries to take it from you, you must swallow it,' put in Pen.

'Swallow it, sir?'

'Pay no heed to my friend!' said Piers hastily. 'There! Be off with you, and remember that I depend upon your fidelity!'

Lucy curtseyed herself out of the room. Piers looked at Pen, still hugging her knees on the window-seat, and said severely: 'I suppose you flatter yourself you have been helpful!'

Impish lights danced in her eyes. 'Oh, I have! Only think if you had had to turn back to fetch the love-birds, which very likely you would have had to do if I had not reminded the abigail about them!'

He could not help grinning. 'Pen, if she does bring them, I'll – I'll turn back just to wring your neck! Now I must go to arrange for the hire of a chaise, and four fast horses.'

'Where will you find them?' she asked.

'There is a posting-house at Keynsham where they keep very tolerable cattle. I shall drive over there immediately.'

'Famous! Go where you are known, and let the news of your wanting a chaise for midnight spread all over the countryside within three hours!'

He checked. 'I had not thought of that! The devil! This means I must go into Bristol, and I can ill spare the time, with so much to attend to.'

'Nothing of the sort!' said Pen, jumping up. 'Now I will be helpful indeed! I will drive to Keynsham with you, and *I* will order the chaise.'

His brow cleared. 'Oh Pen, will you? But Sir Richard! Will he not object, do you think? Of course, I would take every care of you, but –'

'No, no, he will not object, I assure you! I shall not tell him anything about it,' said Pen ingenuously.

'But that would not be right! And I should not wish to do anything –'

'I will leave a message for him with the landlord,' promised Pen. 'Did you walk into the village, or have you a carriage here?'

'Oh, I drove in! The gig is in the yard now. I confess, if you feel it would not be wrong of you to go with me, I should be glad of your help.'

'Only wait while I get my hat!' Pen said, and darted off in search of it.

Twelve

*M*iss Creed and Mr Luttrell, partaking of midday refreshment in Keynsham's best inn, and exhaustively discussing the details of the elopement, were neither of them troubled by doubts of the wisdom of the gentleman's whisking his betrothed off to Scotland at a moment when that lady had become entangled in a case of murder. Indeed, Mr Luttrell, a single-minded young man, was in a fair way to forgetting that he had ever had Beverley Brandon to stay with him. He had left his mother trying to write a suitable letter to Lady Saar, and if he thought about the unfortunate affair at all it was to reflect comfortably that Lady Luttrell would do everything that was proper. His conversation was confined almost exclusively to his own immediate problems, but he digressed several times animadvert on Pen's unconventional exploits.

'Of course,' he conceded, 'it is not so shocking now that you are betrothed to Wyndham, but I own it does surprise me that he – a man of the world! – should have countenanced such a prank. But these Corinthians delight in oddities, I believe! I daresay no one will wonder at it very much. If you were not betrothed it would be different, naturally!'

Pen's clear gaze met his steadily. 'I think you make a great bustle about nothing,' she said.

'My dear Pen!' He gave a little laugh. 'You are such a child! I believe you haven't the smallest notion of the ways of the world!'

She was obliged to admit that this was true. It occurred to her that since Piers seemed to be well-informed on this subject she might with advantage learn a little from him. 'If I were not going to marry Richard, would it be very dreadful?' she asked.

'Pen! What things you do say!' he exclaimed. 'Only think of your situation, travelling all the way from London in Wyndham's company, without even your maid to go with you! Why, you *must* marry him now!'

She tilted her chin. 'I don't see that I must at all.'

'Depend upon it, if you do not, he does. I must say, I think it excessively strange that a man of his years and – and *milieu* – should have wished to marry you, Pen.' He realized his speech was scarcely complimentary, and hastened to add: 'I don't mean *that* precisely, only you are so much younger than he is, and such a little innocent!'

She pounced on this. 'Well, that is one very good reason why I need not marry him!' she said. 'He is so much older than I am that I daresay no one would think it in the smallest degree odd that we should have taken this journey together.'

'Good Gad, Pen, he is not as old as that! What a strange girl you are! Don't you wish to marry him?'

She stared at him with puckered brows. She thought of Sir Richard, of the adventures she had encountered in his company, and of the laughter in his eyes, and of the teasing note in his voice. Suddenly she flushed rosily, and the tears started to her own eyes. 'Yes. Oh, yes, I do!' she said.

'Well! But what is there to cry over?' demanded Piers. 'For a moment I quite thought – Now, don't be silly, Pen!'

She blew her nose defiantly, and said in somewhat watery accents: 'I'm not crying!'

'Indeed, I can't conceive why you should. I think Wyndham a very good sort of man – a famous fellow! I suppose you will become very fashionable, Pen, and cut the deuce of a dash in town!'

Pen, who could see no future beyond a life spent within the walls of her aunt's respectable house, agreed to this, and made haste to direct the conversation into less painful channels.

Although Keynsham was situated only a few miles distant from Queen Charlton, it was close on the dinner-hour when Piers set Pen down at the George Inn again. By this time, a post-chaise had been hired, and four good horses chosen to draw it, the whole being appointed to arrive at a rendezvous outside the gates of Crome Hall at half-past eleven that evening. Beyond a certain degree of anxiety concerning the extent of the baggage his betrothed would wish to bring with her, and some fears that her flight might be intercepted at the outset, Mr Luttrell had nothing further to worry about, as his guide and mentor frequently assured him.

Pen would have liked to have been present at the fatal hour, but this offer Piers declined. They bade each other farewell, therefore, at the door of the George Inn, neither suffering the smallest pang at the notion that each was about to be joined in wedlock to another.

Having waved a last good-bye to her old playmate, Pen went into the inn, and was met by Sir Richard, who looked her up and down, and said: 'Abominable brat, you had better make a clean breast of the whole! Where have you been, and what mischief have you done?'

'Oh, but I left a message for you!' Pen protested. 'Did they not give it to you, sir?'

'They did. But the intelligence that you had gone off with young Luttrell merely filled me with misgiving. Confess!'

She twinkled up at him. 'Well, perhaps you will not be *quite* pleased, but indeed I did it all for the best, Richard!'

'This becomes more and more ominous. I am persuaded you have committed some devilry.'

She passed into the parlour, and went to the mirror above the fireplace to pat her crisp, dishevelled curls into order. 'Not *devilry*, precisely,' she demurred.

Sir Richard who had been observing her in some amusement, said: 'I am relieved. Yes, I think the sooner you put on your petticoats again the better, Pen. That is a very feminine trick, let me tell you.'

She coloured, laughed, and turned away from the mirror. 'I forgot. Well, it doesn't signify, after all, for it seems to me that I have reached the end of my adventure.'

'Not quite,' he replied.

'Yes, I have. You do not know!'

'You look extremely wicked. Out with it!'

'Piers and Lydia are going to elope to-night!'

The laugh died out of his eyes. 'Pen, is this your doing?'

'Oh no, indeed it is not, sir! In fact, I had quite a different plan, only I dared not tell you, and, as a matter of fact, Piers did not think well of it. I wanted to abduct Lydia, so that Piers could rescue her from me, and so soften her Papa's heart. However, I daresay you would not have approved of that.'

'I should not,' said Sir Richard emphatically.

'No, that's why I said nothing to you about it. In the end Lydia decided to elope.'

'You mean that you bullied the wretched girl –'

'I did not! You are most unjust, sir! On my honour, I did not! I don't say that I didn't perhaps put the notion into her head, but it was all the Major's doing. He threatened to take her to Lincolnshire to-morrow morning and of course she could not support life there! Oh, here comes the waiter! I will tell you the whole story presently.'

She retired to her favourite seat in the window while the covers were laid, and Sir Richard, standing with his back to the mighty fireplace, watched her. The waiter took his time over the preparations for dinner, and during one of his brief absences from the parlour, Pen said abruptly: 'You were quite right: he has changed, sir. Only you were wrong about one thing: he does not think I have changed at all.'

'I did not suspect him to be capable of paying you so pretty a compliment,' said Sir Richard, raising his brows.

'Well, I don't think he meant it to be a compliment,' said Pen doubtfully.

He smiled but said nothing. The waiter came back into the room with a laden tray, and began to set various dishes on the table. When he had withdrawn, Sir Richard pulled a chair out for Pen, and said: 'You are served, brat. Hungry?'

'Not very,' she replied, sitting down.

He moved to his own place. 'Why, how is this?'

'Well, I don't know. Piers is going to elope with Lydia at midnight.'

'I trust that circumstance has not taken away your appetite?'

'Oh no! I think they will deal famously together, for they are both very silly.'

'True. What had you to do with their elopement?'

'Oh, very little, I assure you, sir! Lydia made up her mind to do it without any urging from me. All I did was to hire the post-chaise for Piers, on account of his being well-known in Keynsham.'

'I suppose that means that we shall be obliged to sustain another visit from Major Daubenay. I seem to be plunging deeper and deeper into a life of crime.'

She looked up enquiringly. 'Why, sir? You have done nothing!'

'I am aware. But I undoubtedly should do something.'

'Oh no, it is all arranged! There is truly nothing left to do.'

'You don't think that I – as one having reached years of discretion – might perhaps be expected to nip this shocking affair in the bud?'

'Tell the Major, do you mean?' Pen cried. 'Oh, Richard, you would not do such a cruel thing? I am persuaded you could not!'

He refilled his glass. 'I could, very easily, but I won't. I am not, to tell you the truth, much interested in the affairs of a pair of lovers whom I have found, from the outset, extremely tiresome. Shall we discuss instead our own affairs?'

'Yes, I think we ought to,' she agreed. 'I have been so busy to-day I had almost forgot the stammering-man. I do trust, Richard, we shall not be arrested!'

'Indeed, so do I!' he said, laughing.

'It's very well to laugh, but I could see that Mr Philips did not like us at all.'

'I fear that your activities disarranged his mind. Fortunately, news has reached him that a man whom I suspect of being none other than the egregious Captain Trimble has been taken up by the authorities in Bath.'

'Good gracious, I never thought he would be caught! Pray, had he the necklace?'

'That, I am as yet unable to tell you. It is to be hoped that Luttrell and his bride will not prolong their honeymoon, since I fancy Lydia will be wanted to identify the prisoner.'

'If she knew that, I dare say she would never come back at all,' said Pen.

'A public-spirited female,' commented Sir Richard.

She giggled. 'She has no spirit at all. I *told* you so, sir! Will the – the authorities wish to see me?'

'I hardly think so. In any event, they are not going to see you.'

'No, I must say I feel it might be excessively awkward if I were forced to appear,' remarked Pen. 'In fact, sir, I think – I think I had better go home, don't you?'

He looked at her. 'To your Aunt Almeria, brat?'

'Yes, of course. There is nowhere else for me to go.'

'And Cousin Fred?'

'Well, I hope that after all the adventures I have gone through he will not want to marry me any more,' said Pen optimistically. 'He is very easily shocked, you know.'

'Such a man would not be at all the husband for you,' he said, shaking his head. 'You must undoubtedly choose some one who is not at all easily shocked.'

'Perhaps I had better mend my ways,' said Pen, with a swift unhappy smile.

'That would be a pity, for your ways are delightful. I have a better plan than yours, Pen.'

She got up quickly from the table. 'No, no! Please no, sir!' she said in a choking voice.

He too rose, and held out his hand. 'Why do you say that? I want you to marry me, Pen.'

'Oh Richard, I wish you would not!' she begged, retreating to the window. 'Indeed, I don't want you to offer for me. It is extremely obliging of you, but I could not!'

'Obliging of me! What nonsense is this?'

'Yes, yes, I know why you have said it!' she said distressfully. 'You feel that you have compromised me, but indeed you haven't, for no one will ever know the truth!'

'I detect the fell hand of Mr Luttrell,' said Sir Richard rather grimly. 'What pernicious rubbish has he been putting into your head, my little one?'

This term of endearment made Pen wink away a sudden tear. 'Oh no! Only I was stupid not to think of it before. Really, I have no more sense than Lydia! But you are so much older than I am that it truly did not occur to me – until Piers came, and that you told him, to save my face, that we were betrothed! *Then* I saw what a little fool I had been! But it does not signify, sir, for Piers will never breathe a word, even to Lydia, and Aunt Almeria need not know that I have been with you all the time.'

'Pen, will you stop talking nonsense? I am not in the least chivalrous, my dear: you may ask my sister, and she will tell you that I am the most selfish creature alive. I never do anything to please anyone but myself.'

'That I know to be untrue!' Pen said. 'If your sister thinks it, she doesn't know you. And I am not talking nonsense. Piers was shocked to find me with you, and you *did* think he had reason, or you would not have said what you did.'

'Oh yes!' he responded. 'I am well aware of what the world would think of this escapade, but, believe me, my little love, I don't offer marriage from motives of chivalry. To be plain with you, I started on this adventure because I was drunk, and because I was bored, and because I thought I had to do something which was distasteful to me. I stayed in it because I found myself enjoying it as I have not enjoyed anything for years.'

'You did not enjoy the stagecoach,' she reminded him.

'No, but we need not make a practice of travelling by the stagecoach, need we?' he said, smiling down at her. 'Briefly, Pen, when I met you I was about to contract a marriage of convenience. Within twelve hours of making your acquaintance, I knew that no matter what might happen, I would not contract *that* marriage. Within twenty-four hours, my dear, I knew that I had found what I had come to believe did not exist.'

'What was that?' she asked shyly.

His smile was a little twisted. 'A woman – no, a chit of a girl! An impertinent, atrocious, audacious brat – whom I am very sure I cannot live without.'

'Oh!' said Pen, blushing furiously. 'How *kind* of you to say that to me! I know just why you do, and indeed I am very grateful to you for putting it so prettily!'

'And you don't believe a word of it!'

'No, for I am very sure you would not have thought of marrying me if Piers had not been in love with Lydia Daubenay,' she said simply. 'You are sorry for me, because of that, and so –'

'Not in the least.'

'I think you are a little, Richard. And I quite see that to a person like you – for it is no use to pretend to me that you are selfish, because I know that you are nothing of the sort – to a person like you, it must seem that you are bound in honour to marry me. Now, confess! That is true, is it not? Don't – *please* don't tell me polite lies!'

'Very well,' he replied. 'It is true that having embroiled you in this situation I ought in honour to offer you the protection of my name. But I am offering you my heart, Pen.'

She searched feverishly for her handkerchief, and mopped her brimming eyes with it. 'Oh, I *do* thank you!' she said in a muffled voice. 'You have such beautiful manners, sir!'

'Pen, you impossible child!' he exclaimed. 'I am trying to tell you that I love you, and all you will say is that I have beautiful manners!'

'You cannot fall in love with a person in three days!' she objected.

He had taken a step towards her, but he checked himself at that. 'I see.'

She gave her eyes a final wipe, and said apologetically: 'I beg your pardon! I didn't mean to cry, only I think I am a little tired, besides having had a shock, on account of Piers, you know.'

Sir Richard, who had been intimately acquainted with many women, thought that he did know. 'I was afraid of that,' he said. 'Did you care so much, Pen?'

'No, but I thought I did, and it is all very lowering, if you understand what I mean, sir.'

'I suppose I do. I am too old for you, am I not?'

'I am too young for you,' said Pen unsteadily. 'I dare say you think I am amusing – in fact, I know you do, for you are for ever laughing at me – but you would very soon grow tired of laughing, and – and perhaps be sorry that you had married me.'

'I am never tired of laughing.'

'Please do not say any more!' she implored. 'It has been such a splendid adventure until Piers came, and forced you to say what you did! I – I would rather that you didn't say any more, Richard, if you please!'

He perceived that his careful strategy in allowing her to meet her old playfellow before declaring himself had been mistaken. There did not seem to be any way of explaining this. No doubt, he thought, she had from the outset regarded him in an avuncular light. He wondered how deeply her affections had been rooted in the dream-figure of Piers Luttrell, and, mis-reading her tears, feared that her heart had indeed suffered a severe wound. He wanted very much to catch her up in his arms, overbearing her resistance and her scruples, but her very trust in him set up a barrier between them. He said, with a shadow of a smile: 'I have given myself a hard task, have I not?'

She did not understand him, and so said nothing. Not until Piers had shown her a shocked face, and Sir Richard had claimed her as his prospective wife, had she questioned her own heart. Sir Richard had been merely her delightful travelling companion, an immensely superior personage on whom one could place one's dependence. The object of her journey had obsessed her thoughts to such a degree that she had never paused to ask herself whether the entrance into her life of a Corinthian had not altered the whole complexion of her adventure. But it had; and when she had encountered Piers, it had been suddenly borne in upon her that she did not care two pins for him. The Corinthian had ousted him from her mind and heart. Then Piers had turned the adventure into a faintly sordid intrigue, and Sir Richard had made his declaration, not because he had wanted to (for if he had, why should he have held his tongue till then?) but because honour had forced the words out of him. It was absurd to think that a man of fashion, nearing his thirtieth year, could have fallen head-over-ears in love with a miss scarcely out of the schoolroom, however easily the miss might have tumbled into love with him.

'Very well, Miss Creed,' said Sir Richard. 'I will woo you in form, and according to all the dictates of convention.'

The ubiquitous waiter chose this moment to come into the parlour to clear the table. Turning to gaze out of the window, Miss Creed reflected that in a more perfect world no servant would intrude upon his legitimate business at unreasonable moments. While the waiter, who seemed from his intermittent sniffs to be suffering from a cold in the head, shuffled about the room, clattering plates and dishes together on a tray, she resolutely winked away another tear, and fixed her attention on a mongrel dog, scratching for fleas in the middle of the street. But this object of interest was presently sent scuttling to cover by the approach of a smart curricle drawn by a pair of fine bays, and driven by a young blood in a coat of white drab cloth, with as many as fifteen capes, and two tiers of pockets. A Belcher handkerchief protruded from an inner pocket, and the coat was flung open to display an astonishing view of a kerseymere waistcoat, woven in stripes of blue and yellow, and a cravat of white muslin spotted with black. A bouquet was stuck in a button-hole of the driving-coat, and a tall hat with a conical crown and an Allen brim was set at a rakish angle on the head of this exquisite.

The equipage drew up outside the George, and a small Tiger jumped down from the back of the curricle, and ran to the horses' heads. The exquisite cast aside the rug that covered his legs, and alighted, permitting Miss Creed a glimpse of white corduroy breeches, and short boots with very long tops. He passed into the inn while she was still blinking at such a vision, and set up a shout for the landlord.

'Good gracious, sir, such an odd creature has arrived! I wish you could have seen him!' Pen exclaimed. 'Only fancy! He has a blue-and-yellow striped waistcoat, and a spotted tie!'

'I wear them myself sometimes,' murmured Sir Richard apologetically.

She turned, determined to keep the conversation to such unexceptionable subjects. 'You, sir? I cannot believe such a thing to be possible!'

'It sounds remarkably like the insignia of the Four-Horse Club,' he said. 'But what in the name of all that's wonderful should one of our members be doing in Queen Charlton?'

A confused sound of conversation reached them from the entrance-parlour. Above it the landlord's voice, which was rather high-pitched, said clearly: 'My best parlour is bespoke by Sir Richard Wyndham, sir, but if your honour would condescend –'

'*What?*'

There was no difficulty at all in hearing the monosyllable, for it was positively shouted.

'Oh, my God!' said Sir Richard, and turned to run a quick eye over Miss Creed. 'Careful now, brat! I fancy I know this traveller. What in the world have you done to that cravat? Come here!'

He had barely time to straighten Miss Creed's crumpled tie when the same penetrating voice uttered: 'Where? In there? Don't be a fool, man! I know him well!' and hasty footsteps were heard crossing the entrance-parlour.

The door was flung open; the gentleman in the fifteen-caped driving-coat strode in, and, upon setting eyes on Sir Richard, cast his hat and gloves from him, and started forward, exclaiming: '*Ricky!* Ricky, you dog, what are you doing here?'

Pen, effacing herself by the window, watched the tall young man wring Sir Richard's hand, and wondered where she could have seen him before. He seemed vaguely familiar to her, and the very timbre of his reckless voice touched a cord of memory.

'Well, upon my soul!' he said. 'If this don't beat all! I don't know what the deuce you're doing here, but you're the very man I want to see. Ricky, does that offer of yours hold good? Damme, if it does, I'm off to the Peninsula by the first boat! There's the devil and all to pay in the family this time!'

'I know it,' Sir Richard said. 'I take it you have heard the news about Beverley?'

'My God, don't tell me *you've* heard it?'

'I found him,' Sir Richard said.

The Honourable Cedric clapped a hand to his head. 'Found him? What, *you* weren't looking for him, Ricky, were you? How many more people know about it? Where's that damned necklace?'

'Unless the law-officers have now got it, I fancy it is in one Captain Trimble's pocket. It was once in my possession, but I handed it over to Beverley, to – er – restore to your father. When he was murdered –'

Cedric recoiled, his jaw dropping. 'What's that? Murdered? Ricky, not Bev?'

'Ah!' said Sir Richard, 'so you *didn't* know?'

'Good God!' Cedric said. His roving eye alighted on the decanter and the glasses which the waiter had left upon the table. He poured himself out a glass, and tossed it off. 'That's better. So Bev's been murdered, has he? Well, I came here with a little notion of murdering him myself. Who did it?'

'Trimble, I imagine,' Sir Richard replied.

Cedric paused in the act of refilling his glass, and looked up quickly. 'For the sake of the necklace?'

'Presumably.'

To Pen's astonishment, Cedric broke into a shout of laughter. 'Oh, by God, but that's rich!' he gasped. 'Oh, blister me, Ricky, that's hell's own jest!'

Sir Richard put up his eyeglass, surveying his young friend through it with faint surprise. 'I did not, of course, expect the news to prostrate you with grief, but I confess I was hardly prepared –'

'Paste, dear old boy! nothing but paste!' said Cedric, doubled up over a chair-back.

The eyeglass dropped. 'Dear me!' said Sir Richard. 'Yes, I ought to have thought of that. Saar?'

'Years ago!' Cedric said, wiping his streaming eyes with the Belcher handkerchief. 'Only came out when I – I, mark you, Ricky! – set the Bow Street Runners on to it! I thought m'father was devilish lukewarm over the affair. Never guessed, however! There was m'mother sending messenger upon messenger up to Brook Street, and the girls nagging at me, so off I went to Bow Street. Fact is, my head's never at its best in the morning. No sooner had I set the bloodhounds on to the damned necklace than I began to think the thing over. I told you Bev was a bad man, Ricky. I'll lay you a monkey he stole the necklace.'

Sir Richard nodded. 'Quite true.'

'Damme, I call that going too far! M'mother had a secret hiding-place made for it in her chaise. M'father knew. I knew. Bev knew. Dare say the girls knew. But no one else, d'ye mark me? Thought it all out at White's. Nothing like brandy for clearing the head! Then I remembered that Bev took himself off to Bath last week. Never could imagine why! Thought I'd better look into things m'self. Just made up my mind to take a little journey to Bath, when in walked m'father in a deuce of a pucker. He'd heard from Melissa that I'd been to Bow Street. Pounced on me, looking as queer as Dick's hatband, and wanting to know what the devil I meant by setting the Runners on to it. Now, Ricky, dear boy, would you say I was a green 'un? Give you my word I never guessed what was coming! Always thought m'father meant to stick to the diamonds! He sold 'em three years ago when he had that run of bad luck! Had 'em copied, so that no one was the wiser, not even my mother! He was as mad as Bedlam with me, and damme, I don't blame him, for if my

Runner ran the necklace to earth there'd be the devil to pay, and no pitch hot! So that's why I'm here. But what beats me is, what in thunder brought *you* here?'

'You told me to run,' murmured Sir Richard.

'So I did, but to tell you the truth I never thought you would, dear boy. But why here? Out with it, Ricky! You never came here in search of Bev!'

'No, I didn't. I came upon purely – er – family affairs. I fancy you have never met my young cousin, Pen Brown?'

'Never knew you had a cousin of that name. Who is he?' said Cedric cheerfully.

Sir Richard made a slight movement, indicating Pen's presence. The room was deeply shadowed, for the waiter had not yet brought in the candles, and the twilight was fading. Cedric turned his head, and stared with narrowed eyes towards the window-seat, where Pen had been sitting, half hidden by the curtains. 'Damme, I never saw you!' he exclaimed. 'How d'ye do?'

'Mr Brandon, Pen,' Sir Richard explained.

She came forward to shake hands, just as the waiter entered with a couple of chandeliers. He set them down upon the table, and moved across the room to draw the curtains. The sudden glow of candlelight for a moment dazzled Cedric, but as he released Pen's hand his vision cleared, and became riveted on her guinea-gold curls. A portentous frown gathered on his brow, as he struggled with an erratic memory. 'Hey, wait a minute!' he said. 'I haven't seen you before, have I?'

'No, I don't think so,' replied Pen in a small voice.

'That's what I thought. But there's something about you – did you say he was a cousin of yours, Ricky?'

'A distant cousin,' amended Sir Richard.

'Name of Brown?'

Sir Richard sighed. 'Is it so marvellous?'

'Damme, dear boy, I've known you from m'cradle, but I never heard of any relative of yours called Brown! What's the game?'

'If I had guessed that you were so interested in the ramifications of my family, Cedric, I would have informed you of Pen's existence.'

The waiter, interested, but unable to prolong his labours in the parlour, slowly and sadly withdrew.

'Something devilish queer about this!' pronounced Cedric, with a shake of his head. 'Something at the back of my mind, too. Where's that burgundy?'

'Well, I thought at first that I had met you before,' offered Pen. 'But that was because of your likeness to the stam – to the other Mr Brandon.'

'Don't tell me you knew him!' exclaimed Cedric.

'Not very well. We happened to meet him here.'

'I'll tell you what, my lad: he was no fit company for a suckling like you,' said Cedric severely. He frowned upon her again, but apparently abandoned the effort to recall the errant memory, and turned back to Sir Richard. 'But your cousin don't explain your being here, Ricky. Damme, what *did* bring you to this place?'

'Chance,' replied Sir Richard. 'I was – er – constrained to escort my cousin to this neighbourhood, upon urgent family affairs. Upon the way, we encountered an individual who was being pursued by a Bow Street Runner – your Runner, Ceddie – and who slipped a certain necklace into my cousin's pocket.'

'You don't mean it! But did you know Bev was here?'

'By no means. That fact was only revealed to me when I overheard him exchanging somewhat unguarded recriminations with the man whom I suppose to have murdered him. To be brief with you, there were three of them mixed up in this lamentable affair, and one of the three had bubbled the other two. I restored the necklace to Beverley, on the understanding that it should go back to Saar.'

Cedric cocked an eyebrow. 'Steady now, Ricky, steady! I'm not cork-brained, dear old boy! Bev never consented to give the diamonds back – unless he was afraid you were going to mill his canister. Devilish lily-livered, Bev! Was that the way of it?'

'No,' said Sir Richard. 'That was not the way of it.'

'Ricky, you fool, don't tell me you bought him off!'

'I didn't.'

'Promised to, eh? I warned you! I warned you to have nothing to do with Bev! However, if he's dead there's no harm done! Go on!'

'There is really very little more to tell you. Beverley was found – by me – dead, in a spinney not far from here, last night. The necklace had vanished.'

'The devil it had! Y'know, Ricky, this is a damned ugly business! And, the more I think of it the less I understand why you left town in such a hurry, and without a word to anyone. Now, don't tell me you came on urgent family affairs, dear boy! You were disguised that night! Never seen you so foxed in my life! You said you were going to walk home, and by what the porter told George you had it fixed in your head your house was somewhere in the direction of Brook Street. Well, I'll lay anyone what odds they like you did not go to serenade Melissa! Damme, what did happen to you?'

'Oh, I went home!' said Sir Richard placidly.

'Yes, but where did this young sprig come into it?' demanded Cedric, casting a puzzled glance at Pen.

'On my doorstep. He had come to find me, you see.'

'No, damn it, Ricky, that won't do!' protested Cedric. 'Not at three in the morning, dear boy!'

'Of course not!' interposed Pen. 'I had been awaiting him – oh, for hours!'

'On the doorstep?' said Cedric incredulously.

'There were reasons why I did not wish the servants to know that I was in town,' explained Pen, with a false air of candour.

'Well, I never heard such a tale in my life!' said Cedric. 'It ain't like you, Ricky, it ain't like you! I called to see you myself next morning, and I found Louisa and George there, and the whole house in a pucker, with not a man-jack knowing where the devil you'd got to. Oh, by Jupiter, and George would have it you had drowned yourself!'

'Drowned myself! Good God, why?'

'Melissa, dear boy, Melissa!' chuckled Cedric. 'Bed not slept in – crumpled cravat in the grate – lock of –' He broke off, and jerked his head round to stare at Pen. 'By God, I have it! *Now* I know what was puzzling me! That hair! It was yours!'

'Oh, the devil!' said Sir Richard. 'So that was found, was it?'

'One golden curl under a shawl. George would have it it was a relic of your past. But hell and the devil confound it, it don't make sense! You never went to call on Ricky in the small hours to get your hair cut, boy!'

'No, but he said I wore my hair too long, and that he would not go about with me looking *so*,' said Pen desperately. 'And he didn't like my cravat either. He was drunk, you know.'

'He wasn't as drunk as that,' said Cedric. 'I don't know who you are, but you ain't Ricky's cousin. In fact, it's my belief you ain't even a boy! Damme, you're Ricky's past, that's what you are!'

'I am not!' said Pen indignantly. 'It is quite true that I'm not a boy, but I never saw Richard in my life until that night!'

'Never saw him until that night?' repeated Cedric, dazed.

'No! It was all chance, wasn't it, Richard?'

'It was,' agreed Sir Richard, who seemed to be amused. 'She dropped out of a window into my arms, Ceddie.'

'She dropped out of – give me some more burgundy!' said Cedric.

Thirteen

*H*aving fortified himself from the decanter, Cedric sighed, and shook his head. 'No use, it still seems devilish odd to me. Females don't drop out of windows.'

'Well, I didn't drop out precisely. I climbed out, because I was escaping from my relations.'

'I've often wanted to escape from mine, but I never thought of climbing out of a window.'

'Of course not!' said Pen scornfully. 'You are a man!'

Cedric seemed dissatisfied. 'Only females escape out of windows? Something wrong there.'

'I think you are excessively stupid. I escaped out of the window because it was dangerous to go by the door. And Richard happened to be passing at the time, which was a very fortunate circumstance because the sheets were not long enough, and I had to jump.'

'Do you mean to tell me you climbed down the sheets?' demanded Cedric.

'Yes, of course. How else could I have got out, pray?'

'Well, if that don't beat all!' he exclaimed admiringly.

'Oh, that was nothing! Only when Sir Richard guessed that I was not a boy he thought it would not be proper for me to journey to this place alone, so he took me to his house, and cut my hair more neatly at the back, and tied my cravat for me, and – and *that* is why you found those things in his library!'

Cedric cocked an eye at Sir Richard. 'Damme, I knew you'd

shot the cat, Ricky, but I never guessed you were as bosky as that!'

'Yes,' said Sir Richard reflectively, 'I fancy I must have been rather more up in the world than I suspected.'

'Up in the world! Dear old boy, you must have been clean raddled! And how the deuce did you get here? For I remember now that George said your horses were all in the stables. You never travelled in a hired chaise, Ricky!'

'Certainly not,' said Sir Richard. 'We travelled on the stage.'

'On the – on the –' Words failed Cedric.

'That was Pen's notion,' Sir Richard explained kindly. 'I must confess I was not much in favour of it, and I still consider the stage an abominable vehicle, but there is no denying we had a very adventurous journey. Really, to have gone post would have been sadly flat. We were over-turned in a ditch; we became – er – intimately acquainted with a thief; we found ourselves in possession of stolen goods; assisted in an elopement; and discovered a murder. I had not dreamt life could hold so much excitement.'

Cedric, who had been gazing at him open-mouthed, began to laugh. 'Lord, I shall never get over this! *You*, Ricky! Oh Lord, and there was Louisa ready to swear you would never do anything unbefitting a man of fashion, and George thinking you at the bottom of the river, and Melissa standing to it that you had gone off to watch a mill! Gad, she'll be as mad as fire! Out-jockeyed, by Jupiter! Piqued, repiqued, slammed, and capotted!' He once more mopped his eyes with the Belcher handkerchief. 'You'll have to buy me that pair of colours, Ricky: damme, you owe it to me, for I told you to run, now, didn't I?'

'But he did not run!' Pen said anxiously. 'It was *I* who ran. Richard didn't.'

'Oh yes, I did!' said Sir Richard, taking snuff.

'No, no, you know you only came to take care of me; you said I could not go alone!'

Cedric looked at her in a puzzled way. 'Y'know, I can't make this out at all! If you only met three nights ago, you can't be eloping!'

'Of course we're not eloping! I came here on – on a private matter, and Richard pretended to be my tutor. There is not a question of eloping!'

'Tutor? Lord! I thought you said he was your cousin?'

'My dear Cedric, do try not to be so hidebound!' begged Sir Richard. 'I have figured as a tutor, an uncle, a trustee, *and* a cousin.'

'You seem to me to be a sad romp!' Cedric told Pen severely. 'How old are you?'

'I am seventeen, but I do not see that it is any concern of yours.'

'Seventeen!' Cedric cast a dismayed glance at Sir Richard. 'Ricky, you madman! You're in the basket now, the pair of you! And what your mother and Louisa will say, let alone that sour-faced sister of mine – ! When is the wedding?'

'That,' said Sir Richard, 'is the point we were discussing when you walked in on us.'

'Better get married quietly somewhere where you ain't known. You know what people are!' Cedric said, wagging his head. 'Damme, if I won't be best man!'

'Well, you won't,' said Pen, flushing. 'We are not going to be married. It is quite absurd to think of such a thing.'

'I know it's absurd,' replied Cedric frankly. 'But you should have thought of that before you started jauntering about the country in this crazy fashion. There's nothing for it now: you'll have to be married!'

'I won't!' Pen declared. 'No one need ever know that I am not a boy, except you, and one other, who doesn't signify.'

'But my dear girl, it won't do! Take it from me, it won't do! If you don't know that, I'll be bound Ricky does. I daresay you don't fancy the notion, but he's a devilish fine catch, you know. Blister it, we were looking to him to bring our family fortunes about, so we were!' he added, with an irrepressible chuckle.

'I think you are vulgar and detestable!' said Pen. 'I have got a great deal of money of my own; in fact, I'm an heiress, and I have a very good mind not to marry anyone!'

'But only think what a waste!' protested Cedric. 'If you are an heiress, and you can't stomach the notion of marrying Ricky, for which I won't blame you, for the Lord knows he's no lady's man! – a hardened case, m'dear: never looked seriously at a female in his life! – I suppose you wouldn't make shift with your humble servant?'

'Your conversation, my dear Cedric, is always edifying,' said Sir Richard icily.

But Pen, instead of being offended, giggled. 'No, thank you. I shouldn't like to marry you at all.'

'I was afraid you wouldn't. You'll have to take Ricky, then: nothing else for it! But you're too young for him: no getting away from that! Damme, if I know what maggot got into your heads to set you off on this crazy adventure!'

'You are labouring under a misapprehension, Cedric,' said Sir Richard. 'There is nothing I desire more than to marry Pen.'

'Well, of all things!' gasped Cedric. 'And here was I thinking you a hopeless case!'

'I am going to bed,' stated Pen.

Sir Richard moved across the door to open it for her. 'Yes my child: go to bed. But pray do not let Cedric's artless chatter prejudice you! For addle-pated folly I have never met his equal.' He possessed himself of her hand, as he spoke, and lifted it to his lips. 'Pleasant dreams, brat,' he said softly.

She felt a lump rise in her throat, achieved a tremulous smile, and fled, but not before she had heard Cedric exclaim in tones of the liveliest surprise: 'Ricky, you ain't really in love with that chit, are you?'

'I think,' said Sir Richard, closing the door, 'that we shall be more usefully employed in discussing the circumstances which brought you here, Cedric.'

'Oh, by all means!' Cedric said hastily. 'Beg pardon! No intention of prying into your affairs, dear boy; not the least in the world! Now, don't get into a miff! You know how it is with me! Never could keep a discreet tongue in my head!'

'That is what I am afraid of,' Sir Richard said dryly.

'Mum as an oyster!' Cedric assured him. 'But that you of all men, Ricky – ! That's what beats me! However, no concern of mine! What's all this you were telling me about Bev?'

'He's dead. That seems to be the most important thing.'

'Well, it's no good expecting me to pull a long face over it. He was a bad man, take my word for it! What was he doing in this spinney you talk of?'

'As a matter of fact, he went there to meet me,' said Sir Richard.

Cedric frowned at him. 'More in this than meets the eye. Why, Ricky?'

'To be plain with you, he had hit upon the notion of extorting money from me by threatening to make known the fact that my supposed cousin was a girl in disguise.'

'Yes, that's Bev all over,' nodded Cedric, quite unsurprised. 'Offered to pay his debts, didn't you?'

'Oh, I had offered that earlier in the day! Unfortunately Captain Trimble learned of my appointment with Beverley in the spinney, and went there before me. I fancy he had nothing more than robbery in mind. There was a witness to the meeting, who described how a quarrel sprang up, and how Trimble struck Beverley down, searched his pockets, and made off. Possibly he thought he had merely stunned him. When I found him his neck was broken.'

'Jupiter!' said Cedric, giving a whistle of consternation. 'It's worse than I thought, then! The devil! There will be no hushing this up. They don't suspect you of having a hand in it, do they, Ricky?'

'I am fast acquiring a most unsavoury reputation in this neighbourhood, but so far I have not been arrested for murder. What precise object had you in coming here?'

'Why, to choke the truth out of Bev, of course! Couldn't get it out of my head he was at the bottom of that robbery. He was badly dipped, y'know. M'father wants my bloodhound called off, too, but I'm damned if I can come up with any trace of him. If you met the fellow on the Bristol road, that would account for my missing him. I went to Bath. Last I heard of Bev was that he was there, with Freddie Fotheringham. Freddie told me Bev had gone off to stay with some people called Luttrell, living at a place near here. So I saw m'mother, got the full story of the robbery out of her, and came on here. *Now* what's to do?'

'You had better make the acquaintance of the local magistrate. A man who might well be Trimble was taken up in Bath to-day, but whether the necklace was on him I know not.'

'Must lay my hands on that plaguey necklace!' frowned Cedric. 'Won't do if the truth about that were to come out. But what are you going to do, Ricky? It seems to me you're in the deuce of a coil too.'

'I shall no doubt be able to answer that question when I have talked the matter over with Pen to-morrow,' Sir Richard replied.

But Sir Richard was not destined to have the opportunity of talking over any matter with Miss Creed upon the morrow. Miss Creed, going dejectedly up to bed, sat for a long time at the open window of her room, and gazed blindly out upon the moonlit scene. She had spent, she decided, quite the most miserable day of her life, and the sudden incursion of Cedric Brandon had done nothing to alleviate her heaviness of heart. It was apparent that Cedric considered her adventure only one degree less fantastic than the notion that she was to marry Sir Richard. According to his own words, he had known Sir Richard from the cradle, so that it was fair to assume that he was very well acquainted with him. He gave it as his opinion that she must marry Sir Richard, which was tantamount to saying, she reflected, that she had put Sir Richard into the uncomfortable position of being obliged to offer for her. It was most unjust, Pen thought, for Sir Richard had not been sober when he had insisted on accompanying her into Somerset, and he had, moreover, done it out of sheer solicitude for her safety. It had not occurred to her that a gentleman so many years her senior could be supposed to compromise her, or to engage his own honour so disastrously. She had liked him from the moment of setting eyes on him; she had plunged into terms of intimacy with him in the shortest possible time; and had, indeed, felt as though she had known him all her life. She thought herself more stupid even than Lydia Daubenay not to have realized before ever they had reached Queen Charlton, that she had tumbled headlong in love with him. She had refused to look beyond her meeting with Piers, yet she could not but admit to herself now that she had been by no means anxious to summon Piers to her side when she had arrived at the George. By the time she did come face to face with him, he would have had to have been a paragon indeed to have won her from Sir Richard.

His conduct had been anything rather than that of a paragon. He had spoiled everything, Pen thought. He had accused her of impropriety, and had forced Sir Richard into making a declaration he had surely not wanted to make.

'Because I don't suppose he loves me at all,' Pen argued to herself. 'He never said so until Piers was so odious: in fact, he treated me just as if he really was a trustee, or an uncle, or somebody years and years older than I am, which I dare say was what made it all seem quite proper to me, and not in the least scandalous. Only then we fell into so many adventures, and he was obliged to fob off Aunt Almeria, and then the stammering-man guessed I was a girl, and Piers was disagreeable, and I got into a scrape through Lydia's folly, and the Major came, and now this other Mr Brandon knows about me, and the end of it is I have placed poor Richard in the horridest situation imaginable! There is only one thing for it: I shall have to run away.'

This decision, however, made her feel so melancholy that several large tears brimmed over her eyelids and rolled down her cheeks. She wiped them away, telling herself it was stupid to cry. 'Because if he doesn't want to marry me, I don't want to marry him – much; and if he does, I dare say he will come to visit me at Aunt's house. No, he won't. He'll forget all about me, or very likely be glad that he is rid of a badly behaved, tiresome ch-charge! Oh dear!'

So sunk in these dismal reflections did she become that it was a long time before she could rouse herself sufficiently to prepare for bed. She even forgot the elopement she had helped to arrange, and heard the church-clock strike midnight without so much as recalling that Lydia should now be stepping up into the hired post-chaise, with or without a cage of love-birds.

She spent a miserable night, disturbed by unquiet dreams, and tossing from side to side in a way that soon untucked all the sheets and blankets, and made the bed so uncomfortable that by six in the morning, when she finally awoke to find the room full of sunlight, she was very glad to leave it.

A considerable portion of her waking hours had been spent in considering how she could run away without Sir Richard's knowing anything about it. A carrier was used to go into Bristol on certain days, she remembered, and she made up her mind either to buy a seat on his wagon, or, if it was not one of his days, to walk to Bristol, and there book a seat on the London stage-coach. Bristol was not more than six or seven miles distant from Queen Charlton, and there was, moreover, a reasonable hope of being offered a lift in some conveyance bound for the town.

She dressed herself, and very nearly started to cry again when she struggled with the folds of the starched muslin cravat, because it was one of Sir Richard's. Once dressed, she packed her few belongings in the cloak-bag he had lent her, and tiptoed downstairs to the parlour.

The servants, though she could hear them moving about in the coffee-room, and the kitchen, had not yet come into the parlour to draw back the blinds, and to set the room to rights. In its untidy, overnight state it looked dispiriting. Pen pulled the blinds apart, and sat down at the writing-table to compose a letter of farewell to Sir Richard.

It was a very difficult letter to write, and seemed to entail much nose-blowing, and many watery sniffs. When she had at last finished it, Pen read it through rather dubiously, and tried to erase a blot. It was not a satisfactory letter, but there was no time to write another, so she folded, and sealed it, wrote Sir Richard's name on it and propped it up on the mantelpiece.

In the entrance-parlour she encountered the pessimistic

waiter who had served them on the previous evening. His eyes seemed even duller than usual, and beyond staring in a ruminative fashion at her cloak-bag, he evinced no interest in Pen's early rising.

She explained to him glibly that she was obliged to go into Bristol, and asked if the carrier would be passing the George. The waiter said that he would not be passing, because Friday was not his day. 'If you had wanted him yesterday, it would have been different,' he added reproachfully.

She sighed. 'Then I shall be obliged to walk.'

The waiter accepted this without interest, but just as she reached the door he bethought him of something, and said in a voice of unabated gloom: 'The missus is going to Bristol in the trap.'

'Do you think she would take me with her?'

The waiter declined to offer an opinion, but he volunteered to go and ask the missus. However, Pen decided to go herself, and, penetrating to the yard at the back of the inn, found the landlord's wife packing a basket into the trap, and preparing to mount into it herself.

She was surprised at Pen's request, and eyed the cloak-bag with suspicion, but she was a stout, good-natured woman, and upon Pen's assuring her mendaciously that Sir Richard was well-aware of her projected expedition, she allowed her to get into the trap, and to stow the cloak-bag under the seat. Her son, a phlegmatic young man, who chewed a straw throughout the journey, took the reins, and in a few minutes the whole party was proceeding up the village street at a sober but steady pace.

'Well, I only hopes, sir, as I'm not doing wrong,' said Mrs Hopkins, as soon as she had recovered from the exertion of hoisting her bulk into the trap. 'I'm sure I was never one to pry into other folks' business, but if you *was* running away from the gentleman which has you in charge, I should get into trouble, that's what.'

'Oh no, indeed you won't!' Pen assured her. 'You see, we have not our own carriage with us, or – or I should not have been obliged to trouble you in this way.'

Mrs Hopkins said that she was not one to grudge trouble, and added that she was glad of company. When she discovered Pen had had no breakfast, she was very much shocked, and after much tugging and wheezing, pulled out the basket from under the seat, and produced out of it a large packet of sandwiches, a pie wrapped in a napkin, and a bottle of cold tea. Pen accepted a sandwich, but refused the pie, a circumstance which made Mrs Hopkins say that although the young gentleman would have been welcome to it, it was, in point of fact, a gift for her aunt, who lived in Bristol. She further disclosed that she was bound for the town to meet her sister's second girl, who was coming down on the London stage to work as a chambermaid at the George. The ball of conversation having been set rolling in this easy fashion, the journey passed pleasantly enough, Mrs Hopkins furnishing Pen with so exhaustive an account of the various trials and vicissitudes which had befallen every member of her family, that by the time the trap drew up at an inn in the centre of Bristol, Pen felt that there could be little she did not know about the good lady's relatives.

The stage was not due to arrive in Bristol until nine o'clock, at which hour the coach setting out for London would leave the inn. Mrs Hopkins set off to visit her aunt, and Pen, having booked a seat on the stage, and deposited the cloak-bag at the inn, sallied forth to lay out her last remaining coins on provisions to sustain her during the journey.

The streets were rather empty at such an early hour, and some of the shops had not yet taken down their shutters, but after walking for a few minutes and observing with interest the changes which, in five years, had taken place in the town, Pen found a cook-shop that was open. The smell of freshly baked pies made her feel hungry, and she went into the shop, and made a careful selection of the viands offered for sale.

When she came out of the shop, there was still half-an-hour to while away before the coach was due to start, and she wandered into the market-place. Here there were quite a number of people already busy about the day's business. Pen caught sight of Mrs

Hopkins bargaining with a salesman over the price of a length of calico, but since she did not feel that she wanted to learn any more details about the Hopkins family, she avoided her, and pretended to be interested in a clockmaker's shop. So intent was she on avoiding Mrs Hopkins's motherly eye, that she was blissfully unaware that she herself was being closely scrutinized by a thickset man in a duffle coat, and a wide-brimmed hat, who, after gazing fixedly at her for some moments, stepped up to her, and, laying a heavy hand on her shoulder, said deeply: 'Got you!'

Pen jumped guiltily, and looked round in sudden alarm. The voice sounded familiar; to her dismay she found herself staring up into the face of the Bow Street Runner who had overtaken Jimmy Yarde at the inn near Wroxham.

'Oh!' she said faintly. 'Oh! Are you not the – the man I met – the other day? Good – good-morning! A fine day, isn't – isn't it?'

'That's so, young sir,' said the Runner, in a grim tone. 'And a werry complete hand you be, and no mistake! I've been wanting another touch at you. Ah, and when Nat Gudgeon wants a touch at a cove, he gets it, and no mistake about that neither! You come along with me!'

'But I haven't done anything wrong! Indeed I haven't!' said Pen.

'If you haven't, then there's no call for you to be scared of me,' said Mr Gudgeon, with what seemed to her a fiendish leer. 'But what I been thinking, young sir, is, that you and that fine gentleman what was with you loped off mighty quick from that there inn. Why, anyone might have thought, so they might, as how you had took an unaccountable dislike to me!'

'No, no, we didn't! But there was nothing to stay for, and we were already much delayed.'

'Well,' said Mr Gudgeon, shifting his grip to her arm, and grasping this firmly above the elbow, 'I've got a fancy to question you more particular, young sir. Now, don't you make the werry great mistake of trying to struggle with me, because it won't do you no good. Maybe you ain't never heard tell on a cove by the name o' Yarde: likewise you wouldn't reckernize a set o'

208

sparklers if you was to see one. Lor'! if I had a brace of meggs for every green-looking young chub like you which I've took up – ah, and shut up in the Whit just as snug as you please – I'd be a werry rich man, so I would. You come along of me, and stop trying to gammon me, because I've got a werry strong notion you know a deal more about a certain set o' sparklers nor what you're wishful I should get wind of.'

By this time, the attention of several persons had been attracted, and a small crowd was beginning to gather. Pen cast a hunted look around. She saw the aghast face of Mrs Hopkins, but no means of escape, and gave herself up for lost. Mr Gudgeon evidently meant to march her off to the gaol, or at any rate to some place of safe-keeping, where her sex, she suspected, would soon be discovered. Meanwhile, the crowd was swelling, several members of it loudly demanding to know what the young gentleman had done, and one knowledgeable individual explaining to his neighbours that that was one of they Bow Street Runners from London, that was. Nothing would serve her, Pen decided, but a certain measure of frankness. Accordingly, she made no attempt to break away from the Runner's hold, but said in as calm a tone as she was able to assume: 'Indeed, I do not mind going with you at all. In fact, I know just what you want, and I dare say I can furnish you with some very valuable information.'

Mr Gudgeon, who was not accustomed to be met with any appearance of sang-froid, was not in the least softened by this speech. He said in a shocked voice: 'There's a sauce! Ay, you're a rare gager, young as you be! Why, you young warmint, and you with your mother's milk not dry on your lips! You come along, and no bamming, now!'

A section of the crowd showed a disposition to accompany them, but Mr Gudgeon addressed these gentry in such fierce accents that they dispersed in a hurry, and left him to escort his captive out of the market-place in lonely state.

'You are making a great mistake,' Pen told the Runner. 'You are searching for the Brandon diamonds, are you not? Well, I know all about them, and, as a matter of fact, Mr Brandon wishes you to stop searching for them.'

'Ho!' said Mr Gudgeon, with deep meaning. 'He does, does he? Dang me, if ever I see the equal of you for sauce!'

'I wish you will listen to me! I know who has the diamonds, and, what is more, he murdered the other Mr Brandon to get them!'

Mr Gudgeon shook his head in speechless wonder.

'He *did*, I tell you!' Pen said desperately. 'His name is Trimble, and he was in a plot with Jimmy Yarde to steal the necklace! Only it went awry, and the necklace was restored to Mr Beverley Brandon, and then Captain Trimble killed him, and made off with the diamonds. And Mr Cedric Brandon is searching for you high and low, and if you will only go to Queen Charlton you will find him there, and he will tell you that what I say is true!'

'I never heard the like!' gasped Mr Gudgeon, affronted. 'A werry thorough-going young rascal you be, and no mistake about that! And how might you come to know such a powerful deal about these sparklers, might I take the liberty of asking?'

'I know Mr Brandon well,' answered Pen. '*Both* Mr Brandons! And I was in Queen Charlton when the murder was committed. Mr Philips, the magistrate, knows all about me, I assure you!'

Mr Gudgeon was a little shaken by this announcement, and said more mildly: 'I don't say as I disbelieve you, nor I don't say as I believe you neither; but it's an unaccountable queer story you're telling me, young sir, and that's a fact.'

'Yes, I dare say it may seem so to you,' Pen agreed. She felt his grip slacken on her arm, and decided to press home her advantage. 'You had better come with me to Queen Charlton at once, because Mr Brandon wants to see you, and I expect Mr Philips will be very glad of your help in finding Captain Trimble.'

Mr Gudgeon looked at her sideways. 'Either I've been mistook,' he said slowly, 'or you're the most precious young warmint I ever did see. Maybe I will go to this place you talks about, and maybe while I'm gone you'll sit waiting for me where you won't do no harm.'

They had turned into a broad thoroughfare with streets leading off from it on either side. Pen, who had no intention of returning to Queen Charlton, or of being locked up in Bristol gaol, made up her mind, now that Mr Gudgeon's grasp on her arm had become little more than perfunctory, to try the chances of escape. She said airily: 'Just as you please, only I warn you, Mr Brandon will be excessively angry if he hears that you have molested me. Naturally, I do not wish to – Oh, look, look! Quick!'

They were abreast of one of the side streets by this time, and Pen's admirable start brought the Runner to a dead halt. She clasped his arm with her free hand, and exclaimed: 'Over there, just turning into that road! It was he! Captain Trimble! He must have seen me, for he set off running at once! oh, do be quick!'

'Where?' demanded Mr Gudgeon, taken off his guard, and looking round wildly.

'*There!*' panted Pen, and tore herself free from his hold, and ran like a deer down the side-street.

She heard a shout behind her, but wasted no time in looking back. A woman engaged in scrubbing her front doorstep set up a cry of Stop, thief! and an errand boy with a large basket on his arm, gave a shrill cat-call. Pen reached the end of the street with the sound of the hue and cry behind her, turned the corner, saw an alley leading to a huddle of mean dwellings, and sped down it.

It led her into a labyrinth of narrow streets, with dirty gutters, and crazy cottages, and backyards noisome with the refuse left to rot in them. She had never penetrated into this part of the town before, and was soon quite lost. This circumstance did not trouble her much, however, for the noise of the chase had died away in the rear. She did not think that anyone had seen her dive into the alley so that she was able to entertain a reasonable hope of shaking off the pursuit. She stopped running, and began to walk, rather breathlessly, in what she trusted was an easterly direction. After traversing a number of unknown streets, she came at last to a more respectable part of the town, and ventured to enquire the way to the inn where she had left her cloak-bag. She discovered that she had overshot it, and, further, that the time was now a few minutes after nine. She looked so dismayed that her informant, a stout man in corduroys and a frieze coat, who was just preparing to climb into a gig, asked her whether she wanted the London stagecoach. Upon her admitting that she did, he said philosophically: 'Well, you've missed it.'

'Oh dear, what shall I do?' said Pen, foreseeing a day spent in skulking about the town to escape discovery by Mr Gudgeon.

The farmer, who had been looking her over in a ruminative fashion, said: 'Be you in a hurry?'

'Yes, yes! That is, I have paid for my seat, you see.'

'Well, I'm going to Kingswood myself,' said the farmer. 'You can get up alongside me in the gig, if you like. You'll likely catch up with the stage there.'

She accepted this offer gratefully, for she thought that even if she did not succeed in overtaking the stage she would be safer from Mr Gudgeon at Kingswood than in Bristol. Happily, however, the farmer was driving a fast-trotting young horse, and they reached the main London road before the heavy stage had drawn out of the town. The farmer set Pen down in Kingswood, at the door of the inn, and having ascertained that the coach had not yet called there, bade her a cheerful farewell, and drove off.

Feeling that she had escaped disaster by no more than a hair's breadth, Pen sat down upon the bench outside the inn to await the arrival of the stage. It was late in coming, and the guard, when Pen handed him her ticket, seemed to take it as a personal affront that she had not boarded it in Bristol. He told her, with malign satisfaction, that her cloak-bag had been left behind at the 'Talbot' Inn, but after a good deal of grumbling he admitted that she had a right to a seat in the coach, and let down the steps for her to mount into it. She squeezed herself into a place between a fat man, and a woman nursing a peevish infant; the door was shut, the steps let up again, and the vehicle resumed its ponderous journey to London.

Fourteen

Sir Richard Wyndham was not an early riser, but he was roused from sleep at an unconscionably early hour upon the morning of Pen's flight by the boots, who came into his room with a small pile of his linen, which had been laundered in the inn, and his top-boots, and told him diffidently that he was wanted belowstairs.

Sir Richard groaned, and enquired what time it was. With even greater diffidence, the boots said that it was not quite eight o'clock.

'What the devil?' exclaimed Sir Richard, bending a pained glance upon him.

'Yes, sir,' agreed the boots feelingly, 'but it's that Major Daubenay, sir, in such a pucker as you never did see!'

'Oh!' said Sir Richard. 'It is, is it? The devil fly away with Major Daubenay!'

The boots grinned, but awaited more precise instructions. Sir Richard groaned again, and sat up. 'You think I ought to get up, do you? Bring me my shaving water, then.'

'Yessir!'

'Oh, ah! Present my compliments to the Major, and inform him that I shall be with him shortly!'

The boots went off to execute these commands, and Sir Richard, surveying the beauty of the morning with a jaundiced eye, got out of bed.

When the boots came back with a jug of hot water, he found Sir Richard in his shirt and breeches, and reported that the

Major was pacing up and down the parlour more like a wild beast in a circus than a Christian gentleman.

'You appal me,' said Sir Richard unemotionally. 'Just hand me my boots, will you? Alas! Biddle, I never realized your worth until I was bereft of you!'

'Beg pardon, sir?'

'Nothing,' said Sir Richard, inserting his foot into one of the boots, and pulling hard.

Half an hour later he entered the parlour to find his matutinal guest fuming up and down the floor with a large watch in his hand. The Major, whose cheeks were unbecomingly flushed, and whose eyes started quite alarmingly, stabbed at this time-piece with one quivering finger, and said in a suppressed roar: 'Forty minutes, sir! Forty minutes since I entered this room!'

'Yes, I have even surprised myself,' said Sir Richard, with maddening nonchalance. 'Time was when I could not have achieved this result under an hour, but practice, my dear sir, practice, you know, is everything!'

'An hour!' gobbled the Major. 'Practice! Bah, I say! Do you hear me, sir?'

'Yes,' said Sir Richard, flicking a speck of dust from his sleeve. 'And I imagine I am not the only one privileged to hear you.'

'You are a dandy!' uttered the Major, with loathing. 'A dandy, sir! That's what you are!'

'Well, I am glad that the haste with which I dressed has not obscured that fact,' replied Sir Richard amiably. 'But the correct term is Corinthian.'

'I don't care a fig what the correct term may be!' roared the Major, striking the table with his fist. 'It's all the same to me: dandy, Corinthian, or pure popinjay!'

'If I lose my temper with you, which, however, I should be loth to do – at all events, at this hour of the morning – you will discover that you are mistaken,' said Sir Richard. 'Meanwhile, I presume that you did not bring me out of my bed to exchange compliments with me. What, sir, do you want?'

'Don't take that high and mighty tone with me, sir!' said the

Major. 'That whelp of yours has made off with my daughter!'

'Nonsense!' said Sir Richard calmly.

'Nonsense, is it? Then let me tell you that she has gone, sir! Gone, do you hear me? And her maid with her!'

'Accept my condolences,' said Sir Richard.

'Your condolences! I don't want your damned condolences, sir! I want to know what you mean to do!'

'Nothing at all,' replied Sir Richard.

The Major's eyes positively bulged, and a vein stood out on his heated brow. 'You stand there, and say that you mean to do nothing, when your scoundrel of a cousin has eloped with my daughter?'

'Not at all. I mean to do nothing because my cousin has not eloped with your daughter. You must forgive me if I point out to you that I am getting a little weary of your parental difficulties.'

'How dare you, sir? how dare you?' gasped the Major. 'Your cousin meets my daughter by stealth in Bath, lures her out at dead of night here, deceives her with false promises, and now – *now,* to crown all, makes off with her, and you say – you say that you are weary of *my* difficulties!'

'Very weary of them. If your daughter has left your roof – and who shall blame her? – I advise you not to waste your time and my patience here, but to enquire at Crome Hall whether Mr Piers Luttrell is at home, or whether he also is missing.'

'Young Luttrell! By God, if it were so I should be glad of it! Ay, glad of it, and glad that any man rather than that vicious, scoundrelly whelp of yours, had eloped with Lydia!'

'Well, that is a fortunate circumstance,' said Sir Richard.

'It is nothing of the kind! You know very well it is not young Luttrell! She herself confessed that she had been in the habit of meeting your cousin, and the young dog said in this very room – in this very room, mark you, with you standing by –'

'My good sir, your daughter and my cousin talked a great deal of nonsense, but I assure you they have not eloped together.'

'Very well, sir, very well! Where then is your cousin at this moment?'

'In his bed, I imagine.'

'Then send for him!' barked the Major.

'As you please,' Sir Richard said, and strolled over to the bell, and pulled it.

He had scarcely released it when the door opened, and the Honourable Cedric walked in, magnificently arrayed in a brocade dressing-gown of vivid and startling design. 'What the deuce is the matter?' he asked plaintively. 'Never heard such an ungodly racket in my life! Ricky, dear old boy, you ain't *dressed*?'

'Yes,' sighed Sir Richard. 'It is a great bore, however.

'But, my dear fellow, it ain't nine o'clock!' said Cedric in horrified tones. 'Damme if I know what has come over you! You can't start the day at this hour: it ain't decent!'

'I know, Ceddie, but when in Rome, one – er – is obliged to cultivate the habits of the Romans. Ah, allow me to present Major Daubenay – Mr Brandon!'

'Servant, sir!' snapped the Major, with the stiffest of bows.

'Oh, how d'ye do?' said Cedric vaguely. 'Deuced queer hours you keep in the country!'

'I am not here upon a visit of courtesy!' said the Major.

'Now, don't tell me you've been quarrelling, Ricky!' begged Cedric. 'It sounded devilish like it to me. Really, dear boy, you might have remembered I was sleeping above you. Never at my best before noon, y'know. Besides, it ain't like you!'

He lounged, yawning, across the room to an armchair by the fireplace, and dropped into it, stretching his long legs out before him. The Major glared at him, and said pointedly that he had come to see Sir Richard upon a private matter.

This hint passed over Cedric's head. 'What we want is some coffee – strong coffee!' he said.

A maid-servant in a mobbed cap came in just then, and seemed astonished to find the room occupied. 'Oh, I beg pardon, sir! I thought the bell rang!'

'It did,' said Sir Richard. 'Have the goodness to tap on Mr Brown's door, and to request him to step downstairs as soon as he shall have dressed. Major Daubenay wishes to speak to him.'

'Hey, wait a minute!' commanded Cedric. 'Bring some coffee first, there's a good girl!'

'Yes, sir,' said the maid, looking flustered.

'Coffee!' exploded Major Daubenay.

Cedric cocked an intelligent eyebrow. 'Don't like the notion? What shall it be? Myself, I think it's too early for brandy, but if you fancy a can of ale, say the word!'

'I want nothing, sir! Sir Richard, while we waste time in such idle fripperies as these, that young dog is abducting my daughter!'

'Fetch Mr Brown,' Sir Richard told the servant.

'Abduction, by Jupiter!' said Cedric. 'What young dog?'

'Major Daubenay,' said Sir Richard, 'is labouring under the delusion that my cousin eloped last night with his daughter.'

'Eh?' Cedric blinked. An unholy gleam stole into his eyes as he glanced from Sir Richard to the Major; he said unsteadily: 'No, by Jove, you don't mean it? You ought to keep him in better order, Ricky!'

'Yes!' said the Major. 'He ought indeed! But instead of that he has – I will not say *abetted* the young scoundrel – but adopted an attitude which I can only describe as callous, sir, and supine!'

Cedric shook his head. 'That's Ricky all over.' His gravity broke down. 'Oh lord, what the deuce put it into your head your daughter had gone off with his cousin? I'll tell you what, it's the richest jest I've heard in months! Ricky, if I don't roast you for this for years to come!'

'You are going to the Peninsula, Ceddie,' Sir Richard said, with a lurking smile.

'You are amused, sir!' the Major said, bristling.

'Lord, yes, and so would you be if you knew as much about Wyndham's cousin as I do!'

The maid-servant came back into the room. 'Oh, if you please, sir! Mr Brown's not in his room,' she said, dropping a curtsey.

The effect of this pronouncement was startling. The Major gave a roar like that of a baffled bull; Cedric's laughter was cut short; and Sir Richard let his eyeglass fall.

'I knew it! Oh, I knew it!' raged the Major. 'Now, sir!'

Sir Richard recovered himself swiftly. 'Pray do not be absurd, sir!' he said, with more asperity than Cedric ever remembered to have heard in his voice before. 'My cousin has in all probability stepped out to enjoy the air. He is an early riser.'

'If you please, sir, the young gentleman has taken his cloak-bag with him.'

The Major seemed to be having considerable difficulty in holding his fury within bounds. Cedric, observing his gobblings with a sapient eye, begged him to be careful. 'I knew a man once who got into just such a taking. He burst a blood-vessel. True as I sit here!'

The maid-servant, upon whom the Honourable Cedric's charm of manner had not fallen unappreciated, smothered a giggle, and twisted one corner of her apron into a screw. 'There was a letter for your honour upon the mantelshelf when I did the room out,' she volunteered.

Sir Richard swung round on his heel, and went to the fireplace. Pen's note, which she had propped up against the clock, had fallen down, and so missed his. eye. He picked it up, a little pale of countenance, and retired with it to the window.

'*My dear Richard,*' Pen had written. '*This is to say goodbye to you, and to thank you very much for all your kindness. I have made up my mind to return to Aunt Almeria, for the notion of our being obliged to marry is preposterous. I shall tell her some tale that will satisfy her. Dear sir, it was truly a splendid adventure. Your very obliged servant, Penelope Creed.*
P.S. I will send back your cravats and the cloak-bag, and indeed I thank you, dear Richard.'

Cedric, watching his friend's rigid face, dragged himself out of his chair, and lounged across to lay a hand on Sir Richard's shoulder. 'Ricky, dear boy! Now, what is it?'

'I demand to see that letter!' barked the Major.

Sir Richard folded the sheet, and slipped it into his inner

pocket. 'Be content, sir: my cousin has not eloped with your daughter.'

'I don't believe you!'

'If you mean to give me the lie –' Sir Richard checked himself, and turned to the abigail. 'When did Mr Brown leave this place?'

'I don't know, sir. But Parks was downstairs – the waiter, sir.'

'Fetch him.'

'If your cousin has not gone off with my daughter, show me that letter!' demanded the Major.

The Honourable Cedric let his hand fall from Sir Richard's shoulder, and strolled into the middle of the room, an expression of disdain upon his aristocratic countenance. 'You, sir – Daubenay, or whatever your name may be – I don't know what maggot's got into your head, but damme, I'm tired of it! For the lord's sake, go away!'

'I shall not stir from this room until I know the truth!' declared the Major. 'I should not be surprised if I found that you were both in league with that young whippersnapper!'

'Damme, there's something devilish queer about the air of this place!' said Cedric. 'It's my belief you're all mad!'

At this moment the gloomy waiter came into the room. His disclosure that Pen had gone to Bristol with Mrs Hopkins made Sir Richard's face assume a more mask-like expression than ever, but they could not fail to assuage one at least of the Major's alarms. He mopped his brow, and said gruffly that he saw that he had made a mistake.

'That's what we've been telling you,' Cedric pointed out. 'I'll tell you another thing, sir: I want my breakfast, and I'll be damned if I'll sit down to it with you dancing about the room, and shouting in my ear. It ain't restful!'

'But I don't understand!' complained the Major in a milder tone. 'She said she went out to meet your cousin, sir!'

'I have already told you, sir, that your daughter and my cousin both talked a deal of nonsense,' said Sir Richard, over his shoulder.

'You mean she said it to make me believe – to throw dust in my eyes? Upon my soul!'

'Now, don't start that again!' begged Cedric.

'She has gone off with young Luttrell!' exploded the Major. 'By God, I'll break every bone in his body!'

'Well, we don't mind that,' said Cedric. 'You go and do it, sir! Don't waste a moment! Waiter, the door!'

'Good God, this is terrible!' exclaimed the Major, sinking into a chair, and clapping a hand to his brow. 'Depend upon it, they are half-way to the Scottish border by now! As though that were not enough! But there is Philips wanting me to take that wretched girl to Bath this morning, to see whether she can recognize some fellow they have caught there! What am I to say to him? The scandal! My poor wife! I left her prostrate!'

'Run back to her at once!' urged Cedric. 'You have not a moment to spare! Tell me, though, had this fellow the diamonds upon him?'

The Major made a gesture as of one brushing aside a gnat. 'What should I care for that? It is my misguided child I am thinking about!'

'I dare say you don't care, but I do. The man who was murdered was my brother, and those diamonds belong to my family!'

'Your brother? Good Gad, sir, I am astonished!' said the Major, glaring at him. 'No one – no one, believe me! – would credit you with having sustained such a loss! Your levity, your –'

'Never mind my levity, old gentleman! Has that damned necklace been found?'

'Yes, sir, I understand that the prisoner had a necklace in his possession. And if that is your only concern in this appalling affair –'

'Ricky, I must get my hands on that necklace. I hate to leave you, dear boy, but there's nothing for it! Where the devil's that coffee? Can't go without my breakfast!' He caught sight of the waiter, who had reappeared in the doorway. 'You there! What the devil do you mean by standing gaping? Breakfast, you gaby!'

'Yes, sir,' said the waiter, sniffing. 'And what will I tell the lady, sir, if you please?'

'Tell her we ain't receiving! – What lady?'

The waiter proffered a tray with a visiting card upon it. 'For Sir Richard Wyndham,' he said lugubriously. 'She would be obleeged by the favour of a word with him.'

Cedric picked up the card, and read aloud: 'Lady Luttrell. Who the deuce is Lady Luttrell, Ricky?'

'Lady Luttrell!' said the Major, starting up. 'Here? Ha, is this some dastardly plot?'

Sir Richard turned, a look of surprise in his face. 'Show the lady in!' he said.

'Well, I always knew country life would never do for me,' remarked Cedric, 'but damme, I never realized one half of it till now! Not nine o'clock, and the better part of the county paying morning calls! Horrible, Ricky, horrible!'

Sir Richard had turned away from the window, and was watching the door, his brows slightly raised. The waiter ushered in a good-looking woman of between forty and fifty years of age, with brown hair flecked with grey, shrewd, humorous eyes, and a somewhat masterful mouth and chin. Sir Richard moved to meet her, but before he could say anything the Major had burst into speech.

'So, ma'am! So!' he shot out. 'You wish to see Sir Richard Wyndham, do you? You did not expect to meet me here, I dare say!'

'No,' agreed the lady composedly. 'I did not. However, since we shall be obliged, I understand, to meet one another in future with an appearance at least of complaisance, we may as well make a start. How do you do, Major?'

'Upon my word, you are mighty cool, ma'am! Pray, are you aware that your son has eloped with my daughter?'

'Yes,' replied Lady Luttrell. 'My son left a letter behind to inform me of this circumstance.'

Her calm seemed to throw the Major out of his stride. He said rather lamely: 'But what are we to do?'

She smiled. 'We have nothing to do but to accept the event with as good a grace as we can. You do not like the match, and nor do I, but to pursue the young couple, or to show the world our disapproval, will only serve to make us both ridiculous.' She looked him over with a rather mocking light in her eyes, but he seemed so much taken aback, that she relented, and held out her hand to him. 'Come, Major! We may as well bury the hatchet. I cannot be estranged from my only son; you, I am persuaded, would be equally loth to disown your daughter.'

He shook hands with her, not very graciously. 'I do not know what to say! I am utterly confounded! They have behaved very ill towards us, very ill indeed!'

'Oh yes!' she sighed. 'But did we perhaps behave ill towards them?'

This was plainly going too far for the Major, whose eyes began to bulge again. Cedric intervened hastily: 'Don't set him off again, ma'am, for lord's sake!'

'Hold your tongue, sir!' snapped the Major. 'But you came here to see Sir Richard Wyndham, ma'am! How is this?'

'I came to see Sir Richard Wyndham upon quite another matter,' she replied. Her glance dwelled for an instant on Cedric, and travelled past him to Sir Richard. 'And you, I think, must be Sir Richard Wyndham,' she said.

He bowed. 'I am at your service, ma'am. Permit me to present Mr Brandon to you!'

She looked quickly towards Cedric. 'Ah, I thought your face familiar! Sir, I hardly know what to say to you, except that I am more deeply distressed than I am well able to express to you.'

Cedric looked startled. 'Nothing to be distressed about on my account, ma'am, nothing in the world! Must beg your ladyship to excuse my appearance! The fact is, these early hours, you know, put a man out!'

'Lady Luttrell refers, I apprehend, to Beverley's death,' said Sir Richard dryly.

'Bev? Oh, of course, yes! Shocking affair! Never was more surprised in my life!'

'It is a source of profound dismay to me that such a thing should have happened while your brother was a guest in my house,' said Lady Luttrell.

'Don't give it a thought, ma'am!' begged Cedric. 'Not your fault – always thought he would come to a bad end – might have happened anywhere!'

'Your callousness, sir, is disgusting!' proclaimed the Major, picking up his hat. 'I will not remain another instant to be revolted by such a display of heartless unconcern!'

'Well, damme, who wants you to?' demanded Cedric. 'Haven't I been trying to get you to go away this past half-hour? Never met such a thick-skinned fellow in my life!'

'Escort Major Daubenay to the door, Ceddie,' Sir Richard said. 'I understand that Lady Luttrell wishes to see me upon a private matter.'

'Private as you please, dear boy! Ma'am, your very obedient! *After* you, Major!' He bowed the Major out with a flourish, winked at Sir Richard, and went out himself.

'What an engaging scapegrace!' remarked Lady Luttrell, moving forward into the middle of the parlour. 'I confess, I much disliked his brother.'

'Your dislike was shared by most of his acquaintance, ma'am. Will you not be seated?'

She took the chair he offered, and looked him over rather penetratingly. 'Well, Sir Richard,' she said, perfectly mistress of the situation, 'you are wondering, I dare say, why I have come to call upon you.'

'I think I know,' he replied.

'Then I need not beat about the bush. You are travelling with a young gentleman who is said to be your cousin, I understand. A young gentleman who, if my maid is to be believed, answers to the somewhat unusual name of Pen.'

'Yes,' said Sir Richard. 'We should have changed that.'

'Pen Creed, Sir Richard?'

'Yes, ma'am! Pen Creed.'

Her gaze did not waver from his impassive countenance. 'A trifle odd, sir, is it not?'

'The word, ma'am, should have been fantastic. May I know how you came by your information?'

'Certainly you may. I have lately supported a visit from Mrs Griffin and her son, who seemed to expect to find Pen with me. They told me that she had left their roof in her cousin's second-best suit of clothes, by way of the window. That sounded very like Pen Creed to me. But she was not with me, Sir Richard. It was not until this morning that my maid told me of a golden-haired boy who was putting up with his cousin – yourself, Sir Richard – at this inn. That is why I came. I am sure that you will appreciate that I felt a certain degree of anxiety.'

'Perfectly,' he said. 'But Pen is no longer with me. She left for Bristol this morning, and is now, I must suppose, a passenger on the London stagecoach.'

She raised her brows. 'Still more surprising! I hope that you mean to satisfy my curiosity, sir?'

'Obviously I must do so,' he said, and in a cool, expressionless voice, recounted to her all that had happened since Pen had dropped from her rope of sheets into his arms.

She heard him in attentive silence, and all the time watched him. When he had done, she did not say anything for a moment, but looked thoughtfully at him. After a pause, she said: 'Was Pen very much distressed to find my son head over ears in love with Lydia Daubenay?'

'I did not think so.'

'Oh! And my son, I think you said, showed himself to be shocked at the seeming impropriety of her situation?'

'Not unnaturally, though I could have wished that he had not shown his disapproval quite so plainly. She is very young, you see. It had not occurred to her that there was anything amiss.'

'Piers had never the least tact,' she said. 'I expect he told her that you were in honour bound to marry her.'

'He did, and he spoke no less than the truth.'

'Forgive me, Sir Richard, but did you offer for Pen because you felt your honour to be involved?'

'No, I asked her to marry me because I loved her, ma'am.'

'Did you tell her so, Sir Richard?'

'Yes. But she did not believe me.'

'Perhaps,' suggested Lady Luttrell, 'you had not previously given her reason to suppose that you had fallen in love with her?'

'Madam,' said Sir Richard, with a touch of impatience, 'she was in my care, in a situation of the utmost delicacy! Would you have expected me to abuse her confidence by making love to her?'

'No,' she said, smiling. 'From the little I have seen of you, I should have expected you to have treated her just as I imagine you did: as though you were indeed her uncle.'

'With the result,' he said bitterly, 'that that is how she regards me.'

'Is it indeed?' she said tartly. 'Let me tell you, Sir Richard, that men of twenty-nine, with your air, countenance, and address, are not commonly regarded by young females in the light of uncles!'

He flushed, and smiled a little wryly. 'Thank you! But Pen is not like other young females.'

'Pen,' said Lady Luttrell, 'must be a very odd sort of a female if she spent all this while in your company and not succumbed to a charm of manner which you must be so well aware that you possess that I do not scruple to mention it. I consider that your conduct in aiding the chit to escape was disgraceful, but since you were drunk at the time I suppose one must overlook that. I do not blame you for anything you have done since you found yourself in the stagecoach: indeed, you have behaved in a manner that would, if I were twenty-years younger, make me envy Pen exceedingly. Finally, if she did not spend the better part of last night crying her eyes out, I know nothing about my own sex! Where is the letter she left for you? May I see it?'

He drew it from his pocket. 'Pray read it, if you wish. It contains nothing, alas, that may not be read by other eyes than mine.'

She took it from him, read it, and handed it back. 'Just as I thought! Breaking her heart, and determined you shall not know it! Sir Richard, for a man of experience, which I judge you to be, you are a great fool! You never kissed her!'

An unwilling laugh was dragged out of him at this unexpected accusation. 'How could I, situated as we were? She recoiled from the very thought of marriage!'

'Because she thought you had asked her to marry you out of pity! Of course she recoiled!'

'Lady Luttrell, are you serious? Do you indeed think —'

'Think! I know!' said her ladyship. 'Your scruples were very fine, I make no doubt, but how should a chit of Pen's age understand what you were about? She would not care a fig for your precious honour, and I dare say — indeed, I am sure! — that she thought your forbearance mere indifference. And the long and the short of it is that she has gone back to her aunt, and will very likely be bullied into marrying her cousin!'

'Oh no, she will not!' said Sir Richard, with a glance at the clock on the mantelshelf. 'I am desolated to be obliged to leave you, ma'am, but if I am to overtake that stagecoach this side of Chippenham, I must go.'

'Excellent!' she said, laughing. 'Do not waste a thought on me! But having caught the stage, what do you propose to do with Pen?'

'Marry her, ma'am! What else?'

'Dear me, I hope you do not mean to join my foolish son at Gretna Green! I think you had better bring Pen to Crome Hall.'

'Thank you, I will!' he said, with the smile which she privately thought irresistible. 'I am very much in your debt, ma'am.'

He raised her hand to his lips, and kissed it, and left the room, calling for Cedric.

Cedric, who had been partaking of breakfast in the coffee-room, lounged out into the entrance-parlour. 'The devil take you, Ricky, you're as restless as that plaguey friend of yours! What's the matter now?'

'Ceddie, were you driving your own horses yesterday?'

'Dear old boy, of course I was, but what has that to say to anything?'

'I want 'em,' said Sir Richard.

'But, Ricky, I've got to go back to Bath to get hold of that necklace before it's discovered to be made of paste!'

'Take the landlord's gig. I must have a fast pair immediately.'

'The landlord's gig!' gasped Cedric, reeling under the shock. 'Ricky, you *must* be mad!'

'I am not in the least mad. I am going after the London stage, to recover that brat of mine. Be a good fellow, now, and tell them to harness the horses at once!'

'Oh, very well!' Cedric said. 'If that's the way it is! But I'll be satisfied with nothing less than a cavalry regiment, mind!'

'You shall have anything you like!' promised Sir Richard, already half-way up the stairs.

'Mad, quite mad!' said Cedric despairingly, and set up a shout for an ostler.

Ten minutes later, the bays were harnessed to the curricle, and Sir Richard had stepped out into the yard, pulling on his gloves. 'Famous!' he said. 'I hoped you were driving your bays.'

'If you lame 'em –'

'Ceddie, are you – is it possible that you are going to tell me how to drive?' asked Sir Richard.

Cedric, who was still clad in his exotic dressing-gown, leaned against the door-post, and grinned. 'You'll spring 'em. I know you!'

'If I lame them, I will make you a present of my own greys!' said Sir Richard, gathering up the reins.

'Part with your greys?' exclaimed Cedric. 'No, no, you'd never bring yourself to do that, Ricky!'

'Don't disturb yourself: I shan't have to.'

Cedric made a derisive sound, and lingered to watch him mount on to the box-seat. A commotion behind him distracted his attention, and he turned in time to see Mrs Hopkins enter the inn through the front-door, closely followed by a thick-set man in a frieze coat, and a broad-brimmed hat. Mrs Hopkins was labouring under great agitation, and sank immediately into a chair, volubly explaining to the bewildered landlord that she had never had such a turn in her life, and did not expect to recover from her palpitations for a twelvemonth. 'Took up by a Bow Street Runner, Tom!' she panted. 'And him so innocent-seeming as never was!'

'Who?' demanded her spouse.

'That poor young gentleman which is Sir Richard's cousin! Under my very eyes, Tom, and me not dreaming of such a thing! And then if he didn't break away, the which I can't but be glad of, whatever any one may say, Mr Gudgeon not excepted, for a nicer-spoken young gentleman I never did see, and I'm a mother myself, and I have a heart, though others may not, naming no names, and meaning no offence!'

'My God, here's a pretty coil!' exclaimed Cedric, grasping with remarkable swiftness the gist of her remarks. 'Hi Ricky, wait!'

The bays were dancing with impatience. 'Stand away from their heads!' commanded Sir Richard.

'And here's Mr Gudgeon himself, wishful to see Sir Richard and Mr Brandon very particular, which I was obliged to take him up in the trap, though little I want Bow Street Runners, or the like, in my house, as you well know, Tom!'

'*Ricky!*' shouted Cedric, striding out into the yard. 'Wait, man! That bloodhound of mine is here, and there's the devil to pay!'

'Fob him off, Ceddie, fob him off!' called Sir Richard over his shoulder, and swept out of the yard into the street.

'Ricky, you madman, hold a minute!' roared Cedric.

But the curricle had bowled out of sight. The ostler enquired whether he should run after it.

'Run after my bays?' said Cedric scornfully. 'You'd need wings, not legs, to catch them, my good fool!'

He turned back to the inn, encountering in the doorway Lady Luttrell, who had come out to see what all the shouting was about.

'What is the matter, Mr Brandon?' she asked. 'You seem very much put out.'

'Matter, ma'am! Why, here's Richard gone off after the London Stage, and that crazy girl of his taken up by the Bow Street Runner in Bristol!'

'Good God, this is horrible!' she exclaimed. 'Sir Richard must be recalled at all costs! The child must be rescued!'

'Well, by all accounts she seems to have rescued herself,' said Cedric. 'But where she may be now, the Lord only knows! However, I'm glad that Runner has arrived: I was getting deuced tired of hunting for him.'

'But is it impossible to stop Sir Richard?' she asked urgently.

'Lord, ma'am, he's half-way to the London road by now!' said Cedric.

This pronouncement was not strictly accurate. Sir Richard, driving out of Queen Charlton at very much the same time as Miss Creed was boarding the Accommodation coach at Kingswood, chose to take the road to Bath rather than that which led to Keynsham, and thence, due north, through Oldland to join the Bristol road at Warmley. His experience of Accommodation coaches was not such as to induce him to place much confidence in their being likely to cover more than eight miles an hour, and he calculated that if the stage had left Bristol at nine o'clock, which seemed probable, it would not reach the junction of the Bath and Bristol roads until noon at the earliest. The Honourable Cedric's bays, drawing a light curricle, might be depended upon to arrive at Chippenham considerably in advance of that hour, and the Bath road had the advantage of being well known to Sir Richard.

The bays, which seemed to have been fed exclusively on oats, were in fine fettle, and the miles flashed by. They were not, perhaps, an easy pair to handle, but Sir Richard, a notable whip, had little trouble with them, and was so well satisfied with their pace and stamina that he began to toy seriously with the idea of making the Honourable Cedric a handsome offer for them. He was obliged to rein them in to a sedate pace whilst threading his way through the crowded streets of Bath, but once clear of the town he was able to give them their heads on the long stretch to Corsham, and arrived finally in Chippenham to learn that the Accommodation coach from Bristol was not due there for nearly another hour. Sir Richard repaired to the best posting-inn, superintended the disposal of the sweating bays, and ordered breakfast. When he had consumed a dish of ham-and-eggs, and drunk two cups of coffee, he had the bays put-to again, and drove westward along the Bristol road, at a leisurely pace, until he came to a fork, where a weather-beaten signpost pointed northward to Nettleton and Acton Turville, and westward to Wroxham, Marshfield, and Bristol. Here he reined in, to await the approach of the stage.

It was not long in putting in an appearance. It rounded a bend in the deserted road ahead, a green-and-gold monstrosity, rocking and swaying top-heavily in the centre of the road, with half a dozen outside passengers on the roof, the boot piled high with baggage, and the guard sitting up behind with the yard of tin in his hand.

Sir Richard drew the curricle across the road, hitched up his reins, and jumped lightly down from the box-seat. The bays were quiet enough by this time, and except for some fidgeting, showed no immediate disposition to bolt.

Finding his way barred, the stagecoach-man pulled up his team, and demanded aggrievedly what game Sir Richard thought he was playing.

'No game at all!' said Sir Richard. 'You have a fugitive aboard, and when I have taken him into custody, you are at liberty to proceed on your way.'

'Ho, I am, am I?' said the coachman, nonplussed, but by no means mollified. 'Fine doings on the King's Highway! Ah, and so you'll find afore you're much older!'

One of the inside passengers, a red-faced man with very bushy whiskers, poked his head out of the window to discover the reason for the unexpected halt; the guard climbed down from the roof to argue with Sir Richard; and Pen, squashed between a fat farmer, and a woman with a perpetual sniff, had a sudden fear that she had been overtaken by the Bow Street Runner. The sound of the guard's voice, saying: 'There, and if I didn't suspicion him from the werry moment I set eyes on him at Kingswood!' did nothing to allay her alarms. She turned a white, frightened face towards the door, just as it was pulled open, and the steps let down.

The next instant, Sir Richard's tall, immaculate person filled the opening, and Pen, uttering an involuntary sound between a squeak and a whimper, turned first red, and then white, and managed to utter the one word: '*No!*'

'Ah!' said Sir Richard briskly. 'So there you are! Out you come, my young friend!'

'Well, I never did in all my life!' gasped the woman beside Pen. 'Whatever has he been and gone and done, sir?'

'Run away from school,' replied Sir Richard, without a moment's hesitation.

'I haven't! It isn't t-true!' stammered Pen. 'I won't go with you, I w-won't!'

Sir Richard, leaning into the coach, and grasping her hand, said: 'Oh, won't you, by Jove? Don't you dare to defy me, you – brat!'

'Here, guv'nor, steady!' expostulated a kindly man in the far corner. 'I don't know when I've taken more of a fancy to a lad, and there's no call for you to bully him, I'm sure! Dare say there's many of us have wanted to run away from school in our time, eh?'

'Ah,' said Sir Richard brazenly, 'but you do not know the half of it! You think he looks a young innocent, but I could tell you a tale of his depravity which would shock you.'

'Oh, how dare you?' said Pen indignantly. 'It isn't true! Indeed, it isn't!'

The occupants of the coach had by this time ranged themselves into two camps. Several persons said that they had suspected the young varmint of running away from the start, and Pen's supporters demanded to know who Sir Richard was, and what right he had to drag the poor young gentleman out of the coach.

'Every right!' responded Sir Richard. 'I am his guardian. In fact, he is my nephew.'

'I am not!' stated Pen.

His eyes looked down into hers, with so much laughter in them that she felt her heart turn over. 'Aren't you?' he said. 'Well, if you are not my nephew, brat, *what are you?*'

Aghast, she choked: 'Richard, you – you – *traitor!*'

Even the kindly man in the corner seemed to feel that Sir Richard's question called for an answer. Pen looked helplessly round, encountered nothing but glances either of disapproval, or of interrogation, and raised her wrathful eyes to Sir Richard's face.

'Well?' said Sir Richard inexorably. '*Are* you my nephew?'

'Yes – no! Oh, you are abominable! You wouldn't *dare!*'

'Yes, I would,' said Sir Richard. 'Are you going to get out, or are you not?'

A man in a plum-coloured coat recommended Sir Richard to dust the young rascal's jacket for him. Pen stared up at Sir Richard, read the determination behind the amusement in his face, and allowed herself to be pulled to her feet, and out of the stuffy coach.

'P'raps when you've quite finished, your honour, you'll be so werry obliging as to move that curricle of yourn!' said the coachman sardonically.

'Richard, I can't go back!' Pen said in a frantic undertone. 'That Runner caught me in Bristol, and I only just contrived to escape!'

'Ah, that must have been what Cedric was trying to tell me!' said Sir Richard, walking up to the bays, and backing them to the side of the road. 'So you were arrested, were you? What a splendid adventure for you, my little one!'

'And I have left your cloak-bag behind, and it's no use trying to drag me away with you, because I won't go! I won't, I won't!'

'Why won't you?' asked Sir Richard, turning to look down at her.

She found herself unable to speak. There was an expression in Sir Richard's eyes which brought the colour rushing into her cheeks again, and made her feel as though the world were whirling madly round her. Behind her, the guard, having let up the steps, and shut the door, climbed, grumbling, on to the roof again. The coach began to move ponderously forward. Pen paid no heed to it, though the wheels almost brushed her coat. 'Richard, you – you don't want me! You *can't* want me!' she said uncertainly.

'My darling!' he said. 'Oh, my precious, foolish little love!'

The coach lumbered on down the road; as it reached the next bend, the roof-passengers, looking back curiously to see the last of a very odd couple, experienced a shock that made one of them nearly lose his balance. The golden-haired stripling was locked in the Corinthian's arms, being ruthlessly kissed.

'Lawks a-mussy on us! whatever is the world a-coming to?' gasped the roof-passenger, recovering his seat. 'I never did in all my born days!'

'Richard, Richard, they can see us from the coach!' expostulated Pen, between tears and laughter.

'Let them see!' said the Corinthian.

233